THE
MALLOREON
VOLUME TWO

By David Eddings

THE BELGARIAD

Book One: *Pawn of Prophecy*
Book Two: *Queen of Sorcery*
Book Three: *Magician's Gambit*
Book Four: *Castle of Wizardry*
Book Five: *Enchanters' End Game*

THE MALLOREON

Book One: *Guardians of the West*
Book Two: *King of the Murgos*
Book Three: *Demon Lord of Karanda*
Book Four: *Sorceress of Darshiva*
Book Five: *The Seeress of Kell*

THE ELENIUM

Book One: *The Diamond Throne*
Book Two: *The Ruby Knight*
Book Three: *The Sapphire Rose*

THE TAMULI

Book One: *Domes of Fire*
Book Two: *The Shining Ones*
Book Three: *The Hidden City*

BELGARATH THE SORCERER

POLGARA THE SORCERESS

THE REDEMPTION OF ALTHALUS

THE RIVAN CODEX

REGINA'S SONG

THE MALLOREON

VOLUME TWO

DAVID EDDINGS

BALLANTINE BOOKS

NEW YORK

2005 Del Rey Trade Paperback Edition

Sorceress of Darshiva copyright © 1989 by David Eddings
The Seeress of Kell copyright © 1991 by David Eddings
Preface copyright © 2005 by David Eddings

Published in the United States by Del Rey Books, an imprint of The Random House
Publishing Group, a division of Random House, Inc., New York.

Del Rey is a registered trademark and the Del Rey colophon is a trademark of Random
House, Inc.

Originally published in two separate volumes in the United States by Del Rey Books,
an imprint of The Random House Publishing Group, a division of Random House, Inc.,
as *Sorceress of Darshiva* in 1989 and *The Seeress of Kell* in 1991.

ISBN 0-345-48387-1

Printed in the United States of America

www.delreybooks.com

9 8 7 6 5

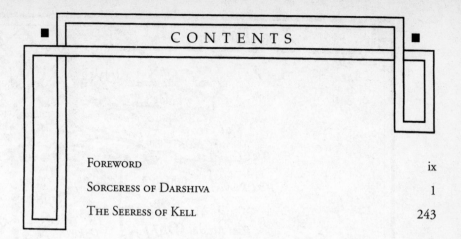

CONTENTS

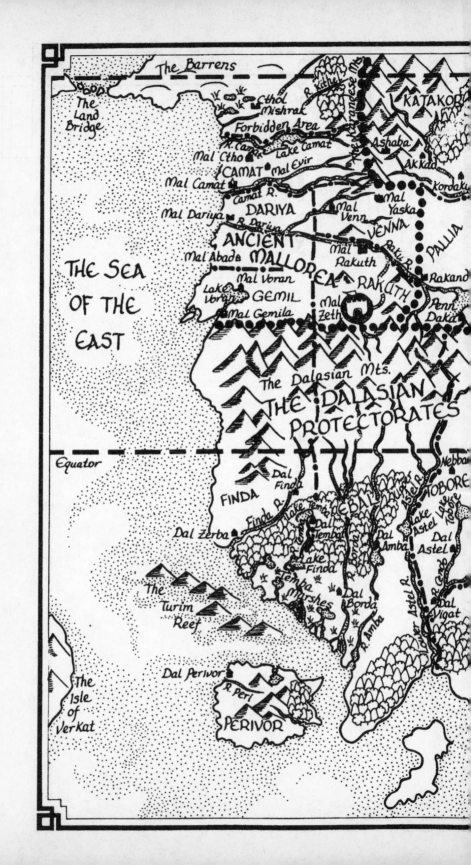

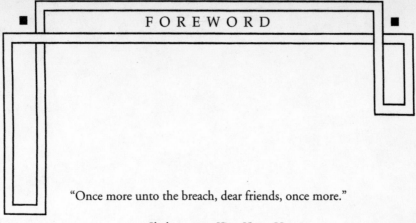

FOREWORD

"Once more unto the breach, dear friends, once more."

—Shakespeare, *King Henry V*

Now we have a two-volume Malloreon to accompany the earlier two-volume Belgariad. You will note that The Malloreon is significantly longer than The Belgariad. Certain restrictions were relaxed after the success of The Belgariad.

When we add the two prequels, *Belgarath the Sorcerer* and *Polgara the Sorceress,* we have the traditional twelve-book format established by Homer in *The Iliad* and *The Odyssey.* He was closely followed by Virgil in *The Aeneid,* and not quite so closely by Milton in *Paradise Lost.* (Take notes, I may give a test later.)

As we mentioned in *The Rivan Codex,* when we met Lester and Judy-Lynn Del Rey, I told him that I thought that there was more story left to tell after The Belgariad was completed. Lest agreed (and Judy-Lynn wanted to write a contract on the back of the menu in the restaurant where we were having dinner).

The Malloreon gave us the chance to get the smell of bubble gum out of my typewriter. Garion (and Ce'Nedra) grow up, so they're now adults and rule the Isle of the Winds. Then, as was fairly common in medieval Europe, we have a kidnapping, and that starts the ball rolling (through five more books). We got to introduce new villains, new heroes, and new allies.

There were many, many things that we didn't explain in these two pentologies, and that's what produced the two prequels, and that carried us into the standard twelve-book format. My unindicted coconspirator suggested several things that show up at the end of *Polgara the Sorceress* that links that book to *Pawn of Prophecy* (Book One of The Belgariad). In effect, the reader can go directly from the end of *Polgara* to the beginning of *Pawn.* The whole story, thus, becomes a circle that's approximately 4,600 pages long. I suppose that there might be readers out there who have been reading their way around that circle for the last twenty years or so, and thus we have the literary equivalent of peddling dope.

Ah well,
David Eddings

SORCERESS OF DARSHIVA

For Oscar William Patrick Janson-Smith:
Welcome to our world!
Much love,
Dave and Leigh

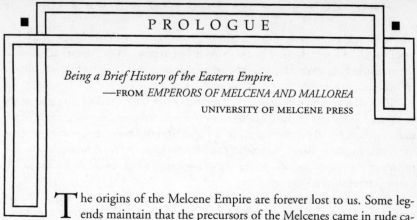

Being a Brief History of the Eastern Empire.
—FROM *EMPERORS OF MELCENA AND MALLOREA*
UNIVERSITY OF MELCENE PRESS

The origins of the Melcene Empire are forever lost to us. Some legends maintain that the precursors of the Melcenes came in rude canoes out of the vast sea lying east of the Melcene Islands; others contend that the ancestral Melcene was an offshoot of that curious culture existing in Dalasia. Whatever the source, however, Melcena stands as the oldest civilization on the earth.

Melcena has always been closely allied with the sea, and her original home lay in the islands off the east coast of the Mallorean continent. The capital at Melcena was a city of light and culture when Tol Honeth was a rude village and Mal Zeth was only a shabby cluster of tents. Only Kell stood in contemplation of the heavens to rival the ancestral home of the Melcenes.

It was the advent of a catastrophe which caused Melcena to abandon its splendid isolation. At a time estimated to be five thousand years ago, a disaster occurred far to the west. The Angaraks and Alorns blame this on a theological dispute between the Gods. Such explanation is not to be taken seriously, but it does give some insight into the gropings of primitive minds to explain the forces of nature.

Whatever the source, the cataclysm involved a great split in the protocontinent and engendered colossal tidal waves. The seas first fell, then rose, and ultimately came to rest at more or less the present shoreline. For Melcena, this was disastrous. Fully half the land area of ancient Melcena was lost to the sea. Although the loss of property was enormous, the bulk of the people were saved. This left a pitifully overcrowded population clinging to the remnants of their former islands. The capital at Melcena had been a fair city in the mountains, where affairs could be managed without the debilitating effects of the climate in the tropical lowlands. Following the catastrophe, Melcena was a shattered city, destroyed by earthquake and flood, lying no more than a league from the new coast.

After a period of rebuilding, it became clear that the shrunken homeland could no longer support the population. Thus the Melcenes turned to the mainland. Southeastern Mallorea lay closest, a region populated by peoples of their own racial stock with a compatible, though corrupted, language; to that region the Melcenes turned their attention. There were five primitive kingdoms in the area—Gandahar, Darshiva, Celanta, Peldane, and Rengel. These were quickly overrun by the technologically superior Melcenes and were absorbed into their growing empire.

The dominating force in the Melcene Empire was the bureaucracy. While there were drawbacks to a bureaucratic form of government, it provided the advantages of continuity and a clear-eyed pragmatism more concerned with finding the most practical way to get the job done than with whim, prejudice, and egocentricity, which so frequently move other forms of government. Melcene bureaucracy was practical almost to a fault. The concept of "an aristocracy of talent" dominated Melcene thinking. If one bureau ignored a talented individual, another was almost certain to snap him up.

The various departments of the Melcene government rushed into the newly conquered mainland provinces to winnow through the population in search of genius. The conquered peoples were thus absorbed directly into the mainstream of the life of the empire. Always pragmatic, the Melcenes left the royal houses of the five mainland provinces in place, preferring to operate through established lines of authority rather than set up new ones.

For the next fourteen hundred years, the Melcene Empire prospered, far removed from the theological and political squabbles of the western continent. Melcene culture was secular, civilized, and highly educated. Slavery was unknown, and trade with the Angaraks and their subject peoples in Karanda and Dalasia was extremely profitable. The old capital at Melcena became a major center of learning. Unfortunately, some Melcene scholars turned toward the arcane. Their summoning of evil spirits went far beyond the mumbo jumbo of the Morindim or the Karandese and began to delve into darker and more serious areas. They made progress in witchcraft and necromancy. But the major interest lay in the field of alchemy.

The first encounter with the Angaraks took place during this period. Although victorious in that first meeting, the Melcenes realized that eventually the Angaraks would overwhelm them by sheer weight of numbers.

While the Angaraks bent most of their efforts to the establishment of the Dalasian Protectorates, there was a wary, tentative peace. The trade contacts between the two nations yielded a somewhat better understanding of each other, though the Melcenes were amused by the preoccupation with religion of even the most worldly Angarak. Over the next eighteen hundred years, relations between the two nations deteriorated into little wars, seldom lasting more than a year or two. Both sides scrupulously avoided committing their full forces, obviously not wishing all-out confrontation.

To gain more information about each other, the two nations developed a tradition of exchanging the children of various leaders for certain periods of time. The sons of high-ranking Melcene bureaucrats were sent to Mal Zeth to live with the families of Angarak generals, and the generals' sons were sent to the imperial capital to be raised. The result was a group of young men with cosmopolitanism which later became the norm for the ruling class of the Mallorean Empire.

One such exchange toward the end of the fourth millennium ultimately resulted in the unification of the two peoples. At about the age of twelve, a youth named Kallath, son of a high-ranking Angarak general, was sent to Melcena to spend his formative years in the household of the Imperial Minister of Foreign Affairs. The minister had frequent official and social contacts with the imperial family, and Kallath soon became a welcome guest at the imperial palace. Emperor Molvan was an elderly man with but one surviving child, a daughter named Danera, perhaps a year younger than Kallath. Matters between the two youngsters progressed in a not uncommon fashion until Kallath was recalled at eighteen to Mal Zeth to begin his military career. Kallath rose meteorically through the ranks to the position of Governor-General of the District of Rakuth by the time he was twenty-eight, thereby becoming the youngest man ever elevated to the General Staff. A year later he journeyed to Melcene, where he and Princess Danera were married.

In the years that followed, Kallath divided his time between Melcena and Mal Zeth, building a power base in each, and when Emperor Molvan died in 3829, he was ready. There had been others in line for the throne, but most of these had died—frequently under mysterious circumstances. It was, nonetheless, over the violent objections of many noble families of Melcena that Kallath was declared Emperor of Melcena in 3830; these objections were quieted with brutal efficiency by Kallath's cohorts. Danera had produced seven healthy children to insure that Kallath's line would continue.

Journeying to Mal Zeth the following year, Kallath brought the Melcene army to the border of Delchin, where it stood poised. At Mal Zeth, Kallath delivered an ultimatum to the General Staff. His forces comprised the army of his own district of Rakuth and of the eastern principalities in Karand, where the Angarak military governors had sworn allegiance to him. Together with the army on the Delchin border, these gave him absolute military supremacy. His demand was to be appointed OverGeneral of the armies of Angarak. There were precedents. In the past, an occasional general had been granted that office, though it was far more common for the General Staff to rule jointly. But Kallath's demand brought something new into the picture. His position as emperor was hereditary, and he insisted that the Over-Generalship of Angarak also be passed to his heirs. Helplessly, the generals acceded to his demands. Kallath stood supreme on the continent as Emperor of Melcene and Commander in Chief of Angarak.

The integration of Melcene and Angarak was turbulent, but in the end, Melcene patience won out over Angarak brutality, as it became evident over the years that the Melcene bureaucracy was infinitely more efficient than Angarak military administration. The bureaucracy first moved on such mundane matters as standards and currency. From there it was but a short step to establishing a continental Bureau of Roads. Within a few hundred years, the bureaucracy ran virtually every aspect of life on the continent. As always, it gathered up talented men and women from every corner of Mallorea, regardless of race; soon administrative units comprised of Melcenes, Karands, Dalasians, and Angaraks were not at all uncommon. By 4400, the bureaucratic ascendancy was complete. In the interim, the title of OverGeneral had begun to fall into disuse, perhaps because the bureaucracy customarily addressed all communications to "the Emperor." There appears to have been no specific date when the Emperor of Melcena became the Emperor of Mallorea, and such usage was never formally approved until after the disastrous adventure in the West which ended in the Battle of Vo Mimbre.

The conversion of Melcenes to the worship of Torak was at best superficial. They pragmatically accepted the *forms* of Angarak worship out of political expediency, but the Grolims were unable to command the abject submission to the Dragon God which had always characterized the Angaraks.

In 4850, Torak himself suddenly emerged from his eons of seclusion at Ashaba. A vast shock ran through Mallorea as the living God, his maimed face concealed behind a polished steel mask, appeared at the gates of Mal Zeth. The Emperor was disdainfully set aside, and Torak assumed full authority as "Kal"—King and God. Messengers were dispatched to Cthol Murgos, Mishrak ac Thull, and Gar og Nadrak, and a council of war was held at Mal Zeth in 4852. The Dalasians, Karands, and Melcenes were stunned by the appearance of a figure they had always thought purely mythical, and their shock was compounded by the presence of Torak's disciples.

Torak was a God and did not speak, except to issue commands. But the Disciples, Ctuchik, Zedar, and Urvon, were men and they probed and examined everything with a kind of cold disdain. They saw at once that Mallorean society had become almost totally secular—and took steps to rectify the situation. A reign of terror descended upon Mallorea. Grolims were everywhere, and secularism was a form of heresy to them. The sacrifices, long virtually unknown, were renewed with fanatic enthusiasm; soon not a village in all Mallorea did not have its altar and reeking bonfire. In one stroke, Torak's disciples overturned millennia of military and bureaucratic rule and returned absolute dominion to the Grolims. Soon there was not one facet of Mallorean life that did not bow abjectly to the will of Torak.

The mobilization of Mallorea in preparation for the war with the West virtually depopulated the continent, and the disaster at Vo Mimbre wiped out an entire generation. The catastrophic campaign, coupled with the apparent death of Torak at the hands of the Rivan Warder, utterly demoralized Mallorea. The doddering old emperor emerged from retirement to try to rebuild the shattered bureaucracy. Grolim efforts to maintain control were met with universal hatred. Without Torak, they had no real power. Most of the emperor's sons had perished at Vo Mimbre, but one gifted child remained, a boy of seven, the son of his old age. The emperor spent his few remaining years instructing and preparing his son for the task of ruling. When age finally rendered the emperor incompetent, Korzeth, then about fourteen, callously deposed his father and ascended the imperial throne.

After the war, Mallorean society had fractured back to its original components of Melcena, Karanda, Dalasia, and Mallorea Antiqua. There was even a movement to disintegrate further into the prehistoric kingdoms which had existed before the coming of the Angaraks. This movement was particularly strong in the principality of Gandahar in southern Melcena, in Zamad and Voresebo in Karanda, and in Perivor in the Dalasian Protectorates. Deceived by Korzeth's youth, these regions rashly declared independence from the imperial throne at Mal Zeth, and other principalities gave indications that they would soon follow suit. Korzeth moved immediately to stem the tide of revolution. The boy emperor spent the rest of his life on horseback in perhaps the greatest bloodbath in history; but when he was done, he delivered a reunified Mallorea to his successor to the throne.

The descendants of Korzeth brought a different kind of rule to the continent. Before the disastrous war, the Emperor of Mallorea had often been little more than a figurehead, and power had largely rested with the bureaucracy. But now the imperial throne was absolute. The center of power shifted from Melcena to Mal Zeth in keeping with the military orientation of Korzeth and his descendants. As is usual when power rests in the hands of one supreme ruler, intrigue became commonplace. Plots and conspiracies abounded as various functionaries schemed to discredit rivals and gain imperial favor. Rather than trying to stop these palace intrigues, Korzeth's descendants encouraged them, perceiving that men divided by mutual distrust could never unite to challenge the power of the throne.

The present emperor, 'Zakath, assumed the throne during his eighteenth year. Intelligent, sensitive, and capable, he gave early promise of enlightened rule. A personal tragedy, however, turned him from that course and made him a man feared by half the world. Now he is obsessed with the concept of power; the idea of becoming Overking of all the Angaraks has dominated his thoughts for the past two decades. Only time will determine if 'Zakath will succeed in asserting dominance over the Western Angarak Kingdoms, but if he succeeds, the history of the entire world may be profoundly altered.

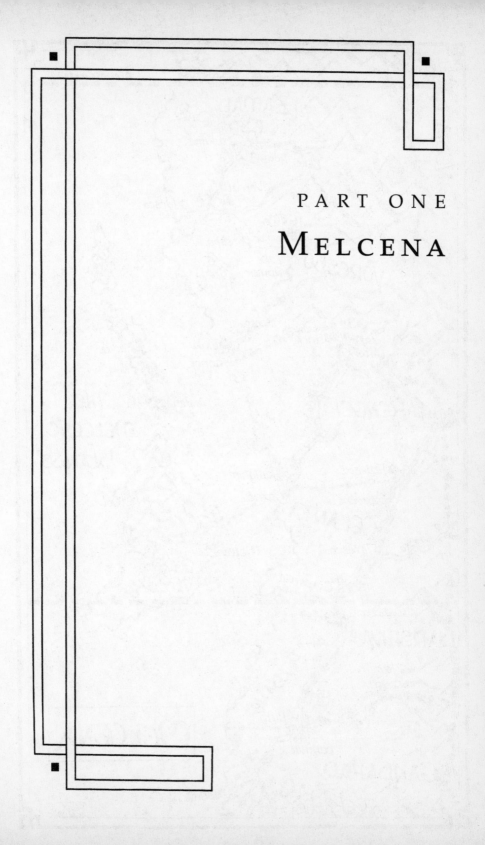

PART ONE

MELCENA

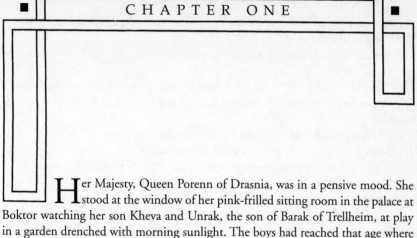

Her Majesty, Queen Porenn of Drasnia, was in a pensive mood. She stood at the window of her pink-frilled sitting room in the palace at Boktor watching her son Kheva and Unrak, the son of Barak of Trellheim, at play in a garden drenched with morning sunlight. The boys had reached that age where sometimes it seemed almost possible to see them growing, and their voices wavered uncertainly between boyish soprano and manly baritone. Porenn sighed, smoothing the front of her black gown. The Queen of Drasnia had worn black since the death of her husband. "You would be proud of him, my dear Rhodar," she whispered sadly.

There was a light knock at her door.

"Yes?" she replied, not turning.

"There's a Nadrak here to see you, your Majesty," the aged butler at the door reported. "He says you know him."

"Oh?"

"He says his name is Yarblek."

"Oh, yes. Prince Kheldar's associate. Show him in, please."

"There's a woman with him, your Majesty," the butler said with a disapproving expression. "She uses language your Majesty might prefer not to hear."

Porenn smiled warmly. "That must be Vella," she said. "I've heard her swear before. I don't know that she's really all that serious about it. Show them both in, if you would, please."

"At once, your Majesty."

Yarblek was as shabby as ever. At some point, the shoulder seam of his long black overcoat had given way and had been rudimentarily repaired with a piece of rawhide thong. His beard was coarse and black and scraggly, his hair was unkempt, and he looked as if he didn't smell very good. "Your Majesty," he said grandly, attempting a bow which was marred a bit by an unsteady lurch.

"Drunk already, Master Yarblek?" Porenn asked him archly.

"No, not really, Porenn," he replied, unabashed. "It's just a little carry-over from last night."

The queen was not offended by the Nadrak's use of her first name. Yarblek's grip on formality had never been very firm.

The woman who had entered with him was a stunningly beautiful Nadrak with blue-black hair and smoldering eyes. She was dressed in tight-fitting leather trousers and a black leather vest. A silver-hilted dagger protruded from each of her boot tops, and two more were tucked under the wide leather belt about her waist.

She bowed with infinite grace. "You're looking tired, Porenn," she observed. "I think you need more sleep."

Porenn laughed. "Tell that to the people who bring me stacks of parchment every hour or so."

"I made myself a rule years ago," Yarblek said, sprawling uninvited in a chair. "Never put anything down in writing. It saves time as well as keeping me out of trouble."

"It seems to me that I've heard Kheldar say the same thing."

Yarblek shrugged. "Silk's got a good grip on reality."

"I haven't seen you two for quite some time," Porenn noted, also sitting.

"We've been in Mallorea," Vella told her, wandering around the room and looking appraisingly at the furnishings.

"Isn't that dangerous? I've heard that there's plague there."

"It's pretty much confined to Mal Zeth," Yarblek replied. "Polgara persuaded the Emperor to seal up the city."

"Polgara?" Porenn exclaimed, coming to her feet. "What's she doing in Mallorea?"

"She was going in the general direction of a place called Ashaba the last time I saw her. She had Belgarath and the others with her."

"How did they get to Mallorea?"

"By boat, I'd imagine. It's a long swim."

"Yarblek, am I going to have to drag every single scrap of information out of you?" Porenn demanded in exasperation.

"I'm getting to it, Porenn," he said, sounding a little injured. "Do you want the story first or the messages? I've got lots of messages for you, and Vella's got a couple more that she won't even talk about—at least not to me."

"Just start at the beginning, Yarblek."

"Any way you want it." He scratched at his beard. "The way I got the story is that Silk and Belgarath and the others were in Cthol Murgos. They got captured by the Malloreans, and 'Zakath took them all to Mal Zeth. The young fellow with the big sword—Belgarion, isn't it? Anyway, he and 'Zakath got to be friends—"

"Garion and 'Zakath?" Porenn asked incredulously. "How?"

"I wouldn't know. I wasn't there when it happened. To make it short, they were friends, but then the plague broke out in Mal Zeth. I managed to sneak Silk and the others out of the city, and we went north. We separated before we got to Venna. They wanted to go to this Ashaba place, and I had a caravan load of goods I wanted to get to Yar Marak. Made a fairly good profit, actually."

"Why were they going to Ashaba?"

"They were after some woman named Zandramas—the one who abducted Belgarion's son."

"A *woman?* Zandramas is a woman?"

"So they told me. Belgarath gave me a letter for you. It's all in there. I told him that he shouldn't write it down, but he wouldn't listen to me." Yarblek unwound himself from his chair, fished around inside his overcoat, and handed a rumpled and none-too-clean piece of parchment to the queen. Then he strolled to the window and looked out. "Isn't that Trellheim's boy down there?" he asked. "The husky one with the red hair?"

Porenn was reading the parchment. "Yes," she said absently, trying to concentrate on the message.

"Is he here? Trellheim, I mean?"

"Yes. I don't know if he's awake yet, though. He stayed up rather late last night and he was a little tipsy when he went to bed."

Yarblek laughed. "That's Barak, all right. Has he got his wife and daughters with him, too?"

"No," Porenn said. "They stayed in Val Alorn, making the preparations for his oldest daughter's wedding."

"Is she that old already?"

"Chereks marry young. They seem to think it's the best way to keep a girl out of trouble. Barak and his son came here to get away from all the fuss."

Yarblek laughed again. "I think I'll go wake him up and see if he's got anything to drink." He touched his forefinger to the spot between his eyes with a pained look. "I'm feeling a little delicate this morning, and Barak's a good man to get well with. I'll stop back when I'm feeling better. Besides, you've got your mail to read. Oh," he said, "I almost forgot. Here are some others." He started rummaging around inside his shabby coat. "One from Polgara." He tossed it negligently on the table. "One from Belgarion. One from Silk, and one from the blond girl with the dimples—the one they call Velvet. The snake didn't send anything—you know how snakes are. Now, if you'll excuse me, I'm *really* not feeling too good." He lurched to the door and went out.

"That is the most exasperating man in the world," Porenn declared.

"He does it on purpose." Vella shrugged. "He thinks it's funny."

"Yarblek said that you have some messages for me, too," the queen said. "I suppose I should read them all at once—get all the shocks over with at one time."

"I've only got one, Porenn," Vella replied, "and it isn't in writing. Liselle—the one they call Velvet—asked me to tell you something when we were alone."

"All right," Porenn said, putting down Belgarath's letter.

"I'm not sure how they found out about this," Vella said, "but it seems that the King of Cthol Murgos is *not* the son of Taur Urgas."

"What are you saying, Vella?"

"Urgit isn't even related to that frothing lunatic. It seems that a number of years ago, a certain Drasnian businessman paid a visit to the palace in Rak Goska. He and Taur Urgas' second wife became friendly." She smiled with one eyebrow slightly raised. "Very friendly. I've always had that suspicion about Murgo women. Anyway, Urgit was the result of that friendship."

A terrible suspicion began to dawn on Queen Porenn.

Vella grinned impishly at her. "We all knew that Silk had royal connections," she said. "We just didn't know how many royal families he was connected to."

"No!" Porenn gasped.

Vella laughed. "Oh, yes. Liselle confronted Urgit's mother with it, and the lady confessed." The Nadrak girl's face grew serious. "The whole point of Liselle's message is that Silk doesn't want that bony fellow, Javelin, to find out about it. Liselle felt that she had to report it to somebody. That's why she told me to pass it on to you. I guess *you're* supposed to decide whether to tell Javelin or not."

"How very kind of her," Porenn said drily. "Now they want me to keep secrets from the chief of my own intelligence service."

Vella's eyes twinkled. "Liselle's in a kind of difficult situation, Porenn," she said. "I know that I drink too much and I swear a lot. That makes people think that I'm stupid, but I'm not. Nadrak women know the world, and I have very good eyes. I didn't actually catch them at it, but I'd be willing to wager half the money I'll get when Yarblek sells me that Silk and Liselle are keeping company."

"Vella!"

"I couldn't prove it, Porenn, but I know what I saw." The Nadrak girl sniffed at her leather vest and made a sour face. "If it's not too much trouble, I would really like to take a bath. I've been in the saddle for weeks. Horses are nice enough animals, I suppose, but I really don't want to smell like one."

Porenn's mind was working very fast now; to give herself time to think, she rose and approached the wild Nadrak girl. "Have you ever worn satin, Vella?" she asked. "A gown, perhaps?"

"Satin? Me?" Vella laughed coarsely. "Nadraks never wear satin."

"Then you might be the very first." Queen Porenn reached out her small white hands and lifted Vella's wealth of blue-black hair into a tumbled mass atop her head. "I'd give my soul for hair like that," she murmured.

"I'll trade you," Vella offered. "Do you know what price I could bring if I were blond?"

"Hush, Vella," Porenn said absently. "I'm trying to think." She twined the girl's hair loosely about her hands, startled at how alive it felt. Then she reached out, lifted Vella's chin, and looked into her huge eyes. Something seemed to reach out and touch the Queen of Drasnia, and she suddenly knew the destiny of this half-wild child before her. "Oh, my dear," she almost laughed, "what an amazing future you have in store for you. You'll touch the sky, Vella, the very sky."

"I really don't know what you're talking about, Porenn."

"You will." Porenn looked at the perfect face before her. "Yes," she said, "satin, I think. Lavender would be nice."

"I prefer red."

"No, dear," Porenn told her. "Red just wouldn't do. It definitely has to be lavender." She reached out and touched the girl's ears. "And I think amethyst here and here."

"What are you up to?"

"It's a game, child. Drasnians are very good at games. And when I'm done, I'll double your price." Porenn was just a bit smug about it. "Bathe first, then let's see what we can do with you."

Vella shrugged. "As long as I can keep my daggers."

"We'll work that out."

"Can you really do something with a lump like me?" Vella asked, almost plaintively.

"Trust me," Porenn said, smiling. "Now go bathe, child. I have letters to read and decisions to make."

After the Queen of Drasnia had read the letters, she summoned her butler and issued a couple of orders. "I want to speak with the Earl of Trellheim," she said, "before he gets any drunker. I also need to talk with Javelin just as soon as he can get to the palace."

It was perhaps ten minutes later when Barak appeared in her doorway. He was a bit bleary-eyed, and his vast red beard stuck out in all directions. Yarblek came with him.

"Put away your tankards, gentlemen," Porenn said crisply. "There's work to be done. Barak, is the *Seabird* ready to sail?"

"She's always ready," he said in an injured tone.

"Good. Then round up your sailors. You have a number of places to go. I'm calling a meeting of the Alorn Council. Get word to Anheg, Fulrach, and Brand's son Kail at Riva. Stop off in Arendia and pick up Mandorallen and Lelldorin." She pursed her lips. "Korodullin's not well enough to travel, so bypass Vo Mimbre. He'd get out of his deathbed to attend if he knew what was going on. Go to Tol Honeth instead and get Varana. I'll send word to Cho-Hag and Hettar myself. Yarblek, you go to Yar Nadrak and get Drosta. Leave Vella here with me."

"But—"

"No buts, Yarblek. Do exactly as I say."

"I thought you said this was a meeting of the Alorn Council, Porenn," Barak objected. "Why are we inviting the Arends and the Tolnedrans—and the Nadraks?"

"We've got an emergency on our hands, Barak, and it concerns everybody."

They stood staring stupidly at her.

She clapped her hands together sharply. "Quickly, gentlemen, quickly. We don't have any time to waste."

Urgit, High King of Cthol Murgos, sat on his garish throne in the Drojim Palace in Rak Urga. He was dressed in his favorite purple doublet and hose, he had one leg negligently cocked over the arm of the throne, and he was absently tossing his crown back and forth between his hands as he listened to the droning voice of Agachak, the cadaverous-looking Hierarch of Rak Urga. "It's going to have to wait, Agachak," he said finally. "I'm getting married next month."

"This is a command of the Church, Urgit."

"Wonderful. Give the Church my regards."

Agachak looked taken a bit aback. "You don't believe in anything now, do you, my King?"

"Not very much, no. Is this sick world we live in ready for atheism yet?"

For the first time in his life, Urgit saw doubt on the face of the Hierarch. "Atheism's a clean place, Agachak," he said, "a flat, gray, empty place where man makes his own destiny, and let the Gods go hang. I didn't make them; they didn't make me; and we're quits on all of that. I wish them well, though."

"This is unlike you, Urgit," Agachak said.

"No, not really. I'm just tired of playing the clown." He stretched out his leg and tossed his crown at his foot like a hoop. He caught it and kicked it back again. "You don't really understand, do you, Agachak?" he said as he caught the crown out of midair.

The Hierarch of Rak Urga drew himself up. "This is not a request, Urgit. I'm not *asking* you."

"Good. Because I'm not going."

"I *command* you to go."

"I don't think so."

"Do you realize to whom you're talking?"

"Perfectly, old boy. You're the same tiresome old Grolim who's been boring me to tears ever since I inherited the throne from that fellow who used to chew on the carpets back in Rak Goska. Listen carefully, Agachak. I'll use short words and simple sentences so that I don't confuse you. I am *not* going to Mallorea. I've never had any intention of going to Mallorea. There's nothing I want to see in Mallorea. There's nothing I want to do there. I most definitely do not intend to put myself anywhere near Kal Zakath, and he's gone back to Mal Zeth. Not only that, they have demons in Mallorea. Have you ever seen a demon, Agachak?"

"Once or twice," the Hierarch replied sullenly.

"And you're *still* going to Mallorea? Agachak, you're as crazy as Taur Urgas was."

"I can make you king of all of Angarak."

"I don't *want* to be king of all of Angarak. I don't even want to be King of Cthol Murgos. All I want is to be left alone to contemplate the horror that's about to descend on me."

"Your marriage, you mean?" Agachak's face grew sly. "You could evade that by coming to Mallorea with me."

"Have I been going too fast for you, Agachak? A wife is bad enough. Demons are much worse. Did anybody ever tell you what that thing did to Chabat?" Urgit shuddered.

"I can protect you."

Urgit laughed scornfully. "You, Agachak? You couldn't even protect yourself. Even Polgara had to have help from a God to deal with that monster. Do you plan to resurrect Torak to give you a hand? Or maybe you could appeal to Aldur. He's the one who helped Polgara. I don't really think He'd like you, though. *I* don't even like you, and I've known you all my life."

"You go too far, Urgit."

"No. Not far enough, Agachak. For centuries—eons, probably—you Grolims have held the upper hand in Cthol Murgos, but that was when Ctuchik was still alive, and Ctuchik is dead now. You did know about that, didn't you, old boy? He tried his hand against Belgarath, and Belgarath disassembled him right down to the floor. I may be the only Murgo alive who's ever met Belgarath and lived to talk about it. We're actually on fairly good terms. Would you like to meet him? I could probably arrange an introduction, if you'd like."

Agachak visibly shrank back.

"Much better, Agachak," Urgit said smoothly. "I'm delighted at your grasp of the realities of the situation. Now, I'm certain that you can raise your hand and wiggle your fingers at me, but now I know how to recognize that sort of thing. I watched Belgarion rather closely while we were trotting across Cthaka last winter. If your hand moves even a fraction of an inch, you're going to get about a bushel basket full of arrows right in the middle of the back. The archers are already in place, and their bows are already drawn. Give it some thought, Agachak—while you're leaving."

"This is not like you, Urgit," Agachak said, his nostrils white with fury.

"I know. Delightful, isn't it? You may go now, Agachak."

The Hierarch spun on his heel and started toward the door.

"Oh, by the way, old boy," Urgit added. "I've had news that our dear brother Gethel of Thulldom recently died—probably something he ate. Thulls eat almost anything that swims, flies, crawls, or spawns on rotten meat. It's a pity, actually. Gethel was one of the few people in the world I could bully. Anyway, he's been succeeded on the throne by his half-wit son, Nathel. I've met Nathel. He has the mentality of an earthworm, but he's a true Angarak king. Why don't you see if *he* wants to go to Mallorea with you? It might take you a while to explain to him where Mallorea is, since I think he believes that the world is flat, but I have every confidence in you, Agachak." Urgit flipped his hand at the fuming Hierarch. "Run along now," he said. "Go back to your temple and gut a few more Grolims. Maybe you can even get the fires started in your sanctum again. If nothing else, I'm sure it will calm your nerves."

Agachak stormed out, slamming the door behind him.

Urgit doubled over, pounding on the arm of his throne and howling in glee.

"Don't you think you might have gone just a bit too far, my son?" Lady Tamazin asked from the shadowy alcove where she had been listening.

"Perhaps so, mother," he agreed, still laughing, "but wasn't it fun?"

She limped into the light and smiled fondly at him. "Yes, Urgit," she agreed, "it was, but don't push Agachak too far. He can be a dangerous enemy."

"I've got lots of enemies, mother," Urgit said, tugging unconsciously at his long, pointed nose. "Most of the people in the world hate me, but I've learned to live with that. It's not as if I had to run for reelection, you know."

The bleak-faced seneschal, Oskatat, also came out of the shadowed alcove. "What are we going to do with you, Urgit?" he said wryly. "What did Belgarion teach you, anyway?"

"He taught me how to be a king, Oskatat. I may not last very long, but by the Gods, as long as I'm here, I'm going to *be* a king. They're going to kill me anyway, so I might as well enjoy myself while I can."

His mother sighed, then raised her hands helplessly. "There's no reasoning with him, Oskatat," she said.

"I suppose not, my Lady Tamazin," the gray-haired man agreed.

"Princess Prala wants to speak with you," Tamazin said to her son.

"I am at her immediate disposal," Urgit said. "Not only immediate, but perpetual, if I understand the terms of the marriage contract."

"Be nice," Tamazin chided.

"Yes, mother."

The Princess Prala of the House of Cthan swept in through a side door. She wore a riding habit consisting of a calf-length black skirt, a white satin blouse and polished boots. Her heels hit the marble floor like little hammers. Her long black hair swayed at her back, and her eyes were dangerous. She held a parchment scroll in her hands.

"Will you assist me, my Lord Oskatat?" Lady Tamazin asked, holding one hand out to the seneschal.

"Of course, my Lady," he replied, offering his arm to Urgit's mother with tender solicitude. The two of them withdrew.

"Now what?" Urgit warily asked his bride-to-be.

"Am I disturbing your Majesty?" Prala asked. She did not bother to curtsy. The princess had changed. She was no longer a properly submissive Murgo lady. The time she had spent with Queen Ce'Nedra and the Margravine Liselle had definitely corrupted her, Urgit felt, and the unwholesome influence of Polgara the sorceress showed in her every move and gesture. She was, however, Urgit concluded, absolutely adorable now. Her black eyes flashed, her delicate white skin seemed to reflect her mood, and her wealth of black hair seemed almost alive as it flowed down her back. Rather surprisingly, Urgit found that he was very fond of her.

"You always disturb me, my beloved," he answered her question, spreading his arms extravagantly.

"Stop that," she snapped. "You sound like your brother."

"It runs in the family."

"Did you put this in here?" she demanded, waving the scroll at him like a club.

"Did I put what in where?"

"This." She unrolled the scroll. " 'It is agreed that Princess Prala of the House of Cthan shall be his majesty's most favored wife,' " she read. "Most favored wife" came out from between clenched teeth.

"What's wrong with that?" he asked, a little surprised at the girl's vehemence.

"The implication is that there will be others."

"It's the custom, Prala. I didn't make the rules."

"You're the king. Make different rules."

"Me?" He swallowed hard.

"There will *be* no other wives, Urgit—or royal concubines." Her usually gentle voice seemed to crackle. "You are *mine,* and I'm not going to share you with anybody."

"Do you really feel that way?" he asked, a bit amazed.

"Yes, I do." She lifted her chin.

"Nobody's ever felt that way about me before."

"Get used to it." Her voice was flat and had the overtone of daggers in it.

"We'll amend the passage," he agreed quickly. "I don't need more than one wife anyway."

"Definitely not, my Lord. A very wise decision."

"Naturally. All royal decisions are wise. It says so in the history books."

She tried very hard not to smile, but finally gave up, laughed, and hurled herself into his arms. "Oh, Urgit," she said burrowing her face into his neck, "I do love you."

"You do? What an amazing thing." Suddenly an idea came to him, and its sheer purity almost blinded him. "What's your feeling about a double wedding, love?" he asked her.

She pulled her face back from where she had been grazing on his neck. "I don't quite follow you," she admitted.

"I'm the king, right?"

"A little more than you were before you met Belgarion," she admitted.

He let that pass. "I've got this female relative," he said. "I'm going to be busy being married."

"*Very* busy, my love," she agreed.

He coughed nervously. "Anyway," he rushed on. "I'm not really going to have all that much time to look after this certain female relative, am I? Wouldn't it be better if I married her off to some deserving fellow who's always held her in the highest regard?"

"I don't quite follow you, Urgit. I didn't think you had any female relatives."

"Only one, my princess," he grinned. "Only one."

She stared at him. "Urgit!" she gasped.

He gave her a rat-faced little grin. "I'm the king," he said grandly. "I can do anything I want to do, and my mother's been alone for far too long, wouldn't you say? Oskatat's loved her since she was a girl, and she's at least fond of him—although I think it might go a little farther than that. If I order them to get married, they'd have to do it, wouldn't they?"

"That's absolutely brilliant, Urgit," she marveled.

"It comes from my Drasnian heritage," he admitted modestly. "Kheldar himself couldn't have come up with a neater scheme."

"It's perfect," she almost squealed. "This way I won't have a mother-in-law interfering when I start changing you."

"Changing?"

"Just a few little things, love," she said sweetly. "You have a few bad habits, and your taste in clothing is terrible. Whatever possessed you to start wearing purple?"

"Anything else?"

"I'll bring the list with me next time I visit."

Urgit began to have second thoughts at that point.

His Imperial Majesty, Kal Zakath of Mallorea, had a busy morning that day. Most of the time, he was closeted with Brador, Chief of the Bureau of Internal Affairs, in a small, blue-draped office on the second floor of the palace.

"It's definitely subsiding, your Majesty," Brador reported when the subject of the plague came up. "There hasn't been a new case in the past week, and a surprising number of people are actually recovering. The plan of walling off each separate district of the city seems to have worked."

"Good," 'Zakath said. He turned to another matter. "Is there any further word out of Karanda?"

Brador shuffled through the papers he was holding. "Mengha hasn't been seen for several weeks now, your Majesty." The Chief of the Bureau of Internal Affairs smiled briefly. "That particular plague also seems to be subsiding. The demons appear to have left, and the fanatics are losing heart." He tapped one of the papers against his pursed lips. "This is only an educated guess, your Majesty, since I can't get any agents into the region, but the turmoil appears to have shifted to the east coast. Shortly after Mengha disappeared, large bodies of Karandese irregular troops, along with Urvon's Temple Guardsmen and his Chandim, crossed the Mountains of Zamad, and all communications out of Voresebo and Rengel have broken down."

"Urvon?" 'Zakath asked.

"It appears so, your Majesty. I'd say that the Disciple is moving into position for a final confrontation with Zandramas. One is tempted to suggest that we just let them fight it out. I don't think that the world would miss either of them very much."

A faint, icy smile touched 'Zakath's lips. "You're right, Brador," he said. "It *is* tempting, but I don't think we should encourage that sort of thing—just as a matter of policy. Those principalities are a part of the empire and they're entitled to imperial protection. It might start some ugly rumors if we were to just stand idly by and let Urvon and Zandramas rip up the countryside. If anybody brings military force to bear in Mallorea, it's going to be me." He leafed through the papers on the table in front of him, picked one up, and frowned at it. "I suppose we'd better deal with this," he said. "Where have you got Baron Vasca?"

"He's in a cell with a splendid view," Brador replied. "He can look out at the executioner's block. I'm sure it's been most educational."

'Zakath remembered something then. "Demote him," he said.

"That's a novel word for the procedure," Brador murmured.

"That's not exactly what I meant," 'Zakath said with another chill smile. "Persuade him to tell us where he hid all the money he extorted from the people he dealt with. We'll transfer the funds to the imperial treasury." He turned to look at the large map on the wall of his study. "Southern Ebal, I think."

"Your Majesty?" Brador looked puzzled.

"Assign him to the post of Minister of Trade in southern Ebal."

"There isn't any trade in southern Ebal, your Majesty. There aren't any seaports, and the only thing they raise in the Temba marshes is mosquitoes."

"Vasca's inventive. I'm sure he'll come up with something."

"Then you don't want him—" Brador made a suggestive gesture across his throat with one hand.

"No," 'Zakath said. "I'm going to try something Belgarion suggested. I may need Vasca again someday and I don't want to have to dig him up in pieces." A faintly pained look crossed the Emperor's face. "Has there been any word about him?" he asked.

"Vasca? I just—"

"No. Belgarion."

"They were seen shortly after they left Mal Zeth, your Majesty. They were traveling with Prince Kheldar's Nadrak partner, Yarblek. Not long after that, Yarblek sailed for Gar og Nadrak."

"It was all a ruse, then," 'Zakath sighed. "All Belgarion really wanted was to get back to his own country. That wild story of theirs was made up out of whole cloth."

'Zakath passed a weary hand before his eyes. "I really liked that young man, Brador," he said sadly. "I should have known better."

"Belgarion didn't go back to the West, your Majesty," Brador informed him, "at least not with Yarblek. We always check that fellow's ships rather closely. So far as we're able to determine, Belgarion has not left Mallorea."

'Zakath leaned back with a genuine smile on his face. "I'm not sure why, but that makes me feel better. The thought that he'd betrayed me was quite painful for some reason. Any idea about where he's gone?"

"There was some turmoil in Katakor, your Majesty—up around Ashaba. It was the sort of thing one might associate with Belgarion—strange lights in the sky, explosions, that sort of thing."

'Zakath laughed out loud, a delighted kind of laugh. "He *can* be a little ostentatious when he's irritated, can't he? He blew the whole wall out of my bedchamber in Rak Hagga one time."

"Oh?"

"He was trying to make a point."

There was a respectful rap on the door.

"Come," 'Zakath replied shortly.

"General Atesca has arrived, your Majesty," one of the red-garbed guards at the door reported.

"Good. Send him in."

The broken-nosed general entered and saluted smartly. "Your Majesty," he said. His red uniform was travel-stained.

"You made good time, Atesca," 'Zakath said. "It's good to see you again."

"Thank you, your Majesty. We had a good following wind, and the sea was calm."

"How many men did you bring with you?"

"About fifty thousand."

"How many men do we have now?" 'Zakath asked Brador.

"Something in excess of a million, your Majesty."

"That's a solid number. Let's stage up the troops and get ready to move." He rose and went to the window. The leaves had begun to turn, filling the garden below with bright reds and yellows. "I want to quiet things down on the east coast," he said, "and it's turning into autumn now, so I think we want to move the troops before the weather starts to deteriorate. We'll go on down to Maga Renn and send out scouting parties from there. If the circumstances are right, we'll march. If not, we can wait at Maga Renn for more troops to come back from Cthol Murgos."

"I'll get started on that immediately, your Majesty." Brador bowed and quietly left the room.

"Sit down, Atesca," the Emperor said. "What's happening in Cthol Murgos?"

"We're going to try to hold the cities we've already taken, your Majesty," Atesca reported, drawing up a chair. "We've gathered the bulk of our forces near Rak Cthan. They're waiting there for transport to bring them back to Mallorea."

"Any chance that Urgit might try a counterattack?"

"I wouldn't think so, your Majesty. I don't believe he'll gamble his army in open country. Of course, you never know what a Murgo might do."

"That's true," 'Zakath agreed. He kept his knowledge that Urgit was not actually a Murgo to himself. He leaned back. "You captured Belgarion for me once, Atesca," he said.

"Yes, your Majesty."

"I'm afraid you're going to have to do it again. He managed to get away. Careless of me, I suppose, but I had a lot on my mind at the time."

"We'll just have to pick him up again then, won't we, your Majesty?"

The Alorn Council met at Boktor that year. Somewhat uncharacteristically, Queen Porenn took charge. The tiny blond queen of Drasnia, dressed in her usual black, walked quietly to the head of the table in the red-draped council chamber in the palace and took the chair normally reserved for the Rivan King. The others stared at her in astonishment.

"Gentlemen," she began crisply, "I recognize the fact that this flies in the face of tradition, but our time is limited. Certain information has come to me that I think you should be made aware of. We have decisions to make and very little time in which to make them."

Emperor Varana leaned back in his chair with an amused twinkle in his eyes. "We will now pause while the Alorn kings go into collective apoplexy," he said.

King Anheg scowled at the curly-haired emperor for a moment, then laughed. "No, Varana," he said wryly. "We all got that out of our systems when Rhodar persuaded us to follow Ce'Nedra into Mishrak ac Thull. It's Porenn's house; let her run things."

"Why, thank you, Anheg." The Queen of Drasnia actually sounded a little surprised. She paused, gathering her thoughts. "As I'm sure you've noticed, our gathering this year includes kings who would not normally attend. The matter before us, however, concerns us all. I've recently received communications from Belgarath, Belgarion, and the others."

There was an excited stir in the room. Porenn held up one hand. "They're in Mallorea, close on the trail of the abductor of Belgarion's son."

"That young man can move faster than the wind sometimes," King Fulrach of Sendaria observed. The years had given Fulrach a tendency toward portliness, and his brown beard was now streaked with silver.

"How did they get to Mallorea?" King Cho-Hag asked in his quiet voice.

"It seems that they were captured by Kal Zakath," Porenn replied. "Garion and 'Zakath became friends, and 'Zakath took them with him when he returned to Mal Zeth."

" 'Zakath actually became *friends* with somebody?" King Drosta of Gar og Nadrak demanded incredulously in his shrill voice. "Impossible!"

"Garion has a way about him, sometimes," Hettar murmured.

"The friendship, however, may have run its course," Porenn continued. "Late one night, Garion and his friends slipped out of Mal Zeth without saying good-bye to the Emperor."

"With the whole imperial army on their trail, I'd imagine," Varana added.

"No," Porenn disagreed. " 'Zakath can't leave Mal Zeth just now. Tell them, Yarblek."

Silk's rangy partner rose to his feet. "They've got plague in Mal Zeth," he said. " 'Zakath has sealed up the city. No one can go in or out."

"Prithee," Mandorallen asked, "how then was it possible for our friends to make good their escape?"

"I'd picked up an itinerant comedian," Yarblek said sourly. "I didn't think much of him, but he amused Vella. She's fond of bawdy stories."

"Be careful, Yarblek," the Nadrak dancer warned. "You still have your health, but I can fix that for you." She put one hand suggestively on a dagger hilt. Vella wore a stunning lavender gown. There were a few concessions to Nadrak customs in her dress, however. She still wore polished leather boots—with daggers in their tops—and the customary wide leather belt about her waist was still adorned with similar knives. The men in the room, however, had all been surreptitiously eyeing her since she had entered. No matter how she was dressed, Vella still had the power to attract every eye.

"Anyway," Yarblek hurried on, "the fellow knew of a tunnel that runs from the palace to an abandoned quarry outside the city. It got us all out of Mal Zeth with no one the wiser."

" 'Zakath won't like that," Drosta said. "He hates to let people go once he's caught them."

"There's been an uprising of some sort in the Seven Kingdoms of Karanda in northern Mallorea," Porenn went on. "I understand that there are demons involved."

"Demons?" Varana said skeptically. "Oh, come now, Porenn."

"That's what Belgarath reports."

"Belgarath has a warped sense of humor, sometimes," Varana scoffed. "He was probably just joking. There's no such thing as a demon."

"You're wrong, Varana," King Drosta said with uncharacteristic soberness. "I saw one once—up in Morindland when I was a boy."

"What did it look like?" Varana did not sound convinced.

Drosta shuddered. "You really don't want to know."

"At any rate," Porenn said, " 'Zakath has ordered the bulk of his army back from Cthol Murgos to put down this uprising. It won't be very long until he floods the entirety of Karanda with troops, and that's the area where our friends are. That's why I've called this meeting. What are we going to do about it?"

Lelldorin of Wildantor came to his feet. "We'll need fast horses," he said to Hettar.

"Why?" Hettar asked.

"To get to their aid, of course." The young Asturian's eyes were flashing with excitement.

"Uh—Lelldorin," Barak said gently, "the Sea of the East is between here and Mallorea."

"Oh," Lelldorin said, looking slightly abashed. "I didn't know that. We'll need a boat, too, won't we?"

Barak and Hettar exchanged a long look. "Ship," Barak corrected absently.

"What?"

"Never mind, Lelldorin," Barak sighed.

"We can't," King Anheg said flatly. "Even if we could get through, we'd destroy Garion's chances of winning in the fight with the Child of Dark. That's what the Seeress told us at Rheon, remember?"

"But this is different," Lelldorin protested, tears standing in his eyes.

"No," Anheg said. "It's not. This is exactly what we were warned against. We can't go near them until this is over."

"But—"

"Lelldorin," Anheg said. "I want to go as much as you do, but we can't. Would Garion thank us if we were responsible for the loss of his son?"

Mandorallen rose to his feet and began to pace up and down, his armor clinking. "Methinks thy reasoning is aright, your Majesty," he said to Anheg. "We may not join with our friends, lest our presence imperil their quest, and we would all give up our lives to prevent that. We *may*, however, journey straightaway to Mallorea and, without going near them, place ourselves between them and the hordes of Kal Zakath. We can thereby bring the unfriendly advance of the Malloreans to a precipitous halt and thus allow Garion to escape."

Barak stared at the great knight, whose face shone with unthinking zeal. Then he groaned and buried his face in his hands.

"There, there," Hettar murmured, patting the big man sympathetically on the shoulder.

King Fulrach rubbed at his beard. "Why does it seem that we've done this before?" he asked. "It's the same as last time. We have to create a diversion to help our friends get through. Any ideas?"

"Invade Mallorea," Drosta said eagerly.

"Sack 'Zakath's coastline," Anheg said just as eagerly.

Porenn sighed.

"We could invade Cthol Murgos," Cho-Hag suggested thoughtfully.

"Yes!" Hettar agreed fiercely.

Cho-Hag held up his hand. "Only as a ruse, my son," he said. " 'Zakath has committed forces to the conquest of Cthol Murgos. If the armies of the West moved into that region, he'd almost be obliged to try to counter us, wouldn't he?"

Varana slid lower in his chair. "It's got possibilities," he admitted, "but it's already autumn, and the mountains of Cthol Murgos are brutal in the winter. It's a bad time to move troops around down there. An army can't move very fast on frozen feet. I think we might be able to accomplish the same thing by diplomacy—without risking a single toe."

"Trust a Tolnedran to be devious," Anheg growled.

"Do you *like* freezing, Anheg?" Varana asked.

Anheg shrugged. "It's something to do in the wintertime," he said.

Varana rolled his eyes ceilingward. "Alorns," he said.

"All right," Anheg said by way of apology. "I was only joking. What's this brilliantly devious plan of yours?"

Varana looked across the room at Javelin. "How good is the Mallorean intelligence service, Margrave Khendon?" he asked bluntly.

Javelin rose to his feet, straightening his pearl-gray doublet. "By himself, Brador is very good, your Imperial Majesty," he replied. "His people are sometimes awkward and obvious, but he has a lot of them. He has unlimited money to work with." He cast a slightly reproachful glance at Queen Porenn.

"Be nice, Khendon," she murmured. "I'm on a tight budget."

"Yes, ma'am." He bowed with a faint smile, then straightened and spoke in a crisp, businesslike manner. "Mallorean intelligence is crude by our standards, but Brador has the resources to put as many agents in the field as he needs. Neither Drasnian nor Tolnedran intelligence has that luxury. Brador sometimes loses a hundred people in the process, but he can usually get the information." He sniffed disdainfully. "I prefer a neater type of operation, personally."

"Then this Brador has operatives in Rak Urga?" Varana pressed.

"Almost certainly," Javelin replied. "I have four in the Drojim Palace at this time myself—and your Majesty's service has two that I know of."

"I didn't know that," Varana said with an innocent look.

"Really?"

Varana laughed. "All right," he went on, "what would 'Zakath do if word reached Mal Zeth that the Kingdoms of the West were about to conclude a military alliance with the King of Murgodom?"

Javelin began to pace up and down. "It's very hard to know exactly what 'Zakath will do in any given situation," he mused. "A lot depends on just how serious his domestic problems are, but an alliance between the Murgos and the West would pose a major threat to Mallorea. He'd almost have to come back immediately and make an all-out effort to crush the Murgos before our troops could reinforce them."

"Ally ourselves with the Murgos?" Hettar exclaimed. "Never!"

"Nobody's suggesting a real alliance, my Lord Hettar," Kail, the son of the Rivan Warder, told him. "All we want to do is distract 'Zakath for long enough to give Belgarion the time to slip past him. The negotiations can drag on and then fall apart later on."

"Oh," Hettar said, looking a bit abashed, "that's different, then—I suppose."

"All right," Varana went on crisply. "Perhaps we can persuade 'Zakath that we're about to conclude an alliance with Urgit—if we do it right. Javelin, have your people kill a few Mallorean agents in the Drojim Palace—not all of them, mind you—just enough to convince Mal Zeth that this is a serious diplomatic effort."

"I understand perfectly, your Majesty." Javelin smiled. "I have just the man—a recently recruited Nyissan assassin named Issus."

"Good. A possible alliance will serve the same purpose as a real one. We can distract 'Zakath without the loss of a single man—unless we count this Issus fellow."

"Don't worry about Issus, your Majesty," Javelin assured him. "He's a survivor."

"I think we're missing something," Anheg growled. "I wish Rhodar were here."

"Yes," Porenn agreed in a voice near to tears.

"Sorry, Porenn," Anheg said, engulfing her tiny hand in his huge one, "but you know what I mean."

"I have a diplomat in Rak Urga," Varana continued. "He can make the overtures to King Urgit. Do we know anything useful about the King of the Murgos?"

"Yes," Porenn said firmly. "He'll be amenable to the suggestion."

"How do you know, your Majesty?"

Porenn hesitated. "I'd rather not say," she said with a quick glance at Javelin. "Just take my word for it."

"Of course," Varana agreed.

Vella rose and walked to the window, her satin gown filling the room with its music. "You people of the West always want to complicate things," she said critically. " 'Zakath's your problem. Send somebody to Mal Zeth with a sharp knife."

"You should have been a man, Vella." Anheg laughed. She turned and looked at him with smoldering eyes. "Do you really think so?" she asked.

"Well," he hesitated, "maybe not."

She leaned disconsolately against the window casing. "I wish I had my juggler here to entertain me," she said. "Politics always give me a headache." She sighed. "I wonder whatever happened to him."

Porenn smiled, watching the girl intently and remembering the sudden insight she had when the Nadrak girl first arrived in Boktor. "Would you be terribly disappointed to find out that your juggler was not who he seemed to be?" she asked. "Belgarath mentioned him in his letter."

Vella looked at her sharply.

"Belgarath would have known him, of course," Porenn went on. "It was Beldin."

Vella's eyes went wide. "The hunchbacked sorcerer?" she exclaimed. "The one who can fly?"

Porenn nodded.

Vella said a number of things that no genteel lady would have said. Even King Anheg turned slightly pale at her choice of language. Then she drew a dagger and advanced on Yarblek, her breath hissing between her teeth. Mandorallen, clad all in steel, stepped in front of her, and Hettar and Barak seized her from behind and wrested the knife from her grasp.

"You idiot!" she shrieked at the cringing Yarblek. "You absolute idiot! You could have sold me to him!" Then she collapsed weeping against Barak's fur-clad chest, even as Hettar prudently relieved her of her other three daggers.

Zandramas, the Child of Dark, stood gazing across a desolate valley where shattered villages smoked and smoldered under a lead-gray sky. The eyes of the Child of Dark were hooded, and she looked unseeing at the devastation spread before her. A lusty wail came from behind her, and she set her teeth together. "Feed him," she said shortly.

"As you command, mistress," the man with white eyes said quickly in a mollifying tone.

"Don't patronize me, Naradas," she snapped. "Just shut the brat up. I'm trying to think."

It had been a long time. Zandramas had worked everything out so very carefully. Now she had come half around the world, and, despite her best efforts, the Godslayer with his dreadful sword was but a few days behind her.

The sword. The flaming sword. It filled her sleep with nightmares—and the burning face of the Child of Light terrified her even more. "How *does* he stay so close behind?" she exploded. "Will nothing slow him?"

She thrust her hands out in front of her and turned them palms-up. A myriad of tiny points of light seemed to swirl beneath the skin of her hands—swirling, glittering like a constellation of minuscule stars spinning in her very flesh. How long would it be until those constellations invaded her entire body and she ceased even to be human? How long until the dreadful spirit of the Child of Dark possessed her utterly? The child wailed again.

"I told you to shut him up!" she half shouted.

"At once, mistress," Naradas said.

The Child of Dark went back to the contemplation of the starry universe enclosed in her flesh.

Eriond and Horse rode out at the first light before the others had awakened, cantering across a mountain meadow in the silvery dawn-light. It was good to ride alone, to feel the surge and flow of Horse's muscles under him and the wind against his face without the distraction of talk.

He reined in atop a knoll to watch the sun rise, and that was good, too. He looked out over the sun-touched mountains of Zamad, drinking in the beauty and solitude, then gazed at the fair sight of the bright green fields and forests. Life was good here. The world was filled with loveliness and with people he loved.

How could Aldur have forced Himself to leave all this? Aldur had been the God who must have loved this world above all things, since He had refused to take a people to worship Him, but had chosen to spend His time alone to study this fair world. And now He could only visit occasionally in spiritual form.

But Aldur had accepted the sacrifice. Eriond sighed, feeling that perhaps no sacrifice could be truly unbearable if it were made out of love. Eriond took comfort in that belief.

Then he sighed again and slowly rode back toward the little lake and the cluster of tents where the others slept.

CHAPTER TWO

They rose late that morning. The turmoil of the past several weeks seemed finally to have caught up with Garion, and, even though he could tell by the light streaming in through the front of the tent that the sun was already high, he was reluctant to move. He could hear the clinking of Polgara's cooking utensils and the murmur of voices. He knew that he was going to have to get up soon anyway. He considered trying to doze off to catch a last few moments of sleep, but he decided against it. He moved carefully to avoid waking Ce'Nedra as he slid out from under their blankets. He leaned over and gently kissed her hair, then he pulled on his rust-colored tunic, picked up his boots and sword, and ducked out of the tent.

Polgara, in her gray traveling dress, was by her cook-fire. As usual, she hummed softly as she worked. Silk and Belgarath were talking quietly nearby. Silk had, for some reason, changed clothes and he now wore the soft, pearl-gray doublet which marked him as a prosperous businessman. Belgarath, of course, still wore his rust-colored tunic, patched hose, and mismatched boots. Durnik and Toth were fishing, lacing the blue surface of the little mountain lake with their lines, and Eriond was brushing the gleaming chestnut coat of his stallion. The rest of their friends had apparently not arisen yet.

"We thought you were going to sleep all day," Belgarath said as Garion sat on a log to pull on his boots.

"I gave it some thought," Garion admitted. He stood up and looked across the sparkling lake. There was a grove of aspens on the far side, their trunks the color of new snow. The leaves had begun to turn and they shimmered in the morning sun like beaten gold. The air was cool and slightly damp. Suddenly he wished that they could stay here for a few days. He sighed and walked over to join his grandfather and Silk near the fire. "Why the fancy clothes?" he asked the rat-faced little Drasnian.

Silk shrugged. "We're moving into an area where I'm fairly well known," he replied. "We might be able to take advantage of that—as long as people recognize me. Are you absolutely sure the trail goes toward the southeast?"

Garion nodded. "There was a little confusion right at first, but I got it sorted out."

"Confusion?" Belgarath asked.

"The Sardion was here, too—a long time ago. For a few moments, the Orb seemed to want to follow both trails at the same time. I had to speak with it rather firmly about that." Garion draped the sword belt over his shoulder and buckled it. Then he shifted the scabbard slightly until it was more comfortable. The Orb on the pommel of the sword was glowing a sullen red color.

"Why's it doing that?" Silk asked curiously.

"Because of the Sardion," Garion told him. He looked over his shoulder at the glowing stone. "Stop that," he said.

"Don't hurt its feelings," Silk warned. "We could be in a great deal of trouble if it decides to start sulking."

"What lies off to the southeast?" Belgarath asked the little man.

"Voresebo," Silk replied. "There isn't much there except some caravan tracks and a few mines up in the mountains. There's a seaport at Pannor. I land there sometimes on my way back from Melcena."

"Are the people there Karands?"

Silk nodded. "But they're even cruder than the ones back in the central kingdoms—if that's possible."

The blue-banded hawk came spiraling out of a bright morning sky, flared, and shimmered into the form of Beldin as soon as the talons touched the ground. The hunchbacked little sorcerer was dressed in his usual rags tied on with bits of thong, and twigs and straw clung to his hair and beard. He shivered. "I *hate* to fly when it's cold," he grumbled. "It makes my wings ache."

"It's not really that cold," Silk said.

"Try it a couple thousand feet up." Beldin pointed toward the sky, then turned, and spat out a couple of soggy gray feathers.

"Grazing again, uncle?" Polgara asked from her cook-fire.

"Just a bite of breakfast, Pol," he replied. "There was a pigeon that got up too early this morning."

"You didn't have to do that, you know." She tapped meaningfully on the side of her bubbling pot with a long-handled wooden spoon.

Beldin shrugged. "The world isn't going to miss one pigeon."

Garion shuddered. "How can you stand to eat them raw like that?"

"You get used to it. I've never had much luck trying to build a cook-fire with my talons." He looked at Belgarath. "There's some trouble up ahead," he said, "a lot of smoke and groups of armed men wandering around."

"Could you see who they were?"

"I didn't get that close. There's usually a bored archer or two in any crowd like that, and I'd prefer not to have my tail feathers parted with an arrow just because some idiot wants to show off his skill."

"Has that ever happened?" Silk asked curiously.

"Once—a long time ago. My hip still aches in cold weather."

"Did you do something about it?"

"I had a chat with the archer. I asked him not to do it any more. He was breaking his bow across his knee when I left." He turned back to Belgarath. "Are we sure the trail goes on down to that plain?"

"The Orb is."

"Then we'll have to chance it." The little man looked around. "I thought you'd have struck the tents by now."

"I decided it might not hurt to let everybody get some sleep. We've been traveling hard and we're going to have to do it some more, I think."

"You always want to pick these idyllic spots for your rest stops, Belgarath," Beldin observed. "I think you're secretly a romantic."

Belgarath shrugged. "Nobody's perfect."

"Garion," Polgara called.

"Yes, Aunt Pol?"

"Why don't you wake the others? Breakfast's almost ready."

"Right away, Aunt Pol."

After breakfast, they broke camp and started out about midmorning with Beldin flying on ahead to scout out possible trouble. It was pleasantly warm now, and there was the pungent smell of evergreens in the air. Ce'Nedra was strangely quiet as she rode along beside Garion with her dark gray cloak pulled tightly around her.

"What's the matter, dear?" he asked her.

"She didn't have Geran with her," the little queen murmured sadly.

"Zandramas, you mean? No, she didn't, did she?"

"Was she really there, Garion?"

"In a way, but in a way she wasn't. It was sort of the way Cyradis was here and not here at the same time."

"I don't understand."

"It was more than a projection, but less than actually being there. We talked it over last night, and Beldin explained it. I didn't understand very much of what he said. Beldin's explanations get a little obscure sometimes."

"He's very wise, isn't he?"

Garion nodded. "But he's not a very good teacher. He gets impatient with people who can't keep up with him. Anyway, this business of being somewhere between a projection and the real thing makes Zandramas very dangerous. We can't hurt her, but she can hurt us. She came very close to killing you yesterday, you know—until Poledra stopped her. She's very much afraid of Poledra."

"That's the first time I've ever seen your grandmother."

"No, actually it's not. She was there at Aunt Pol's wedding, remember? And she helped us in Ulgoland when we had to fight the Eldrak."

"But one time she was an owl, and the other time she was a wolf."

"In Poledra's case, I don't think that really matters."

Ce'Nedra suddenly laughed.

"What's so funny?"

"When this is all over and we're back home with our baby, why don't you change into a wolf for a while?" she suggested.

"Why?"

"It might be nice having a big gray wolf lying before the fire. And then on cold nights, I could burrow my feet into your fur to keep them warm."

He gave her a long steady look.

"I'd scratch your ears for you, Garion," she offered by way of inducement, "and get you nice bones from the kitchen to chew on."

"Never mind," he said flatly.

"But my feet get cold."

"I've noticed."

Just ahead of them as they rode up through a shady mountain pass, Silk and Sadi were engaged in a heated discussion. "Absolutely not," Silk said vehemently.

"I really think you're being unreasonable about this, Kheldar," Sadi protested. The eunuch had discarded his iridescent silk robe and now wore western-style tunic and hose and stout boots. "You have the distribution system already in place, and I have access to unlimited supplies. We could make millions."

"Forget it, Sadi. I won't deal in drugs."

"You deal in everything else, Kheldar. There's a market out there just waiting to be tapped. Why let scruples stand in the way of business?"

"You're Nyissan, Sadi. Drugs are a part of your culture, so you wouldn't understand."

"Lady Polgara uses drugs when she treats the sick," Sadi pointed out defensively.

"That's different."

"I don't see how."

"I could never explain it to you."

Sadi sighed. "I'm very disappointed in you, Kheldar. You're a spy, an assassin, and a thief. You cheat at dice, you counterfeit money, and you're unscrupulous with married women. You swindle your customers outrageously and you soak up ale like a sponge. You're the most corrupt man I've ever known, but you refuse to transport a few harmless little compounds that would make your customers very happy."

"A man has to draw the line somewhere," Silk replied loftily.

Velvet shifted in her saddle to look back at them. "That was one of the more fascinating conversations I've ever heard, gentlemen," she complimented them. "The implications in the field of comparative morality are absolutely staggering." She gave them a sunny smile with her dimples flashing into view.

"Uh—Margravine Liselle," Sadi said. "Do you happen to have Zith again?"

"Why, yes, Sadi, as a matter of fact, I do." The honey-blond girl held up one hand to head off his objections. "*But* I didn't steal her this time. She crawled into my tent in the middle of the night and crept into her favorite hiding place all on her own. The poor dear was actually shivering."

Silk turned slightly pale.

"Would you like to have her back?" Velvet asked the shaved-headed eunuch.

"No," Sadi sighed, rubbing his hand over his scalp, "I suppose not. As long as she's happy where she is, we might as well leave her there."

"She's very happy. In fact, she's purring." Velvet frowned slightly. "I think you should watch her diet just a bit, Sadi," she said critically. "Her little tummy seems to be getting bigger." She smiled again. "We wouldn't want a fat snake on our hands, would we?"

"Well, excuse me!" Sadi said, sounding very offended.

There was a large snag at the top of the pass, and the blue-banded hawk perched on a dead limb, busily preening his feathers with his hooked beak. As they approached, he swooped down, and Beldin stood in the trail in front of them, muttering curses.

"Something wrong, uncle?" Polgara asked him.

"I got caught in a crosswind," he growled. "It scrambled my feathers a bit. You know how that goes."

"Oh, goodness yes. It happens to me all the time. Night breezes are so unpredictable."

"Your feathers are too soft."

"I didn't design the owl, uncle, so don't blame me about the feathers."

"There's a crossroads tavern just up ahead," Beldin said to Belgarath. "Did you want to stop and see if we can find out what's going on down there on the plain?"

"That might not be a bad idea," Belgarath agreed. "Let's not ride into trouble if we don't have to."

"I'll wait for you inside then," Beldin said and soared away again.

Polgara sighed. "Why must it *always* be a tavern?" she complained.

"Because people who've been drinking like to talk, Pol," Belgarath explained in a reasonable tone. "You can gather more information in five minutes in a tavern than you can in an hour in a tearoom."

"I knew you'd be able to find a reason for it."

"Naturally."

They crossed over the top of the wooded pass and on down the shade-splotched trail to the tavern. It was a low building made of logs crudely chinked with mud. The roof was low, and its shingles had curled with the weather and the passage of years. Buff-colored chickens scratched at the dirt in the dooryard, and a large speckled sow lay in a mud puddle, nursing a litter of happily grunting piglets. There were a few spavined nags tied to a hitch rail in front of the tavern, and a Karand dressed in moth-eaten furs snored on the front stoop.

Polgara reined in her horse as they approached the tavern and the first whiff of its reeking interior reached her nostrils. "I think, ladies, that we might prefer to wait over there in the shade."

"There *is* a certain fragrance coming out that door, isn't there?" Velvet agreed.

"You, too, Eriond," Polgara said firmly. "There's no need for you to start picking up bad habits this early in life." She rode over toward a grove of tall fir trees some distance away from the tavern and dismounted in the shade. Durnik and Toth exchanged a quick glance, then joined her there with Velvet, Ce'Nedra, and Eriond.

Sadi started to dismount in front of the tavern. Then he sniffed once and gagged slightly. "This is not my sort of place, gentlemen," he said. "I think I'll wait outside as well. Besides, it's Zith's feeding time."

"Suit yourself," Belgarath shrugged, dismounting and leading the way toward the building. They stepped over the snoring Karand on the stoop and went on inside. "Split up and spread out," the old man muttered. "Circulate and talk to as many as you can." He looked at Silk. "We're not here to make a career out of this," he cautioned.

"Trust me," Silk said, moving away.

Garion stood just inside the door, blinking to let his eyes adjust to the dimness. The tavern showed no signs of ever having been cleaned. The floor was covered with moldy straw that reeked of spilled beer, and scraps of rotting food lay in heaps in the corners. A crudely built fireplace smoked at the far end, adding its fumes to the generally unpleasant odor of the place. The tables consisted of rough-hewn planks laid on trellises, and the benches were half logs with sticks drilled into their undersides for legs. Garion saw Beldin talking with several Karands over in one corner and he started over to join him.

As he passed one of the tables, his foot came down on something soft. There was a protesting squeal and a sudden scramble of hoofed feet.

"Don't step on my pig," the bleary-eyed old Karand sitting at the table said belligerently. "I don't step on your pig, do I?" He pronounced it "peg," and Garion had a little trouble sorting out his dialect.

"Watch yer fate," the Karand said ominously.

"Fate?" Garion shrank back from that word just a bit.

"Fate. Them thangs you got on the end of yer laigs."

"Oh. Feet."

"That's what I just said—fate."

"Sorry," Garion apologized. "I didn't quite understand."

"That's the trouble with you outlanders. You can't even understand the language when she's spoke to you plain as day."

"Why don't we have a tankard of ale?" Garion suggested. "I'll apologize to your pig just as soon as he comes back."

The Karand squinted at him suspiciously. The old man was bearded and he wore clothing made of poorly tanned furs. He wore a hat made from the whole skin of a badger—with the legs and tail still attached. He was very dirty, and Garion could clearly see the fleas peeking out of his beard.

"I'm buying," Garion offered, sitting down across the table from the pig's owner.

The old Karand's face brightened noticeably.

They had a couple of tankards of ale together. Garion noticed that the stuff had a raw, green flavor to it, as if it had been dipped from the vat a week or so too soon. His host, however, smacked his lips and rolled his eyes as if this were the finest brew in the world. Something cold and wet touched Garion's hand, and he jerked it away. He looked down into a pair of earnest blue eyes fenced in by bristly white eyelashes. The pig had recently been to the wallow and he carried a powerful odor with him.

The old Karand chortled. "That's just my peg," he said. "He's a good-natured young peg, and he don't hold no grudges." The fur-clad fellow blinked owlishly. "He's a orphan, y'know."

"Oh?"

"His ma made real good bacon, though." The old man snuffled and wiped his nose on the back of his hand. "Sometimes I miss her real bad," he admitted. He squinted at Garion. "Say, that's a mighty big knife you got there."

"Yes," Garion agreed. He absently scratched the half-grown pig's ears, and the animal closed his eyes in bliss, laid his head in Garion's lap, and grunted contentedly.

"We were coming down the trail out of the mountains," Garion said, "and we saw a lot of smoke out on the plain. Is there some kind of trouble out there?"

"The worst kinda trouble there is, friend," the old man said seriously. He squinted at Garion again. "You're not one of them Mal-or-eens, are you?"

"No," Garion assured him, "not Mallorean. I come from farther west."

"I didn't know there *was* anythin' to the west of the Malor-eens. Anyhow, there's whole bunches of people down there on the plains havin' some kind of an argument about religion."

"Religion?"

"I don't hold much with it myself," the Karand admitted. "There's them as do and them as don't, and I'm one of them as don't. Let the Gods take care of theirselves, I say. I'll take care of me and mine, and we're quits on the whole business."

"Seems like a good way," Garion said carefully.

"Glad you see it like that. Anyhow, there's this Grolim named Zandramas down in Dar-sheeva. This Zandramas, she come up into Voresebo and started talkin' about this here new God of Angarak—Torak bein' dead an' all, y'know. Now, I'm just about as interested in all that as my peg is. He's a smart peg and he knows when people is talkin' nonsense."

Garion patted the pig's muddy flank, and the plump little animal made an ecstatic sound. "Good pig," Garion agreed. "Peg, that is."

"I'm fond of him. He's warm and good to snuggle up against on a cold night— and he don't hardly snore none at all. Well, sir, this Zandramas, she come up here and started preachin' and yellin' and I don't know what all. The Grolims all gives out a moan and falls down on their faces. Then, a while back, a whole new bunch of Grolims comes over the mountains, and they says that this Zandramas is dead wrong. They says that there's gonna be a new God over Angarak, right enough, but that this Zandramas don't have the straight of it. That's what all the smoke down there on the plains is about. Both sides is a-burnin' and a-killin' and a-preachin' about *their* idea of who the new God's gonna be. I'm not gonna have anythin' to do with either side. Me and my peg are gonna go back up in the mountains and let them folks kill each other. When they get it all sorted out, we'll come back and nod at whichever altar comes out on top as we go by."

"You keep calling this Zandramas 'she,' " Garion noted.

"Would you believe it's a *woman*?" the Karand snorted. "That's the foolishest thing I ever heard tell of. Women got no business mixin' up in men's affairs."

"Have you ever seen her?"

"Like I say, I don't mess around in religious stuff. Me and my peg, we just kinda keep to ourselves when it comes to that."

"Good way to get along," Garion said to him. "My friends and I have to go through that plain down there, though. Are Grolims all we need to worry about?"

"I can see you're a stranger," the Karand said, suggestively looking down into his empty tankard.

"Here," Garion said, "let's get another one." He fished another coin out of the pouch at his waist and signaled the servingman.

"The whole thang, friend," the garrulous owner of the pig went on, "is that in this part of the country, them Grolims always has troops with 'em. The ones as follows Zandramas, they got the army of the king of Voresebo with 'em. The old king, he didn't hold with none of this religious stuff, but he got hisself de-posed. His son decided the old man was gettin' too silly to run the country, so he set his pa aside and took the throne for hisself. The son's a squinty-eyed sort and he's lookin' to put hisself on the side most likely to win. He's throwed in with Zandramas, but then this Urvon fella, he comes along, and he's got this whole army out of Jenno and Ganesia and folks in armor and some real ugly big black dogs with him—not to mention all the Grolims. It's mean down there on the plains, friend. They're killin' and burnin' and sacrificin' prisoners on this altar or that. If it was me, I'd go a long way around all that foolishness."

"I wish I could, friend," Garion told him sincerely. "We heard that there were demons up in Jenno—off toward Callida. Have any of them shown up around here?"

"Demons?" The Karand shuddered, making the sign against evil. "None that I ever heard of. If I had, me and my peg would already be so far back in the mountains that they'd have to ship daylight in to us by pack train."

Despite himself, Garion found that he liked this gabbly old fellow. There was an almost musical flow to his illiterate speech, a kind of warm inclusiveness that paid no attention to any kind of social distinctions, and a shrewd, even penetrating, assessment of the chaos around him. It was almost with regret that Garion briefly acknowledged Silk's jerk of the head in the direction of the door. Gently, he removed the pig's head from his lap. The animal made a small, discontented sound. "I'm afraid I'm going to have to go now," he told the Karand as he rose to his feet. "I thank you for your company—and the loan of your pig."

"Peg," the Karand corrected.

"Peg," Garion agreed. He stopped the servingman who was going by and handed him a coin. "Give my friend and his peg whatever they'd like," he said.

"Why, thank you, my young friend." The old Karand grinned expansively.

"My pleasure," Garion said. He looked down. "Have a nice day, pig," he added.

The pig grunted rather distantly and clattered around the table to his master.

Ce'Nedra wrinkled her nose as he approached the shady spot where the ladies had been waiting. "What on earth have you been doing, Garion?" she asked. "You smell awful."

"I was getting acquainted with a pig."

"A pig?" she exclaimed. "Whatever for?"

"You almost had to have been there."

As they rode along exchanging the information they had gleaned, it became evident that the owner of the pig had offered a surprisingly complete and succinct perception of the situation in Voresebo. Garion repeated the conversation, complete with dialect.

"He didn't *really* talk that way, did he?" Velvet giggled incredulously.

"Why, no'm," Garion said, exaggerating just a bit, "when you get right down to the core of it, he didn't. There was 'theses' and 'thoses' and 'themses' that I can't quite get the hang of. Me and the pig got along good, though."

"Garion," Polgara said a bit distantly, "do you suppose you could ride back there a ways?" She gestured toward the rear of the column. "Several hundred yards or so, I'd say."

"Yes, ma'am," he said. He reined Chretienne in. The big gray horse, he noted, also seemed a bit offended by something in the air.

By general request, Garion bathed that night in a shockingly cold mountain stream. When he returned, shivering, to the fire, Belgarath looked at him and said, "I think you'd better put your armor back on. If half of what your friend with the pig said is true, you might need it."

"Peg," Garion corrected.

"What?"

"Never mind."

The next morning dawned clear and definitely chilly. The mail coat felt clammy even through the padded tunic Garion always wore under it, and it was heavy and uncomfortable. Durnik cut him a lance from a nearby thicket and leaned it against a tree near where the horses were picketed.

Belgarath came back from a small hilltop where he had been surveying the plains below. "From what I can see, the turmoil is fairly general down there, so there isn't much point in trying to avoid people. The quicker we get past Voresebo, the better, so we might as well ride straight on through. We'll try to talk our way out of any difficulties first; and, if that doesn't work, we'll do it the other way."

"I suppose I'd better go find another club," Sadi sighed.

They rode out with Garion jingling along in the lead. His helmet was in place, and his shield was strapped to his left arm. The butt of his lance rested beside his foot in his stirrup, and he affected a menacing scowl. The sword strapped across his back pulled steadily at him, indicating that they were still on the trail of Zandramas. When they reached the edge of the foothills, the winding mountain track became a narrow, rutted road stretching off toward the southeast. They picked up their pace and moved along the road at a brisk trot.

A few miles out onto the plain, they passed a burning village set back about a half mile from the road. They did not stop to investigate.

About noon, they encountered a party of armed men on foot. There were about fifteen of them, and they wore clothing which vaguely resembled uniforms.

"Well?" Garion said back over his shoulder, tightening his grip on his lance.

"Let me talk to them first," Silk said, moving his horse forward. "Try to look dangerous." The little man walked his horse toward the strangers. "You're blocking the road," he told them in a flat, unfriendly tone.

"We have orders to check everyone who passes," one of them said, looking at Garion a little nervously.

"All right, you've checked us. Now stand aside."

"Which side are you on?"

"Now, that's a stupid question, man," Silk replied. "Which side are *you* on?"

"I don't have to answer that."

"Then neither do I. Use your eyes, man. Do I look like a Karand—or a Temple Guardsman—or a Grolim?"

"Do you follow Urvon or Zandramas?"

"Neither one. I follow money, and you don't make money by getting mixed up in religion."

The roughly dressed soldier looked even more uncertain. "I have to report which side you're on to my captain."

"That's assuming that you've seen me," Silk told him, bouncing a purse suggestively on the palm of his hand. "I'm in a hurry, friend. I have no interest in your religion. Please do me the same courtesy."

The soldier was looking at the purse in Silk's hand with undisguised greed.

"It would be worth quite a bit to me not to be delayed," Silk suggested slyly. He theatrically wiped his brow. "It's getting hot out here," he said. "Why don't you and your men go find some shade to rest in? I'll 'accidentally' drop this purse here, and you can 'find' it later. That way, you make a nice profit, and I get to move along without interference and without having someone in authority find out that I've passed."

"It *is* getting warm out here," the soldier agreed.

"I thought you might have noticed that."

The other soldiers were grinning openly.

"You won't forget to drop the purse?"

"Trust me," Silk said.

The soldiers trooped across the field toward a grove of trees. Silk negligently tossed the purse into the ditch beside the road and motioned for the others to come ahead. "We might want to move right along," he suggested.

"Another purse full of pebbles?" Durnik grinned.

"Oh, no, Durnik. The purse has real money in it—Mallorean brass half-pennies. You can't buy very much with them, but they're real money, right enough."

"What if he'd asked to see what was inside?"

Silk grinned and held up his cupped hand. Tightly wedged between the folds of skin in his palm were several silver coins. "I like to be ready for eventualities," he said. Then he looked back over his shoulder. "I think we should leave now. The soldiers are coming back to the road."

The next encounter was a bit more serious. Three Temple Guardsmen blocked the road. Their shields were in front of them and their lances were at the ready. Their faces were devoid of thought. "My turn," Garion said, settling his helmet more firmly in place and shifting his shield. He lowered his lance and thumped Chretienne with his heels. As he charged, he could hear another horse pounding along behind him, but he did not have time to look back. It was all so stupid, but he felt that surge in his blood again. "Idiocy," he muttered. Then he easily unhorsed the Guardsman in the center. Durnik, he noted, had cut his lance perhaps two feet longer than was standard. With a quick flick of his shield, he deflected the lances of the other two Guardsmen and thundered on between them. Chretienne's hooves slammed down into the still-tumbling body of the fallen Guardsman. Garion reined in sharply and whirled the big gray to face the two he had left behind. But there was no need. The man riding behind him was Toth, and the two Guardsmen had already tumbled limply from their saddles.

"I could find work for you in Arendia, Toth," he said to the huge man. "Somewhere there has to be someone to convince them that they're not invincible."

Toth grinned at him in a soundless laugh.

Central Voresebo was in total chaos. Pillars of smoke rose from burning villages and farms. Crops had been put to the torch, and bands of armed men savagely attacked each other. One such skirmish was taking place in a burning field, and both sides were caught up in such a frenzy that they paid no attention to the wall of flame sweeping down on them.

Mutilated bodies seemed to be everywhere, and there was no way Garion could shield Ce'Nedra from the horrors littering the ditches and even the road itself.

They galloped on.

As dusk descended over the stricken countryside, Durnik and Toth turned aside from the road to seek shelter for the night. They returned to report that they had discovered a low thicket lying in a gully a mile or so back from the road. "We won't be able to build any fires," Durnik said soberly, "but if we stay fairly quiet, I don't think anybody's going to find us."

The night was not pleasant. They took a cold supper in the thicket and tried for what scant shelter they could make out of what was available, since they could not erect their tents in the dense brush. Autumn was in the air, and it was cold, once the sky turned dark. As the first light of dawn touched the eastern horizon, they rose, ate a hasty breakfast, and rode on.

The cold, miserable night and the senseless slaughter all around them made Garion angry, and he grew angrier with each passing mile. About midmorning he saw a black-robed Grolim standing beside an altar several hundred yards out in a field to the right of the road. A band of roughly dressed soldiers were dragging three terrified villagers toward the altar by ropes tied about the victims' necks. Garion did not even stop to think. He discarded his lance, drew Iron-grip's sword, cautioned the Orb to avoid display, and then charged.

The Grolim was apparently so caught up in his religious frenzy that he neither heard nor saw Garion bearing down on him. He screamed once as Chretienne thundered over the top of him. The soldiers took one startled look at Garion, threw away their weapons, and fled. That did not seem to satisfy his anger, however. Implacably, he pursued them. His anger was not so great, though, as to goad him into killing unarmed men. Instead, he simply rode them down one by one. When the last had tumbled beneath the big gray's hooves, Garion wheeled, freed the prisoners, and cantered back to the road.

"Don't you think that was a little excessive?" Belgarath demanded angrily.

"Not under the circumstances, no," Garion snapped back. "At least I'm fairly sure that *one* group of soldiers in this stinking country won't be dragging civilians to the altar—at least not until all the broken bones mend."

Belgarath snorted in disgust and turned away.

Still enraged, Garion glared belligerently at Polgara. "Well?" he demanded.

"I didn't say anything, dear," she said mildly. "Next time, though, don't you think you should let your grandfather know what you're planning? These little surprises set his teeth on edge sometimes."

Beldin came flaring in. "What happened out there?" he asked curiously when he had resumed his own form. He pointed at the groaning soldiers dotting the nearby field.

"My horse needed some exercise," Garion said flatly. "Those soldiers got in his way."

"What's got you so foul-tempered this morning?"

"This is all so stupid."

"Of course it is, but get ready for some more of it. The border of Rengel is just ahead, and things are just as bad down there as they are here."

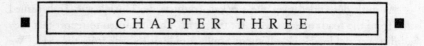

CHAPTER THREE

They paused at the border to consider their alternatives. The guardpost at the boundary was deserted, but black columns of smoke rose from burning villages, and they could clearly see large groups of men moving across the landscape, looking tiny in the distance.

"Things are a little more organized down here," Beldin reported. "About all we saw in Voresebo were fairly small bands, and they were more interested in loot than fighting. The groups are bigger on up ahead, and there's a certain semblance of discipline. I don't think we'll be able to bluff our way through Rengel the way we did Voresebo."

Toth made a series of obscure gestures.

"What did he say?" Belgarath asked Durnik.

"He suggests that we travel at night," Durnik replied.

"That's an absurd notion, Toth," Sadi protested. "If things are dangerous in the daytime, they'll be ten times more dangerous at night."

Toth's hands began to move again. For some reason, Garion found that he could almost understand what the huge mute was trying to say.

"He says that you looked at the idea too fast, Sadi," Durnik translated. "We've got certain advantages." The smith frowned slightly, and he looked back at his friend. "How did you find out about that?" he asked.

Toth gestured again.

"Oh," Durnik nodded. "I guess she *would* know, wouldn't she?" He turned to the others. "He says that Belgarath, Pol, and Garion can lead the way in their other forms. The darkness wouldn't be that big a problem for a pair of wolves and an owl."

Belgarath tugged thoughtfully at one earlobe. "It's got possibilities," he said to Beldin. "We could avoid just about anybody out there that way. Soldiers don't move around in the dark very much."

"They post sentries, though," the hunchback pointed out.

"Garion, Pol, and I wouldn't have much trouble locating them and leading the rest of you around them."

"It's going to be slow going," Velvet said. "We won't be able to travel at a gallop, and we'll have to detour around every sentry we come across."

"You know," Silk said, "now that I think about it, it's not such a bad idea. I sort of like it."

"You always enjoy sneaking around in the dark, Kheldar," Velvet said to him. "Don't you?"

"Well—" Then she smiled at him. "I suppose I do, yes—but then, I'm a Drasnian, too."

"It would take too long," Ce'Nedra protested. "We're only a little way behind Zandramas. If we try to sneak, she'll get ahead again."

"I don't see that we've got much choice, Ce'Nedra," Garion told her gently. "If we just try to plow our way across Rengel, sooner or later we're going to run into more soldiers than we can handle."

"You're a sorcerer," she said accusingly. "You could wave your hand and just knock them out of our way."

"There are limits to that, Ce'Nedra," Polgara said. "Both Zandramas and Urvon have Grolims in the region. If we tried to do it that way, everybody in Rengel would know exactly where we were."

Ce'Nedra's eyes filled with tears, and her lower lip began to tremble. She turned and ran blindly away from the road, sobbing.

"Go after her, Garion," Polgara said. "See if you can get her calmed down."

They took shelter for the rest of the day in a grove of beech trees about a mile from the road. Garion tried to sleep, knowing that the night ahead of them would be very long; but after about an hour, he gave up and wandered restlessly about the camp. He shared Ce'Nedra's impatience. They were so close to Zandramas now, and moving at night would slow their pace to a crawl. Try though he might, however, he could think of no alternative.

As the sun was going down, they struck camp and waited at the edge of the beech grove for it to get dark.

"I think I've just hit a flaw in the plan," Silk said.

"Oh?" Belgarath asked.

"We need the Orb to be able to follow Zandramas. If Garion turns into a wolf, the Orb won't be able to tell him which way to go—or will it?"

Belgarath and Beldin exchanged a long look. "I don't know," Belgarath admitted. "Do you?"

"I haven't got the slightest idea," Beldin said.

"Well, there's only one way to find out," Garion said. He handed Chretienne's reins to Durnik and went some distance away from the horses. Carefully, he created the image of the wolf in his mind, then he began to focus his will upon the image. He seemed, as always, to go through a peculiar sensation of melting, and then it was done. He sat on his haunches for a moment, checking himself over to make sure everything was there.

His nose suddenly caught a familiar fragrance. He turned his head and looked back over his shoulder. Ce'Nedra stood there, her eyes very wide and the fingertips of one hand to her lips. "I-is that still really you, Garion?" she stammered.

He rose to his feet and shook himself. There was no way he could answer her. Human words would not fit in the mouth of a wolf. Instead, he padded over to her and licked her hand. She sank to her knees, wrapped her arms about his head, and laid her cheek against his muzzle. "Oh, Garion," she said in a tone of wonder.

On an impulse born out of sheer mischief, he deliberately licked her face from chin to hairline. His tongue was quite long—and quite wet.

"Stop that," she said, giggling in spite of herself and trying to wipe her face. He momentarily touched his cold nose to the side of her neck. She flinched away. Then he turned and loped off toward the road where the trail was. He paused in the bushes beside the road and carefully peered out, his ears alert and his nose searching for the scent of anyone in the vicinity. Then, satisfied, he slipped out of the bushes with his belly low to the ground to stand in the middle of the road.

It was not the same, of course. There was a subtle difference to the pulling sensation, but it was still there. He felt a peculiar satisfaction and had to restrain an urge to lift his muzzle in a howl of triumph. He turned then and loped back toward where the others were hidden. His toenails dug into the turf, and he exulted in a wild sense of freedom. It was almost with regret that he changed back into his own shape.

"Well?" Belgarath asked as he walked toward them in the gathering dusk.

"No problem," Garion replied, trying to sound casual about it. He suppressed the urge to grin, knowing that his offhand manner would irritate his grandfather enormously.

"Are you really sure we need him along on this trip?" Belgarath asked his daughter.

"Ah—yes, father," she said. "He is sort of necessary."

"I was afraid you might feel that way about it." He looked at the others. "All right," he said. "This is the way it works. Pol and Durnik can keep in touch with each other over quite some distance, so he'll be able to warn you if we run across any soldiers—or if the trail moves off the road. Move at a walk to keep down the noise, and be ready to take cover on short notice. Garion, keep your mind in contact with Pol's and don't forget that you've got a nose and ears as well as eyes. Swing back to the road from time to time to make sure we're still on the trail. Does anybody have any questions?"

They all shook their heads.

"All right then, let's go."

"Do you want me to go along?" Beldin offered.

"Thanks all the same, uncle," Polgara declined, "but hawks don't really see all that well in the dark. You wouldn't be much help after you'd flown head-on into a few trees."

It was surprisingly easy. The first impulse of any group of soldiers when setting up for the night is to build fires, and the second is to keep them going until the sun comes up. Guided by these cheery beacons, Garion and Belgarath were able to locate the night encampments of all the bands of troops in the area and to sniff out the sentries. As luck had it, in most cases the troops had set up some distance from the road, and the party was able to ride through undetected.

It was well into the night. Garion had crept to the top of a hill to survey the next valley. There were a fair number of campfires out there, winking at him in the darkness.

"Garion?" Ce'Nedra's voice seemed right on top of him. With a startled yelp, he jumped high in the air.

It took him a moment to regain his composure. "Ce'Nedra," he whined plaintively, "*please* don't do that. You almost scared me out of my fur."

"I just wanted to be sure you were all right," she said defensively. "If I have to wear this amulet, I may as well get some use out of it."

"I'm fine, Ce'Nedra," he said in a patient tone. "Just don't startle me like that. Wolves are edgy animals."

"Children," Polgara's voice cut in firmly. "You can play some other time. I'm trying to hear Durnik, and you're drowning him out with all this chatter."

"Yes, Aunt Pol," Garion replied automatically.

"I love you, Garion," Ce'Nedra whispered by way of farewell.

They traveled by night and sought cover as dawn began to stain the eastern sky for the next several days. It all became so easy that finally Garion grew careless. He was padding through a thicket on the fourth night and accidentally stepped on a dry twig.

"Who's there?" The voice was downwind of him, and the soldier's scent had not reached his nostrils. The fellow came pushing into the thicket, making a great deal of noise. He was warily holding a spear out in front of him. Angry more at himself than at the clumsy sentry, Garion shouldered the spear aside, raised up on his hind legs, and put his forepaws on the terrified man's shoulders. Then he swore at some length, his oaths coming out as a horrid growling and snarling.

The soldier's eyes bulged as Garion's awful fangs snapped within inches of his face. Then he screamed and fled. Garion slunk guiltily out of the thicket and loped away.

Polgara's voice came to him. "What was that?"

"Nothing important," he replied, more than a little ashamed of himself. "Tell Durnik and the others to swing out to the west for a while. This group of soldiers is camped fairly close to the road."

It was nearly dawn on the following night when the night breeze brought the smell of frying bacon to Garion's nostrils. He crept forward through the tall grass, but before he could get near enough to see who was cooking, he encountered his grandfather.

"Who is it?" he asked in the manner of wolves.

"A couple hundred soldiers," Belgarath replied, "and a whole herd of pack mules."

"They're right on the road, aren't they?"

"I don't think that's going to be a problem. I heard a couple of them talking. It seems that they work for Silk."

"Silk's got his own army?" Garion asked incredulously.

"So it would seem. I wish that little thief wouldn't keep secrets from me." Garion felt the old man's thought reaching out. "Pol, tell Durnik to send Silk up here." Then he looked at Garion. "Let's go back to the road. I want to have a little talk with the pride of Drasnia."

They loped back to the road, resumed their own shapes, and intercepted Silk. Belgarath, Garion thought, showed enormous restraint. "There's a large group of soldiers wearing blue tunics just up ahead," he said in a level tone. "Would you by any chance know who they are?"

"What are they doing here?" Silk asked with a puzzled frown. "They've been told to avoid any area where there's trouble."

"Maybe they didn't hear you." Belgarath's tone was sarcastic.

"It's a standing order. I'm definitely going to talk with the captain about this."

"You've got a private army?" Garion asked the little man.

"I don't know that I'd call it an army, exactly. Yarblek and I hired some mercenaries to guard our caravans, is all."

"Isn't that terribly expensive?"

"Not nearly as expensive as losing those caravans would be. Highway robbery is a cottage industry in Karanda. Let's go talk with them."

"Why don't we?" Belgarath's tone was flat—even unfriendly.

"You're not taking this very well, old friend."

"Don't crowd it, Silk. I've been slinking through wet grass for five nights running. I've got burrs in my coat and a snarl in my tail that's going to take me a week to chew out, and all this time you've had an armed escort within shouting distance."

"I didn't know they were here, Belgarath," Silk protested. "They're not supposed to be here."

Belgarath stalked away muttering curses under his breath.

The muleteers in the camp had begun to load their animals when Silk, with Garion walking on one side of him and Belgarath on the other, rode in. A hardbitten-looking man with a pockmarked face and thick wrists approached them and saluted. "Your Highness," he said to Silk, "we didn't know that you were in this part of Mallorea."

"I move around a lot," Silk said. "Is it all right if we join you, Captain Rakos?"

"Of course, your Highness."

"The rest of our party will be along shortly," Silk told him. "What are we having for breakfast this morning?"

"Bacon, fried eggs, chops, hot bread, jam—the usual, your Highness."

"No gruel?"

"I can have the cook mix some up for you, if you'd like, your Highness," Rakos replied.

"No, thanks, Captain," Silk said. "I think I can live without gruel, for today anyway."

"Would your Highness care to inspect the troops?"

Silk made a face, then sighed. "They sort of expect it, don't they?"

"It's good for morale, your Highness," Rakos assured him. "An uninspected trooper begins to feel unappreciated."

"Right you are, Captain," Silk said, dismounting. "Fall them in if you would please, and I'll boost their morale."

The captain turned and bellowed an order.

"Excuse me," Silk said to Belgarath and Garion. "Certain formalities are the price of command." He smoothed down his hair with the palm of his hand and carefully adjusted his clothing. Then he followed Captain Rakos toward the ranks of soldiers standing at attention beside the road. His manner was grand as he inspected his troops, and he rather meticulously pointed out missing buttons, unshaved faces, and boots not polished to perfection. Durnik, Polgara, and the others arrived while he was progressing down the last rank. Belgarath quickly explained the situation to them.

When Silk returned, he had a certain self-satisfied look on his face.

"Was all that really necessary?" Velvet asked him.

"It's expected." He shrugged. He looked rather proudly at his men. "They look good, don't they? I may not have the biggest army in Mallorea, but I've got the sharpest. Why don't we go have some breakfast?"

"I've eaten soldiers' rations before," Beldin told him. "I think I'll go look for another pigeon."

"You're jumping to conclusions, Beldin," the little man assured him. "Bad food is the greatest cause of dissatisfaction in the ranks in any army. Yarblek and I are very careful to hire only the best cooks and to provide them with the finest food available. Dry rations might be good enough for Kal Zakath's army, but not for mine."

Captain Rakos joined them for breakfast. Rakos was obviously a field soldier and he had certain difficulties with his utensils.

"Where's the caravan bound?" Silk asked him.

"Jarot, your Highness."

"What are we carrying?"

"Beans."

"Beans?" Silk sounded a little startled.

"It was your order, your Highness," Rakos said. "Word came from your factor in Mal Zeth before the plague broke out that you wanted to corner the market in beans. Your warehouses in Maga Renn are overflowing with them, so lately we've been transferring them to Jarot."

"Why would I do that?" Silk said, scratching his head in bafflement.

" 'Zakath was bringing his army back from Cthol Murgos," Garion reminded him. "He was going to mount a campaign in Karanda. You wanted to buy up all the beans in Mallorea so that you could gouge the Bureau of Military Procurement."

"Gouge is such an ugly word, Garion," Silk protested with a pained look. He frowned. "I thought I'd rescinded that order."

"Not that I've heard, your Highness," Rakos said. "You've got tons of beans pouring into Maga Renn from all over Delchin and southern Ganesia."

Silk groaned. "How much longer is it going to take us to reach Jarot?" he asked. "I've got to put a stop to this."

"Several days, your Highness," Rakos replied.

"And the beans will just keep piling up the whole time."

"Probably, your Highness."

Silk groaned again.

They rode on down through the remainder of Rengel with no further incidents. Silk's professional soldiers apparently had a wide reputation in the region, and the poorly trained troops of the varying factions there gave them a wide berth. Silk rode at the head of the column like a field marshal, looking about with a lordly manner.

"Are you going to let him get away with that?" Ce'Nedra asked Velvet after a day or so.

"Of course not," Velvet replied, "but let him enjoy it for now. Time enough to teach him the realities of the situation later on."

"You're terrible," Ce'Nedra giggled.

"Naturally. But didn't you do the same thing to our hero here?" Velvet looked pointedly at Garion.

"Liselle," Polgara said firmly, "you're giving away secrets again."

"Sorry, Lady Polgara," Velvet replied contritely.

The trail of Zandramas was soon joined by the sullen scarlet trail of the Sardion, and both proceeded down across Rengel to the River Kallahar and the border of Celanta. The trails also seemed to be going toward Jarot.

"Why is she going toward the sea?" Garion worriedly asked Belgarath.

"Who knows?" the old man replied shortly. "She's read the Ashabine Oracles, and I haven't. It could be that she knows where she's going, and I'm just floundering along in the rear."

"But what if—"

"Please don't 'what if' me, Garion," Belgarath said. "I've got enough problems already."

They crossed the River Kallahar aboard a cluster of ferries that seemed to belong to Silk and arrived in the port city of Jarot on the Celanta side. As they rode through the cobbled streets, crowds came out to cheer. Silk rode at the head of the column graciously waving his acknowledgment of the cheers.

"Have I missed something?" Durnik asked.

"His people love him very much," Eriond explained.

"*His* people?"

"Who owns a man, Durnik?" the blond young man asked sadly. "The one who rules him, or the one who pays him?"

Silk's offices in Jarot were opulent—even ostentatious. Mallorean carpets lay thick upon the floors, the walls were paneled in rare, polished woods, and officials in costly livery were everywhere.

"One sort of has to keep up appearances," the little man explained apologetically as they entered. "The natives are so impressed by show."

"Of course," Belgarath said drily.

"Surely you don't think—"

"Just let it pass, Silk."

"But it's all so much fun, Belgarath." Silk grinned.

Belgarath then did something Garion had never thought he would see him do. He raised his hands imploringly, assumed a tragic expression, and said, "Why me?"

Beldin chortled.

"Well?" Belgarath said crossly to him.

"Nothing," Beldin replied.

Silk's factor in Jarot was a baggy-eyed Melcene named Kasvor. Kasvor walked as if he had the weight of the world on his shoulders and he sighed often. He came wearily into the office where Silk sat as if enthroned behind a very large writing desk and the rest of them lounged in comfortable chairs along the walls. "Prince Kheldar," Kasvor said, bowing.

"Ah, Kasvor," Silk said.

"I've seen to the rooms your Highness wanted." Kasvor sighed. "The inn is called the Lion. It's two streets over. I've taken the entire top floor for you."

Durnik leaned over and whispered to Garion. "Wasn't that inn we stayed at in Camaar also called the Lion?" he asked. "The place where Brendig arrested us that time?"

"I'd imagine that you could find a Lion Inn in just about every city in the world," Garion replied.

"Capital, Kasvor. Capital," Silk was saying.

Kasvor smiled faintly.

"How's business?" Silk asked.

"We're showing a fair profit, your Highness."

"How fair?"

"About forty-five percent."

"Not bad. I need to talk to you about something else, though. Let's stop buying beans."

"I'm afraid it's a little late for that, your Highness. We own just about every bean in Mallorea already."

Silk groaned and buried his face in his hands.

"The market's up ten points, though, your Highness."

"It is?" Silk sounded startled, and his eyes brightened. "How did that happen?"

"There have been all manner of rumors going about and some tentative inquiries from the Bureau of Military Procurement. Everyone's been scrambling around trying to buy up beans, but we've got them all."

"Ten points, you say?"

"Yes, your Highness."

"Sell," Silk said.

Kasvor looked startled.

"We bought up the bean crop in the expectation of an imperial military campaign in Karanda. There won't be one now."

"Can your Highness be sure?"

"I have access to certain sources of information. When the word gets out, the market in beans is going to sink like a rock, and we don't really want several million tons of beans on our hands, do we? Have there been any offers?"

"The Melcene consortium has expressed some interest, your Highness. They're willing to go two points above the market."

"Negotiate with them, Kasvor. When they get to three points above the market price, sell. I don't want to have to eat all those beans myself."

"Yes, your Highness."

Belgarath cleared his throat meaningfully.

Silk glanced at the old man and nodded. "We just came down through Voresebo and Rengel," he said. "Things are a bit chaotic up there."

"So I've heard, your Highness," Kasvor replied.

"Is there unrest anywhere else in the region? We have some things to do in this part of the world and we don't want to have to do them in a war zone if we don't have to."

Kasvor shrugged. "Darshiva's in an uproar, but there's nothing new about that. Darshiva's been in an uproar for the past dozen years. I took the liberty of pulling all our people out of that principality. There's nothing left there that's worth our while." He looked toward the ceiling in mock piety. "May Zandramas grow a boil on her nose," he prayed.

"Amen," Silk agreed fervently. "Is there any place else we ought to avoid?"

"I've heard that northern Gandahar is a bit nervous," Kasvor answered, "but that doesn't affect us, since we don't deal in elephants."

"Smartest decision we ever made," Silk said to Belgarath. "Do you have any idea how much an elephant can eat?"

"Peldane is also reported to be in turmoil just now, your Highness," Kasvor reported. "Zandramas is spreading her infection in all directions."

"Have you ever seen her?" Silk asked him.

Kasvor shook his head. "She hasn't come this far east yet. I think she's trying to consolidate her position before she comes this way. The Emperor won't mourn the loss of Darshiva, Rengel, and Voresebo very much, and Peldane and Gandahar are more trouble than they're worth. Celanta—and certainly Melcena—are altogether different matters, though."

"Truly," Silk agreed.

Kasvor frowned. "I did hear something, though, your Highness," he said.

"There's a rumor going around the waterfront that Zandramas' cohort, Naradas, hired a ship for Melcena a few days ago."

"Naradas?"

"Your Highness may never have seen him, but he's fairly easy to pick out of a crowd. He has absolutely white eyes." Kasvor shuddered. "Gruesome-looking fellow. Anyway, he's reputed to have been with Zandramas since the beginning and, as I understand it, he's her right arm. There are some other rumors as well, but I don't think I should repeat them in the presence of the ladies." He looked apologetically at Polgara, Ce'Nedra, and Velvet.

Silk tapped his forefinger thoughtfully on his chin. "So Naradas went to Melcena," he said. "I think I'd like to get a few more details about that."

"I'll circulate some people around the waterfront, your Highness," Kasvor said. "I'm sure we'll be able to find someone who can give us more information."

"Good," Silk said, rising to his feet. "If you find someone, send him to me at the Lion Inn. Tell him that I'll be very generous."

"Of course, your Highness."

Silk hefted the leather pouch at his belt. "I'll need some money," he noted.

"I'll see to it at once, Prince Kheldar."

As they left the building and walked down the polished stone steps toward their horses, Beldin made a disgusted sound. "It's unwholesome," he muttered.

"What is?" Belgarath asked him.

"How lucky you are."

"I don't quite follow you."

"Isn't it remarkable that Kasvor just *happened* to remember the one thing you really had to know? He threw it out almost as an afterthought."

"The Gods have always been fond of me," Belgarath replied complacently.

"You think of luck as a God? Our Master would put you on bread and water for several centuries if he heard you talking like that."

"It may not have been entirely luck," Durnik said thoughtfully. "This prophecy of ours has nudged people a bit now and then. I remember one time in Arendia when Ce'Nedra was supposed to give a speech. She was so terrified she was almost sick until a drunken young nobleman insulted her. Then she got angry, and her speech set fire to the whole crowd. Pol said that maybe the prophecy had made him get drunk so that he'd insult Ce'Nedra in order to make her angry enough to give the speech. Couldn't this have been sort of like that? Fate instead of luck?"

Beldin looked at the smith, his eyes suddenly alight. "This man is a jewel, Belgarath," he said. "I've been looking for someone to talk philosophy with for centuries now, and here he is, right under my nose." He put his large, gnarled hand on Durnik's shoulder. "When we get to that inn, my friend," he said, "you and I are going to begin a very long conversation. It might just go on for several centuries."

Polgara sighed.

The Lion Inn was a large building with walls of yellow brick and a red tile roof. A broad stairway led up to an imposing main door attended by a liveried footman.

"Where are the stables?" Durnik asked, looking about.

"Probably around back," Silk replied. "Melcene architecture is a bit different from the style in the West."

As they dismounted, two grooms came trotting around the building to take their horses. Silk mounted the stairs, and the footman at the door bowed deeply to him. "This house is honored by your presence, Prince Kheldar," he said. "My master's waiting inside to greet you."

"Why, thank you, my good man," Silk replied, giving him a coin. "There may be someone along later to see me. It's possible that he'll be a sailor or a longshoreman. When he arrives, would you be so good as to send him to me immediately?"

"Of course, your Highness."

The top floor of the inn was palatial. The rooms were large and deeply carpeted. The walls were covered with white mortar, and the windows were draped with blue velvet. The furnishings were massive and comfortable-looking. The doorways were arched.

Durnik wiped his feet carefully before entering. He looked around.

"They seem to be awfully fond of arches," he noted. "I've always preferred post-and-lintel construction myself. For some reason, I just don't quite trust an arch."

"It's perfectly sound, Durnik," Silk assured him.

"I know the theory," Durnik said. "The trouble is that I don't know the man who built the arch, so I don't know if he can be trusted."

"Do you still want to talk philosophy with him?" Belgarath said to Beldin.

"Why not? Solid practicality has a place in the world, too, and sometimes my speculations get a little airy."

"I think the word is windy, Beldin. Windy."

"You didn't really have to say that, did you?"

Belgarath looked at him critically. "Yes," he replied. "I think I did."

Polgara, Ce'Nedra, and Velvet retired to an elaborate bath that was even larger than those in their quarters in the imperial palace at Mal Zeth.

While the ladies were bathing, Silk excused himself. "There are a few other things I need to attend to," he explained. "I won't be very long."

It was after bath time, but before suppertime, when a wiry little fellow in a tar-smeared canvas smock was escorted into the main sitting room. "I was told that there was a Prince Kheldar as was wantin' words with me," he said, looking around. He spoke in a brogue almost identical to Feldegast's.

"Ah—" Garion floundered, "the prince has stepped out for a moment."

"I surely don't have all day to sit around coolin' me heels, me boy," the little fellow objected. "I've things to do an' people to see, don't y' know."

"I'll handle this, Garion," Durnik said mildly.

"But—"

"It's no problem at all," Durnik said just a bit more firmly. He turned to the little dockhand. "The prince just had a few questions, is all," he said in an almost lazy tone. "It's nothing that you and I can't take care of without bothering his Highness." He laughed. "You know how these highborn people are—excitable."

"Now that's the truth, surely. There's nothin' like a title t' rob a man of his good sense."

Durnik spread his hands. "What can I say?" he said. "Why don't we sit down and talk a bit? Would you take a spot of ale?"

"I've been known t' take a sup from time t' time." The little fellow grinned. "Yer a man after me own heart, me friend. What trade is it ye follow?"

Durnik held out his calloused and burn-scarred hands. "I'm a blacksmith," he admitted.

"Whoosh!" the dockhand exclaimed. " 'Tis a hot an' heavy line o' work ye've chose fer yerself. I labor on the docks, meself. 'Tis heavy enough, but at least it's out in the open air."

"It is indeed," Durnik agreed in that same easygoing fashion. Then he turned and snapped his fingers at Belgarath. "Why don't you see if you can find some ale for my friend and me?" he suggested. "Get some for yourself, too—if you're of a mind."

Belgarath made a number of strangling noises and went to the door to talk to the servant waiting outside.

"A relative of my wife's," Durnik confided to the tar-smeared man. "He's not quite bright, but she insists that I keep him on. You know how that goes."

"Oh, by the Gods, yes. Me own dear wife's got cousins by the score who can't tell one end of a shovel from another. They kin surely find the ale barrel an' supper table, though."

Durnik laughed. "How's the work?" he asked. "On the docks, I mean?"

" 'Tis cruel hard. The masters keep all the gold fer theirselves, and we git the brass."

Durnik laughed ironically. "Isn't that always the way of it?"

"It is indeed, me friend. It is indeed."

"There's no justice in the world," Durnik sighed, "and a man can only bow to the ill winds of fortune."

"How truly ye speak. I see that ye've suffered under unkind masters yerself."

"A time or two," Durnik admitted. He sighed. "Well," he said, "on to the business at hand, then. The prince has got a certain interest in a fellow with white eyes. Have you ever seen him?"

"Ah," the dockhand said, "*that* one. May he sink in a cesspool up to the eyebrows."

"You've met him, I take it."

"An' the meetin' gave me no pleasure, I kin tell ye."

"Well, then," Durnik said smoothly, "I can see that we're of the same opinion about this fellow."

"If it's in yer mind t' kill him, I'll lend ye me cargo hook."

"It's a thought." Durnik laughed.

Garion stared in amazement at his honest old friend. This was a side of Durnik he had never seen before. He glanced quickly to one side and saw Polgara's eyes wide with astonishment.

At that moment, Silk came in, but stopped as Velvet motioned him to silence.

"However," Durnik went on slyly, "what better way to upset somebody that we both dislike than to overturn a scheme he's been hatching for a year or more?"

The dockhand's lips peeled back from his teeth in a feral grin. "I'm listenin', me friend," he said fervently. "Tell me how to spoke the white-eyed man's wheel, an' I'm with ye to the end." He spat in his hand and held it out.

Durnik also spat on his palm, and the two of them smacked their hands together in a gesture as old as time. Then the smith lowered his voice confidentially. "Now," he said, "we've heard that this white-eyed one—may all of his teeth fall out—hired a ship for Melcena. What we need to know is when he left, on what ship, who went with him, and where he was to land."

"Simplicity in itself," the dockhand said expansively, leaning back in his chair.

"You, there," Durnik said to Belgarath, "is that ale on the way?"

Belgarath made a few more strangling noises.

"It's so hard to get good help these days." Durnik sighed.

Polgara tried very hard to stifle a laugh.

"Well, now," the dockhand said, leaning forward in that same confidential manner, "this is what I seen with me own two eyes, so I'm not handin' along second-hand information. I seen this white-eyed one come to the docks on a mornin' about five days ago. 'Twas about daybreak, it was, an' one of them cloudy mornin's when ye can't tell the difference between fog an' smoke, an' ye don't want to breathe too deep of either. Anyway, the white-eyed one, he had a woman with him in a black satin robe with a hood coverin' her head, an' she had a little boy with her."

"How do you know it was a woman?" Durnik interrupted.

"Have ye no eyes, man?" the dockhand laughed. "They don't walk the same as we do. There's a certain swayin' of the hips that no man alive could imitate. 'Twas a woman, right enough, an' ye have me word on that. An' the little boy was as fair as a mornin' sunrise, but he seemed a little sad. Sturdy little lad he was, an' looked fer all the world as if he wished he could put his hands on a sword to rid hisself of them as he didn't like too much. Anyway, they went aboard ship, an' the ship, she slipped her hawsers an' rowed off into the fog. Word was that they was bound fer the city of Melcena—or some well-hid cove nearby, smugglin' not bein' unknown in these parts, don't y' know."

"And this was five days ago?" Durnik asked.

"Five or four. Sometimes I lose track of the days."

Durnik seized the man's tar-smeared hand warmly. "My friend," he said, "between us, we'll kick all the spokes out of the white-eyed man's wheel yet."

"I'd surely like to help with the kickin'," the dockhand said a bit wistfully.

"You have, friend," Durnik said. "You definitely have. I'll kick a time or two for you myself. Silk," the smith said very seriously, "I think our friend here should have something to pay him for his trouble."

Silk, looking a bit awed, shook a few coins out of his purse.

"Is that the best you can do?" Durnik asked critically.

Silk doubled the amount. Then, after a glance at Durnik's disapproving expression, doubled that in gold.

The dockhand left, his fist clutched protectively around his coins.

Velvet rose wordlessly to her feet and curtsied to Durnik with profound respect.

"Where did you learn how to do that?" Silk demanded.

Durnik looked at him with some surprise. "Haven't you ever traded horses at a country fair before, Silk?" he asked.

"As I told ye, me old friend," Beldin said gaily, "the old speech has not died out yet altogether, an' 'tis music to me ears t' hear it again."

"Must you?" Belgarath said in a highly offended tone. He turned to Durnik. "What was all that folksy business?"

Durnik shrugged. "I've met that sort of man many times," he explained. "They can be very helpful, if you give them a reason to be—but they're very touchy, so you have to approach them just right." He smiled. "Given a little time, I could have sold that fellow a three-legged horse—and convinced him that he'd got the best of the bargain."

"Oh, my Durnik," Polgara said, throwing her arms about the smith's neck. "What would we ever do without you?"

"I hope we never have to find out," he said.

"All right," Belgarath said, "now we know that Zandramas went to Melcena. The question is why."

"To get away from us?" Silk suggested.

"I don't think so, Kheldar," Sadi disagreed. "Her center of power is in Darshiva. Why should she run off in the other direction?"

"I'll work on that."

"What's in Melcena?" Velvet asked.

"Not too much," Silk replied, "unless you count all the money in Melcena itself—most of the world's supply, last time I heard."

"Would Zandramas be interested in money?" the blond girl asked.

"No," Polgara said very firmly. "Money would have no meaning to her—not at this point. It's something else."

"The only thing that means anything to Zandramas right now is the Sardion, isn't it?" Garion said. "Could the Sardion be out there in the islands someplace?"

Beldin and Belgarath exchanged a look. "What *does* that phrase mean?" Beldin demanded in exasperation. "Think, Belgarath. What does it mean when they say the 'Place Which Is No More'?"

"You're smarter than I am," Belgarath retorted. "You answer the riddle."

"I hate riddles!"

"I think about all we can do at this point is trail along behind and find out," Silk said. "Zandramas seems to know where she's going, and we don't. That doesn't leave us much choice, does it?"

"The Sardion came to Jarot as well," Garion mused. "It was a long time ago, but the Orb picked up its trail just outside of town. I'll go down to the docks and see if both trails are still running together. It's possible that Zandramas has some way of following the Sardion, the same as we do. She might not really know where it's going. Maybe she's just following it."

"He's got a point there," Beldin said.

"If the Sardion is hidden somewhere out there in Melcena, this could all end before the week is out," Garion added.

"It's too early," Polgara said flatly.

"Too early?" Ce'Nedra exclaimed. "Lady Polgara, my baby's been gone for over a year now. How can you say it's too early?"

"It has nothing to do with that, Ce'Nedra," the sorceress replied. "You've waited a year for the return of your baby. I waited a thousand years and more for Garion. Fate and time and the Gods pay no attention to our years, but Cyradis said at Ashaba that we still had nine months until the final meeting, and it hasn't been that long yet."

"She might have been wrong," Ce'Nedra objected.

"Perhaps—but only by a second or so either way."

<hr />

CHAPTER FOUR

It was foggy in the harbor the next morning, one of those thick early autumn fogs that always hovers on the verge of rain. As they were loading the horses, Garion glanced up and found that he could see no more than a few feet up the masts of the ship they were boarding. Silk stood on the aft deck talking with the ship's captain.

"It should clear off when we get a few leagues out to sea, your Highness," the captain was saying as Garion approached. "There's a fairly steady wind that always blows down the passage between the coast and Melcena."

"Good," Silk said. "I wouldn't want to run into anything. How long is it likely to take us to get to Melcena?"

"Most of the day, your Highness," the captain replied. "It's a fair distance, but the prevailing wind works to our advantage. The return voyage takes several days, though."

"We'll be all loaded shortly," Silk told him.

"We can leave any time you're ready, your Highness."

Silk nodded and joined Garion at the rail. "Are you feeling any better?" he asked.

"I don't quite follow you."

"You were just a bit grumpy when you got up this morning."

"Sorry. I've got a lot on my mind."

"Spread it around," Silk suggested. "Worries get lighter when you've got people to share them with you."

"We're getting closer," Garion said. "Even if this meeting doesn't happen out here in the islands, it's still only a matter of a few more months."

"Good. I'm getting a little tired of living out of a saddlebag."

"But we don't know what's going to happen yet."

"Of course we do. You're going to meet Zandramas, divide her down the middle with that big knife of yours, and take your wife and son back to Riva where they belong."

"But we don't *know* that, Silk."

"We didn't know you were going to win the duel with Torak either, but you did. Anyone who goes around picking fights with Gods has very little to fear from a second-rate sorceress."

"How do we know she's second-rate?"

"She's not a disciple, is she? Or would the word be disciple-ess?"

"How would I know?" Garion smiled faintly, then grew serious again. "I think Zandramas has stepped over discipleship. She's the Child of Dark, and that makes her a bit more serious than an ordinary disciple." He banged his fist down on the rail. "I *wish* I knew what I'm supposed to do. When I went after Torak, I knew. This time I'm not sure."

"You'll get instructions when the time comes, I'm sure."

"But if I knew, I could sort of get ready."

"I get the feeling that this is not the sort of thing you can get ready for, Garion." The little man glanced over the rail at the garbage bobbing in the water beside the ship. "Did you follow the trail all the way to the harbor last night?" he asked.

Garion nodded. "Yes—both of them. Both Zandramas and the Sardion left from here. We're fairly sure that Zandramas is going to Melcena. Only the Gods know where the Sardion went."

"And probably not even they."

A large drop of water fell from the rigging lost in the fog overhead and landed with a splat on Silk's shoulder.

"Why is it always me?" the little man complained.

"What?"

"Anytime something wet falls out of the sky, it lands on me."

"Maybe somebody's trying to tell you something," Garion grinned.

Toth and Durnik led the last of the horses up the gangway and on down into the hold.

"That's the lot, Captain," Silk called. "We can leave any time now."

"Yes, your Highness," the captain agreed. He raised his voice and started shouting orders.

"I've been meaning to ask you about something," Garion said to Silk. "Always before, you acted almost as if you were ashamed of your title. Here in Mallorea, though, you seem to want to wallow in it."

"What a fascinating choice of words."

"You know what I mean."

Silk tugged at one earlobe. "In the West, my title's an inconvenience. It attracts too much attention, and it gets in my way. Things are different here in Mallorea. Here, nobody takes you seriously unless you've got a title. I've got one, so I use it. It opens certain doors for me and permits me to have dealings with people who wouldn't have time for Ambar of Kotu or Radek of Boktor. Nothing's really changed, though."

"Then all of that posturing and pomposity—pardon the terms—are just for show?"

"Of course they are, Garion. You don't think I've turned into a complete ass, do you?"

A strange thought came to Garion. "Then Prince Kheldar is as much a fiction as Ambar and Radek, isn't he?"

"Of course he is."

"But where's the real Silk?"

"It's very hard to say, Garion." Silk sighed. "Sometimes I think I lost him years ago." He looked around at the fog. "Let's go below," he said. "Murky mornings always seem to start off these gloomy conversations."

A league or so beyond the breakwater, the sky turned a rusty color, and the fog began to thin. The sea lying to the east of the coast of Mallorea rolled in long, sullen swells that spoke of vast stretches of uninterrupted water. The ship ran before the prevailing wind, her prow knifing through the swells, and by late afternoon the coast of the largest of the Melcene Islands was clearly visible on the horizon.

The harbor of the city of Melcena was crowded with shipping from all over Mallorea. Small and large, the vessels jostled against each other in the choppy water as Silk's captain carefully threaded his way toward the stone quays thrusting out from the shore. It was dusk by the time they had unloaded, and Silk led them through the broad streets toward the house he maintained there. Melcena appeared to be a sedate, even stuffy city. The streets were wide and scrupulously clean. The houses were imposing, and the inhabitants all wore robes in sober hues. There was none of the bustle here that was evident in other cities. The citizens of Melcena moved through the streets with decorum, and the street hawkers did not bawl their wares in those strident voices that helped so much to raise that continual shouted babble that filled the streets of less reserved cities. Although Melcena lay in tropic latitudes, the prevailing breeze coming in off the ocean moderated the temperature enough to make the climate pleasant.

Silk's house here was what might more properly be called a palace. It was constructed of marble and was several stories high. It was fronted by a large formal garden and flanked by stately trees. A paved drive curved up through the garden to a porch lined with columns, and liveried servants stood attentively at the entryway.

"Opulent," Sadi noted as they dismounted.

"It's a nice little place," Silk admitted in an offhand way. Then he laughed. "Actually, Sadi, it's mostly for show. Personally, I prefer shabby little offices in back streets, but Melcena takes itself very seriously, and one has to try to fit in, if one plans to do business here. Let's go inside."

They went up the broad steps and through an imposing door. The foyer inside the door was very large, and the walls were clad with marble. Silk led them on through the foyer and up a grand staircase. "The rooms on the ground floor are given over to offices," he explained. "The living quarters are up here."

"What sort of business do you do here?" Durnik asked. "I didn't see anything that looked like a warehouse."

"There aren't many warehouses in Melcena," Silk said as he opened a door and led them into a very large, blue-carpeted sitting room. "The decisions are made here, of course, but the goods are normally stored on the mainland. There's not much point in shipping things here and then turning around and shipping them back again."

"That makes sense," Durnik approved.

The furnishings of the room they had entered were ornate. Divans and comfortable chairs were clustered in little groupings here and there, and wax candles burned in sconces along the wood-paneled walls.

"It's a little late to be wandering around the streets looking for Zandramas," Silk observed. "I thought we might have something to eat, get a good night's sleep, and then Garion and I can start out early in the morning."

"That's probably the best way to go at it," Belgarath agreed, sinking down onto a well-upholstered divan.

"Could I offer you all something to drink while we're waiting for dinner?" Silk asked.

"I thought you'd never ask," Beldin growled, sprawling in a chair and scratching his beard.

Silk tugged at a bellpull, and a servant entered immediately. "I think we'll have some wine," Silk told him.

"Yes, your Highness."

"Bring several varieties."

"Have you got any ale?" Beldin asked. "Wine sours my stomach."

"Bring ale for my messy friend as well," Silk ordered, "and tell the kitchen that there'll be eleven of us for dinner."

"At once, your Highness." The servant bowed and quietly left the room.

"You have bathing facilities, I assume?" Polgara asked, removing the light cloak she had worn on the voyage.

"You bathed just last night in Jarot, Pol," Belgarath pointed out.

"Yes, father," she said dreamily. "I know."

"Each suite has its own bath," Silk told her. "They're not quite as large as the ones in 'Zakath's palace, but they'll get you wet."

She smiled and sat on one of the divans.

"Please, everybody, sit down," Silk said to the rest of them.

"Do you think any of your people here might know what's going on in the world?" Belgarath asked the little man.

"Naturally."

"Why naturally?"

"My boyhood occupation was spying, Belgarath, and old habits die hard. All of my people are instructed to gather information."

"What do you do with it?" Velvet asked him.

He shrugged. "I sort through it. I get almost as much pleasure from handling information as I do from handling money."

"Do you forward any of this information to Javelin in Boktor?"

"I send him a few crumbs now and then—just to remind him that I'm still alive."

"I'm sure he knows that, Silk."

"Why don't you send for someone who can bring us up to date?" Belgarath suggested. "We've been out of touch for quite a while, and I'd sort of like to know what certain people are up to."

"Right," Silk agreed. He tugged the bellpull again, and another liveried servant responded. "Would you ask Vetter to step in here for a moment?" Silk asked.

The servant bowed and left.

"My factor here," Silk said, taking a seat. "We lured him away from Brador's secret police. He's got a good head for business and he's had all that training in the intelligence service."

Vetter proved to be a narrow-faced man with a nervous tic in his left eyelid. "Your Highness wanted to see me?" he asked respectfully as he entered the room.

"Ah, there you are, Vetter," Silk said. "I've been back in the hinterlands and I was wondering if you could fill me in on what's been happening lately."

"Here in Melcena, your Highness?"

"Perhaps a bit more general than that."

"All right." Vetter paused, gathering his thoughts. "There was a plague in Mal Zeth," he began. "The Emperor sealed the city to prevent the spread of the disease, so, for a time, we couldn't get any information out of the capital. The plague has subsided, however, so the gates have been opened again. The Emperor's agents are moving freely around Mallorea now.

"There was an upheaval in central Karanda. It appeared to have been fomented by a former Grolim named Mengha. The Karands all believed that there were demons involved, but Karands think that there's a demon behind any unusual occurrence. It does appear, though, that there were at least a few supernatural events in the region. Mengha hasn't been seen for quite some time, and order is being gradually restored. The Emperor took the business seriously enough to summon the army back from Cthol Murgos to put down the uprising."

"Has he rescinded that order yet?" Silk asked. "If things are quieting down in Karanda, he's not going to need all those troops, is he?"

Vetter shook his head in disagreement. "The troops are still landing at Mal Gemila," he reported. "The word we've been getting out of Mal Zeth is that the Emperor has lost his enthusiasm for the conquest of Cthol Murgos. He had personal reasons for the campaign in the first place, and those reasons don't seem to be as pressing any more. His major concern at the moment seems to be the impending confrontation between the Disciple Urvon and Zandramas the Sorceress. That situation is about to come to a head. Urvon seems to be suffering from some form of mental instability, but his subordinates are moving large numbers of people into the region in preparation for something fairly major. Zandramas is also marshaling her forces. Our best assessment of the situation is that it's only going to be a matter of time before the Emperor moves his forces out of Mal Zeth to restore order. There have been reports of supplies being stockpiled at Maga Renn. It's apparent that Kal Zakath intends to use it as a staging area."

"Were we able to capitalize on that in any way?" Silk asked intently.

"To some degree, your Highness. We sold a part of our bean holdings to the Bureau of Military Procurement just today."

"What was the price?"

"About fifteen points above what we paid."

"You'd better get word to Kasvor in Jarot," Silk said with a sour expression. "I told him to sell at thirteen. The Melcene consortium has been making offers. Is the price likely to go higher?"

Vetter spread one hand and rocked it back and forth uncertainly.

"Let the word get out that we sold at fifteen and tell Kasvor to hold out for that figure. Even if the price goes to sixteen, we'll have still taken most of the profit out of the transaction."

"I'll see to it, your Highness." Vetter frowned a bit. "There's something going on in Dalasia," he continued his report. "We haven't been able to get the straight of it yet, but the Dalasians all seem to be very exited about it. Kell has been sealed off, so we can't get anybody there to investigate, and Kell is the source of just about everything that goes on in Dalasia."

"Any news from the West?" Garion asked.

"Things are still stalemated in Cthol Murgos," Vetter replied. "Kal Zakath is reducing his forces there and he's called all his generals home. He's still holding the cities in eastern Cthol Murgos, but the countryside is reverting. It's not certain whether King Urgit is going to take advantage of the situation. He has other things on his mind."

"Oh?" Silk asked curiously.

"He's getting married. A princess from the House of Cthan, as I understand it." Silk sighed.

"King Gethel of Mishrak ac Thull died," Vetter went on, "and he was succeeded by his son, Nathel. Nathel's a hopeless incompetent, so we can't be sure how long he'll last." Vetter paused, scratching at his chin. "We've had reports that there was a meeting of the Alorn Council at Boktor. The Alorns get together once a year, but it's usually at Riva. About the only other thing unusual about it was the fact that a fair number of non-Alorn monarchs attended."

"Oh?" Belgarath said. "Who?"

"The king of the Sendars, the Emperor of Tolnedra, and King Drosta of Gar og Nadrak. The king of Arendia was ill, but he sent representatives."

"*Now* what are they up to?" Belgarath muttered.

"We weren't able to get our hands on the agenda," Vetter told him, "but not long afterward, a delegation of diplomats from their kingdoms went to Rak Urga. There are rumors that some fairly serious negotiations are going on."

"What are they *doing*?" Belgarath demanded in an exasperated voice.

"I've told you over and over not to go off and leave the Alorns untended," Beldin said. "If there's any way at all for them to do something wrong, they'll do it."

"The price of gold is up," Vetter continued, "and the price of Mallorean crowns is down. Melcene imperials are holding steady, but the diamond market is fluctuating so wildly that we've withdrawn our investments in that commodity. That's more or less what's current, your Highness. I'll have a more detailed report on your desk first thing in the morning."

"Thank you, Vetter," Silk replied. "That's all for right now."

Vetter bowed and quietly left.

Belgarath began to pace up and down, swearing to himself.

"There's nothing you can do about it, father," Polgara told him, "so why upset yourself?"

"Perhaps they have some reason for what they're doing," Silk suggested.

"What possible reason could they have to be negotiating with the Murgos?"

"I don't know." Silk spread his hands. "I wasn't there when they made the decision. Maybe Urgit offered them something they wanted."

Belgarath continued to swear.

About a half hour later, they adjourned to the dining room and took seats near one end of a table that could easily have accommodated a half a hundred. The linen was snowy white, the knives and forks were solid silver, and the porcelain plates were edged in gold. The service was exquisite, and the meal was of banquet proportions.

"I must talk with your cook," Polgara said as they lingered over dessert. "He appears to be a man of talent."

"I should hope so," Silk replied. "He's costing me enough."

"I'd say you can afford it," Durnik noted, looking around at the luxurious furnishings.

Silk leaned back in his chair, toying with the stem of a silver goblet. "It doesn't really make much sense to maintain a place like this when I only come here about twice a year," he admitted, "but it's expected, I guess."

"Doesn't Yarblek use it, too?" Garion asked him.

Silk shook his head. "No. Yarblek and I have an agreement. I give him free rein in the rest of world as long as he stays out of Melcena. He doesn't really fit in here, and he insists on taking Vella with him everyplace he goes. Vella really shocks the Melcenes."

"She's a good wench, though," Beldin said, grinning. "When this is all over, I might just buy her."

"That's disgusting!" Ce'Nedra flared.

"What did I say?" Beldin looked confused.

"She's not a cow, you know."

"No. If I wanted a cow, I'd buy a cow."

"You can't just buy people."

"Of course you can," he said. "She's a Nadrak woman. She'd be insulted if I didn't try to buy her."

"Just be careful of her knives, uncle," Polgara cautioned. "She's very quick with them."

He shrugged. "Everybody has a few bad habits."

Garion did not sleep well that night, although the bed he shared with Ce'Nedra was deep and soft. At first he thought that might be part of the problem. He had been sleeping on the ground for weeks now, and it seemed reasonable that he was just not used to a soft bed. About midnight, however, he realized that the bed had nothing to do with his sleeplessness. Time was moving on inexorably, and his meeting with Zandramas marched toward him with a measured, unstoppable pace. He still knew little more than he had at the beginning. He was, to be sure, closer to her than he had been at the start—no more than a week at most behind, if the reports were correct—but he was still trailing after her and he still did not know where she was leading him. Darkly, he muttered a few choice oaths at the madman who had written the Mrin Codex. Why did it all have to be so cryptic? Why couldn't it have been written in plain language?

"Because if it had been, half the world would be waiting for you when you got to the place of the meeting," the dry voice in his mind told him. *"You're not the only one who wants to find the Sardion, you know."*

"I thought you'd left for good."

"Oh, no, I'm still around."

"How far behind Zandramas are we?"

"About three days."

Garion felt a wild surge of hope.

"Don't get too excited," the voice said, *"and don't just dash off as soon as you find the trail again. There's something else that has to be done here."*

"What?"

"You know, better than to ask that, Garion. I can't tell you, so quit trying to trick me into answering."

"Why can't you just tell me?"

"Because if I tell you certain things, the other spirit will be free to tell other things to Zandramas—like the location of the Place Which Is No More, for instance."

"You mean she doesn't know?" Garion asked incredulously.

"Of course she doesn't know. If she knew, she'd be there by now."

"Then the location isn't written down in the Ashabine Oracles?"

"Obviously. Pay attention tomorrow. Somebody's going to say something in passing that's very important. Don't miss it."

"Who's going to say it?"

But the voice was gone.

It was breezy the following morning when Silk and Garion set out, wearing long robes of a sober blue color. At Silk's suggestion, Garion had detached the Orb from the hilt of his sword and carried it concealed beneath his robe. "Melcenes rarely wear arms inside the city," the little man had explained, "and your sword is very conspicuous." They did not take their horses, but rather walked out into the street to mingle with the citizens of Melcena.

"We might as well start along the waterfront," Silk suggested. "Each wharf is owned by a different group of businessmen, and if we can find out which wharf Zandramas landed on, we'll know whom to question for more information."

"Sounds reasonable," Garion said shortly, striding off toward the harbor.

"Don't run," Silk told him.

"I'm not."

"You're moving too fast," the little man said. "People in Melcena go at a more stately pace."

"You know, Silk, I really don't care what the people here think of me. I'm not here to waste time."

Silk took hold of his friend's arm with a firm grip. "Garion," he said seriously, "we know that Zandramas and her underling have come here. She knows that we're after her, and there are people in Melcena who can be hired for various kinds of mischief. Let's not make it easy for them by standing out in the crowd."

Garion looked at him. "All right," he said. "We'll do it your way."

They walked at an infuriatingly slow pace down a broad avenue. At one point, Silk stopped with a muttered oath.

"What's wrong?" Garion asked him.

"That fellow just ahead—the one with the big nose—he's a member of Brador's secret police."

"Are you sure?"

Silk nodded. "I've known him for quite some time." The little man squared his shoulders. "Well, there's no help for it, I guess. He's already seen us. Let's move along."

But the man with the large, bulbous nose moved forward to stand in their path. "Good morning, Prince Kheldar," he said, bowing slightly.

"Rolla," Silk replied distantly.

"And your Majesty," Rolla added, bowing more deeply to Garion. "We weren't expecting you to appear here in Melcena. Brador will be very surprised."

"Surprises are good for him." Silk shrugged. "An unsurprised man gets complacent."

"The Emperor was most put out with you, your Majesty," Rolla said reproachfully to Garion.

"I'm sure he'll survive it."

"In Mallorea, your Majesty, it's the ones who offend Kal Zakath who need to be concerned about survival."

"Don't make threats, Rolla," Silk warned. "If his Majesty here decides that your report to the Chief of the Bureau of Internal Affairs would be embarrassing, he might decide to take steps to keep you from ever writing it. His Majesty is an Alorn, after all, and you know how short-tempered they can be."

Rolla stepped back apprehensively.

"Always nice talking with you, Rolla," Silk said in a tone of dismissal. Then he and Garion walked on. Garion noticed that the big-nosed man had a slightly worried look on his face as they passed him.

"I love to do that to people," Silk smirked.

"You're easily amused," Garion said. "You do know that when his report gets to Mal Zeth, 'Zakath's going to flood this whole region with people trying to find us."

"Do you want me to go back and kill him for you?" Silk offered.

"Of course not!"

"I didn't think so. If you can't do something about a situation, there's no point in worrying about it."

When they reached the harbor, Garion tightened his grip on the Orb. The pulling of Iron-grip's sword had sometimes been quite strong, and Garion had no desire to have the stone jump out of his hand. They walked northward along the wharves with the salt tang of the sea in their nostrils. The harbor of Melcena, unlike that of most of the port cities in the world, was surprisingly clear of floating garbage. "How do they keep it so clean?" Garion asked curiously. "The water, I mean?"

"There's a heavy fine for throwing things in the harbor," Silk replied. "Melcenes are compulsively tidy. They also have workmen with nets in small boats patrolling the waterfront to scoop up any floating debris. It helps to maintain full employment." He grinned. "It's a nasty job and it's always assigned to people who aren't interested in finding regular work. A few days in a small boat full of garbage and dead fish increases their ambition enormously."

"You know," Garion said, "that's really a very good idea. I wonder if—" The Orb suddenly grew very warm in his hand. He pulled his robe open slightly and looked at it. It was glowing a sullen red.

"Zandramas?" Silk asked.

Garion shook his head. "The Sardion," he replied.

Silk nervously tugged at his nose. "That's a sort of dilemma, isn't it? Do we follow the Sardion or Zandramas?"

"Zandramas," Garion said. "She's the one who's got my son."

"It's up to you." Silk shrugged. "That's the last wharf just up ahead. If we don't pick up the trail there, we'll go on and check the north gate."

They passed the last wharf. The Orb gave no indication of interest.

"Could they have landed on one of the other islands?" Garion asked with a worried frown.

"Not unless they changed course once they were at sea," Silk replied. "There are plenty of other places to land a ship along this coast. Let's go have a look at the north gate."

Once again they moved through the streets at that frustratingly leisurely pace. After they had crossed several streets, Silk stopped. "Oh, no," he groaned.

"What is it?"

"That fat man coming this way is Viscount Esca. He's one of the senior members of the Melcene Consortium. He's bound to want to talk business."

"Tell him we have an appointment."

"It wouldn't do any good. Time doesn't mean that much to Melcenes."

"Why, there you are, Prince Kheldar," the fat man in a gray robe said, waddling up to them. "I've been looking all over the city for you."

"Viscount Esca," Silk said, bowing.

"My colleagues and I have stood in awe of your recent venture into the commodities market," Esca said admiringly.

Silk's eyes grew sly, and his long nose twitched. Then he assumed a pained expression. "A blunder, actually, my dear Viscount," he said mournfully. "There's little profit to be made in something as bulky as farm produce."

"Have you been keeping abreast of the market?" Esca asked, his face taking on a transparent cast of neutrality, but his eyes filled with undisguised greed.

"No," Silk lied, "not really. I've been upcountry, and I haven't had the chance to talk with my factor as yet. I left instructions for him to take the first offer that comes along, though—even if we have to take a loss. I need my warehouses, and they're all filled to the rafters with beans."

"Well, now," Esca said, rubbing his hands together, "I'll speak with my colleagues. Perhaps we can make you a modest offer." He had begun to sweat.

"I couldn't let you do that, Esca. My holdings are virtually worthless. Why don't we let some stranger take the loss? I couldn't really do that to a friend."

"But, my dear Prince Kheldar," Esca protested in a tone verging on anguish, "we wouldn't really expect to make a *vast* profit. Our purchase would be more in the nature of long-term speculation."

"Well," Silk said dubiously, "as long as you're fully aware of the risks involved—"

"Oh, we are, we are," Esca said eagerly.

Silk sighed. "All right, then," he said. "Why don't you make your offer to Vetter? I'll trust you not to take advantage of my situation."

"Oh, of course, Kheldar, of course." Esca bowed hastily. "I really must be off now. Pressing business, you understand."

"Oh," Silk said, "quite."

Esca waddled off at an unseemly rate of speed.

"Hooked him!" Silk chortled. "Now I'll let Vetter land him."

"Don't you ever think about anything else?" Garion asked.

"Of course I do, but we're busy right now and we didn't have all morning to listen to him babble. Let's move along, shall we?"

A thought occurred to Garion. "What if Zandramas avoided the city?" he asked.

"Then we'll get our horses and check the coastline. She had to have landed somewhere."

As they approached the north gate of Melcena, the press in the street grew noticeably heavier. Carriages and people on horseback began to become more frequent, and the normally sedate citizens began to move more rapidly. Garion and Silk found it necessary to push their way through the throng.

"Anything?" Silk asked.

"Not yet," Garion replied, taking a firmer grip on the Orb. Then, as they passed a side street, he felt the now-familiar pulling. "She's been here," he reported. "She came out of that street—or went into it. I can't quite tell which yet." He went a few steps up the side street. The Orb tried to push him back. He turned around and rejoined his rat-faced friend. The steady pull of the Orb drew him toward the gate. "She went out this way," he reported as they reached the arched opening.

"Good," Silk said. "Let's go back and get the others. And then maybe we can find out why Zandramas came to Melcena."

CHAPTER FIVE

It seemed somehow that Garion's impatience had communicated itself to Chretienne. The big gray stallion was restive as they left Silk's house and rode into the street and he flicked his ears in irritation as Garion tried to curb him with the reins. Even the sound of his steel-shod hooves on the cobblestones came as a kind of restless staccato. As Garion leaned forward to lay a calming hand on the arched gray neck, he could feel the nervous quivering of his horse's muscles under the sleek skin. "I know," he said. "I feel the same way, but we have to wait until we're outside the city before we can run."

Chretienne snorted and then made a plaintive whinnying sound.

"It won't take that long," Garion assured him.

They rode in single file through the busy streets with Silk in the lead. The breeze swirling through the streets carried with it the dusty smell of autumn.

"What are all those buildings over there?" Eriond called ahead to Silk. The blond young man pointed toward a large complex of structures that seemed to be set in the center of a lush green park.

"The University of Melcena," Silk replied. "It's the largest institution of higher learning in the world."

"Even bigger than the one in Tol Honeth?" Garion asked.

"Yes, much. The Melcenes study everything. There are branches of learning at that university that the Tolnedrans won't even admit exist."

"Oh? Such as what?"

"Applied alchemy, astrology, necromancy, fundamentals of witchcraft, that sort of thing. They've even got an entire college devoted to the reading of tea leaves."

"You're not serious."

"I'm not, but they are."

Garion laughed and rode on.

The streets of Melcena grew even busier, but there was a decorum to the bustle. No matter how urgent his affairs might be, a Melcene businessman was never so preoccupied that he didn't have time for a friendly chat with one of his competitors. The snatches of conversation Garion heard as they rode along the boulevards ranged in subject from the weather to politics to flower arrangement. The major concentration that morning, however, seemed to be centered on the price of beans.

When they reached the north gate, the great sword strapped across Garion's back began to pull at him. Despite Silk's critical look, Garion had decided that he was not going out into the countryside without the sword. Zandramas had a way of leaving traps behind her, and Garion definitely did not want to walk into one of them unprepared. As they passed through the gate, he nudged Chretienne forward to ride beside Silk. "The trail seems to be following this road," he said, pointing up a broad highway stretching off to the north.

"At least it doesn't go across open country," Silk said. "The ground gets a little marshy in spots up here, and I hate to ride through mud."

Belgarath had said nothing since they had left Silk's house, but had ridden along with an irritated expression on his face. Now he came forward to join Silk and Garion. He looked around to make sure that none of the local citizens were close enough to overhear what they were saying and then spoke to Garion. "Let's go over it again—step by step this time. Exactly what did your friend say?"

"Well," Garion replied, "he started out by saying that all the prophecies are cryptic in order to keep the information out of the wrong hands."

"That makes a certain amount of sense, Belgarath," Beldin said from just behind them.

"It might make sense," Belgarath said, "but it doesn't make things any easier."

"Nobody promised you easy."

"I know. I just wish they'd stop going out of their way to make it difficult. Go ahead, Garion."

"Then he said that we're only three days behind Zandramas," Garion told him.

"That means that she's left the island," Silk noted.

"How did you arrive at that conclusion?" Belgarath asked.

"Melcena's a big island, but not that big. You can ride from one end of it to the other in two days. She might have gone on to one of the northern islands, but if we're three days behind her, she isn't on this one any more."

Belgarath grunted. "What else did he say?" he asked Garion.

"He said that there's something else we have to do here—besides finding the trail, I mean."

"I gather he wasn't very specific."

"No. He explained why not, though. He said if he told me what it was, the other prophecy could tell Zandramas certain things she didn't know yet. That's when he told me that she doesn't know where the Place Which Is No More is, and that the location's not in the Ashabine Oracles."

"Did he give you any clues at all about this task of ours?"

"Only that somebody's going to say something to us today that's very important."

"Who?"

"He wouldn't tell me. All he said was that somebody was going to say something in passing that we shouldn't miss. He said that we should be alert for that kind of thing."

"Anything else?"

"No. That's when he left."

The old man started to swear.

"I felt pretty much the same way myself," Garion agreed.

"He's done as much as he can, Belgarath," Beldin said. "The rest is up to us."

Belgarath made a wry face. "I suppose you're right."

"Of course I'm right. I'm always right."

"I wouldn't go that far. Well, first things first, I guess. Let's find out where Zandramas went. Then we can start analyzing every casual remark we hear." He turned in his saddle. "Keep your ears open today, all of you." Then he nudged his mount into a trot.

A rider in sober blue galloped past, going toward the city with uncharacteristic haste. Silk began to laugh after the man had passed them.

"Who was that?" Durnik asked.

"A member of the Consortium," Silk replied gaily. "It appears that Viscount Esca's called an emergency session."

"Is this something I ought to know about?" Belgarath asked.

"Not unless you're interested in the market price of beans."

"*Will* you keep your mind on what we're here for and stop playing?"

"It was sort of necessary, Grandfather," Garion came to his friend's defense. "The Viscount stopped us in the street while we were looking for the trail. He'd have talked all day if Silk hadn't sent him off on a fool's errand."

"Did he say anything at all that might be what we're looking for?"

"No. He just talked about beans."

"Did you meet anybody else today? Share these little encounters with us, Garion."

"We ran into one of Brador's secret policemen. I'd imagine that his messenger is already on the way to Mal Zeth."

"Did *he* say anything?"

"He made a few veiled threats, is all. I guess Emperor 'Zakath's a little unhappy with us. The policeman recognized me, but I suppose that's only natural. Silk was going to kill him, but I said no."

"Why?" Beldin asked bluntly.

"We were in the middle of a busy street for one thing. Killing somebody's the sort of thing you ought to do in private, wouldn't you say?"

"You were a much nicer boy before you developed this clever mouth," Beldin snapped.

Garion shrugged. "Nothing ever stays the same, uncle."

"Be polite, Garion," Polgara called from behind.

"Yes, ma'am."

A black carriage rattled by. The team of white horses drawing it was moving at a dead run and they were flecked with foam.

"Another bean buyer?" Belgarath asked.

Silk smirked and nodded.

Durnik had been looking around. "I don't see any signs that this land is being farmed," he said.

Silk laughed. "Land in Melcena's too valuable to be wasted on farming, Durnik. The people here import all their food from the mainland. About all we'll find out here are the estates of the very wealthy—retired businessmen, nobles, that sort of thing. The whole countryside's one huge park. Even the mountains have been landscaped."

"That doesn't seem very practical," Durnik said disapprovingly.

"The people who live on the estates spent a great deal of money for them, so I guess they can do what they like with the land."

"It still seems wasteful."

"Of course it is. That's what rich people do best—waste things."

The green hills to the north of the city were gently rolling and were dotted with artistically placed groves of trees. Many of the trees had been carefully pruned to accentuate their pleasing shapes. Garion found this tampering with nature somehow offensive. It appeared that he was not alone in this feeling. Ce'Nedra rode with a stiff look of disapproval on her face and frequently made little sounds of disgust, usually at the sight of a well-trimmed oak tree.

They moved into a canter, following the trail north along a road surfaced with gleaming white gravel. The road curved gently from hillside to hillside and in level spots it frequently made wide bends, evidently for no other purpose than to relieve the monotony of long straight stretches. The houses set far back from the road were universally constructed of marble and were usually surrounded by parks and gardens. It was a sunny autumn day, and the prevailing breeze carried with it the smell of the sea, a smell Garion found very familiar. He suddenly felt a sharp pang of homesickness for Riva.

As they cantered past one estate, a large number of gaily dressed people crossed the road ahead of them at a gallop, chasing after a pack of barking dogs. The people jumped fences and ditches with what appeared to be reckless abandon.

"What are they doing?" Eriond called to Silk.

"Fox hunting."

"That doesn't really make any sense, Silk," Durnik objected. "If they don't farm, they don't raise chickens. Why are they worried about foxes?"

"It makes even less sense in view of the fact that the fox isn't native to these islands. They have to be imported."

"That's ridiculous!"

"Of course it is. Rich people are always ridiculous, and their sports are usually exotic—and often cruel."

Beldin gave an ugly little chuckle. "I wonder how sporting they'd find chasing a pack of Algroths—or maybe an Eldrak or two."

"Never mind," Belgarath told him.

"It wouldn't really take much effort to raise a few, Belgarath." The hunchback grinned. "Or maybe some Trolls," he mused. "Trolls are great fun, and I'd love to see the look on the face of one of those overdressed butterflies when he jumped a fence and came face to face with a full-grown Troll."

"Never mind," Belgarath repeated.

The road forked at one point, and the Orb pulled toward the left. "She's headed toward the ocean again," Silk noted. "I wonder what it is that makes her so fond of water. She's been hopping from island to island ever since we started out after her."

"Maybe she knows that the Orb can't follow her over water," Garion said.

"I don't think that would be her major concern at this point," Polgara disagreed. "Time's running out—for her as well as us. She doesn't have the leisure for side trips."

The road they were following led down toward the cliffs, and finally the Orb pulled Garion onto a long, paved drive that curved down toward an imposing house set at the very edge of a precipitous drop and overlooking the ocean far below. As they rode toward the house, Garion loosened his sword in its scabbard.

"Expecting trouble?" Silk asked.

"I just like to be ready," Garion replied. "That's a big house up ahead, and a lot of people could be hiding inside."

The men who came out of the cliff-top villa, however, were not armed and they were all garbed in purple livery. "May I ask your business?" one of them asked. He was tall and thin and had an imposing mane of snowy white hair. He carried himself with an air of self-importance, that kind of air usually assumed by senior servants accustomed to ordering grooms and maids about.

Silk pushed forward. "My friends and I have been out for a morning ride," he said, "and we were struck by the beauty of this house and its location. Is the owner about perhaps?"

"His Lordship, the Archduke, is away at present," the tall man replied.

"What a shame," Silk said. He looked around. "I'm really taken with this place," he said. Then he laughed. "Maybe it's as well that he's not at home. If he were, I might be tempted to make him an offer for his house."

"I don't know that his Grace would be very interested," the servant said.

"I don't believe I know his Grace," Silk said artfully. "Do you suppose you could tell me his name?"

"He's the Archduke Otrath, sir," the servant answered, puffing himself up slightly. "He's a member of the imperial family."

"Oh?"

"He's the third cousin—twice removed—of his Imperial Majesty, Kal Zakath."

"Really? What an amazing thing. I'm so sorry to have missed him. I'll tell his Majesty that I stopped by the next time I see him, though."

"You know his Majesty?"

"Oh, yes. We're old friends."

"Might I ask your name, honored sir?"

"Oh, sorry. How very stupid of me. I'm Prince Kheldar of Drasnia."

"*The* Prince Kheldar?"

"I certainly hope there aren't any others." Silk laughed. "I can get into enough trouble all by myself."

"His Grace will be very sorry to have missed you, your Highness."

"I'll be in Melcena for several weeks," Silk said. "Perhaps I can call again. When do you expect his Grace to return?"

"That's very hard to say, your Highness. He left not three days ago with some people from the mainland." The white-haired servant paused thoughtfully. "If you and your friends wouldn't mind waiting for a few moments, Prince Kheldar, I'll go advise her Grace, the Archduke's wife, that you're here. Her Grace has so few visitors out here, and she loves company. Won't you please come inside? I'll go to her at once and tell her that you're here."

They dismounted and followed him into a broad entryway. He bowed rather stiffly and went off down a corridor lined with tapestries.

"Very smooth, Kheldar," Velvet murmured admiringly.

"They don't call me Silk for nothing," he said, polishing his ring on the front of his pearl-gray doublet.

When the tall servant returned, he had a slightly pained look on his face. "Her Grace is a bit indisposed at the moment, your Highness," he apologized to Silk.

"I'm sorry to hear that," Silk replied with genuine regret. "Perhaps another time, then."

"Oh, no, your Highness. Her Grace insists on seeing you, but please forgive her if she seems a bit—ah—disoriented."

One of Silk's eyebrows shot up.

"It's the isolation, your Highness," the servant confided, looking embarrassed. "Her Grace is not happy in this somewhat bucolic locale, and she's resorted to a certain amount of reinforcement in her exile."

"Reinforcement?"

"I trust I can count on your Highness' discretion?"

"Of course."

"Her Grace takes some wine from time to time, your Highness, and this appears to be one of those times. I'm afraid she's had a bit more than is really good for her."

"This early in the morning?"

"Her Grace does not keep what one might call regular hours. If you'll come with me, please."

As they followed the servant down a long corridor, Silk murmured back over his shoulder to the rest of them. "Follow my lead on this," he said. "Just smile and try not to look too startled at what I say."

"Don't you just love it when he gets devious?" Velvet said admiringly to Ce'Nedra.

The archduchess was a lady in her mid-thirties. She had luxurious dark hair and very large eyes. She had a pouting lower lip and an ever-so-slightly overgenerous figure which filled her burgundy gown to the point of overflowing. She was also as drunk as a lord. She had discarded her goblet and now drank directly from a decanter. "Prince Kheldar," she hiccuped, trying to curtsy. Sadi moved sinuously to catch her arm to prevent a disaster.

" 'Scuse me," she slurred to him. "So nice of you."

"My pleasure, your Grace," the eunuch said politely.

She blinked at him several times. "Are you really bald—or is that an affectation?"

"It's a cultural thing, your Grace," he explained, bowing.

"How disappointing," she sighed, rubbing her hand over his head and taking another drink from the decanter. "Could I offer you all something to drink?" she asked brightly.

Most of them declined with faint headshakes. Beldin, however, stumped forward with his hand extended. "Why not?" the grotesque little man said. "Let's try a rip of that, me girl." For some reason he had lapsed into Feldegast's brogue.

Belgarath rolled his eyes ceilingward.

The archduchess laughed uproariously and passed over the decanter.

Beldin drained it without stopping for breath. "Very tasty," he belched, tossing the decanter negligently into a corner, "but ale's me preference, y'r Ladyship. Wine's hard on the stomach so early of a morning."

"Ale it shall be, then," she crowed happily. "We'll all sit around and swill ourselves into insensibility." She fell back on a couch, exposing a great deal of herself in the process. "Bring ale," she commanded the embarrassed servant, "lots and lots of ale."

"As your Grace commands," the tall man replied stiffly, withdrawing.

"Nice enough fellow," the archduchess slurred, "but he's so terribly stuffy sometimes. He absolutely refuses to take a drink with me." Her eyes suddenly filled with tears. "Nobody wants to drink with me," she complained. She held out her arms imploringly to Beldin, and he enfolded her in an embrace. "*You* understand, don't you, my friend?" she sobbed, burying her face in his shoulder.

"Of course I do," he said, patting her shoulder. "There, there, me little darlin'," he said, " 'twill all be right again soon."

The noblewoman regained her composure, sniffed loudly, and fished for a handkerchief. "It's not that I *want* to be like this, your Highness," she apologized, trying to focus her eyes on Silk. "It's just that I'm so absolutely *bored* out here. Otrath has all the social grace of an oyster, so he's imprisoned me out here in the hinterlands with nothing but the booming of the surf and the screeching of gulls for company. I so miss the balls and the dinner parties and the conversation in Melcena. What am I to do with myself out here?"

" 'Tis cruel hard, me darlin'," Beldin agreed. He took the small cask of ale the servant cringingly brought, placed it between his knees, and bashed in the top with his gnarled fist. "Would ye care fer a sup, sweeting?" he asked the duchess politely, holding out the cask.

"I'd drown if I tried to drink out of that," she protested with a silly little laugh.

"Right y' are," he agreed. "You there," he said to Belgarath. "Get the poor girl a cup or somethin'."

Belgarath scowled at his gnarled brother, then wordlessly fetched a silver tankard from a sideboard.

Beldin dipped deeply into the cask with the tankard, wiped off the bottom with his sleeve, and offered it to their hostess. "To yer good health, me darlin'," he said, drinking from the cask.

"You're *so* kind," she hiccuped. Then she drained off about half the tankard with foamy ale spilling out of the corners of her mouth and down the front of her gown.

"We were very sorry to have missed his Grace," Silk said, obviously a little non-plussed by Beldin's rough-and-ready approach to a highborn, though tipsy, lady.

"You didn't miss a thing, your Highness," she burped, politely covering her mouth. "My husband's a fat green toad with all the charm of a dead rat. He spends his time trying to decipher his proximity to the imperial throne. Kal Zakath has no heir, so all the imperial cousins sit around waiting for one another to die and trying to cement alliances. Have you ever been in Mal Zeth, your Highness? It's an absolutely ghastly place. Frankly, imperial crown or no, I'd sooner live in Hell." She drained her tankard and handed it wordlessly back to Beldin. Then she looked around brightly, her eyes slightly unfocused. "But my dear Prince Kheldar," she said, "you haven't introduced me to your friends as yet."

"How terribly forgetful of me, your Grace," he exclaimed, slapping his hand to his forehead. He rose formally to his feet. "Your Grace, I have the honor to present her Grace, the Duchess of Erat." He held his hand out grandly to Polgara, who rose and curtsied.

"Your Grace," she murmured.

"Your Grace," the archduchess replied, trying to rise, but not quite succeeding.

"There, there, me darlin'," Beldin said, pressing down on her shoulder to keep her more or less in place. " 'Tis early, an' we're all friends. There's no need at all fer us t' be goin' through all these tiresome formalities."

"I *like* him," the noblewoman said, pointing at Beldin with one hand and dipping out more ale with the other. "Can I keep him?"

"Sorry, your Grace," Belgarath said. "We might need him later on."

"So grim a face," she observed, looking at the ancient sorcerer. She grinned roguishly. "I'll wager I could make you smile."

Silk rushed on. "Her Highness, Princess Ce'Nedra of the House of Borune," he said, "and the Margravine Liselle of Drasnia. The young man with the sword is known as the Lord of the Western Sea—an obscure title, I'll grant you, but his people are an obscure sort of folk."

Garion bowed deeply to the tipsy archduchess.

"So great a sword you have, my Lord," she said.

"It's a family heirloom, your Grace," he replied. "I'm more or less obliged to carry it."

"The others have no titles they care to acknowledge," Silk said. "They're business associates, and we don't worry about titles where money is concerned."

"Do *you* have a title?" the lady asked Beldin.

"Several, me little darlin'," he replied in an offhand way, "but none from any land ye'd be recognizin' the name of—most of 'em havin' disappeared long ago." He raised the cask again and drank noisily.

"What a dear little man you are," she said in a smoldering sort of voice.

" 'Tis me charm, darlin'," he replied with a resigned sort of sigh. " 'Tis always been me bane, this charmin' quality about me. Sometimes I must actually hide myself t' keep off the maids overpowered with unreasonin' passion." He sighed again, then belched.

"We might want to talk about that one of these days," she suggested.

Silk was obviously out of his depth here. "Ah—" he said lamely, "—as I was saying, we're sorry to have missed the archduke."

"I can't for the life of me think why, your Highness," the lady said bluntly. "My husband's an unmitigated ass, and he doesn't bathe regularly. He has wild aspirations about the imperial throne and very little in the way of prospects in that direction." She held out her tankard to Beldin. "Would you, dear?"

He squinted down into the cask. "It could just be that we'll need another, me darlin'," he suggested.

"I've got a cellar full," she sighed happily. "We can go on like this for days, if you'd like."

Belgarath and Beldin exchanged a long look. "Never mind," Belgarath said.

"But—"

"Never mind."

"You were saying that your husband has imperial ambitions, your Grace," Silk floundered on.

"Can you imagine that idiot as emperor of Mallorea?" She sneered. "Half the time he can't even get his shoes on the right feet. Fortunately, he's a long way down the line of succession."

Garion suddenly remembered something. "Has anyone ever suggested anything to him that might have encouraged these ambitions?" he asked.

"*I* certainly didn't," she declared. She frowned blearily at the far wall. "Now that you mention it, though, there *was* a fellow who came through here a few years ago—a fellow with white eyes. Have you ever seen anybody with eyes like that? It makes your blood run cold. Anyway, he and the archduke went off to my husband's study to talk." She snorted derisively. "Study! I don't think my idiot husband can even read. He can barely talk to me, but he calls the room his study. Isn't that absurd? Well, at any rate, that happened at a time when I was still curious about the oaf's affairs. I'd had one of the footmen drill a hole through the wall so I could watch—and hear—what the fool was up to." Her lower lip began to tremble. "Not long after that, I saw him in there with the upstairs maid." She threw her arms out tragically, sloshing ale on Beldin. "Betrayed!" she cried. "In my own house!"

"What were they talking about?" Garion asked her gently. "Your husband and the white-eyed man, I mean?"

"White-eyes told my husband that somebody named Zandramas could guarantee him succession to the throne in Mal Zeth. That name sounds familiar for some reason. Has anybody ever heard it before?" She looked around, trying to focus her eyes.

"Not that I recall," Silk lied blandly. "Have you ever seen this white-eyed man again?"

The archduchess was busily trying to dip the last bit of ale out of the cask. "What?" she asked.

"The white-eyed man," Belgarath said impatiently. "Did he ever come back?"

"Of course." The lady leaned back and lustily drained her tankard. "He was here just a few days ago. He came here with some woman in a black satin robe and a little boy." She belched modestly. "Could you give that bellpull over there a bit of a jerk, my twisted little friend?" she asked Beldin. "I think we've used up all of this cask, and I'm still sort of thirsty."

"I'll see to it at once, me darlin'!" The hunchback stumped to the bellpull.

"It's so very nice to have friends about," the archduchess said dreamily. Then her head drooped to one side and she began to snore.

"Wake her up, Pol," Belgarath said.

"Yes, father."

It was a very light surge, but the tipsy noblewoman's eyes popped open immediately. "Where was I?" she asked.

"Ah—you were telling us about the visit of the white-eyed man a few days back, your Grace," Silk supplied.

"Oh, yes. He came in about dusk—him and that hag in black satin."

"Hag?" Silk asked.

"She must have been a hag. She went to a lot of trouble to keep her face covered. The little boy was adorable, though—reddish-blond curls and the bluest eyes you ever saw. I got some milk for him, because he was hungry. Anyway, White-eyes and the hag went off along with my husband, and then they all took horses and rode off. The toad, my husband, told me that he was going to be gone for a while and that I should send for my dressmaker—something about a gown suitable for an imperial coronation. I forget exactly."

"What happened to the little boy?" Ce'Nedra asked in a very tense voice.

The archduchess shrugged. "Who knows? As far as I know, they did take him with them." She sighed. "I'm suddenly so sleepy," she murmured.

"Did your husband give you any hint about where they were going?" Silk asked her.

She waved her hands helplessly. "I stopped listening to him years ago," she said. "We have a small yacht in a cove about a mile from here. It's gone, so I think they took that. My husband was saying something about those commercial wharves south of the city." She looked around. "Has that other cask of ale got here yet?" she asked drowsily.

" 'Twill only be a moment or two, me darlin'," Beldin assured her in a gentle voice.

"Oh, good."

"You need anything more?" Silk quietly asked Belgarath.

"I don't think so." The old man turned to his daughter. "Put her to sleep again, Pol," he said.

"There's no need, father," she replied. She looked rather sadly at the lush-bodied noblewoman, who had once again wrapped her arms about Beldin's neck, burrowed her face into his shoulder, and was lightly snoring. Gently, the dwarfed hunchback disengaged her arms and laid her softly on the couch. He straightened her gown, then crossed the room, picked up a comforter from a divan, returned, and covered her with it. "Sleep well, my Lady," he murmured, touching her face with one sad hand. Then he turned and glared pugnaciously at Belgarath. "Well?" he demanded in the tone of a man ready to fight.

"I didn't say anything," Belgarath said to him.

Wordlessly, Ce'Nedra rose, went to the hideous little man, embraced him, and kissed him on the cheek.

"What was that all about?" he asked suspiciously.

"I didn't say anything either," she replied, absently picking a few pieces of straw out of his beard and handing them to him.

CHAPTER SIX

As they emerged from the house, Garion went immediately to Chreti-enne and swung up into his saddle.

"What have you got in mind?" Silk asked him.

"I'm going to stay on the trail," Garion replied.

"Why? All it's going to do is run down to that cove the lady mentioned and then go out to sea again."

Garion looked at him helplessly.

"I'd say that the best thing for us to do right now is get back to Melcena as quickly as possible. I have a lot of people working for me there. I'll saturate those commercial wharves with men—the same way we did in Jarot. Naradas won't be hard to follow."

"Why don't I just take the Orb and go down to the wharves myself?" Garion protested.

"Because all you'll find out that way is which wharf she sailed from. We need more than that." Silk looked sympathetically at his friend. "I know you're impatient, Garion—we all are—but my way's going to be faster, actually. My people can find out when Zandramas sailed and where she was going. That's the thing we really have to know."

"All right, then," Belgarath said, "let's ride."

They mounted quickly and rode at a canter back up the drive to the road. Then they went south toward Melcena at a gallop.

It was about noon when they reached the north gate and not long after that when they dismounted in front of Silk's house. They went inside and on up the stairs to the sitting room. "Would you ask Vetter to come up?" the little man asked a passing servant as they entered the room.

"At once, your Highness."

"I'd say we'd better pack again," Silk suggested, removing his businessman's robe. "As soon as we find out where Zandramas is going, I think we'll be leaving again."

Sadi smiled faintly. "Poor Zith," he murmured. "She's getting very tired of traveling."

"She's not the only one," Velvet said a bit ruefully. "When this is all over, I don't think I'll ever want even to *look* at another horse."

There was a polite knock at the door, and Vetter opened it. "You wanted to see me, your Highness?" he asked.

"Yes, Vetter. Come in, please." Silk was pacing up and down, his eyes deep in thought. "We've been looking for some people," he said.

"I surmised as much, your Highness."

"Good. We know that these people came to Melcena not too long back. Then they left again about three days ago. We need to know where they went."

"Very well, your Highness. Can you give me a description?"

"I was just getting to that. There were two men, a woman, and a small boy. One of the men was the Archduke Otrath. Do you know him?"

Vetter nodded. "I can give our people an accurate description of him, yes."

"Very good, Vetter. The other man is named Naradas."

"I've heard the name, your Highness, but I don't think I've ever seen him."

"You wouldn't have forgotten him. His eyes are totally white."

"He's a blind man?"

"No, but his eyes have no color to them."

"That should make things simpler."

"I thought it might. The woman's been going to some trouble to keep her face covered, but she'll be with the archduke and Naradas. We've picked up the information that they may have sailed from one of the commercial wharves to the south of the city. Start out by concentrating the search there. Send every man you can put your hands on down there. Have them talk with everybody on those wharves. We need information and we need it fast. Spread money around if you have to. I want to know when they left, on which ship, and where they were going. If the ship happens to be back in port, bring me one of the sailors—or even better yet, the captain. Speed is essential, Vetter."

"I'll see to it at once, your Highness. I'll have several hundred men on those wharves within the hour and I'll keep you posted about the progress of the search. Will there be anything else?"

Silk frowned. "Yes," he decided. "We came to Melcena aboard one of our own ships. It should still be down in the harbor. Send someone to the captain and tell him to make ready to sail again. We'll be leaving as soon as we get the information."

"I'll attend to it." Vetter bowed and quietly left the room.

"He seems like a good man," Beldin noted.

"One of the best," Silk agreed. "He gets things done and he never gets excited." The little man smiled. "I've heard that Brador's been trying to lure him back, but I've got more money than Brador has."

Beldin grunted and looked at Belgarath. "We've got some things to sort out," he said. "Why is Zandramas saddling herself with this archduke? This whole side trip of hers didn't make any sense at all."

"Of course it did."

"I'm sure you'll explain that to me—sometime in the next week or so."

Belgarath fished around inside his tunic and pulled out a tattered scrap of paper. He looked at it. "This is it," he grunted. He held the paper out in front of him. " 'Behold:' " he read. " 'In the days which shall follow the ascension of the Dark God into the heavens shall the King of the East and the King of the South do war upon each other, and this shall be a sign unto ye that the day of the meeting is at hand. Hasten therefore unto the Place Which Is No More when battles do rage upon the plains of the South. Take with thee the chosen sacrifice and a King of Angarak to bear witness to what shall come to pass. For lo, whichever of ye cometh into the presence of Cthrag Sardius with the sacrifice and an Angarak king shall be exalted above all the rest and shall have dominion over them. And know further that in the moment of sacrifice shall the Dark God be reborn, and he shall triumph over the Child of Light in the instant of his rebirth.' "

"What a fascinating piece of gibberish," Beldin said. "Where did you come by it?"

"We picked it up in Cthol Murgos." Belgarath shrugged. "It's a part of the Grolim Prophecies of Rak Cthol. I told you about it before."

"No," Beldin disagreed, "as a matter of fact, you didn't."

"I must have."

"I'm sorry, Belgarath," the grubby little man said from between clenched teeth, "you didn't."

"What an amazing thing." Belgarath frowned. "It must have completely slipped my mind."

"We knew it was going to happen eventually, Pol," Beldin said. "The old boy's finally slipped over the line into senility."

"Be nice, uncle," she murmured.

"Are you *positive* I didn't tell you about this?" Belgarath said a little plaintively.

"There's no such thing as positive," Beldin replied, automatically, it seemed.

"I'm awfully glad you said that," Belgarath said just a bit smugly.

"Stop that."

"Stop what?"

"Don't try to use my own prejudices against me. Where does this Grolim insanity put us?"

"Grolims obey orders beyond the point of reason."

"So do we, when you get down to it."

"Perhaps, but at least we question the orders now and then. Grolims don't. They follow instructions blindly. When we were in Rak Urga, we saw the Hierarch Agachak bullying King Urgit about this. Agachak knows that he has to have an Angarak king in tow if he's going to have any chance at all when he gets to this place of the final meeting. He's going to take Urgit, even if he has to drag him by the hair. Up until now, Zandramas hasn't bothered herself about the requirement."

"She must be planning to kill 'Zakath, then," Durnik said, "and then put this archduke on the throne in his place."

"She won't even have to do that, Durnik. All you need to be called a king in Angarak society is a hint of royal blood, a coronation ceremony, and recognition by a major Grolim priest. Back in the old days, every clan-chief was a king. It didn't really matter that much, because all the power was in the hands of Torak anyway. They all had crowns and thrones, though. Anyway, Zandramas is a recognized Grolim priest—or priestess, in this case. Otrath is of royal blood. A coronation, spurious or not, would qualify him as a King of Angarak, and that would satisfy the prophecy."

"It still seems a little questionable to me," Durnik said.

"This comes from a man whose people elected a rutabaga farmer as their first king," Beldin said.

"Actually, Fundor the Magnificent wasn't a bad king," Belgarath said. "At least, once he got the hang of it all. Farmers always make good kings. They know what's important. At any rate, Otrath will be king enough to fulfill the prophecy, and that means that Zandramas has everything she needs now. She has Geran and an Angarak king."

"Do we need one, too?" Durnik asked. "An Angarak king, I mean?"

"No. We'd need an Alorn King. I think Garion qualifies."

"It wasn't this complicated last time, was it?"

"Actually it was. Garion was already the Rivan King as well as the Child of Light. Torak was both king and God, *and* he was the Child of Dark."

"Who was the sacrifice, then?"

Belgarath smiled affectionately at the good man. "You were, Durnik," he said gently. "Remember?"

"Oh," Durnik said, looking a bit embarrassed. "I forget about that sometimes."

"I wouldn't be at all surprised," Beldin growled. "Getting killed is the sort of thing that might tend to make one's memory wander just a bit."

"That's enough of that, uncle," Polgara said dangerously, putting a protective arm about Durnik's shoulders.

Garion suddenly realized that not one of them had ever spoken with Durnik about that terrible time between the moment Zedar had killed him and the moment when the Orb and the Gods had returned him to life. He had the very strong feeling that Polgara fully intended to keep it that way.

"She's completed all her tasks then, hasn't she?" Ce'Nedra asked sadly. "Zandramas, I mean. She has my son and an Angarak king. I do so wish I could see him one more time before I die."

"Die?" Garion asked incredulously. "What do you mean, die?"

"One of us is going to," she said simply. "I'm sure it's going to be me. There's no other reason for me being along, is there? We all have tasks to perform. Mine is to die, I think."

"Nonsense!"

"Really?" She sighed.

"Actually, Zandramas still has several more tasks," Belgarath told her. "She has to deal with Urvon at the very least."

"And Agachak, I think," Sadi added. "He wants to play, too, as I recall."

"Agachak's in Cthol Murgos," Silk objected.

"So were we—until some months back," the eunuch pointed out. "All it takes to get to Mallorea from Cthol Murgos is a boat and a little luck with the weather."

"Zandramas has one other thing she has to do as well," Velvet said, moving over until she was beside Ce'Nedra and wrapping her arms about the sad little queen.

"Oh?" Ce'Nedra said without much interest. "What's that?"

"The prophecy told Garion that she still doesn't know where the Place Which Is No More is. She can't go there until she finds out, can she?"

Ce'Nedra's face brightened just a bit. "That's true, isn't it?" she conceded. "I suppose it's something," she said, laying her head against Velvet's shoulder.

"Zandramas isn't the only one with things left to do," Belgarath said. "I still have to find an unmutilated copy of the Ashabine Oracles." He looked at Silk. "How long do you think it's going to take your men to find out what we need to know?"

Silk spread his hands. "It's a little hard to say," he admitted. "A lot could depend on luck. A day at the most, I'd imagine."

"How fast is that ship of yours?" Garion asked him. "I mean, can it go any faster than it did when we were coming here?"

"Not by very much," Silk replied. "Melcenes are better shipbuilders than Angaraks, but that ship was built to carry cargo, not to win races. If the wind gets too strong, the captain's going to have to shorten his sails."

"I'd give a lot to have a Cherek warship right now," Garion said. "A fast boat could make up for a lot of lost time." He gazed thoughtfully at the floor. "It wouldn't really be too hard, would it?" he suggested. He looked at Belgarath. "Maybe you and I could put our heads together, and—" He made a kind of vague gesture with his hand.

"Uh—Garion," Durnik interrupted him, "even if you did have a Cherek boat, who would you find to sail her? I don't think the sailors here would understand what's involved."

"Oh," Garion said glumly. "I hadn't thought about that, I guess."

There was a light rap at the door, and Vetter entered carrying a sheaf of parchments. "The men have been dispatched to the south wharves, your Highness," he reported. "You suggested that the matter was of some urgency, so I took the liberty of posting couriers on fast horses to central locations near the waterfront. As soon as anyone gets news of any kind, the word should reach us here within five minutes." He glanced at Ce'Nedra. "I hope that will relieve some of her Majesty's anxiety," he added.

"Her—" Silk burst out, then controlled himself. He stared at his factor for a moment, then burst out laughing. "How did you find out, Vetter?" he asked. "I didn't introduce anybody."

"Please, your Highness," Vetter replied with a pained look. "You didn't engage me in this position to be stupid, did you? I've maintained certain contacts with my former associates in Mal Zeth, so I more or less know who your guests are and what your mission is. You chose not to mention the matter, so I didn't make an issue of it, but you aren't paying me to keep my eyes and ears closed, are you?"

"Don't you just love Melcenes?" Velvet said to Sadi.

Sadi, however, was already looking at Vetter with a certain interest. "It may just happen that in time I'll be able to resolve the slight misunderstanding I presently have with my queen," he said delicately to Silk's factor. "Should that happen, I might want to make you aware of certain employment opportunities in Sthiss Tor."

"Sadi!" Silk gasped.

"Business is business, Prince Kheldar," Sadi said blandly.

Vetter smiled. "There are these few documents, your Highness," he said to Silk, handing over the parchments he carried. "As long as you're waiting, I thought you might want to glance at them. A few require your signature."

Silk sighed. "I suppose I might as well," he agreed.

"It does save time, your Highness. Sometimes it takes quite a while for things to catch up with you."

Silk riffled through the stack. "This all seems fairly routine. Is there anything else of note going on?"

"The house is being watched, your Highness," Vetter reported. "A couple of Rolla's secret policemen. I imagine they'll try to follow you when you leave."

Silk frowned. "I'd forgotten about him. Is there some way to get them off our trail?"

"I think I can manage that for your Highness."

"Nothing fatal, though," Silk cautioned. "The Rivan King here disapproves of random fatalities." He grinned at Garion.

"I think we'll be able to deal with the situation without bloodshed, your Highness."

"Anything else I should know about?"

"The Consortium will make an offer on our bean holdings tomorrow morning," Vetter replied. "They'll start at three points below market and go as high as five above it."

"How did you find that out?" Silk looked amazed.

"I've bribed one of the members." Vetter shrugged. "I promised to give him a quarter point commission on everything over ten—a bit generous, perhaps, but we may need him again sometime, and now I'll have a hold on him."

"That's worth a quarter of a point right there."

"I thought so myself, your Highness." Vetter laughed suddenly. "Oh, one other thing, Prince Kheldar. We have this investment opportunity."

"Oh?"

"Actually, it's more in the nature of a charitable contribution."

"I gave at the office," Silk said with an absolutely straight face. Then his nose twitched slightly. "It wouldn't hurt to hear about it, though, I guess."

"There's a very grubby little alchemist at the university," Vetter explained. "He absolutely swears that he can turn brass into gold."

"Well, now." Silk's eyes brightened.

Vetter held up a cautioning hand. "The cost, however, is prohibitive at this time. It doesn't make much sense to spend two pieces of gold to get back one."

"No, I wouldn't say so."

"The little clubfoot maintains that he can reduce the cost, though. He's been approaching every businessman in Melcena about the project. He needs a rich patron to underwrite the cost of his experiments."

"Did you look into the matter at all?"

"Of course. Unless he's a very skilled trickster, it appears that he actually *can* turn brass into gold. He has a rather peculiar reputation. They say that he's been around for centuries. He's got a bad temper and he smells awful—the chemicals he uses, I understand."

Belgarath's eyes suddenly went very wide. "What did you call him?" he demanded.

"I don't believe I mentioned his name, Ancient One," Vetter replied. "He's called Senji."

"I don't mean his name. Describe him."

"He's short and mostly bald. He wears a beard—though most of his whiskers have been singed off. Sometimes his experiments go awry, and there have been explosions. Oh, and he has a clubfoot—the left one, I believe."

"That's it!" Belgarath exclaimed, snapping his fingers.

"Don't be cryptic, father," Polgara said primly.

"The prophecy told Garion that somebody was going to say something to us in passing today that was very important. This is it."

"I don't quite—"

"At Ashaba, Cyradis told us to seek out the clubfooted one because he'd help us in our search."

"There are many men with clubfeet in the world, father."

"I know, but the prophecy went out of its way to introduce this one."

"Introduce?"

"Maybe that's the wrong word, but you know what I mean."

"It does sort of fit, Pol," Beldin said. "As I remember, we were talking about the Ashabine Oracles when Cyradis told us about this clubfoot. She said that Zandramas has one uncut copy, Nahaz has another, and that this clubfoot has the third—or knows where it is."

"It's pretty thin, Belgarath," Durnik said dubiously.

"We've got time enough to chase it down," the old man replied. "We can't go anywhere until we find out where Zandramas is going anyway." He looked at Vetter. "Where do we find this Senji?"

"He's on the faculty of the College of Applied Alchemy at the university, Ancient One."

"All right, I'll take Garion and we'll go there. The rest of you might as well get ready to leave."

"Grandfather," Garion protested, "I have to stay here.
I want to hear the word about Zandramas with my own ears."

"Pol can listen for you. I might need you along to help persuade the alchemist to talk to me. Bring the Orb, but leave the sword behind."

"Why the Orb?"

"Let's just call it a hunch."

"I'll come with you," Beldin said, rising to his feet.

"There's no need of that."

"Oh, yes there is. Your memory seems to be failing a bit, Belgarath. You forget to tell me things. If I'm there when you locate the Oracles, I'll be able to save you all the time and trouble of trying to remember."

CHAPTER SEVEN

The University of Melcena was a sprawling complex of buildings situated in a vast park. The buildings were old and stately, and the trees dotting the close-clipped lawns were gnarled with age. There was a kind of secure serenity about the place that bespoke a dedication to the life of the mind. A calm came over Garion as he walked with the two old sorcerers across the green lawn, but there was a kind of melancholy as well. He sighed.

"What's the problem?" Belgarath asked him.

"Oh, I don't know, Grandfather. Sometimes I wish I might have had the chance to come to a place like this. It might be kind of nice to study something for no reason except that you want to know about it. Most of my studying has been pretty urgent—you know, find the answer, or the world will come to an end."

"Universities are overrated places," Beldin said. "Too many young men attend simply because their fathers insist, and they spend more time carousing than they do studying. The noise is distracting to the serious student. Stick to studying alone. You get more done." He looked at Belgarath. "Have you got even the remotest idea where we're going to find this Senji?"

"Vetter said that he's a member of the faculty of the College of Applied Alchemy. I'd imagine that's the place to start."

"Logic, Belgarath? You? The next question that pops to mind is where we're going to find the College of Applied Alchemy."

Belgarath stopped a robed scholar who was walking across the lawn with an open book in his hand. "Excuse me, learned sir," he said politely, "but could you direct me to the College of Applied Alchemy?"

"Umm?" the scholar said, looking up from his book.

"The College of Applied Alchemy. Could you tell me where I could find it?"

"The sciences are all down that way," the scholar said, "near the theology department." He waved rather vaguely toward the south end of the campus.

"Thank you," Belgarath said. "You're too kind."

"It's a scholar's duty to provide instruction and direction," the fellow replied pompously.

"Ah, yes," Belgarath murmured. "Sometimes I lose sight of that."

They walked on in the direction the scholar had indicated.

"If he doesn't give his students any more specific directions than that, they probably come out of this place with a rather vague idea of the world," Beldin observed.

The directions they received from others gradually grew more precise, and they finally reached a blocky-looking building constructed of thick gray rock and solidly buttressed along its walls. They went up the steps in front and entered a hallway that was also shored up with stout buttresses.

"I don't quite follow the reason for all the interior reinforcement," Garion confessed.

As if in answer to his question, there came a thunderous detonation from behind a door partway up the hall. The door blew outward violently, and clouds of reeking smoke came pouring out.

"Oh," Garion said. "Now I understand."

A fellow with a dazed look on his face and with his clothes hanging from his body in smoking tatters came staggering out through the smoke. "Too much sulfur," he was muttering over and over again. "Too much sulfur."

"Excuse me," Belgarath said, "do you by any chance know where we might find the alchemist Senji?"

"Too much sulfur," the experimenter said, looking blankly at Belgarath.

"Senji," the old man repeated. "Could you tell us where to find him?"

The tattered fellow frowned. "What?" he said blankly.

"Let me," Beldin said. "Can you tell us where to find Senji?" he bellowed at the top of his lungs. "He's got a clubfoot."

"Oh," the man replied, shaking his head to clear his befuddlement. "His laboratory's on the top floor—down toward the other end."

"Thank you," Beldin shouted at him.

"Too much sulfur. That's the problem, all right. I put in too much sulfur."

"Why were you shouting at him?" Belgarath asked curiously as the three of them went on down the hall.

"I've been in the middle of a few explosions myself." The hunchback shrugged. "I was always deaf as a post for a week or two afterward."

"Oh."

They went up two flights of stairs to the top floor. They passed another door that had only recently been exploded out of its casement. Belgarath poked his head through the opening. "Where can we find Senji?" he shouted into the room.

There was a mumbled reply.

"Last door on the left," the old man grunted, leading the way.

"Alchemy seems to be a fairly dangerous occupation," Garion noted.

"Also fairly stupid," Beldin growled. "If they want gold so badly, why don't they just go dig it up?"

"I don't think that's occurred to very many of them," Belgarath said. He stopped before the last door on the left, a door showing signs of recent repair. He knocked.

"Go away," a rusty-sounding voice replied.

"We need to talk with you, Senji," Belgarath called mildly.

The rusty voice told him at some length what he could do with his need to talk. Most of the words were very colorful.

Belgarath's face grew set. He gathered himself up and spoke a single word. The door disappeared with a shocking sound.

"Now that's something you don't see around here very much," the grubby little man sitting in the midst of the splintered remains of his door said in a conversational tone. "I can't remember the last time I saw a door blow *in*." He started picking splinters out of his beard.

"Are you all right?" Garion asked him.

"Of course, just a little surprised is all. When you've been blown up as many times as I have, you sort of get used to the idea. Does one of you want to pull this door off me?"

Beldin stumped forward and lifted the remains of the door.

"You're an ugly one, aren't you?" the man on the floor said.

"You're no beauty yourself."

"I can live with it."

"So can I."

"Good. Are you the one who blew my door in?"

"He did." Beldin pointed at Belgarath and then helped the fellow to his feet.

"How did you manage that?" the grubby little man asked Belgarath curiously. "I don't smell any chemicals at all."

"It's a gift," Belgarath replied. "You're Senji, I take it?"

"I am. Senji the clubfoot, senior member of the faculty of the College of Applied Alchemy." He thumped on the side of his head with the heel of his hand. "Explosions always make my ears ring," he noted. "You—my ugly friend," he said to Beldin. "There's a barrel of beer over there in the corner. Why don't you bring me some? Get some for yourself and your friends as well."

"We're going to get along fairly well," Beldin said.

Senji limped toward a stone table in the center of the room. His left leg was several inches shorter than his right, and his left foot was grotesquely deformed. He leafed through several sheets of parchment. "Good," he said to Belgarath. "At least your explosion didn't scatter my calculations all over the room." He looked at them. "As long as you're here, you might as well find something to sit down on."

Beldin brought him a cup of beer, then went back to the corner where the barrel was and filled three more cups.

"That is *really* an ugly fellow," Senji noted, hauling himself up and sitting on top of the table. "I sort of like him, though. I haven't met anybody quite like that for almost a thousand years."

Belgarath and Garion exchanged a quick look. "That's quite a long time," Belgarath said cautiously.

"Yes," Senji agreed, taking a drink from his cup. He made a face. "It's gone flat again," he said. "You there," he called to Beldin. "There's an earthenware jar on the shelf just above the barrel. Be a good fellow and dump a couple handfuls of that powder into the beer. It wakes it up again." He looked back at Belgarath. "What was it you wanted to talk about?" he asked. "What's so important that you have to go around blowing doors apart?"

"In a minute," Belgarath said. He crossed to where the little clubfoot sat. "Do you mind?" he asked. He reached out and lightly touched his fingertips to the smelly man's bald head.

"Well?" Beldin asked.

Belgarath nodded. "He doesn't use it very often, but it's there. Garion, fix the door. I think we'll want to talk in private."

Garion looked helplessly at the shattered remains of the door. "It's not in very good shape, Grandfather," he said dubiously.

"Make a new one then."

"Oh. I guess I forgot about that."

"You need some practice anyway. Just make sure that you can get it open later. I don't want to have to blow it down again when the time comes to leave."

Garion gathered in his will, concentrated a moment, pointed at the empty opening, and said, "Door." The opening was immediately filled again.

"Door?" Beldin said incredulously.

"He does that sometimes," Belgarath said. "I've been trying to break him of the habit, but he backslides from time to time."

Senji's eyes were narrow as he looked at them. "Well, now," he said. "I seem to have some talented guests. I haven't met a real sorcerer in a long, long time."

"How long?" Belgarath asked bluntly.

"Oh, a dozen centuries or so, I guess. A Grolim was here giving lectures in the College of Comparative Theology. Stuffy sort of fellow, as I recall, but then, most Grolims are."

"All right, Senji," Belgarath said, "just how old *are* you?"

"I think I was born during the fifteenth century," Senji replied. "What year is it now?"

"Fifty-three seventy-nine," Garion told him.

"Already?" Senji said mildly. "Where does the time go?" He counted it up on his fingers. "I guess that would make me about thirty-nine hundred or so."

"When did you find out about the Will and the Word?" Belgarath pressed.

"The what?"

"Sorcery."

"Is that what you call it?" Senji pondered a bit. "I suppose the term is sort of accurate, at that," he mused. "I like that. The Will and the Word. Has a nice ring to it, doesn't it?"

"When did you make the discovery?" Belgarath repeated.

"During the fifteenth century, obviously. Otherwise I'd have died in the normal course of time, like everybody else."

"You didn't have any instruction?"

"Who was around in the fifteenth century to instruct me? I just stumbled over it."

Belgarath and Beldin looked at each other. Then Belgarath sighed and covered his eyes with one hand.

"It happens once in a while," Beldin said. "Some people just fall into it."

"I know, but it's so discouraging. Look at all the centuries our Master took instructing us, and this fellow just picks it up on his own." He looked back at Senji. "Why don't you tell us about it?" he suggested. "Try not to leave too much out."

"Do we really have time, Grandfather?" Garion asked.

"We have to *make* time," Beldin told him. "It was one of our Master's final commandments. Any time we come across somebody who's picked up the secret spontaneously, we're supposed to investigate. Not even the Gods know how it happens."

Senji slid down from the table and limped over to an overflowing bookcase. He rummaged around for a moment and finally selected a book that looked much the worse for wear. "Sorry about the shape it's in," he apologized. "It's been blown up a few times." He limped back to the table and opened the book. "I wrote this during the twenty-third century," he said. "I noticed that I was starting to get a little absentminded, so I wanted to get it all down while it was still fresh in my memory."

"Makes sense," Beldin said. "My grim-faced friend over there has been suffering from some shocking lapses of memory lately—of course, that's to be expected from somebody who's nineteen thousand years old."

"Do you mind?" Belgarath said acidly.

"You mean it's been longer?"

"Shut up, Beldin."

"Here we are," Senji said. Then he began to read aloud.

" 'For the next fourteen hundred years the Melcene Empire prospered, far removed from the theological and political squabbles of the western part of the continent. Melcene culture was secular, civilized, and highly educated. Slavery was unknown, and trade with the Angaraks and their subject peoples in Karanda and Dalasia was extremely profitable. The old imperial capital at Melcena became a major center of learning.' "

"Excuse me," Belgarath said, "but isn't that taken directly from *Emperors of Melcena and Mallorea?*"

"Naturally," Senji replied without any embarrassment. "Plagiarism is the first rule of scholarship. Please don't interrupt."

"Sorry," Belgarath said.

" 'Unfortunately,' " Senji read on, " 'some of the thrust of Melcene scholarship turned toward the arcane. Their major field of concentration lay in the field of alchemy.' " He looked at Belgarath. "This is where it gets original," he said. He cleared his throat. " 'It was a Melcene alchemist, Senji the clubfooted, who inadvertently utilized sorcery during the course of one of his experiments.' "

"You speak of yourself in the third person?" Beldin asked.

"It was a twenty-third-century affectation," Senji replied. "Autobiography was considered to be in terribly bad taste—immodest, don't you know. It was a very boring century. I yawned all the way through it." He went back to reading. " 'Senji, a fifteenth-century practitioner of alchemy at the university in the imperial city, was notorious for his ineptitude.' " He paused. "I might want to edit that part just a bit," he noted critically. He glanced at the next line. "And this just won't do at all," he added. " 'To be quite frank about it,' " he read with distaste, " 'Senji's experiments more often turned gold into lead than the reverse. In a fit of colossal frustration at the failure of his most recent experiment, Senji accidentally converted a half ton of brass plumbing into solid gold. An immediate debate arose, involving the Bureau of Currency, the Bureau of Mines, the Department of Sanitation, the faculty of the College of Applied Alchemy, and the faculty of the College of Comparative Theology about which organization should have control of Senji's discovery. After about three hundred years of argumentation, it suddenly occurred to the disputants that Senji was not merely talented, but also appeared to be immortal. In the name of scientific experimentation, the varying bureaus, departments, and faculties agreed that an effort should be made to have him assassinated to verify that fact.' "

"They didn't!" Beldin said.

"Oh, yes," Senji replied with a grim smugness. "Melcenes are inquisitive to the point of idiocy. They'll go to any lengths to prove a theory."

"What did you do?"

Senji smirked so hard that his long nose and pointed chin almost touched. " 'A well-known defenestrator was retained to throw the irascible old alchemist from a high window in one of the towers of the university administration building,' " he read. " 'The experiment had a threefold purpose. What the curious bureaus wished to find out was: (A) if Senji *was* in fact unkillable, (B) what means he would take to save his life while plummeting toward the paved courtyard, and (C) if it might be possible to discover the secret of flight by giving him no other alternative.' " The clubfooted alchemist tapped the back of his hand against the text. "I've always been a little proud of that sentence," he said. "It's so beautifully balanced."

"It's a masterpiece," Beldin approved, slapping the little man on the shoulder so hard that it nearly knocked him off the table. "Here," he said, taking Senji's cup, "let me refill that for you." His brow creased, there was a surge, and the cup was full again. Senji took a sip and fell to gasping.

"It's a drink that a Nadrak woman of my acquaintance brews," Beldin told him. "Robust, isn't it?"

"Very," Senji agreed in a hoarse voice.

"Go on with your story, my friend."

Senji cleared his throat—several times—and went on.

" 'What the officials and learned men actually found out as a result of their experiment was that it is extremely dangerous to threaten the life of a sorcerer—even one as inept as Senji. The defenestrator found himself suddenly translocated to a position some fifteen hundred meters above the harbor, five miles distant. At one instant he had been wrestling Senji toward the window; at the next, he found himself standing on insubstantial air high above a fishing fleet. His demise occasioned no particular sorrow—except among the fishermen, whose nets were badly damaged by his rapid descent.' "

"That was a masterful passage," Beldin chortled, "but where did you discover the meaning of the word 'translocation'?"

"I was reading an old text on the exploits of Belgarath the Sorcerer, and I—" Senji stopped, going very pale, turned, and gaped at Garion's grandfather.

"It's a terrible letdown, isn't it?" Beldin said. "We always told him he ought to try to look more impressive."

"You're in no position to talk," the old man said.

"You're the one with the earthshaking reputation." Beldin shrugged. "I'm just a flunky. I'm along for comic relief."

"You're really enjoying this, aren't you, Beldin?"

"I haven't had so much fun in years. Wait until I tell Pol."

"You keep your mouth shut, you hear me?"

"Yes, O mighty Belgarath," Beldin said mockingly.

Belgarath turned to Garion. "Now you understand why Silk irritates me so much," he said.

"Yes, Grandfather, I think I do."

Senji was still a little wild-eyed.

"Take another drink, Senji," Beldin advised. "It's not nearly so hard to accept when your wits are half-fuddled."

Senji began to tremble. Then he drained his cup in one gulp without so much as a cough.

"Now there's a brave lad," Beldin congratulated him. "Please read on. Your story is fascinating."

Falteringly, the little alchemist continued. " 'In an outburst of righteous indignation, Senji then proceeded to chastise the department heads who had consorted to do violence to his person. It was finally only a personal appeal from the emperor himself that persuaded the old man to desist from some fairly exotic punishments. After that, the department heads were more than happy to allow Senji to go his own way unmolested.

" 'On his own, Senji established a private academy and advertised for students. While his pupils never became sorcerers of the magnitude of Belgarath, Polgara, Ctuchik, or Zedar, some of them were, nonetheless, able to perform some rudimentary applications of the principle their master had inadvertently discovered. This immediately elevated them far above the magicians and witches practicing *their* art forms within the confines of the university.' " Senji looked up. "There's more," he said, "but most of it deals with my experiments in the field of alchemy."

"I think that's the crucial part," Belgarath said. "Let's go back a bit. What were you feeling at the exact moment that you changed all that brass into gold?"

"Irritation," Senji shrugged, closing his book. "Or maybe more than that. I'd worked out my calculations so very carefully, but the bar of lead I was working on just lay there not doing anything. I was infuriated. Then I just sort of pulled everything around me inside, and I could feel an enormous power building up. I shouted 'Change!'—mostly at the lead bar, but there were some pipes running through the room as well, and my concentration was a little diffused."

"You're lucky you didn't change the walls, too," Beldin told him. "Were you ever able to do it again?"

Senji shook his head. "I tried, but I never seemed to be able to put together that kind of anger again."

"Are you always angry when you do this sort of thing?" the hunchback asked.

"Almost always," Senji admitted. "If I'm not angry, I can't be certain of the results. Sometimes it works and sometimes it doesn't."

"That seems to be the key to it, Belgarath," Beldin said. "Rage is the common element in every case we've come across."

"As I remember, I was irritated the first time I did it as well," Belgarath conceded.

"So was I," Beldin said. "With you, I think."

"Why did you take it out on that tree, then?"

"At the last second I remembered that our Master was fond of you, and I didn't want to hurt his feelings by obliterating you."

"That probably saved your life: If you'd said 'be not,' you wouldn't be here now."

Beldin scratched at his stomach. "That might explain why we find so few cases of spontaneous sorcery," he mused. "When somebody's enraged at something, his first impulse is usually to destroy it. This might have happened many, many times, but the spontaneous sorcerers probably annihilated themselves in the moment of discovery."

"I wouldn't be at all surprised that you've hit it," Belgarath agreed.

Senji had gone pale again. "I think there's something I need to know here," he said.

"It's the first rule," Garion told him. "The universe won't let us unmake things. If we try, all the force turns inward, and we're the ones who vanish." With a shudder he remembered the obliteration of Ctuchik. He looked at Beldin. "Did I get that right?" he asked.

"Fairly close. The explanation is a little more complex, but you described the process pretty accurately."

"Did that by any chance happen to any of your students?" Belgarath asked Senji.

The alchemist frowned. "It might have," he admitted. "Quite a few of them disappeared. I thought they'd just gone off someplace, but maybe not."

"Are you taking any more students these days?"

Senji shook his head. "I don't have the patience for it any more. Only about one in ten could even grasp the concept, and the rest stood around whining and sniveling and blaming me for not explaining it any better. I went back to alchemy. I almost never use sorcery any more."

"We were told that you can actually do it," Garion said. "Turn brass or lead into gold, I mean."

"Oh, yes," Senji replied in an offhand way. "It's really fairly easy, but the process is more expensive than the gold is worth. That's what I'm trying to do now—simplify the process and substitute less expensive chemicals. I can't get anyone to fund my experiments, though."

Garion felt a sudden throbbing against his hip. Puzzled, he looked down at the pouch in which he was carrying the Orb. There was a sound in his ears, an angry sort of buzz that was unlike the shimmering sound the Orb usually made.

"What's that peculiar sound?" Senji asked.

Garion untied the pouch from his belt and opened it. The Orb was glowing an angry red.

"Zandramas?" Belgarath asked intently.

Garion shook his head. "No, Grandfather. I don't think so."

"Does it want to take you someplace?"

"It's pulling."

"Let's see where it wants to go."

Garion held the Orb out in his right hand and it drew him steadily toward the door. They went out into the corridor with Senji limping along behind them, his face afire with curiosity. The Orb led them down the stairs and out the front door of the building.

"It seems to want to go toward that building over there," Garion said, pointing toward a soaring tower of pure white marble.

"The College of Comparative Theology," Senji sniffed. "They're a sorry group of scholars with an inflated notion of their contribution to the sum of human knowledge."

"Follow it, Garion," Belgarath instructed.

They crossed the lawn. Startled scholars scattered before them like frightened birds after one look at Belgarath's face.

They entered the ground floor of the tower. A thin man in ecclesiastical robes sat at a high desk just inside the door. "You're not members of this college," he said in an outraged voice. "You can't come in here."

Without even slowing his pace, Belgarath translocated the officious doorman some distance out onto the lawn, desk and all.

"It does have its uses, doesn't it?" Senji conceded. "Maybe I should give it a little more study. Alchemy's beginning to bore me."

"What's behind this door?" Garion asked, pointing.

"That's their museum." Senji shrugged. "It's a hodgepodge of old idols, religious artifacts, and that sort of thing."

Garion tried the handle. "It's locked."

Beldin leaned back and kicked the door open, splintering the wood around the lock.

"Why did you do that?" Belgarath asked him.

"Why not?" Beldin shrugged. "I'm not going to waste the effort of pulling in my will for an ordinary door."

"You're getting lazy."

"I'll put it back together, and you can open it."

"Never mind."

They went into the dusty, cluttered room. There were rows of glass display cases in the center, and the walls were lined with grotesque statues. Cobwebs hung from the ceiling and dust lay everywhere.

"They don't come in here very often," Senji noted. "They'd rather cook up addlepated theories than look at the real effects of human religious impulses."

"This way," Garion said as the Orb continued to pull steadily at his hand. He noticed that the stone was glowing redder and redder, and it was getting uncomfortably warm.

Then it stopped before a glass case where a rotting cushion lay behind the dusty panes. Aside from the cushion, the case was empty. The Orb was actually hot now, and its ruddy glow filled the entire room.

"What was in this case?" Belgarath demanded.

Senji leaned forward to read the inscription on the corroded brass plate attached to the case. "Oh," he said, "now I remember. This is the case where they used to keep Cthrag Sardius—before it was stolen."

Suddenly, without any warning, the Orb seemed to jump in Garion's hand, and the glass case standing empty before them exploded into a thousand fragments.

■ CHAPTER EIGHT ■

"How long was it here?" Belgarath asked the shaken Senji, who was gaping in awe first at the still sullenly glowing Orb in Garion's hand, then at the shattered remains of the case.

"Senji," Belgarath said sharply, "pay attention."

"Is that what I think it is?" the alchemist asked, pointing at the Orb with a trembling hand.

"Cthrag Yaska," Beldin told him. "If you're going to play this game, you may as well learn what's involved. Now answer my brother's question."

Senji floundered. "I'm not—" he began. "I've always been just an alchemist. I'm not interested in—"

"It doesn't work that way," Belgarath cut him off. "Like it or not, you're a member of a very select group. Stop thinking about gold and other nonsense, and start paying attention to what's important."

Senji swallowed hard. "It was always just a kind of game," he quavered. "Nobody ever took me seriously."

"We do," Garion told him, holding out the Orb to the now-cringing little man. "Do you have any idea of the kind of power you've stumbled over?" He was suddenly enormously angry. "Would you like to have me blow down this tower—or sink the Melcene Islands back into the sea—just to show you how serious we are?"

"You're Belgarion, aren't you?"

"Yes."

"The Godslayer?"

"Some people call me that."

"Oh, my God," Senji whimpered.

"We're wasting time," Belgarath said flatly. "Start talking. I want to know just where Cthrag Sardius came from, how long it was here, and where it went from here."

"It's a long story," Senji said.

"Abbreviate it," Beldin told him, kicking aside the glass shards on the floor. "We're a little pressed for time right now."

"How long was the Sardion here?" Belgarath asked.

"Eons," Senji replied.

"Where did it come from?"

"Zamad," the alchemist responded. "The people up there are Karands, but they're a little timid about demons. I think a few of their magicians were eaten alive. Anyway—or so the legends say—at about the time of the cracking of the world some five thousand years or so ago . . ." he faltered again, staring at the two dreadful old men facing him.

"It was noisy," Beldin supplied distastefully. "A lot of steam and earthquakes. Torak was always ostentatious—some kind of character defect, I think."

"Oh, my God," Senji said again.

"Don't keep saying that," Belgarath told him in a disgusted tone. "You don't even know who your God is."

"But you will, Senji," Garion said in a voice that was not his own, "and once you have met Him, you will follow Him all the days of your life."

Belgarath looked at Garion with one raised eyebrow.

Garion spread his hands helplessly. "Get on with this, Belgarath," the voice said through Garion's lips. "Time isn't waiting for you, you know."

Belgarath turned back to Senji. "All right," he said. "The Sardion came to Zamad. How?"

"It's said to have fallen out of the sky."

"They always do," Beldin said. "Someday I'd like to see something rise up out of the earth—just for the sake of variety."

"You get bored too easily, my brother," Belgarath told him.

"I didn't see you sitting over Burnt-face's tomb for five hundred years, my brother," Beldin retorted.

"I don't think I can stand this," Senji said, burying his face in his trembling hands.

"It gets easier as you go along," Garion said in a comforting tone. "We're not really here to make your life unpleasant. All we need is a little information and then we'll go away. If you think about it in the right way, you might even be able to make yourself believe that this is all a dream."

"I'm in the presence of three demigods, and you want me to pass it off as a dream?"

"That's a nice term," Beldin said. "Demigod. I like the sound of it."

"You're easily impressed by words," Belgarath told him.

"Words are the core of thought. Without words there *is* no thought."

Senji's eyes brightened. "Now, we might want to talk about that a little bit," he suggested.

"Later," Belgarath said. "Get back to Zamad—and the Sardion."

"All right," the clubfooted little alchemist said. "Cthrag Sardius—or the Sardion, whatever you want to call it—came out of the sky into Zamad. The barbarians up there thought that it was holy and built a shrine to it and fell down on their faces and worshipped it. The shrine was in a valley up in the mountains, and there was a grotto and an altar and that sort of thing."

"We've been there," Belgarath said shortly. "It's at the bottom of a lake now. How did it get to Melcena?"

"That came years later," Senji replied. "The Karands have always been a troublesome people, and their social organization is fairly rudimentary. About three thousand years ago—or maybe a little longer—a King of Zamad began to feel ambitious, so he assimilated Voresebo and started looking hungrily south. There were a series of raids in force across the border into Rengel. Of course, Rengel was a part of the Melcene Empire, and the emperor decided that it was time to teach the Karands a lesson. He mounted a punitive expedition and marched into Voresebo and then Zamad at the head of a column of elephant cavalry. The Karands had never seen an elephant before and they fled in panic. The emperor systematically destroyed all the towns and villages up there. He heard about the holy object and its shrine and he went there and took Cthrag Sardius—more I think to punish the Karands than out of any desire to possess the stone for himself. It's not really very attractive, you know."

"What does it look like?" Garion asked him.

"It's fairly large," Senji said. "It's sort of oval-shaped and about so big." He indicated an object about two feet in diameter with his hands. "It's a strange reddish sort of color, and kind of milky-looking—like certain kinds of flint. Anyway, as I said, the emperor didn't really want the thing, so when he got back to Melcena, he donated it to the university. It was passed around from department to department, and it finally ended up here in this museum. It lay in that case for thousands of years, collecting dust, and nobody really paid any attention to it."

"How did it leave here?" Belgarath asked.

"I was just getting to that. About five hundred years ago there was a scholar in the College of Arcane Learning. He was a strange sort who heard voices. At any rate, he became absolutely obsessed with Cthrag Sardius. He used to sneak in here at night and sit for hours staring at it. I think he believed that it was talking to him."

"It's possible," Beldin said. "It could probably do that."

"This scholar grew more and more irrational and he finally came in here one night and stole Cthrag Sardius. I don't think anyone would have noticed that it was missing, but the scholar fled the island as if all the legions of Melcena were on his heels. He took ship and sailed south. His ship was last seen near the southern tip of Gandahar, and it seemed to be bound in the direction of the Dalasian Protectorates. The ship never came back, so it was generally assumed that she went down in a storm somewhere in those waters. That's all I really know about it."

Beldin scratched reflectively at his stomach. "It sort of fits together, Belgarath. The Sardion has the same kind of power that the Orb has. I'd say that it's been taking conscious steps to move itself from place to place—probably in response to certain events. It's my guess that if we pinned it down, we'd find that this Melcene emperor took it out of Zamad at just about the time that you and Bear-shoulders went to Cthol Mishrak to steal back the Orb. Then that scholar Senji mentioned stole it from here at just about the time of the Battle of Vo Mimbre."

"You speak as if it were alive," Senji objected.

"It is," Beldin told him, "and it can control the thoughts of people around it. Obviously it can't get up and walk by itself, so it has men do the picking and carrying."

"It's pretty speculative, Beldin," Belgarath said.

"That's what I do best. Shall we move along? We've got a boat to catch, you know. We can sort all this out later."

Belgarath nodded and looked at Senji. "We've been advised that you might be able to help us," he said.

"I can try."

"Good. Someone told us that you might be able to put your hands on an uncut copy of the Ashabine Oracles."

"Who said so?" Senji asked warily.

"A Dalasian seeress named Cyradis."

"Nobody believes anything the seers say," Senji scoffed.

"I do. In seven thousand years, I've never known a seer to be wrong—cryptic, sometimes, but never wrong."

Senji backed away from him.

"Don't be coy, Senji," Beldin told him. "Do you know where we can find a copy of the Oracles?"

"There used to be one in the library of this college," the alchemist replied evasively.

"Used to be?"

Senji looked around nervously. Then he lowered his voice to a whisper. "I stole it," he confessed.

"Does it have any passages cut out of it?" Belgarath asked intently.

"Not that I could see, no."

Belgarath let his breath out explosively. "Well, finally," he said. "I think we just beat Zandramas at her own game."

"You're going up against Zandramas?" Senji asked incredulously.

"Just as soon as we can catch up with her," Beldin told him.

"She's terribly dangerous, you know."

"So are we," Belgarath said. "Where's this book you stole?"

"It's hidden in my laboratory. The university officials are very narrow about people from one department pilfering from other people's libraries."

"Officials are always narrow." Beldin shrugged. "It's one of the qualifications for the job. Let's go back to your laboratory. My ancient friend here has to read that book."

Senji limped toward the door and back out into the hallway again.

The thin man in ecclesiastical robes had somehow managed to get his desk back where it belonged and he sat at it again. Garion noticed that his eyes were a little wild.

"We'll be leaving now," Belgarath told him. "Any objections?"

The thin man shrank back.

"Wise decision," Beldin said.

It was late afternoon by now, and the autumn sun streamed down on the well-maintained lawn.

"I wonder if the others have traced down Naradas yet," Garion said as they walked back toward the College of Applied Alchemy.

"More than likely," Belgarath replied. "Silk's people are very efficient."

They entered the reinforced building again to find the halls full of smoke and several more splintered doors lying in the corridor.

Senji sniffed at the smoke. "They're putting in too much sulfur," he noted professionally.

"A fellow we ran into was saying exactly the same thing," Garion told him. "It was right after he blew himself up, I think."

"I've told them over and over again," Senji said. "A little sulfur is necessary, but put in too much and—poof!"

"It looks as if there's been a fair amount of poofing going on in here," Beldin said, fanning at the smokey air in front of his face with one hand.

"That happens frequently when you're an alchemist," Senji replied. "You get used to it." He laughed. "And you never know what's going to happen. One idiot actually turned glass into steel."

Belgarath stopped. "He did what?"

"He turned glass into steel—or something very much like it. It was still transparent, but it wouldn't bend, break, or splinter. It was the hardest stuff I've ever seen."

Belgarath smacked his palm against his forehead.

"Steady," Beldin told him. Then he turned to Senji. "Does this fellow happen to remember the process?"

"I doubt it. He burned all his notes and then went into a monastery."

Belgarath was making strangling noises.

"Do you have any idea what a process like that would be worth?" Beldin asked Senji. "Glass is just about the cheapest stuff in the world—it's only melted sand, after all—and you can mold it into any shape you want. That particular process might just have been worth more than all the gold in the world."

Senji blinked.

"Never mind," Beldin said to him. "You're a pure scholar, remember? You're not interested in money, are you?"

Senji's hands began to shake.

They climbed the stairs and reentered Senji's cluttered laboratory. The alchemist closed and locked the door, then limped to a large cabinet near the window. Grunting, he moved it out from the wall a few inches, knelt, and reached behind it.

The book was not thick and it was bound in black leather. Belgarath's hands were shaking as he carried it to a table, sat, and opened it.

"I couldn't really make very much out of it," Senji confessed to Beldin. "I think whoever wrote it might have been insane."

"He was," the hunchback replied.

"You know who he was?"

Beldin nodded. "Torak," he said shortly.

"Torak's just a myth—something the Angaraks dreamed up."

"Tell that to him," Beldin said, pointing at Garion.

Senji swallowed hard, staring at Garion. "Did you really—I mean—?"

"Yes," Garion answered sadly. Oddly enough, he found that he still regretted what had happened at Cthol Mishrak over a dozen years ago.

"It's uncut!" Belgarath exclaimed triumphantly. "Somebody copied from the original before Torak had time to mutilate it. The missing passages are all here. Listen to this: 'And it shall come to pass that the Child of Light and the Child of Dark shall meet in the City of Endless Night. But that is not the place of the final meeting, for the choice will not be made there, and the Spirit of Dark shall flee. Know, moreover, that a new Child of Dark shall arise in the east.'"

"Why would Torak cut that passage?" Garion asked, puzzled.

"The implications of it aren't good—at least not for him," Belgarath replied. "The fact that there was going to be a new Child of Dark hints rather strongly that he wouldn't survive the meeting at Cthol Mishrak."

"Not only that," Beldin added, "even if he did survive, he was going to be demoted. That might have been just a little hard for him to swallow."

Belgarath quickly leafed through several pages.

"Are you sure you're not missing things?" Beldin asked him.

"I know what that copy at Ashaba said, Beldin. I have a very good memory."

"Really?" Beldin's tone was sardonic.

"Just let it lie." Belgarath read another passage rapidly. "I can see why he cut this one," he said. "'Behold, the stone which holds the power of the Dark Spirit will not reveal itself to that Child of Dark who shall come to the City of Endless Night, but will yield instead only to Him who is yet to come.'" He scratched at his beard. "If I'm reading this right, the Sardion concealed itself from Torak because he wasn't intended to be the ultimate instrument of the Dark Prophecy."

"I imagine that hurt his ego just a little." Beldin laughed.

But Belgarath had already moved on. His eyes suddenly widened, and his face paled slightly. "'For lo,'" he read, "'only one who hath put his hand to Cthrag Yaska shall be permitted to touch Cthrag Sardius. And in the moment of that touch, all that he is or might have become shall be sacrificed, and he shall become the Vessel of the Spirit of Dark. Seek ye, therefore, the son of the Child of Light, for he shall be our champion in the Place Which Is No More. And should he be chosen, he shall rise above all others and shall bestride the world with Cthrag Yaska in one hand and Cthrag Sardius in the other, and thus shall all that was divided be made one again, and he will have lordship and dominion over all things until the end of days.'"

Garion was thunderstruck. "So *that's* what they mean by the word 'sacrifice'!" he exclaimed. "Zandramas *isn't* going to kill Geran."

"No," Belgarath said darkly. "She's going to do something worse. She's going to turn him into another Torak."

"It goes a little further than that, Belgarath," Beldin growled. "The Orb rejected Torak—and burned off half his face in the process. The Sardion didn't even let Torak know that it was around. But the Orb *will* accept Geran, and so will the Sardion. If he gets his hands on both those stones, he'll have absolute power. Torak was a baby compared to what he'll be." He looked somberly at Garion. "That's why Cyradis told you at Rheon that you might have to kill your son."

"That's unthinkable!" Garion retorted hotly.

"Maybe you'd better start thinking about it. Geran won't be your son any more. Once he touches the Sardion, he'll be something totally evil—and he'll be a God."

Bleakly, Belgarath read on. "Here's something," he said. " 'And the Child of Dark who shall bear the champion to the place of choosing shall be possessed utterly by the Dark Spirit, and her flesh shall be but a husk, and all the starry universe shall be contained therein.' "

"What does that mean?" Garion asked.

"I'm not sure," Belgarath admitted. He leafed through a couple more pages. He frowned. " 'And it shall come to pass that she who gave birth unto the champion shall reveal unto ye the place of the final meeting, but ye must beguile her ere she will speak.' "

"Ce'Nedra?" Garion asked incredulously.

"Zandramas has tampered with Ce'Nedra before," Belgarath reminded him. "We'll have Pol keep an eye on her." He frowned again. "Why would Torak cut out that passage?" he asked with a baffled look.

"Torak wasn't the only one with a sharp knife, Belgarath," Beldin said. "That's a fairly crucial bit of information. I don't think Zandramas would have wanted to leave it behind, do you?"

"That confuses the issue, doesn't it," Belgarath said sourly. "I read a book at Ashaba that had two editors. I'm surprised there was anything left of it at all."

"Read on, old man," Beldin said, glancing at the window. "The sun's going down."

"Well, finally," Belgarath said after reading for a moment more. "Here it is. 'Behold, the place of the final meeting shall be revealed at Kell, for it lies hidden within the pages of the accursed book of the seers.' " He thought about it. "Nonsense!" he burst out. "I've read parts of the Mallorean Gospels myself, and there are dozens of copies scattered all over the world. If this is right, *anybody* could have picked up the location."

"They're not all the same," Senji murmured.

"*What?*" Belgarath exploded.

"The copies of the Mallorean Gospels aren't all the same," the alchemist repeated. "I used to look through all these holy books. Sometimes the ancients ran across things that could prove helpful in my experiments. I've gathered up a fair library of that sort of thing. That's why I stole the book you've got in your hands."

"I suppose you've even got a copy of the Mrin Codex," Beldin said.

"Two, actually, and they're identical. That's the peculiar thing about the Mallorean Gospels. I've got three sets, and no two copies are the same."

"Oh, fine," Belgarath said. "I knew there was a reason not to trust the seers."

"I think they do it on purpose." Senji shrugged. "After I started running across discrepancies, I went to Kell, and the seers there told me that there are secrets in the Gospels that are too dangerous to have out there for just anyone to read. That's why every copy is different. They've all been modified to hide those secrets—except for the original, of course. That's always been kept at Kell."

Beldin and Belgarath exchanged a long look. "All right," Beldin said flatly, "we go to Kell."

"But we're right behind Zandramas," Garion objected.

"And that's where we'll stay if we don't go to Kell," Beldin told him. "*Behind* her. Going to Kell is the only way we can get ahead of her."

Belgarath had turned to the last page of the Oracles. "I think this is a personal message, Garion," he said in an awed sort of voice, holding out the book.

"What?"

"Torak wants to talk to you."

"He can talk all he wants. I'm not going to listen to him. I almost made that mistake once—when he tried to tell me he was my father, remember?"

"This is a little different. He's not lying this time."

Garion took hold of the book, and a deathly chill seemed to run up through his hands and into his arms.

"Read it," Belgarath said implacably.

Compelled—driven, even—Garion lowered his eyes to the spidery script on the page before him. " 'Hail, Belgarion,' " he read aloud in a faltering voice. " 'If it should ever come to pass that thine eyes fall upon this, then it means that I have fallen beneath thy hand. I mourn that not. I will have cast myself into the crucible of destiny, and, if I have failed, so be it. Know that I hate thee, Belgarion. For hate's sake I will throw myself into the darkness. For hate's sake will I spit out my last breath at thee, my damned brother.' " Garion's voice failed him. He could actually feel the maimed God's towering hatred reaching down to him through the eons. He now understood the full import of what had happened in the terrible City of Endless Night.

"Keep reading," Belgarath told him. "There's more."

"Grandfather, this is more than I can bear."

"Read!" Belgarath's voice was like the crack of a whip.

Helplessly, Garion again lifted the book. " 'Know that we *are* brothers, Belgarion, though our hate for each other may one day sunder the heavens. We are brothers in that we share a dreadful task. That thou art reading my words means that thou hast been my destroyer. Thus must I charge *thee* with the task. What is foretold in these pages is an abomination. Do not let it come to pass. Destroy the world. Destroy the universe if need be, but do not permit this to come to pass. In thy hand is now the fate of all that was; all that is; and all that is yet to be. Hail, my hated brother, and farewell. We will meet—or have met—in the City of Endless Night, and there will our dispute be concluded. The task, however, still lies before us in the Place Which Is No More. One of us must go there to face the ultimate horror. Should it be thou, fail us not. Failing all else, thou must reave the life from thine only son, even as thou hath reft mine from me.' "

The book fell from Garion's hands as his knees failed and he sank to the floor, weeping uncontrollably. He howled a wolflike howl of absolute despair and hammered at the floor with both his fists and with tears streaming openly down his face.

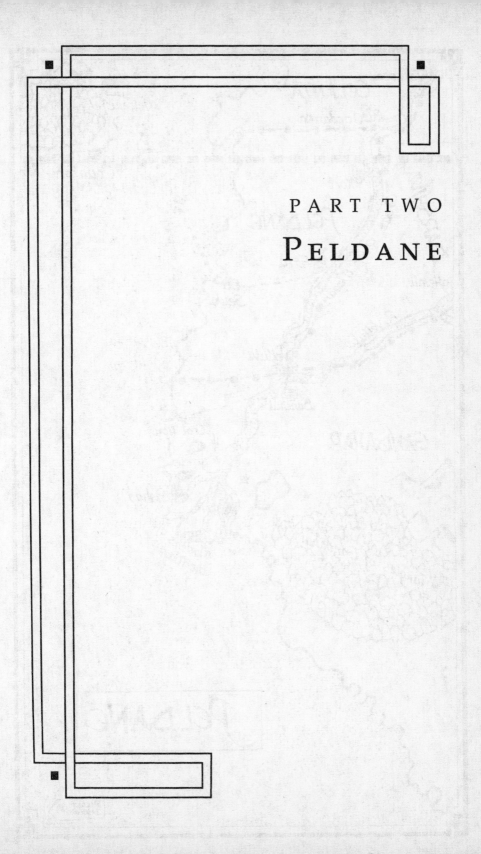

PART TWO
PELDANE

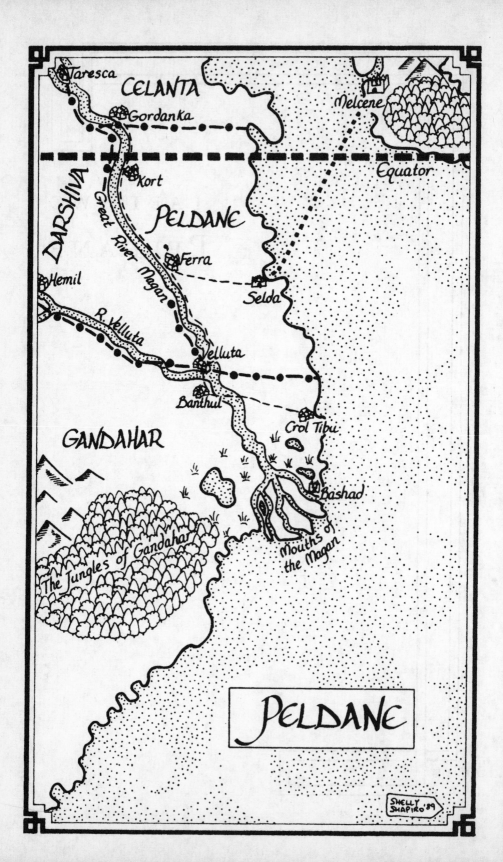

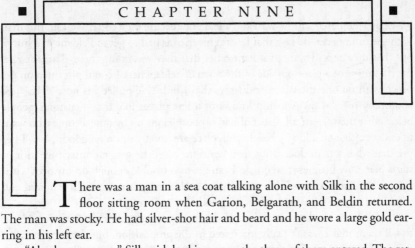

T here was a man in a sea coat talking alone with Silk in the second floor sitting room when Garion, Belgarath, and Beldin returned. The man was stocky. He had silver-shot hair and beard and he wore a large gold earring in his left ear.

"Ah, there you are," Silk said, looking up as the three of them entered. The rat-faced little man had changed clothes and now wore plain doublet and hose of a nondescript brown. "This is Captain Kadian. He's the one who took our friends to the mainland." He looked back at the seaman. "Why don't you tell them what you just told me, Captain?" he suggested.

"If you want me to, your Highness," Kadian agreed. He had that rusty sort of voice seafaring men often have—the result of bad weather and strong drink, Garion surmised. He took a swallow from the silver tankard he was holding. "Well, sir," he began, "it was three days ago when it happened. I'd just come up from Bashad in Gandahar. It's down by the mouth of the Magan." He made a face. "It's an unhealthy sort of a place—all swamps and jungles. Anyhow, I'd carried a cargo of ivory up here for the Consortium, and we'd just off-loaded, so I was sort of looking around for a cargo. A ship doesn't make any money for her owner when she's tied up to a wharf, y'know. I went to a certain tavern I know of. The tavern keeper's an old friend of mine—we was shipmates when we was younger—and he sort of keeps his ear to the ground for me. Well sir, I no sooner got there and set myself down, when my friend, he comes over to me and he asks me if I'd be interested in a short, easy voyage at a good price. I says to him that I'm always interested in that kind of proposition, but that I'd want to know what kind of cargo was involved before I made up my mind. There's some things I don't like to carry—cattle, for instance. They can dirty up the hold of a ship to the point where it takes weeks to get it clean again. Well, my friend, he says to me that there wouldn't be no cargo involved at all. It was just some people as wanted passage to the mainland. I says that it wouldn't hurt none to talk with them, and so he takes me into this room in the back of the tavern where four people was sitting at a table—two men, a woman, and a little boy. One of the men was dressed in expensive clothes—a nobleman of some kind, I think—but it was the other one as did all the talking."

"Was there anything unusual about that one?" Silk prompted.

"I was just getting to that. He was wearing ordinary clothes, but that wasn't what caught my attention. At first I thought he was blind—because of his eyes, you understand—but it seems that he can see well enough, even though his eyes don't have no color at all. I had a ship's cook one time, and one of his eyes was the same way. Foul-tempered sort he was, and a real poor excuse for a cook. Well sir, this man with the funny eyes, he says that he and his friends had to get to Peldane in a hurry, but that they sort of wanted it kept quiet that they was going there. Then he asks me if I knows of a place outside of the town of Selda where I could put them on the beach with no one the wiser, and I says that I did." He pulled his nose slyly. "Just about any man as owns a ship knows of a few places like that—customs people being what they are an' all. I sort of had my suspicions up by now. People who want to end a voyage on a lonely beach someplace are usually up to no good. Now, I figure that what a man does is his own concern, but if he gets me mixed up in it, it starts being my business real quick. I can get into trouble enough on my own without no help from others." He paused and took a long drink from his tankard and wiped his mouth with the back of his hand.

"Like I say, I had my suspicions about these people by now and I was just about to tell them that I wasn't really interested in the proposition, but then the woman, she says something I didn't hear to the one as was doing the talking. She was wearing a kind of long cloak or robe of some kind made out of black satin. She kept the hood of it up the whole time, so I never saw her face, but she was keeping a real tight grip on the little boy. Anyhow, the one with the white eyes, he pulls out a purse and spills it out on the table, and that purse was full of gold, my friends, more than I'd make in a dozen voyages along these coasts. That put a whole new light on the situation, let me tell you. Well sir, to make it short, we struck the bargain right then and there, and I asks them when they wanted to leave, and the fellow as was doing the talking, he says they'd come down to my ship just as soon as it gets dark. I saw right off that my suspicions wasn't too far off the mark. You don't find very many as is honest who want to sail out of a harbor in the dark of night, but we'd already struck our bargain, and I had his purse tucked under my belt, so it was too late to back out. We sailed that very night and got to the coast of Peldane on the next afternoon."

"Tell them about the fog," Silk said intently.

"I was just about to, your Highness," Kadian said. "That coast down there is sunk in fog almost all spring, and the day we got there wasn't no exception. It was thicker than a wool cloak, but the people in Selda, they're used to it, so they always light beacons on the city walls to guide ships into their harbor on foggy days. I took my bearings on those beacons and I didn't have no trouble finding the beach I wanted. We hove to a few hundred yards offshore, and I sent my passengers toward the beach in a small boat with my bo'sun in charge. We hung a lantern from the mainmast to guide him back through the fog, and I put some men to banging on pots and pans to help him find the way. Anyhow, after some time passed, we could hear the sound of the oarlocks out there in the fog near the beach, and we knowed the bo'sun's coming back. And then, all of a sudden, I seen the light of a fire coming through the fog all sort of misty, like. I heard some screaming, and then everything got quiet. We waited for a bit, but the bo'sun, he never came back. I didn't like the smell of things, so I ordered the anchor up, and we sort of eased on back out to sea. I don't know what happened and I wasn't going to stay around to find out. There was things going on that made me real nervous."

"Oh," Beldin said, "such as what?"

"Well sir, one time in the main cabin, this woman as the white-eyed man and the aristocrat had with them, she reached out to take hold of the little boy, him acting kind of restless and all, and I seen her hand. Now, it might have been bad light in the cabin or some such—I don't spend all that much on lamp oil or candles. But—and strike me blind if I'm wrong—it seemed to me that there was sparkles under the skin of her hand."

"Sparkles?" Belgarath asked him.

"Yes, sir. I seen it with my own eyes, and they was moving—all these little tiny sparkles moving around in her flesh, almost like fireflies on a summer's evening."

"As if all the starry universe were contained therein?" Beldin asked intently, quoting from the obscure passage in the Ashabine Oracles.

"Now that you put it that way, that's exactly how it was," Kadian agreed. "I knowed right off that these wasn't no ordinary folks and, after I seen that fire in the fog, I didn't really want to stay around to find out just how *un*-ordinary they was."

"That might just have saved your life, Captain," Belgarath told him. "Have you ever heard of Zandramas?"

"The witch? Everybody's heard of her."

"I think she was your glittering passenger, and Zandramas is a firm believer in the old notion that dead people can't tell stories. So far as we know, she's drowned three ships and fed several people to the lions. I expect it was only the fog that saved you. If she'd have been able to see you, you wouldn't be here now."

Captain Kadian swallowed hard.

"Do you need any more?" Silk asked.

"No," Belgarath replied. "I think that covers everything." He looked at the captain. "We thank you, Kadian. Can you sketch us a map of the beach where you dropped off these passengers of yours?"

"I can indeed," Kadian replied bleakly. "Is it in your mind to chase down the witch?"

"We were sort of thinking along those lines, yes."

"When you burn her, throw on a few logs of wood in memory of my bo'sun and his oarsmen."

"You have my word on that, Captain," Garion told him.

"Green logs," Kadian added. "They don't burn so fast."

"We'll keep that in mind."

Silk stood up and handed the captain a leather pouch.

Kadian bounced it on his palm a few times, and it gave forth a jingling sound. "You're very generous, your Highness," he said, also rising to his feet. "Is there pen and ink handy? I'll draw you that chart."

"Right over on that table," Silk said, pointing.

The captain nodded and crossed the room.

"Where's Aunt Pol," Garion asked, "and the others?"

"They're changing clothes," Silk replied. "I sent word to our ship just as soon as one of Vetter's men came back and told us that they'd found Captain Kadian. She's waiting in the harbor for us right now." He looked closely at Garion. "Aren't you feeling well?" he asked. "You're looking a little pale."

"I got a message that had some bad news in it."

Silk gave Belgarath a puzzled look.

"We found the Ashabine Oracles," the old man explained tersely. "Torak left a message for Garion on the last page. It wasn't very pleasant. We can talk about it once we get on board ship."

Captain Kadian came back holding a sheet of parchment. "This is Selda," he said, pointing at his drawing. "There's a headland to the south, and the beach I was telling you about is just south of that. I can't tell you exactly where the witch landed because of the fog, but this place marked with the X should be fairly close."

"Thanks again, Captain," Silk said.

"My pleasure, your Highness, and good hunting." Kadian turned and left the room with the rolling gait of a man who spends little time on shore.

It was only a few moments later when Polgara and the others joined them. Ce'Nedra and Velvet were both wearing plain gray dresses much like the one Polgara always wore when she was traveling. Gray, Garion noticed, was not a good color for Ce'Nedra. It made her skin look very pale, and the only touch of color about her was her flaming wealth of copper-colored hair.

Durnik and the other men—except for Toth, who still wore only his unbleached blanket and loincloth—were dressed in the same nondescript brown that Silk wore.

"Well, father?" Polgara asked as she entered, "did you find what we wanted?"

He nodded. "Why don't we talk about that after we get on board ship, though? We've done what we came to do in Melcena and we can talk while our ship's moving." He led the way out and down the stairs.

It was a silvery evening. The full moon had risen early and it filled the streets of Melcena with its pale light. Candles glowed golden in the windows of the houses they passed, and hundreds of lanterns winked from the rigging of the ships anchored in the harbor. Garion rode in silence, his melancholy thoughts still on the dreadful communication Torak had left for him thousands of years ago.

They boarded their ship quickly and went immediately below to the cramped cabin beneath the aft deck.

"All right," Belgarath said to them after Durnik had closed the door, "we found the Oracles and we also found the place where the Sardion was kept until just about the time of the battle of Vo Mimbre."

"That was a profitable trip, wasn't it?" Silk noted. "Is Senji really as old as they say?"

Beldin grunted. "Older."

"Wouldn't that mean that he's a sorcerer?" Ce'Nedra asked. Perhaps it was the somber gray dress, but she seemed a bit disconsolate as she sat on an ornately carved bench under a swinging oil lamp.

Belgarath nodded. "He's not very good at it, but he does have the ability, yes."

"Who was his instructor?" Polgara wanted to know. She sat down beside Ce'Nedra and laid one arm affectionately across the little queen's shoulders.

"Nobody," Belgarath said with a certain disgust. "Would you believe that he just stumbled over it on his own?"

"Did you look into that?"

"Yes. Beldin's got a theory. He can explain it to you later. At any rate, the Sardion was brought to the university here several thousand years ago. They kept it in a museum. I don't think anybody knew what it really was. Then, about five hundred years ago, one of the scholars stole it and took it around the southern tip of Gandahar and sailed off in the general direction of the Dalasian Protectorates. Nobody knows for sure what happened to it after that. Anyway, Senji had an unmutilated copy of the Ashabine Oracles."

"What did it say?" Velvet asked intently.

"A great deal. We found out why Zandramas abducted Geran."

"As a sacrifice?" she said.

"Only in an obscure sense of the word. If the Dark Prophecy wins out, Geran is going to be the new God of Angarak."

"My baby?" Ce'Nedra exclaimed.

"He won't be your baby any more, I'm afraid," the old man told her bleakly. "He'll be Torak."

"Or worse," Beldin added. "He'll have the Orb in one hand and the Sardion in the other. He'll have dominion over everything that exists, and I don't think he'll be a kindly God."

"We have to stop her!" Ce'Nedra cried. "We can't let this happen!"

"I think that's the general idea, your Majesty," Sadi told her.

"What else did it say, father?" Polgara asked.

"It said something about Zandramas that's a little obscure. For some reason her body's being gradually taken over by some kind of light. The sea captain who carried her to Selda caught a glimpse of her hand and he said that there are moving lights under her skin. The Oracles said it was going to happen."

"What does it mean?" Durnik asked.

"I haven't got the faintest idea," Belgarath admitted. He looked at Garion and moved his fingers slightly. —*I don't think we need to tell Ce'Nedra what the book said about her, do you?*—

Garion shook his head.

"Anyway, we're going to have to go to Kell."

"Kell?" Polgara's voice was startled. "What for?"

"The location of the place we're looking for is in the copy of the Mallorean Gospels the seers keep there. If we go to Kell, we can get to this meeting place before Zandramas does."

"That might be a nice change," Silk said. "I'm getting a little tired of tagging along behind her."

"But we'll lose the trail," Ce'Nedra protested.

"Little girl," Beldin said to her gruffly, "if we know where Zandramas is going, we won't *need* the trail. We can just go directly to the Place Which Is No More and wait for her to show up."

Polgara's arm curled more tightly about Ce'Nedra's shoulders in a protective fashion. "Be gentle with her, uncle. She was brave enough to kiss you at the archduke's house, and I'd imagine that was quite a shock to her sensibilities."

"Very funny, Pol." The ugly hunchback dropped heavily into a chair and scratched vigorously at one armpit.

"Was there anything else, father?" Polgara asked.

"Torak wrote something to Garion," Belgarath replied. "It was fairly bleak, but it appears that even he knew how bad things would get if Zandramas succeeds. He told Garion to stop her at all costs."

"I was going to do that anyway," Garion said quietly. "I didn't need any suggestions from Torak."

"What are we going to be up against in Peldane?" Belgarath asked Silk.

"More of what we ran into in Voresebo and Rengel, I'd imagine."

"What's the fastest way to get to Kell?" Durnik asked.

"It's in the Protectorate of Likandia," Silk replied, "and the shortest way there is right straight across Peldane and Darshiva and then down through the mountains."

"What about Gandahar?" Sadi asked. "We could avoid all that unpleasantness if we sailed south and went through there." Somehow Sadi looked peculiar in hose and a belted tunic. Once he had discarded his iridescent robe, he seemed more like an ordinary man and less like a eunuch. His scalp, however, was freshly shaved.

Silk shook his head. "It's all jungle down in Gandahar, Sadi," he said. "You have to chop your way through."

"Jungles aren't all that bad, Kheldar."

"They are if you're in a hurry."

"Could you send for those soldiers of yours?" Velvet asked.

"It's possible, I suppose," Silk answered, "but I'm not sure they'd be all that much help. Vetter says that Darshiva's crawling with Grolims and Zandramas' troops, and Peldane's been in chaos for years. My troops are good, but not that good." He looked at Belgarath. "I'm afraid you're going to get more burrs in your fur, old friend."

"Are we just going to ignore the trail, then," Garion asked, "and make straight for Kell?"

Belgarath tugged at one earlobe. "I've got a suspicion that the trail is going to lead in the general direction of Kell anyway," he said. "Zandramas read the Ashabine Oracles, too, you know, and she knows that Kell's the only place where she can get the information she needs."

"Will Cyradis let her look at the Gospels?" Durnik asked.

"Probably. Cyradis is still neutral and she's not likely to show any favoritism."

Garion rose to his feet. "I think I'll go up on deck, Grandfather," he said. "I've got some thinking to do, and sea air helps to clear my head."

The lights of Melcena twinkled low on the horizon behind them, and the moon laid a silvery path across the surface of the sea. The ship's captain stood at the tiller on the aft deck, his hands steady and sure.

"Isn't it a little hard to know which way you're going at night?" Garion asked him.

"Not at all," the captain replied. He pointed up toward the night sky. "Seasons come and go, but the stars never change."

"Well," Garion said, "we can hope, I guess." Then he walked forward to stand in the bow of the ship.

The night breeze that blew down the strait between Melcena and the mainland was erratic, and the sails first bellied and then fell slack, their booming sounding like a funeral drum. That sound fitted Garion's mood. For a long time he stood toying with the end of a knotted rope and looking out over the moon-touched waves, not so much thinking as simply registering the sights and sounds and smells around him.

He knew she was there. It was not merely the fragrance he had known since his earliest childhood, but also the calm sense of her presence. With a peculiar kind of abstraction he sought back through his memories. He had, it seemed, always known exactly where she was. Even on the darkest of nights he could have started from sleep in a strange room in some forgotten town and pointed unerringly to the place where she was. The captain of this ship was guided by the lights in the sky, but the star that had led Garion for his entire life was not some far-distant glimmer on the velvet throat of night. It was much closer, and much more constant.

"What's troubling you, Garion?" she asked, laying a gentle hand on his shoulder.

"I could hear his voice, Aunt Pol—Torak's voice. He hated me thousands of years before I was even born. He even knew my name."

"Garion," she said very calmly, "the universe knew your name before that moon up there was spun out of the emptiness. Whole constellations have been waiting for you since the beginning of time."

"I didn't want them to, Aunt Pol."

"There are those of us who aren't given that option, Garion. There are things that have to be done and certain people who have to do them. It's as simple as that."

He smiled rather sadly at her flawless face and gently touched the snowy white lock at her brow. Then, for the last time in his life, he asked the question that had been on his lips since he was a tiny boy. "Why me, Aunt Pol? Why me?"

"Can you possibly think of anyone else you'd trust to deal with these matters, Garion?"

He had not really been prepared for that question. It came at him in stark simplicity. Now at last he fully understood. "No," he sighed, "I suppose not. Somehow it seems a little unfair, though. I wasn't even consulted."

"Neither was I, Garion," she answered. "But we didn't have to be consulted, did we? The knowledge of what we have to do is born in us." She put her arms around him and drew him close. "I'm so very proud of you, my Garion," she said.

He laughed a bit wryly. "I suppose I didn't turn out too badly after all," he conceded. "I can get my shoes on the right feet at least."

"And you have no idea how long that took to explain to you," she replied with a light laugh. "You were a good boy, Garion, but you'd never listen. Even Rundorig would listen. He didn't usually understand, but at least he'd listen."

"I miss him sometimes. Him and Doroon and Zubrette." Garion paused. "Did they ever get married? Rundorig and Zubrette, I mean?"

"Oh, yes. Years and years ago, and Zubrette is up to her waist in children—five or so. I used to get a message every autumn, and I'd have to go back to Faldor's farm to deliver her newest baby."

"You did that?" He was amazed.

"I certainly wouldn't have let anyone else do it. Zubrette and I disagreed about certain things, but I'm still very fond of her."

"Is she happy?"

"I think she is, yes. Rundorig's easy to manage, and she has all those children to keep her mind occupied." She looked at him critically. "Are you a little less moody now?" she asked.

"I feel better," he replied. "I always feel better when you're around."

"That's nice."

He remembered something. "Did Grandfather get a chance to tell you what the Oracles said about Ce'Nedra?"

"Yes," she said. "I'll keep an eye on her. Why don't we go below now? The next few weeks might be hectic, so let's get all the sleep we can while we have the chance."

The coast of Peldane was engulfed in fog just as Captain Kadian had predicted, but the beacon fires burning on the walls of Selda provided reference points, and they were able to feel their way carefully along the coast until the ship's captain estimated that they were near the beach shown on Kadian's chart.

"There's a fishing village about a mile south of here, your Highness," the captain advised Silk. "It's deserted now, because of all the troubles in the area, but there's a dock there—or at least there was the last time I sailed past this coast. We should be able to unload your horses there."

"Excellent, Captain," Silk replied.

They crept along through the fog until they reached the deserted village and its shaky-looking dock. As soon as Chretienne reached the shore, Garion saddled him, then mounted and rode slowly back along the beach with Iron-grip's sword resting on the pommel of his saddle. After he had gone perhaps a mile and a half, he felt the familiar pull. He turned and rode back.

The others had also saddled their horses and led them to the edge of the fog-shrouded fishermen's village. Their ship was moving slowly out to sea, a dim shape in the fog with red and green lanterns marking her port and starboard sides and with a lone sailor astride her bowsprit blowing a melancholy foghorn to warn other ships away.

Garion dismounted and led his big gray stallion to where the others waited.

"Did you find it?" Ce'Nedra asked intently in a hushed little voice. Garion had noticed that for some reason, fog always made people speak quietly.

"Yes," he replied. Then he looked at his grandfather. "Well?" he asked. "Do we just ignore the trail and take the shortest route to Kell or what?"

Belgarath scratched at his beard and looked first at Beldin, then at Polgara. "What do you think?" he asked them.

"The trail was going inland, wasn't it?" Beldin asked Garion.

Garion nodded.

"Then we don't have to make the decision yet," the hunchback said. "As long as Zandramas is going in the same direction we want to go, we can keep on following her. If she changes direction later on, then we can decide."

"It makes sense, father," Polgara agreed.

"All right, we'll do it that way, then." The old man looked around. "This fog should hide us just as well as darkness would. Let's go pick up the trail, and then Garion, Pol, and I can scout on ahead." He squinted up into the murky sky. "Can anybody make a guess about the time?"

"It's about midafternoon, Belgarath," Durnik told him after a momentary consultation with Toth.

"Let's go find out which way she's going, then."

They rode along the beach, following Chretienne's tracks until they reached the spot where Garion's sword swung in his hand to point inland.

"We should be able to gain some time on her," Sadi noted.

"Why's that?" Silk asked him.

"She came ashore in a small boat," the eunuch replied, "so she didn't have horses."

"That's no real problem for her, Sadi," Polgara told him. "She's a Grolim, and she can communicate with her underlings over long distances. I'm sure she was on horseback within an hour of the time her foot touched the sand."

The eunuch sighed. "I forget about that from time to time," he admitted. "It's very convenient for us to have that advantage, but not nearly so convenient when the other side has it, too."

Belgarath swung down from his horse. "Come along, Garion. You, too, Pol. We might as well get started." He looked over at Durnik. "We'll stay in close touch," he told the smith. "This fog could make things a little tricky."

"Right," Durnik agreed.

Garion took Polgara's arm to help her through the soft sand and followed his grandfather up the beach to the line of driftwood at the high-water mark.

"This should do it," the old man decided. "Let's make the change here, and then Garion and I can scout on ahead. Pol, try to keep the others more or less in sight. I don't want them straying."

"Yes, father," she said even as she began to shimmer and change.

Garion formed the image in his mind, pulled in his will, and once again felt that curious melting sensation. He looked himself over carefully as he always did. On one occasion he'd made the change in a hurry and had forgotten his tail. A tail does not mean very much to a two-legged animal, but it is distinctly necessary for a four-legged one.

"Stop admiring yourself," he heard Belgarath's voice in the silences of his mind. "We've got work to do."

"I was just making sure that I had everything, Grandfather."

"Let's go. You won't be able to see very much in the fog, so use your nose."

Polgara was perched sedately on a bone-white limb jutting up from a driftwood log. She was meticulously preening her snowy feathers with her hooked beak.

Belgarath and Garion effortlessly hurdled over the driftwood and loped off into the fog. "It's going to be a wet day," Garion noted soundlessly as he ran alongside the great silver wolf.

"Your fur won't melt."

"I know, but my paws get cold when they're wet."

"I'll have Durnik make you some little booties."

"That would be absolutely ridiculous, Grandfather," Garion said indignantly. Even though he had only recently made the change, the wolf's enormous sense of decorum and propriety had already begun to permeate his consciousness.

"There are some people just ahead," Belgarath said, sniffing at the air. "Tell your aunt."

They separated and moved off into the tall, fog-wet marsh grass. "Aunt Pol." Garion cast the words into the foggy silence around him.

"Yes, dear?"

"Tell Durnik and the others to rein in. There are some strangers up ahead."

"All right, Garion. Be careful."

Garion slunk low to the ground through the wet grass, setting each paw down carefully.

"Will it never lift?" he heard a voice somewhere off to his left demand irritably.

"The local people say that it's always foggy around here in the spring," another voice replied.

"It's not spring."

"It is here. We're south of the line. The seasons are reversed."

"That's a stupid sort of thing."

"It wasn't my idea. Talk to the Gods if you want to register a complaint."

There was a long silence. "Have the Hounds found anything yet?" the first voice asked.

"It's very hard to sniff out a trail after three days—even for the Hounds—and all the wet from this fog isn't making it any easier."

Garion froze. "Grandfather!" he hurled the thought into the fog.

"Don't shout."

"There are two men talking just up ahead. They have some of the Hounds with them. I think they're trying to find the trail, too."

"Pol." The old man's thought seemed to crackle. "Come up here."

"Yes, father."

It was no more than a few minutes, but it seemed like hours. Then in the murky fog overhead, Garion heard the single stroke of soft wings.

"There are some men over there to the left," Belgarath's voice reported. "I think they might be Grolims. Have a look, but be careful."

"All right," she replied. There was another soft wing beat in the fog. Again there was that interminable wait.

Then her voice came back quite clearly. "You're right, father," she said. "They're Chandim."

A muttered oath came out of the stillness. "Urvon," Belgarath's voice said.

"And probably Nahaz as well," Polgara added.

"This complicates things," the old man said. "Let's go back and talk with the others. We might have to make the decision sooner than Beldin thought."

CHAPTER TEN

They gathered not far from the driftwood-littered beach. The fog had slipped imperceptibly from white to gray as evening settled slowly over this misty coast.

"That's it, then," Beldin said after Belgarath had told them what lay ahead. "If the Chandim and the Hounds are out there trying to sniff out Zandramas' trail the same as we are, we're bound to run into them sooner or later."

"We've dealt with them before," Silk objected.

"I'll grant that," Beldin replied, "but why risk that sort of thing if we don't have to? The trail of Zandramas isn't really important to us now. What we really need to do at this point is to get to Kell."

Belgarath was pacing up and down. "Beldin's right," he said. "There's no point in taking risks over something that doesn't really matter any more."

"But we're so close," Ce'Nedra protested.

"If we start running into Chandim—and Hounds—we won't *stay* very close," Beldin told her.

Sadi had put on a western-style traveler's cloak and had turned the hood up to ward off the dampness of the fog. The covering of his shaved scalp peculiarly altered his appearance. "What's Zandramas likely to do when she finds out that the Chandim are trailing her?" he asked.

"She'll put every Grolim and every soldier she can lay her hands on in their path," Polgara replied.

"And they'll just bring in more force to counter that, won't they?"

"That's the logical assumption," Durnik agreed.

"That sort of means that things are going to come to a head here fairly soon, wouldn't you say—even if neither side would particularly have chosen this place for a major confrontation?"

"What are you getting at, Sadi?" Silk asked him.

"If Urvon and Zandramas are concentrating on each other, they won't really pay that much attention to us, will they? About all we have to do is get out of this general vicinity, and then we should be able to make straight for Kell without much in the way of interference."

"What lies to the south of us?" Beldin asked Silk.

"Nothing major." Silk shrugged. "At least not until you get to Gandahar."

Beldin nodded. "But we've got a city just to the north of here, don't we?"

"Selda," Silk supplied.

"Urvon's probably there already, but if we go south, we should be able to avoid him—and Zandramas as well. Sadi's right. They'll be so busy with each other they won't have time to look for us."

"Anybody want to add anything?" Belgarath asked them.

"A fire maybe?" Durnik said.

"I don't quite follow you."

"We've got all this fog," Durnik explained, "and night's coming on. The Chandim are out there ahead of us, and we need something to distract their attention while we slip around them. There's all that driftwood along the upper edge of the beach. A bonfire on a foggy night lights up the whole sky. You can see it for miles. If we build a few fires, the Chandim are going to think that something serious is going on behind them and they'll all rush back to investigate. That ought to clear the way for us."

Beldin grinned and clapped a gnarled hand on the smith's shoulder. "You made a good choice, Pol," he chortled. "This is a rare fellow here."

"Yes," she murmured. "I saw that almost immediately."

They rode back along the beach to the abandoned fishing village. "Do you want me to do it, Grandfather?" Garion offered. "Set fire to the driftwood, I mean?"

"No," the old man replied, "I'll take care of it. You and Pol take the others on down along the shoreline. I'll catch up in a bit."

"Do you want these?" Durnik asked, offering the old man his flint and steel.

Belgarath shook his head. "I'll do it the other way," he said. "I want to give the Chandim some noise to listen to, as well as the fire to watch. That should get their undivided attention." He strode off into the fog, heading back up the beach.

"Come along, Garion," Polgara said, pushing back the hood of her cloak. "We'll scout ahead again. I think we'll want to move fairly fast."

The two of them walked a short distance down the beach and made the change once more. "Keep your mind awake as well as your ears and nose," Polgara's voice silently instructed. "With this fog, the Chandim will probably be watching with their thoughts rather than their eyes."

"Yes, Aunt Pol," he replied, loping toward the upper end of the beach. Sand was different underfoot than grass or turf. It gave slightly under his paws and it slowed him a bit. He decided that he did not really like running in sand. He ran along for a couple of miles without any encounters, then he heard and felt a shockingly loud surge coming from somewhere behind him. He flinched and glanced back over his shoulder. The fog was illuminated by a sooty orange glow. There was another surge that sounded almost like a detonation, then another, and another.

"Tacky, father," he heard Polgara say disapprovingly. "Why are you being so ostentatious?"

"I just wanted to be sure they heard me, is all," the old man replied.

"They probably heard you in Mal Zeth. Are you coming back now?"

"Let me start a few more fires first. The Chandim have a limited attention span. Besides, the smoke should confuse the Hounds' sense of smell."

There were several more detonations.

"That should do it." Belgarath's thought had a note of self-satisfaction in it.

About twenty minutes later, the great silver wolf came out of the fog like a ghost. "Oh, there you are," Belgarath said to Garion in the way of wolves. "Let's spread out a bit and move right along. Durnik and the others are right behind us."

"Did the Chandim go back to the beach to see what was happening?"

"Oh, yes." Belgarath's tongue lolled out in the wolf's version of a grin. "They were definitely curious. There were quite a few of them. Shall we go?"

They ran along for about another hour before Garion's nostrils caught the scent of a horse and rider coming from somewhere ahead. He loped on through the fog, ranging back and forth until he pinpointed the man's location. Then he ran forward.

It was a solitary Temple Guardsman who was galloping northward toward the towering fires Belgarath had ignited. Garion rushed him, snarling terribly. The Guardsman's horse squealed in panic, rearing up onto his hind legs and dumping his startled rider into a bleached pile of driftwood. The horse fled, and the Guardsman groaned as he lay tangled up in the white logs and branches half-buried in the sand.

"Trouble?" Belgarath's thought came out of the fog.

"A Guardsman," Garion replied. "He fell off his horse. I think he may have broken some things."

"Was he alone?"

"Yes, Grandfather. Where are you?"

"Just a ways ahead of you. There are some woods up here. This looks like as good a place as any to turn west. I don't think we need to go all the way down to Gandahar."

"I'll tell Aunt Pol to pass the word to Durnik."

The woods were quite extensive, and there was very little undergrowth. At one point, Garion passed the embers of a campfire still glowing in the foggy dark. The campsite, however, was deserted, and there were signs that whoever had been there had departed in some haste. The track of churned loam on the forest floor indicated that the people had galloped off toward the fires on the beach.

Garion ran on.

Near the edge of the woods, a faint breeze carried a sharp canine reek. Garion stopped. "Grandfather," he sent his thought out urgently, "I smell a dog up ahead."

"Only one?"

"I think so." He crept forward, his ears and nose alert. "I can only smell one," he reported.

"Stay put. I'll be right there."

Garion dropped to his haunches and waited. A few moments later, the silver wolf joined him.

"Is he moving around at all?" Belgarath asked.

"No, Grandfather. He seems to be just sitting in one place. Do you think we can slip around him?"

"You and I could, but I don't think that Durnik and the others would be able to. The Hounds can hear and smell almost as well as wolves can."

"Can we frighten him off?"

"I doubt it. He's bigger than we are. Even if we did, he'd just go for help—and we definitely don't want a pack of the Hounds on our trail. We're going to have to kill him."

"Grandfather!" Garion gasped. For some reason, the thought of deliberately killing another canine profoundly shocked him.

"I know," Belgarath agreed. "The notion's repugnant, but we don't have any choice. He's blocking our way out of this area, and we have to be clear of here by daylight. Now listen carefully. The Hounds are big, but they're not very agile. They particularly aren't very good at turning around in a hurry. I'll confront him head-on. You run in behind him and hamstring him. You know how to do that?"

That knowledge was instinctive in wolves, and Garion found, almost with surprise, that he knew precisely what to do. "Yes," he replied. The speech of wolves is limited in its emotional range, so he could not indicate how uncomfortable this impending encounter made him.

"All right," Belgarath continued, "once you cut his hamstrings, get back out of the range of his teeth. He'll try to turn on you. That's instinctive, so he won't be able to stop himself. That's when I'll take his throat."

Garion shuddered at the deliberateness of the plan. Belgarath was proposing not a fight, but a cold-blooded killing. "Let's get it over with, Grandfather," he said unhappily.

"Don't whine, Garion," Belgarath's thought came to him. "He'll hear you."

"I don't like this," Garion thought back.

"Neither do I, but it's the only thing we can do. Let's go."

They crept among the fog-dimmed tree trunks with the smell of the Hound growing stronger in their nostrils. It was not a pleasant smell, since dogs will eat carrion, while wolves will not. Then Garion saw the Hound outlined black against the fog beyond the edge of the trees. Belgarath paused, indicating that he also saw their intended victim. Then the two wolves separated and moved in the slow, deliberate pace of the hunt, setting each paw carefully and noiselessly down on the damp forest loam.

It was over in a shockingly short time. The Hound screamed once when Garion's fangs ripped the tendons of his hind legs, but the scream died into a hideous rattling gurgle as Belgarath's jaws closed on his throat. The huge black body twitched a few times with its front paws scratching convulsively at the dirt. Then it shuddered and went limp. The dead Hound blurred peculiarly, and then there was a Grolim lying on the ground before them with his throat torn out.

"I didn't know they did that," Garion said, fighting down a surge of revulsion.

"Sometimes they do." Then Belgarath sent out his thought. "It's clear now, Pol. Tell Durnik to bring them on through."

As dawn turned the fog opalescent, they took shelter in a ruined village. There had been a wall around it, and part of it was still standing. The houses had been made of stone. Some were still more or less intact—except for the roofs. Others had been tumbled into the narrow streets. In places, smoke still rose from the shattered debris.

"I think we can risk a fire," Durnik suggested, looking at the smoke.

Polgara looked around. "A hot breakfast wouldn't hurt," she agreed. "It might be some time before we get another chance for one. Over there, I think," she added, "in what's left of that house."

"In just a moment, Durnik," Belgarath said. "I'll need you to translate for me." He looked at Toth. "I assume you know how to get to Kell from here?" he asked the huge mute.

Toth shifted the unbleached wool blanket he wore draped over one shoulder and nodded.

"In Melcena, we heard that Kell has been sealed off," the old man continued. "Will they let us through?"

Toth made a series of those obscure gestures.

"He says that there won't be any problem—as long as Cyradis is still at Kell," Durnik translated. "She'll instruct the other seers to let us through."

"She's there, then?" Belgarath asked.

The gestures came more rapidly.

"I didn't quite follow that," Durnik told his friend.

Toth gestured again, slower this time.

Durnik frowned. "This is a little complicated, Belgarath," he said. "As closely as I can make out what he says, she's there and yet not there at the same time—sort of the way she was when we saw Zandramas that time. But she's also there and not there in several other places as well—and in several different times."

"That's a neat trick," Beldin said. "Did he tell you where these other places and times are?"

"No. I think he'd rather not."

"We can respect that," Belgarath said.

"It doesn't diminish the curiosity, though," Beldin said. He brushed a few twigs out of his beard, then pointed at the sky. "I'm going up there," he added. "I think we ought to know how far this fog extends and what we're likely to run into once we get past it." He stopped, spread his arms, shimmered, and swooped away.

Durnik led the way into the ruined house and built a small fire in the fireplace while Silk and Sadi prowled through the shattered village. After a short while they returned with a very thin Melcene in the brown robe of a bureaucrat. "He was hiding in a cellar," Silk reported.

The bureaucrat was trembling visibly, and his eyes were wild.

"What's your name?" Belgarath asked him.

The Melcene stared at the old man as if he didn't understand.

"I think he's had a bad time lately," Silk said. "We weren't able to get a word out of him."

"Can you give him something to calm his nerves?" Belgarath asked Sadi.

"I was just about to suggest that myself, Ancient One." Sadi went to his red leather case and took out a small glass vial filled with amber liquid. He took a tin cup from the table and poured some water into it. Then he carefully measured a few drops of the amber liquid into the water and swirled it around. "Why don't you drink this?" he said, handing the trembling Melcene the cup.

The fellow seized the cup gratefully and drained it in several noisy gulps.

"Give it a few moments to take effect," Sadi said quietly to Belgarath.

They watched the terrified man until his trembling subsided. "Are you feeling any better now, friend?" Sadi asked him.

"Y-yes," the thin fellow replied. He drew in a long shuddering breath. "Thank you," he said. "Have you any food? I'm very hungry."

Polgara gave him some bread and cheese. "This should tide you over until breakfast," she said.

"Thank you, Lady." He hungrily took the food and began to wolf it down.

"You look as if you've been through quite a lot lately," Silk said.

"And none of it pleasant," the bureaucrat told him.

"What did you say your name was?"

"Nabros. I'm with the Bureau of Roads."

"How long have you been in Peldane?"

"It seems like forever, but I suppose it's only been twenty years or so."

"What's going on here?" The rat-faced man gestured around at the shattered houses.

"Absolute chaos," Nabros replied. "Things have been in an upheaval for several years now, but last month Zandramas annexed Peldane."

"How did she do that? I'd heard that she was somewhere in the western part of the continent."

"So had I. Maybe she just got word back to her generals. Nobody's seen her for several years now."

"You seem to be fairly well informed, Nabros," Silk suggested.

Nabros shrugged. "It goes with being a member of the bureaucracy." He smiled a bit wanly. "Sometimes I think we spend more time gossiping than we do working."

"What have you heard about Zandramas lately?" Belgarath asked.

"Well," the fellow replied, rubbing at his unshaven cheek, "just before I fled the bureau offices in Selda, a friend of mine from the Bureau of Commerce came by. He said that there's supposed to be a coronation of some kind in Hemil—that's the capital of Darshiva, you know. My friend told me that they're going to crown some archduke from Melcena as Emperor of Mallorea."

"Mallorea's already got an emperor," Velvet objected.

"I think that may be part of the idea. My friend from Commerce is a fairly shrewd fellow, and he was speculating a bit after he told me what they were planning. Kal Zakath's been in Cthol Murgos for years now, but he recently returned to Mal Zeth. Most of his army is still in the west, however, so he can't put great masses of troops in the field. My friend seemed to think that Zandramas ordered this coronation in order to infuriate the Emperor to the point that he'll do something rash. It's my guess that she hopes to lure him out of Mal Zeth so her forces can fall on him. If she succeeds in killing him, this archduke from Melcena will actually *be* the emperor."

"What's the point of that?" Silk asked him.

"You've heard of Urvon, haven't you?"

"The Disciple?"

"That's the one. He's been sitting for centuries in Mal Yaska, but what's been going on in this part of the world has finally lured him out. It's because of Zandramas, you see. She's a direct challenge to him. Anyway, he marched across Karanda gathering up an enormous army. The Karands even believe he has demons aiding him. That's nonsense, of course, but Karands will believe anything. That's why Zandramas—or her people—have to get control of the imperial throne. She needs to bring the Mallorean army back from Cthol Murgos to match Urvon's forces. Otherwise, he'll destroy everything she's worked for." The suddenly talkative bureaucrat sighed deeply, and his head began to nod.

"I think he'll sleep now," Sadi murmured to Belgarath.

"That's all right," the old man replied. "I've got what I need."

"Not quite yet," Polgara said crisply from her cook-fire. "There are some things that I need as well." She carefully stepped across the littered floor of the half-ruined house and lightly touched one hand to the dozing bureaucrat's face. His eyes opened, and he looked at her a bit blankly. "How much do you know about Zandramas?" she asked him. "I think I'd like to hear the full story—if you know it. How did she gain so much power?"

"That's a long story, Lady."

"We have time."

The thin Melcene rubbed at his eyes and stifled a yawn. "Let me see," he said, half to himself, "where did it all start?" He sighed. "I came here to Peldane about twenty years ago. I was young and very enthusiastic. It was my first post, and I wanted very much to make good. Peldane's not such a bad place, really. We had Grolims here, naturally, but they were a long way from Urvon and Mal Yaska, and they didn't take their religion very seriously. Torak had been dormant for five hundred years, and Urvon wasn't interested in what was going on out here in the hinterlands.

"Over in Darshiva, though, things were different. There had been some kind of a schism in the Temple in Hemil, the capital, and it ended up in a bloodbath." He smiled faintly. "One of the few times Grolims have ever put their knives to good use, I suppose. The upshot of the affair was that a new archpriest gained control of the Temple—a man named Naradas."

"Yes," Polgara said. "We've heard of him."

"I've never actually seen him, but I'm told he has very strange eyes. Anyway, among his followers there was a young Grolim priestess named Zandramas. She must have been about sixteen then, and very beautiful, I've heard. Naradas reintroduced the old forms of worship, and the altar in the Temple at Hemil ran with blood." He shuddered. "It seems that the young priestess was the most enthusiastic participant in the Grolim rite of sacrifice—either out of an excess of fanaticism, or innate cruelty, or because she knew that this was the best way to attract the eye of the new archpriest. There are rumors that she attracted his eye in other ways as well. She'd unearthed a very obscure passage in the *Book of Torak* that seemed to say that the rite of sacrifice should be performed unclad. They say that Zandramas has a striking figure, and I guess the combination of blood and her nakedness completely inflamed Naradas. I've heard that things used to happen in the sanctum of the Temple during the rite that cannot be described in the presence of ladies."

"I think we can skip over that part, Nabros," Polgara told him primly, glancing at Eriond.

"Anyhow," Nabros continued, "all Grolims *claim* to be sorcerers, but from what I gather, the ones in Darshiva weren't very skilled. Naradas could manage a few things, but most of his followers resorted to charlatanism—sleight of hand and other forms of trickery, you understand.

"At any rate, not long after Naradas had consolidated his position, word reached us here that Torak had been killed. Naradas and his underlings went into absolute despair, but something rather profound seems to have happened to Zandramas. She walked out of the Temple at Hemil in a kind of a daze. My friend from the Bureau of Commerce was there at the time and he saw her. He said that her eyes were glazed and that she had an expression of inhuman ecstasy on her face. When she reached the edge of the city, she stripped off her clothes and ran naked into the forest. We all assumed that she'd gone completely mad and that we'd seen the last of her.

"Once in a while, though, travelers would report having seen her in that wilderness near the border of Likandia. Sometimes, she'd run away from them, and other times, she'd stop them and speak to them in a language no one could understand. They listened, though—perhaps because she still hadn't managed to find any clothes.

"Then one day after a few years, she showed up at the gates of Hemil. She was wearing a black Grolim robe made of satin, and she seemed to be totally in control of herself. She went to the Temple and sought out Naradas. The archpriest had given himself wholly over to the grossest kind of debauchery in his despair, but after he and Zandramas spoke together privately, he seems to have had a reconversion of some kind. Since that time, he's been the follower. He'll do anything Zandramas tells him to do.

"Zandramas spent a short time in the Temple, then she began to move about in Darshiva. At first she spoke only with Grolims, but in time she went out and talked with ordinary people as well. She always told them the same thing—that a new God of Angarak was coming. After a time, word of what she was doing got back to Mal Yaska, and Urvon sent some very powerful Grolims to Darshiva to stop her. I'm not sure what happened to her out there in that wilderness, but whatever it was seems to have filled her with enormous power. When Urvon's Grolims tried to stop her from preaching, she simply obliterated them."

"Obliterated?" Belgarath exclaimed in astonishment.

"That's about the only word I can use. Some of them she consumed with fire. Others were blasted to bits by bolts of lightning that shot down out of a cloudless sky. Once, she opened the earth, dropped five of them into a pit, and then closed the earth on them again. Urvon began to take her very seriously at that point, I guess. He sent more and more Grolims to Darshiva, but she destroyed them all. The Darshivan Grolims who chose to follow her were given *real* powers, so they didn't have to resort to trickery any more."

"And the ones who didn't?" Polgara asked.

"None of them survived. I understand that a few of them tried deception— pretending to accept her message—but I guess she could see right through them and took appropriate steps. It probably wasn't really necessary, though. She spoke as if inspired, and no one could resist her message. Before long, all of Darshiva— Grolims and secular people alike—groveled at her feet.

"She moved north from Darshiva into Rengel and Voresebo, preaching as she went and converting whole multitudes. The archpriest Naradas followed her blindly and he was also enormously eloquent and appears to have only slightly less power than she does. For some reason, she never came across the River Magan into Peldane—until recently."

"All right," Polgara said, "she converted Rengel and Voresebo. Then what?"

"I really can't say." Nabros shrugged. "About three years ago, both she and Naradas disappeared. I think they went off to the west someplace, but I don't know for sure. About the last thing she told the crowds before she left was that she was going to be the bride of this new God she's been talking about. Then, a month ago, her forces came across the Magan and invaded Peldane. That's about all I know, really."

Polgara stepped back. "Thank you, Nabros," she said gently. "Why don't you see if you can get some sleep now? I'll save some breakfast for you."

He sighed, and his eyelids began to droop. "Thank you, Lady," he said drowsily, and a moment later he was fast asleep. Polgara gently covered him with a blanket.

Belgarath motioned to them, and they all went back over to the fire again. "It's all beginning to fit together now, isn't it?" he said. "When Torak died, the Dark Spirit took over Zandramas and made her the Child of Dark. That's what that business in the wilderness was all about."

Ce'Nedra had been muttering to herself under her breath. Her eyes were dangerous and her face angry. "You'd better do something about this, old man," she said threateningly to Belgarath.

"About what?" He looked a little baffled.

"You heard what that man said. He told us that Zandramas plans to be the bride of this new God."

"Yes," he said mildly, "I heard him."

"You're not going to let something like that happen, are you?"

"I hadn't planned to, no. What's got you so upset, Ce'Nedra?"

Her eyes flashed. "I will *not* have Zandramas for a daughter-in-law," she declared hotly, "no matter what happens."

He stared at her for a moment, then he began to laugh.

■ CHAPTER ELEVEN ■

By midafternoon the wan dish of the sun had begun to burn through the pervading mist, and Beldin returned. "The fog's completely cleared away about a league west of here," he told them.

"Are there any signs of movement out there?" Belgarath asked him.

"Some," Beldin replied. "A few detachments of troops that are all headed north. Otherwise it's as empty as a merchant's soul. Sorry, Kheldar, it's just an old expression."

"That's all right, Beldin," Silk forgave him grandly. "These little slips of the tongue are common in the very elderly."

Beldin gave him a hard look and then continued. "The villages up ahead all seem to be deserted and mostly in ruins. I'd say that the villagers have fled." He glanced at the sleeping Melcene. "Who's your guest?" he asked.

"He's with the Bureau of Roads," Belgarath replied. "Silk found him hiding in a cellar."

"Is he really all that sleepy?"

"Sadi gave him something to calm his nerves."

"I'd say it worked pretty good. He looks very calm."

"Would you like something to eat, uncle?" Polgara asked.

"Thanks all the same, Pol, but I had a fat rabbit an hour or so ago." He looked back at Belgarath. "I think we'll still want to travel at night," he advised. "You don't have whole regiments out there, but there are enough to give us trouble if they happen to surprise us."

"Any idea of whose troops they are?"

"I didn't see any Guardsmen or Karands. I'd guess that they belong to Zandramas—or to the King of Peldane. Whoever they are, they're going north toward that battle that's about to begin."

"All right," Belgarath said, "we'll travel at night, then—at least until we get past the soldiers."

They moved along at a fair rate of speed that night. They had passed the woods, and the watchfires of the soldiers encamped on the plain made them easy to avoid. Then, just before dawn, Belgarath and Garion stopped atop a low hill and looked down at a camp that seemed quite a bit larger than those they had passed earlier. "About a battalion, Grandfather," Garion surmised. "I think we've got a problem here. The country around here's awfully flat. This is the only hill we've seen for miles, and there isn't very much cover. No matter how we try to hide, their scouts are going to see us. It might be safer if we turned around and went back a ways."

Belgarath laid back his ears in irritation. "Let's go back and warn the others," he growled. He rose to his feet and led Garion back the way they had come.

"There's no point in taking chances, father," Polgara said after she had drifted in on silent wings. "The country was more broken a few miles back. We can go back there and find shelter."

"Were the cooks making breakfast?" Sadi asked.

"Yes," Garion replied. "I could smell it—some kind of porridge and bacon."

"They're not likely to move or send out scouts until after they eat, are they?"

"No," Garion told him. "Troops get very surly if you make them start marching before you feed them."

"And were the sentries all wearing the standard military cloak—the ones that look more or less like these?" He plucked at the front of his traveler's cloak.

"The ones I saw were," Garion said.

"Why don't we pay them a visit, Prince Kheldar?" The eunuch suggested.

"What have you got in mind?" Silk asked suspiciously.

"Porridge is so bland, don't you think? I have a number of things in my case that can spice it up just a bit. We can walk through the encampment like a pair of sentries who've just been relieved and go directly to the cook-fires for a bite of breakfast. I shouldn't have much trouble seasoning the kettles with certain condiments."

Silk grinned at him.

"No poison," Belgarath said firmly.

"I hadn't considered poison, Ancient One," Sadi protested mildly. "Not out of any sense of morality, mind you. It's just that soldiers tend to grow suspicious when their messmates turn black in the face and topple over. I have something much more pleasant in mind. The soldiers will all be deliriously happy for a short while, then they'll fall asleep."

"For how long?" Silk asked.

"Several days," Sadi shrugged. "A week at the very most."

Silk whistled. "Is it dangerous at all?"

"Only if one has a weak heart. I've used it on myself on occasion—when I was particularly tired. Shall we go, then?"

"Teaming those two together may have been a moral blunder," Belgarath mused as the two rogues walked off in the darkness toward the twinkling watchfires.

It was about an hour later when the little Drasnian and the eunuch returned. "It's safe now," Sadi reported. "We can go on through their camp. There's a low range of hills a league or so farther on where we can take shelter until night."

"Any trouble at all?" Velvet asked.

"Not a bit," Silk smirked. "Sadi's very good at that sort of thing."

"Practice, my dear Kheldar," the eunuch said deprecatingly. "I've poisoned a fair number of people in my time." He grinned mirthlessly. "Once I gave a banquet for a group of my enemies. Not a single one of them saw me season the soup course, and Nyissans are very observant when it comes to that sort of thing."

"Didn't they get suspicious when you didn't eat any soup?" Velvet asked curiously.

"But I did, Liselle. I'd spent an entire week dosing myself with the antidote." He shuddered. "Vile-tasting stuff, as I recall. The poison itself was quite tasty. A number of my guests even complimented me on the soup before they left." He sighed. "Those were the good old days," he mourned.

"I think we can reminisce later on," Belgarath said. "Let's see if we can reach those hills before the sun gets much higher."

The soldiers' encampment was silent, except for an occasional snore. The troops were all smiling happily as they slept.

The following night was cloudy, and the air smelled strongly of incipient rain. Garion and Belgarath had no trouble finding the encampments of the soldiers in their path, and a few overheard snatches of conversation revealed the fact that these troops were members of the royal army of Peldane, and further that they were approaching the impending battle with a great deal of reluctance. About morning, Garion and his grandfather trotted back to rejoin the others with Polgara ghosting just above them on silent wings.

"A sound is still a sound," Durnik was saying stubbornly to Beldin. The two were riding side by side.

"But if there's nobody to hear it, how can we call it a sound?" Beldin argued.

Belgarath shook himself into his own form. "The noise in the woods again, Beldin?" he said in a tone of profoundest disgust.

The hunchback shrugged. "You've got to start somewhere."

"Can't you think of anything new? After we argued the question for a thousand years, I thought you might have gotten tired of it."

"What's this?" Polgara asked, walking through the tall grass to join them in the shadowless light of dawn.

"Beldin and Durnik are discussing a very tired old philosophical question." Belgarath snorted. "If there's a noise in the woods, and there's nobody around to hear it, is it really a noise?"

"Of course it is," she replied calmly.

"How did you reach that conclusion?" Beldin demanded.

"Because there's no such thing as an empty place, uncle. There are always creatures around—wild animals, mice, insects, birds—and they can all hear."

"But what if there weren't? What if the woods are truly empty?"

"Why waste your time talking about an impossibility?"

He stared at her in frustration.

"Not only that," Ce'Nedra added just a bit smugly, "you're talking about woods, so there are trees there. Trees can hear, too, you know."

He glared at her. "Why are you all taking sides against me?"

"Because you're wrong, uncle." Polgara smiled.

"Wrong, Polgara?" He spluttered. *"Me?"*

"It happens to everybody once in a while. Why don't we all have some breakfast?"

The sun rose while they were eating, and Belgarath looked up, squinting into the morning rays. "We haven't seen any soldiers since midnight," he said, "and all we've seen so far are troops of the army of Peldane. They're not really anything to worry about, so I think it's safe to ride on a little farther this morning." He looked at Silk. "How far is it to the border of Darshiva?"

"Not really all that far, but we haven't been making very good time. It's spring, so the nights are getting shorter, and we lose time when we have to circle around those troops." He frowned. "We might have a bit of a problem at the border, though. We're going to have to cross the River Magan, and if everyone has fled the area, we could have some trouble finding a boat."

"Is the Magan really as big as they say?" Sadi asked.

"It's the biggest river in the world. It runs for a thousand leagues and more, and it's so wide that you can't see the far shore."

Durnik rose to his feet. "I want to check over the horses before we go any farther," he said. "We've been riding them in the dark, and that's always a little dangerous. We don't want any of them pulling up lame."

Eriond and Toth also rose, and the three of them went through the tall grass to the place where the horses were picketed.

"I'll go on ahead," Beldin said. "Even if the troops are Peldanes, we still don't need any surprises." He changed form and flew off toward the west, spiraling up into the cloudless morning sky.

Garion stretched his legs out in front of him and leaned back on his elbows.

"You must be tired," Ce'Nedra said, sitting beside him and touching his face tenderly.

"Wolves don't really get that tired," he told her. "I get the feeling that I could run for a week if I really had to."

"Well, you don't have to, so don't even consider it."

"Yes, dear."

Sadi had risen to his feet with his red leather case in his hands. "As long as we're stopped, I think I'll find something to feed Zith," he said. A small frown touched his brow. "You know, Liselle," he said to Velvet, "I think you were right back in Zamad. She definitely looks as if she's gained a few ounces."

"Put her on a diet," the blond girl suggested.

"I'm not sure about that." He smiled. "It's very hard to explain to a snake why you're starving her, and I wouldn't want her to get cross with me."

They rode out not long afterward, following Toth's gestured directions.

"He says that we can probably find a village south of the big town on the river," Durnik told them.

"Ferra," Silk supplied.

"I suppose so. I haven't looked at a map for a while. Anyway, he says that there are quite a few villages on this side where we might be able to hire a boat to get us across to Darshiva."

"That's assuming that they aren't all deserted," Silk added.

Durnik shrugged. "We'll never know until we get there."

It was a warm morning, and they rode across the rolling grasslands of southern Peldane under cloudless skies. About midmorning, Eriond rode forward and fell in beside Garion. "Do you think Polgara would mind if you and I took a little gallop?" he asked. "Maybe to that hill over there?" He pointed at a large knoll off to the north.

"She probably would," Garion said, "unless we can come up with a good reason."

"You don't think she'd accept the idea that Horse and Chretienne need to run once in a while?"

"Eriond, you've known her for a long time. Do you really think she'd listen if we tried to tell her that?"

Eriond sighed. "No, I suppose not."

Garion squinted at the hilltop. "We really ought to keep an eye out to the north, though," he said thoughtfully. "That's where the trouble's going to break out. We sort of need to know what's happening up there, don't we? That hilltop would be a perfect place to have a look."

"That's very true, Belgarion."

"It's not as if we'd actually be lying to her."

"I wouldn't dream of lying to her."

"Of course not. Neither would I."

The two young men grinned at each other. "I'll tell Belgarath where we're going," Garion said. "We'll let him explain it to her."

"He's the perfect one to do it," Eriond agreed.

Garion dropped back and touched his half-dozing grandfather's shoulder. "Eriond and I are going to ride over to that hill," he said. "I want to see if there are any signs that the fighting's started yet."

"What? Oh, good idea." Belgarath yawned and closed his eyes again.

Garion motioned to Eriond, and the two of them trotted off into the tall grass at the side of the trail.

"Garion," Polgara called, "where are you going?"

"Grandfather can explain it, Aunt Pol," he shouted back. "We'll catch up again in just a bit." He looked at Eriond. "Now let's get out of earshot in a hurry."

They went north, first at a gallop and then at a dead run with the grass whipping at their horses' legs. The chestnut and the gray matched stride for stride, plunging along with their heads thrust far forward and their hooves pounding on the thick turf. Garion leaned forward in his saddle, surrendering to the flow and surge of Chretienne's muscles. Both he and Eriond were laughing with delight when they reined in on the hilltop.

"That was good," Garion said, swinging down from his saddle. "We don't get the chance to do that very often any more, do we?"

"Not often enough," Eriond agreed, also dismounting. "You managed to arrange it very diplomatically, Belgarion."

"Of course. Diplomacy's what kings do best."

"Do you think we fooled her?"

"Us?" Garion laughed. "Fool Aunt Pol? Be serious, Eriond."

"I suppose you're right." Eriond made a wry face. "She'll probably scold us, won't she?"

"Inevitably, but the ride was worth a scolding, wasn't it?"

Eriond smiled. Then he looked around, and his smile faded. "Belgarion," he said sadly, pointing to the north.

Garion looked. Tall columns of black smoke rose along the horizon. "It looks as if it's started," he said bleakly.

"Yes." Eriond sighed. "Why do they have to do that?"

Garion crossed his arms on Chretienne's saddle and leaned his chin pensively on them. "Pride, I suppose," he replied, "and the hunger for power. Revenge, too, sometimes. I guess. Once in Arendia, Lelldorin said that very often it's because people just don't know how to stop it, once it's started."

"But it's all so senseless."

"Of course it is. Arends aren't the only stupid people on earth. Any time you have two people who both want the same thing badly enough, you're going to have a fight. If the two people have enough followers, they call it a war. If a couple of ordinary men have that kind of disagreement, there might be a broken nose and some missing teeth, but when you start getting armies involved, people get killed."

"Are you and 'Zakath going to have a war, then?"

It was a troubling question, and Garion wasn't sure he knew the answer. "I don't really know," he admitted.

"He wants to rule the world," Eriond pointed out, "and you don't want him to. Isn't that the sort of thing that starts a war?"

"It's awfully hard to say," Garion replied sadly. "Maybe if we hadn't left Mal Zeth when we did, I might have been able to bring him around. But we had to leave, so I lost the chance." He sighed. "I think it's finally going to be up to him. Maybe he's changed enough so that he'll abandon the whole idea—but then again, maybe he hasn't. You can never tell with a man like 'Zakath. I *hope* he's given up the notion. I don't want a war—not with anybody; but I'm not going to bow to him, either. The world wasn't meant to be ruled by one man—and certainly not by somebody like 'Zakath."

"But you like him, don't you?"

"Yes, I do. I wish I could have met him before Taur Urgas ruined his life." He paused, and his face grew set. "Now there's a man I'd have rather cheerfully gone to war with. He contaminated the whole world just by living in it."

"But it wasn't really his fault. He was insane, and that excuses him."

"You're a very forgiving young man, Eriond."

"Isn't it easier to forgive than to hate? Until we learn how to forgive, that sort of thing is going to keep on happening." He pointed at the tall pillars of smoke rising to the north. "Hate is a sterile thing, Belgarion."

"I know." Garion sighed. "I hated Torak, but in the end I guess I forgave him—more out of pity than anything else. I still had to kill him, though."

"What do you think the world would be like if people didn't kill each other any more?"

"Nicer, probably."

"Why don't we fix it that way then?"

"You and I?" Garion laughed. "All by ourselves?"

"Why not?"

"Because it's impossible, Eriond."

"I thought you and Belgarath had settled the issue of impossible a long time ago."

Garion laughed again. "Yes, I suppose we did. All right, let's drop impossible. Would you accept extremely difficult instead?"

"Nothing that's really worthwhile should be easy, Belgarion. If it's easy, we don't value it; but I'm certain we'll be able to find an answer." He said it with such shining confidence in his face that for a moment Garion actually believed that the wild notion might indeed be feasible.

Then he looked out at the ugly columns of smoke again, and the hope died. "I suppose we should go back and let the others know what's happening out there," he said.

It was about noon when Beldin returned. "There's another detachment of troops about a mile ahead," he told Belgarath. "A dozen or so."

"Are they going toward that battle to the north?"

"No, I'd say this particular group is running away from it. They look as if they were fairly well mauled recently."

"Could you tell which side they're on?"

"That doesn't really matter, Belgarath. A man gives up his allegiances when he deserts."

"Sometimes you're so clever you make me sick."

"Why don't you have Pol mix you up something to cure it?"

"How long has that been going on?" Velvet asked Polgara.

"Which was that, dear?"

"That constant wrangling between those two?"

Polgara closed her eyes and sighed. "You wouldn't believe it, Liselle. Sometimes I think it started at about the beginning of time."

The soldiers they encountered were wary, even frightened. They stood their ground, however, with their hands on their weapons. Silk made a quick motion to Garion, and the two of them rode forward at an unthreatening walk.

"Good day, gentlemen," Silk greeted them conversationally. "What in the world is happening around here?"

"You mean you haven't heard?" a wiry fellow with a bloody bandage around his head asked.

"I haven't found anybody to tell me," Silk replied. "What happened to all the people who used to live in this part of Peldane? We haven't seen a soul in the last four days."

"They all fled," the bandaged man told him. "The ones who were still alive did, at any rate."

"What were they fleeing from?"

"Zandramas," the fellow replied with a shudder. "Her army marched into Peldane about a month ago. We tried to stop them, but they had Grolims with them, and ordinary troops can't do much against Grolims."

"That's the truth, certainly. What's all that smoke up to the north?"

"There's a big battle going on." The soldier sat down on the ground and began to unwind the bloodstained bandage from around his head.

"It's not like any battle *I've* ever seen," another soldier supplied. His left arm was in a sling, and he looked as if he had just spent several days lying in the mud. "I've been in a few wars, but nothing like this. When you're a soldier, you takes your chances—swords and arrows and spears and the like, y'know—but when they starts throwing horrors at me, I begins to feel it's time to find another line of work."

"Horrors?" Silk asked him.

"They's got demons with 'em, friend—both sides of 'em has—monstrous big demons with snaky arms and fangs and claws and suchlike."

"You're not serious!"

"I seen 'em with my own eyes. You ever seen a man get et alive? Makes your hair stand on end, it does."

"I don't quite follow this," Silk confessed. "Who's involved in this battle? I mean, ordinary armies don't keep tame demons with them to help with the fighting."

"That's the honest truth," the muddy man agreed. "A ordinary soldier's likely to leave the service if they expect him to march alongside something that looks at him as if he was something to eat. I never did get the straight of it, though." He looked at the man with the wounded head. "Did you ever find out who was fighting, Corporal?"

The corporal was wrapping a clean bandage around his head. "The captain told us before he got killed," he said.

"Maybe you'd better start at the beginning," Silk said. "I'm a little confused about this."

"Like I told you," the corporal said, "about a month ago the Darshivans and their Grolims invaded Peldane. Me and my men are in the Royal Army of Peldane, so we tried to hold them back. We slowed them some on the east bank of the Magan, but then the Grolims come at us, and we had to retreat. Then we heard that there was another army coming down out of the north—Karands and soldiers in armor and more Grolims. We figured that we was really in for it at that point, but as it turns out, this new army isn't connected with the Darshivans. It seems that it's working for some High Grolim from way off to the west. Well, this Grolim, he sets up along the coast and don't come inland at all. It's like he's waiting for something. We had our hands full with the Darshivans, so we wasn't too interested in what it was he was waiting for. We was doing a lot of what our officers called 'maneuvering'—which is officer talk for running away."

"I take it that the Grolim finally decided to come inland after all," Silk observed.

"He surely did, friend. He surely did. It was just a few days ago when he struck inland just as straight as a tight string. Either he knew exactly where he was going or he was following something, I don't know exactly which. Anyway, the Darshivans, they stopped chasing us and rushed in to try to block his way, and that's when he called in the demons Vurk here was talking about. At first, the demons charged right through the Darshivans, but then their Grolims—or maybe it was Zandramas herself—they conjured up *their* demons, and that's when the big fight commenced. The demons, they went at each other for all they was worth and they trampled over anybody unlucky enough to get in the way. There we was, caught right in the middle of it all and getting trampled on by first one set of demons and then the other. That's when me and Vurk and these others put our heads together and decided to find out what the weather's like in Gandahar."

"Hot this time of year," Silk told him.

"Not near as hot as it is north of here, friend. You ever see a demon breathe fire? I seen one of them armored soldiers get roasted alive right inside his chain mail. Then the demon picked him out of his armor piece by piece and et him while he was still smoking." The corporal knotted the ends of his fresh bandage. "That ought to hold it," he said, rising to his feet again. He looked up into the noon sky, squinting slightly. "We can make some more miles before the sun goes down, Vurk," he said to his muddy friend. "Get the men ready to march. If that battle starts to spread out, we could get caught in the middle of it again, and none of us want that."

"I'll do 'er, Corporal," Vurk replied.

The corporal looked at Silk again, his eyes narrowed appraisingly. "You and your friends are welcome to come along," he offered. "A few men on horseback might be a help in case we run into trouble."

"Thanks all the same, Corporal," Silk declined, "but I think we'll ride over to the Magan and see if we can find a boat. We could be at the mouth of the river in a week or so."

"I'd advise riding hard, then, my friend. Demons can run awful fast when they're hungry."

Silk nodded. "Good luck in Gandahar, Corporal," he added.

"I think I'll stop being a corporal," the fellow said ruefully. "The pay wasn't bad, but the work's getting dangerouser and dangerouser, and all the pay in the world won't do a man much good once he takes up residence inside a demon." He turned to his friend. "Let's move out, Vurk," he ordered.

Silk wheeled his horse and rode back to where the others were waiting, Garion close behind him.

"It's more or less what we thought," the little man reported, dismounting. "The battle up north is between Urvon and Zandramas, and both sides have demons now."

"She went *that* far?" Polgara asked incredulously.

"She didn't really have that much choice, Polgara," Silk told her. "Nahaz was leading his hordes of demons into the ranks of her troops, and her army was being decimated. She had to do something to stop him. Being captured by a demon is no joke—not even for the Child of Dark."

"All right," Durnik said soberly, "what do we do now?"

"The corporal in charge of those troops made an interesting suggestion," Silk told him.

"Oh? What was that?"

"He recommended that we get out of Peldane as fast as we possibly can."

"Corporals usually have good sense," Durnik noted. "Why don't we follow his advice?"

"I was hoping someone would say that," Silk agreed.

CHAPTER TWELVE

Vella was feeling melancholy. It was an unusual emotion for her, but she found that she rather liked it. There was much to be said for sweet, languorous sadness. She went with quiet dignity through the stately, marble-clad corridors of the palace in Boktor, and everyone gave way to her pensive expression. She chose not to consider the fact that her daggers may have played a certain part in this universal respect. In point of fact, Vella had not drawn a dagger on anyone for almost a week now—the last having been a slightly overfamiliar serving man who had mistaken her bluff camaraderie for an offer of a more intimate friendship. But she had not hurt him very much, and he had forgiven her almost before the bleeding had stopped.

Her destination that early morning was the sitting room of the Queen of Drasnia. In many ways Queen Porenn baffled Vella. She was petite and imperturbable. She carried no daggers and seldom raised her voice, but all of Drasnia and the other Alorn kingdoms held her in universal regard. Vella herself, not knowing exactly why, had acceded to the tiny queen's suggestion that she should customarily garb herself in gowns of lavender satin. A gown is a cumbersome thing that tangles up one's legs and confines one's bosom. Always before, Vella had preferred black leather trousers, boots, and a leather vest. The garb was comfortable and utilitarian. It was sturdy, and yet it provided opportunities for Vella to display her attributes to those whom she wished to impress. Then, on special occasions, she had customarily donned an easily discardable wool dress and a fine diaphanous undergown of rose-colored Mallorean silk that clung to her as she danced. Satin, on the other hand, rustled disturbingly, but felt good against her skin, and it made Vella uncomfortably aware of the fact that there was more to being a woman than a couple pair of daggers and a willingness to use them.

She tapped lightly on Porenn's door.

"Yes?" Porenn's voice came to her.

Did the woman never sleep?

"It's me, Porenn—Vella."

"Come in, child."

Vella set her teeth. She was not, after all, a child. She had been abroad in the world since her twelfth birthday. She had been sold—and bought—a half-dozen times, and she had been married for a brief, deliriously happy year to a lean Nadrak trapper named Tekk, whom she had loved to distraction. Porenn, however, seemed to prefer to look upon her as some half-gentled colt in sore need of training. In spite of herself, that thought softened Vella's resentment. The little blond Queen of Drasnia had in some strange way become the mother she had never known, and thoughts of daggers and of being bought and sold slid away under the influence of that wise, gentle voice.

"Good morning, Vella," Porenn said as the Nadrak girl entered her room. "Would you like some tea?" Although the queen always wore black in public, her dressing gown that morning was of the palest rose, and she looked somehow very vulnerable in that soft color.

"Hullo, Porenn," Vella said. "No tea, thanks." She flung herself into a chair beside the blond queen's divan.

"Don't flop, Vella," Porenn told her. "Ladies don't flop."

"I'm not a lady."

"Not yet, perhaps, but I'm working on it."

"Why are you wasting your time on me, Porenn?"

"Nothing worthwhile is ever a waste of time."

"Me? Worthwhile?"

"More than you could possibly know. You're early this morning. Is something troubling you?"

"I haven't been able to sleep. I've been having the strangest dreams lately."

"Don't let dreams bother you, child. Dreams are sometimes the past, sometimes the future, but mostly they're only that—dreams."

"Please don't call me 'child,' Porenn," Vella objected. "I think if we got right down to it, I'm almost as old as you are."

"In years, perhaps, but years aren't the only way to measure time."

There was a discreet rap at the door.

"Yes?" Porenn replied.

"It's me, your Majesty," a familiar voice said.

"Come in, Margrave Khendon," the queen said.

Javelin had not changed since Vella had last seen him. He was still bone-thin and aristocratic and had a sardonically amused twist to his lips. He wore, as was his custom, a pearl-gray doublet and tight-fitting black hose. His skinny shanks were not shown to any particular advantage by the latter. He bowed rather extravagantly. "Your Majesty," he greeted the queen, "and my Lady Vella."

"Don't be insulting, Javelin," Vella retorted. "I don't have a title, so don't 'my Lady' me."

"Haven't you told her yet?" Javelin mildly asked the queen.

"I'm saving it for her birthday."

"What's this?" Vella demanded.

"Be patient, dear," Porenn told her. "You'll find out about your title all in due time."

"I don't need a Drasnian title."

"Everybody needs a title, dear—even if it's only 'ma'am.' "

"Has she always been like this?" Vella bluntly asked the Chief of Drasnian Intelligence.

"She was a little more ingenuous when she still had her baby teeth," Javelin replied urbanely, "but she got to be more fun when she developed her fangs."

"Be nice, Khendon," Porenn told him. "How was Rak Urga?"

"Ugly—but then, most Murgo cities are."

"And how is King Urgit?"

"Newly married, your Majesty, and a little distracted by the novelty of it."

Porenn made a face. "I didn't send a gift," she fretted.

"I took the liberty of attending to that, your Majesty," Javelin said. "A rather nice silver service I picked up in Tol Honeth—at a bargain price, of course. I have this limited budget, you understand."

She gave him a long, unfriendly look.

"I left the bill with your chamberlain," he added with not even the faintest trace of embarrassment.

"How are the negotiations going?"

"Surprisingly well, my queen. The King of the Murgos seems not to have yet succumbed to the hereditary disorder of the House of Urga. He's very shrewd, actually."

"I somehow thought he might be," Porenn replied just a bit smugly.

"You're keeping secrets, Porenn," Javelin accused.

"Yes. Women do that from time to time. Are the Mallorean agents in the Drojim keeping abreast of things?"

"Oh, yes." Javelin smiled. "Sometimes we have to be a little obvious in order to make sure that they're getting the point, but they're more or less fully aware of the progress of the negotiations. We seem to be making them a bit apprehensive."

"You made good time on your return voyage."

Javelin shuddered slightly. "King Anheg put a ship at our disposal. Her captain is that pirate Greldik. I made the mistake of telling him I was in a hurry. The passage through the Bore was ghastly."

There was another polite knock on the door.

"Yes?" Porenn answered.

A servant opened the door. "The Nadrak Yarblek is here again, your Majesty," he reported.

"Show him in, please."

Yarblek had a tight look on his face that Vella recognized all too well. Her owner was in many respects a transparent man. He pulled off his shabby fur cap. "Good morning, Porenn," he said without ceremony, tossing the cap into a corner. "Have you got anything to drink? I've been in the saddle for five days and I'm perishing of thirst."

"Over there." Porenn pointed at a sideboard near the window.

Yarblek grunted, crossed the room, and filled a large goblet from a crystal decanter. He took a long drink. "Javelin," he said then, "have you got any people in Yar Nadrak?"

"A few," Javelin admitted cautiously.

"You'd better have them keep an eye on Drosta. He's up to something."

"He's always up to something."

"That's no lie, but this might be a little more serious. He's reopened lines of communication with Mal Zeth. He and 'Zakath haven't been on speaking terms since he changed sides at Thull Mardu, but now they're talking again. I don't like the smell of it."

"Are you sure? None of my people have reported it."

"They're probably in the palace, then. Drosta doesn't conduct serious business there. Have them go to a riverside tavern in the thieves' quarter. It's called the One-Eyed Dog. Drosta goes there to amuse himself. The emissary from Mal Zeth's been meeting with him in an upstairs room there—that's when Drosta can drag himself away from the girls."

"I'll put some people on it right away. Could you get any idea at all of what they're discussing?"

Yarblek shook his head and dropped wearily into a chair. "Drosta's ordered his guards to keep me out of the place." He looked at Vella. "You're looking a little pecky this morning," he observed. "Did you drink too much last night?"

"I almost never get drunk any more," she told him.

"I knew it was a mistake to leave you here in Boktor," he said glumly. "Porenn's a corrupting influence. Did you get over your irritation with me yet?"

"I suppose so. It's not really your fault that you're stupid."

"Thanks." He looked her up and down appraisingly. "I like the dress," he told her. "It makes you look more like a woman, for a change."

"Did you ever have any doubts, Yarblek?" she asked him archly.

Adiss, the Chief Eunuch in the palace of Eternal Salmissra, received the summons early that morning and he approached the throne room with fear and trembling. The queen had been in a peculiar mood of late, and Adiss painfully remembered the fate of his predecessor. He entered the dimly lit throne room and prostrated himself before the dais.

"The Chief Eunuch approaches the throne," the adoring chorus intoned in unison. Even though he himself had been until recently a member of that chorus, Adiss found their mouthing of the obvious irritating.

The queen dozed on her divan, her mottled coils moving restlessly with the dry hiss of scales rubbing against each other. She opened her soulless serpent's eyes and looked at him, her forked tongue flickering. "Well?" she said peevishly in the dusty whisper that always chilled his blood.

"Y-you summoned me, Divine Salmissra," he faltered.

"I'm aware of that, you idiot. Do not irritate me, Adiss. I'm on the verge of going into molt, and that always makes me short-tempered. I asked you to find out what the Alorns are up to. I am waiting for your report."

"I haven't been able to find out very much, my Queen."

"That is not the answer I wanted to hear, Adiss," she told him dangerously. "Is it possible that the duties of your office are beyond your capabilities?"

Adiss began to tremble violently. "I-I've sent for Droblek, your Majesty—the Drasnian Port Authority here in Sthiss Tor. I thought he might be able to shed some light on the situation."

"Perhaps so." Her tone was distant, and she gazed at her reflection in the mirror. "Summon the Tolnedran Ambassador as well. Whatever the Alorns are doing in Cthol Murgos also involves Varana."

"Forgive me, Divine Salmissra," Adiss said, feeling a trifle confused, "but why should the activities of the Alorns and Tolnedrans concern us?"

She swung her head about slowly, her sinuous neck weaving in the air. "Are you a total incompetent, Adiss?" she asked him. "We may not like it, but Nyissa is a part of the world, and we must always know what our neighbors are doing—and why." She paused, her tongue nervously tasting the air. "There is a game of some kind afoot, and I want to find out exactly what it is before I decide whether or not to become involved in it." She paused again. "Have you ever found out what happened to that one-eyed fellow, Issus?"

"Yes, your Majesty. He was recruited by Drasnian intelligence. At last report, he was in Rak Urga with the Alorn negotiators."

"How very curious. I think this entire business is reaching the point where I must have detailed information—and very, very soon. Do not fail me, Adiss. Your position is not all that secure, you know. Now you may kiss me." She lowered her head, and he stumbled to the dais to touch his cringing lips to her cold forehead.

"Very well, Adiss," she said. "Leave now." And she went back to gazing at her reflection in the mirror.

King Nathel of Mishrak ac Thull was a slack-lipped, dull-eyed young man with lank, mud-colored hair and a profound lack of anything even remotely resembling intelligence. His royal robes were spotted and wrinkled, and his crown did not fit him. It rested atop his ears and quite often slid down over his eyes.

Agachak, the cadaverous Hierarch of Rak Urgo, could not stand the young King of the Thulls, but he forced himself to be civil to him during their current discussions. Civility was not one of Agachak's strong points. He much preferred peremptory commands backed up by threats of dreadful retribution for failure to comply, but a careful assessment of Nathel's personality had persuaded him that the young Thull would collapse on the spot if he were suddenly given any kind of threat or ultimatum. And so it was that Agachak was forced to rely on cajolery and wheedling instead.

"The prophecy clearly states, your Majesty," he tried again, "that whichever king accompanies me to the place of the meeting will become Overking of all of Angarak."

"Does that mean I get Cthol Murgos and Gar og Nadrak, too?" Nathel asked, a faint glimmer coming into his uncomprehending eyes.

"Absolutely, your Majesty," Agachak assured him, "and Mallorea as well."

"Won't that make Kal Zakath unhappy with me? I wouldn't want him to feel that way. He had my father flogged once, did you know that? He was going to crucify him, but there weren't any trees around."

"Yes, I'd heard about that, but you don't have to worry. 'Zakath would have to genuflect to you."

" 'Zakath genuflect—to me?" Nathel laughed. It was a sound frighteningly devoid of thought.

"He would have no choice, your Majesty. If he were to refuse, the New God would blast him to atoms on the spot."

"What's an atom?"

Agachak ground his teeth. "A very small piece, your Majesty," he explained.

"I wouldn't mind making Urgit and Drosta bow to me," Nathel confessed, "but I don't know about 'Zakath. Urgit and Drosta think they're so smart. I'd like to take them down a peg or two. 'Zakath, though—I don't know about that." His eyes brightened again. "That means I'd get all the gold in Cthol Murgos and Gar og Nadrak, doesn't it? And I could make them dig it out of the ground for me, too." His crown slipped down over his eyes again, and he tilted his head back so that he could peer out from under its rim.

"And you'd get all the gold in Mallorea, too, and the jewels, and the silks and carpets—and they'd even give you your own elephant to ride."

"What's an elephant?"

"It's a very large animal, your Majesty."

"Bigger than a horse, even?"

"Much bigger. Besides, you'd also get Tolnedra and you know how much money they've got. You'd be the king of the world."

"Even bigger than an ox? I've seen some awful big oxes sometimes."

"Ten times as big."

Nathel smiled happily. "I bet that would make people sit up and take notice."

"Absolutely, your Majesty."

"What is it I have to do again?"

"You must go with me to the Place Which Is No More."

"That's the part I don't understand. How can we go there if it's not there any more?"

"The prophecy will reveal that to us in time, your Majesty."

"Oh. I see. Have you got any idea about where it is?"

"The clues I've been getting indicate that it's somewhere in Mallorea."

Nathel's face suddenly fell. "Now that's a real shame," he said petulantly.

"I don't quite—"

"I'd really like to go with you, Agachak. Truly I would—what with all the gold and carpets and silks and stuff—and making Urgit and Drosta and maybe even 'Zakath bow down to me and all, but I just can't."

"I don't understand. Why not?"

"I'm not allowed to leave home. My mother'd punish me something awful if I did. You know how that goes. I couldn't even think of going as far away as Mallorea."

"But you're the king."

"That doesn't change a thing. I still do what mother says. She tells everybody that I'm the best boy ever when it comes to that."

Agachak resisted a powerful urge to change this half-wit into a toad or perhaps a jellyfish. "Why don't I talk with your mother?" he suggested. "I'm sure I can persuade her to give you her permission."

"Why, that's a real, real good idea, Agachak. If mother says it's all right, I'll go with you quick as lightning."

"Good," Agachak said, turning.

"Oh, Agachak?" Nathel's voice sounded puzzled.

"Yes?"

"What's a prophecy?"

They had gathered at Vo Mandor, far from the watchful eyes of their kings, to discuss something that was very private and very urgent. It was also just a trifle on the disobedient side, and there is a very ugly word men use to describe those who disobey their kings.

Barak was there, and also Hettar, Mandorallen, and Lelldorin. Relg had just arrived from Maragor, and Barak's son Unrak sat on a high-backed bench by the window.

The Earl of Trellheim cleared his throat by way of calling them to order. They had gathered in the tower of Mandorallen's keep, and the golden autumn sunlight streamed in through the arched window. Barak was huge and resplendent in a green velvet doublet. His red beard was combed, and his hair was braided. "All right," he rumbled, "let's get started. Mandorallen, are you sure the stairway leading up here is guarded? I wouldn't want anybody to overhear us."

"Of a certainty, my Lord of Trellheim," the great knight replied earnestly. "I vouchsafe it upon my life to thee." Mandorallen wore mail and his silver-trimmed blue surcoat.

"A simple yes would have been enough, Mandorallen." Barak sighed. "Now," he continued briskly, "we've been forbidden to ride along with Garion and the others, right?"

"That's what Cyradis said at Rheon," Hettar replied softly. He wore his usual black horsehide, and his scalplock was caught in a silver ring. He lounged in a chair with his long legs thrust far out in front of him.

"All right, then," Barak continued. "We can't go with them, *but* there's nothing to stop us from going to Mallorea on business of our own, is there?"

"What kind of business?" Lelldorin asked blankly.

"We'll think of something. I've got a ship. We'll run on down to Tol Honeth and load her with a cargo of some kind. Then we'll go to Mallorea and do some trading."

"How do you plan to get the *Seabird* across to the Sea of the East?" Hettar asked. "That could be a long portage, don't you think?"

Barak winked broadly. "I've got a map," he said. "We can sail around the southern end of Cthol Murgos and right on into the eastern sea. From there to Mallorea is nothing at all."

"I thought the Murgos were very secretive about maps of their coastline," Lelldorin said, a frown creasing his open young face.

"They are," Barak grinned, "but Javelin's been in Rak Urga and he managed to steal one."

"How did you get it away from Javelin?" Hettar asked. "He's even more secretive than the Murgos."

"He sailed back to Boktor aboard Greldik's ship. Javelin's not a good sailor, so he wasn't feeling very well. Greldik pinched the map and had his cartographer make a copy. Javelin never even knew he'd been robbed."

"Thy plan is excellent, my Lord," Mandorallen said gravely, "but methinks I detect a flaw."

"Oh?"

"As all the world knows, Mallorea is a vast continent, thousands of leagues across and even more thousands from the south to the polar ice of the far north. It could well take us our lifetimes to locate our friends, for I perceive that to be the thrust of thy proposal."

Barak slyly laid one finger aside his nose. "I was just coming to that," he said. "When we were in Boktor, I got Yarblek drunk. He's shrewd enough when he's sober, but once you get a half keg of ale into him, he gets talkative. I asked him a few questions about the operation of the business he and Silk are running in Mallorea, and I got some very useful answers. It seems that the two of them have offices in every major city in Mallorea, and those offices keep in constant touch with each other. No matter what else he's doing, Silk's going to keep an eye on his business interests. Every time he gets near one of those offices, he'll find some excuse to stop by to see how many millions he's made in the past week."

"That's Silk, all right," Hettar agreed.

"All we have to do is drop anchor in some Mallorean seaport and look up the little thief's office. His people will know approximately where he is, and where Silk is, you're going to find the others."

"My Lord," Mandorallen apologized, "I have wronged thee. Canst thou forgive me for underestimating thy shrewdness?"

"Perfectly all right, Mandorallen," Barak replied magnanimously.

"But," Lelldorin protested, "we're still forbidden to join Garion and the others."

"Truly," Mandorallen agreed. "We may not approach them lest we doom their quest to failure."

"I think I've worked that part out, too," the big man said. "We can't ride along with them, but Cyradis didn't say anything about how far we have to stay away from them, did she? All we're going to be doing is minding our own business—a league or so away—or maybe a mile. We'll be close enough so that if they get into any kind of trouble, we'll be able to lend a hand and then be on our way again. There's nothing wrong with that, is there?"

Mandorallen's face came suddenly alight. "'Tis a duty, my Lord," he exclaimed, "a moral obligation. The Gods look with great disfavor upon those who fail to come to the aid of travelers in peril."

"Somehow I knew you'd see it that way," Barak said, slapping his friend on the shoulder with one huge hand.

"Sophistry," Relg said with a note of finality in his harsh voice. The Ulgo zealot now wore a tunic that looked very much like the one Durnik customarily wore. His once-pale skin was now sun-browned, and he no longer wore a cloth across his eyes. The years of working out of doors near the house he had built for Taiba and their horde of children had gradually accustomed his skin and eyes to sunlight.

"What do you mean, sophistry?" Barak protested.

"Just what I said, Barak. The Gods look at our intent, not our clever excuses. You want to go to Mallorea to aid Belgarion—we all do—but don't try to fool the Gods with these trumped-up stories."

They all stared at the zealot helplessly.

"But it was such a good plan," Barak said plaintively.

"Very good," Relg agreed, "but it's disobedient, and disobedience of the Gods—and of prophecy—is sin."

"Sin again, Relg?" Barak said in disgust. "I thought you'd gotten over that."

"Not entirely, no."

Barak's son Unrak, who at fourteen was already as big as a grown man, rose to his feet. He wore a mail shirt and had a sword belted at his side. His hair was flaming red, and his downy beard had already begun to cover his cheeks. "Let's see if I've got this right," he said. Unrak's voice no longer cracked and warbled, but had settled into a resonant baritone. "We have to obey the prophecy, is that it?"

"To the letter," Relg said firmly.

"Then I *have* to go to Mallorea," Unrak said.

"That went by a little fast," his father said to him.

"It's not really all that complicated, father. I'm the hereditary protector of the heir to the Rivan Throne, aren't I?"

"He's got a point there," Hettar said. "Go ahead, Unrak. Tell us what you've got in mind."

"Well," the young man said, blushing slightly under the scrutiny of his elders, "if Prince Geran's in Mallorea and in danger, I have to go there. The prophecy says so. Now, I don't know where he is, so I'm going to have to follow King Belgarion until he finds his son so that I can protect him."

Barak grinned broadly at his son.

"But," Unrak added, "I'm a little inexperienced at this protection business, so I might need a little guidance. Do you suppose, father, that I might be able to persuade you and your friends to come with me? Just to keep me from making any mistakes, you understand."

Hettar rose and shook Barak's hand. "Congratulations," he said simply.

"Well, Relg," Barak said, "does that satisfy your sense of propriety?"

Relg considered it. "Why yes," he said, "as a matter of fact, I think it does." Then he grinned the first grin Barak had ever seen on his harsh face. "When do we leave?" he asked.

His Imperial Majesty, Kal Zakath of Mallorea, stood at a window in a high tower in Maga Renn, looking out at the broad expanse of the great River Magan. A huge armada of river craft of all sizes dotted the surface of the river upstream of the city and moved down in orderly progression to the wharves where the imperial regiments waited to embark.

"Have you had any further news?" the Emperor asked.

"Things are a bit chaotic down there, your Imperial Majesty," Brador, the brown-robed Chief of the Bureau of Internal Affairs, reported, "but it appears that the major confrontation between Urvon and Zandramas is going to take place in

Peldane. Urvon has been moving down from the north, and Zandramas annexed Peldane last month to put a buffer between him and Darshiva. She's been rushing her forces into Peldane to meet him."

"What's your assessment, Atesca?" 'Zakath asked.

General Atesca rose and went to the map hanging on the wall. He studied it for a moment, then stabbed one blunt finger at it. "Here, your Majesty," he said, "the town of Ferra. We move down in force and occupy that place. It's a logical forward base of operations. The River Magan is about fifteen miles wide at that point, and it shouldn't be too difficult to interdict any further movement across it from Darshiva. That will eliminate Zandramas' reinforcements. Urvon will have numerical superiority when they meet, and he'll crush her army. He'll take casualties, though. Both sides are fanatics, and they'll fight to the death. After he wipes out Zandramas' army, he'll stop to lick his wounds. That's when we should hit him. He'll be weakened, and his troops will be exhausted. Ours will be fresh. The outcome ought to be fairly predictable. Then we can cross the Magan and mop up in Darshiva."

"Excellent, Atesca," 'Zakath said, a faint smile touching his cold lips. "There's a certain ironic charm to your plan. First we have Urvon eliminate Zandramas for us, then we eliminate him. I like the idea of having the Disciple of Torak do my dirty work for me."

"With your Majesty's permission, I'd like to lead the forward elements and oversee the occupation of Ferra," the general said. "Zandramas will almost have to counterattack, since we'll have cut her army in two. We'll need to fortify the town. I'll also need to put out patrols on the river to keep her from trying to slip her troops into Peldane around our flanks. It's a fairly crucial part of the operation, and I'd like to supervise it myself."

"By all means, Atesca," 'Zakath gave his consent. "I wouldn't really trust anyone else to do it anyway."

Atesca bowed. "Your Majesty is very kind," he said.

"If I may, your Imperial Majesty," Brador said, "we're getting some disturbing reports from Cthol Murgos. Our agents there report that there are some fairly serious negotiations going on between Urgit and the Alorns."

"The Murgos and the Alorns?" 'Zakath asked incredulously. "They've hated each other for eons."

"Perhaps they've found a common cause," Brador suggested delicately.

"Me, you mean?"

"It does seem logical, your Majesty."

"We have to put a stop to that. I think we'll have to attack the Alorns. Give them something close to home to worry about so they won't have time for any adventures in Cthol Murgos."

Atesca cleared his throat. "May I speak bluntly, your Majesty?" he asked.

"I've never heard you speak any other way, Atesca. What's on your mind?"

"Only an idiot tries to fight a war on two fronts, and only a madman tries to fight one on three. You have this war here in Peldane, another in Cthol Murgos, and now you're contemplating a third in Aloria. I advise against it in the strongest possible terms."

'Zakath smiled wryly. "You're a brave man, Atesca," he said. "I can't recall the last time somebody called me an idiot and a madman in the same breath."

"I trust your Majesty will forgive my candor, but that's my honest opinion of the matter."

"That's all right, Atesca." 'Zakath waved one hand as if brushing it aside. "You're here to advise me, not to flatter me, and your plain language definitely got my attention. Very well, we'll hold off on going to war with the Alorns until we finish up here. I'll go as far as idiocy; lunacy is something else. The world had enough of that with Taur Urgas." He began to pace up and down. "Curse you, Belgarion!" he burst out suddenly. "What *are* you up to?"

"Uh—your Majesty," Brador interposed diffidently, "Belgarion isn't in the West. He was seen just last week in Melcena."

"What's he doing in Melcena?"

"We weren't able to determine that, your Majesty. It's fairly certain that he left the islands, however. We think that he's somewhere in this general vicinity."

"Adding to the confusion, no doubt. Keep an eye out for him, Atesca. I really want to have a long talk with that young man. He stalks through the world like a natural disaster."

"I'll make a point of trying to locate him for your Majesty," Atesca replied. "Now, with your Majesty's permission, I'd like to go supervise the loading of the troops."

"How long is it going to take you to get to Ferra?"

"Perhaps three or four days, your Majesty. I'll put the troops to manning the oars."

"They won't like that."

"They don't have to like it, your Majesty."

"All right, go ahead. I'll be along a few days behind you."

Atesca saluted and turned to go.

"Oh, by the way, Atesca," 'Zakath said as an afterthought, "why don't you take a kitten on your way out?" He pointed at a number of prowling, half-grown cats on the far side of the room. His own mackerel-striped tabby was perched high on the mantelpiece with a slightly harried expression on her face.

"Ah . . ." Atesca hesitated. "I'm overwhelmed with gratitude, your Majesty, but cat fur makes my eyes swell shut, and I think I'll need my eyes during the next few weeks."

'Zakath sighed. "I understand, Atesca," he said. "That will be all."

The general bowed and left the room.

'Zakath considered it. "Well," he said, "if he won't take a kitten, I suppose we'll have to give him a field marshal's baton instead—but *only* if this campaign of his is successful, you understand."

"Perfectly, your Majesty," Brador murmured.

The coronation of the Archduke Otrath as Emperor of Mallorea went off quite smoothly. Otrath, of course, was an unmitigated ass and he had to be led by the hand through the ceremony. When it was over, Zandramas installed him on an ornate throne in the palace at Hemil and left instructions that he be flattered and fawned over. Then she quietly left.

Prince Geran was in the simple room Zandramas had chosen for herself in the temple. A middle-aged Grolim priestess had been watching over him. "He's been very good this morning, Holy Zandramas," the priestess advised.

"Good, bad—what difference does it make?" Zandramas shrugged. "You can go now."

"Yes, Holy Priestess." The middle-aged woman genuflected and left the room. Prince Geran looked at Zandramas with a grave expression on his little face.

"You're quiet this morning, your Highness," Zandramas said ironically.

The child's expression did not change. Though they had been together for over a year, Geran had never shown the slightest sign of affection for her and, perhaps even more disturbing, he had never shown fear either. He held up one of his toys. "Ball," he said.

"Yes," she replied, "I suppose so." Then, perhaps because his penetrating gaze disturbed her, she crossed the room to stand before her mirror. She pushed back her hood and gazed intently at her reflection. It had not touched her face yet. That was something at least. She looked with distaste at the whirling, sparkling lights beneath the skin of her hands. Then, quite deliberately, she opened the front of her robe and gazed at her nude reflection. It was spreading, there could be no question about that. Her breasts and belly were also underlaid with those selfsame whirling points of light.

Geran had come silently up to stand beside her. "Stars," he said, pointing at the mirror.

"Just go play, Geran," the Child of Dark told him, closing her robe.

CHAPTER THIRTEEN

As they rode west that afternoon, they could see a heavy, dark purple cloudbank building up ahead of them, rising higher and higher and blotting out the blue of the sky. Finally Durnik rode forward. "Toth says that we'd better find shelter," he told Belgarath. "These spring storms in this part of the world are savage."

Belgarath shrugged. "I've been rained on before."

"He says that the storm won't last long," Durnik said, "but it's going to be very intense. It should blow through by morning. I really think we should listen to him, Belgarath. It's not only the rain and wind. He says that there's usually hail as well, and the hailstones can be as big as apples."

Belgarath peered toward the blue-black clouds towering up into the western sky with lightning bolts staggering down from their centers. "All right," he decided. "We wouldn't be able to go much farther today anyway. Does he know of any shelter nearby?"

"There's a farm village a league or so ahead," Durnik told him. "If it's like the others we've passed, there won't be anybody there. We ought to be able to find a house with enough roof left to keep the hailstones off our heads."

"Let's aim for there then. That storm's moving fast. I'll call in Beldin and have him take a look." He lifted his face, and Garion could feel his thought reaching out.

They rode at a gallop into a mounting wind that whipped their cloaks about them and carried with it an unpleasant chill and vagrant spatters of cold rain.

When they crested the hill above the deserted village, they could see the storm front advancing like a wall across the open plain.

"It's going to be close," Belgarath shouted above the wind. "Let's make a run for it."

They plunged down the hill through wildly tossing grass and then across a broad belt of plowed ground that encircled the village. The place was walled, but the gate was off its hinges, and many houses showed signs of recent fires. They clattered along a rubble-littered street with the wind screaming at them. Garion heard a loud pop. Then another. Then several more in a growing staccato. "Here comes the hail!" he shouted.

Velvet suddenly cried out and clutched at her shoulder. Silk, almost without thinking, it seemed, pulled his horse in beside hers and flipped his cloak over her, tenting it protectively with his arm.

Beldin stood in the dooryard of a relatively intact house. "In here!" he called urgently. "The stable doors are open! Get the horses inside!"

They swung out of their saddles and quickly led their mounts into a cavernlike stable. Then they pushed the doors shut and dashed across the yard to the house.

"Did you check the village for people?" Belgarath asked the hunchbacked sorcerer as they entered.

"There's nobody here," Beldin told him, "unless there's another bureaucrat hiding in a cellar somewhere."

The banging sound outside grew louder until it became a steady roar. Garion looked out the door. Great chunks of ice were streaking out of the sky and smashing themselves to bits on the cobblestones. The chill grew more intense moment by moment. "I think we made it just in time," he said.

"Close the door, Garion," Polgara told him, "and let's get a fire going."

The room into which they had come showed signs of a hasty departure. The table and the chairs had been overturned, and there were broken dishes on the floor. Durnik looked around and picked up a stub of candle from the corner. He righted the table, set the candle on a piece of broken plate, and reached for his flint, steel, and tinder.

Toth went to the window and opened it. Then he reached out, pulled the shutters closed, and latched them.

Durnik's candle guttered a bit, then its flame grew steady, casting a golden glow through the room. The smith went to the fireplace. Despite the litter on the floor and the disarray of the furniture, the room was pleasant. The walls had been white-washed, and the overhead beams were dark and had been neatly adzed square. The fireplace was large and it had an arched opening. A number of pothooks jutted from its back wall, and a pile of firewood was neatly stacked beside it. It was a friendly kind of place.

"All right, gentlemen," Polgara said to them. "Let's not just stand there. The furniture needs to be put right, and the floor needs to be swept. We'll need more candles, and I'll want to check the sleeping quarters."

The fire Durnik had built was catching hold. He gave it a critical look; satisfied, he rose to his feet. "I'd better see to the horses," he said. "Do you want the packs in here, Pol?"

"Just the food and the cooking things for now, dear. But don't you think you should wait until the hail lets up?"

"There's a sort of covered walkway along the side of the house," he replied. "I'd guess that the people who built the place knew about this sort of weather." He went out with Toth and Eriond close behind him.

Garion crossed the room to where Velvet sat on a rude bench with her hand laid protectively over her right shoulder. Her face was pale, and her brow was dewed with sweat.

"Are you all right?" he asked her.

"It surprised me, that's all," she replied. "It's nice of you to ask, though."

"Nice my foot!" He was suddenly angry. "You're like a sister to me, Liselle, and if you let yourself get hurt, I'll take it as a personal insult."

"Yes, your Majesty," she said, her smile suddenly lighting up the room.

"Don't play with me, Velvet. Don't try to be brave. If you're hurt, say so."

"It's only a little bruise, Belgarion," she protested. Her large brown eyes conveyed a world of sincerity, mostly feigned.

"I'll spank you," he threatened.

"Now, that's an interesting notion." She laughed.

He didn't even think about it. He simply leaned forward and kissed her on the forehead.

She looked a little surprised. "Why, your Majesty," she said in mock alarm. "What if Ce'Nedra had seen you do that?"

"Ce'Nedra can cope with it. She loves you as much as I do. I'll have Aunt Pol look at that shoulder."

"It's really fine, Belgarion."

"Do you want to argue about that with Aunt Pol?"

She thought about it. "No," she said, "I don't really think so. Why don't you send Kheldar over to hold my hand?"

"Anything else?"

"You could kiss me again, if you'd like."

With a certain clinical detachment, Polgara opened the front of Velvet's gray dress and carefully examined the large purple bruise on the blond girl's shoulder. Velvet blushed and modestly covered her more salient features.

"I don't think anything's broken," Polgara said, gently probing the bruised shoulder. "It's going to be very painful, though."

"I noticed that almost immediately," Velvet said, wincing.

"All right, Sadi," Polgara said briskly, "I need a good analgesic. What would you suggest?"

"I have oret, Lady Polgara," the eunuch answered.

She thought about it. "No," she said. "Oret would incapacitate her for the next two days. Do you have any miseth?"

He looked a bit startled. "Lady Polgara," he protested. "Miseth is an excellent painkiller, but—" He looked at the suffering Velvet. "There are those side effects, you know."

"We can control her if necessary."

"What side effects?" Silk demanded, hovering protectively over the blond girl.

"It tends to rouse a certain—ah, shall we say—ardor," Sadi replied delicately. "In Nyissa it's widely used for that purpose."

"Oh," Silk said, flushing slightly.

"One drop," Polgara said. "No. Make that two."

"Two?" Sadi exclaimed.

"I want it to last until the pain subsides."

"Two drops will do that, all right," Sadi said, "but you'll have to confine her until it wears off."

"I'll keep her asleep if I need to."

Dubiously, Sadi opened his red case and removed a vial of deep purple liquid. "This is against my better judgment, Lady Polgara," he said.

"Trust me."

"It always makes me nervous when somebody says that," Belgarath said to Beldin.

"A lot of things make you nervous. We can't go anywhere until the girl's better. Pol knows what she's doing."

"Maybe," Belgarath replied.

Sadi carefully measured two drops of the purple medication into a cup of water and stirred the mixture with his finger. Then he rather carefully dried his hand on a piece of cloth. He handed the cup to Velvet. "Drink it slowly," he instructed. "You'll begin to feel very strange almost immediately."

"Strange?" she asked suspiciously.

"We can talk about it later. All you need to know now is that it's going to make the pain go away."

Velvet sipped at the cup. "It doesn't taste bad," she observed.

"Of course not," the eunuch replied, "and you'll find that it tastes better and better as you get toward the bottom of the cup."

Velvet continued to take small sips of the liquid. Her face grew flushed. "My," she said, "isn't it warm in here all of a sudden?"

Silk sat down on the bench beside her. "Is it helping at all?" he asked.

"Hmm?"

"How's the shoulder?"

"Did you see my bruise, Kheldar?" She pulled her dress open to show it to him. She showed him—and everyone else in the room—other things as well. "Oops," she said absently, not bothering to cover herself.

"I think you'd better take those steps you mentioned, Lady Polgara," Sadi said. "The situation is likely to get out of hand any minute now."

Polgara nodded and put one hand briefly on Velvet's brow. Garion felt a light surge.

"Suddenly I feel so very drowsy," Velvet said. "Is the medicine doing that?"

"In a manner of speaking," Polgara replied.

Velvet's head drooped forward, and she laid it on Silk's shoulder.

"Bring her along, Silk," Polgara told the little man. "Let's find a bed for her."

Silk picked the sleeping girl up and carried her from the room with Polgara close beside him.

"Does that stuff always have that effect?" Ce'Nedra asked Sadi.

"Miseth? Oh yes. It could arouse a stick."

"And does it work on men, too?"

"Gender makes no difference, your Majesty."

"How very interesting." She gave Garion a sly, sidelong glance. "Don't lose that little bottle, Sadi," she said.

"Never mind," Garion told her.

It took them perhaps a quarter of an hour to tidy up the room. Polgara was smiling when she and Silk returned. "She'll sleep now," she said. "I looked into the other rooms, too. The woman of the house appears to have been a very neat sort of person," she said. "This is the only room that was seriously disturbed when the family left." She set her candle down and smoothed the front of her gray dress with a satisfied expression. "The house will do very nicely, uncle," she told Beldin.

"I'm glad you approve," he replied. He was sprawled on a high-backed bench by the window and was carefully retying the thong that held his ragged left sleeve in place.

"How far are we from the river?" Belgarath asked him.

"It's still a ways—a good day's hard riding at least. I can't be much more exact than that. When the wind came up, it almost blew off my feathers."

"Is the country on up ahead still empty?"

"It's hard to be sure. I was up fairly high, and if there are any people out there, they'd all have taken cover from this storm."

"We'll have to have a look in the morning." Belgarath leaned back in his chair and stretched his feet out toward the hearth. "That fire was a good idea," he said. "There's a definite chill in the air."

"That happens sometimes when you pile three or four inches of ice on the ground," Beldin told him. The ugly little man squinted thoughtfully. "If this sort of storm is a regular afternoon occurrence around here, we'll need to cross the Magan during the morning hours," he noted. "Getting caught in a hailstorm in an open boat isn't my idea of fun."

"Now you stop that!" Sadi said sharply to Zith's earthenware bottle.

"What's the trouble?" Ce'Nedra asked.

"She was making a funny little noise," Sadi replied. "I wanted to see if she was all right, and she hissed at me."

"She does that every now and then, doesn't she?"

"This was a bit different. She was actually warning me to stay away from her."

"Could she be ill?"

"I wouldn't think so. She's a fairly young snake, and I've been very careful about what I feed her."

"Perhaps she needs a tonic." Ce'Nedra looked questioningly at Polgara.

Polgara laughed helplessly. "I'm sorry, Ce'Nedra," she said, "but I have no experience with the illnesses of reptiles."

"Do you suppose we could talk about something else?" Silk asked plaintively. "Zith is a nice enough little animal, I suppose, but she's still a snake."

Ce'Nedra whirled on him, her eyes suddenly flashing. "How can you say that?" she snapped angrily. "She's saved all our lives twice—once in Rak Urga when she nipped that Grolim, Sorchak, and again at Ashaba when she bit Harakan. Without her, we wouldn't be here. You might show at least a little bit of gratitude."

"Well . . ." he said a little uncertainly. "You could be right, I suppose, but hang it all, Ce'Nedra, I can't abide snakes."

"I don't even think of her as a snake."

"Ce'Nedra," he said patiently, "she's long and skinny, she wriggles, she doesn't have any arms or legs, and she's poisonous. By definition, she's a snake."

"You're prejudiced," she accused.

"Well—yes, I suppose you could say that."

"I'm bitterly disappointed in you, Prince Kheldar. She's a sweet, loving, brave little creature, and you're insulting her."

He looked at her for a moment, then rose to his feet and bowed floridly to the earthenware bottle. "I'm dreadfully sorry, dear Zith," he apologized. "I can't think what came over me. Can you possibly find it in your cold little green heart to forgive me?"

Zith hissed at him, a hiss ending in a curious grunt.

"She says to leave her alone," Sadi told him.

"Can you really understand what she's saying?"

"In a general sort of way, yes. Snakes have a very limited vocabulary, so it's not all that difficult to pick up a few phrases here and there." The eunuch frowned. "She's been swearing a great deal lately, though, and that's not like her. She's usually a very ladylike little snake."

"I can't believe I'm actually involved in this conversation," Silk said, shaking his head and going off down the hall toward the back of the house.

Durnik returned with Toth and Eriond. They were carrying the packs containing Polgara's utensils and the food. Polgara looked critically at the fireplace and its facilities. "We've been eating some rather sketchy meals lately," she noted. "We have a fairly adequate kitchen here, so why don't we take advantage of it?" She opened the food pack and rummaged through it. "I wish I had something besides travel rations to work with," she said half to herself.

"There's a hen roost out back, Pol," Beldin told her helpfully.

She smiled at him. "Durnik, dear," she said in an almost dreamy tone of voice.

"I'll see to it at once, Pol. Three, maybe?"

"Make it four. Then we'll be able to carry some cold chicken with us when we leave. Ce'Nedra, go with him and gather up all the eggs you can find."

Ce'Nedra stared at her in astonishment. "I've never gathered eggs before, Lady Polgara," she protested.

"It's not hard, dear. Just be careful not to break them, that's all."

"But—"

"I thought I'd make a cheese omelette for breakfast."

Ce'Nedra's eyes brightened. "I'll get a basket," she said quickly.

"Splendid idea, dear. Uncle, are there any other interesting things about this place?"

"There's a brewhouse at the back of the building." He shrugged. "I didn't have time to look into it."

Belgarath rose to his feet. "Why don't we do that right now?" he suggested.

"People in farm villages don't make very good beer, Belgarath."

"Maybe this one's an exception. We'll never know until we try it, will we?"

"You've got a point there."

The two old sorcerers went off toward the back of the house while Eriond piled more wood on the fire.

Ce'Nedra returned, frowning and a little angry. "They won't give me their eggs, Lady Polgara," she complained. "They're sitting on them."

"You have to reach under them and take the eggs, dear."

"Won't that make them angry?"

"Are you afraid of a chicken?"

The little queen's eyes hardened, and she left the room purposefully.

A root cellar behind the house yielded a store of vegetables, and Belgarath and Beldin brought a cask of beer in from the brewhouse. While the chickens were roasting, Polgara rummaged through the canisters and bins in the kitchen. She found flour and a number of other staples, and she rolled up her sleeves in a businesslike way, mixed up a large batch of dough, and began to knead it on a well-scrubbed cutting board near the fire. "We can have some biscuits tonight, I think," she said, "and I'll bake some fresh bread in the morning."

The supper was the best Garion had eaten in months. There had been banquets and adequate meals in inns and the like, but there was a certain indefinable quality to his Aunt Pol's cooking that no other cook in the world could hope to match. After he had eaten more perhaps than was really good for him, he pushed his plate away with a sigh and leaned back in his chair.

"I'm glad you decided to leave some for the rest of us," Ce'Nedra said in a slightly snippy tone.

"Are you cross with me for some reason?" he asked her.

"No, I suppose not, Garion. I'm just a little irritated, that's all."

"Why?"

"A chicken bit me." She pointed at the remains of a roasted hen lying on a large platter. "That one," she added. She reached out, wrenched a drumstick off the chicken and bit into it rather savagely with her small white teeth. "There," she said in a vengeful tone. "How do you like it?"

Garion knew his wife, so he knew better than to laugh.

After supper, they all lingered at the table in a kind of happy contentment as the storm outside abated.

Then there was a light, almost diffident rap on the door. Garion sprang to his feet, reaching over his shoulder for his sword.

"I don't mean to disturb you," a querulous old voice came from the other side of the door. "I just wanted to be sure you have everything you need."

Belgarath rose from his chair, went to the door, and opened it.

"Holy Belgarath," the man outside said with a bow of the profoundest respect. He was very old, with snowy white hair and a thin, lined face.

He was also a Grolim.

Belgarath stared at him warily. "You know me?" he asked.

"Of course. I know you all. I've been waiting for you. May I come in?"

Wordlessly, Belgarath stepped aside for him, and the aged Grolim tottered into the room, aided by a twisted cane. He bowed to Polgara. "Lady Polgara," he murmured. Then he turned to Garion. "Your Majesty," he said, "may I beg your forgiveness?"

"Why?" Garion replied. "You've never done anything to me."

"Yes I have, your Majesty. When I heard about what had happened in the City of Endless Night, I hated you. Can you forgive that?"

"There's nothing to forgive. It was only natural for you to feel that way. You've had a change of heart, I take it?"

"It was changed for me, King Belgarion. The New God of Angarak will be a kindlier, gentler God than was Torak. I live now only to serve that God and I abide against the day of his coming."

"Sit down, my friend," Belgarath told him. "I assume you've had a religious experience of some kind?"

The old Grolim sank into a chair with a beatific smile on his lined face. "My heart has been touched, Holy Belgarath," he said simply. "I had devoted all of my life to the service of Torak in the temple in this village. I grieved more than you can know when I learned of His death, for I served Him without question. Now I have removed His likeness from the Temple wall and I decorate the altar with flowers instead of the blood of sacrificial victims. Bitterly I repent the times when I myself held the knife during the rite of sacrifice."

"And what was it that so changed you?" Polgara asked him.

"It was a voice that spoke to me in the silences of my soul, Lady Polgara, a voice that filled me with such joy that it seemed that all the world was bathed in light."

"And what did the voice say to you?"

The old priest reached inside his black robe and withdrew a parchment sheet. "I took great care to inscribe the words exactly as the voice spoke them to me," he said, "for such was the instruction I received. A man may misconstrue what he is told, or change it if it is not to his liking or if he fails to understand." He smiled gently. "What I have written is for the benefit of others, though, for the words are engraved upon my heart far more indelibly than upon this sheet." He lifted the parchment and read from it in a quavering voice. " 'Behold:' " he read, " 'In the days which shall follow the meeting of the Child of Light and the Child of Dark in the City of Endless Night shall a great despair fall over the Priests of the Dark God, for He shall have been laid low and shall come no more among His people. But lift up thine heart, for thy despair is but the night which shall be banished by the rising of a new sun. For verily I say to thee, Angarak shall have a new birth with the coming of her true God—He who was purposed to lead her since the Beginning of Days. For lo, the Dark God was born out of nothingness in the instant of the EVENT which divided all creation, and it was not He who was foreordained to guide and protect Angarak. In the last meeting of the Child of Dark and the Child of Light shall the *true* God of Angarak be revealed, and ye shall render up unto Him your hearts and your devotion.

" 'And the course which Angarak shall follow shall be determined by the CHOICE, and once the CHOICE is made, it may not be unmade and shall prevail eternally for good or for ill. For harken, *two* shall stand in the Place Which Is No More, but only one shall be chosen. And the Child of Light and the Child of Dark shall surrender up the burden of the spirits which guide them to the two who shall stand in expectation of the CHOICE. And should the CHOICE fall to the one hand, the world shall be drowned in darkness, but should it fall to the other hand, shall all be bathed in light, and that which was ordained since before the beginning of time shall come to pass.

" 'Abide in hope, therefore, and treat thy fellow creatures kindly and with love, for this is pleasing to the true God, and should He prevail and be chosen, He shall bless thee and shall lay but a gentle yoke upon thee.' " The old Grolim lowered the sheet and bowed his head prayerfully. "Thus spoke the voice which filled my heart with joy and banished my despair," he said simply.

"We're grateful that you shared this with us," Belgarath told him. "Might we offer you something to eat?"

The Grolim shook his head. "I do not eat meat any more," he said. "I would not offend my God. I have cast away my dagger and will shed no more blood for all the days of my life." He rose to his feet. "I will leave you now," he said. "I came but to reveal to you the words the voice spoke to me, and to assure you that one at least in all of Angarak shall pray for your success."

"We thank you," Belgarath said sincerely. He went to the door and held it open for the gentle old man.

"That was fairly specific, wasn't it?" Beldin said after the Grolim had left. "It's the first time I heard a prophecy that got straight to the point."

"You mean to say that he's really a prophet?" Silk asked.

"Of course he is. It's an almost classic case. He had all the symptoms—the ecstasy, the radical change of personality, all of it."

"There's something wrong here, though," Belgarath said, frowning. "I've spent eons reading prophecies, and what he said didn't have the same tone as any that I've ever come across—either ours or the others." He looked at Garion. "Can you get in touch with your friend?" he asked. "I need to talk with him."

"I can try," Garion replied. "He doesn't always come when I call, though."

"See if you can reach him. Tell him that it's important."

"I'll see what I can do, Grandfather." Garion sat down and closed his eyes. *"Are you in there?"* he asked.

"Please don't shout, Garion," the voice responded in a pained tone. *"It hurts my ears."*

"Sorry," Garion apologized. *"I didn't realize I was talking so loud. Grandfather wants to talk with you."*

"All right. Open your eyes, Garion. I can't see when they're closed."

As had happened occasionally in the past, Garion felt himself shunted off into some quiet corner of his mind, and the dry voice took over. *"All right, Belgarath,"* it said through Garion's lips. *"What is it this time?"*

"I've got a couple of questions," the old man replied.

"There's nothing new about that. You've always got questions."

"Did you hear what the Grolim said?"

"Naturally."

"Was it you? I mean, were you the voice that came to him?"

"No, as a matter of fact, I wasn't."

"Then it was the other spirit?"

"No. It wasn't him either."

"Then who was it?"

"Sometimes I can't believe that Aldur chose you as his first disciple. Are your brains packed in wool?"

"You don't have to be insulting." Belgarath sounded a bit injured, but Beldin laughed an ugly, cackling kind of laugh.

"All right," the voice sighed, *"I'll go through it carefully. Try not to miss too much. My counterpart and I came into existence when Destiny was divided. Have you got that part?"*

"I knew that already."

"And you even managed to remember it? Amazing."

"Thanks," Belgarath said in a flat tone.

"I'm working with Garion's vocabulary. He's a peasant, so he can be a little blunt sometimes. Now, doesn't it seem logical that when Destiny is reunited, there should be a new voice? My counterpart and I will have served our purpose, so there won't be any further need for us. Millions of years of enmity between us have warped our perceptions a bit."

Belgarath looked startled at that.

"Think, old man," the voice told him. *"I'm not suited to deal with a united universe. I've got too many old grudges. The new voice can start out fresh without any preconceptions. It's better that way, believe me."*

"I think I'm going to miss you."

"Don't get sentimental on me, Belgarath. I don't think I could bear that."

"Wait a minute. This new voice will come into existence after the meeting, right?"

"At the instant of the meeting, actually."

"Then how did it speak to the old Grolim, if it's not in existence yet?"

"Time doesn't really mean that much to us, Belgarath. We can move backward and forward in it without any particular difficulty."

"You mean the voice was speaking to him from the future?"

"Obviously." Garion felt a faint, ironic smile cross his lips. *"How do you know I'm not speaking to you from the past?"*

Belgarath blinked.

"Now we've got you," Beldin said triumphantly. *"We're going to win, aren't we?"*

"We can hope so, but there's no guarantee."

"The voice that spoke to the Grolim represents a kindlier God, doesn't it?"

"Yes."

"If the Child of Dark wins, the New God isn't going to be very kindly, is he?"

"No."

"Then the simple fact that the voice came to him from out of the future—after the choice—indicates that the Child of Light is going to win, doesn't it?"

The voice sighed. *"Why do you always have to complicate things, Beldin? The voice that spoke to the Grolim is the* possibility *of the new spirit. It's simply reaching back in time to make certain preparations so that things will be ready in the eventuality that it comes out on top. The Choice still hasn't been made yet, you know."*

"Even the possibility *of existence has that kind of power?"*

"Possibility has enormous power, Beldin—sometimes even more than actuality."

"And the possibility of the other spirit could be making its own preparations as well, couldn't it?"

"I wouldn't be at all surprised. You have an enormous grasp of the obvious."

"Then we're right back where we started from. We're still going to have two spirits wrestling across time and the universe for dominance."

"No. The Choice will eliminate one of the possibilities once and for all."

"I don't understand," Beldin confessed.

"I didn't think you would."

"What preparations was this new voice making?" Polgara asked suddenly.

"The Grolim who came to you here will be the prophet and the first Disciple of the New God—assuming that the Child of Light is chosen, of course."

"A Grolim?"

"The decision wasn't mine to make. The new God will be a God of Angarak, though, so it does make sense, I suppose."

"That might take a bit of getting adjusted to."

"You have as many prejudices as I do, Polgara," the voice laughed, *"but I think in the long run, you're more adaptable—and certainly more so than these two stubborn old men are. You'll come to accept it in time. Now, if there aren't any more questions, I still have some things to attend to—in another part of time."*

And then the voice was gone.

CHAPTER FOURTEEN

The sun was just going down, staining the purple cloudbank to the west with a jaundiced yellow as it broke through an opening in the approaching storm. Garion crested a long hill and looked down into the next valley. There was a complex of buildings there, a complex so familiar that he dropped onto his haunches and stared at it in amazement for a moment. Then he rose on all fours again and moved cautiously through the tall grass toward the farmstead. He saw no smoke, and the large gate was open, but he didn't see any point in taking chances. Farmers have an automatic aversion to wolves, and Garion did not particularly want to dodge arrows shot at him from concealment.

He stopped at the edge of the cleared area surrounding the farm, dropped to his belly in the grass, and looked at the farm for quite some time. It seemed to be deserted. He ran forward and slunk cautiously through the open gate. The compound was quite nearly as large as Faldor's farm, half a world away.

He slipped through an open shed door and stood inside with one forepaw slightly raised as his nose and ears intently sought for any evidence that he was not alone. The farmstead was silent, save for the complaining moan of an udder-heavy cow lowing to be milked in the barn across the central yard. The smells of people were here, of course, but they were all many days old.

Garion slipped out of the shed and trotted cautiously from door to door, opening each in turn by twisting the handle with his jaws. The place in many respects was so strikingly familiar that it brought him a sharp pang of a homesickness he thought he had long since put behind him. The storage rooms were all almost the same as at Faldor's. The smithy was so like Durnik's that Garion could almost hear the steely ring of his friend's hammer on the anvil. He was quite certain that he could close his eyes and pad unerringly across the yard to the kitchen.

Methodically, he entered each room around the lower floor of the farmstead, then scrambled up the stairs leading to the gallery with his toenails scratching at the wooden steps.

All was deserted.

He returned to the yard and poked an inquiring nose into the barn. The cow bawled in panic, and Garion backed out through the door to avoid causing her further distress.

"Aunt Pol," he sent his thought out.

"Yes, dear?"

"There's nobody here, and it's a perfect place."

"Perfect is an extravagant word, Garion."

"Wait until you see it."

A few moments later, Belgarath trotted through the gateway, sniffed, looked around, and blurred into his own form. "It's like coming home, isn't it?" He grinned.

"I thought so myself," Garion replied.

Beldin came spiraling in. "It's about a league to the river," he said even as he changed. "If we move right along, we can make it by dark."

"Let's stay here instead," Belgarath said. "The riverbanks might be patrolled, and there's no point in creeping around in the dark if we don't have to."

The hunchback shrugged. "It's up to you."

Then Polgara, as pale and silent as a ghost, drifted over the wall, settled on the tailgate of a two-wheeled cart in the center of the yard, and resumed her own form. "Oh, my," she murmured, stepping down and looking around. "You were right, Garion. It *is* perfect." She folded her cloak across her arm and crossed the yard to the kitchen door.

About five minutes later, Durnik led the others into the yard. He also looked around, then suddenly laughed. "You'd almost expect Faldor himself to come out that door," he said. "How's it possible for two places so far apart to look so much alike?"

"It's the most practical design for a farm, Durnik," Belgarath told him, "and sooner or later, practical people the world over are going to arrive at it. Can you do something about that cow? We won't get much sleep if she bawls all night long."

"I'll milk her right away." The smith slid down from his saddle and led his horse toward the barn.

Belgarath looked after him with an affectionate expression. "We may have to drag him away from here in the morning," he noted.

"Where's Polgara?" Silk asked, looking around as he helped Velvet down from her horse.

"Where else?" Belgarath pointed toward the kitchen. "Getting her out of there may be even harder than dragging Durnik out of the smithy."

Velvet looked around with a slightly dreamy expression on her face. The drug Sadi had given her the previous night had not yet entirely worn off, and Garion surmised that Polgara was keeping her under rigid control. "Very nice," she said, leaning involuntarily toward Silk. "Sort of homey."

Silk's expression was wary, like that of a man about ready to bolt.

They ate well again that evening, sitting around a long table in the beamed kitchen with the golden light of wax candles filling the room and winking back from the polished copper bottoms of kettles hung on the wall. The room was snug and warm, even though the storm which had been building up all afternoon raged outside, filling the night with thunder and wind and driving rain.

Garion felt oddly at peace, a peace he had not known for more than a year now, and he accepted this time of renewal gratefully, knowing that it would strengthen him in the climactic months ahead.

"Oh, my goodness!" Sadi exclaimed. After he had finished eating, the eunuch had taken his red case to the far end of the kitchen and had been trying to coax Zith from her little home with a saucer of fresh, warm milk.

"What is it, Sadi?" Velvet said, seeming to shake off the effects of the drug and Polgara's insistence that she remain calm.

"Zith had a little surprise for us," Sadi replied in a delighted tone. "Several little surprises, in fact."

Velvet went curiously to his side. "Oh," she said with a little catch in her voice, "aren't they adorable?"

"What is it?" Polgara asked.

"Our dear little Zith is a mother," Velvet said.

The rest of them rose and went to the other end of the room to look at the new arrivals. Like their mother, they were all bright green with the characteristic red stripe running from nose to tail. There were five of them, and they were no larger than angleworms. They all had their chins on the edge of the saucer and they were lapping up warm milk with their forked little tongues, purring all the while. Zith hovered over them protectively, somehow managing to look demure.

"That would explain why she's been so bad-tempered lately," Sadi said. "Why didn't you tell me, Zith? I could have helped you with the delivery."

"I'm not sure I'd want to be a midwife to a snake," Silk said. "Besides, I thought reptiles laid eggs."

"Most of them do," Sadi admitted. "Some kinds are live-bearers, though. Zith happens to be one of those kinds."

"And here I thought she was just getting fat," Velvet said, "and all the time she was pregnant."

Durnik was frowning. "Something doesn't quite fit here," he said. "Isn't Nyissa the only place where her species is found?"

"Yes," Sadi said, "and they're very rare even in Nyissa."

"Then how . . ." Durnik flushed slightly. "What I'm getting at is, how did this happen? We've been away from Nyissa for a long time. Where did she meet the father?"

Sadi blinked. "That's true, isn't it? This is impossible. Zith, what have you been up to?"

The little green snake ignored him.

"It's really not such a mystery, Sadi," Eriond told him, smiling slightly. "Don't you remember what Cyradis said to Zith at Ashaba?"

"Something about something being delayed. I didn't really pay that much attention. We were in the middle of something fairly distracting at the moment, if I remember right."

"She said, 'Be tranquil, little sister, for the purpose of all thy days is now accomplished, and that which was delayed may now come to pass.' This is what she was talking about. This is what was delayed."

"You know," Beldin said to Belgarath, "I think he's right. This isn't the first time the prophecy's tampered with things in order to get the job done. That business about the 'purpose of all her days' simply means that Zith was born for one thing—to bite Harakan. Once she'd done that, things went back to normal again." Then the hunchback looked at Eriond. "How is it that you remembered exactly what she said? We were all fairly excited there in Urvon's throne room."

"I always try to remember what people say," Eriond replied. "It may not always make sense at the time they say it, but sooner or later it always seems to fit together."

"This is a strange boy, Belgarath," Beldin said.

"We've noticed that on occasion."

"Is it really possible?" Sadi asked the old sorcerer. "That sort of intervention, I mean?"

"That's the wrong question to ask my grandfather." Garion laughed. "He doesn't believe that anything's impossible."

Silk was standing a safe distance away from Zith and her new brood. His eyebrow was raised slightly. "Congratulations, Zith," he said finally to the little green mother. Then he looked sternly at the others. "This is all very nice, I suppose," he added, "but if anybody calls them little nippers, I'll just scream."

They had bathed and gone to bed, but Ce'Nedra was restless, and she tossed and turned. Suddenly she sat up. "I wonder if that milk's still warm," she murmured. She tossed back the blanket and padded on little bare feet to the door. "Do you want some, too?" she asked Garion.

"No, thanks all the same, dear."

"It would help you sleep."

"I'm not the one who's having trouble sleeping."

She stuck her tongue out at him and went out into the hallway.

When she returned a few moments later with her glass of milk, she was stifling a naughty little giggle.

"What's so funny?" he asked her.

"I saw Silk."

"So?"

"He didn't see me, but I saw him. He was going into a bedroom."

"He can go in and out of his bedroom if he wants to."

She giggled again and hopped into bed. "That's the point, Garion," she said. "It wasn't *his* bedroom."

"Oh." Garion coughed in embarrassment. "Drink your milk."

"I listened at the door for a moment," she said. "Don't you want to hear what they were saying?"

"Not particularly, no."

She told him anyway.

The rain had passed on through, although there were still rumbles of thunder far to the west, and jagged sheets of lightning raked the western horizon. Garion awoke suddenly and sat upright in bed. There was a different kind of rumble outside, and it was occasionally accompanied by a shrill bellowing noise. He slipped softly out of bed and went out onto the balcony that encircled the farmyard. A long line of torches was slowly moving out there in the darkness, perhaps a half mile to the west. Garion peered out through the tag end of the storm, then began to form up the image of the wolf in his mind. This was definitely something that needed to be investigated.

The torches moved at a peculiarly slow pace; as Garion loped closer to them, he noticed that they seemed much higher than they would have been if the torch-bearers were mounted on horses. The slow rumbling sound and the peculiar bellowing continued. Then he stopped beside a bramble thicket and sat down on his haunches to watch and listen. A long line of huge gray beasts was plodding through the night in a northeasterly direction. Garion had seen the image, at least, of an elephant on the Isle of Verkat in Cthol Murgos when his Aunt Pol had routed the mad hermit in the forest. An image of an elephant is one thing, however, but the reality is quite something else. They were enormous, far larger than any animal Garion had ever seen, and there was a kind of ponderous implacability about their steady pace. Their foreheads and flanks were covered with skirts of chain mail, and Garion shuddered inwardly at the thought of such vast weight, though the elephants moved as if the mail were as insubstantial as cobwebs. Their sail-like ears swayed as they walked, and their pendulous trunks drooped down before them. Occasionally, one of them would curl his trunk up, touching it to his forehead, and give vent to a shattering trumpet sound.

Men in crude body armor were mounted on the huge, plodding beasts. One, bearing a torch, sat cross-legged atop each huge neck. Those riding behind were armed with javelins, slings, and short-limbed bows. At the head of the column, riding astride the neck of a beast fully a yard taller than the ones in his wake, was a man wearing the black robe of a Grolim.

Garion rose and slunk closer, his careful paws making no sound in the rain-wet grass. Although he was certain that the elephants could easily catch his scent, he reasoned that beasts so large would pay little attention to a predator who posed no real threat to them. In the presence of such immensity, he felt small, even flealike. He did not particularly like the feeling. His own bulk approached two hundred pounds, but an elephant's weight was measured in tons, not in pounds.

He ranged on silent paws along the column, maintaining a distance of perhaps fifty yards and keeping his nose and eyes alert. His attention was concentrated on the black-robed Grolim astride the neck of the lead animal.

The elephants moved on, and Garion trotted alongside the column, maintaining his distance.

Then there appeared in the track ahead of the lead elephant a figure robed in shiny black satin that gleamed in the torchlight. The column halted, and Garion slunk closer.

The satin-robed figure pushed back her hood with a hand that seemed filled with swirling light. At Ashaba and again in Zamad, Garion had briefly seen the face of his son's abductor, but the confrontations with the Darshivan sorceress had been so charged with danger and dread that he had not really had time to let the features of the Child of Dark register on his memory. Now, slinking still closer, he looked upon her torchlit face.

Her features were regular, even beautiful. Her hair was a lustrous black, and her skin was very nearly as pale as that of Garion's cousin Adara. The similarity ended there, however. Zandramas was a Grolim, and her dark eyes had that peculiar angularity common to all Angaraks, her nose was slightly aquiline, and her forehead was broad and unlined. Her chin was pointed, which made her face seem oddly triangular.

"I have been awaiting thee, Naradas," she said in her harshly accented voice. "Where hast thou been?"

"Forgive me, mistress," the Grolim astride the neck of the massive lead bull apologized. "The herdsmen were farther south than we had been told." He pushed back his hood. His face was cruel, and his white eyes gleamed in the flickering torchlight. "How fares the struggle with the Disciple's minions?"

"Not well, Naradas," she replied. "His Guardsmen and his Chandim and the rabble out of Karanda outnumber our forces."

"I have a regiment of elephant cavalry behind me, mistress," Naradas informed her. "They will turn the tide of battle. The grass of central Peldane will be well watered with the blood of Urvon's Guardsmen, Chandim, and Karands. We will roll them back and make Darshiva secure once and for all."

"I care nothing for Darshiva, Naradas. I seek the world, and the fate of one small principality on the eastern edge of Mallorea is a matter of sublime indifference to me. Let it stand or let it fall. I care not. It hath served its purpose, and now I am weary of it. How long will it take you to deliver your beasts to the field of battle?"

"Two days at most, mistress."

"Do so then. Put them under the command of my generals and then follow me to Kell. I will return to Hemil and gather up Otrath and Belgarion's brat. We will await thee in the shadow of the holy mountain of the seers."

"Is it true that Urvon brought the Demon Lord Nahaz and his hordes with him, mistress?"

"He did, but that no longer concerns us. Demons are not so difficult to raise, and Nahaz is not the only Demon Lord in Hell. Lord Mordja consented to aid us with *his* hordes. There hath long been enmity between Mordja and Nahaz. They do war upon each other now with no concern for ordinary forces."

"Mistress!" Naradas exclaimed. "Surely you would not consort with such creatures!"

"I would consort with the King of Hell himself in order to triumph in the Place Which Is No More. Mordja hath feigned flight and hath lured Nahaz away from the battlefield. Take thy beasts there so that they may destroy Urvon's hosts. Nahaz and his minions shall not be there to delay thee. Then come with all possible speed to Kell."

"I shall, mistress," Naradas promised submissively.

A slow rage had been building up in Garion. His son's abductor was no more than seconds away from him, and he knew that there was no way she could gather in her will before his fangs were into her flesh, and then it would be too late. He curled his lips back from his dreadful teeth and slunk closer, one step at a time, his hackles erect and his belly low to the ground. He thirsted for blood, and his hatred burned like a fire in his brain. Quivering in awful anticipation, he bunched his muscles, and a low, rumbling growl filled his throat.

It was that sound that ultimately brought him to his senses. The thought that had seared his brain was the thought of a wolf, and it considered nothing beyond the immediate moment. If Zandramas indeed stood no more than a few bounds away, he could rend her flesh and scatter her blood in the tall grass beside the track upon which she stood before the echo of her shrieks had returned from nearby hillsides. But if the figure standing before white-eyed Naradas was but an insubstantial projection, he would clash his curved fangs on nothingness, and the Sorceress of Darshiva would escape his vengeance once again, even as she had at Ashaba.

It was perhaps the thought burning in his brain that alerted her; or perhaps, as Polgara had done so often, she had merely sampled the surrounding region with her mind and had located the others. Whatever it was, the sorceress suddenly hissed in alarm. "Danger!" she snapped to her white-eyed underling. Then she smiled a cruel, mirthless smile. "But I have a form immune to Alorn sorcery." She tensed herself, then blurred, and then the immense shape of the dragon appeared before the suddenly terrified elephants. She spread the vast sails of her wings and launched herself into the damp night air, filling the darkness with her shrieking bellow and her sooty red fire.

"Aunt Pol!" Garion's thought flew out. "The dragon's coming!"

"What?" her answering thought came back.

"Zandramas has changed form! She's flying toward you!"

"Come back here!" she commanded crisply. "Now!"

He spun, his claws digging into the damp turf, and ran toward the farmstead as fast as he could. Behind him he could hear the shrill, panicky trumpeting of the elephants, and overhead the shrieking bellow of the vast dragon. He ran on desperately, knowing that Zandramas was immune to whatever countermeasures Polgara and the others might try, and that only the flaming sword of Iron-grip could drive her away.

It was not far, though the seconds seemed like hours as he bunched and stretched in the running gait of the wolf. Ahead of him he could see the dragon's fiery breath illuminating the storm clouds roiling overhead, a fire eerily accompanied by pale blue lightning that danced in jerky streaks down from the clouds. Then she folded her huge wings and plummeted down toward the farmstead with billows of fire preceding her.

Between bounds, Garion changed and ran on toward the gate with the sword of Iron-grip flaming in the air above his head.

At the last instant, the dragon extended her vast pinions and settled into the farmyard, still belching fire and smoke. She swung her snakelike neck around, sending incandescent billows of flame into the wooden structures surrounding the yard. The seasoned wood began to char and smoke, and here and there small blue flames began to flicker their way up the sides of the door frames.

Garion rushed into the yard, his burning sword aloft. Grimly, he began to flail at the dragon with it. "You may be immune to sorcery, Zandramas," he shouted at her, "but you're *not* immune to this!"

She shrieked, engulfing him in a sheet of flame, but he ignored it and continued to lash her with the blue flame of the Orb and the sword. Finally, unable to bear his relentless strokes any longer, she hurled herself into the air, flapping her great wings frantically. She clawed at the air and finally managed to clear the second-story roof of the farmstead. Then she settled to earth again and continued to bathe the structure in flame.

Garion dashed out through the gateway, fully intending to confront her again. But then he stopped. The dragon was not alone. Glowing with her peculiar nimbus, the blue wolf faced the altered form of the Sorceress of Darshiva. Then, even as Polgara had once expanded into immensity in Sthiss Tor to face the God Issa and as Garion himself had done in the City of Endless Night when he had come at last to his fated meeting with Torak, the blue wolf swelled into vastness.

The meeting of the two was the sort of thing nightmares are made of. The dragon fought with flame, and the wolf with her terrible fangs. Since the wolf was insubstantial—except for her teeth—the dragon's flame had no effect; and though the teeth of the wolf were very sharp, they could not penetrate the dragon's scaly hide. Back and forth they raged in titanic but inconclusive struggle. Then Garion thought he detected something. The light was not good. The sky overhead was still obscured by the last tattered clouds of the evening's storm, and the sullen flickers of lightning seemed to obscure more than they revealed, but it appeared that each time the wolf lunged, the dragon flinched visibly. Then it came to him. Though the wolf's teeth could not injure the dragon, her blue nimbus could. It seemed in some way to be akin to the glow of the Orb and the fire of Iron-grip's sword. Somehow the blue glow surrounding Poledra, when she assumed the shape of the wolf, partook of the power of the Orb, and Garion had discovered that even in the form of the invincible dragon, Zandramas feared the Orb and anything connected with it. Her flinching became more visible, and Poledra pressed her advantage with savage, snarling lunges. Then, suddenly, they both stopped. A wordless agreement seemed to pass between them and each blurred back into her natural form. Their eyes flashing with implacable hatred, Zandramas and Poledra faced each other as two women.

"I've warned you about this, Zandramas," Poledra said in a deadly voice. "Each time you try to thwart the purpose of the Destiny which controls us all, I will block you."

"And I have told thee, Poledra, that I do not fear thee," the sorceress retorted.

"Fine, then," Poledra almost purred. "Let us summon the seeress of Kell and let her make the choice here and now and based upon the outcome of *this* meeting."

"Thou art not the Child of Light, Poledra. Thou hast no part in the ordained meeting."

"I can stand in Belgarion's stead, if need be," Poledra replied, "for the meeting between you and him is not the meeting upon which the fate of creation hinges. In that last meeting you will no longer be the Child of Dark, and he will no longer be the Child of Light. Others are destined to take up those burdens, so let the meeting between you and me come now and in this place."

"Thou wilt turn all to chaos, Poledra," Zandramas screamed.

"Not *all*, I think. You have far more to lose than I. Belgarion is the Child of Light and he will go from here to the Place Which Is No More. You are the Child of Dark, but if we have our meeting here and now, and if you are the one to fall, who will assume your burden? Urvon, perhaps, or Agachak? Or some other? You, however, will not be the exalted one, and I think that thought might be more than you can bear. Consider it, Zandramas, and then choose."

The two stood facing each other with the last flickers of lightning from the evening's storm playing luridly among the clouds to the west, bathing their faces in an eerie light.

"Well, Zandramas?"

"We will surely meet, Poledra, and all shall be decided—but not here. This is not the place of my choosing." Then the Child of Dark shimmered and vanished, and Garion heard and felt the rushing surge of her translocation.

CHAPTER FIFTEEN

She walked toward him with a stately, unhurried step, her golden eyes a mystery. "Put your sword away, Garion," she told him. "There's no need for it now."

"Yes, Grandmother." He reached back over his shoulder and inserted the tip of his blade into the sheath and let it slide home of its own weight.

"You heard, I suppose?"

"Yes, Grandmother."

"Then you understand?"

"Not entirely, no."

"I'm sure you will in time. Let's go inside. I need to talk with my husband and my daughter."

"All right." Garion was not entirely sure about the proprieties and he was just a bit unsure of what his reaction might be should he attempt to assist her, only to discover that she had no substance. Good manners, however, dictated that a gentleman help a lady across uneven ground, and so he set his teeth, reached out, and took her elbow.

She was as solid as he was. That made him feel better.

"Thank you, Garion." She smiled a bit whimsically at him. "Did you really think your hand would pass right through me?"

He flushed. "You knew what I was thinking."

"Of course." She laughed a low, warm laugh. "It's not really all that miraculous, Garion. You're a wolf in your other form, and wolves are very open about their thoughts. You were speaking them out loud in a hundred little moves and gestures you weren't even aware you were making."

"I didn't know that."

"There's a great deal of charm about it. Puppies do it all the time."

"Thanks," he said drily as the two of them passed through the gateway into the yard of the farmstead.

Durnik and Toth were extinguishing the last flickers of flame from the scorched wall of a first-floor shed with buckets full of water carried to them by Silk, Eriond, and Sadi. The dragon had not had enough time to ignite the structures fully with her searing breath, and so none of the fires were very serious.

Polgara crossed the yard gravely with Ce'Nedra and Velvet close behind her. "Mother," she said simply.

"You're looking well, Polgara," the tawny-haired woman replied as if they had spoken together only last week. "Married life agrees with you."

"I rather like it." Polgara smiled.

"I rather thought you might. Is *he* around? I need to talk with him as well as with you."

"He's in one of the upstairs rooms. You know how he feels about these meetings."

"Would you fetch him for me, Garion? I have only so much time, and there are things he has to know. He's going to have to put his feelings aside this time."

"Right away, Grandmother." He turned and went quickly up the wooden steps to the second floor gallery and the door his Aunt Pol had indicated.

Belgarath sat on a rumpled cot. His elbows were on his knees, and his face was buried in his hands.

"Grandfather," Garion said gently.

"What?"

"She wants to talk with you."

Belgarath lifted his face. His expression was one of mute suffering.

"I'm sorry, Grandfather, but she says it's very important."

Belgarath set his jaw, then sighed in resignation. "All right," he said, rising to his feet. "Let's go, then."

As the two of them started down the steps, they saw Durnik bowing a bit awkwardly to Poledra. "Ma'am," the smith was saying. Garion suddenly realized that this was probably the first time the two had been formally introduced.

"So stiff and proper, Durnik?" she replied. She reached out and lightly touched his face with one hand. Then she embraced him. "You've made my daughter very happy, Durnik," she told him. "Thank you." Then she turned and looked directly at Belgarath. "Well?" she said. There was a challenge in her voice.

"You haven't changed a bit," he said in a voice thick with emotion.

"Oh, I've changed all right," she replied wryly, "in ways not even you could imagine."

"It doesn't show."

"It's nice of you to say so. Did you hear the little exchange between the witch and me?"

He nodded. "You were taking chances, Poledra. What if she'd taken up your challenge?"

"Wolves enjoy taking chances." She shrugged. "It adds a certain zest to their lives. It really wasn't all that risky, though. Zandramas is the Child of Dark, and the Dark Spirit is gradually taking over her body as well as her soul; it's not going to gamble at this particular time. It takes too long to train replacements, and there's not that much time left before the final meeting. All right, let's get down to business. Zandramas has her Angarak king now."

Belgarath nodded. "We'd heard about that."

"You always were good at ferreting out secrets. The coronation ceremony was fairly grotesque. Zandramas followed the ancient Angarak ritual. Torak was supposed to be present, but she worked her way around that. It involved a certain amount of fakery, but the image of Him she conjured up was convincing enough to deceive the gullible." Poledra smiled. "It certainly persuaded Archduke Otrath," she added. "He fainted on three separate occasions during the ceremony. I think the oaf actually believes that he really *is* the emperor now—a delusion Kal Zakath's headsman will relieve him of shortly if Otrath is unlucky enough to fall into his cousin's hands. At any rate, Zandramas has only one more major task."

"Oh?" Belgarath said. "What's that?"

"The same as yours. She has to find out where the meeting's supposed to take place. Don't dally on your way to Kell. You've still got a long way to go. Time's getting short, and you have to get across the Magan before 'Zakath gets here."

" 'Zakath?" He sounded startled.

"You mean you didn't know? He moved his army into place around Maga Renn some weeks back. He sent out advance elements a few days ago, and he left Maga Renn with the bulk of his army just yesterday. He plans to blockade the river from the northern end of the Dalasian Mountains to the jungles of Gandahar. If he gets that blockade in place, you might have some difficulty getting across the river." Then she looked at Beldin. "You haven't changed much, my crooked friend," she noted.

"Did you expect me to, Poledra?" He grinned at her.

"I thought you might at least have changed that disreputable old tunic—or that it might have rotted off your back by now."

"I patch it from time to time." He shrugged. "Then I replace the patches when they wear out. It's a comfortable tunic and it fits me. The original is probably only a memory, though. Is there anything else you think we need to know? Or are we going to stand around discussing my wardrobe?"

She laughed. "I've missed you," she told him. "Oh, one of the hierarchs of Cthol Murgos has landed at Finda on the west coast of the Dalasian Protectorates."

"Which one?"

"Agachak."

"Does he have an Angarak king with him?" Silk asked eagerly.

"Yes."

"Urgit—the King of the Murgos?"

She shook her head. "No. Apparently Urgit defied Agachak and refused to make the journey."

"Urgit defied Agachak? Are you sure? Urgit's afraid of his own shadow."

"Not any more, it seems. Your brother's changed quite a bit since you last saw him, Kheldar. His new wife may have had something to do with that. She's a very determined young woman, and she's making him over to fit her conception of him."

"That's terribly depressing," Silk mourned.

"Agachak brought the new king of the Thulls instead—a cretin named Nathel." Poledra looked at her husband. "Be very careful when you get to Dalasia," she told him. "Zandramas, Urvon, and Agachak will all be converging on you. They hate each other, but they all know that you're the common enemy. They may decide to put aside their feelings in order to join forces against you."

"When you add 'Zakath and the whole Mallorean army to that, the Place Which Is No More might be just a little crowded when we get there," Silk observed wryly.

"Numbers will mean absolutely nothing in that place, Kheldar. There will only be three who matter there—the Child of Light, the Child of Dark, and the Seeress of Kell, who will make the choice." She looked at Eriond then. "Do you know what it is you have to do?" she asked him.

"Yes," he replied simply. "It's not such a difficult thing, really."

"Perhaps not," Poledra told him, "but you're the only one who can do it."

"I'll be ready when the time comes, Poledra."

Then the tawny-haired woman looked again at Belgarath. "Now I think it's finally time for you and me to have that little talk you've been avoiding since our daughters were born," she said very firmly.

The old man started.

"In private," she added. "Come with me."

"Yes, Poledra," he replied meekly.

Purposefully she walked toward the gate of the farmstead with Belgarath trailing behind her like a schoolboy anticipating a scolding—or worse.

"At last," Polgara sighed with relief.

"What's going on, Lady Polgara?" Ce'Nedra asked in a baffled little voice.

"My mother and father are going to be reconciled," Polgara replied happily. "My mother died—or perhaps didn't—when my sister Beldaran and I were born. My father always blamed himself because he wasn't there to help her. He and Bearshoulders and the others had gone to Cthol Mishrak to steal the Orb back from Torak. Mother never blamed him because she knew how important what they were doing was. Father doesn't forgive himself that easily, however, and he's been punishing himself about it for all these centuries. Mother's finally gotten tired of it, so she's going to take steps to correct the situation."

"Oh," Ce'Nedra said with that odd little catch in her voice. "That's just beautiful." Her eyes filled with sudden tears.

Wordlessly, Velvet drew a flimsy little bit of a handkerchief from her sleeve, dabbed at her own eyes, then passed it to Ce'Nedra.

It was perhaps an hour later when Belgarath returned. He was alone, but there was a gentle smile on his face and a youthful twinkle in his eye. No one saw fit to ask him any questions. "What time of night would you say it is?" he asked Durnik.

The smith squinted up at the sky where the last remnants of cloud were being swept off to the east by the prevailing wind to reveal the stars. "I'd guess about two hours until first light, Belgarath," he replied. "The breeze has come up, and it sort of smells like morning."

"I don't think we'll get any more sleep tonight," the old man said. "Why don't we load the packs and saddle the horses while Pol fixes some of those eggs for breakfast?"

Polgara looked at him with a slightly raised eyebrow.

"You weren't planning to let us leave without feeding us first, were you, Pol?" he asked her roguishly.

"No, father," she said, "as a matter of fact, I wasn't."

"I didn't think so." Then he laughed and threw his arms about her. "Oh, my Pol," he said exuberantly.

Ce'Nedra's eyes filled with tears again, and Velvet reached for her handkerchief once more.

"Between them, they're going to wear that little thing out," Silk noted clinically.

"That's all right," Garion replied. "I've got a couple of spares in my pack." Then he remembered something. "Grandfather," he said, "in all the excitement, I almost forgot something. Before she changed into the dragon, I heard Zandramas talking with Naradas."

"Oh?"

"He's been in Gandahar and he's taking a regiment of elephant cavalry to the battlefield."

"That won't matter very much to the demons."

"The demons aren't there any more. Zandramas raised another Demon Lord—Mordja, his name is—and he's managed to lure Nahaz away from the battlefield. They've gone off someplace else to fight."

Belgarath scratched at one bearded cheek. "Just how good is that elephant cavalry out of Gandahar?" he asked Silk.

"Pretty close to invincible," Silk replied. "They drape them in chain mail, and they trample wide paths through opposing armies. If the demons have left the field, Urvon's army hasn't got a chance."

"There are too many people involved in this race anyway," Belgarath grunted. "Let's get across the Magan and leave all these armies to their own devices."

They ate breakfast and rode out from the farmstead as the first light of dawn began to creep slowly up out of the eastern horizon. Oddly, Garion felt no particular weariness despite a night significantly short on sleep. A great deal had happened since the sun had gone down, and he had much to think about.

The sun had risen when they reached the great River Magan. Then, following Toth's gestured directions, they rode slowly southward, looking for a village where they might find a boat large enough to carry them across to Darshiva. The day was warm, and the grass and trees had all been washed clean by the previous night's storm.

They came to a small settlement of mud-smeared shacks standing on stilts, with rickety docks thrusting out into the river. A lone fisherman sat at the end of one of the docks negligently holding a long cane pole.

"Talk to him, Durnik," Belgarath said. "See if he knows where we can hire a boat."

The smith nodded and reined his horse around. On an impulse, Garion followed him. They dismounted at the landward end of the dock and walked out toward the fisherman.

He was a stumpy-looking little fellow, dressed in a homespun tunic and with muddy, baglike shoes on his feet. His bare legs were laced with knotty, purple veins, and they were not very clean. His face was tanned, and he was not so much bearded as unshaven.

"Any luck?" Durnik asked him.

"See fer yerself," the fisherman said, pointing at the wooden tub at his side. He did not turn, but rather kept his eyes intently on the floating red stick to which his line was attached and which dangled his baited hook down into the murky water of the river. The tub was half-full of water, and several foot-long trout swam in circles in it. The fish had angry-looking eyes and jutting lower jaws.

Durnik squatted down beside the fisherman, his hands on his knees. "Nice-looking fish," he observed.

"A fish is a fish." The stumpy fellow shrugged. "They look better on the plate than they do in the tub."

"That's why we catch them," Durnik agreed. "What are you using for bait?"

"Tried angleworms earlier," the fellow replied laconically. "Didn't seem to interest 'em, so I switched over to fish roe."

"I don't think I've ever tried that," Durnik admitted. "How does it work?"

"Caught them five in the last half hour. Sometimes it makes 'em so excited, you got to go behind a tree to bait your hook to keep 'em from chasin' you right up onto the bank."

"I'll have to try it," Durnik said, eyeing the water wistfully. "Have you got any idea of where we might be able to hire a boat? We've got to go across the river."

The fisherman turned and stared at the smith incredulously. "To the Darshiva side?" he exclaimed. "Man, are you out of your mind?"

"Is there some trouble over there?"

"Trouble? That don't even *begin* to describe what's happenin' over there. You ever hear tell of what they call a demon?"

"A few times."

"You ever seen one?"

"Once, I think."

"There's no *think* about it, friend. If you seen one, you'd know." The fellow shuddered. "They're just plain awful. Well, sir, the whole of Darshiva's just crawlin' with 'em. There's this Grolim, he come down from the north with a whole pack of 'em snappin' an' growlin' at his heels. Then there's this other Grolim—a woman, if you can believe that—Zandramas, her name is, an' she stepped back an' cast a spell an' hauled some of her own out of wherever it is they come from, an' them demons is fightin' each other over there in Darshiva."

"We'd heard that there was fighting to the north of here in Peldane."

"Those are just ordinary troops, and what they're fightin' is an ordinary war with swords an' axes an' burnin' pitch an' all. The demons, they all went across the river lookin' fer fresh ground to tear up an' fresh people to eat. They do that, y' know—demons I mean. They eat folks—alive, most of the time."

"I'm afraid we still have to go over there," Durnik told him.

"I hope yer a good swimmer then. Yer gonna have no luck at all findin' a boat. Ever'body from here jumped on anythin' as would float an' headed downriver t'ward Gandahar. Guess they figgered them wild elephants down there was a whole lot preferable to demons."

"I think you're getting a bite," Durnik said politely, pointing at the floating stick on the stumpy man's line. The stick was submerging and popping back to the surface again.

The fisherman jerked his pole straight up into the air and then swore. "Missed 'im," he said.

"You can't catch them all," Durnik said philosophically.

"You can sure try, though." The fellow laughed, pulling in his line and rebaiting his hook with a dripping gobbet of fish roe he took from an earthenware bowl at his side.

"I'd try under the dock, myself," Durnik advised. "Trout always seem to like shade."

"That's the good thing about usin' fish roe fer bait," the fisherman said sagely. "They kin smell it, an' they'll go fer it even if they gotta climb a fence to get there." He cast his line out again and absently wiped his hand on the front of his tunic.

"How is it that you stayed behind?" Durnik asked. "I mean, if there's so much trouble around here, why didn't you go to Gandahar with the other people who left here?"

"I never lost nothin' in Gandahar. Them folks is all crazy down there. They spend all their time chasin' elephants. I mean, what y' gonna do with a elephant once y' catch 'im? An' the fish down there aren't worth the bait. Besides, this is the first time I've had this dock all to myself in the last five years. Most of the time I can't even get my line in the water, there's so many out here."

"Well," Durnik said, rising to his feet a little regretfully, "I suppose we'd better push on. We're going to have to find a boat somewhere."

"I'd sure advise stayin' away from the Darshiva side, friend," the fisherman said seriously. "You'd be better off t' cut yerself a pole an' sit right here with me until all the trouble blows over."

"I certainly wish I could," Durnik sighed. "Good luck, friend."

"Just bein' here with my line in the water is the best luck in the world." The fellow shrugged, turning his eyes back to the floating stick on his line. "If you go over to the Darshiva side, try not t' get et by demons."

"I'll make a special point of it," Durnik promised.

As Garion and his friend walked back along the rickety dock to where their horses were tethered, Durnik smiled. "They talk differently in this part of the world, don't they?"

"Yes," Garion agreed, remembering the gabby old man and his pig in the wayside tavern above the plains of Voresebo.

"I sort of like it, though," Durnik admitted. "It's kind of free and relaxed and easy, somehow."

"I wouldn't necessarily try to imitate it, though, if I were you," Garion advised. "Aunt Pol might wash your mouth out with soap if you did."

"Oh," Durnik smiled, "I don't think she'd really do that, Garion."

Garion shrugged. "She's your wife—and it's your mouth."

Belgarath was waiting for them atop the grassy hill rising above the village on the riverbank. "Well?" he asked.

"The fish are biting," Durnik told him seriously.

Belgarath stared at him for a moment, then rolled his eyes heavenward and groaned. "I meant in Darshiva," he said from between clenched teeth.

"I couldn't really say for sure about that, Belgarath, but if they're biting on this side, it only stands to reason that they'd be biting over there, too, doesn't it?" Durnik's face was very sincere, and his tone was earnest.

Belgarath turned and stamped away, muttering to himself.

When they rejoined the others, Garion briefly repeated the information he and Durnik had gleaned from the solitary man at the end of the dock.

"That puts a whole new complexion on things, doesn't it?" Silk said. "Now what?"

"If you don't mind a suggestion, Ancient One," Sadi said to Belgarath. "I think we might be wise to follow the example of the villagers Belgarion mentioned and go on downriver to Gandahar and find a boat there. It might take us a little longer, but we'll avoid the demons."

Toth shook his head. The huge mute's usually impassive face had a worried frown on it. He made a quick series of those obscure gestures to Durnik.

"He says we don't have time," the smith translated.

"Is there some kind of special time when we have to get to Kell?" Silk asked.

Toth gestured again, his big hands moving rapidly.

"He says that Kell has been sealed off from the rest of Dalasia," Durnik told them. "Cyradis has made arrangements for us to get through, but once she leaves, the other seers will seal it off again."

"Leaves?" Belgarath said with some surprise. "Where's she going?"

Durnik looked inquiringly at Toth, and the mute gestured some more.

"Oh," Durnik said, "I see." He turned back to Belgarath. "She needs to go to the place of the meeting soon. She has to be there when it happens so that she can make the choice."

"Couldn't she just travel with us?" Velvet asked.

Toth shook his head again, and his gestures became more emphatic.

"I'm not sure I got all that," Durnik confessed. "Tell me if I make any mistakes." He turned once more. "He says that something's supposed to happen before we get to Kell, but if it doesn't, she'll have to travel alone."

"Did he say what this something is going to be?" Polgara asked her husband.

"The way I understand it, he doesn't know, Pol."

"Does he know *where* it's going to happen?" Belgarath asked intently.

Toth spread his hands.

"That young lady's really beginning to irritate me." The old man looked at Beldin. "What do you think?"

"I don't see that we have much choice, Belgarath. If this event's supposed to happen in Darshiva and we avoid the place, it might not happen at all, and the whole business could hinge on that."

"All right," Belgarath said. "We go to Darshiva then. We've dodged demons before. The main thing right now is to get across the river before 'Zakath gets here."

"We're going to need a boat," Durnik said.

"I'll go see if I can find one," Beldin said, crouching and spreading his arms.

"You don't have to be too selective," Belgarath said. "Anything that floats should do it."

"I'll keep that in mind," Beldin replied and soared away.

PART THREE

DARSHIVA

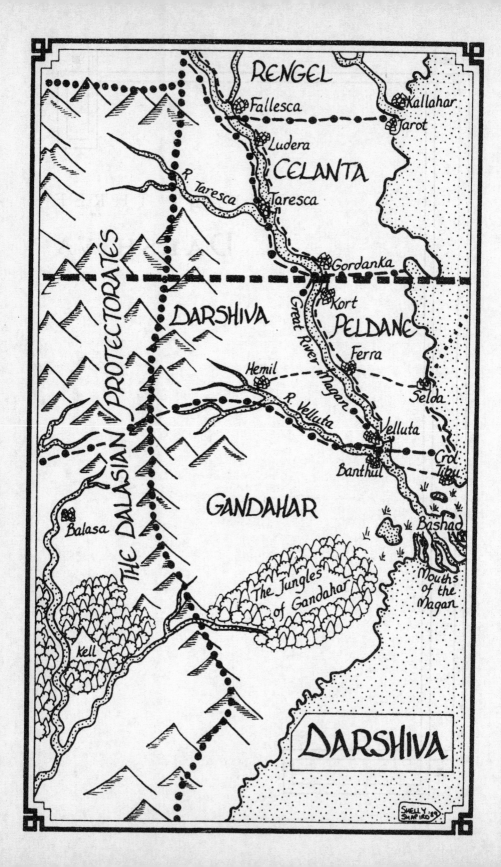

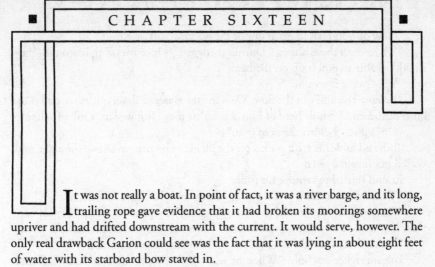

It was not really a boat. In point of fact, it was a river barge, and its long, trailing rope gave evidence that it had broken its moorings somewhere upriver and had drifted downstream with the current. It would serve, however. The only real drawback Garion could see was the fact that it was lying in about eight feet of water with its starboard bow staved in.

"What do you think, Belgarath?" Beldin asked.

"A boat that's already been sunk once doesn't inspire much confidence," the old man said.

"How would you like to try swimming? There's not even a raft for ten miles in either direction."

Durnik stood squinting down into the cloudy water of the river. "It might be all right," he said.

"Durnik," Silk objected, "it's got a big hole in the front of it."

"I can fix that—provided it hasn't been down there long enough to start rotting." He pulled off his rust-colored tunic and his boots. "Well," he said, "there's one way to find out." He waded out into the river, sank beneath the surface, and swam down to the wreck. He went hand over hand down one side, stopping every few feet to dig at the wood with his knife. After what seemed an eternity, he came up for air.

"Well?" Belgarath called to him.

"That side seems all right," Durnik replied. "Let me check the other." He dove down again through the greenish water and went up along the other side. He came up briefly, then went back down to look over the interior of the barge. Then he inspected the gaping hole in the bow. He was breathing hard when he came back up. "It's sound," he reported as he came dripping out of the river, "and whatever it ran into didn't damage anything major. I think I can fix it well enough to get us across the river. We'll have to unload it first, though."

"Oh?" Silk's nose twitched with curiosity. "What kind of cargo was it carrying?"

"Beans," Durnik replied, "bags of them. Most of the bags burst when the beans swelled up, though."

Silk groaned.

"Maybe they belonged to someone else, Kheldar," Velvet said consolingly.

"Are you trying to be funny?"

"I'll help you, Durnik," Garion offered, starting to pull off his plain tunic.

"Ah . . ." Durnik hesitated. "Thanks all the same, Garion, but I've seen you swim. You'd better stay on the bank. Toth and I can manage."

"How do you plan to get it out of the water?" Sadi asked.

"We have all these horses." Durnik shrugged. "Once we swing it around, they should be able to pull it up on the bank."

"Why swing it around?"

"Because the hole's in the bow. We want the water to drain out as we pull it up onto the beach. A whole herd of horses couldn't move it if we left it full of water."

"Oh. I guess I didn't think of that."

Toth laid aside his staff, pulled off the blanket he wore across one shoulder, and waded out into the river.

Eriond started to remove his tunic.

"Where do you think you're going, young man?" Polgara asked him.

"I'm going to help unload the boat, Polgara," he replied earnestly. "I swim very well. I've had lots of practice, remember?" Then he, too, waded out into the water.

"I'm not sure I caught the significance of that," Velvet admitted.

Polgara sighed ruefully. "When he was a little boy, he lived with Durnik and me in the Vale. There was a river nearby, and he used to fall into it regularly."

"Oh. That explains it, I guess."

"All right," Belgarath said crisply. "They're going to need lumber to patch that hole. We passed a shed about a half mile upstream. Let's go back and tear it apart."

It was well after sundown by the time Durnik got the foundered barge up onto the beach. For once, nature cooperated, and there was no hailstorm that evening. They built a fire on the beach to provide light, and the smith, Toth, and Eriond got down to work.

Silk walked mournfully around the barge. "It's mine, all right," he sighed.

"You keep well-equipped barges, Silk," Durnik said, carefully measuring a board. "This one had everything I need right in the bow—nails, a barrel of tar, and even a fairly good saw. We'll have it afloat before morning."

"I'm glad you approve," Silk said sourly. He made a wry face. "This is unnatural," he complained.

"What's the problem, Kheldar?" Velvet asked him.

"Usually, when I want a boat, I steal one. Using one of my own seems immoral somehow."

She laughed gaily and patted his cheek. "Poor, poor dear," she said. "It must be terrible to be burdened with so delicate a conscience."

"All right, ladies," Polgara said then, "let's see to supper."

While Durnik, Toth, and Eriond worked on the patch and Polgara, Ce'Nedra, and Velvet prepared supper, Garion and the others fetched more lumber and began to fashion crude oars. They continued to work, even as they ate. Somehow, everything seemed right to Garion. All his friends were around him and they were all busy. Although the repairing of the boat was of vital importance, the simple chores involved seemed almost mundane, and Garion could lose himself in the tasks at hand with no sense of the urgency which had attended the things he had been forced to do lately. It was almost soothing.

After the ladies had finished with supper, they carried canvas buckets of water from the river and heated the water with hot rocks. Then they retired behind a screen of tenting to bathe.

About midnight, Garion went down to the water's edge to dip his sore hands into the river. Ce'Nedra sat not far away, idly letting handfuls of sand trickle out from between her fingers. "Why don't you see if you can get some sleep, Ce'Nedra?" Garion asked her.

"I can stay awake as long as you can," she replied.

"I'm sure you can, but why?"

"Don't patronize me, Garion. I'm not a child."

"You know," he said slyly, "I've noticed that myself on any number of occasions."

"Garion!" she gasped, and then she suddenly blushed.

He laughed, rose to his feet, and went over and kissed her soundly. "Go get some sleep, dear," he told her.

"What are you doing over there?" she asked, looking up the beach to where the others still worked.

"We're making oars. If we just push that barge out into the river, the current's going to take us all the way down into Gandahar."

"Oh. All right then. Have a pleasant night." She stretched and yawned. "Why don't you get me a blanket before you go back to building oars?"

It took Durnik and Toth most of the night to nail a rough, tar-smeared patch over the hole in the bow, while the others fashioned crude oars fixed on long poles. Several hours before daylight, fog began to rise in misty tendrils from the surface of the river. After Durnik had liberally applied hot tar to the inside and the outside of the patch, he stepped back and critically examined his handiwork.

"I think it's going to leak," Silk predicted.

"All boats leak." Durnik shrugged. "We can bail the water out."

It took a great deal of effort and some fairly exotic rigging to get the barge back into the river again. Durnik leaped aboard and went forward with a torch to examine the patch. "A little trickle is all," he said with some satisfaction. "It's nothing we can't keep ahead of."

The fog grew steadily thicker as they loaded their packs aboard the barge. It was spring in this part of the world, and frogs sang lustily of love in the rushes at the river's edge just upstream. It was a pleasant, drowsy sound. Durnik scouted several hundred yards downstream and found a shallow bank where the current had cut away the soil. He fashioned a ramp from the remaining lumber. They towed the barge down to the cut bank and loaded the horses on board.

"Let's wait until we have a little more light," the smith suggested. "Fog's bad enough, but when you add darkness to it, it's almost impossible to see where you're going. Rowing this thing isn't going to be so enjoyable that we need to paddle around in circles just for the entertainment of it."

"Couldn't we rig a sail of some sort?" Silk asked hopefully.

"Easily," Durnik replied. He wet one finger with his tongue and held it up. "I'll do that just as soon as you work out a way to make the wind blow."

Silk's face fell.

"While you're doing that, I need to go talk with Ce'Nedra." He went back up the beach and gently shook Garion's sleeping wife awake.

"You know? Sometimes he has a very warped sense of humor," Silk observed.

When the first light of day began to tinge the misty eastern horizon, they pushed out into the fog and took their places at the oars.

"I don't want to seem critical, Goodman," Sadi said to Durnik, who stood in the stern with his hands gripping the tiller, "but I've seen a lot of fog in Nyissa, and, once it's fully daylight, you won't have the faintest idea of where the sun is. How do you plan to keep your course?"

"Ce'Nedra's taking care of that," the smith replied, pointing toward the bow.

The Rivan Queen was leaning over the portside intently watching a floating piece of wood attached to a long cord.

"What's she doing?" Sadi asked, sounding a bit perplexed.

"She's watching the current. We'll be quartering it, but as long as that cord stays at the same angle from the boat, we'll be right on course. I put a mark on the rail to show her what the angle ought to be."

"You think of everything, don't you?" Sadi said, continuing to pull his oar.

"I try. You can usually avoid problems if you think your way completely through a job."

Ce'Nedra raised one arm and pointed imperiously to starboard. She seemed to be taking her job very seriously. Durnik obediently moved the tiller.

Once the eastern shore of the great river vanished in the fog, it seemed to Garion that time had stopped entirely. There was no real sense of motion, though he bent his back over his oar with monotonous regularity.

"Tiresome, isn't it?" Silk said.

"Rowing always is," Garion replied.

Silk looked around, then spoke quietly. "Do you notice a change in Durnik?" he asked.

"No. Not really."

"What I'm getting at is that usually he's so self-effacing that you almost forget that he's around, but back there on the beach, he just sort of took charge."

"He's always been like that, Silk. When we're doing something he doesn't know all that much about, he just follows along and keeps his eyes open; but when we come to something he knows about, he steps in and does what has to be done." Garion smiled affectionately back over his shoulder at his old friend. Then he looked slyly at Silk. "He also learns very fast. By now, he's probably at least as good a spy as you are, and he watched you very closely while you were manipulating the bean market back there in Melcena. If he ever decides to go into business, I think you and Yarblek had better start keeping a close count of your tail feathers."

Silk looked a bit worried. "He wouldn't really do that, would he?"

"He might. You never really know about Durnik, do you?"

As the sun rose higher, the fog diffused its light, and the world around them became a monochrome—white fog and black water with no hint at all that they were making any progress or, if they were, that it was in the right direction. Garion felt a bit strange, knowing that they were entirely at Ce'Nedra's mercy. It was only her eyes on that cord lightly lying across an angled mark on the rail that kept them on course. He loved her, but he knew that she was sometimes flighty, and her judgment was not always the best. Her insistent little gestures to port or to starboard, however, showed no sign of hesitancy or lack of certainty, and Durnik obeyed them implicitly. Garion sighed and kept on rowing.

About midmorning, the fog began to thin, and Beldin drew in his oar. "Can you manage here without me?" he asked Belgarath. "I think we ought to know just exactly what we're running into. There's all sorts of unpleasantness going on in Darshiva, and I don't think we'll want to come ashore right in the middle of it."

"And you're getting tired of rowing, right?" the old man replied sarcastically.

"I could row all the way around the world if I wanted to," the gnarled-looking little hunchback replied, flexing his oak-stump arms, "but this might be more important. Do you really want to beach this tub and find Nahaz waiting for you on the sand?"

"Do whatever you think is right."

"I always do, Belgarath—even if it makes you unhappy sometimes." The grimy little gnome went forward toward the bow. "Excuse me, me little darlin'," he said to Ce'Nedra in an exaggerated brogue, "but I must be off now."

"I need you at that oar," she objected. "How can I keep the course if everybody runs away?"

"I'm sure y' kin manage, me little darlin'," he said, patting her cheek; then, leaving a ghostly laugh behind him, he disappeared into the fog.

"You come back here!" she shouted after him, but he was already gone.

There was the faintest touch of a breeze then. Garion could feel it brushing across the back of his sweaty neck as he rowed. The fog eddied and swirled slightly, thinning even more.

And then there were looming black shapes all around them.

"Garion!" Ce'Nedra exclaimed.

A number of triumphant shouts came out of the rapidly dissipating fog. They were surrounded by ships that moved purposefully to block them.

"Do we make a run for it?" Silk asked in a tense, hoarse whisper.

Belgarath looked at the ships moving to surround them, his eyes like flint. "Run?" he said. "In this tub? Don't be ridiculous."

A boat had moved directly in front of them, and, as they drifted closer, Garion could see the oarsmen. "Mallorean soldiers," he noted quietly. " 'Zakath's army."

Belgarath muttered a few choice oaths. "Let's sit tight for a bit. They may not know who we are. Silk, see if you can talk us out of this."

The little man rose and went to the bow of their barge. "We're certainly glad to see imperial troops in this region, Captain," he said to the officer commanding the boat blocking their path. "Maybe you can put a stop to all the insanity that's been going on around here."

"I'll need your name," the officer replied.

"Of course," Silk said, slapping his forehead. "How stupid of me. My name is Vetter. I work for Prince Kheldar. Perhaps you've heard of him?"

"The name's familiar. Where are you going?"

"Actually, we're bound for Balasa down in the Dalasian Protectorates. Prince Kheldar has interests there—that's assuming we can make our way across Darshiva. Things are in turmoil there." He paused. "I wonder, Captain, do you suppose you could spare us a few soldiers to act as an escort? I'm authorized to pay quite handsomely."

"We'll see," the officer said.

Then an even larger ship emerged from the fog and moved alongside their patched and leaky vessel. A familiar face looked over the rail. "It's been quite some time, hasn't it, King Belgarion?" General Atesca said in a pleasant, conversational tone. "We really ought to try to stay in touch." Atesca wore his customary scarlet cloak and a burnished steel helmet embossed with gold.

Garion's heart sank. Subterfuge was quite out of the question now. "You knew we were out here," he said accusingly.

"Of course. I had people watching you on the Peldane side." The red-clad general sounded a bit smug about that.

"I felt no presence," Polgara declared, pulling her blue cloak about her.

"I'd have been very surprised if you had, my Lady," Atesca replied. "The men who were watching you are imbeciles. Their minds are as vacant as the minds of mushrooms." He looked distastefully out across the river. "You have no idea of how long it took me to explain to them what they were supposed to do. Every army has a few men like that. We try to weed them out, but even gross stupidity has its uses, I suppose."

"You're very clever, General Atesca," she said in a tight voice.

"No, Lady Polgara," he disagreed. "I'm just a plain soldier. No officer is more clever than his intelligence service. Brador's the clever one. He's been gathering information about your peculiar gifts from various Grolims since the battle of Thull Mardu. Grolims pay very close attention to your exploits, my Lady, and over the years they've amassed a great deal of information about your abilities. As I understand it—although I'm certainly no expert—the more acute a mind is, the more easily you can detect its presence. That's why I sent those human turnips out to watch you." He looked critically at their boat. "That's really a wretched thing, you know. Are you keeping it afloat by sorcery?"

"No," Durnik told him in a flat, angry tone of voice, "by skill."

"I bow to your skill, Goodman Durnik," Atesca said a bit extravagantly. "You could probably work out a way to make a rock float—if you really wanted to." He paused and looked at Belgarath. "I assume we're going to be civilized about this, Ancient One?" he asked.

"I'm willing to listen," Belgarath replied warily.

"His Imperial Majesty feels a strong need to discuss certain matters with you and your companions, Holy Belgarath," Atesca said, "and I think I should advise you that you're paddling this wreck of yours directly into the middle of a hornet's nest. Sensible people are avoiding Darshiva right now."

"I've never pretended to be sensible."

Atesca laughed ruefully. "I haven't either," he admitted. "At the moment, I'm trying to map out a military campaign to invade that most insensible region. May I offer you gentlemen—and your ladies—the hospitality of my ship?" He paused. "I think I'll have to insist," he added regretfully. "Orders, you understand. Besides, we might want to pool our information while we await the arrival of his Imperial Majesty."

"Is 'Zakath coming here?" Garion asked.

"I doubt that he's more than a day behind me, your Majesty," Atesca replied, "and he's aflame with the desire to have a long, long talk with you."

—*What do we do, Grandfather?*—Garion's fingers asked.

—*I don't think we've got much choice at the moment. Beldin's out there somewhere. I'll let him know what's happening. He'll come up with something.*—"All right, General," he said aloud. "I was getting a little tired of rowing anyway."—*Pass the word to the others*—He motioned to Garion.—*Let's seem to go along—at least until we get to the Darshiva side.*—

Atesca's ship, while not opulent, was comfortable. They gathered in the forward cabin, a room littered with maps and various-sized bits and pieces of parchment. As always, General Atesca was polite, but firm. "Have you had breakfast yet?" he inquired.

"We were a little rushed," Belgarath told him.

"I'll send word to the cook, then," Atesca said. He went to the door and spoke with one of the red-garbed guards posted outside. Then he came back. "While we're waiting, why don't we share that information I was talking about? I'd heard that you were going to Ashaba when you left Mal Zeth. Then you suddenly surface in Melcena, and now you're halfway across the Magan to Darshiva. You people certainly move around."

—*He already knows what we're doing.*—Silk's fingers said to Belgarath.—*There's no point in trying to hide it.*—

"Please, Prince Kheldar," Atesca said in a pained tone, "don't do that. It's very impolite, you know."

Silk laughed. "Either your eyes are very sharp, General, or advancing age is making my fingers clumsy. In point of fact, I was merely suggesting to Belgarath that we'd made no secret of our reason for coming to Mallorea. Kal Zakath knew why we were here, so there's no point in being coy about it." He gave Belgarath an inquiring look, and the old man nodded. Silk's face grew serious, even bleak. "We went to Ashaba in pursuit of Zandramas—and King Belgarion's son. Then we followed her across Karanda and on down to Jarot in northern Celanta. Her trail led to Melcena, so we followed her there. Then we came back to the continent."

"And you're still on her trail?" Atesca asked intently.

"More or less," Silk lied smoothly. Then he sidestepped the issue. "We discovered at Ashaba that Urvon is totally mad now. I'm sure Kal Zakath will be interested in that. Anyhow, Urvon's under the control of a Demon Lord named Nahaz. Zandramas has raised another Demon Lord named Mordja, and the two are fighting each other in Darshiva. I'd think a long time before I invaded that region, General. Nahaz and Mordja might prefer not to be interrupted."

"What happened to Mengha?" Atesca asked suddenly. "I thought he was the one who was raising demons."

Silk smiled wryly. "Mengha was actually a Chandim priest named Harakan. He was Urvon's underling for centuries."

"Was?"

"I'm afraid he's no longer with us. He met a little green snake named Zith and he lost interest in things shortly after that."

Atesca threw back his head and laughed. "I'd heard about your pet, your Excellency," he said to Sadi. "Do you suppose she'd accept a medal—Heroine of the Empire or something?"

"I don't think she'd really be interested, General Atesca," Sadi replied coolly. "Besides, if somebody tried to pin a medal to her, she might misunderstand."

"You've got a point there," Atesca said. He looked around a little nervously. "You *do* have her confined, don't you?"

"Of course, General," Velvet assured him with a dimpled smile. "At the moment, she's taking care of her babies. They're absolutely adorable. Why don't you show them to the General, Sadi?"

"Ah . . ." Atesca hesitated. "Some other time, perhaps."

"All right, General Atesca," Belgarath said, "we've told you what we've been doing. Now I think it's time for you to share a bit of information with us."

"We haven't really made a secret of our activities either, Ancient Belgarath. The Emperor's forces moved out of Mal Zeth, and we used Maga Renn as a staging area. I was instructed to lead the advance elements of the army down the Magan and to occupy Ferra. The idea was to cut off Zandramas' reinforcements out of Darshiva so that Urvon's army could annihilate the troops she had in Peldane. Then we planned to fall on Urvon—heavily. After that, we were going to cross the river and deal with whatever force Zandramas had left."

"Good plan," Silk said.

"Unfortunately, it didn't work. We've got Darshiva cut off, but one of Zandramas' underlings went down into Gandahar and hired a sizable body of elephant cavalry." Atesca frowned. "I think I'll speak with his Imperial Majesty about that. I don't really object to mercenaries, but the elephant herders of Gandahar are just a bit unselective when it comes to hiring themselves out. At any rate, there was a battle in central Peldane yesterday, and elephants did what elephants usually do. Urvon's army fled, but instead of running back toward Celanta, they outflanked the elephants and the rest of the Darshivan army, and they're driving straight toward the Magan. If they get across into Darshiva, I'll have my work cut out for me. I'll have demons and Grolims and Chandim and Hounds and elephants and Karands and the whole army of Darshiva to deal with." He sighed mournfully. "This is not, I'm afraid, going to be the short, easy campaign I'd anticipated."

"Why not just let Urvon and Zandramas fight it out?" Silk suggested.

"Policy, Prince Kheldar. The Emperor does not want to appear timid—or powerless—and he most certainly doesn't want any army in Mallorea except his own to win any kind of a victory. It sets a bad precedent and it might give others certain ideas. Mallorea is not as monolithic a society as it might appear from the outside. Overwhelming imperial force is the only thing that holds us together."

"I approve of the reasoning," Silk agreed. "Stability is good for business."

"Speaking of that," Atesca said. "One of these days you and I are going to have to have a long talk about beans."

"Are you buying or selling, General Atesca?" Silk asked impudently.

"Let's get down to cases, gentlemen," Polgara said. "General Atesca, what are the Emperor's plans concerning us?"

"That's for him to decide, my Lady," Atesca replied. "His Majesty doesn't always confide in me. He was, however, quite distressed about the way you chose to abuse his hospitality in Mal Zeth."

"He knew where we were going," Garion said flatly, "and why."

"That's likely to be one of the things he'll want to discuss with your Majesty. It's possible that the two of you might be able to work out an accommodation of some kind."

"Possible, but not very probable."

"That's up to his Imperial Majesty, isn't it?"

The fog had lifted, but the sky over Darshiva was heavily overcast. As Garion stood in the bow of Atesca's ship, he caught a scent that was hauntingly familiar. It was a compound of damp rust, stagnant water, and the musty smell of fungus. He peered ahead and saw a forest composed of dead white snags. His heart sank.

Atesca quietly joined him. "I hope your Majesty isn't offended with me," he said. "I seem to be making a habit of apprehending you and your friends."

"You're only following orders, General," Garion said shortly. "My quarrel is with your Emperor, not with you."

"You're a very tolerant man, your Majesty."

"Not really, General, but I don't waste my time holding grudges against people who are only doing what they're told to do."

Atesca looked toward the Darshivan shore, less than a mile away. "I expect that overcast will burn off by noon," he said, smoothly changing the subject.

"I wouldn't count on it, Atesca," Garion said somberly. "Did you ever visit Cthol Mishrak?"

"Military people don't have much reason to visit uninhabited ruins, your Majesty."

"Cthol Mishrak wasn't uninhabited," Garion told him. "The Chandim were there, and the Hounds, and other things I can't even put names to."

"Religious fanatics," Atesca shrugged. "They do things for strange reasons. I'm told it was an unhealthy sort of place."

Garion pointed at the Darshivan shore. "You're looking at another one, I'm afraid. I know that Melcenes are almost as skeptical as Tolnedrans, so I don't know how much you'll believe of what I'm going to tell you. Do you smell that peculiar odor in the air?"

Atesca sniffed, then wrinkled his nose. "Not very pleasant, is it?"

"Cthol Mishrak smelled exactly the same way. I'd guess that the cloud cover over Darshiva has been there for a dozen years at least."

"I find that a bit hard to accept."

"Look at those trees." Garion pointed at the snags. "What do you think it would take to kill a whole forest?"

"Some kind of disease, I suppose."

"No, General. Seedlings would have sprouted by now, and there's not even any undergrowth there. The trees died from lack of sunlight. The only thing growing out there now is fungus. It rains from time to time, and the rain water collects in pools. The sun doesn't come out to evaporate the water, so it just lies there and stagnates. That's a part of what you're smelling."

"I seem to smell rust, too. Where's that coming from?"

"I really don't know. At Cthol Mishrak it came from the ruins of Torak's iron tower. Darshiva's shrouded in perpetual gloom because it's the home of the Child of Dark."

"I've heard the term before. Who is this Child of Dark?"

"Zandramas—at least for the time being. Are you really sure you want to land your troops there?"

"I have my orders, King Belgarion. My troops are well trained. They'll build a fortified enclave on that shore whether the sun shines or not. Then we'll wait for the Emperor. He has a number of decisions to make—not the least of which is what he's going to do about you."

■ | CHAPTER SEVENTEEN | ■

They waited on board Atesca's ship while the soldiers went ashore and began to build the enclave. The Mallorean troops were quite nearly as efficient as the legions of Imperial Tolnedra, and in a very short period of time, they had cleared several acres of ground and erected a neat, orderly city of tents. It was surrounded on the inland side by breastworks, catapults, and a deep ditch bristling with sharpened stakes. A palisade of sharpened poles lined the river's edge, and a number of floating docks extended out into the water.

It was midafternoon when Garion and the others disembarked and were escorted to a large, guarded pavilion in the center of the enclave and politely, but firmly, asked to remain inside.

"Have you been able to contact Beldin?" Silk asked Belgarath in a whisper.

The old man nodded. "He's working on something."

"I hope he doesn't take too long," the little man said. "I expect that once 'Zakath gets here, he'll decide that we need slightly more secure quarters—probably a place involving stout walls and locked doors." He made a sour face. "I hate jails."

"Don't you think you're exaggerating, Prince Kheldar?" Ce'Nedra asked. " 'Zakath's always behaved like a perfect gentleman."

"Oh, of course," he replied with heavy sarcasm. "Why don't you tell that to all those Murgos he crucified on the plains of Hagga? He can be polite when it doesn't inconvenience him too much, but we've seriously irritated him. If we're not gone by the time he gets here, I expect he'll show us just how irritated he really is."

"You're wrong, Prince Kheldar," Eriond said gravely. "He just doesn't know what he's supposed to do yet, that's all."

"What's that supposed to mean?"

"Back in Cthol Murgos, Cyradis told him that he was going to come to a crossroads in his life. This is it, I think. Once he makes the right choice, we can be friends again."

"Just like that?"

"More or less, yes."

"Polgara, would you please make him stop that?"

The tent was familiar. It was a Mallorean officer's pavilion with the usual red carpeting, and furniture which could be easily disassembled. They had been housed in this same kind of pavilion many times in the past. Garion looked around without much interest, then he sprawled on a bench.

"What's the matter, Garion?" Ce'Nedra asked, coming over to sit beside him.

"Isn't it obvious? Why don't they just leave us alone?"

"I think you worry too much," she told him. She reached out and touched his forehead with one little finger. "Your friend in there isn't going to let anything happen that's not supposed to happen, so stop brooding about this. We're supposed to go to Kell, and 'Zakath couldn't stop us, even if he brought his whole army back from Cthol Murgos and piled them in our path."

"You're taking this all awfully calmly."

"I have to believe, Garion," she replied with a little sigh. "If I didn't, I'd go insane." She leaned forward and kissed him. "Now get that grumpy look off your face. You're starting to look exactly like Belgarath."

"Of course I am. He's my grandfather, after all."

"The resemblance shouldn't start to show up for several thousand years yet, though," she said tartly.

Two soldiers brought them a supper consisting of standard military rations. Silk opened one of the metal pots and looked inside. He sighed. "I was afraid of that."

"What's the trouble, Kheldar?" Sadi asked him.

"Beans," Silk replied, pointing at the pot.

"I thought you liked beans."

"Not to eat, I don't."

Because they had not slept the previous night, they retired early. Garion tossed restlessly for a while and then finally dropped off.

The following morning they all slept late, and Garion emerged from the curtained-off compartment he shared with Ce'Nedra to find Silk pacing up and down restlessly. "Finally," the little man said with some relief. "I thought everybody was going to sleep till noon."

"What's your problem?" Garion asked him.

"I need somebody to talk to, that's all."

"Lonesome?"

"No. Edgy. 'Zakath's probably going to show up today. Do you suppose we ought to wake Belgarath?"

"Why?"

"To find out if Beldin's come up with a way to get us out of here, naturally."

"You worry too much."

"My, aren't *we* complacent this morning?" Silk snapped.

"Not really, but there's not much point in chewing off all our fingernails over something that's out of our hands, is there?"

"Garion, why don't you go back to bed?"

"I thought you were lonesome."

"Not that lonesome."

"Has Atesca come by this morning?"

"No. He's probably fairly busy. He's going to have some sort of campaign mapped out by the time 'Zakath gets here." The little man flung himself into one of the folding chairs. "No matter what Beldin comes up with, we're very likely to have at least a regiment hot on our heels when we ride out of here," he predicted, "and I hate being chased."

"We've had people chasing us ever since the night we left Faldor's farm. You should be used to it by now."

"Oh, I am, Garion. I still don't like it, though."

Perhaps an hour or so later, the others began to wake up, and not long after that, the same red-garbed soldiers brought them breakfast. The two men were the only people they had seen since they had been confined in the pavilion.

They spent the rest of the morning in desultory conversation. By unspoken agreement, no one mentioned their present situation.

About noon, General Atesca entered the tent. "His Imperial Majesty will arrive shortly," he announced. "His ships are approaching the docks."

"Thank you, General," Belgarath replied.

Atesca bowed stiffly and went back out.

Polgara rose to her feet. "Come along, ladies," she said to Ce'Nedra and Velvet. "Let's go make ourselves presentable."

Sadi looked down at his plain tunic and hose. "Hardly suitable for an imperial audience," he said. "Do you think we ought to change?"

"Why bother?" Belgarath shrugged. "Let's not give 'Zakath the impression that we take him seriously."

"Don't we?"

"Maybe, but we don't need to let him know about it."

Not much later, the Emperor of Mallorea entered with General Atesca and the Chief of the Bureau of Internal Affairs. As was his custom, 'Zakath wore a plain linen robe, but he had a scarlet military cape draped across his shoulders. His eyes were once again melancholy, and his pallid lips expressionless. "Good day, your Majesty," he said to Garion in a flat, emotionless tone. "You've been well, I trust?"

"Tolerably, your Majesty," Garion replied. If 'Zakath wanted formality, Garion would give him formality.

"Your extensive travels must have been fatiguing," 'Zakath said in that same flat tone, "particularly for the ladies. I'll see to it that your return journey to Mal Zeth is made in easy stages."

"Your Majesty is very kind, but we're not going back to Mal Zeth."

"You're wrong, Belgarion. You *are* going back to Mal Zeth."

"Sorry. I've got a pressing engagement elsewhere."

"I'll convey your regrets to Zandramas when I see her."

"I'm sure she'd be overjoyed to hear that I'm not coming."

"Not for very long, she won't. I fully intend to have her burned as a witch."

"Good luck, your Majesty, but I don't think you'll find that she's very combustible."

"Aren't you gentlemen being just a little silly?" Polgara asked then. She had changed into a blue dress and she sat at a table, calmly mending a pair of Eriond's socks.

"Silly?" 'Zakath snapped, his eyes suddenly flashing.

"You're still friends and you both know it. Now stop behaving like a couple of schoolboys."

"I think you go too far, Lady Polgara," 'Zakath told her in a frigid tone.

"Really?" she replied. "I thought I'd described the situation rather accurately. You're not going to put Garion in chains, and he's not going to turn you into a radish, so stop trying to bully each other."

"I think we can continue this discussion some other time," 'Zakath said curtly. He bowed slightly to Polgara and left the tent.

"Wasn't that perhaps a trifle abrupt, Lady Polgara?" Sadi asked her.

"I don't think so," she replied. "It cut through a lot of nonsense." She carefully folded the socks she had been mending. "Eriond, I think it's time for you to trim your toenails again. You're cutting your way out of your socks faster than I can mend them."

"He's gone back to being the way he was before, hasn't he?" Garion said sadly. " 'Zakath, I mean."

"Not entirely," Polgara disagreed. "Most of that was a pose to conceal his real feelings." She looked at Belgarath. "Well, father, has Uncle Beldin come up with anything yet?"

"He was working on something this morning. I can't talk to him right now because he's chasing a rabbit. We'll get back in touch after he finishes his lunch."

"Can't he concentrate on business?"

"Oh, come now, Pol. I've known you to go out of your way for a fat rabbit on occasion."

"You don't!" Ce'Nedra gasped to Polgara, her eyes wide with sudden horror.

"I really don't think you'd understand, dear," Polgara told her. "Why don't you bring me your gray dress? I noticed a rip in the hem and I've already got my sewing box out."

They waited out the remainder of the afternoon; after supper, they sat around talking quietly.

Silk squinted toward the door of the tent, beyond which the guards were posted. "Any luck with Beldin yet?" he whispered to Belgarath.

"He's working on something—something fairly exotic, I'd imagine, knowing Beldin. He's still hammering out the details. He'll tell me the whole thing once he gets it put together."

"Wouldn't it be better if the two of you worked on it together?"

"He knows what he has to do. I'd just get in his way if I tried to stick my oar in, too." The old man stretched and yawned. Then he stood up. "I don't know about the rest of you," he said, "but I think I'll go to bed."

The next morning, Garion rose quietly, dressed, and slipped out of the curtained-off chamber, leaving Ce'Nedra still asleep.

Durnik and Toth were seated at the table in the main part of the pavilion with Belgarath.

"Don't ask me how he did it," Belgarath was saying. "All he told me was that Cyradis agreed to come here when Toth summoned her."

Durnik and Toth exchanged a few gestures. "He says he can do that," the smith translated. "Do you want her to come here now?"

Belgarath shook his head. "No, let's wait until 'Zakath is in here with us. I know how much it tires her to project her image over long distances." He made a face. "Beldin suggests that we let the conversation get to a climax before we send for her. Beldin has urges in the direction of melodrama sometimes. We've all talked to him about it over the years, but he backslides from time to time. Good morning, Garion."

Garion nodded briefly to each of them, then sat at the table. "What's Cyradis going to be able to do that we can't?" he asked.

"I'm not sure," Belgarath replied. "We all know that she has a peculiar effect on 'Zakath, though. He tends to lose his grip on things every time he sees her. Beldin wouldn't tell me exactly what he's got in mind, but he sounded disgustingly pleased with himself. Do you feel up to some theatricality this morning?"

"Not really, but I suppose I can manage something."

"You're supposed to goad 'Zakath a little—not too much, mind, but push him into making some threats. That's when we're supposed to call Cyradis. Don't be too obvious about it. Sort of lead him into it gradually." The old man looked at Toth. "Keep your eyes on me when Garion and 'Zakath start arguing," he instructed. "I'll cover my mouth and cough. That's when we'll need your mistress."

Toth nodded.

"Are we going to tell the others?" Garion asked.

Belgarath squinted. "No," he decided. "Their reactions might be more natural if they don't know what's going on."

Durnik smiled slightly. "I'd say that Beldin isn't the only one with a flair for the dramatic."

"I used to be a professional storyteller, Durnik," Belgarath reminded him. "I can play an audience like a lute."

After the others had awakened and breakfast had been served, General Atesca came into the tent. "His Imperial Majesty instructs that you make ready. You'll be departing for Mal Zeth within the hour."

Garion moved quickly to head that off. "Tell his Imperial Majesty that we're not going anyplace until we finish the conversation we started yesterday."

Atesca looked momentarily startled, then recovered. "People do not speak so to the Emperor, your Majesty," he declared.

"He might find it refreshing, then."

Atesca drew himself up. "The Emperor is otherwise occupied at the moment."

Garion leaned back in his chair and crossed his legs. "We'll wait," he said flatly. "That will be all, General."

Atesca's face grew tight, then he bowed stiffly, turned, and went out without another word.

"Garion!" Ce'Nedra gasped, "We're at 'Zakath's mercy, and you were being deliberately rude."

"He hasn't been overly polite to me." Garion shrugged. "I told him we weren't going back to Mal Zeth, and he ignored me. It appears that sometimes it takes a bit to get his attention."

Polgara was looking narrowly at Garion. Then she turned to Belgarath. "What are you two up to, father?" she asked.

He winked at her, but did not reply.

It took Kal Zakath approximately two minutes to arrive. He burst into the tent with his eyes wild and his face beet red. "What do you mean?" he almost screamed at Garion.

"What do you mean, what do I mean?"

"I gave you an imperial command!"

"So? I'm not one of your subjects."

"This is intolerable!"

"You'll get used to it. You should know by now that I always do what I set out to do. I thought I'd made that point when we left Mal Zeth. I told you we were going to Ashaba, and that's exactly what we did."

With some effort, the Emperor got himself under control. "I was trying to protect you and your friends, you idiot," he said from between clenched teeth. "You were riding directly into Mengha's path."

"We didn't have any particular problem with Mengha."

"Atesca told me that you'd killed him. I didn't get the details, though." 'Zakath seemed to have recovered his composure to some degree.

"Actually, I'm not the one who did it. Margravine Liselle killed him."

'Zakath looked with one raised eyebrow at the dimpled Velvet.

"His Majesty is perhaps overgenerous," she murmured with a little curtsy. "I had some help."

"Help? From whom?"

"Zith, actually. Mengha was very surprised."

"Will someone *please* tell me what happened without all this clever repartee?"

"It was really fairly simple, your Majesty," Silk said smoothly. "We were having a little disagreement with the Chandim and some others in Torak's old throne room at Ashaba. Mengha was shouting orders to his men, and Liselle pulled Zith out of her bodice and threw the little green darling right into his face. Zith nipped him a few times, he stiffened up like a plank, and he was dead before he hit the floor."

"You don't actually carry that snake down the front of your dress, do you?" 'Zakath asked Velvet incredulously. "How can you?"

"It took a bit of getting used to," she admitted, placing one modest hand on her bodice.

"It didn't *really* happen that way, did it?"

"Prince Kheldar's description of what took place was fairly accurate, your Imperial Majesty," Sadi assured him. "Zith was very put out. I think she was asleep when the Margravine threw her at Mengha, and being awakened suddenly always makes her cross."

"As it turns out, 'Zakath," Belgarath said, "Mengha was really one of the Chandim and Urvon's chief underlings."

"Yes, so Atesca told me. That puts Urvon behind what was going on in Karanda, doesn't it?"

"Only marginally," Belgarath replied. "Urvon isn't sane enough to be behind much of anything. He's completely under the domination of a Demon Lord named Nahaz, and consorting with demons usually unhinges a man's mind. Urvon's totally convinced that he's a God now."

"If he's that mad, who's running his campaign here? Atesca said that his out-flanking of the Darshivan army and their elephant cavalry was a stroke of tactical genius."

"It's my guess that Nahaz is more or less in command, and Demon Lords pay very little attention to casualties. They also have ways of making people run very fast."

"I've never gone to war with a Demon Lord before," 'Zakath mused. "What's his objective?"

"The Sardion," Garion replied. "Everybody wants to get his hands on it—me included."

"To raise a new God over Angarak?"

"That's its purpose, I suppose."

"I don't think I'd like that. You liberated us from Torak, and I don't propose to see his replacement enthroned at either Mal Zeth or Mal Yaska. Angarak doesn't need a God. It has me. Who's your candidate?"

"I don't know yet. They haven't told me."

"What am I going to do with you, Belgarion?" 'Zakath sighed.

"You're going to let us go so we can do what we're supposed to do. You might not like the idea of a New God, but I think you'll find my choice a lot more prefer-able to anything Zandramas or Urvon or Agachak might come up with."

"Agachak?"

"The Hierarch of Rak Urga. He's here in Mallorea as well."

"I'll deal with him, too, then. That still leaves you, I'm afraid."

"I just told you what to do about me."

A faint smile touched 'Zakath's lips. "I don't think I really like your proposal. You're a little undependable."

"What's your goal in all this?" Belgarath asked him.

"I'm going to restore order in Mallorea, even if I have to depopulate whole dis-tricts to do it. Since this Sardion is the thing that's got everyone so agitated, I'd guess that my best course would be to find it and destroy it."

"Good," Garion said, rising to his feet. "Let's go, then."

"Oh, no, your Majesty." 'Zakath's tone was once again coldly imperial. "I don't trust you any more. I made that mistake once already. I can eliminate at least one of the people trying to reach the Sardion by sending you and your friends back to Mal Zeth under heavy guard. Then I can concentrate on looking for the Sardion my-self."

"Where do you plan to start looking?" Garion asked him bluntly. The conver-sation, he decided, had moved around to the point where the goading Belgarath had suggested seemed to be in order. "You don't even know what you're looking for and you haven't got the faintest idea of where to start. You're just floundering around."

"I don't think I care for that, Belgarion."

"That's too bad. The truth is sometimes painful, isn't it?"

"And I suppose you do know where it is?"

"I can find out."

"If you can, so can I, and I'm sure you'll give me a few clues."

"Not a chance."

"You'll grow more cooperative once I put a few of your friends on the rack. I'll even let you watch."

"You'd better hire an expendable torturer, then. Haven't you realized yet just what I'm capable of? And all this time I thought you were intelligent."

"I think that's quite enough, Belgarion," 'Zakath snapped. "Make ready. You're leaving for Mal Zeth; and to make sure you behave yourself, I'm going to separate all of you people. That should give me plenty of hostages in the event you decide to do something rash. I think that covers everything. This conversation is concluded."

Belgarath covered his mouth with one hand and coughed. Toth nodded and lowered his head.

'Zakath stepped back in startled amazement as a shimmering apparition suddenly appeared directly in front of him. He glared at Garion. "Is this some kind of trick?" he demanded.

"No tricks, 'Zakath," Garion replied. "She has some things to tell you. I suggest that you listen."

"Wilt thou hear my words, 'Zakath?" the glowing form of the blindfolded Seeress of Kell asked him.

'Zakath's face was still taut with suspicion. "What is it, Cyradis?" he asked bluntly.

"My time with thee must needs be short, Emperor of Mallorea. I spoke to thee once concerning a crossroad in thy life. Thou hast reached that point now. Put aside thine imperious manner and submit willingly to the task which I must lay upon thee. Thou hast spoken here of hostages."

He drew himself up. "A custom, Cyradis," he told her. "It's a simple means of insuring good behavior."

"Dost thou indeed feel so feeble that thou must threaten the innocent to impose thy will upon others?" Her tone was lightly touched with scorn.

"Feeble? Me?"

"Why else wouldst thou choose so cowardly a course? But hear me well, Kal Zakath, for thy life hangs in the balance. In the instant that thou dost raise thy hand against the Child of Light or any of his companions, thy heart shall burst, and thou shalt die between two breaths."

"So be it then. I rule in Mallorea, and to change or falter because of any threat—even yours—is to become as nothing in my own eyes, and I will not do that."

"Then shalt thou surely die, and in thy death shall thy mighty empire crumble into dust." She said it with a dreadful finality.

He stared at her, his pale face growing even more livid.

"Thou wilt not hear my warnings, Emperor of Mallorea, so I will make thee an offer instead. If thou dost require a hostage, *I* will be thy hostage. The Child of Light doth know that should I depart from this life ere my task is complete, his quest will surely fail. What better restraint canst thou place upon him?"

"I will not threaten you, Holy Seeress," he said, sounding a bit less sure of himself.

"And why not, mighty 'Zakath?"

"It would not be appropriate," he said shortly. "Was that all you had to say to me? I have certain duties to attend to."

"They are of no moment. Thine only true duties are to me and to the task which I shall lay upon thee. The completion of that task is the purpose of thy life. It was for that and for that only that thou wast born. Shouldst thou refuse it, thou wilt not live to see another winter."

"That's the second time you've threatened my life since you arrived, Cyradis. Do you hate me so much?"

"I do not hate thee, 'Zakath, and I made no threats. I merely revealed unto thee that which fate has in store for thee. Wilt thou accept thy task?"

"Not until I know a little more about it."

"Very well, then. I will reveal unto thee the first part of thy task. Thou must come to me at Kell, where I shall submit to thee. I shall be thy hostage, but thou art also surely mine. Come thou then to Kell with the Child of Light and his other chosen companions; for, as hath been foretold since the beginning of days, thou art of their company."

"But—"

She held up one slim hand. "Leave behind thee thy retinue and thine army and thy symbols of power. They will be of no use to thee." She paused. "Or art thou fearful, O mighty 'Zakath, to go about in thy vast realm without thy soldiers clustered about thee to compel the stubborn knee to bend and to coerce the rebellious to submit to thy will?"

'Zakath flushed angrily. "I fear nothing, Holy Seeress," he replied in a cold voice, "not even death."

"Death is a small thing, Kal Zakath. Methinks it is *life* which thou dost fear. As I have said, thou art my hostage, and I command thee to come to me at Kell and there to take up thy burden."

The Emperor of Mallorea began to tremble. Garion knew this man and he knew that 'Zakath would normally reject Cyradis' imperious command instantly, but he appeared seized by some overpowering compulsion. His trembling grew more violent, and his pale face broke out in a sweat.

Cyradis, despite her blindfolded eyes, seemed to be aware of the turmoil which had seized her "hostage." "Thy choice is well made, Kal Zakath," she declared. "Thou wilt submit to me willingly—or with reluctance—but thou *must* submit, for it is thy destiny." She drew herself up. "Speak now, Emperor of Mallorea, for thy fate requires thine acceptance of it. Wilt thou come to me at Kell?"

He seemed to choke on it. "I will come," he croaked.

"So be it then. Take thy foreordained place at Belgarion's side and come to the Holy City. There shall I instruct thee further in thy task and tell thee why it is not merely thy life which doth hinge upon it, but the life of all this world." She turned slightly so that her blindfolded eyes seemed to be looking at Garion. "Bring him to me, Child of Light," she told him, "for all of this is a part of what must come to pass ere the final meeting."

She stretched out her hand to Toth in a gesture of longing.

And then she vanished.

"And now we are twelve," Sadi murmured.

The most recent recruit to their company, however, stood ashen-faced in the center of the tent, and Garion was astonished to see unshed tears standing in the eyes of the Emperor of Mallorea.

CHAPTER EIGHTEEN

"The Empty One," Eriond said with a slight note of satisfaction in his voice. "It's almost complete now."

"I don't quite follow you," Sadi confessed.

"Cyradis came to us at Rheon," the young man explained. "She told us who would come with us to the Place Which Is No More. I've been wondering who the Empty One would be. Now I know."

"And how did she describe me?" the eunuch asked.

"Are you really sure you want to know?"

"I have a certain curiosity about it, yes."

"She called you the Man Who Is No Man."

Sadi winced. "That's direct enough, isn't it?"

"You did ask."

Sadi sighed. "It's all right, Eriond," he said. "The procedure took place when I was a baby, so I've never known what it might be like to be different. Actually, I find all this interest in that particular function slightly amusing. Mine is a much less complicated way of life."

"Why did they do it to you?"

Sadi shrugged, rubbing his hand over his shaved scalp. "My mother was poor," he replied. "It was the only gift she could give me."

"Gift?"

"It gave me the chance for employment in Queen Salmissra's palace. Otherwise, I'd have probably been a street beggar like the rest of my family."

"Are you all right?" Garion asked the ashen-faced 'Zakath.

"Just leave me alone, Garion," 'Zakath muttered.

"Why don't you let me deal with it, dear?" Polgara suggested to Garion. "This is very difficult for him."

"I can understand that. It didn't come too easily for me, either."

"And we broke it to you gently. Cyradis didn't have time to be gentle. I'll talk with him."

"All right, Aunt Pol." Garion walked away and left her alone with the shaken 'Zakath. This particular turn of events gave him some misgivings. Although he liked the Mallorean Emperor personally, he could foresee any number of difficulties arising from the inclusion of this man in their party. Quite often in the past, their very survival had depended entirely upon the absolute oneness of purpose of every member of the group, and 'Zakath's motives were never really clear.

"Garion," the voice in his mind said wearily, *"don't tamper with things you don't understand. 'Zakath has to go with you, so you might as well get used to the idea."*

"But—"

"No buts. Just do it."

Garion muttered a few oaths under his breath.

"And don't swear at me, either."

"This is an absurdity!" 'Zakath burst out, slumping into a chair.

"No," Polgara disagreed. "You just have to get used to looking at the world in a different way, that's all. For most people, that's not necessary. You're a member of a very select group now, and different rules apply."

"Rules have *never* applied to me, Lady Polgara. I make my own rules."

"Not any more."

"Why me?" 'Zakath demanded.

"That's always the first question they ask," Belgarath said drily to Silk.

"Has anybody ever answered it?"

"Not to my knowledge, no."

"We can instruct you as we go along," Polgara assured 'Zakath. "The only important thing right now is whether or not you intend to honor your commitment to Cyradis."

"Of course I do. I gave my word. I don't like it, but I don't have any choice. How can she possibly manipulate me the way she does?"

"She has very strange powers."

"She does it by sorcery, you mean?"

"No. By truth."

"Did you understand any of that gibberish she was speaking?"

"Some of it, but certainly not all. I told you that we look at the world in a different way. The seers look at it in yet another. No one who does not share their vision can fully understand it."

'Zakath stared at the floor. "I suddenly feel very helpless," he admitted, "and I don't like the feeling. I've been rather effectively dethroned, you know. This morning I was the Emperor of the largest nation on earth; this afternoon, I'm going to be a vagabond."

"You might find it refreshing," Silk told him lightly.

"Shut up, Kheldar," 'Zakath said almost absently. He looked back at Polgara. "You know something rather peculiar?"

"What's that?"

"Even if I hadn't given my word, I'd still have to go to Kell. It's almost like a compulsion. I feel as if I'm being driven, and my driver is a blindfolded girl who's hardly more than a child."

"There are rewards," she told him.

"Such as what?"

"Who knows? Happiness, perhaps."

He laughed ironically. "Happiness has never been a driving ambition of mine, Lady Polgara, not for a long time now."

"You may have to accept it anyway." She smiled. "We aren't allowed to choose our rewards any more than we are our tasks. Those decisions are made for us."

"Are *you* happy?"

"Why, yes, as a matter of fact, I am."

He sighed.

"And why so great a sigh, Kal Zakath?"

He held up his thumb and forefinger spread an inch or so apart. "I was that close to becoming the master of the entire world."

"Why would you want to be?"

He shrugged. "No one's ever done it before, and power has its satisfactions."

"You'll find other satisfactions, I'm sure," she smiled, laying one hand on his shoulder.

"It's settled?" Belgarath asked the Mallorean.

"Nothing is ever really settled, Belgarath," 'Zakath replied. "Not until we're in our graves; but yes, I'll go to Kell with you."

"Why don't you send for Atesca, then? You'll need to tell him where you're going, so he can at least cover our rear. I don't like having people sneak up behind me. Has Urvon made it across the Magan as yet?"

"That's very hard to say. Have you looked outside today, Belgarath?"

"The tent door is guarded, and Atesca's soldiers don't encourage sight-seeing."

"The fog's so thick you could walk on it. Urvon could be anyplace out there."

Polgara rose and quickly crossed to the tent flap. She opened it, and one of the guards outside said something to her sharply.

"Oh, don't be silly," she told him. Then she took several deep breaths and closed the flap. "It's not natural, father," she said soberly. "It doesn't smell right."

"Grolims?"

"I think so, yes. Probably Chandim trying to conceal Urvon's forces from Atesca's patrol boats. They should be able to cross the Magan without much difficulty."

"Once they get across, the trip to Kell might just turn into a horse race."

"I'll talk to Atesca," 'Zakath said. "He might be able to delay them a bit." He looked speculatively at the old man.

"I know why I'm going to Kell," he said, "but why are *you*?"

"I have to read the Mallorean Gospels to find out what our ultimate destination is."

"You mean you don't know?"

"Not yet, no. I know what it's called, though. They keep calling it the Place Which Is No More."

"Belgarath, that's pure gibberish."

"I didn't come up with the name, so don't blame me."

"Why didn't you say something back at Mal Zeth? I have a copy of the Gospels in my library."

"In the first place, I didn't know about it when I was at Mal Zeth. I only found out recently. In the second place, your copy wouldn't have done me any good. They're all different, I'm told, and the only one that contains the passage I need is at Kell."

"It all sounds very complicated."

"It is. These things usually are."

'Zakath went to the door of the tent and spoke briefly with one of the guards posted there. Then he came back. "I've sent for Atesca and Brador," he said. He smiled a bit ruefully. "I wouldn't be surprised if they objected rather violently to this whole thing."

"Don't give them time to object," Garion advised.

"They're both Melcenes, Garion," 'Zakath pointed out. "Melcenes object to things out of habit." He frowned. "Speaking of that, why did you go to Melcena? Wasn't it a bit out of your way?"

"We were following Zandramas," Garion replied.

"Why did *she* go there?"

"She had to pick up your cousin, Archduke Otrath."

"That silly ass? What for?"

"She took him to Hemil and crowned him Emperor of Mallorea."

"She did *what?*" 'Zakath's eyes bulged.

"She needs an Angarak king with her when she gets to the Place Which Is No More. As I understand it, the coronation ceremony had a certain validity."

"Not after I get my hands on Otrath, it won't!" 'Zakath's face was scarlet with anger.

"There was another reason for our going to Melcena—although we didn't know it at the time," Belgarath said. "There was an unmutilated copy of the Ashabine Oracles there. I had to read that in order to find out that our next step is the trip to Kell. I'm following a trail that was laid down for me thousands of years ago."

Atesca and Brador entered. "You sent for us, your Majesty?" Atesca said with a crisp salute.

"Yes," 'Zakath replied. He looked at the two of them speculatively. "Please listen carefully," he instructed, "and try not to argue with me." Oddly he said it not so much in the tone of imperial command, but rather as a man appealing to two old friends. "There's been a change of plans," he went on. "Certain information has come into my possession, and it's absolutely imperative that we not interfere with Belgarion and his friends. Their mission is vital to the security of Mallorea."

Brador's eyes came alight with curiosity. "Shouldn't I perhaps be briefed on this matter, your Imperial Majesty?" he asked. "State security is my responsibility, after all."

"Ah—no, Brador," 'Zakath said regretfully, "I'm afraid not. It might require too great an adjustment in your thinking. You're not ready for that. As a matter of fact, I'm not sure I am, either. At any rate, Belgarion and these others absolutely *must* go to Dalasia." He paused. "Oh, one other thing," he added. "I'll be going with them."

Atesca stared incredulously at his Emperor. Then, with some effort, he got himself under control. "I'll notify the commander of the Imperial Guard, your Majesty," he said stiffly. "They'll be ready to leave within the hour."

"Don't bother," 'Zakath told him. "They won't be going with us. I'll be going with Belgarion alone."

"Alone?" Atesca exclaimed. "Your Majesty, that's unheard of."

'Zakath smiled wanly. "You see," he said to Garion. "What did I tell you?"

"General," Belgarath said to Atesca, "Kal Zakath is simply following orders. I'm sure you can understand that. He was told not to bring any troops along. Troops wouldn't do him any good where we're going anyway."

"Orders?" Atesca said in amazement. "Who has the authority to give his Majesty orders?"

"It's a long story, Atesca," the old man told him, "and we're pressed for time."

"Ah—your Imperial Majesty," Brador said diffidently, "if you're going to Dalasia, that means you'll have to cross the whole of Darshiva. Might I remind you that Darshiva is hostile territory at the moment? Is it wise to risk the imperial person under such circumstances? Might not an escort at least as far as the border be prudent?"

'Zakath looked at Belgarath.

The old man shook his head. "Let's just do it the way we were told to," he said.

"Sorry, Brador," 'Zakath said. "We can't take an escort with us. I think I'll need some armor, though, and a sword."

"Your Majesty has not held a sword for years," Atesca objected.

"Belgarion can give me some instruction." 'Zakath shrugged. "I'm sure I'll pick it up again. Now then, Urvon's going to cross the Magan. I have it on very good authority that there won't be very much we can do to stop him. I imagine that the Darshivan Army won't be very far behind him, and they have elephant cavalry with them. I want you to keep all those people off my back. Delay Urvon long enough for the Darshivans to catch up with him. After that, they can annihilate each other, for all I care. Once those two armies are fully engaged, pull back your forces. Don't get any more of my soldiers killed than you absolutely have to."

Atesca frowned. "Then the policy we discussed at Maga Renn is no longer in force?" he asked.

'Zakath shrugged. "Policy changes from time to time," he said. "At this point, I'm militantly indifferent about who wins an unimportant battle in this corner of the world. That may give you some idea of just how vital Belgarion's mission is." He looked at Garion. "Does that cover everything?"

"Except for the demons," Garion replied. "They're here in Darshiva, too."

'Zakath frowned. "I'd forgotten about them. They'll come to Urvon's aid, won't they?"

"Nahaz will," Belgarath told him. "Mordja will help the Darshivans."

"You're going a little fast for me."

"When Urvon showed up with Nahaz in tow, Zandramas raised a Demon Lord of her own," the old man explained. "She went a little far afield for him, actually. Mordja is Lord over the demons in Morindland. He and Nahaz are evenly matched, and they've hated each other for all eternity."

"Then it still appears to be a stalemate. Both sides have an army and they both have demons."

"Demons are grossly unselective in their choice of victims, 'Zakath," Polgara said. "They'll kill anything that moves, and your own army's here in Darshiva."

"I hadn't thought of that," he conceded. He looked around. "Any suggestions?"

Belgarath and Polgara exchanged a long look. "I suppose it's worth a try," the old sorcerer shrugged. "He's not fond of Angaraks, but He's even less fond of demons. I think we'll have better luck with Him if we go outside the camp, though."

"Exactly who are we talking about?" 'Zakath asked curiously.

"Aldur," Belgarath replied. He scratched at his cheek. "Would it be safe to tell Him that you'd be very reluctant to go with us if your army was in danger?" he asked.

"I think you could say that, yes." 'Zakath's eyes widened. "Are you trying to say you can actually summon a God?" he asked incredulously.

"I'm not sure if summon is exactly the right word. We can talk with Him, though. We'll see what He says."

"You're not really going to try subterfuge, are you, father?" Polgara asked the old man.

"Aldur knows what I'm doing," he replied. "I couldn't deceive Him if I tried. 'Zakath's reluctance just gives us a starting point for the conversation. Aldur's reasonable, but He's always liked a good argument. You should know that, Pol. He helped to educate you, after all. Let's see if we can talk with Him."

"Would it be all right if I came along?" Eriond asked. "I need to talk with Him, too."

Belgarath looked a bit surprised at that. He looked for a moment as if he were about to refuse, but then he seemed to change his mind. "Suit yourself," he shrugged. "Atesca, could you have your guards escort us as far as that ditch around the outside of the camp? We'll go on from there alone."

Atesca spoke with the guards at the door of the tent, and the three were allowed to leave without challenge.

"I'd give a great deal to witness this meeting," Brador murmured. "Have you ever seen Aldur, Prince Kheldar?"

"A couple of times, yes," Silk replied in an offhand manner. "Once in the Vale and then again at Cthol Mishrak when He and the other Gods came to claim the body of Torak after Garion killed Him."

"I'd imagine that He took a certain satisfaction in that," 'Zakath said. "Aldur and Torak were sworn enemies."

"No," Garion disagreed sadly. "No one took any pleasure in the death of Torak. He and Aldur were brothers. I think UL grieved the most, though. Torak was His son, after all."

"There seem to be some fairly huge gaps in Angarak theology," 'Zakath mused. "I don't think the Grolims even admit the existence of UL."

"They would if they ever saw Him," Silk said.

"Is He really that impressive-looking?" Brador asked.

"It's not so much the way He looks." Silk shrugged.

"It's the sense of His presence. It's overwhelming."

"He was very nice to *me*," Ce'Nedra objected.

"Everybody's nice to you, Ce'Nedra," Silk told her. "You have that effect on people."

"Most of the time," Garion corrected.

"I suppose we'd better start packing," Durnik suggested. "I think Belgarath's going to want to leave just as soon as he gets back." He looked at Atesca. "Do you suppose we could get a few things from your stores?" he asked. "It's a long way to Kell, and I don't think we'll be able to pick up much in the way of supplies here in Darshiva."

"Of course, Goodman Durnik," the general replied.

"I'll make out a list of the things we'll need, then."

As Durnik sat down at the table to draw up his list, Atesca gave Silk a penetrating look. "We never did get the chance to talk about your recent venture in the commodities market, did we, your Highness?" he said.

"Are you considering a second career, Atesca?" 'Zakath asked him.

"Hardly, your Majesty. I'm quite happy as a soldier. Prince Kheldar recently did a bit of speculation in this year's bean crop. The Bureau of Military Procurement went into a state of anguished consternation when they found out his asking price."

Brador suddenly chuckled. "Good for you, Kheldar," he said.

"That's a peculiar attitude, Brador," 'Zakath reproved him. "How would you like it if I took Prince Kheldar's excess profits out of your budget?"

"Actually, your Majesty, Kheldar's venture didn't cost your treasury a thing. The members of the Bureau of Military Procurement are the greatest unhanged scoundrels in the empire. Some years ago, while you were busy in Cthol Murgos, they sent you a rather innocuous-looking document having to do with standardizing the prices of all the items they purchase for the army."

"I remember it—vaguely. Their argument seemed to be that it would provide a basis for long-range planning."

"That was on the surface, your Majesty. In actuality, fixing those prices provided them with a golden opportunity to line their own pockets. They could buy at below the fixed price, sell to the army at the legal rate, and keep the difference for themselves."

"What is the fixed rate on beans?"

"Ten half-crowns per hundredweight, your Majesty."

"That doesn't seem unreasonable."

"When they're buying at three half-crowns?"

'Zakath stared at him.

Brador held up one hand. "However," he said, "by law, they *have* to sell to the army at ten—no matter what price they have to pay, so they have to make up the difference out of their own pockets. That might account for the anguish General Atesca mentioned."

'Zakath suddenly grinned a wolfish sort of grin. "What price were you asking, Kheldar?" he asked.

"I sold out to the Melcene Consortium at fifteen." The little man shrugged, buffing his nails on the front of his tunic. "I'd imagine that they added a few points to that—reasonable profit, you understand."

"And you controlled the entire bean crop?"

"I certainly tried."

"I feel fairly sure that your Majesty will receive several letters of resignation from members of the Bureau," Brador said. "I'd advise not accepting them until *after* all accounts are settled."

"I'll keep that in mind, Brador." 'Zakath looked speculatively at Silk. "Tell me, Kheldar," he said, "how much would you take to suspend operations here in Mallorea?"

"I don't really believe your Majesty's treasury has that much money," Silk replied blandly. "Besides, I've become a sort of necessity. The Mallorean economy was stagnant until I got here. You could almost say that I'm working for you."

"Did that make any sense?" 'Zakath asked Brador.

"Yes, your Majesty," Brador sighed. "In a peculiar way, it does. Our tax revenues have been rising steadily since Kheldar and his scruffy-looking partner began doing business here in the empire. If we were to expel him, it's entirely possible that the economy would collapse."

"Then I'm at his mercy?"

"To some degree, yes, your Majesty."

'Zakath sighed mournfully. "I wish I hadn't gotten out of bed this morning," he said.

Both Belgarath and Polgara looked troubled when they returned with Eriond close behind them. The blond young man, however, looked as unconcerned as always.

"What did He say?" Garion asked.

"He didn't like it too much," Belgarath said, "but He finally agreed. General Atesca, how many troops do you have here in Darshiva?"

"Several hundred thousand. They're in enclaves like this one up and down the east bank of the Magan. The bulk of our forces are across the river in Peldane. We can summon them on short notice."

"Leave them where they are. Once you've delayed Urvon long enough to allow the Darshivan army to catch up with him, withdraw all your men to this enclave."

"It's hardly big enough for that many men, Ancient One," Atesca pointed out.

"You'd better expand it, then. Aldur has agreed to protect this enclave. He didn't say anything about any of the others. Bring your men here. He'll keep the demons away."

"How?" Brador asked curiously.

"Demons can't bear the presence of a God. Neither Nahaz nor Mordja will come within ten leagues of this place."

"He's actually going to be here?"

"Only in a rather peculiar sense of the word. Once the enclave is expanded, that ditch of yours is going to be filled with a kind of blue light. Tell your men to stay out of it. Aldur's still not fond of Angaraks, and peculiar things might happen to any soldier who strays into that light." The old man suddenly grinned at 'Zakath. "You might find it interesting to know that your whole army here in Darshiva will be at least nominally subject to Aldur for a while," he said. "He's never had an army before, so it's a little hard to say what he might decide to do with one."

"Is your grandfather always like this?" 'Zakath asked Garion.

"Usually, yes." Garion stood up, moving his fingers slightly. Then he crossed to the far side of the tent. Belgarath followed him. "What happened out there, Grandfather?" Garion whispered.

Belgarath shrugged. "We talked with Aldur, and He promised to protect 'Zakath's army."

Garion shook his head. "No," he said, "something else happened, too. Both you and Aunt Pol were looking very strange when you came back—and why did Eriond go with you?"

"It's a long story," the old man replied evasively.

"I've got time. I think I'd better know what's going on."

"No, as a matter of fact, you'd better not. Aldur was quite emphatic about that. If you know what's happening, it might interfere with what you have to do."

"I thought we'd exhausted that tired old excuse a long time ago. I'm grown now. You don't have to try to keep me stupid."

"I'll tell you what, Garion. Since you're the Child of Light, why don't you go talk with Aldur yourself? He might even decide to tell you, but that's up to Him. He told me to keep my mouth shut, and I'm not going to disobey my Master, whether you like it or not." And he turned and went back to rejoin the others.

CHAPTER NINETEEN

"I still don't understand why I have to look so shabby," 'Zakath said as he reentered the pavilion. He wore a battered breastplate over a mail shirt and a rust-splotched helmet devoid of any kind of decoration. A patched brown cloak was draped over his shoulders, and a plain, leather-bound sword hung at his side.

"Explain it to him, Silk," Belgarath said. "You're the expert at this sort of thing."

"It's really not all that complicated," Silk told the Emperor. "It's fairly standard practice for travelers to hire a few mercenary soldiers to act as armed guards. Mercenaries don't usually spend all that much time taking care of their equipment, so we had to make you look a bit down at the heels. All you and Garion have to do is wear armor and ride in front looking dangerous."

A faint smile touched the Mallorean's pallid features. "I didn't think anonymity would require such pains."

Silk grinned at him. "Actually, it's harder to be anonymous than it is to be a grand duke. Now, please don't be offended, 'Zakath, but we're all going to forget we know how to say 'your Majesty.' Someone might make a slip at the wrong time."

"That's perfectly all right, Kheldar," 'Zakath replied. "All the 'Majesties' grate on my ears sometimes anyway."

Silk looked closely at their newest recruit's face. "You really ought to spend more time outside, you know. You're as pale as a sheet."

"I can take care of that, Silk," Polgara said. "I'll mix up something to make him look suitably weather-beaten."

"Oh, one other thing," Silk added. "Your face is on every coin in Mallorea, isn't it?"

"You should know. You've got most of them, haven't you?"

"Well, I've picked up a few here and there," Silk said modestly. "Let's cover up that famous face with whiskers. Stop shaving."

"Kheldar, I haven't shaved my own face since my beard sprouted. I wouldn't even know how to hold a razor."

"You let somebody else near your throat with a razor? Isn't that a trifle imprudent?"

"Does that more or less cover everything?" Belgarath asked the little Drasnian.

"That covers the basics," Silk replied. "I can coach him on the finer details as we go along."

"All right, then." The old man looked around at them. "We're likely to encounter people out there. Some of them might be hostile, but most of them will probably just be trying to stay out of harm's way, so they won't bother a group of ordinary travelers." He looked directly at 'Zakath. "Silk should be able to talk us out of most situations, but if we get into any serious confrontations, I want you to fall back a bit and let the rest of us handle things. You're out of practice with your weapons, and I didn't go to all the trouble of finding you to lose you in some meaningless skirmish."

"I can still carry my own weight, Belgarath."

"I'm sure you can, but let's not risk it right at first. Cyradis might be very unhappy if we don't have you with us in one piece when we get to Kell."

'Zakath shrugged, walked over, and sat on the bench beside Garion. The Rivan King was dressed in his mail shirt and he was sliding the snug-fitting leather sleeve over the hilt of Iron-grip's sword. 'Zakath was actually grinning, and the unaccustomed expression made him look ten years younger. Garion was uncomfortably reminded of Lelldorin. "I think you're actually enjoying this, aren't you?" he asked.

"For some reason, I feel almost like a young man again," 'Zakath replied. "Is it always like this—subterfuge and a little danger and this wild sense of exhilaration?"

"More or less," Garion replied. "Sometimes there's more than just a little danger, though."

"I can live with that. My life's been tediously secure so far."

"Even when Naradas poisoned you back in Cthol Murgos?"

"I was too sick to know what was going on," 'Zakath said. "I envy you, Garion. You've had a wildly exciting life." He frowned slightly. "Something rather peculiar is happening to me," he confessed. "Ever since I agreed to meet Cyradis at Kell, I've felt as if some vast weight had been lifted off me. The whole world looks fresh and new now. I have absolutely no control over my life, and yet I'm as happy as a fish in deep water. It's irrational, but I can't help it."

Garion looked rather closely at him. "Don't misunderstand," he said. "I'm not deliberately trying to be mystical about this, but you're probably happy because you're doing what you're supposed to do. It happens to all of us. It's a part of that different way of looking at things Aunt Pol mentioned earlier, and it's one of the rewards she talked about."

"That's a little obscure for me," 'Zakath admitted.

"Give it some time," Garion told him. "It comes to you gradually."

General Atesca entered the tent with Brador close behind him. "The horses are ready, your Majesty," he reported in a neutral tone. Garion could tell by Atesca's expression that he still strongly disapproved of this whole business. The General turned to Durnik. "I've added a few more pack animals, Goodman," he said. "Yours were fairly well loaded down."

"Thank you, General," Durnik replied.

"I'm going to be out of touch, Atesca," 'Zakath said, "so I'm leaving you in charge here. I'll try to get word to you from time to time, but there may be long periods when you won't hear from me."

"Yes, your Majesty," Atesca replied.

"You know what to do, though. Let Brador handle civil matters, and you deal with the military situation. Get the troops back here to this enclave as soon as Urvon and the Darshivans are engaged. And keep in touch with Mal Zeth." He tugged a large signet ring off his finger. "Use this if you need to seal any official documents."

"Such documents require your Majesty's signature," Atesca reminded him.

"Brador can forge it. He writes my name better than I do myself."

"Your Majesty!" Brador protested.

"Don't play innocent with me, Brador. I've known about your experiments in penmanship. Take care of my cat while I'm gone, and see if you can find homes for the rest of those kittens."

"Yes, your Majesty."

"Anything else that needs my attention before I leave?"

"Ah—one thing, your Majesty," Atesca said. "A disciplinary matter."

"Can't you take care of it?" 'Zakath asked a bit irritably. He was obviously impatient to be off.

"I can, your Majesty," Atesca said, "but you've sort of placed the man under your personal protection, so I thought I'd consult with you before I took action."

"Whom am I protecting?" 'Zakath looked puzzled.

"It's a corporal from the Mal Zeth garrison, your Majesty—a man named Actas. He was drunk on duty."

"Actas? I don't recall—"

"It was that corporal who'd been demoted just before we arrived in Mal Zeth," Ce'Nedra reminded him. "The one whose wife was making such a scene in that side street."

"Oh, yes," 'Zakath said. "Now I remember. Drunk, you say? He's not supposed to drink any more."

"I doubt if he could drink any more, your Majesty," Atesca said with a faint smile, "at least not right now. He's as drunk as a lord."

"Is he nearby?"

"Just outside, your Majesty."

'Zakath sighed. "I guess you'd better bring him in," he said. He looked at Belgarath. "This should only take a moment or two," he apologized.

Garion remembered the scrawny corporal as soon as the fellow staggered into the tent. The corporal tried to come to attention, without much success. Then he attempted to bang his breastplate in a salute, but hit himself in the nose with his fist instead. "Yer Imperrl Majeshy," he slurred.

"What am I going to do with you, Actas," 'Zakath said wearily.

"I've made a beash of myshelf, yer Majeshy," Actas confessed, "an absholute beash."

"Yes," 'Zakath agreed, "you have." He turned his head away. "Please don't breathe on me, Actas. Your mouth smells like a reopened grave. Take him out and sober him up, Atesca."

"I'll personally throw him in the river, your Majesty." Atesca was trying to suppress a grin.

"You're enjoying this, aren't you?"

"Me, your Majesty?"

'Zakath's eyes narrowed slyly. "Well, Ce'Nedra?" he said. "He's your responsibility, too. What do we do with him?"

She waved one little hand negligently. "Hang him," she said in an indifferent tone. She looked more closely at her hand. "Great Nedra!" she exclaimed. "I've broken another fingernail!"

Corporal Actas' eyes were bulging and his mouth was suddenly agape. Trembling violently, he fell to his knees. "Please, your Majesty," he begged, suddenly cold sober. "Please!"

'Zakath squinted at the Rivan Queen, who sat mourning the broken nail. "Take him outside, Atesca," he said. "I'll give you orders for his final disposition in a moment."

Atesca saluted and hauled the blubbering Actas to his feet.

"You weren't really serious, were you, Ce'Nedra?" 'Zakath asked after the two men had left.

"Oh, of course not," she said. "I'm not a monster, 'Zakath. Clean him up and send him back to his wife." She tapped one finger thoughtfully on her chin. "*But* erect a gibbet in the street in front of his house. Give him something to think about the next time he gets thirsty."

"You actually *married* this woman?" 'Zakath exclaimed to Garion.

"It was sort of arranged by our families," Garion replied with aplomb. "We didn't have much to say about it."

"Now, be nice, Garion," Ce'Nedra said with unruffled calm.

They mounted their horses outside the pavilion and rode through the camp to the drawbridge spanning the deep, stake-studded ditch that formed a part of the outer fortifications. When they reached the far side of the ditch, 'Zakath let out an explosive breath of relief.

"What is it?" Garion asked him.

"I was half afraid that somebody might have found a way to keep me there." He glanced a bit apprehensively back over his shoulder. "Do you think we could possibly gallop for a ways?" he asked. "I'd hate to have them catch up with me."

Garion began to have misgivings at that point. "Are you sure you're all right?" he asked suspiciously.

"I've never felt better—or more free—in my entire life," 'Zakath declared.

"I was afraid of that," Garion muttered.

"What?"

"Just keep moving at a canter, 'Zakath. There's something I need to discuss with Belgarath. I'll be right back." He reined Chretienne in and rode back to where his grandfather and his aunt rode side by side, deep in conversation. "He's absolutely out of control," he told them. "What's happened to him?"

"It's the first time in his entire life that he hasn't had the weight of half the world on his shoulders, Garion," Polgara replied calmly. "He'll settle down. Just give him a day or so."

"Do we have a day or so? He's acting exactly the way Lelldorin would—or maybe even Mandorallen. Can we afford that?"

"Talk to him," Belgarath suggested. "Just keep talking. Recite the *Book of Alorn* to him if you have to."

"But I don't know the *Book of Alorn,* Grandfather," Garion objected.

"Yes, you do. It's in your blood. You could have recited it letter-perfect in your cradle. Now get back up there before he gets completely out of hand."

Garion swore and rode back to rejoin 'Zakath.

"Trouble?" Silk asked him.

"I don't want to talk about it."

Beldin was waiting for them around the next bend in the road. "Well," the grotesque little hunchback said. "It seems to have worked, but why did you bring him along?"

"Cyradis persuaded him to come with us," Belgarath replied. "What gave you the idea of going to her?"

"It was worth a try. Pol told me about a few of the things she said to him back in Cthol Murgos. She seems to have some sort of interest in him. I didn't really think he was supposed to join us, though. What did she say to him?"

"She told him that he'd die if he didn't come with us."

"I imagine that got his attention. Hello, 'Zakath."

"Do we know each other?"

"I know you—by sight, anyway. I've seen you parading through the streets of Mal Zeth a few times."

"This is my brother Beldin," Belgarath introduced the misshapen dwarf.

"I didn't know you had any brothers."

"The relationship's a bit obscure, but we serve the same Master, so that makes us brothers in a peculiar sort of way. There used to be seven of us, but there are only four of us left now."

'Zakath frowned slightly. "Your name rings a bell, Master Beldin," he said. "Aren't you the one whose picture is posted on every tree for six leagues in any direction from Mal Yaska?"

"I believe that's me, all right. I make Urvon a little nervous. He seems to think that I want to split him up the middle."

"Do you?"

"I've thought about it a time or two. I think what I'd really like to do, though, is yank out his guts, hang them on a thornbush, and invite in some vultures. I'm sure he'd find watching them eat very entertaining."

'Zakath blanched slightly.

"Vultures have to eat, too." The hunchback shrugged. "Oh, speaking of eating, Pol, do you have anything decent around? All I've had in the last few days was a very scrawny rat and a nest full of crow's eggs. I don't think there's a rabbit or a pigeon left in the whole of Darshiva."

"This is a very unusual fellow," 'Zakath said to Garion.

"He gets more unusual the more you get to know him." Garion smiled slightly. "He frightened Urvon almost into sanity at Ashaba."

"He was exaggerating, wasn't he—about the vultures, I mean?"

"Probably not. He fully intends to gut Torak's last Disciple like a butchered hog."

'Zakath's eyes grew bright. "You think he might want some help?" he asked eagerly.

"Were any of your ancestors possibly Arendish?" Garion asked suspiciously.

"I don't understand the question."

"Never mind." Garion sighed.

Beldin squatted in the dirt at the roadside, tearing at the carcass of a cold roast chicken. "You burnt it, Pol," he accused.

"I didn't cook it, uncle," she replied primly.

"Why not? Did you forget how?"

"I have a wonderful recipe for boiled dwarf," she told him. "I'm almost sure I could find someone willing to eat that sort of thing."

"You're losing your edge again, Pol," he said, wiping his greasy fingers on the front of his ragged tunic. "Your mind's getting as flabby as your bottom."

Garion restrained 'Zakath with one hand when the Mallorean Emperor's face grew outraged. "It's a personal thing," he cautioned. "I wouldn't interfere. They've been insulting each other for thousands of years. It's a peculiar kind of love, I think."

"Love?"

"Listen," Garion suggested. "You might learn something. Alorns aren't like Angaraks. We don't bow very often and we sometimes hide our feelings with jokes."

"Polgara is an Alorn?" 'Zakath sounded surprised.

"Use your eyes, man. Her hair's dark, I'll grant you, but her twin sister was as blond as a wheat field. Look at her cheekbones and her jaw. I rule a kingdom of Alorns and I know what they look like. She and Liselle could be sisters."

"Now that you mention it, they do look a bit alike, don't they? How is it I never saw that before?"

"You hired Brador to be your eyes," Garion replied, shifting his mail shirt. "I don't trust other peoples' eyes all that much."

"Is Beldin an Alorn, too?"

"Nobody knows what Beldin is. He's so deformed that you can't put a name to him."

"Poor fellow."

"Don't waste your pity on Beldin," Garion replied. "He's six thousand years old and he could turn you into a frog if he felt like it. He can make it snow or rain, and he's far, far smarter than Belgarath."

"But he's so grubby," 'Zakath said, eyeing the filthy dwarf.

"He's grubby because he doesn't care," Garion said. "This is the form he uses to go among us. It's ugly, so he doesn't waste time on it. His other form is so magnificent it would blind you."

"Other form?"

"It's a peculiarity of ours. Sometimes a human form isn't practical for some of the things we have to do. Beldin likes to fly, so he spends most of his time as a blue-banded hawk."

"I'm a falconer, Garion. I don't believe there is such a bird."

"Tell *him* that." Garion pointed at the ugly dwarf ripping the chicken apart with his teeth by the roadside.

"You could have cut it up first, uncle," Polgara said.

"Why?" He took another huge bite.

"It's more polite."

"Pol, I taught you how to fly and how to hunt. Don't you try to teach me how to eat."

"I don't think 'eat' is the right word, uncle. You're not an eater; you're a ravener."

"We all do it our own way, Pol." He belched. "You do it with a silver fork off a porcelain plate, and I do it with my talons and beak in a ditch beside the road. It all gets to the same place no matter how you do it." He raked a patch of burned skin off the chicken leg he was holding in one hand. "This isn't too bad," he conceded, "at least not after you get down to the real meat."

"Anything up ahead?" Belgarath asked him.

"A few troops, some terrified civilians, and a Grolim now and then. That's about it."

"Any demons?"

"I didn't see any. Of course that doesn't mean they're not lurking around somewhere. You know how it is with demons. Are you going to travel at night again?"

Belgarath thought about it. "I don't think so," he decided. "It takes too long to do it that way, and time's running out on us. Let's just make a run for it."

"Suit yourself." Beldin discarded the remains of the chicken and stood up. "I'll keep an eye out up ahead and let you know when you're about to run into trouble." The hunchback bent, spread his arms, and soared up into the murky sky.

"Torak's teeth!" 'Zakath exclaimed. "He *is* a blue-banded hawk!"

"He invented it himself," Belgarath said. "He didn't like the regular colors. Let's move along."

Although it was nearly summer, there was a dreary chill hanging over Darshiva. Garion could not be certain if it was the result of the prevailing overcast or if it derived from some other, more ominous, source. The white snags of dead trees lined the road, and the air was thick with the reek of fungus, decay, and stagnant water. They passed long-deserted villages tumbled now into ruins. A roadside temple seemed to huddle mournfully with fungus creeping up its walls like some loathesome disease. Its doors gaped open, and the polished steel mask of the face of Torak, which should have surmounted them, was gone. Belgarath reined in his horse and dismounted. "I'll be right back," he said. He went up the steps of the temple and looked inside. Then he turned and came back. "I thought they might have done that," he said.

"Done what, father?" Aunt Pol asked him.

"They've taken Torak's face down from the wall behind the altar. There's a blank mask there now. They're waiting to see what the New God looks like."

They took shelter for the night beside the half-tumbled wall of a ruined village. They built no fire and traded off standing watch. At first light the next morning, they pushed on. The countryside grew more bleak and foreboding with each passing mile.

About midmorning, Beldin swooped in, flared his wings, and settled to earth. He shimmered into his own form and stood waiting for them. "There are some troops blocking the road about a mile ahead," he announced.

"Any chance of getting around them?" Belgarath asked.

"I doubt it. The country's pretty flat there, and all the vegetation's been dead for years."

"How many are there?" Silk asked.

"Fifteen or so. They've got a Grolim with them."

"Any idea which side they're on?" Belgarath said.

"They're not that distinctive."

"Do you want me to see if I can talk our way past them?" Silk offered.

Belgarath looked at Beldin. "Are they deliberately blocking the road, or are they just camped on it?"

"They've built a barricade out of dead logs."

"That answers that, then. Talk isn't going to do us any good." He mulled it over.

"We could wait until dark and then slip around them," Velvet suggested.

"We'd lose a whole day that way," Belgarath replied. "I don't see any help for it. We're going to have to go through them. Try not to kill any more of them than you absolutely have to."

"That gets right to the point, doesn't it?" 'Zakath said wryly to Garion.

"There's no sense in trying to surprise them, I suppose?" Belgarath asked Beldin.

The dwarf shook his head. "They'll see you coming for at least a half a mile." He went to the side of the road, wrenched a half-rotten stump out of the ground, and pounded it against a rock until all the decayed wood had been knocked loose. The gnarled taproot made a fearsome-looking cudgel.

"Well, I guess we'd better go have a look," Belgarath said bleakly.

They rode on to the crest of the hill and looked down the road toward the barricade and the troops standing behind it. 'Zakath peered at them. "Darshivans," he said.

"How can you tell from this distance?" Silk asked him.

"By the shape of their helmets." The Mallorean narrowed his eyes. "Darshivan soldiers are not notoriously brave and they get very little in the way of training. Do you think there might be some way we can lure them out from behind that barricade?"

Garion looked down at the soldiers crouched behind their logs. "I'd say they've been told not to let anybody past," he said. "What if we charge them and then at the last minute swing out and around them? They'll run for their horses. Then we turn around and charge back at them. They'll be confused and milling around, and we'll be able to pin them up against their own barricade. It shouldn't be too hard to put a fair number of them on the ground. The rest should run at that point."

"That's not a bad plan, Garion. You're quite a tactician. Have you had any formal military training?"

"No. I just picked it up."

In a land of brittle, dead trees, a lance was quite out of the question, so Garion strapped his shield to his left arm and drew his sword.

"All right," Belgarath said, "let's give it a try. It might hold down the casualties."

"One other thing," Silk added. "I think we should make a special point of not letting any of them get on a horse. A man on foot can't go for help very fast. If we run off their horses, we can be out of the area before they can bring in reinforcements."

"I'll take care of that," Belgarath said. "All right. Let's go."

They urged their horses into a gallop and charged down the road toward the barricade, brandishing their weapons. As they pounded down the hill, Garion saw 'Zakath pulling a curious-looking leather half-glove clad with steel onto his right hand.

Just before they reached the barricade and the alarmed soldiers standing behind it, they veered sharply to the left, then galloped around the obstruction and back onto the road.

"After them!" a black-robed Grolim screamed at the startled troops. "Don't let them escape!"

Garion rode on past the soldiers' picketed horses, then wheeled Chretienne around. He charged back with the others close on his heels and rode full into the face of the confused Darshivans. He did not really want to kill any of them, so he laid about him with the flat of the blade rather than the edge. He put three of them down as he crashed through their ranks; behind him he could hear the sound of blows and cries of pain. The Grolim rose before him, and he could feel the black-robed man drawing in his will. He did not falter, but simply rode the priest down. Then he wheeled again. Toth was laying about him with his heavy staff, and Durnik was busily caving in helmets with the butt of his axe. 'Zakath, however, was leaned far over in his saddle. He had no weapon in his hand but rather was smashing his metal-clad fist into the faces of the Darshivan soldiers. The glove appeared to be quite effective.

Then, from where the soldiers' horses were picketed, there came a blood-curdling howl. The great silver wolf was snapping and snarling at the horses. They lunged back in panic, the picket rope snapped, and they fled.

"Let's go!" Garion shouted to his friends, and they galloped once again through the center of the Darshivans and on down the road to rejoin Polgara, Ce'Nedra, Velvet, and Eriond. Belgarath loped after them, then changed into his own form and walked back to his horse.

"It seems to have worked more or less the way we'd planned," 'Zakath noted. He was panting, and his forehead was dewed with sweat. "I seem to be a bit out of condition, though," he added.

"Too much sitting down," Silk said. "What's that thing you've got on your hand?"

"It's called a cestus," the Mallorean replied, pulling it off. "I'm a little rusty with my sword, so I thought this might work just as well—particularly since Belgarath wanted to keep down the fatalities."

"Did we kill anybody?" Durnik asked.

"Two," Sadi admitted. He held up his small dagger. "It's a little hard to unpoison a knife."

"And one other," Silk told the smith. "He was running up behind you with a spear, so I threw a knife at him."

"It couldn't be helped," Belgarath said. "Now let's get out of here."

They continued at a gallop for several miles, then slowed back to a canter again.

They took shelter that night in a sizable stand of dead trees. Durnik and Toth dug a shallow pit and built a small fire in it. After the tents were pitched, Garion and 'Zakath walked to the edge of the trees to keep watch on the road.

"Is it always like this?" 'Zakath asked quietly.

"Like what?"

"All this sneaking and hiding?"

"Usually. Belgarath tries to avoid trouble whenever he can. He doesn't like to risk people in random skirmishes. Most of the time we're able to avoid the kind of thing that happened this morning. Silk—and Sadi, too, for that matter—have lied us out of some very tight spots." He smiled faintly. "Up in Voresebo, Silk bribed our way past a group of soldiers with a pouchful of brass Mallorean half-pennies."

"But they're virtually worthless."

"That's what Silk said, but we were quite a ways past the soldiers before they opened the pouch."

Then they heard a chilling howl.

"A wolf?" 'Zakath asked. "Belgarath again?"

"No. That wasn't a wolf. Let's go back. I think Urvon's managed to outflank General Atesca."

"What makes you think so?"

"That was a Hound."

CHAPTER TWENTY

They walked carefully through the forest of dead snags, avoiding as best they could the litter of fallen limbs and twigs on the ground. The faint glow from Durnik's sunken fire guided them, and Garion knew it would serve as a dim beacon for the Hounds as well. 'Zakath's euphoria seemed to have evaporated. His expression now was wary, and he walked with his hand on his sword hilt.

They entered the small clearing where the others were seated around the fire pit. "There's a Hound out there," Garion said quietly. "It howled once."

"Could you make out what it was saying?" Belgarath asked, his voice tense.

"I don't speak its language, Grandfather. It seemed to be some kind of a call, though."

"Probably to the rest of the pack," the old man grunted. "The Hounds don't hunt alone very often."

"The glow from our fire is fairly visible," Garion pointed out.

"I'll take care of that right away," Durnik said, starting to shovel dirt into the fire pit.

"Could you pinpoint the Hound's location at all?" Belgarath asked.

"It was some distance away," Garion replied. "I think it's out there on the road."

"Following our trail?" Silk asked.

"It's following something. I could pick up that much."

"If the Hound is following us, I can divert it with some of that powder I used back at Ashaba," Sadi suggested.

"What do you think?" Belgarath asked Beldin.

The dwarf squatted on the ground, absently scratching an obscure diagram in the dirt with a broken stick. "It wouldn't work," he said finally. "The Hounds aren't entirely dogs, so they're not going to just blindly follow the one in the lead. Once they pinpoint our location, they'll spread out and come at us from all sides. We're going to have to come up with something else."

"Fairly soon, I'd think," Silk added, looking around nervously.

Polgara removed her blue cloak and handed it to Durnik. "I'll deal with it," she said calmly.

"What have you got in mind, Pol?" Belgarath asked suspiciously.

"I haven't decided yet, Old Wolf. Maybe I'll just make it up as I go along—the way you do sometimes." She drew herself up, and the air around her shimmered with an odd luminescence. She was winging her way off among the dead white trees even before the light had faded.

"I hate it when she does that," Belgarath muttered.

"You do it all the time," Beldin said.

"That's different."

'Zakath was staring at the ghostly shape of the disappearing white owl. "That's uncanny," he shuddered. Then he looked at Garion. "I can't say that I understand all this concern," he confessed. "You people—at least some of you—are sorcerers. Can't you just . . . ?" He left it hanging.

"No," Garion shook his head.

"Why not?"

"It makes too much noise. Not the sort of noise ordinary people can hear—but we can hear it, and so can the Grolims. If we tried to do it that way, we'd have every Grolim in this part of Darshiva down our necks. Sorcery's an overrated thing, 'Zakath. I'll grant you we can do things that other people can't, but there are so many restrictions on us that sometimes it's not worth the trouble—unless you're in a hurry."

"I didn't know that," 'Zakath admitted. "Are the Hounds as big as they say they are?"

"Probably even bigger," Silk replied. "They're about the size of small horses."

"You're a droll fellow, Kheldar," 'Zakath said, "so I think I'd have to see that to believe it."

"You'd better hope that you don't get that close."

Belgarath looked narrowly at the Mallorean. "You don't believe in very much, do you?" he asked.

"What I can see." 'Zakath shrugged. "I've had most of the belief washed out of me over the years."

"That could prove to be a problem," the old man said, scratching at his cheek. "A time might come when we'll have to do something in a hurry and we won't have time for explanations—and *you* won't have time to stand around gaping in astonishment. I think this might be a good time to fill you in on a few things."

"I'll listen to you," 'Zakath said. "I don't promise to believe everything you say, though. Go ahead."

"I'll let Garion do it. I want to keep in touch with Pol. Why don't you two go back to the edge of the woods and keep watch? Garion can fill you in there. Try not to be skeptical just on principle."

"We'll see," 'Zakath replied.

During the next hour, as Garion and 'Zakath crouched behind a fallen tree at the edge of the woods, the Emperor of Mallorea had his credulity stretched to the limits. Garion spoke in a half whisper even as he kept his eyes and ears alert. He began by briefly sketching in the *Book of Alorn,* then went on to a few salient points from the Mrin Codex. Then, so far as he knew it, he described the early life of Belgarath the sorcerer. And then he got down to business. He explained the possibilities and the limitations of the Will and the Word, covering such matters as projections, translocation, shape-change, and so on. He covered the mysterious sound that accompanies the use of what common people call sorcery, the exhaustion that comes over a sorcerer after its use, and the single absolute prohibition—that of unmaking. "That's what happened to Ctuchik," he concluded. "He was so afraid of what would happen if I got my hands on the Orb that he forgot he was stepping over the line when he tried to destroy it."

Out in the darkness, the Hound howled again, and there was an answering howl from a different direction. "They're getting closer," Garion whispered. "I hope Aunt Pol hurries."

'Zakath, however, was still mulling over the things Garion had told him. "Are you trying to tell me that it was the Orb that killed Ctuchik and not Belgarath?" he whispered.

"No. It wasn't the Orb. It was the universe. Do you really want to get into theology?"

"I'm even more skeptical in that direction."

"That's the one thing you can't afford, 'Zakath," Garion said seriously. "You *have* to believe. Otherwise, we'll fail, and, if we fail, the world fails—forever."

The Hound howled again, even closer this time.

"Keep your voice down," Garion warned in a tense whisper. "The Hounds have very sharp ears."

"I'm not afraid of a dog, Garion, no matter how big it is."

"That could be a mistake. Being afraid is one of the things that keeps us alive. All right. As closely as I understand it, this is the way it went. UL created the universe."

"I thought it was just spun out of nothingness."

"It was, but UL was the spinner. Then he joined his thought with the awareness of the universe, and the Seven Gods were born."

"The Grolims say it was Torak who made everything."

"That's what Torak wanted them to believe. That's one of the reasons I had to kill him. He thought he owned the universe and that he was more powerful than UL. He was wrong, and nobody owns the universe. She owns herself, and she makes the rules."

"She?"

"Of course. She's the mother of everything—you, me, that rock, and even this dead tree we're hiding behind. We're all related, I suppose, and the universe won't permit unmaking." Garion pulled off his helmet and scratched at his sweaty hair. He sighed. "I'm awfully sorry, 'Zakath. I know this is coming at you very fast, but we don't have time for subtlety. For some reason, we're caught up in this—you and I." He smiled wryly. "We're both woefully unsuited for the task, I'm afraid, but our mother needs us. Are you up to it?"

"I'm up to most things, I suppose," 'Zakath replied in an indifferent tone. "Regardless of what Cyradis said back there, I don't really expect to come out of this alive anyway."

"Are you sure you're not Arendish?" Garion asked suspiciously. "The whole idea is to live, 'Zakath, not to die. Dying defeats the purpose. Don't do it. I might need you later on. The voice told me that you're supposed to be a part of this. I think we're walking directly into the ultimate horror. You might have to hold me up when we get there."

"Voice?"

"It's in here," Garion tapped his forehead. "I'll explain that later. You've got enough to think about for now."

"You hear voices? There's a name for people who hear voices, you know."

Garion smiled. "I'm not really crazy, 'Zakath," he said. "I get a little distracted once in a while, but I've still got a fairly firm grip on reality."

There was a sudden, shocking sound that echoed through Garion's head like an explosion.

"What was that?" 'Zakath exclaimed.

"You heard it, too?" Garion was amazed. "You shouldn't have been able to hear it!"

"It shook the earth, Garion. Look there." 'Zakath pointed off toward the north where a huge pillar of fire was soaring up toward the murky, starless sky. "What is it?"

"Aunt Pol did something. She's *never* that clumsy. Listen!"

The baying of the Hound, which had been coming closer and closer as they had been speaking, had broken off into a series of pained yelps. "It probably hurt his ears," Garion said. "I know it hurt mine."

The Hound took up his baying again, and his howls were soon joined by others. The sound began to fade off toward the north and the boiling column of fire.

"Let's go back," Garion said. "I don't think we need to keep watch here any more."

Belgarath and Beldin were both pale and shaken, and even Durnik seemed awed.

"She hasn't done anything that noisy since she was about sixteen," Beldin said, blinking in astonishment. He looked suspiciously at Durnik. "Have you gone and got her pregnant?"

Even in the faint light from the overcast sky Garion could see his friend blushing furiously.

"What would that have to do with it?" Belgarath asked.

"It's only a theory of mine," Beldin said. "I can't prove it, because Polgara's the only sorceress I know right now, and she's never been in that condition."

"I'm sure you'll get around to explaining it—eventually."

"It's not that complicated, Belgarath. A woman's body gets a little confused when she's carrying a child. It does some peculiar things to her emotions and her thought processes. Focusing the Will takes control and concentration. A pregnant woman might just lose her grip on that sort of thing. You see—" He went on at some length to describe the physical, emotional, and intellectual changes involved in pregnancy. He spoke in matter-of-fact, even graphic, terms. After a moment, Ce'Nedra and Velvet withdrew, firmly taking Eriond with them. A moment later, Durnik joined them.

"Did you work this out all by yourself?" Belgarath asked.

"It gave me something to speculate about while I was watching the cave where Zedar had hidden Torak."

"It took you five hundred years, then?"

"I wanted to be sure I'd covered all the possibilities." Beldin shrugged.

"Why didn't you just ask Pol? She could have told you immediately."

Beldin blinked. "I never thought of that," he admitted.

Belgarath walked away, shaking his head.

Some time later, they heard a sudden, screeching bellow coming from the west through the murky sky.

"Everybody get down!" Belgarath hissed. "And keep quiet!"

"What is it?" 'Zakath exclaimed.

"Be still!" Beldin snapped. "She'll hear you!"

From overhead there came the flap of vast wings and a sooty orange billow of fire. Then the huge beast flew on, screeching and belching out flames.

"What was it?" 'Zakath repeated.

"Zandramas," Garion whispered. "Keep your voice down. She might come back."

They waited.

"She seems to be going toward all the noise Pol kicked up," Belgarath said in a low voice.

"At least she's not looking for us," Silk said with some relief.

"Not yet, anyway."

"That wasn't actually a dragon, was it?" 'Zakath asked the old man.

"No, not really. Garion was right. It was Zandramas. That's her other form."

"Isn't it just a bit ostentatious?"

"Zandramas seems to have urges in that direction. She can only go for so long without doing something spectacular. It might have something to do with the fact that she's a woman."

"I heard that, Belgarath," Ce'Nedra's voice came threateningly from the far side of the clearing.

"Maybe it didn't come out exactly the way I'd intended," he half apologized.

The snowy owl came drifting through the forest of dead trees. She hovered for a moment near the fire, then shimmered back into her own form.

"What did you do out there, Pol?" Belgarath asked her.

"I found a dormant volcano," she replied, taking her cloak from Durnik and wrapping it around her shoulders. "I reignited it. Did the Hounds go off to investigate?"

"Almost immediately," Garion assured her.

"So did Zandramas," Silk added.

"Yes, I saw her." She smiled faintly. "It worked out rather well, actually. When she gets there, she'll probably find the Hounds slinking around and decide to do something about them. I don't think they'll be bothering us any more, and I'm sure Zandramas would be filled with chagrin if she found out that she's helping us."

"Were you that clumsy on purpose, Pol?" Beldin asked her.

"Of course. I wanted to make enough noise to draw off the Hounds—and any Grolims who might be in the area. Zandramas was just a bonus. Could you build up the fire again, dear?" she said to Durnik. "I think it's safe now to start thinking about supper."

They broke camp early the next morning. Polgara's volcano was still belching smoke and ash high into the air, where they mingled with the pervading overcast to cause a sullen kind of gloom. The murky air reeked of sulfur.

"Flying in that isn't going to be very enjoyable," Beldin said sourly.

"We need to know what's ahead," Belgarath told him.

"I know that," Beldin replied. "I'm not stupid, you know. I was just making an observation." He bent slightly, changed form, and drove himself into the air with powerful strokes of his wings.

"I'd pay a fortune to have a hawk like that," 'Zakath said wistfully.

"You might have trouble training him," Belgarath said. "He's not the most tractable bird in the world."

"And the first time you tried to hood him, he'd probably rip off one of your fingers," Polgara added.

It was nearly noon when Beldin returned, flying hard. "Get ready!" he shouted almost before he had completed the change. "Temple Guardsmen—about ten— just over that rise! They're coming this way and they've got a Hound with them!"

Garion reached for his sword, and he heard 'Zakath's blade come whistling out of its sheath. "No!" he said sharply to the Mallorean. "Stay out of it!"

"Not a chance," 'Zakath replied.

"I'll take care of the dog," Sadi said, reaching into the pouch at his belt for some of the powder he had used so effectively in Karanda.

They spread out with their weapons in their hands as Eriond led the women to the rear.

The Hound came over the hill first, and it stopped when it saw them. Then it wheeled and loped back.

"That's it," Belgarath said. "They know we're here now."

The Guardsmen came over the top of the hill at a rolling trot. Garion noticed that they weren't carrying lances, but each mail-clad man held a sword and wore a shield. They paused for a moment to assess the situation, then they charged. The Hound came first, running smoothly and with his lips peeled back from his teeth in a fearful snarl. Sadi spurred forward to meet him, holding a fistful of the powder. When the Hound reared up on his hind legs to drag the eunuch from his saddle, Sadi coolly hurled the powder full into the animal's face. The Hound shook his massive head, trying to clear his eyes. Then he sneezed once. His eyes grew wide, and his snarl turned into a terrified whimper. He shrieked suddenly, a dreadful, half-human sound. Then he turned and fled, howling in terror.

"Let's go!" Garion barked, and he charged toward the oncoming Guardsmen. These were more serious opponents than the Darshivan soldiers had been, so the choices in dealing with them were greatly reduced. One, somewhat larger than his fellows and astride a heavy-bodied warhorse, was leading the charge, and Garion cut him out of his saddle with a single stroke of Iron-grip's great sword.

Garion heard the sound of steel on steel off to his left, but he dared not take his eyes off the still-charging Guardsmen. He chopped two more from their saddles, and Chretienne crashed into the horse of a third, sending the rider and his mount tumbling. Then Garion was through the ranks of their enemies, and he wheeled around.

'Zakath was being hard pressed by two mailed men. He had, it appeared, already felled a third; but then the other two had come at him, one from either side. Garion kicked at Chretienne's flanks, intending to go to his friend's aid, but Toth was already there. With one huge hand he plucked one of 'Zakath's attackers from his saddle and hurled him headfirst at a large boulder at the side of the road. 'Zakath turned on his other enemy, deftly parried a couple of strokes, then smoothly ran the man through.

Silk's daggers were already doing their deadly work. One Guardsman was aimlessly riding around in a circle, doubled over in his saddle and clutching at the dagger hilt protruding from his stomach. The acrobatic little Drasnian then leaped from his horse and landed behind the saddle of a confused Guardsman. With a wide sweep of his arm, Silk drove a dagger into the side of the man's neck. Blood gushed from the Guardsman's mouth as he fell to the ground.

The remaining two armored men tried to flee, but Durnik and Beldin were already on them, clubbing at them with cudgel and axe. They tumbled senselessly from their horses and lay twitching in the dirt of the road.

"Are you all right?" Garion asked 'Zakath.

"I'm fine, Garion." The Mallorean was breathing hard, though.

"Your training seems to be coming back to you."

"I had a certain amount of incentive." 'Zakath looked critically at the bodies littering the road. "When this is all over, I think I'll order this organization disbanded," he said. "The notion of private armies offends me for some reason."

"Did any of them get away?" Silk asked, looking around.

"Not a one," Durnik told him.

"Good. We wouldn't want somebody going for help." Silk frowned. "What were they doing this far south?" he asked.

"Probably trying to stir up enough trouble to draw the Darshivan troops away from Urvon's main body," Belgarath replied. "I think we'll have to be alert from now on. This whole area could be crawling with soldiers at any time now." He looked at Beldin. "Why don't you have a look around?" he said. "See if you can find out what Urvon's up to and where the Darshivans are. We don't want to get caught between them."

"It's going to take a while," the hunchback replied. "Darshiva's a fairly large place."

"You'd better get started, then, hadn't you?"

They took shelter that night in the ruins of another village. Belgarath and Garion scouted the surrounding region, but found it to be deserted. The following morning, the two wolves ranged out ahead of the rest of the party, but again they encountered no one.

It was almost evening when Beldin returned. "Urvon outflanked your army," he told 'Zakath. "He's got at least one general who knows what he's doing. His troops are in the Dalasian Mountains now, and they're coming south at a forced march. Atesca had to stay near the coast to meet the Darshivans and their elephants."

"Did you see Urvon?" Belgarath asked him.

Beldin cackled an ugly little laugh. "Oh, yes. He's absolutely mad now. He's got two dozen soldiers carrying him on a throne and he's doing parlor tricks to demonstrate his divinity. I doubt if he could focus enough of his will right now to wilt a flower."

"Is Nahaz with him?"

Beldin nodded. "Right beside him, whispering in his ear. I'd say he needs to keep a tight grip on his plaything. If Urvon starts giving the wrong orders, his army could wind up wandering around in those mountains for a generation."

Belgarath frowned. "This doesn't exactly fit," he said. "Every bit of information we picked up pointed to the probability that Nahaz and Mordja were concentrating on each other."

"Maybe they've already had it out," the hunchback shrugged, "and Mordja lost."

"I doubt it. That sort of thing would have made a lot of noise, and we'd have heard it."

"Who knows why demons do anything?" Beldin scowled, scratching at his matted hair. "Let's face it, Belgarath," he said. "Zandramas knows that she has to go to Kell, and so does Nahaz. I think this is turning into a race. We're all trying to be the first one to get to Cyradis."

"I get the feeling that I'm overlooking something," Belgarath said. "Something important."

"You'll think of it. It might take you a couple of months, but you'll think of it."

Belgarath ignored that.

The heavy pall of smoke and ash began to subside as evening drew on, but the prevailing gloom of thick overcast remained. Darshiva was still a land of dead trees, fungus, and stagnant water. Increasingly, that last became a problem. The supplies of water they had carried with them from the Mallorean camp on the shores of the Magan had long since been exhausted. As night fell, the others continued along the road, and Belgarath and Garion ranged ahead as wolves again, searching this time not so much for trouble as for fresh water. Their sharp noses easily detected the stale reek of long-standing pools, and they passed them without slowing.

It was in a blasted forest of long-dead trees that Garion encountered another wolf. She was gaunt and bedraggled, and she limped painfully on her left front paw. She looked at him warily, baring her teeth in warning.

He sat down on his haunches to show his peaceable intent.

"What is it you do here?" she asked him in the language of wolves.

"I am going from one place to another place," he replied politely. "I have no intention to hunt in the place which is yours. I seek only clean water to drink."

"Clean water comes from the ground on the other side of that high place." She glanced toward a hill deeper in the forest. "Drink your fill."

"I have others with me as well," he told her.

"Your pack?" She came cautiously closer to him and sniffed. "You have the scent of the man-things about you," she accused.

"Some of those in my pack are man-things," he admitted. "Where is your pack?"

"Gone," she told him. "When there were no longer creatures to hunt in this place, they went into the mountains." She licked at her injured foot. "I could not follow."

"Where is your mate?"

"He no longer runs or hunts. I visit his bones sometimes." She said it with such simple dignity that a lump caught in Garion's throat.

"How do you hunt with that hurt in your paw?"

"I lie in wait for unwary things. All are very small. I have not eaten my fill for many seasons."

"Grandfather," Garion sent his thought out. "I need you."

"Trouble?" the old man's thought came back.

"Not that kind. Oh, I found water, by the way, but don't come in here running. You'll frighten her."

"Her?"

"You'll understand when you get here."

"To whom were you speaking?" she asked.

"You heard?" He was startled.

"No, but your manner was that of one who was speaking."

"We can talk of that after some time has passed. My pack-leader is coming to this place. He must make the decisions."

"That is only proper." She lay down on her belly and continued to lick at her paw.

"How did you come to be hurt?"

"The man-things conceal things beneath the leaves. I stepped on one of those things, and it bit my paw. Its jaws were very strong."

Belgarath came trotting through the dead forest. He stopped and dropped to his haunches, his tongue lolling out.

The she-wolf laid her muzzle submissively on the ground in a gesture of respect.

"What's the problem?" Belgarath's thought came to Garion.

"She caught her foot in a trap. Her pack left her behind, and her mate died. She's crippled and starving."

"It happens sometimes."

"I'm not going to leave her behind to die."

Belgarath gave him a long, steady look. "No," he replied. "I don't imagine you would—and I'd think less of you if you did." He approached the she-wolf. "How is it with you, little sister?" he asked in the language of wolves, sniffing at her.

"Not well, revered leader," she sighed. "I will not hunt much longer, I think."

"You will join my pack, and we will see to your hurt. We will bring you such meat as you require. Where are your young? I can smell them on your fur."

Garion gave a startled little whine.

"There is but one remaining," the she-wolf replied, "and he is very weak."

"Take us to him. We will make him strong again."

"As you decide, revered leader," she said with automatic obedience.

"Pol," Belgarath sent out his thought. "Come here. Take your mother's form." The note of command in his voice was incisive and far more wolflike than human.

There was a startled silence. "Yes, father," Polgara replied. When she arrived a few moments later, Garion recognized her from the characteristic white streak above her left brow. "What is it, father?" she asked.

"Our little sister here is hurt," he replied. "It's her left front paw. Can you fix it?"

She approached the she-wolf and sniffed at the paw. "It's ulcerated," she said with her thought. "Nothing seems to be broken. Several days with a poultice ought to do it."

"Fix it, then. She also has a puppy. We'll need to find him as well."

She looked at him, a question in her golden eyes.

"She and her puppy are joining our pack. They'll be going with us." Then he sent his thought to her. "It's Garion's idea, actually. He refuses to leave her behind."

"It's very noble, but is it practical?"

"Probably not, but it's his decision. He thinks it's the right thing to do, and I more or less agree with him. You're going to have to explain some things to her, though. She doesn't have much reason to trust man, and I don't want her to go into a panic when the others catch up with us." He turned to the she-wolf. "Everything will be well again, little sister," he told her. "Now, let us go find your young one."

CHAPTER TWENTY-ONE

The half-grown pup was so emaciated that it could not stand, so Polgara resorted to the simple expedient of picking it up by the scruff of its neck between her jaws and carrying it out of the den.

"Go meet the others," she instructed Garion. "Don't let them get too close until I've had time to talk with our little sister here. Bring back food, though. Put as much as you can carry in a sack and come right back."

"Yes, Aunt Pol." He loped back toward the road, changed into his own form, and waited for his friends.

"We've got a little bit of a problem," he told them when they arrived. "We've found an injured female just up ahead in those woods. She's starving, and she has a young one as well."

"A baby?" Ce'Nedra exclaimed.

"Not exactly," he said, going to one of the food packs and beginning to load a stout canvas bag with meat and cheese.

"But you just said—"

"It's a puppy, Ce'Nedra. The female is a she-wolf."

"What?"

"It's a wolf. She got her paw caught in a trap. She can't run, so she can't hunt. She'll be coming with us—at least until her paw heals."

"But—"

"No buts. She's coming with us. Durnik, can you work out some way we can carry her without having the horses go wild?"

"I'll think of something," the smith replied.

"Under the circumstances, don't you think this altruism might be misplaced?" Sadi asked mildly.

"No," Garion said, tying the top of the sack shut, "I don't. There's a hill in the middle of those woods. Stay on this side of it until we can persuade her that we don't mean to harm her. There's water there, but it's too close to her den. We'll have to wait a bit before we can water the horses."

"What's got you so angry?" Silk asked him.

"If I had the time, I'd look up the man who set that trap and break his leg—in several places. I've got to go back now. She and the puppy are very hungry." He slung the sack over his shoulder and stalked off. His anger was, he knew, irrational, and there had not really been any excuse for being surly with Ce'Nedra and the others, but he could not have helped himself. The wolf's calm acceptance of death and her mourning for her lost mate had torn at his heart, and anger kept the tears out of his eyes.

The sack was awkward to carry, once he had changed form, and it kept throwing him off balance, but he stumbled on with his head high to keep his burden from dragging on the ground.

Polgara and Belgarath were talking with the she-wolf when he reached the den again. The injured wolf had a skeptical expression in her eyes as she listened.

"She can't accept it," Polgara said.

"Does she think you're lying?" Garion asked, dropping the sack.

"Wolves don't understand the meaning of that word. She thinks we're mistaken. We're going to have to show her. She met you first, so she might trust you a little more. Change back. You'll need your hands to untie the knot in that sack, anyway."

"All right." He drew his own image in his imagination and changed.

"How remarkable," the she-wolf said in amazement.

Belgarath looked at her sharply. "Why did you say that?" he asked her.

"Did you not find it so?"

"I am accustomed to it. Why did you choose those particular words?"

"They came to me. I am no pack-leader, and I have no need to choose my words with care in order to protect my dignity."

Garion had opened the sack and he laid meat and cheese on the ground in front of her. She began to eat ravenously. He knelt beside the starving pup and began to feed him, being careful to keep his fingers away from the needle-sharp teeth.

"A little bit at a time," Polgara cautioned. "Don't make him sick."

When the she-wolf had eaten her fill, she limped to the spring which came bubbling out from between two rocks and drank. Garion picked up the puppy and carried him to the spring so that he could also drink.

"You are not like the other man-things," the she-wolf observed.

"No," he agreed. "Not entirely."

"Are you mated?" she asked.

"Yes."

"To a wolf or to one of the shes of the man-things?"

"To one of the shes of this kind." He tapped his own chest.

"Ah. And does she hunt with you?"

"Our shes do not usually hunt."

"What useless things they must be." The wolf sniffed disdainfully.

"Not altogether."

"Durnik and the others are coming," Polgara said. Then she looked at the she-wolf. "The others of our pack are coming to this place, little sister," she said. "They are the man-things of which I spoke. Do not be afraid of them, for they are like this one." She pointed her nose at Garion. "Our leader here and I will now also change our forms. The presence of wolves alarms the beasts we have with us, and they must drink from your water. If it please you, will you go with this one who fed you, so that our beasts may drink?"

"It shall be as you say," the she-wolf replied.

Garion led the limping wolf away from the spring, carrying the now drowsy puppy in his arms. The puppy raised his muzzle, licked Garion's face once, and then fell asleep.

Durnik and Toth set up their camp near the spring, while Eriond and Silk watered the horses and then took them back to picket them in the woods.

After a while, Garion led the now wary she-wolf toward the fire. "It is time for you to meet the other members of our pack," he told her, "for they are now your packmates as well."

"This is not a natural thing," she said nervously as she limped along at his side.

"They will not harm you," he assured her. Then he spoke to the others. "Please stand very still," he told them. "She'll want to smell each of you so that she can recognize you later. Don't try to touch her and, when you speak, do it quietly. She's very nervous right now." He led the wolf around the fire, allowing her to sniff at each of his companions.

"What's her name?" Ce'Nedra asked as the she-wolf sniffed at her little hand.

"Wolves don't need names."

"We have to call her *something,* Garion. May I hold the puppy?"

"I think she'd rather you didn't just yet. Let her get used to you first."

"This one is your mate," the she-wolf said. "I can smell your scent on her."

"Yes," Garion agreed.

"She's very small. I see now why she can't hunt. Is she fully grown?"

"Yes, she is."

"Has she had her first litter yet?"

"Yes."

"How many puppies?"

"One."

"One only?" The wolf sniffed. "I have had as many as six. You should have chosen a larger mate. I'm sure she was the runt of her litter."

"What's she saying?" Ce'Nedra asked.

"It wouldn't translate," Garion lied.

After the wolf had grown a little more at ease, Polgara boiled a number of herbs in a small pot, mixed them with a paste of soap and sugar, and applied the poultice to the wolf's injured paw. Then she wrapped the paw in a clean white cloth. "Try not to lick this or chew it off, little sister," she instructed. "It will not taste good and it needs to stay where it is to heal your hurt."

"One is grateful," the wolf replied. She looked into the dancing flames of the fire. "That is a comforting thing, is it not?" she observed.

"We find it so," Polgara said.

"You man-things are very clever with your forepaws."

"They're useful," Polgara agreed. She took the sleeping puppy from Garion's arms and nestled him beside his mother.

"I will sleep now," the wolf decided. She laid her muzzle protectively on her puppy's flank and closed her eyes.

Durnik motioned to Garion and led him aside. "I think I've come up with a way to bring her along without frightening the horses," he said. "I can make a sort of sled for her to ride in. I'll put a long enough towrope on it to keep her smell away from them, and I'll cover her and her puppy with an old horse blanket. She might make them a little jumpy at first, but they'll get used to her." The smith looked gravely at his friend. "Why are we doing this, Garion?" he asked.

"I couldn't bear the thought of just leaving the two of them here. They'd have both died before the week was out."

"You're a good man," Durnik said simply, putting his hand on Garion's shoulder. "You're decent as well as brave."

"I'm a Sendar." Garion shrugged. "We're all like that."

"But you're not actually a Sendar, you know."

"That's how I was raised, and that's all that matters, isn't it?"

The sled Durnik contrived for the wolf and her puppy the next morning had wide-set runners and was built low to the ground so there was little chance of its overturning. "It might be better if it had wheels," he admitted, "but I don't have any wheels to work with, and it would take too long to make some."

"I'll ransack the next village we come to," Silk told him. "Maybe I can find a cart of some kind."

They rode out, slowly at first until they saw that the sled ran smoothly on the damp earth of the road, and then they moved on at their usual canter.

Silk was checking a map as he rode along. "There's a fair-sized town just up ahead," he told Belgarath. "I think we could use some up-to-date information about now, don't you?"

"Why is it that you absolutely *have* to go into every town we pass?" Belgarath asked him.

"I'm a city dweller, Belgarath," the little man replied in an offhand manner. "I get edgy if I can't walk on cobblestones every so often. Besides, we need supplies. Garion's wolf eats a great deal. Why don't the rest of you go out in a wide circle around the place, and we'll catch up with you on the other side?"

"We?" Garion asked him.

"You're coming along, aren't you?"

Garion sighed. "I guess so," he said. "You always seem to get into trouble if we let you go off alone."

"Trouble?" Silk said innocently. "Me?"

'Zakath rubbed at his stubbled chin. "I'll come, too," he said. "I don't look that much like the coins any more." He glared briefly at Belgarath. "How can you stand this?" he demanded, scratching vigorously at his face. "The itching is about to drive me wild."

"You get used to it," Belgarath told him. "I wouldn't feel right if my face didn't itch."

The place appeared to be a market town that had at some time in the past been fortified. It crouched atop a hill and it was surrounded by a thick stone wall with watchtowers at each corner. The pervading overcast that seemed to cover all of Darshiva made the town look gray and dismal. The gate was unguarded, and Silk, Garion, and 'Zakath clattered on through into what appeared to be a deserted street.

"Let's see if we can find somebody," Silk said. "If not, we can at least ransack a few shops for the food we'll need."

"Don't you ever pay for anything, Kheldar?" 'Zakath asked with some asperity.

"Not if I don't have to. No honest merchant ever passes up an opportunity to steal. Let's push on, shall we?"

"This is a very corrupt little man; do you know that?" 'Zakath said to Garion.

"We've noticed that from time to time."

They rounded a corner and saw a group of men in canvas smocks loading a wagon under the direction of a sweating fat man.

Silk reined in his horse. "Where are all the people, friend?" he called to the fat man.

"Gone. Fled to either Gandahar or Dalasia."

"Fled? What for?"

"Where have you been, man? Urvon's coming."

"Really? I hadn't heard that."

"Everybody in Darshiva knows it."

"Zandramas will stop him," Silk said confidently.

"Zandramas isn't here." The fat man suddenly bawled at one of his workers. "Be careful with that box!" he shouted. "The things in there are breakable!"

Silk led the others closer. "Where did she go? Zandramas, I mean?"

"Who knows? Who cares? There's been nothing but trouble in Darshiva ever since she gained control of the country." The fat man mopped at his face with a soiled kerchief.

"You'd better not let the Grolims hear you talking like that."

"Grolims," the fat man snorted. "They were the first ones to run. Urvon's army uses Darshivan Grolims for firewood."

"Why would Zandramas leave when her country's being invaded?"

"Who knows why she does anything?" The fat fellow looked around nervously, then spoke in a quiet voice. "Just between you and me, friend, I think she's mad. She held some kind of ceremony at Hemil. She stuck a crown on the head of some archduke from Melcena and said that he's the Emperor of Mallorea. He'll be a head shorter when Kal Zakath catches up with him, I'll wager."

"I'd like to put some money on the same proposition," 'Zakath agreed quietly.

"Then she gave a speech in the temple at Hemil," the fat man went on. "She said that the day is at hand." He sneered. "Grolims of every stripe have been saying that the day is at hand for as long as I can remember. Every one of them seems to be talking about a different day, though. Anyway, she came through here a few days ago and told us all that she was going to the place where the New God of Angarak will be chosen. She held up her hand and said, 'And this is a sign to you that I shall prevail.' It gave me quite a turn at first, let me tell you. There were swirling lights under her skin. I thought for a while that there was really something significant about it, but my friend, the apothecary who keeps the shop next to mine, he told me that she's a sorceress and she can make people see anything she wants them to see. That explains it, I guess."

"Did she say anything else?" Silk asked him intently.

"Only that this New God of hers will appear before the summer is gone."

"Let's hope she's right," Silk said. "That might put an end to all this turmoil."

"I doubt it," the fat man said moodily. "I think we're in for a long siege of trouble."

"Was she alone?" Garion asked him.

"No. She had her bogus emperor with her and that white-eyed Grolim from the temple at Hemil—the one who follows her around like a tame ape."

"Anyone else?"

"Only a little boy. I don't know where she picked him up. Just before she left, she told us that the army of Urvon the Disciple was coming and she ordered the whole populace to go out and block his path. Then she left, going that way." He pointed off toward the west. "Well, my friends and I, we all sort of looked at each other for a while, and then everybody grabbed up whatever he could carry and bolted. We're not stupid enough to throw ourselves in the path of an advancing army, no matter who orders us to."

"How is it that you stayed behind?" Silk asked him curiously.

"This is my shop," the fat man replied in a plaintive tone. "I've worked all my life to build it up. I wasn't going to run off and let the riffraff from the gutters loot it. Now they're all gone, so it's safe for me to make a run for it with whatever I can salvage. A lot of what I'll have to leave behind won't keep anyway, so I'm not losing very much."

"Oh," Silk said, his pointed nose twitching with interest. "What is it you deal in, friend?"

"General merchandise." The fat man looked critically at his workmen. "Stack those boxes closer together!" he shouted. "There's still a lot left to go in that wagon!"

"What sort of general merchandise?" Silk pressed.

"Household goods, tools, bolts of cloth, foodstuffs—that sort of thing."

"Well, now," Silk said, his nose twitching even more violently. "Maybe you and I can do some business. My friends and I have a long way to go, and we're running a little short of supplies. You mentioned foodstuffs. What sort of foodstuffs?"

The merchant's eyes narrowed. "Bread, cheese, butter, dried fruit, hams. I've even got a fresh side of beef. I warn you, though, those things are going to cost you very dearly. Food's scarce in this part of Darshiva."

"Oh," Silk said blandly, "I don't think they'll cost all that much—unless you plan to wait here to greet Urvon when he arrives."

The merchant stared at him in consternation.

"You see, my friend," Silk continued, "you have to leave—and very soon, I think. That wagon of yours won't carry everything you've got in your shop, and your team isn't going to be able to move very fast—not the way you're loading the wagon. My friends and I have fast horses, though, so we can afford to wait a little longer. After you leave, we might just browse through your shop for the things we need."

The merchant's face went suddenly very pale. "That's robbery," he gasped.

"Why, yes," Silk admitted blandly, "I believe some people do call it that." He paused for a moment to allow the merchant time to understand the situation fully. The fat man's face grew anguished. Then Silk sighed. "Unfortunately, I'm cursed with a delicate conscience. I can't bear the thought of cheating an honest man—unless I absolutely have to." He lifted a pouch from his belt, opened it, and peered inside. "I seem to have eight or ten silver half-crowns in here," he said. "What would you say to five of them for everything my friends and I can carry?"

"That's outrageous!" the merchant spluttered.

With some show of regret, Silk closed the pouch and tucked it back under his belt. "I guess we'll just have to wait, then. Do you think you and your men will be much longer?"

"You're robbing me!" the merchant wailed.

"No, not really. The way I see it, what we have here is a buyer's market. That's my offer, friend—five silver half-crowns. Take it or leave it. We'll wait over there across the street while you decide." He turned his horse and led Garion and 'Zakath toward a large house on the other side of the street.

'Zakath was trying very hard to stifle a laugh as they dismounted.

"We're not quite done yet," Silk muttered. "It needs just one more little touch." He went up to the locked door of the house, reached into his boot, and took out a long, pointed needle. He probed at the lock for a moment, and it snapped open with a solid-sounding *click*. "We'll need a table and three chairs," he told them. "Bring them out and set them up in front of the house. I'll rummage around and find the other things we'll need." He went into the house.

Garion and 'Zakath went into the kitchen and carried out a fair-sized table. Then they went back for chairs.

"What's he up to?" 'Zakath asked with a look of bafflement on his face.

"He's playing," Garion said with a certain disgust. "He does that from time to time during his business dealings."

They carried out the chairs and found Silk waiting for them. Several bottles of wine and four goblets sat on the table. "All right, gentlemen," the little Drasnian said. "Seat yourselves and have some wine. I'll be right back. I want to check something I saw at the side of the house." He went around the corner and came back after a few minutes with a broad smirk on his face. He sat, poured himself a goblet of wine, leaned back in his chair, and put his feet up on the table with the air of a man planning to make a long stay of it. "I give him about five minutes," he said.

"Who?" Garion asked.

"The merchant." Silk shrugged. "He'll only be able to watch us sitting here for so long and then he'll start to see things my way."

"You're a cruel, cruel man, Prince Kheldar." 'Zakath laughed.

"Business is business," Silk replied, taking a sip of his wine. "This really isn't bad, you know," he said, holding up his goblet to admire the color of the wine.

"What were you doing around at the side?" Garion asked him.

"There's a carriage house there—with a large lock on the door. You don't flee a town and lock a door unless there's something valuable behind it, do you? Besides, locked doors always pique my curiosity."

"So? What was inside?"

"Rather a nice little cabriolet, actually."

"What's a cabriolet?"

"A two-wheeled carriage."

"And you're going to steal it."

"Of course. I told the merchant over there that we'd take only what we could carry. I didn't tell him how we were going to carry it. Besides, Durnik wanted wheels to make something to carry your wolf in. That little carriage could save him all the trouble of building things. Friends should always help their friends, right?"

As Silk had predicted, the merchant could only bear watching the three of them lounging at the table across from his shop for just so long. As his men finished loading the wagon, he came across the street. "All right," he said sullenly, "five half-crowns—but only so much as you can carry, mind."

"Trust me," Silk told him, counting out the coins on the table. "Would you care for a glass of wine? It's really quite good."

The merchant snatched up the coins and turned without answering.

"We'll lock up for you when we leave," Silk called after him.

The fat man did not look back.

After the merchant and his men had ridden off down the street, Silk led his horse around to the side of the house while Garion and 'Zakath crossed the street to plunder the fat man's shop.

The little two-wheeled carriage had a folding top and a large leather-covered box across its back. Silk's saddle horse looked a bit uncomfortable between the shafts of the carriage, and the sense of being followed by the wheeled thing definitely made him nervous.

The box across the back of the cabriolet held an astonishing amount of supplies. They filled it with cheeses, rolls of butter, hams, slabs of bacon, and several bags of beans. Then they filled up the empty spaces with loaves of bread. When Garion picked up a large bag of meal, however, Silk firmly shook his head. "No," he said adamantly.

"Why not?"

"You know what Polgara makes with ground meal. I'm not deliberately going to volunteer to eat gruel for breakfast every morning for the next month. Let's get that side of beef instead."

"We won't be able to eat all that before it goes bad," Garion objected.

"We have these two new mouths to feed, remember? I've seen your wolf and her puppy eat. The meat won't have time to go bad, believe me."

They rode out of town with Silk idly lounging in the seat of the little carriage with the reins held negligently in his left hand. In his right, he held a wine bottle. "Now this is more like it," he said happily, taking a long drink.

"I'm glad you're enjoying yourself," Garion said a little tartly.

"Oh, I am," Silk replied. "But after all, Garion, fair is fair. I stole it, so I get to ride in it."

CHAPTER TWENTY-TWO

The others were clustered in the yard of an abandoned farmstead a league or so beyond the town. "I see you've been busy," Belgarath observed as Silk drove the little carriage up and stopped.

"We needed something to carry the supplies in," Silk replied glibly.

"Of course."

"I hope you were able to find something beside beans," Sadi said. "Soldiers' rations tend to grow monotonous after a while."

"Silk swindled a shopkeeper," Garion said, opening the leather-covered box at the back of the carriage. "We did rather well, actually."

"*Swindled?*" Silk protested.

"Didn't you?" Garion moved the side of beef so that Polgara could look into the box.

"Well—I suppose so," Silk admitted, "but swindled is such an awkward way to sum it up."

"It's perfectly all right, Prince Kheldar." Polgara almost purred as she took a mental inventory of the items in the box. "To be honest with you, I don't care how you came by all this."

He bowed. "My pleasure, Polgara," he said grandly.

"Yes," she said absently, "I'm sure you enjoyed it."

"What did you find out?" Beldin asked Garion.

"Well, for one thing, Zandramas is ahead of us again," Garion replied. "She went through here a few days ago. She knows that Urvon's army is coming down through the mountains. He might be moving a little faster than we thought, though, because she's ordering the civilian population to delay him. They're more or less ignoring her."

"Wise decision." Beldin grunted. "Anything else?"

"She told them that this is all going to be settled before the summer's over."

"That agrees with what Cyradis told us at Ashaba," Belgarath said. "All right, then. We all know when the meeting's going to happen. The only thing that's left to find out is *where.*"

"That's why we're all in such a hurry to get to Kell," Beldin said. "Cyradis is sitting on that information like a mother hen on a clutch of eggs."

"What *is* it?" Belgarath burst out irritably.

"What's what?"

"I'm missing something. It's something important and it's something you told me."

"I've told you lots of things, Belgarath. You don't usually listen, though."

"This was a while back. It seems to me we were sitting in my tower, talking."

"We've done that from time to time over the last several thousand years."

"No. This was more recent. Eriond was there and he was just a boy."

"That would put it at about ten years or so ago, then."

"Right."

"What were we doing ten years ago?"

Belgarath began to pace up and down, scowling. "I'd been helping Durnik. We were making Poledra's cottage livable. You'd been here in Mallorea."

Beldin scratched reflectively at his stomach. "I think I remember the time. We were sharing a cask of ale you'd stolen from the twins, and Eriond was scrubbing the floor."

"What were you telling me?"

Beldin shrugged. "I'd just come back from Mallorea. I was describing conditions here and telling you about the Sardion—although we didn't know very much about it at that point."

"No," Belgarath shook his head. "That wasn't it. You said something about Kell."

Beldin frowned, thinking back. "It must not have been very important, because neither of us seems to be able to remember it."

"It seems to me it was just something you said in passing."

"I say a lot of things in passing. They help to fill up the blank spaces in a conversation. Are you certain it was all that important?"

Belgarath nodded. "I'm sure of it."

"All right. Let's see if we can track it down."

"Won't this wait, father?" Polgara asked.

"No, Pol. I don't think so. We're right on the edge of it, and I don't want to lose it again."

"Let's see," Beldin said, his ugly face creased with thought. "I came in, and you and Eriond were cleaning. You offered me some of the ale you'd stolen from the twins. You asked me what I'd been doing since Belgarion's wedding, and I told you I'd been keeping an eye on the Angaraks."

"Yes," Belgarath agreed. "I remember that part."

"I told you that the Murgos were in general despair about the death of Taur Urgas, and that the western Grolims had gone to pieces over the death of Torak."

"Then you told me about 'Zakath's campaign in Cthol Murgos and about how he'd added the Kal to his name."

"That actually wasn't my idea," 'Zakath said with a slightly pained look. "Brador came up with it—as a means of unifying Mallorean society." He made a wry face. "It didn't really work all that well, I guess."

"Things do seem a bit disorganized here," Silk agreed.

"What did we talk about then?" Belgarath asked.

"Well," Beldin replied, "as I remember it, we told Eriond the story of Vo Mimbre, and then you asked me what was going on in Mallorea. I told you that things were all pretty much the same—that the bureaucracy's the glue that holds everything together, that there were plots and intrigues in Melcena and Mal Zeth, that Karanda and Darshiva and Gandahar were on the verge of open rebellion, and that the Grolims—" He stopped, his eyes suddenly going very wide.

"Are still afraid to go near Kell!" Belgarath completed it in a shout of triumph. "That's it!"

Beldin smacked his forehead with his open palm. "How could I have been so stupid?" he exclaimed. Then he fell over on his back, howling with laughter and kicking at the ground in sheer delight. "We've got her, Belgarath!" he roared. "We've got them all—Zandramas, Urvon, even Agachak! They *can't* go to Kell!"

Belgarath was also laughing uproariously. "How did we miss it?"

"Father," Polgara said ominously. "This is beginning to make me cross. Will one of you please explain all this hysteria?"

Beldin and Belgarath were capering hand in hand in a grotesque little dance of glee.

"Will you two stop that?" Polgara snapped.

"Oh, this is just too rare, Pol," Beldin gasped, catching her in a bear hug.

"Don't do that! Just talk!"

"All right, Pol," he said, wiping the tears of mirth from his eyes. "Kell is the holy place of the Dals. It's the center of their whole culture."

"Yes, uncle. I know that."

"When the Angaraks overran Dalasia, the Grolims came in to erase the Dalasian religion and to replace it with the worship of Torak—the same way they did in Karanda. When they found out the significance of Kell, they moved to destroy it. The Dals had to prevent that, so they put their wizards to work on the problem. The wizards laid curses on the entire region around Kell." He frowned. "Maybe curses isn't the right word," he admitted. "Enchantments might be closer, but it amounts to the same thing. Anyway, since the Grolims were the real danger to Kell, the enchantments were directed at them. Any Grolim who tries to approach Kell is struck blind."

"Why didn't you tell us about this earlier?" she asked him tartly.

"I've never really paid that much attention to it. I probably even forgot about it. I don't bother to go into Dalasia because the Dals are all mystics, and mysticism has always irritated me. The seers all talk in riddles, and necromancy seems like a waste of time to me. I wasn't even sure if the enchantments really worked. Grolims are very gullible sometimes. A suggestion of a curse would probably work just as well as a real one."

"You know," Belgarath mused, "I think the reason we missed it was because we've been concentrating on the fact that Urvon, Zandramas, and Agachak are all sorcerers. We kept overlooking the fact that they're also Grolims."

"Is this curse—or whatever you call it—aimed specifically at the Grolims," Garion asked, "or would it affect us, too?"

Beldin scratched at his beard. "It's a good question, Belgarath," he said. "That's not the sort of thing you'd want to risk lightly."

"Senji!" Belgarath snapped his fingers.

"I didn't quite follow that."

"Senji went to Kell, remember? And even as inept as he is, he's still a sorcerer."

"That's it, then," Beldin grinned. "*We* can go to Kell, and *they* can't. They'll have to follow us for a change."

"What about the demons?" Durnik asked soberly. "Nahaz is already marching toward Kell, and as far as we know, Zandramas has Mordja with her. Would they be able to go to Kell? What I'm getting at is that even if Urvon and Zandramas can't go there, couldn't they just send the demons instead to get the information for them?"

Beldin shook his head. "It wouldn't do them any good. Cyradis won't let a demon anywhere near her copy of the Mallorean Gospels. No matter what other faults they have, the seers refuse to have anything to do with the agents of chaos."

"Could she prevent either of the demons from just taking what they want, though?" Durnik looked worried. "Let's face it, Beldin. A demon is a fairly awful thing."

"She can take care of herself," Beldin replied. "Don't worry about Cyradis."

"Master Beldin," 'Zakath objected, "she's little more than a child, and with her eyes bound like that, she's utterly helpless."

Beldin laughed coarsely. "Helpless? Cyradis? Man, are you out of your mind? She could probably stop the sun if she needed to. We can't even begin to make guesses about how much power she has."

"I don't understand." 'Zakath looked baffled.

"Cyradis is the focus of all the power of her race, 'Zakath," Polgara explained. "Not only the power of the Dals who are presently alive, but also that of all of them who have ever lived."

"Or who might live in the future, for all we know," Belgarath added.

"That's an interesting idea," Beldin said. "We might want to discuss it some-day. Anyway," he continued to 'Zakath, "Cyradis can do just about anything she has to do to make sure the final meeting takes place at the correct time and the correct place. Demons aren't a part of that meeting, so she'll probably just ignore them; and if they get too troublesome, she'll just send them back where they came from."

"Can you do that?"

Beldin shook his head.

"But she can?"

"I think so, yes."

"I'm having a little trouble with all this," Silk admitted. "If none of the Grolims can go to Kell without going blind, and if the demons aren't going to find out any-thing, even if they do go there, why are they all running toward it? What good's it going to do them?"

"They're putting themselves into a position where they can follow us when we come out," Belgarath replied. "They know we *can* go there and that we'll find out where the meeting is going to take place. They probably plan to tag along behind when we leave."

"That's going to make it very nervous when we leave Kell, isn't it? We'll have half the Grolims in the world right behind us."

"Everything will work out, Silk," Belgarath replied confidently.

"Fatalism does not fill me with confidence at this point, old man," Silk said acidly.

Belgarath's expression became almost beatific. "Trust me," he said.

Silk glared at him, threw his arms in the air, and then stamped away, swearing under his breath.

"You know, I've been wanting to do that to him for years," the old man chuck-led, his blue eyes twinkling. "I think it was actually worth the wait. All right. Let's get things together again and move on."

They transferred some of the supplies from the box across the back of the little carriage to the packhorses, and then Durnik stood considering the vehicle thought-fully. "It's not going to work," he said.

"What's wrong with it?" Silk asked him a bit defensively.

"The horse has to be hitched between those shafts. If we put the wolf on the seat, she'll be right behind him. He'll bolt at that point. Nothing could stop him."

"I suppose I didn't think of that," Silk said glumly.

"It's the smell of the wolf that sends horses into such a panic, isn't it?" Velvet asked.

"That and the snapping and snarling," Durnik replied.

"Belgarion can persuade her not to snap and snarl."

"What about the smell?" Silk asked.

"I'll take care of that." She went to one of the packs and removed a small glass bottle. "I expect you to buy me some more of this, Prince Kheldar," she said firmly. "You stole the wrong kind of carriage, so it's up to you to replace what I have to use to smooth over your blunder."

"What is it?" he asked suspiciously.

"Perfume, Kheldar, and it's dreadfully expensive." She looked at Garion, her smile dimpling her cheeks. "I'll need you to translate for me," she said. "I wouldn't want the wolf to misunderstand when I start to sprinkle this on her."

"Of course."

When the two of them returned from the sledlike contraption the wolf and her puppy were riding in, they found Ce'Nedra firmly ensconced on the front seat of the smart little carriage. "This will do very nicely, Prince Kheldar," she said brightly. "Thank you ever so much."

"But—"

"Was there something?" she asked, her eyes wide.

Silk's expression grew surly, and he wandered away muttering to himself.

"His morning has taken a turn for the worse, hasn't it?" 'Zakath observed to Garion.

"He's doing all right," Garion replied. "He got all the entertainment out of cheating that merchant and stealing the carriage. He gets unbearable if he has too many successes in a row. Ce'Nedra and Liselle usually manage to let the air out of him, though."

"You mean they cooked all that up between them?"

"They didn't have to. They've been doing it for so long now that they don't even have to discuss it any more."

"Do you think Liselle's perfume will work?"

"There's one way to find out," Garion said.

They transferred the injured wolf from the sled to the front seat of the two-wheeled carriage and dabbed some perfume on the bridge of the horse's nose. Then they stepped back and looked closely at the horse while Ce'Nedra held the reins tightly. The horse looked a bit suspicious, but did not panic. Garion went back for the puppy and deposited him in Ce'Nedra's lap. She smiled, patted the she-wolf on the head, and shook the reins gently.

"That's really unfair," Silk complained to Garion as they all moved out in the Rivan Queen's wake.

"Did you want to share that seat with the she-wolf?" Garion asked him.

Silk frowned. "I hadn't thought of that, I guess," he admitted. "She wouldn't really bite me, though, would she?"

"I don't think so, but then, you never know with wolves."

"I think I'll stay where I am, then."

"That might be a good idea."

"Aren't you just a little worried about Ce'Nedra? That wolf could eat her in two bites."

"No. She won't do that. She knows that Ce'Nedra's my mate and she sort of likes me."

"Ce'Nedra's your wife." Silk shrugged. "If the wolf bites her in two, I suppose Polgara could put her back together again."

As they started out, a thought came to Garion. He rode forward and fell in beside 'Zakath. "You're the Emperor of Mallorea, right?"

"How nice of you to notice finally," 'Zakath replied dryly.

"Then how is it that you didn't know about that curse Beldin was talking about?"

"As you may have noticed, Garion, I pay very little attention to the Grolims. I knew that most of them wouldn't go there, but I thought it was just a superstition of some kind."

"A good ruler tries to know everything he can about his kingdom," Garion said, then realized how priggish that sounded. "Sorry, 'Zakath," he apologized. "That didn't come out exactly the way I'd intended it to."

"Garion," 'Zakath said patiently, "your kingdom's a small island. I'd imagine you know most of your subjects personally."

"Well, a lot of them—by sight, anyway."

"I thought you might. You know their problems, their dreams, and their hopes, and you take a personal interest in them."

"Well, yes, I suppose I do."

"You're a good king—probably one of the best in the world—but it's very easy to be a good king when your kingdom is so small. You've seen my empire, though—part of it anyway—and I'm sure you have at least some idea of how many people live here. It would be utterly impossible for me to be a good king. That's why I'm an emperor instead."

"And a God?" Garion asked slyly.

"No. I'll leave that particular delusion to Urvon and Zandramas. People's wits seem to slip a bit when they aspire to divinity, and, believe me, I need all my wits about me. I found that out after I'd wasted half my life trying to destroy Taur Urgas."

"Garion, dear," Ce'Nedra called from the carriage.

"Yes?"

"Could you come back here a moment? The wolf is whimpering a little, and I don't know how to ask her what the trouble is."

"I'll be right back," Garion said to 'Zakath, turning Chretienne around and trotting back to the carriage.

Ce'Nedra sat in the carriage with the wolf pup in her lap. The little creature lay blissfully on his back with all four paws in the air while she scratched his furry tummy.

The she-wolf lay on the seat beside her. The wolf's ears were twitching and her eyes were mournful.

"Are you in pain?" Garion asked her.

"Does this she of yours always talk this much?" she whined.

It was impossible to lie, and evasion was almost as much out of the question. "Yes," he admitted.

"Can you make her stop?"

"I can try." He looked at Ce'Nedra. "The wolf is very tired," he told her. "She wants to go to sleep."

"I'm not stopping her."

"You've been talking to her," he pointed out gently.

"I was only trying to make friends with her, Garion."

"You're already friends. She likes you. Now let her go to sleep."

Ce'Nedra pouted. "I won't bother her," she said, sounding a bit injured. "I'll talk to the puppy instead."

"He's tired, too."

"How can they be so tired in the daytime?"

"Wolves usually hunt at night. This is their normal sleeping time."

"Oh. I didn't know that. All right, Garion. Tell her that I'll be quiet while they sleep."

"Little sister," he said to the wolf, "she promises not to talk to you if your eyes are closed."

The wolf gave him a puzzled look.

"She will think you're sleeping."

The wolf managed to look shocked. "Is it possible in the language of the man-things to say that which is not truth?"

"Sometimes."

"How remarkable. Very well," she said. "If it is the rule of the pack, I will do this. It is, however, very unnatural."

"Yes. I know."

"I will close my eyes," the wolf said. "I will keep them closed all day if it will keep her from chattering at me." She let out a long sigh and closed her eyes.

"Is she asleep?" Ce'Nedra whispered.

"I think so," Garion whispered back. Then he turned and rode back to the head of the column.

The countryside grew more hilly and broken as they rode west. Although the overcast continued to be as heavy as before, there appeared to be some hint of light along the western horizon as afternoon progressed.

They clattered across a stone bridge that arched over a tumbling stream. "It smells clean, Belgarath," Durnik said. "I think it's coming down out of the mountains."

Belgarath squinted up the gully from which the stream emerged. "Why don't you have a look?" he suggested. "See if there's a place to make camp. Good water has been hard to find, so let's not pass any up."

"I was thinking the same thing myself." Then the smith and his towering mute friend rode off upstream.

They set up camp for the night several hundred yards up the gully where a bend in the stream had opened out a kind of curved gravel bench. After they had watered the horses and set up the tents, Polgara began cooking supper. She cut steaks from the side of beef and made a thick soup of dried peas, seasoned with chunks of ham. Then she set a large loaf of dark peasant bread near the fire to warm, humming to herself all the while. As always, cooking seemed to satisfy some deep-seated need in her.

The supper which came from her fire that evening was of near-banquet proportions, and evening was settling in as they finished eating and leaned back contentedly.

"Very good, Pol." Beldin belched. "I guess you haven't lost your touch after all."

"Thank you, uncle." She smiled. Then she looked at Eriond. "Don't get too comfortable," she told him. "At least not until you've finished helping with the dishes."

Eriond sighed and took a bucket down to the stream for water.

"That used to be my job," Garion told 'Zakath. "I'm glad there's someone younger along this time."

"Isn't that women's work?"

"Would you like to tell *her* that?"

"Ah—now that you mention it, perhaps not."

"You learn very fast, 'Zakath."

"I don't believe I've ever washed a dish—not in my entire life."

"I've washed enough for both of us, and I wouldn't say that too loudly. She might decide that it's time for you to learn how." Garion gave Polgara a speculative sidelong glance. "Let's go feed the wolf and her puppy," he suggested. "Idleness in others irritates Aunt Pol for some reason, and she can almost always think of things for people to do."

"Garion, dear," Polgara said sweetly as they rose. "After the dishes are done, we'll need water for bathing."

"Yes, Aunt Pol," he said automatically. "You see?" he muttered to the Emperor of Mallorea, "I knew we hadn't moved quite fast enough."

"Do you always do what she asks? And does she mean me, too?"

Garion sighed. "Yes," he replied, "on both counts."

They rose early the next morning, and Beldin soared off to scout on ahead while the rest ate breakfast, struck camp, and saddled their horses. The damp, sullen chill which had hovered over this desolate countryside was now edged with a drier kind of cold as the prevailing wind swept down from the summits of the Dalasian mountains. Garion pulled his cloak about him and rode on. They had gone only a league or so when Beldin spiraled down out of the overcast sky. "I think you'd better turn south," he advised. "Urvon's just ahead, and his whole army's right behind him."

Belgarath swore.

"There's more," the hunchback told him. "The Darshivans managed to get past Atesca—or through him. They're coming up from behind. The elephants are leading the march. We're right between two armies here."

"How far ahead of us is Urvon?" Belgarath asked him.

"Six or eight leagues. He's in the foothills of the mountains."

"And how far behind us are the elephants?"

"About five leagues. It looks to me as if they're going to try to cut Urvon's column off. There's no help for it, Belgarath. We're going to have to run. We have to get out of the middle of this before the fighting starts."

"Is Atesca pursuing Zandramas' army?" 'Zakath asked intently.

"No. I think he followed your orders and pulled back to that enclave on the bank of the Magan."

Belgarath was still swearing. "How did Urvon get this far south so fast?" he muttered.

"He's killing his troops by the score," Beldin replied. "He's making them run, and Nahaz has demons whipping them along."

"I guess we don't have any choice," Belgarath said. "We'll have to go south. Toth, will you be able to lead us to Kell if we go into the mountains down near the border of Gandahar?"

The big mute nodded, then gestured to Durnik.

"It's going to be more difficult, though," the smith translated. "The mountains are very rugged down there, and there's still a lot of snow at the higher elevations."

"We'll lose a lot of time, Grandfather," Garion said.

"Not as much as we'll lose if we get caught in the middle of a battle. All right. Let's go south."

"In a moment, father," Polgara said. "Ce'Nedra," she called, "come up here." Ce'Nedra shook her reins and drove her carriage up to where they stood.

Polgara quickly explained the situation to her. "Now then," she said, "we need to know exactly what they're doing and what they're planning to do—both armies. I think it's time for you to use my sister's amulet."

"Why didn't I think of that?" Belgarath said, sounding a bit embarrassed.

"You were too busy trying to remember all the swearwords you've ever heard," Beldin suggested.

"Can you do that and drive the carriage at the same time?" Polgara asked the little queen.

"I can try, Lady Polgara." Ce'Nedra sounded a little dubious. She lifted the sleeping puppy out of her lap and laid him beside his mother.

"Let's move out," Belgarath said.

They turned off the road and jolted across an open field through long-dead grass. After they had gone a short distance, Ce'Nedra called to Polgara. "It's not working, Lady Polgara," she said. "I need both hands on the reins on this rough ground."

They reined in.

"It's not that big a problem," Velvet said. "I'll lead the carriage horse, and Ce'Nedra can concentrate on what she's doing."

"It's a little dangerous, Liselle," Belgarath objected. "If that carriage horse shies, he'll jerk you out of the saddle and the carriage will run right over you."

"Have you ever seen me fall off a horse, Ancient One? Don't worry, I'll be perfectly fine." She rode over to the carriage horse and took hold of his reins. They started out slowly and then gradually picked up speed. Polgara rode beside the carriage, and Ce'Nedra, a little frown of concentration on her face, kept her hand on the amulet chained about her throat.

"Anything?" Polgara asked.

"I'm hearing a lot of random conversation, Lady Polgara," the little queen replied. "There are great numbers of people out there. Wait a minute," she said, "I think I've pinpointed Nahaz. That's not the sort of voice you forget." She frowned. "I think he's talking to Urvon's generals. They've had the Hounds out, so they know the elephants are coming."

"Will you be able to come back to them?" Belgarath asked her.

"I think so. Once I find somebody, I can usually locate him again fairly quickly."

"Good. See if you can find out if the Darshivan generals know that Urvon's just ahead of them. If there's going to be a battle, I want to know exactly where it's going to happen."

Ce'Nedra turned slightly, her amulet clenched tightly in her fist. She closed her eyes. After a moment, she opened them. "I *do* wish they'd be still," she fretted.

"Who?" Silk asked her.

"The elephant herders. They babble worse than old women. Wait. There they are. I've got them now." She listened for a few moments as the carriage jolted along over the rough ground. "The Darshivan officers are very worried," she reported. "They know that Urvon's army is somewhere in the mountains, but they don't know his exact location. None of their scouts came back to report."

"The Hounds are probably seeing to that," Silk said.

"What are the Darshivans planning?" Belgarath asked.

"They're undecided. They're going to push on cautiously and send out more scouts."

"All right. Now see if you can go back to Nahaz."

"I'll try." She closed her eyes again. "Oh, that's revolting!" she exclaimed after a moment.

"What is it, dear?" Polgara asked her.

"The Karands have found a narrow gorge. They're going to lure the elephants into it and then roll boulders and burning bushes down on them from the top." She listened for a few moments longer. "Once they've eliminated the elephants, the whole army is going to charge down out of the foothills and attack the rest of the Darshivans."

"Is Urvon there?" Beldin asked, his eyes intent.

"No. He's off to the side someplace. He's raving."

"I think you'd better go find that gorge," Belgarath told the dwarf. "That's where the battle's going to be, and I want to be sure it's behind us and not on up ahead somewhere."

"Right," Beldin agreed, crouching and spreading his arms. "Keep in touch," he suggested even as he began to change form.

They rode along at a careful walk, and Garion buckled on his shield.

"Do you really think that's going to help if we run into an entire army?" 'Zakath asked him.

"It may not help much, but it won't hurt."

Belgarath rode now with his face lifted toward the murky sky. Garion could feel the old man's thought reaching out.

"Not so loud, father," Polgara cautioned. "We've got Grolims all around us."

"Good," he replied. "None of them will be able to tell who's making the noise. They'll all think it's just another Grolim."

They rode on slowly with all of them watching the old sorcerer. "North!" he exploded finally. "Beldin's found the gorge where the ambush is. It's behind us. A little hard riding now and we'll be completely clear of both armies."

"Why don't we just sort of step right along, then?" Silk suggested.

CHAPTER TWENTY-THREE

They galloped south through the desolate countryside of western Darshiva with Velvet once again leading Ce'Nedra's horse. The little queen clung to the side of the carriage with one hand and kept the other on her amulet. "The Darshivans still don't know that Urvon's waiting in ambush for them," she called.

"I'd imagine they'll find out before too long," Silk called back.

"How far is it to the border of Gandahar?" Garion asked 'Zakath.

"I'd guess about twenty leagues."

"Grandfather," Garion said, "do we really have to go that far south?"

"Probably not," the old man replied. "Beldin's on up ahead. As soon as we're well past Urvon's scouts, he'll lead us up into the mountains. I don't have any particular urge to explore Gandahar, do you?"

"Not really, no."

They rode on.

The overcast grew perceptibly thicker, and Garion felt the first drops of a chill rain striking his face.

They crested a hill, and Belgarath rose in his stirrups the better to see what lay ahead. "There," he said, pointing. "He's circling."

Garion peered out across the shallow valley on the far side of the hill. A solitary bird, hardly more than a minuscule black speck in the distance, swung almost lazily in the air. They plunged down the hill, and the bird veered and flew off toward the west with slow strokes of his wings. They turned and followed.

The intermittent rain turned to a chilly drizzle, obscuring the surrounding countryside with its filmy haze.

"Don't you just love to ride in the rain?" Silk said with heavy irony.

"Under the circumstances, yes," Sadi replied. "Rain's not quite as good as fog, but it does cut down the visibility, and there are all manner of people looking for us."

"You've got a point there," Silk admitted, pulling his cloak tighter about him.

The terrain grew increasingly rugged with outcroppings of weathered stone jutting up out of the ground. After about a half hour of hard riding, Beldin led them into a shallow gully. They rode on, and the gully walls grew progressively steeper and higher. Soon they were riding up a narrow, rocky ravine.

It was midafternoon by now, and they were all thoroughly soaked. Garion wiped his face and peered ahead. The sky to the west appeared to be growing lighter, giving promise of clearing. He had perhaps not even been aware of how much the prevailing gloom hanging over Darshiva had depressed him. He urged Chretienne into a run. Somehow he seemed to feel that once they reached the sunlight again, they would be safe.

He rounded a bend in the ravine and saw Beldin standing in the trail ahead of them. The dwarf's matted hair hung in scraggly wet strands about his shoulders, and his beard was dripping. "You'd better slow down," he growled at them. "I could hear you coming for a mile, and we're not alone in these foothills."

Regretfully, Garion reined Chretienne in.

"Exactly where does this ravine lead?" Belgarath asked the hunchback.

"It twists and turns a lot, but eventually it opens out onto a ridge top. The ridge runs north and south. If we follow it north, we'll come to the main caravan route. That's the fastest way down into Dalasia."

"Everybody else knows that, too."

"That's all right. We'll be at least a day ahead of them. They still have a battle to fight."

"Are you going to scout ahead again?"

"Not until the rain lets up. My feathers are wet. It'd take a derrick to get me off the ground again. Oh, one other thing. When we get to that ridge, we're going to have to be careful. A couple leagues north, it runs just a few miles above the spot where Nahaz has his ambush set up."

"Your choice of a route leaves a lot to be desired," Belgarath said. "If someone down there happens to look up, we'll have half of Urvon's army all over us."

"Not unless they can fly. An earthquake went through here a few thousand years ago and it sliced off the side of that ridge. It's a very steep cliff now."

"How high?"

"High enough—a thousand feet or so."

"How far is it to the caravan route?"

"About fifteen leagues from the place where we'll come out on the ridge."

"North of Urvon's army, then?"

"Quite a bit north, yes."

"Why did Nahaz pass it by? Why didn't he just turn west?"

"He probably didn't want the Darshivans and their elephants coming up behind him. Besides, he's a demon. I'd guess he just couldn't bring himself to pass up the chance for a mass slaughter."

"Maybe. Do you think the battle's going to start this afternoon?"

"I doubt it. Elephants don't move all that fast, and the Darshivans are moving cautiously. They'll stop for the night soon. First thing tomorrow morning, though, things are going to start getting noisy."

"Maybe we can get past the place where the ambush is set up during the night."

"I wouldn't advise it. You won't be able to light any torches, and that cliff's a sheer drop. If you ride off the edge of it, you'll bounce all the way back to the Magan."

Belgarath grunted. "Are you sure you can't fly?"

"Not a chance. Right now you couldn't get me into the air with a catapult."

"Why don't you change into a duck?"

"Why don't you mind your own business?"

"All right, Garion," Belgarath said with some resignation, "I guess it's up to us, then." He slid down out of his saddle and walked on up the ravine. Garion sighed, dismounted, and followed him.

They ranged out ahead, searching the soggy terrain with their ears and noses. It was almost evening when the walls of the ravine began to fan out, and they could see the line of the ridge top ahead. They reached it and loped north through the gradually diminishing drizzle.

"Grandfather," Garion said, "I think that's a cave over there." He pointed with his muzzle at an opening in the rock.

"Let's look."

The opening of the cave was narrow, not much more than a wide crack, and the cavern did not open up noticeably inside. It was deep, however, running far back into the rock. It seemed more like a long corridor than a room.

"What do you think?" Garion asked as the two of them stood at the entrance peering back into the darkness.

"It's a place to get in out of the weather, and it's a good place to hide for the night. Go get the others, and I'll see if I can get a fire started."

Garion turned and loped back down the ridge. The rain was definitely slacking off now, but the wind was coming up, and it was getting colder.

The others were coming warily up out of the ravine when Garion reached them.

"Another cave?" Silk said plaintively when Garion told them what he and Belgarath had found.

"I'll hold your hand, Kheldar," Velvet offered.

"I appreciate the gesture, Liselle, but I don't think it's going to help very much. I loathe caves."

"Someday you'll have to tell me why."

"No. I don't think so. I don't like to talk about it. I don't even like to think about it."

Garion led them to the narrow track atop the ridge. Ce'Nedra's carriage jolted over the rocky ground. The smug look that had come over her face when she had expropriated the vehicle had evaporated, and she rode with resignation, wincing at every bump.

"That's not much of a cave," Beldin said critically when they reached the opening in the rock.

"Feel free to sleep outside," Belgarath told him.

"We're going to have to put blinders on the horses to get them inside," Durnik noted. "They'll take one look at that opening and flatly refuse even to try it."

"I feel much the same way myself," Silk said. "Sometimes it's surprising just how intelligent horses really are."

"We're not going to be able to get the carriage inside," Sadi said.

"We can cover it with tent canvas and sprinkle dirt over it," Durnik said. "It won't be really visible—at least not in the dark."

"Let's get started," Belgarath said. "I think we want to be inside before it gets much darker."

It took the better part of half an hour to get the balky horses into the narrow cave. Then Durnik covered the entrance with tent canvas and went back outside to help Eriond and Toth conceal the carriage.

The she-wolf had limped into the cave, followed by her frolicsome pup. Now that he was being fed regularly, the previously listless animal had turned playful. His mother, too, Garion noted, had begun to fill out again, and her fur was glossy and less matted. "An excellent den," she observed. "Will we hunt from here?"

"No, little sister," Polgara replied, stirring the small pot of simmering herbs on the fire. "We have things that must be done in another place. Let me have a look at your hurt."

Obediently, the wolf lay down by the fire and extended her injured paw. Polgara gently unwrapped it and examined the ulcers. "Much better," she said. "It's nearly healed. Does it still cause you pain?"

"Pain is to be endured," the wolf replied indifferently. "It is of no moment."

"The amount of pain, however, tells us how much longer it will be until the hurt is gone."

"That is true," the wolf admitted. "I have observed the same thing myself in times past. The pain is less now. The hurt is going away, I think."

Polgara bathed the injured paw in the pungent juice from her pot, then mixed the pulped herbs with soap and sugar again, packed it over the wound, and replaced the bandage. "We will not have to do this again, little sister," she told her patient. "The hurt is nearly gone."

"I am grateful," the wolf said simply. "Will I be able to walk when it grows light again? The thing which runs on round feet is most uncomfortable to sit in, and the she who makes it run talks much."

"Sit in it one more time while it is light," Polgara advised. "Give the hurt that much more time to go away."

The wolf sighed and laid her chin on her paws.

They carried water from a nearby spring, and Polgara cooked supper. After they had eaten, Belgarath rose to his feet. "Let's have a look around," he said to Garion. "I want to get an idea of what we're dealing with."

Garion nodded and stood up. The two of them went outside the cave, carrying Silk's supper out to him. The little man had volunteered, enthusiastically, Garion thought, to stand watch. "Where are you going?" he asked, sitting down on a rock to eat.

"We're going to nose around a bit," Belgarath replied.

"Good idea. You want me to come along?"

"No. You'd better stay here and keep your eyes open. Warn the others if any-body comes up the ridge." Then the old man led Garion a few hundred feet up the ridge line, and the two of them made the change into their other forms. Garion had changed back and forth so many times in the past few months that at times the dis-tinction between the two shapes had begun to blur and, oftentimes, even when he was in his human form, he found himself thinking in the language of wolves. He loped along behind the great silver wolf, considering this peculiar loss of identity.

Belgarath stopped. "Keep your mind on what we're doing," he said. "Your ears and nose won't be much good to us if you're wool-gathering."

"Yes, revered pack-leader," Garion replied, feeling very embarrassed. Wolves seldom needed reprimanding and they were covered with shame when it happened.

When they reached the spot where the side of the ridge had been sheared away by the earthquake, they stopped. The foothills that sloped down toward the plain were dark. Urvon's army was obviously under orders to build no fires. Out on the plain itself, however, the watch fires twinkled in profusion like small orange stars.

"Zandramas has a big army," Garion sent his thought quietly to his grand-father.

"Yes," the old man agreed. "That battle tomorrow morning might take quite a while. Even Nahaz's demons are going to need a lot of time to kill that many peo-ple."

"The longer the better. They can take all week, if they want to. We could be halfway to Kell by then."

Belgarath looked around. "Let's go on up the ridge a ways and have a look."

"All right."

Despite Beldin's warning that there might be scouts from the two armies here in the higher foothills, the two wolves encountered no one. "They probably went back to report," Garion heard Belgarath's voice speaking in his mind. "They'll be out again first thing in the morning, most likely. Let's go on back to the cave and get some sleep."

They rose early the following morning, long before first light. They were all subdued as they ate breakfast. Although the two armies facing each other below them were composed entirely of enemies, none of them took any particular pleasure in the prospect of the bloodshed the day would bring. After breakfast, they carried out the packs and their saddles and, last of all, they led out the horses.

"You're quiet this morning, Garion," 'Zakath said as the two were saddling their mounts.

"I was just wondering if there might be some way to stop what's going to hap-pen today."

"Not really," 'Zakath told him. "Their positions are too firmly fixed. It's too late to turn it back now. The Darshivans will advance, and Urvon's army will am-bush them. I've organized enough battles to know that at a certain point things be-come inevitable."

"The way Thull Mardu was?"

"Thull Mardu was a blunder," 'Zakath admitted. "I should have gone around Ce'Nedra's army instead of trying to go through it. The Grolims had me convinced that they could hold that fog in place all day. I should have known better than to believe them. And I definitely shouldn't have underestimated the Asturian bowmen. How can they possibly shoot arrows that fast?"

"There's a knack to it. Lelldorin showed me how it's done."

"Lelldorin?"

"An Asturian friend of mine."

"We've always been told that Arends are stupid to the point of imbecility."

"They're not overly bright," Garion admitted. "Maybe that's what makes them such good soldiers. They don't have enough imagination to be afraid." He smiled in the darkness. "Mandorallen can't even conceive of the possibility that he could lose a fight. He'd attack your whole army—all by himself."

"The Baron of Vo Mandor? I know his reputation." 'Zakath laughed wryly. "It's entirely possible that he'd win, you know."

"Don't ever tell him that. He has enough problems as it is." Garion sighed. "I wish he were here, though—and Barak and Hettar and even Relg."

"Relg?"

"He's an Ulgo mystic. He walks through rock."

'Zakath stared at him.

"I don't know how, so don't ask me. I saw him stick a Grolim into a large boulder once. Then he just left him there with only his hands sticking out."

'Zakath shuddered.

They mounted and rode slowly up the ravine with Ce'Nedra's carriage jolting along behind them. The sky gradually grew lighter overhead, and Garion saw that they were approaching the edge of the cliff that overlooked the site of the impending battle.

"Belgarath," 'Zakath said quietly, "would you mind a suggestion?"

"I'll always listen to suggestions."

"This is probably the only place where we'll be able to see what's going on down below. Wouldn't it be a good idea to stop and make sure that the armies down there are fully engaged before we move on? If the Darshivans outflank Urvon's ambush, we'll have them no more than a few leagues behind us. We'll need to run at that point."

Belgarath frowned. "You might be right," he conceded. "It never hurts to know the whole situation." He reined in. "All right," he said, "we'll stop here and go ahead on foot. There's cover enough at the edge of that cliff so that we can watch without being seen." He swung down from his horse.

"The ladies and I will wait here, father," Polgara told him. "We've seen battles before. I don't think we need to watch another one." She glanced at Eriond. "You stay with us, too," she told him.

"Yes, Polgara."

The rest of them moved forward at a crouch and took cover behind the few boulders at the edge of the cliff. The gloomy overcast that hung perpetually over Darshiva covered the blasted and decaying plain below with a sullen twilight. Out on the plain, Garion could make out tiny-appearing figures moving forward at what seemed no more than a crawl.

"I think I've detected a flaw in what was otherwise an excellent plan," 'Zakath said wryly. "They're too far away to make out any details."

"I can take care of that," Beldin growled. "A hawk's eyes are about ten times more acute than a man's. I can circle over them at a few hundred feet and pick out every detail."

"Are you sure your feathers are dry?" Belgarath asked.

"That's why I slept near the fire last night."

"All right. Keep me advised."

"Naturally." The grim hunchback crouched and blurred. With an agile leap the hawk settled atop a boulder, his fierce eyes looking out over the plain. Then he spread his wings and dropped headlong off the cliff.

"You people always take that so casually," 'Zakath noted.

"It's not really that," Sadi murmured, rubbing his scalp. "It's just that we're numb. The first time I saw him do it, my hair stood on end, and for me that's a neat trick."

"Urvon's army's hiding in shallow pits along the ridge tops on either side of that long gorge," Belgarath repeated the silent words of the hawk soaring through the murky air far below them, "and the elephants are moving directly toward the same gorge."

'Zakath leaned out over the edge and looked down.

"Careful," Garion said, catching the Mallorean's arm with one hand.

"It *is* a long way down," 'Zakath agreed. "All right then," he said. "Now I see why the Darshivans are making for that gorge. It branches at the foot of this cliff, and one branch goes north. It probably connects with the main caravan route." He thought about it. "It's actually a good strategy. If Nahaz hadn't driven his troops so hard, the Darshivans would have reached the caravan route first, and they could have set up an ambush of their own." He pulled back away from the edge of the cliff. "That's one of the reasons I always hate to operate in rough terrain. I got a number of very nasty surprises in Cthol Murgos."

"The elephants are starting to form up into a column," Belgarath reported, "and the rest of the Darshivans are strung out behind them."

"Are they putting out scouts?" 'Zakath asked.

"Yes, but they're only scouting along the floor of the gorge. A few of them went up to the ridge tops, but the Hounds eliminated those."

They waited as Beldin circled above the two armies.

"They're committed now," Belgarath said sadly. "The elephants are starting into the gorge."

"I feel a little sorry for the elephants," Durnik said. "They didn't volunteer for this. I wish they didn't plan to use fire on them."

"It's fairly standard, Goodman," 'Zakath said calmly. "Fire's the only thing elephants are really afraid of. They'll stampede back down the gorge."

"Right through the Darshivans," Silk added in a slightly sick voice. "Nahaz should get his fill of blood today."

"Do we really have to watch this?" Durnik asked.

"We have to wait until it gets started," Belgarath replied.

"I think I'll go back and wait with Pol," the smith said, edging back from the cliff top. Then he and Toth went on down the ridge.

"He's a very gentle person, isn't he?" 'Zakath said.

"Usually," Garion replied. "When it's necessary, though, he can do what needs doing."

"You remember the time he chased that Murgo into a quicksand bog," Silk said with a shudder, "and then watched him sink?"

"It shouldn't be too long now," Belgarath said tensely. "The last of the elephants just entered the gorge."

They waited. For some reason, Garion felt suddenly cold.

Then, even though what was happening was more than a league away, they heard a thunderous rumbling sound as Urvon's troops began to roll huge boulders down on the advancing elephants. Faintly they could hear the agonized screams of the huge beasts. Then, smoke and flame began to boil up out of the gorge as the brutish Karands rained huge piles of burning brush down on the helpless animals.

"I think I've seen enough," Sadi said. He rose and went back down the ridge.

The surviving elephants, looking almost like ants in the distance, wheeled and fled in panic back down the gorge, and the agonized squeals of the animals were suddenly accompanied by human screams as the great beasts crushed their way through rank after rank of Darshivan soldiers.

Beldin came soaring up from below and settled back on the boulder from which he had started.

"What's that?" Silk exclaimed. "There at the mouth of the gorge."

There seemed to be some vast disturbance in the murky air at the edge of the plain, a sort of shimmering filled with flickering, rainbow-hued light and sullen flashes of heat lightning. Then, quite suddenly, the disturbance coalesced into a nightmare.

"Belar!" Silk swore. "It's as big as a barn!"

The thing was hideous. It had a dozen or more snakelike arms that writhed and lashed at the air. It had three blazing eyes and a vast muzzle filled with great fangs. It towered over the elephants and kicked them aside contemptuously with huge, clawed feet. Then with thunderous stride, it started up the gorge, walking indifferently through the flames and paying no more attention to the boulders bouncing off its shoulders than it might have to snowflakes.

"What *is* that thing?" 'Zakath asked in a shaken voice.

"That's Mordja," Belgarath told him. "I've seen him before—in Morindland—and that's not the sort of face one forgets."

The demon in the gorge was reaching out with his many arms now, catching whole platoons of Karands in his clawed hands and almost casually hurling them with terrific force against the surrounding rocks.

"It looks to me as if the tide of battle just turned," Silk said. "What's our general feeling about leaving—along about right now?"

The Demon Lord Mordja raised his huge muzzle and thundered something in a language too hideous for human comprehension.

"Stay put!" Belgarath ordered, catching Silk's arm. "This isn't played out yet. That was a challenge, and Nahaz won't be able to refuse it."

Another of those flickering disturbances appeared in the air above the upper end of the gorge, and another towering form appeared out of its center. Garion could not see its face, a fact for which he was profoundly grateful, but it, too, had snaky arms growing in profusion from its vast shoulders. "Thou darest to face me, Mordja?" it roared in a voice which shook the nearby mountains.

"I do not fear thee, Nahaz," Mordja bellowed back. "Our enmity hath endured for a thousand thousand years. Let it end here. I shall carry word of thy death back to the King of Hell and bear thy head with me as proof of my words."

"My head is thine," Nahaz said with a chilling laugh. "Come and take it—if thou canst."

"And thou wouldst bestow the stone of power on the mad Disciple of maimed Torak?" Mordja sneered.

"Thy sojourn in the land of the Morindim hath bereft thee of thy wits, Mordja. The stone of power shall be *mine*, and I shall rule these ants that creep upon the face of this world. I will raise them like cattle and feed upon them when I hunger."

"How wilt thou feed, Nahaz—without thy head? It is I who will rule and feed here, for the stone of power shall lie in my hand."

"That we will soon discover, Mordja. Come. Let us contend for a head and for the stone we both desire." Suddenly Nahaz spun about, his baleful eyes searching the top of the cliff where Garion and his friends lay hidden. A volcanic hiss burst from the demon's distorted lips. "The Child of Light!" he roared. "Praise the name of the King of Hell, who hath brought him within my reach. I will rend him asunder and seize the stone which *he* carries. Thou art doomed, Mordja. That stone in my hand shall be thy undoing." With hideous speed the Demon Lord Nahaz clambered over the tumbled rocks at the foot of the cliff and reached out with his dozens of clawed hands at the sheer rock face. His vast shoulders heaved.

"He's climbing straight up the rock!" Silk exclaimed in a strangled voice. "Let's get out of here!"

The Demon Lord Mordja stood for a moment in stunned chagrin, then he, too, ran forward and began to claw his way up the face of the cliff.

Garion rose to his feet, looking down at the two vast monsters clambering up the sheer rock. He felt a peculiar detachment as he reached back over his shoulder and drew his sword. He untied the leather sleeve covering the hilt and slipped it off. The Orb glowed, and when he took the sword in both hands, the familiar blue flame ran up the blade.

"Garion!" 'Zakath exclaimed.

"They want the Orb," Garion said grimly. "Well, they're going to have to take it, and I may have something to say about that."

But then Durnik was there. His face was calm, and he was stripped to the waist. In his right hand he carried an awesome sledgehammer that glowed as blue as Garion's sword. "Excuse me, Garion," he said in a matter-of-fact tone, "but this is my task."

Polgara had come with him, and her face showed no fear. She had drawn her blue cloak about her, and the snowy lock at her brow glowed.

"What's happening here?" Belgarath demanded.

"Stay out of it, father," Polgara told him. "This is something that has to happen."

Durnik advanced to the edge of the cliff and looked down at the two horrors struggling up the sheer face toward him. "I abjure ye," he said to them in a great voice, "return to the place from whence ye came, lest ye die." Overlaying his voice was another voice, calm, almost gentle, but with a power in it that shook Garion as a tree is shaken by a hurricane. He knew that voice.

"Begone!" Durnik commanded, emphasizing that word with a dreadful blow of his sledge that shattered a boulder into fragments.

The demons clawing their way up the cliff hesitated.

At first it was barely perceptible. At first it seemed that Durnik was only swelling his chest and shoulders in preparation for an impossible struggle. Then Garion saw his oldest friend begin to grow. At ten feet, the smith was awesome. At twenty, he was beyond belief. The great hammer in his hand grew with him, and the blue nimbus about it grew more intense as he expanded and grew, thrusting the sullen air aside with his massive shoulders. The very rocks seemed to cringe back from him as, with long sweeps of his dreadful, glowing hammer, he loosened his arm.

The Demon Lord Mordja paused, clinging to the rock. His bestial face suddenly showed fear. Again Durnik destroyed whole square yards of rock with a single ringing blow.

Nahaz, however, his eyes ablaze and empty of thought, continued to slather and claw his way up the rock face, screeching imprecations in that dreadful language which only demons know.

"So be it, then," Durnik said, and the voice in which he spoke was not his own, but that other, more profound voice, which rang in Garion's ears like the very crack of doom.

The Demon Lord Mordja looked up, his terrible face filled with terror. Then suddenly he released his grip on the face of the rock cliff to topple and tumble to the rocks below. Howling, and with his multitudinous arms covering his scabrous head, he fled.

Nahaz, however, his blazing eyes filled with madness, continued to sink his claws into naked rock and to haul his vast body up the cliff.

Almost politely, it seemed, Durnik stepped back from the awful brink and wrapped both enormous hands about the glowing handle of his sledge.

"Durnik!" Silk cried. "No! Don't let him get his feet under him!"

Durnik did not reply, but a faint smile touched his honest face. Again he tested his vast hammer, swinging it in both hands. The sound of its passage through the air was not a whistle, but a roar.

Nahaz clambered up over the edge of the cliff and rose enormously, clawing at the sky and roaring insanely in the hideous language of the demons.

Durnik spat on his left hand; then on his right. He twisted his huge hands on the handle of his sledge to set them in place, then he swung a vast, overhand blow that took the Demon Lord full in the chest. "Begone!" the smith roared in a voice louder than thunder. The sledge struck fiery sparks from the demon's body, sullen orange sparks that sizzled and jumped on the ground like burning roaches.

Nahaz screamed, clutching at his chest.

Unperturbed, Durnik swung again.

And again.

Garion recognized the rhythm of his friend's strokes. Durnik was not fighting;

he was hammering with the age-old precision of a man whose tools are but an extension of his arms. Again and again the glowing hammer crashed into the body of the Demon Lord. With each blow, the sparks flew. Nahaz cringed, trying to shield his body from those awful, shattering strokes. Each time Durnik struck, he roared, "Begone!" Gradually, like a man splitting a huge rock, he began to hammer Nahaz into pieces. Pythonlike arms fell writhing into the abyss, and great, craterlike holes appeared in the demon's chest.

Unable to watch the dreadful work any longer, Garion averted his eyes. Far below, he saw Urvon's throne. The two dozen bearers who had carried it had fled, and the mad Disciple capered on the rocks howling insanely.

Durnik struck again. "Begone!"

And again. "Begone!"

And again. "Begone!"

Beaten beyond endurance, the Demon Lord Nahaz flinched back, missed his footing, and toppled off the cliff with a howl of rage and despair. Down and down he plunged, glowing with green fire like a streaking comet. As he drove into the earth, one snakelike arm lashed out and caught the last Disciple of Torak in a deathly grip. Urvon, shrieking, was pulled along as Nahaz sank into the earth like a stick into water.

When Garion looked back, Durnik had resumed his normal size. His chest and arms were covered with sweat, and he was breathing hard from his exertions. He held his glowing sledge out at arm's length, and its fire grew brighter and brighter until it was incandescent. Then the fire gradually faded, and the smith was holding a silver amulet in his hand with its chain draped across the backs of his fingers.

The voice which had overlain Durnik's during his awful encounter with the Demon Lord now spoke in no more than a whisper. "Know that this good man is also my beloved Disciple, since he was best suited of all of ye for this task."

Belgarath bowed in the direction the voice was coming from. "It shall be as You say, Master," he said in a voice thick with emotion. "We welcome him as a brother."

Polgara came forward with a look of wonder on her face and gently took the amulet from Durnik's hand. "How very appropriate," she said softly, looking at the silver disc. She lovingly hung the chain around her husband's neck, then she kissed him and held him to her tightly.

"Please, Pol," he objected with flaming cheeks, "we're not alone, you know."

She laughed her warm, rich laugh and held him even tighter.

Beldin was grinning crookedly. "Nice job, brother mine," he said to Durnik. "Hot work though, I'd imagine." He reached out his hand and took a foaming tankard out of the air and handed it to Aldur's newest Disciple.

Durnik drank gratefully.

Belgarath clapped him on the shoulder. "It's been a long, long time since we last had a new brother," he said. Then he quickly embraced Durnik.

"Oh," Ce'Nedra said with a little catch in her voice, "that's just beautiful."

Wordlessly, Velvet handed her the wispy little handkerchief. "What is that on his amulet?" the blond girl asked, sounding just a bit awed.

"It's a hammer," Belgarath told her. "What else could it be?"

"If I might make a suggestion, Ancient One," Sadi said diffidently, "the armies down there on the plain seem to be in a state of total confusion. Wouldn't this be an excellent time to depart—before they regain their wits?"

"My thought exactly," Silk approved, putting his hand on the eunuch's shoulder.

"They're right, Belgarath," Beldin agreed. "We've done what we were sent here to do—or Durnik has, at least." The hunchback sighed and looked over the edge of the cliff. "I really wanted to kill Urvon myself," he said, "but I suppose this is even better. I hope he enjoys his sojourn in Hell."

A shrill laugh suddenly came from the top of the ridge, a laugh of triumph. Garion whirled, then stopped, frozen with surprise. Atop the ridge stood the black-robed figure of the Sorceress of Darshiva. Beside her stood a blond little boy. Geran's features had changed in the year and more since he had been abducted, but Garion knew him instantly. "Ye have done my work well," Zandramas declared. "I myself could not have found a more fitting end for Torak's last Disciple. Now, Child of Light, only thou standest between me and Cthrag Sardius. I will await thy coming in the Place Which Is No More. There shalt thou be a witness when I raise up a New God over Angorak, whose dominion over all the world shall endure until the end of days!"

Geran reached out his hand imploringly to Ce'Nedra, but then he and Zandramas vanished.

"How remarkable," the she-wolf said in surprise.

THE SEERESS
OF KELL

For Lester,

We've been at this for a decade now. About all either of us could have reasonably expected was to come out ten years older, but it appears that we did just a bit more. Between us, I think that we raised a fairly good boy. I hope it was as much fun for you as it was for me, and I think we can both take a certain pride in the fact that we didn't kill each other in the process, a tribute more to the inhuman patience of a pair of special ladies than to any particular virtue of ours, I expect.

All my best,
Dave Eddings

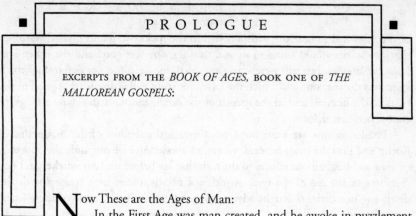

PROLOGUE

EXCERPTS FROM THE *BOOK OF AGES*, BOOK ONE OF *THE MALLOREAN GOSPELS*:

Now These are the Ages of Man:

In the First Age was man created, and he awoke in puzzlement and wonder as he beheld the world about him. And those that had made him considered him and selected from his number those that pleased them, and the rest were cast out and driven away. And some went in search of the Spirit known as UL, and they left us and passed into the west, and we saw them no more. And some denied the Gods, and they went into the far north to wrestle with demons. And some turned to worldly matters, and they went away into the east and built mighty cities there.

But we despaired, and we sat us down upon the earth in the shadow of the mountains of Korim, and in bitterness we bewailed our fate that we had been made and then cast out.

And it came to pass that in the midst of our grief a woman of our people was seized by a rapture, and it was as if she had been shaken by a mighty hand. And she arose from the earth upon which she sat, and she bound her eyes with a cloth, signifying that she had seen that which no mortal had seen before, for lo, she was the first seeress in all the world. And with the touch of her vision still upon her, she spake unto us, saying:

"Behold! A feast hath been set before Those who made us, and this feast shall ye call the Feast of Life. And Those who made us have chosen that which pleased Them, and that which pleased Them not was not chosen.

"Now *we* are the Feast of Life, and ye sorrow that no Guest at the feast hath chosen ye. Despair not, however, for one Guest hath not yet arrived at the feast. The other Guests have taken their fill, but this great Feast of Life awaiteth still the Beloved Guest who cometh late, and I say unto all the people that it is *He* who will choose us. Abide therefore against His coming, for it is certain. Put aside thy grief and turn thy face to the sky and to the earth that thou mayest read the signs written there, for this I say unto all the people. It is upon *ye* that His coming rests. For behold, He may not choose *ye* unless ye choose *Him*. And this is the Fate for which we were made. Rise up, therefore, and sit no more upon the earth in vain and foolish lamentation. Take up the task which lies before ye and prepare the way for Him who will surely come."

Much we marveled at these words, and we considered them most carefully. We questioned the seeress, but her answers were dark and obscure. And so it was that we turned our faces to the sky and bent our ears to the whispers which came from the earth that we might see and hear and learn. And as we learned to read the book of the skies and to hear the whispers within the rocks, we found myriad warnings that *two* spirits would come to us and that the one was good and the other evil. Long we labored, but still were sorely troubled, for we could not determine which spirit was the true one and which the false. For truly, evil is disguised as good in the book of the heavens and in the speech of the earth, and no man is wise enough to choose between them.

Pondering this, we went out from beneath the shadow of the mountains of Korim and into the lands beyond, where we abode. And we put aside the concerns of man and bent all our efforts to the task that lay before us. Our witches and our seers sought the aid of the spirit world, our necromancers took counsel with the dead, and our diviners sought advice from the earth. But lo, none of these knew more than we.

Then gathered we at last upon a fertile plain to bring together all that we had learned. And these are the truths that we have learned from the stars, from the rocks, from the hearts of men and from the minds of the spirits:

Know ye that all adown the endless avenues of time hath division marred all that is—for there is division at the very heart of creation. And some have said that this is natural and will persist until the end of days, but it is not so. Were the division destined to be eternal, then the purpose of creation would be to contain it. But the stars and the spirits and the voices within the rocks speak of the day when the division will end and all will be made one again, for creation itself knows that the day *will* come.

Know ye further that two spirits contend with each other at the very center of time, and these spirits are the two sides of that which hath divided creation. And in a certain time shall those spirits meet upon *this* world, and then will come the time of the Choice. And if the Choice be *not* made, then shall this world vanish, and the Beloved Guest of whom the seeress spoke will never come. For it is this which she meant when she said to us: "Behold, He may not choose *ye* unless ye choose *Him*." And the Choice that we must make is the choice between good and evil, and the division between good and evil, and the reality that will exist after we have made the choice will be a reality of good or a reality of evil, and it will prevail so until the end of days.

Behold also this truth: the rocks of this world and of all other worlds murmur continually of the two stones that lie at the center of the division. Once these stones were one, and they stood at the very center of all of creation, but, like all else, they were divided, and in the instant of division they were rent apart with a force that destroyed whole suns. And where these stones come into the presence of each other again, there surely will be the last confrontation between the two spirits. Now the day will come when all will be made one again, *except* that the division between the two stones is so great that they can never be rejoined. And in the day when the division ends shall one of the stones cease forever to exist, and in that day also shall one of the spirits forever vanish.

These then were the truths that we had gathered, and it was our discovery of these truths that marked the end of the First Age.

Now the Second Age of man began in thunder and earthquake, for lo, the earth herself split apart, and the sea rushed in to divide the lands of men even as creation itself is divided. And the mountains of Korim shuddered and groaned and heaved as the sea swallowed them. And we knew that this would come to pass, for our seers had warned us that it would be so. We went our way, therefore, and found safety before the world was cracked and the sea first rushed away and then rushed back and never departed more.

And in the days that followed the rushing in of the sea, the children of the Dragon God fled from the waters, and they abode to the north of us beyond the mountains. Now our seers told us that the children of the Dragon God would one day come among us as conquerors. And we took counsel with each other and considered how we might least offend the children of the Dragon God when they should come so that they would not interrupt our studies. In the end we concluded that our warlike neighbors would be least apprehensive about simple tillers of the soil living in rude communities on the land, and we so ordered our lives. We pulled down our cities and carried away the stones and we betook ourselves back to the land so that we might not alarm our neighbors nor arouse their envy.

And the years passed and became centuries, and the centuries passed and became eons. And as we had known they would, the children of Angarak came down amongst us and established their overlordship. And they called the lands in which we dwelt Dalasia, and we did what they wished us to do and continued our studies.

Now at about this time it came to pass in the far north that a disciple of the God Aldur came with certain others to reclaim a thing that the Dragon God had stolen from Aldur. And that act was so important that when it was done, the Second Age ended, and the Third Age began.

Now it was in the Third Age that the priests of Angarak, which men call Grolims, came to speak to us of the Dragon God and of His hunger for our love, and we considered what they said even as we considered all things men told us. And we consulted the book of the heavens and confirmed that Torak was the incarnate God-aspect of one of the spirits which contend at the center of time. But where was the other? How might men choose when but one of the spirits came to them? Then it was that we perceived our dreadful responsibility. The spirits would come to us, each in its own time, and each would proclaim that it was good and the other was evil. It was man, however, who would choose. And we took counsel among ourselves, and we concluded that we might accept the *forms* of the worship that the Grolims so urgently pressed upon us. This would give us the opportunity to examine the nature of the Dragon God and make us better prepared to choose when the other God appeared.

In time the events of the world intruded upon us. The Angaraks allied themselves by marriage with the great city-builders of the east, who called themselves Melcene, and between them they built an empire that bestrode the continent. Now the Angaraks were doers of deeds, but the Melcenes were performers of tasks. A deed once done is done forever, but a task returns every day, and the Melcenes came among us to seek out those who might aid them in their endless tasks. Now as it chanced to happen, one of our kinsmen who aided the Melcenes had occasion to journey to the north in performance of one of those tasks. And he came to a place called Ashaba and sought shelter there from a storm that had overtaken him. And the Master of the house at Ashaba was neither Grolim nor Angarak nor any other man. Our kinsman had come unaware upon the house of Torak. Now, Torak was curious about our people, and He sent for the traveler, and our kinsman went in to behold the Dragon God. And in the instant that he looked upon the face of Torak, the Third Age ended, and the Fourth Age began. For lo, the Dragon God of Angarak was *not* one of the Gods for whom we waited. The signs that were upon Him did not lead beyond Him, and our kinsman saw in an instant that Torak was doomed, and that which He was would die with Him.

And then we perceived our error, and we marveled at what we had not seen— that even a God might be but the tool of destiny. For behold, Torak was *of* one of the two fates, but he was not the *entire* fate.

Now it happened that on the far side of the world a king was slain, and all his family with him—save one. And this king had been the keeper of one of the two stones of power, and when word of this was brought to Torak, He exulted, for He believed that an ancient foe was no more. Then it was that He began His preparations to do war upon the kingdoms of the west. But the signs in the heavens and the whispers in the rocks told us that it was not as Torak believed. The stone was still guarded, and the line of the guardian remained unbroken. Torak's war would bring Him to grief.

The preparations of the Dragon God were long, and the tasks He laid upon his people were the tasks of generations. And even as we, Torak watched the heavens to read there the signs that would tell Him when to move against the west. But Torak watched only for the signs He wished to see and He did not read the *entire* message written in the sky. Reading thus but a small part of the signs, He set His forces in motion on the worst possible day.

And, as we had known it must, disaster befell the armies of Torak on a broad plain lying before the city of Vo Mimbre in the far west. And the Dragon God was bound in sleep to await the coming of His enemy.

And then it was that a whisper began to reach us with yet another name. The whisper of that name became clearer to us, and upon the day of his birth the whisper of his name became a great shout. Belgarion the Godslayer had come at last.

And now the pace of events quickened, and the rush toward the awful meeting became so swift that the pages of the book of the heavens became as a blur. And then upon the day that men celebrate as the day the world was made, the stone of power was delivered up to Belgarion; and in the instant that his hand closed upon it, the book of the heavens filled with a great light, and the sound of Belgarion's name rang from the farthest star.

And then we felt Belgarion moving toward Mallorea bearing the stone of power, and we could feel Torak stirring as his sleep grew fitful. And finally there came that dreadful night. As we watched helplessly, the vast pages of the book of the heavens moved so rapidly that we could not read them. And then the book stopped, and we read one terrible line, "Torak is slain," and the book shuddered, and all the light in all of creation went out. And in that awful instant of darkness and silence, the Fourth Age ended, and the Fifth Age began.

And as the Fifth Age began, we found a mystery in the book of the heavens. Before, all had moved toward the meeting between Belgarion and Torak, but now events moved toward a different meeting. There were signs among the stars which told us that the fates had selected yet other aspects for their final encounter, and we could feel the movements of those presences, but we knew not who or what they might be, for the pages of the great book were dark and obscure. Yet we felt a presence shrouded and veiled in darkness, and it moved through the affairs of men, and the moon spoke most clearly, advising us that this dark presence was a woman.

One thing we saw in all the vast confusion that now clouded the book of the heavens. The Ages of man grew shorter as each one passed, and the Events that were the meetings between the two fates were growing closer and closer together. The time for leisurely contemplation had passed, and now we must hasten lest the last Event come upon us all unaware.

We decided that we must goad or deceive the participants in that final Event so that they should both come to the appointed place at the destined time.

And we sent the similitude of She Who Must Make the Choice to the veiled and hooded presence of dark and to Belgarion the Godslayer, and she set them upon the path that would lead them at last to the place of our choosing.

And then we all turned to *our* preparations, for much remained to be done, and we knew that this Event would be the last. The division of creation had endured for too long; and in *this* meeting between the two fates the division would end and all would be made one again.

PART ONE

KELL

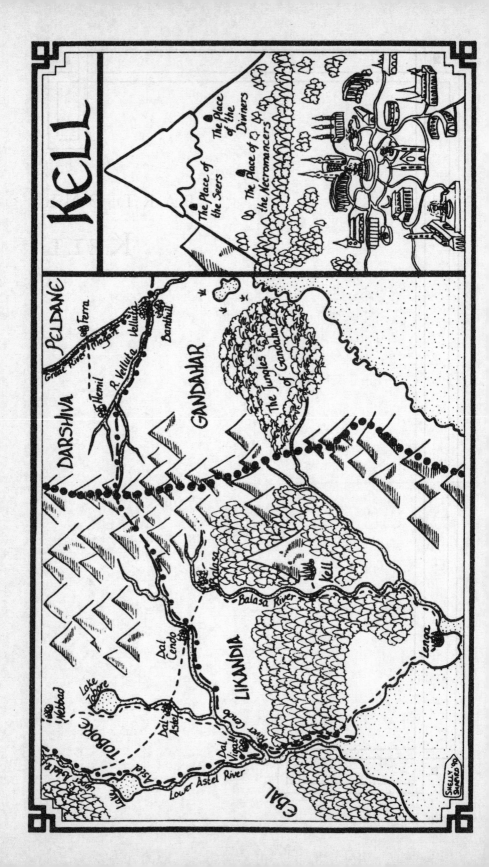

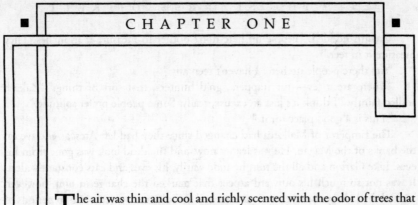

The air was thin and cool and richly scented with the odor of trees that shed no leaves but stood dark green and resinous from one end of their lives to the other. The sunlight on the snowfields above them was dazzling, and the sound of tumbling water seething down and down rocky streambeds to feed rivers leagues below on the plains of Darshiva and Gandahar was constantly in their ears. That tumble and roar of waters rushing to their destined meeting with the great River Magan was accompanied by the soft, melancholy sighing of an endless wind passing through the deep-green forest of pine and fir and spruce which clad hills that reached toward the sky in a kind of unthinking yearning. The caravan route Garion and his friends followed rose up and up, winding along streambeds and mounting the sides of ridges. From atop each ridge they could see yet another, and looming over all was the spine of the continent where peaks beyond imagining soared upward to touch the very vault of heaven, peaks pure and pristine in their mantle of eternal snow. Garion had spent time in mountains before, but never had he seen such enormous peaks. He knew that those colossal spires were leagues and leagues away, but the mountain air was so clear that it seemed he could almost reach out and touch them.

There was an abiding peace here, a peace that washed away the turmoil and anxiety that had beset them all on the plains below and somehow erased care and even thought. Each turn and each ridge top brought new vistas, each filled with more splendor than the last until they could only ride in silence and wonder. The works of man shrank into insignificance here. Man would never, *could* never, touch these eternal mountains.

It was summer, and the days were long and filled with sunlight. Birds sang from the trees beside the winding track, and the smell of sun-warmed evergreens was touched lightly with the delicate odors of the acre upon acre of wildflowers carpeting the steep meadows. Occasionally the wild, shrill cry of an eagle echoed from the rocks. "Have you ever considered moving your capital?" Garion asked the Emperor of Mallorea, who rode beside him. His tone was hushed. To speak in a louder voice would somehow profane what lay around them.

"No, not really, Garion," 'Zakath replied. "My government wouldn't function here. The bureaucracy is largely Melcene. Melcenes appear to be prosaic people, but actually they aren't. I'm afraid my officials would spend about half their time looking at the scenery and the other half writing bad poetry. Nobody would get any work done. Besides, you have no idea what it's like up here in the winter."

"Snow?"

'Zakath nodded. "People up here don't bother to measure it in inches. They measure it in feet."

"Are there people up here? I haven't seen any."

"There are a few—fur trappers, gold hunters, that sort of thing." 'Zakath smiled faintly. "I think it's just an excuse, really. Some people prefer solitude."

"This is a good place for it."

The Emperor of Mallorea had changed since they had left Atesca's enclave on the banks of the Magan. He was leaner now, and the dead look was gone from his eyes. Like Garion and all the rest, he rode warily, his eyes and ears constantly alert. It was not so much his outward aspect that marked the change in him, however. 'Zakath had always been a pensive, even melancholy man, given often to periods of black depression, but filled at the same time with a cold ambition. Garion had often felt that the Mallorean's ambition and his apparent hunger for power were not so much a driving need in him as they had been a kind of continual testing of himself, and, at perhaps a deeper level, deriving from an urge toward self-destruction. It had seemed almost that 'Zakath had hurled himself and all the resources of his empire into impossible struggles in the secret hope that eventually he would encounter someone strong enough to kill him and thereby relieve him of the burden of a life that was barely tolerable to him.

Such was no longer the case. His meeting with Cyradis on the banks of the Magan had forever changed him. A world that had always been flat and stale now seemed to be all new to him. At times, Garion even thought he detected a faint touch of hope in his friend's face, and hope had never been a part of 'Zakath's makeup.

As they rounded a wide bend in the track, Garion saw the she-wolf he had found in the dead forest back in Darshiva. She sat patiently on her haunches waiting for them. Increasingly, the behavior of the wolf puzzled him. Now that her injured paw was healed, she made sporadic sweeps through the surrounding forests in search of her pack, but always returned, seemingly unconcerned about her failure to locate them. It was as if she were perfectly content to remain with them as a member of their most unusual pack. So long as they were in forests and uninhabited mountains, this peculiarity of hers caused no particular problems, but they would not always be in the wilderness, and the appearance of an untamed and probably nervous wolf on the busy street of a populous city would be likely to attract attention, to say the very least.

"How is it with you, little sister?" he asked her politely in the language of wolves.

"It is well," she replied.

"Did you find any traces of your pack?"

"There are many other wolves about, but they are not of my kindred. One will remain with you for yet a while longer. Where is the young one?"

Garion glanced back over his shoulder at the little two-wheeled carriage trundling along behind them. "He sits beside my mate in the thing with round feet."

The wolf sighed. "If he sits much longer, he will no longer be able to run or hunt," she said disapprovingly, "and if your mate continues to feed him so much, she will stretch his belly, and he will not survive a lean season when there is little food."

"One will speak with her about it."

"Will she listen?"

"Probably not, but one will speak with her all the same. She is fond of the young one and takes pleasure in having him near her."

"Soon one will need to teach him how to hunt."

"Yes. One knows. One will explain that to one's mate."

"One is grateful." She paused, looking about a bit warily. "Proceed with some caution," she warned. "There is a creature who dwells here. One has caught his scent several times, though one has not seen him. He is quite large, however."

"How large?"

"Larger than the beast upon which you sit." She looked pointedly at Chretienne. Familiarity had made the big gray stallion less nervous in the presence of the she-wolf, though Garion suspected that he would be much happier if she did not come quite so close.

"One will tell the pack-leader of what you have said," Garion promised. For some reason, the she-wolf avoided Belgarath. Garion surmised that her behavior might reflect some obscure facet of wolfly etiquette of which he was not aware.

"One will continue one's search then," she said, rising to her feet. "It may happen that one will come upon this beast, and then we will know him." She paused. "His scent tells one that he is dangerous, however. He feeds on all things—even on things that we would shun." Then she turned and loped off into the forest, moving swiftly and silently.

"That's really uncanny, you know," 'Zakath observed. "I've heard men talk to animals before, but never in their own language."

"It's a family peculiarity." Garion smiled. "At first I didn't believe it either. Birds used to come and talk to Aunt Pol all the time—usually about their eggs. Birds are awfully fond of talking about their eggs, I understand. They can be very silly at times. Wolves are much more dignified." He paused a moment. "You don't necessarily have to tell Aunt Pol I said that," he added.

"Subterfuge, Garion?" 'Zakath laughed.

"Prudence," Garion corrected. "I have to go talk with Belgarath. Keep your eyes open. The wolf says that there's some kind of animal out there somewhere. She says it's bigger than a horse and very dangerous. She hinted at the fact that it's a man-eater."

"What does it look like?"

"She hasn't seen it. She's smelled it, though, and seen its tracks."

"I'll watch for it."

"Good idea." Garion turned and rode back to where Belgarath and Aunt Pol were deep in a discussion.

"Durnik needs a tower somewhere in the Vale," Belgarath was saying.

"I don't see why, father," Polgara replied.

"All of Aldur's disciples have towers, Pol. It's the custom."

"Old customs persist—even when there's no longer any need for them."

"He's going to need to study, Pol. How can he possibly study with you underfoot all the time?"

She gave him a long, chilly stare.

"Maybe I should rephrase that."

"Take as long as you need, father. I'm willing to wait."

"Grandfather," Garion said, reining in. "I was just talking with the wolf, and she says there's a very large animal out in the forest."

"A bear maybe?"

"I don't think so. She's caught its scent a few times, and she'd probably recognize the smell of a bear, wouldn't she?"

"I'd think so, yes."

"She didn't say it exactly, but I got the impression that it's not too selective about what it eats." He paused. "Is it my imagination, or is she a very strange wolf?"

"How do you mean, exactly?"

"She stretches the language about as far as it will go, and I get the feeling that she still has more to say."

"She's intelligent, that's all. It's an uncommon trait in females, but it's not unheard of."

"What a fascinating turn this conversation has taken," Polgara observed.

"Oh," the old man said blandly, "are you still here, Pol? I thought you'd have found something else to do by now."

Her gaze was icy, but Belgarath seemed totally unperturbed. "You'd better warn the others," he told Garion. "A wolf would pass an ordinary animal without comment. Whatever this thing is, it's unusual, and unusual usually means dangerous. Tell Ce'Nedra to get up here among the rest of us. She's a bit vulnerable trailing along behind the way she is." He considered it. "Don't say anything to alarm her, but have Liselle ride in the carriage with her."

"Liselle?"

"The blond girl. The one with the dimples."

"I know who she is, Grandfather. Wouldn't Durnik—or maybe Toth—be a better idea?"

"No. If either of them got in the carriage with Ce'Nedra, she'd know something was wrong, and that might frighten her. An animal who's hunting can smell fear. Let's not expose her to that kind of danger. Liselle's very well trained, and she's probably got two or three daggers hidden in various places." He grinned slyly. "I'd imagine Silk could tell you where they are," he added.

"Father!" Polgara gasped.

"You mean you didn't know, Pol? My goodness, how unobservant of you."

"One for your side," Garion noted.

"I'm glad you liked it." Belgarath smirked at Polgara.

Garion turned Chretienne so that his aunt would not see his smile.

They took a bit more care setting up camp that night, choosing a small grove of aspens backed by a steep cliff and with a deep mountain river at its front. As the sun sank into the eternal snowfields above them and twilight filled the ravines and gorges with azure shadows, Beldin returned from his wide-ranging vigil. "Isn't it a bit early to be stopping?" he rasped after he had shimmered and changed.

"The horses are tired," Belgarath replied, casting a sidelong glance at Ce'Nedra. "This is a very steep trail."

"Wait a bit," Beldin told him, limping toward the fire. "It gets steeper on up ahead."

"What happened to your foot?"

"I had a little disagreement with an eagle—stupid birds, eagles. He couldn't tell the difference between a hawk and a pigeon. I had to educate him. He bit me while I was tearing out a sizable number of his wing feathers."

"Uncle," Polgara said reproachfully.

"He started it."

"Are there any soldiers coming up behind us?" Belgarath asked him.

"Some Darshivans. They're two or three days behind, though. Urvon's army is retreating. Now that he and Nahaz are gone, there's not much point in their staying."

"That gets at least *some* of the troops off our backs," Silk said.

"Don't be too quick to start gloating," Beldin told him. "With the Guardsmen and the Karands gone, the Darshivans are free to concentrate on us."

"That's true, I suppose. Do you think they know we're here?"

"Zandramas does, and I don't think she'd hide the information from her soldiers. You'll probably hit snow sometime late tomorrow. You might want to be thinking about some way to hide your tracks." He looked around. "Where's your wolf?" he asked Garion.

"Hunting. She's been looking for signs of her pack."

"That brings something up," Belgarath said quietly, looking around to make sure that Ce'Nedra was out of earshot. "The wolf told Garion that there's a large animal of some kind in this area. Pol's going to go out and take a look around tonight, but it might not hurt if you nosed around tomorrow, as well. I'm not in the mood for any surprises."

"I'll see what I can find."

Sadi and Velvet sat on the far side of the fire. They had placed the little earthenware bottle on its side and were trying to coax Zith and her children out with morsels of cheese. "I wish we had some milk," Sadi said in his contralto voice. "Milk is very good for young snakes. It strengthens their teeth."

"I'll remember that," Velvet said.

"Were you planning a career as a snakeherdess, Margravine?"

"They're nice little creatures," she replied. "They're clean and quiet, and they don't eat very much. Besides, they're very useful in emergencies."

He smiled at her affectionately. "We'll make a Nyissan of you yet, Liselle."

"Not if *I* can help it," Silk muttered darkly to Garion.

They had broiled trout for supper that evening. After Durnik and Toth had finished setting up their encampment, they had adjourned to the riverbank with their poles and lures. Durnik's recent elevation to disciplehood had changed him in some ways, but had not lessened his appetite for his favorite pastime. It was no longer necessary for him and his mute friend even to discuss these excursions. Any time they camped in the vicinity of a lake or stream, their reaction was automatic.

After supper, Polgara flew off into the shadowy forest, but when she returned, she reported having seen no sign of the large beast the she-wolf had warned them about.

It was cold the following morning, and there was a trace of frost in the air. The horses' breath steamed in the mountain air as they set out, and Garion and the others rode with their cloaks wrapped tightly about them.

As Beldin had predicted, they reached the snow line late that afternoon. The first windrows of white in the wagon ruts were thin and crusty, but farther on ahead they could see deeper drifts. They made camp below the snow and set out again early the following morning. Silk had devised a sort of yoke for one of the pack-horses, and trailing on ropes behind the yoke were a dozen or so head-sized round rocks. The little man critically examined the tracks the rocks made in the snow as they started up the track into the world of perpetual white. "Good enough," he said in a self-congratulatory tone.

"I don't quite see the purpose of your contrivance, Prince Kheldar," Sadi confessed.

"The rocks leave trails that look about the same as wagon tracks," Silk explained. "Horse tracks by themselves might make the soldiers coming up behind us suspicious. Wagon tracks on a caravan route aren't going to look all that remarkable."

"Clever," the eunuch said, "but why not just cut bushes and drag them behind us?"

Silk shook his head. "If you brush out all the tracks in the snow, it looks even more suspicious. This is a fairly well-traveled route."

"You think of everything, don't you?"

"Sneaking was his major field of study at the academy," Velvet said from the little carriage she shared with Ce'Nedra and the wolf pup. "Sometimes he sneaks just to keep in practice."

"I don't know if I'd go *that* far, Liselle," the little man objected in a pained tone.

"Don't you?"

"Well, yes, I suppose so, but you don't have to come right out and say it—and 'sneak' has such an ugly ring to it."

"Can you think of a better term?"

"Well, 'evasion' sounds a bit nicer, doesn't it?"

"Since it means the same thing, why quibble over terminology?" She smiled winsomely at him, her cheeks dimpling.

"It's a question of style, Liselle."

The caravan track grew steeper, and the snow had piled in deeper and deeper drifts along the sides. Miles-long plumes of snow blew from the mountaintops ahead, and the wind grew stronger with a biting, arid chill to it.

About noon, the peaks ahead were suddenly obscured by an ominous-looking cloudbank rolling in from the west, and the she-wolf came loping down the track to meet them. "One advises that you seek shelter for the pack and your beasts," she said with a peculiar kind of urgency.

"Have you found the creature who dwells here?" Garion asked.

"No. This is more dangerous." She looked meaningfully back over her shoulder at the approaching cloud.

"One will tell the pack-leader."

"That is proper." She pointed her muzzle at 'Zakath. "Have this one follow me. There are trees a short way ahead. He and I will find a suitable place."

"She wants you to go with her," Garion told the Mallorean. "We've got bad weather coming, and she thinks we should take shelter in some trees just ahead. Find a place, and I'll go warn the others."

"A blizzard?" 'Zakath asked.

"I'd guess so. It takes something fairly serious in the way of weather to make a wolf nervous." Garion wheeled Chretienne and rode back down to alert the others. The steep, slippery track made haste difficult, and the chill wind was whipping stinging pellets of snow about them by the time they reached the thicket to which the wolf had led 'Zakath. The trees were slender pine saplings, and they grew very close together. At some time in the not too distant past an avalanche had cut a swath through the thicket and had piled a jumble of limbs and broken trunks against the face of a steep rock cliff. Durnik and Toth went to work immediately even as the wind picked up and the snow grew thicker. Garion and the others joined in, and before long they had erected a latticed frame for a long lean-to against the cliff face. They covered the frame with tent canvas, tying it securely in place and weighting it down with logs. Then they cleared away the interior and led the horses into the lower end of the rude shelter just as the full force of the storm hit.

The wind shrieked insanely, and the thicket seemed to vanish in the swirling snow.

"Is Beldin going to be all right?" Durnik asked, looking slightly worried.

"You don't have to worry about Beldin," Belgarath said. "He's ridden out storms before. He'll either go above it or change back and bury himself in a snowdrift until it passes."

"He'll freeze to death!" Ce'Nedra exclaimed.

"Not under the snow, he won't," Belgarath assured her. "Beldin tends to ignore weather." He looked at the she-wolf, who sat on her haunches at the opening of the lean-to staring out at the swirling snow. "One is grateful for your warning, little sister," he said formally.

"One is a member of your pack now, revered leader," she replied with equal formality. "The well-being of all is the responsibility of all."

"Wisely said, little sister."

She wagged her tail but said nothing else.

The blizzard continued for the rest of the day and then on into the night while Garion and the others sat around the fire Durnik had built. Then, about midnight, the wind died as quickly as it had come. The snow continued to sift down among the trees until morning, and then it, too, abated. It had done its work, however. The snow outside the lean-to reached above Garion's knees. "We're going to have to break a trail, I'm afraid," Durnik said soberly. "It's a quarter of a mile back up to that caravan track, and there are all sorts of things hidden under this fresh snow. This is not a good time—or place—to start breaking the horses' legs."

"What about my carriage?" Ce'Nedra asked him.

"I'm afraid we'll have to leave it behind, Ce'Nedra. The snow's just too deep. Even if we could get it back up onto the road, the carriage horse wouldn't be able to drag it through the drifts."

She sighed. "It was such a nice carriage, too." Then she looked at Silk with a perfectly straight face. "I certainly want to thank you for lending it to me, Prince Kheldar," she told him. "I've finished with it now, so you can have it back."

It was Toth who broke the initial trail up the steep slope to the caravan track. The others followed behind him, trampling the trail wider and searching for hidden logs and branches with their feet. It took nearly two hours to plow out the trail back to the caravan track, and they were all panting from the exertion at this high altitude.

They started back down toward the lean-to where the ladies waited with the horses, but about halfway down, the wolf suddenly laid back her ears and snarled.

"What is it?" Garion said.

"The creature," she growled. "He hunts."

"Get ready!" Garion shouted to the others. "That animal is out there!" He reached back over his shoulder and drew Iron-grip's sword.

It came out of the thicket on the far side of the avalanche track. Its shaggy coat was clotted with snow, and it shuffled along in a brutish half crouch. Its face was hideous and chillingly familiar. It had piglike eyes sunk beneath heavy brow ridges. Its lower jaw jutted out, and two massive yellow tusks curved up over its cheeks. It opened its mouth and roared, pounding on its vast chest with its fists and rising to its full height. It was almost eight feet tall.

"That's impossible!" Belgarath exclaimed.

"What is it?" Sadi demanded.

"It's an Eldrak," Belgarath said, "and the only place the Eldrakyn live is in Ulgoland."

"I think you're wrong, Belgarath," 'Zakath disagreed. "That's what's called an ape-bear. There are a few of them in these mountains."

"Do you gentlemen suppose we could discuss its exact species some other time?" Silk suggested. "The main question now is whether we fight or run."

"We can't run in this snow," Garion said grimly. "We're going to have to fight it."

"I was afraid you might say that."

"The main thing is to keep it away from the ladies," Durnik said. He looked at the eunuch. "Sadi, would the poison on your dagger kill it?"

Sadi looked dubiously at the shaggy beast. "I'm sure it would," he said, "but that thing is awfully large. It would take awhile for the poison to work."

"That's it, then," Belgarath decided. "The rest of us will keep its attention and give Sadi time to get around behind it. After he stabs it, we'll fall back and give the poison time to take effect. Spread out, and don't take any chances." He blurred into the form of a wolf.

They moved into a rough half circle, their weapons at the ready as the monster continued to roar and pound on its chest at the edge of the trees, working itself up into a frenzy. Then it lumbered forward with the snow spraying out from its huge feet. Sadi edged his way uphill, his small dagger held low even as Belgarath and the she-wolf darted in to tear at the beast with their fangs.

Garion's mind was working very clearly as he advanced through the deep snow, swinging his sword threateningly. He saw that this creature was not as quick as Grul the Eldrak had been. It was not able to respond to the sudden darting attacks of the wolves, and the snow around it was soon spotted with its blood. It roared in frustration and rage and made a desperate rush at Durnik. Toth, however, stepped in and drove the tip of his heavy staff squarely into the beast's face. It howled in pain and spread its huge arms wide to catch the big mute in a crushing embrace, but Garion slashed it across one shoulder with his sword even as 'Zakath ducked under the other shaggy arm and gashed it across the chest and belly with whiplike sword strokes.

The creature bellowed, and its blood spurted from its wounds.

"Any time now, Sadi," Silk said urgently, ducking and feinting and trying to get a clean throw with one of his heavy daggers.

The wolves continued their harrying attacks on the animal's flanks and legs as Sadi cautiously advanced on the raging beast's back. Desperately the creature flailed about with its huge arms, trying to keep its attackers away.

Then, with almost surgical precision, the she-wolf lunged in and ripped the heavy muscle at the back of the beast's left knee with her fangs.

The agonized shriek was dreadful—all the more so because it was strangely human. The shaggy beast toppled backward, clutching at its maimed leg.

Garion reversed his great sword, grasping the crosspiece of the hilt, bestrode the writhing body and raised the weapon, intending to drive the point full into the shaggy chest.

"Please!" it cried, its brutish face twisted in agony and terror. "Please don't kill me!"

CHAPTER TWO

It was a Grolim. The huge beast lying in the bloodstained snow blurred and changed even as Garion's friends moved in with their weapons ready to deliver the last fatal strokes.

"Wait!" Durnik said sharply. "It's a man!"

They stopped, staring at the dreadfully wounded priest lying in the snow.

Garion bleakly set the point of his sword under the Grolim's chin. He was terribly angry. "All right," he said in a cold voice, "talk—and I think you'd better be very convincing. Who put you up to this?"

"It was Naradas," the Grolim groaned, "archpriest of the temple at Hemil."

"The henchman of Zandramas?" Garion demanded. "The one with white eyes?"

"Yes. I was only doing what he commanded. Please don't kill me."

"Why did he tell you to attack us?"

"I was supposed to kill one of you."

"Which one?"

"He didn't care. He just said to make sure that one of you died."

"They're still playing that tired old game," Silk noted, sheathing his daggers. "Grolims are so unimaginative."

Sadi looked inquiringly at Garion, holding up his slim little knife suggestively.

"No!" Eriond said sharply.

Garion hesitated. "He's right, Sadi," he said finally. "We can't just kill him in cold blood."

"Alorns." Sadi sighed, rolling his eyes up toward the clearing sky. "You do know, of course, that if we leave him here in this condition, he'll die anyway. And if we try to take him along, he'll delay us—not to mention the fact that he's hardly the sort to be trusted."

"Eriond," Garion said, "why don't you go get Aunt Pol? We'd better get those wounds of his tended before he bleeds to death." He looked at Belgarath, who had changed form again. "Any objections?" he asked.

"I didn't say anything."

"I appreciate that."

"You should have killed him before he changed form on you," a familiar harsh voice came from the thicket behind them. Beldin was sitting on a log, gnawing at something that was uncooked and still had a few feathers clinging to it.

"I suppose it didn't occur to you to give us a hand?" Belgarath asked acidly.

"You were doing all right." The dwarf shrugged. He belched and tossed the remains of his breakfast to the she-wolf.

"One is grateful," she said politely as her jaws crunched into the half-eaten carcass. Garion could not be sure that Beldin understood, though he guessed that the gnarled little man probably did.

"What's an Eldrak doing here in Mallorea?" Belgarath asked.

"It's not exactly an Eldrak, Belgarath," Beldin replied, spitting out a few soggy feathers.

"All right, but how did a Mallorean Grolim even know what an Eldrak looks like?"

"You weren't listening, old man. There are a few of those things up here in these mountains. They're distantly related to the Eldrakyn, but they're not the same. They're not as big, for one thing, and they're not as smart."

"I thought all the monsters lived in Ulgoland."

"Use your head, Belgarath. There are Trolls in Cherek, Algroths range down into Arendia, and the Dryads live in southern Tolnedra. Then there's that dragon. Nobody knows for sure where she lives. There are monsters scattered all over. They're just a little more concentrated in Ulgo, that's all."

"I suppose you're right," Belgarath conceded. He looked at 'Zakath. "What did you call the thing?"

"An ape-bear. It's probably not too accurate, but the people who live up here aren't very sophisticated."

"Where's Naradas right now?" Silk asked the injured Grolim.

"I saw him at Balasa," the Grolim replied. "I don't know where he went from there."

"Was Zandramas with him?"

"I didn't see her, but that doesn't mean she wasn't there. The Holy Sorceress doesn't show herself very often anymore."

"Because of the lights under her skin?" the weasel-faced little man asked shrewdly.

The Grolim's face grew even more pale. "We're forbidden to discuss that—even among ourselves," he replied in a frightened tone of voice.

"That's all right, friend." Silk smiled at him and drew one of his daggers. "You have my permission."

The Grolim swallowed hard and then nodded.

"Stout fellow." Silk patted him on the shoulder. "When did those lights start to appear?"

"I can't say for sure. Zandramas was off in the west with Naradas for a long time. The lights had started to appear when she came back. One of the priests at Hemil used to gossip a great deal. He said it was some kind of plague."

"Used to?"

"She found out about what he'd said and had his heart cut out."

"That's the Zandramas we've come to know and love, all right."

Aunt Pol came up along the path trampling through the snow, followed by Ce'Nedra and Velvet. She tended the Grolim's wounds without comment while Durnik and Toth went back to the lean-to and led out the horses. Then they untied the tent canvas and broke down the frame. When they led the horses up to the place where the wounded Grolim lay, Sadi went to his saddle and opened the red leather case. "Just to be on the safe side," he muttered to Garion, taking out a little vial.

Garion raised one eyebrow.

"It won't hurt him," the eunuch assured him. "It'll make him tractable, though. Besides, since you're in this humanitarian mood, it should also numb the pain of his wounds."

"You don't approve, do you?" Garion said. "That we didn't kill him, I mean?"

"I think it's imprudent, Belgarion," Sadi said seriously. "Dead enemies are safe enemies. Live ones can come back to haunt you. It's your decision, though."

"I'll make a concession," Garion said. "Stay close to him. If he starts getting out of hand, do whatever seems appropriate."

Sadi smiled faintly. "Much better," he approved. "We'll teach you the rudiments of practical politics yet."

They led the horses up the steep hill to the caravan route and mounted. The howling wind that had accompanied the blizzard had scoured most of the snow from the track, although there were deep drifts in sheltered places where the road curved behind bands of trees and rock outcroppings. They made good time when the road was in the open, but it was slow going when they came to the drifts. Now that the storm had passed, the sunlight on the new snow was dazzling, and even though he squinted his eyes nearly shut, Garion found that after about an hour he was beginning to develop a splitting headache.

Silk reined in. "I think it's time for a precaution or two," he announced. He took a light scarf from inside his cloak and bound it across his eyes. Garion was suddenly reminded of Relg and the way the cave-born zealot had always covered his eyes when out in the open.

"A blindfold?" Sadi asked. "Have you suddenly become a seer, Prince Kheldar?"

"I'm not the sort to have visions, Sadi," Silk replied. "The scarf is thin enough so that I can see through it. The idea is to protect the eyes from the glare of sunlight on the snow."

"It *is* rather bright, isn't it?" Sadi agreed.

"It is indeed, and if you look at it long enough, it can blind you—at least temporarily." Silk adjusted the covering on his eyes. "This is a trick the reindeer herders in northern Drasnia came up with. It works fairly well."

"Let's not take any chances," Belgarath said, also covering his eyes with a piece of cloth. He smiled. "Maybe this is how the Dalasian wizards struck the Grolims blind when they tried to go to Kell."

"I'd be terribly disappointed if it was that simple," Velvet said, tying a scarf across her eyes. "I like to have my magic nice and inexplicable. Snow blindness would be such a prosaic thing."

They plowed on through the drifts, climbing now toward a high pass between two towering peaks. It was midafternoon when they reached the pass. The track wound up between massive boulders, but straightened out when they reached the summit. They stopped to rest the horses and to look out over the vast wilderness that lay beyond the pass.

Toth unbound his eyes and gestured to Durnik. The smith pulled down his protective scarf, and the big mute pointed. Durnik's face was suddenly filled with awe. "Look!" he said in a half-choked whisper.

The rest of them also uncovered their eyes.

"Belar!" Silk gasped. "Nothing can be that big!"

The peaks around them that had seemed so enormous shrank into insignificance. Standing quite alone in solitary splendor rose a mountain so huge and high that the mind could not comprehend it. It was perfectly symmetrical, a steep, white cone with sharply sloping sides. Its base was enormous, and its summit soared thousands of feet above nearby peaks. An absolute calm seemed to surround it, as if, having achieved everything that any mountain could, it simply existed.

"It's the highest peak in the world," 'Zakath said very quietly. "The scholars at the University of Melcene have calculated its height and compared that with the heights of peaks on the western continent. It's thousands of feet higher than any other mountain."

"Please, 'Zakath," Silk said with a pained look, "don't tell me how high."

'Zakath looked puzzled.

"As you may have noticed, I'm not really a very large person. Immensity depresses me. I'll admit that your mountain is bigger than I am. I just don't want to know how *much* bigger."

Toth was gesturing to Durnik again.

"He says that Kell lies in the shadow of that mountain," the smith said.

"That's a little unspecific, Goodman," Sadi said wryly. "I'd guess that about half the continent lies in the shadow of that thing."

Beldin came soaring in again. "Big, isn't it?" he said, squinting at the huge white peak looming into the sky.

"We noticed," Belgarath replied. "What's on up ahead?"

"A fair amount of downhill going—at least until you get to the slopes of that monster there."

"I can see that from here."

"Congratulations. I found a place where you can get rid of your Grolim. Several places, actually."

"Exactly how do you mean 'get rid of,' uncle?" Polgara asked suspiciously.

"There are quite a few high cliffs alongside this track on the way down," he replied blandly. "Accidents do happen, you know."

"Out of the question. I didn't treat his wounds just to keep him going until you found time to throw him off a cliff."

"Polgara, you're interfering with the practice of my religion."

She raised one eyebrow.

"I thought you knew. It's an article of the faith: 'Kill every Grolim you come across.' "

"I might even consider converting to that religion," 'Zakath said.

"Are you absolutely *certain* you're not Arendish?" Garion said to him.

Beldin sighed. "Since you're going to be such a spoilsport for this, Pol, I found a group of sheepherders below the snow line."

"Shepherds, uncle," she corrected.

"It means the same thing. If you really look at it, it's even the same word."

"Shepherd sounds nicer."

"Nicer." He snorted. "Sheep are stupid, they smell bad, and they taste worse. Anybody who spends his life tending them is either defective or degenerate."

"You're in rare form this afternoon," Belgarath congratulated him.

"It's been a great day for flying," Beldin explained with a broad grin. "Do you have any idea of how much warm air comes up off new snow when the sun hits it? I flew up so high once that I started getting spots in front of my eyes."

"That's stupid, uncle," Polgara snapped. "You should *never* go up where the air's that thin."

"We're all entitled to a little stupidity now and then." He shrugged. "And the dive from that height is unbelievable. Why don't you join me, and I'll show you."

"Will you never grow up?"

"I doubt it, and I certainly hope not." He looked at Belgarath. "I think you'd better go down a mile or so and make camp."

"It's early yet."

"No. Actually it's late. That afternoon sun is quite warm—even up here. All this snow's starting to get soft. I've seen three avalanches already. If you make a wrong guess up here, you might get down a lot quicker than you want to."

"Interesting point there. We'll get down out of this pass and set up for the night."

"I'll go on ahead." Beldin crouched and spread his arms. "Are you sure you don't want to come along, Pol?"

"Don't be silly."

He left a ghostly chuckle behind him as he soared away.

They set up for the night on a ridge line. Although it exposed them to the constant wind, it was free from the danger of avalanche. Garion slept poorly that night. The wind that raked the exposed ridge set the taut canvas of the tent he shared with Ce'Nedra to thrumming, and the noise intruded itself upon him as he tried again and again to drift off. He shifted restlessly.

"Can't you sleep either?" Ce'Nedra said in the chill darkness.

"It's the wind," he replied.

"Try not to think about it."

"I don't have to think about it. It's like trying to sleep inside a big drum."

"You were very brave this morning, Garion. I was terrified when I heard about that monster."

"We've dealt with monsters before. After a while, you get used to it."

"My, aren't we getting blasé?"

"It's an occupational trait. All of us mighty heroes have it. Fighting a monster or two before breakfast helps to sharpen the appetite."

"You've changed, Garion."

"Not really."

"Yes, you have. When I first met you, you'd never have said anything like that."

"When you first met me, I took everything very seriously."

"Don't you take what we're doing seriously?" She said it almost accusingly.

"Of course I do. It's the little incidental things along the way I sort of shrug off. There's not much point in worrying about something after it's already over, is there?"

"Well, as long as neither of us can sleep anyway—" And she drew him to her and kissed him rather seriously.

The temperature plunged that night, and when they arose, the snow, which had been dangerously soft the previous afternoon, had frozen, and they were able to proceed with little danger of avalanche. Because this side of the summit had taken the full force of the wind during the blizzard, the caravan track had little snow on it, and they made good time going down. By midafternoon they passed the last of the snow and rode down into a world of spring. The meadows were steep and lush and speckled with wildflowers bending in the mountain breeze. Brooks, which came directly out of the faces of glaciers, purled and danced over gleaming stones, and soft-eyed deer watched in gentle astonishment as Garion and the others rode by.

A few miles below the snow line, they began to see herds of sheep grazing with witless concentration, consuming grass and wildflowers with indiscriminate appetite. The shepherds who watched them all wore simple white smocks, and they sat on hillocks or rocks in dreamy contemplation while their dogs did all the work.

The she-wolf trotted sedately beside Chretienne. Her ears twitched occasionally, however, and she watched the sheep, her tawny eyes intent.

"One advises against it, little sister," Garion said to her in the language of wolves.

"One was not really considering it," she replied. "One has encountered these beasts before—and the man-things and dog-things that guard them. It is not difficult to take one of them, but the dog-things grow excited when one does, and their barking disturbs one's meal." Her tongue lolled out in a wolfish sort of grin. "One could make the beasts run, however. All things should know to whom the forest belongs."

"The pack-leader would disapprove, one is afraid."

"Ah," she agreed. "Perhaps the pack-leader takes himself too seriously. One has observed that quality in him."

"What did she say?" 'Zakath asked curiously.

"She was thinking about chasing the sheep," Garion replied, "not necessarily to kill any of them but just to make them run. I think it amuses her."

"Amuses? That's an odd thing to say about a wolf."

"Not really. Wolves play a great deal, and they have a very refined sense of humor."

'Zakath's face grew thoughtful. "You know something, Garion?" he said. "Man thinks he owns the world, but we share it with all sorts of creatures who are indifferent to our overlordship. They have their own societies, and I suppose even their own cultures. They don't even pay any attention to us, do they?"

"Only when we inconvenience them."

"That's a crushing blow to the ego of an emperor." 'Zakath smiled wryly. "We're the two most powerful men on earth, and wolves look upon us as no more than a minor inconvenience."

"It teaches us humility," Garion agreed. "Humility is good for the soul."

"Perhaps."

It was evening when they reached the shepherds' encampment. Since a sheep camp is a more or less permanent thing, it is usually more well organized than the hasty encampments of travelers. The tents were larger, for one thing, and they were stretched over pole frames. The tents lined either side of a street made of logs laid tightly side by side. The corrals for the shepherds' horses were at the lower end of the street, and a log dam had backed up a mountain brook to form a sparkling little pond that provided water for the sheep and horses. The shadows of evening were settling over the little valley where the camp lay, and blue columns of smoke rose straight up from the cook-fires into the calm and windless air.

A tall, lean fellow with a deeply tanned face, snowy white hair, and the simple white smock that seemed to be the common garb of these shepherds came out of one of the tents as Garion and 'Zakath reined in just outside the camp. "We have been advised of your coming," he said. His voice was very deep and quiet. "Will you share our evening meal with us?" Garion looked at him closely, noting his resemblance to Vard, the man whom they had met on the Isle of Verkat, half a world away. There could be no question now that the Dals and the slave race in Cthol Murgos were related.

"We would be honored," 'Zakath responded to the invitation. "We do not wish to impose, however."

"It is no imposition. I am Burk. I will have some of my men care for your mounts."

The others rode up and stopped.

"Welcome all," Burk greeted them. "Will you step down? The evening meal is almost ready, and we have set aside a tent for your use." He looked gravely at the she-wolf and inclined his head to her. It was evident that her presence did not alarm him.

"Your courtesy is most becoming," Polgara said, dismounting, "and your hospitality is quite unexpected this far from civilization."

"Man carries his civilization with him, Lady," Burk replied.

"We have an injured man with us," Sadi told him, "a poor traveler we came across on our way over the mountain. We gave him what aid we could, but our business is pressing, and I'm afraid our pace is aggravating his injuries."

"You may leave him with us, and we will care for him." Burk looked critically at the drugged priest slumped in his saddle. "A Grolim," he noted. "Is your destination perhaps Kell?"

"We have to stop there," Belgarath said cautiously.

"This Grolim would not be able to go with you then."

"We've heard about that," Silk said, swinging down from his horse. "Do they really go blind when they try to go to Kell?"

"In a manner of speaking, yes. We have such a one here in our camp with us now. We found him wandering in the forest when we were bringing the sheep up to summer pasture."

Belgarath's eyes narrowed slightly. "Do you suppose I might be able to talk with him?" he asked. "I've made a study of such things, and I'm always eager to get additional information."

"Of course," Burk agreed. "He's in the last tent on the right."

"Garion, Pol, come along," the old man said tersely and started along the log street. Oddly, the she-wolf accompanied them.

"Why the sudden curiosity, father?" Polgara asked when they were out of earshot.

"I want to find out just how effective this curse the Dals have laid around Kell really is. If it's something that can be overcome, we might run into Zandramas when we get there after all."

They found the Grolim sitting on the floor in his tent. The harsh angularity of his face had softened, and his sightless eyes had lost the burning fanaticism common to all Grolims. His face instead was filled with a kind of wonder.

"How is it with you, friend?" Belgarath asked him gently.

"I am content," the Grolim replied. The word seemed peculiar coming from the mouth of a priest of Torak.

"Why is it that you tried to approach Kell? Didn't you know about the curse?"

"It is not a curse. It is a blessing."

"A blessing?"

"I was ordered by the Sorceress Zandramas to try to reach the holy city of the Dals," the Grolim continued. "She told me that I would be exalted should I be successful." He smiled gently. "It was in her mind, I think, to test the strength of the enchantment to determine if it might be safe for her to attempt the journey."

"I gather that it wouldn't be."

"That is difficult to say. Great benefit might come to her if she tried."

"I'd hardly call going blind a benefit."

"But I am not blind."

"I thought that's what the enchantment was all about."

"Oh, no. I cannot see the world around me, but that is because I see something else—something that fills my heart with joy."

"Oh? What's that?"

"I see the face of God, my friend, and will until the end of my days."

CHAPTER THREE

It was always there. Even when they were in deep, cool forests they could feel it looming over them, still and white and serene. The mountain filled their eyes, their thoughts, and even their dreams. Silk grew increasingly irritable as they rode day after day toward that gleaming white enormity. "How can anyone possibly get anything done in this part of the world with that thing there filling up half the sky?" he burst out one sunny afternoon.

"Perhaps they ignore it, Kheldar," Velvet said sweetly.

"How can you ignore something that big?" he retorted. "I wonder if it knows how ostentatious—and even vulgar—it is."

"You're being irrational," she said. "The mountain doesn't care how we feel about it. It's going to be there long after we're all gone." She paused. "Is that what bothers you, Kheldar? Coming across something permanent in the middle of a transient life?"

"The stars are permanent," he pointed out. "So's dirt, for that matter, but they don't intrude the way that beast does." He looked at 'Zakath. "Has anybody ever climbed to the top of it?" he asked.

"Why would anybody want to?"

"To beat it. To reduce it." Silk laughed. "That's even more irrational, isn't it?"

'Zakath, however, was looking speculatively at the looming presence that filled the southern sky. "I don't know, Kheldar," he said. "I've never considered the possibility of fighting a mountain before. It's easy to beat men. To beat a mountain, though—now that's something else."

"Would it care?" Eriond asked. The young man so seldom spoke that he seemed at times to be as mute as Toth. He had of late, however, seemed even more withdrawn. "The mountain might even welcome you." He smiled gently. "I'd imagine it gets lonesome. It could even want to share what it sees with anyone brave enough to go up there and look."

'Zakath and Silk exchanged a long, almost hungry look. "You'd need ropes," Silk said in a neutral sort of tone.

"And probably certain kinds of tools, as well," 'Zakath added. "Things that would dig into the ice and hold you while you climbed up higher."

"Durnik could figure those out for us."

"Will you two stop that?" Polgara said tartly. "We have other things to think about right now."

"Just speculation, Polgara," Silk said lightly. "This business of ours won't last forever, and when it's over—well, who knows?"

They were all subtly changed by the mountain. Speech seemed less and less necessary, and they all thought long thoughts, which, during quiet times around the campfire at night, they tried to share with each other. It became somehow a time of cleansing and healing, and they all grew closer together as they approached that solitary immensity.

One night Garion awoke with a light as bright as day in his eyes. He slipped out from under the blankets and turned back the flap of the tent. A full moon had arisen, and it filled the world with a pale luminescence. The mountain stood stark and white against the starry blackness of the night sky, glowing with a cool incandescence that seemed almost alive.

A movement caught his eye. Aunt Pol emerged from the tent she shared with Durnik. She wore a white robe that seemed almost a reflection of the moon-washed mountain. She stood for a moment in silent contemplation, then turned slightly. "Durnik," she murmured softly, "come and look."

Durnik emerged from the tent. He was bare-chested, and his silver amulet glittered in the moonlight. He put his arm about Polgara's shoulders, and the two of them stood drinking in the beauty of this most perfect of nights.

Garion was about to call out to them, but something stayed his tongue. The moment they were sharing was too private to be intruded upon. After quite some time, Aunt Pol whispered something to her husband, and, smiling, the two of them turned and went hand in hand back into their tent.

Quietly Garion let the tent flap drop and went back to his blankets.

Slowly, as they continued in a generally southwesterly direction, the forest changed. When they were still in the mountains, the trees had been evergreens interspersed here and there with aspens. As they approached the lowlands at the base of the huge mountain, they increasingly came across groves of beech and elm. And then at last they entered a forest of ancient oaks.

As they rode beneath the spreading branches in sun-dappled shade, Garion was sharply reminded of the Wood of the Dryads in southern Tolnedra. One glance at his little wife's face revealed that the similarity was not lost on her either. A kind of dreamy contentment came over her, and she seemed to be listening to voices that only she could hear.

It was about noon on a splendid summer day that they overtook another traveler, a white-bearded man dressed in clothing made from deerskin. The handles of the tools protruding from the lumpy bundle on the back of his pack mule proclaimed him to be a gold hunter, one of those vagrant hermits who haunt wildernesses the world over. He was riding a shaggy mountain pony so stumpy that its rider's feet nearly touched the ground on either side. "I thought I heard somebody coming up from behind," the gold hunter said as Garion and 'Zakath, both in their mail shirts and helmets, drew alongside him. "Don't see many in these woods— what with the curse and all."

"I thought the curse only worked on Grolims," Garion said.

"Most believe it doesn't pay to take chances. Where are you bound?"

"To Kell," Garion replied. There was no real point in making a secret of it.

"I hope you've been invited. The folk at Kell don't welcome strangers who just take it upon themselves to go there."

"They know we're coming."

"Oh. It's all right then. Strange place, Kell, and strange people. Of course living right under that mountain the way they do would make anybody strange after a while. If it's all right, I'll ride along with you as far as the turnoff to Balasa a couple miles on up ahead."

"Feel free," 'Zakath told him. "Aren't you missing a good time to be looking for gold, though?"

"Got myself caught up in the mountains last winter," the old fellow replied. "Supplies ran out on me. Besides, I get hungry for talk now and then. The pony and the mule listen pretty good, but they don't answer very well, and the wolves up there move around so much that you can't hardly get a conversation started with them." He looked at the she-wolf and then astonishingly spoke to her in her own language. "How is it with you, mother?" he asked. His accent was abominable, and he spoke haltingly, but his speech was undeniably that of a wolf.

"How remarkable," she said with some surprise. Then she responded to the ritual greeting. "One is content."

"One is pleased to hear that. How is it that you go with the man-things?"

"One has joined their pack for a certain time."

"Ah."

"How did you manage to learn the language of wolves?" Garion asked in some amazement.

"You recognized it, then." The old fellow sounded pleased about that for some reason. He leaned back in his saddle. "Spent most of my life up there where the wolves are," he explained. "It's only polite to learn the language of your neighbors." He grinned. "To be honest about it, though, at first I couldn't make much out of it, but if you listen hard enough, it starts to come to you. Spent a winter in a den with a pack of them about five years back. That helped quite a bit."

"They actually let you live with them?" 'Zakath asked.

"It took them awhile to get used to me," the old man admitted, "but I made myself useful, so they sort of accepted me."

"Useful?"

"The den was a little crowded, and I got them there tools." He jerked his thumb at his pack mule. "I dug the den out some larger, and they seemed to appreciate it. Then, after a while, I took to watching over the pups while the rest was out hunting. Good pups they was, too. Playful as kittens. Some time later I tried to make up to a bear. Never had much luck with that. Bears are a standoffish bunch. They keep to theirselves most of the time, and deer are just too skittish to try to make friends with. Give me wolves every time."

The old gold hunter's pony did not move very fast, so the others soon caught up with them.

"Any luck?" Silk asked the old gold hunter, his nose twitching with interest.

"Some," the white-bearded man answered evasively.

"Sorry," Silk apologized. "I didn't mean to pry."

"That's all right, friend. I can see that you're an honest man."

Velvet muffled a slightly derisive chuckle.

"It's just a habit I picked up," the fellow continued. "It's not really too smart to go around telling everybody how much gold you've managed to pick up."

"I can certainly understand that."

"I don't usually carry that much with me when I come down into the low country, though—only to pay for what I need. I leave the rest of it hid back up there in the mountains."

"Why do you do it then?" Durnik asked. "Spend all your time looking for gold, I mean? You don't spend it, so why bother?"

"It's something to do." The fellow shrugged. "And it gives me an excuse to be up there in the mountains. A man feels sort of frivolous if he does that without no reason." He grinned again. "Then, too, there's a certain kind of excitement that comes with finding a pocket of gold in a streambed. Like some say, finding is more fun than spending, and gold's sort of pretty to look at."

"Oh, it is indeed," Silk agreed fervently.

The old gold hunter glanced at the she-wolf and then looked at Belgarath. "I can see by the way she's acting that you're the leader of this group," he noted.

Belgarath looked a bit startled at that.

"He's learned the language," Garion explained.

"How remarkable," Belgarath said, unconsciously echoing the comment of the wolf.

"I was going to pass on some advice to these two young fellows, but you're the one who probably ought to hear it."

"I'll certainly listen."

"The Dals are a peculiar sort, friend, and they've got some peculiar superstitions. I won't go so far as to say they think of these woods as sacred, but they do feel pretty strongly about them. I wouldn't advise cutting any trees—and don't, whatever you do, kill anything or anybody here." He pointed at the wolf. "She knows about that already. You've probably noticed that she won't hunt here. The Dals don't want this forest profaned with blood. I'd respect that, if I were you. The Dals can be helpful, but if you offend their beliefs, they can make things mighty difficult for you."

"I appreciate the information," Belgarath told him.

"It never hurts a man to pass on things he's picked up," the old fellow said. He looked up the track. "Well," he said. "This is as far as I go. That's the road to Balasa just on up ahead. It's been nice talking with you." He doffed his shabby hat politely to Polgara, then looked at the wolf. "Be well, mother," he said, then he thumped his heels against his pony's flanks. The pony broke into an ambling sort of trot and jolted around a bend in the road to Balasa and out of sight.

"What a delightful old man," Ce'Nedra said.

"Useful, too," Polgara added. "You'd better get in touch with Uncle Beldin, father," she said to Belgarath. "Tell him to leave the rabbits and pigeons alone while we're in this forest."

"I'd forgotten about that," he said. "I'll take care of it right now." He lifted his face and closed his eyes.

"Can that old fellow really talk with wolves?" Silk asked Garion.

"He knows the language," Garion replied. "He doesn't speak it very well, but he knows it."

"One is sure he understands better than he speaks," the she-wolf said.

Garion stared at her, slightly startled that she had understood the conversation.

"The language of the man-things is not difficult to learn," she said. "As the man-thing with the white fur on his face said, one can learn rapidly if one takes the trouble to listen. One would not care to speak your language, however," she added critically. "The speech of the man-things would place one's tongue in much danger of being bitten."

A sudden thought came to Garion then, accompanied by an absolute certainty that the thought was entirely accurate. "Grandfather," he said.

"Not now, Garion. I'm busy."

"I'll wait."

"Is it important?"

"I think so, yes."

Belgarath opened his eyes curiously. "What is it?" he asked.

"Do you remember that conversation we had in Tol Honeth—the morning it was snowing?"

"I think so."

"We were talking about the way everything that happened seemed to have happened before."

"Yes, now I remember."

"You said that when the two prophecies got separated, things sort of stopped—that the future can't happen until they get back together again. Then you said that until they do, we'd all have to keep going through the same series of events over and over again."

"Did I really say that?" The old man looked a bit pleased. "That's sort of profound, isn't it? What's the point of this, though? Why are you bringing it up now?"

"Because I think it just happened again." Garion looked at Silk. "Do you remember that old gold hunter we met in Gar og Nadrak when the three of us were on our way to Cthol Mishrak?"

Silk nodded a bit dubiously.

"Wasn't the old fellow we just talked with almost exactly the same?"

"Now that you mention it . . ." Silk's eyes narrowed. "All right, Belgarath, what does it mean?"

Belgarath squinted up at the leafy branches overhead. "Let me think about it for a minute," he said. "There are some similarities, all right," he admitted. "The two of them are the same kind of people, and they both warned us about something. I think I'd better get Beldin back here. This might be very important."

It was no more than a quarter of an hour later when the blue-banded hawk settled out of the sky and blurred into the misshapen sorcerer. "What's got you so excited?" he demanded crossly.

"We just met somebody," Belgarath replied.

"Congratulations."

"I think this is serious, Beldin." Belgarath quickly explained his theory of recurring events.

"It's a little rudimentary," Beldin growled, "but there's nothing remarkable about that. Your hypotheses usually are." He squinted. "It's probably fairly accurate though—as far as it goes."

"Thanks," Belgarath said dryly. Then he went on to describe the two meetings, the one in Gar og Nadrak and the other here. "The similarities are a little striking, aren't they?"

"Coincidence?"

"Shrugging things off as coincidence is the best way I know of to get in trouble."

"All right. For the sake of argument, let's say it wasn't coincidence." The dwarf squatted in the dirt at the roadside, his face twisted in thought. "Why don't we take this theory of yours a step further?" he mused. "Let's look at the notion that these repetitions crop up at significant points in the course of events."

"Sort of like signposts?" Durnik suggested.

"Exactly. I couldn't have found a better term myself. Let's suppose that these signposts point at really important things that are right on the verge of happening—that they're sort of like warnings."

"I'm hearing a lot of 'notions' and 'supposes,'" Silk said skeptically. "I think you're off into the realm of pure speculation."

"You're a brave man, Kheldar," Beldin said sardonically. "Something could be trying to warn you about a potential catastrophe, and you choose to ignore the warning. That's either very brave or very stupid. Of course I'm giving you the benefit of the doubt by using the word 'brave' instead of the other one."

"One for his side," Velvet murmured.

Silk flushed slightly. "But how do we know what it is that's going to happen?" he objected.

"We don't," Belgarath said. "The circumstances just call for some extra alertness, is all. We've been warned. The rest is up to us."

They took some special precautions when they set up their encampment that evening. Polgara prepared supper quickly, and the fire was extinguished as soon as they had finished eating. Garion and Silk took the first watch. They stood atop a knoll behind the camp, peering into the darkness.

"I hate this," Silk whispered.

"Hate what?"

"Knowing that *something* is going to happen without knowing what it is. I wish those two old men would keep their speculations to themselves."

"Do you really like surprises?"

"A surprise is better than living with this sense of dread. My nerves aren't what they used to be."

"You're too high-strung sometimes. Look at all the entertainment you're getting out of anticipation."

"I'm terribly disappointed in you, Garion. I thought you were a nice, sensible boy."

"What did I say?"

"Anticipation. In this situation, that's just another word for 'worry,' and worry isn't good for anybody."

"It's just a way to get us ready in case something happens."

"I'm always ready, Garion. That's how I've managed to live so long, but right now I feel almost as tightly wound as a lute string."

"Try not to think about it."

"Of course," Silk retorted sarcastically. "But doesn't that defeat the purpose of the warning? Aren't we supposed to think about it?"

The sun had not come up yet when Sadi came back to their camp, moving very quietly and going from tent to tent with a whispering warning. "There's somebody out there," he warned after he had scratched on the flap of Garion's tent.

Garion rolled out from under his blankets, his hand automatically reaching for his sword. He paused then. The old gold hunter had warned them against the shedding of blood. Was this event for which they had been waiting? But were they supposed to obey the prohibition, or to step over it in response to some higher need? There was not time now to stand locked in indecision, however. Sword in hand, Garion rushed from the tent.

The light had that peculiar steely tint that comes from a colorless sky before the sun rises. It cast no shadows and what lay beneath the broad-spread oaks was not so much darkness as it was a fainter light. Garion moved quickly, his feet avoiding almost on their own the windrows of years-old dead leaves and the fallen twigs and branches that littered the floor of this ancient forest.

'Zakath stood atop the knoll, holding his sword.

"Where are they?" Garion's voice was not so much a whisper as a breath.

"They were coming up from the south," 'Zakath whispered back.

"How many?"

"It's hard to say."

"Are they trying to sneak up on us?"

"It didn't really look that way. The ones we saw could have hidden back there among the trees, but they just came walking through the forest."

Garion peered out into the growing light. And then he saw them. They were dressed all in white—robes or long smocks—and they made no attempts at concealment. Their movements were deliberate and seemed to have a placid, unhurried calm about them. They came in single file, each following the one in front at a distance of about ten yards. There was something hauntingly familiar about the way they moved through the forest.

"All they need are the torches," Silk said from directly behind Garion. The little man made no attempt to keep his voice down.

"Be still!" 'Zakath hissed.

"Why? They know we're here." Silk laughed a caustic little laugh. "Remember that time on the Isle of Verkat?" he said to Garion. "You and I spent a half hour or so crawling through the wet grass following Vard and his people, and I'm absolutely sure now that they knew we were there all the time. We could have just walked along behind them and saved ourselves all the discomfort."

"What are you talking about, Kheldar?" 'Zakath demanded in a hoarse whisper.

"This is another of Belgarath's repetitions." Silk shrugged. "Garion and I have been through it before." He sighed ruefully. "Life is going to get terribly boring if nothing new ever happens." Then he raised his voice to a shout. "We're over here," he called to the white-robed figures out in the forest.

"Are you mad?" 'Zakath exclaimed.

"Probably not, but then crazy people never really know, do they? Those people are Dals, and I seriously doubt that any Dal has ever hurt anybody since the beginning of time."

The leader of the strange column halted at the foot of the knoll and pushed back the cowl of his white robe. "We have been awaiting you," he announced. "The Holy Seeress has sent us to see you safely to Kell."

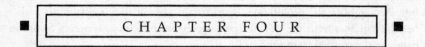

CHAPTER FOUR

King Kheva of Drasnia was irritable that morning. He had overheard a conversation the previous evening between his mother and an emmisary of King Anheg of Cherek, and his irritation grew out of a sort of moral dilemma. To reveal to his mother that he had been eavesdropping would of course be quite out of the question, and so he could not discuss with her what he had heard until she broached the subject herself. It seemed quite unlikely that she would do so, and so Kheva was at an impasse.

It should be stated here that King Kheva was not really the sort of boy who would normally intrude on his mother's privacy. He was basically a decent lad. But he was also a Drasnian. There is a national trait among Drasnians which, for want of a better term, might be called curiosity. All people are curious to a certain degree, but in Drasnians the trait was quite nearly compulsive. Some contended that it was their innate curiosity which has made spying their national industry. Others maintained with equal vigor that generations of spying had honed the Drasnians' natural curiosity to a fine edge. The debate was much like the endless argument about the chicken and the egg, and almost as pointless. Quite early in life, Kheva had trailed unobtrusively along behind one of the official court spies and thereby discovered the closet hidden behind the east wall of his mother's sitting room. Periodically he would slip into that closet in order to keep track of affairs of state and any other matters of interest. He was the king, after all, and thus he had a perfect right to the information. He reasoned that by spying, he could obtain it while sparing his mother the inconvenience of passing it on to him. Kheva was a considerate boy.

The conversation in question had concerned the mysterious disappearance of the Earl of Trellheim, his ship *Seabird,* and a number of other individuals, including Trellheim's son Unrak.

Barak, Earl of Trellheim, was considered in some quarters to be an unreliable sort, and his companions in this vanishing were, if anything, even worse. The Alorn kings were disquieted by the potential for disaster represented by Barak and his cohorts roaming loose in the Gods only knew what ocean.

What concerned young King Kheva, however, was not so much random disasters as it was the fact that his friend Unrak had been invited to participate while he had not. The injustice of that rankled. The fact that he was a king seemed to automatically exclude him from anything that could even remotely be considered hazardous. Everyone went out of his way to keep Kheva safe and secure, but Kheva did not *want* to be kept safe and secure. Safety and security were boring, and Kheva was at an age where he would go to any lengths to avoid boredom.

Clad all in red, he made his way through the marble halls of the palace in Boktor that winter morning. He stopped in front of a large tapestry and made some show of examining it. Then, at least relatively sure that no one was watching—this *was* Drasnia, after all—he slipped behind the tapestry and into the small closet previously mentioned.

His mother was conferring with the Nadrak girl Vella and with Yarblek, Prince Kheldar's shabby partner. Vella always made King Kheva nervous. She aroused certain feelings in him with which he was not yet prepared to cope, and so he customarily avoided her. Yarblek, on the other hand, could be quite amusing. His speech was blunt and often colorful and laced with oaths Kheva was not supposed to know the meaning of.

"They'll turn up, Porenn," Yarblek was assuring Kheva's mother. "Barak just got bored, that's all."

"I wouldn't be so concerned if he'd gotten bored by himself," Queen Porenn replied, "but the fact that this boredom seems to be an epidemic worries me. Barak's companions aren't the most stable men in the world."

"I've met them." Yarblek grunted. "You might just be right." He paced up and down for a moment. "I'll have our people keep an eye out for them."

"Yarblek, I've got the finest intelligence service in the world."

"Perhaps so, Porenn, but Silk and I have more men than you do, and we've got offices and warehouses in places Javelin hasn't even heard of." He looked at Vella. "Do you want to go back to Gar og Nadrak with me?" he asked.

"In the wintertime?" Porenn objected.

"We'll just wear more clothes, that's all." Yarblek shrugged.

"What are you going to do there?" Vella asked. "I'm not really very interested in sitting around listening to you talk business."

"I thought we'd go to Yar Nadrak. Javelin's people don't seem to be having much luck finding out what Drosta's up to." He broke off and looked speculatively at Queen Porenn. "Unless they've picked up something lately I haven't heard about yet," he added.

"Would I keep secrets from you, Yarblek?" she asked with mock innocence.

"Probably, yes. If you've got something, Porenn, share it with me. I don't want to make the trip for nothing, and Yar Nadrak's a miserable place in the winter."

"Nothing yet," she replied seriously.

Yarblek grunted. "I didn't think so. Drasnians look too much like Drasnians to be able to move around in Yar Nadrak without attracting attention." He glanced at Vella. "Well?" he asked.

"Why not?" she agreed. "Don't take this personally, Porenn, but this project of yours—trying to turn me into a lady—is starting to distract me just a little. Would you believe that yesterday I left my room with only one of my daggers? I think I need some fresh air and stale beer to clear my head."

Kheva's mother sighed. "Try not to forget everything I've taught you, Vella."

"I have a very good memory, and I can tell the difference between Boktor and Yar Nadrak. Boktor smells better, for one thing."

"How long will you be gone?" Porenn asked the rangy Yarblek.

"A month or two, I'd imagine. I think we'll want to go to Yar Nadrak by a roundabout route. I don't want to announce to Drosta that I'm coming."

"All right then," the queen agreed. Then she thought of something. "One last thing, Yarblek."

"Yes?"

"I'm very fond of Vella. Don't make the mistake of selling her while you're in Gar og Nadrak. I'd be very put out if you did that."

"Who'd buy her?" Yarblek responded. Then he grinned and skipped out of the way as Vella automatically went for one of her daggers.

Eternal Salmissra looked with some distaste at her current Chief Eunuch, Adiss. In addition to being incompetent, Adiss was slovenly. His iridescent robe was food-spotted, and his scalp and face were sparsely stubbled. He had never, she concluded, been more than an opportunist, and now that he had ascended to the position of Chief Eunuch and felt more or less secure there, he had given himself over to the grossest sorts of debauchery. He consumed staggering quantities of some of the most pernicious drugs available in Nyissa and frequently came into her presence with the vacant-eyed shamble of a sleepwalker. He bathed infrequently, and the combination of the climate of Sthiss Tor and the various drugs he used gave his body a rank, almost rancid, odor. Since the Serpent Queen now sampled the air with her flickering tongue, she could not only smell him but also taste him.

He groveled on the marble floor before the dais, delivering a report on some unimportant matter in a whining, nasal voice. Unimportant matters filled the Chief Eunuch's days. He devoted himself to petty things, since significant things were beyond his capabilities. With the mindless concentration of a man with severely limited talents, he expanded the trivial out of all proportion and reported it as if it were of earthshaking importance. Most of the time, Salmissra suspected, he was blithely ignorant of the things that should really be receiving his full attention.

"That will be all, Adiss," she told him in her sibilant whisper, her coils moving restlessly on her divanlike throne.

"But, my Queen," he protested, the half-dozen or so drugs he had taken since breakfast making him brave, "this matter is of utmost urgency."

"To you, perhaps. I am indifferent to it. Hire an assassin to cut off the Satrap's head and have done with it."

Adiss stared at her in consternation. "B-but, Eternal Salmissra," he squeaked in horror, "the Satrap is of vital importance to the security of the nation."

"The Satrap is a petty time-server who bribes you to keep himself in office. He serves no particular purpose. Remove him and bring me his head as proof of your absolute devotion and obedience."

"H-his head?"

"That's the part that has eyes in it, Adiss," she hissed sarcastically. "Don't make a mistake and bring me a foot instead. Now leave."

He stumbled backward toward the door, genuflecting every step or two.

"Oh, Adiss," she added, "don't ever enter the throne room again unless you've bathed."

He gaped at her in stupid incomprehension.

"You stink, Adiss. Your stench turns my stomach. Now get out of here."

He fled.

"Oh, my Sadi," she sighed half to herself, "where are you? Why have you deserted me?"

Urgit, High King of Cthol Murgos, was wearing a blue doublet and hose, and he sat up straight on his garish throne in the Drojim Palace. Javelin privately suspected that Urgit's new wife had a great deal to do with the High King's change of dress and demeanor. Urgit was not bearing up too well under the stresses of marriage. His face had a slightly baffled look on it as if something profoundly confusing had entered his life.

"That is our current assessment of the situation, your Majesty," Javelin concluded his report. "Kal Zakath has so reduced his forces here in Cthol Murgos that you could quite easily sweep them into the sea."

"That's easy for you to say, Margrave Khendon," Urgit replied a bit petulantly, "but I don't see you Alorns committing any of your forces to assist with the sweeping."

"Your Majesty raises a slightly delicate point," Javelin said, thinking very fast now. "Although we have agreed from the start that we have a common enemy in the Emperor of Mallorea, the eons of enmity between the Alorns and the Murgos cannot be erased overnight. Do you really want a Cherek fleet off your coast or a sea of Algar horsemen on the plains of Cthan and Hagga? The Alorn kings and Queen Porenn will give instructions, certainly, but commanders in the field have a way of interpreting royal commands to suit their own preconceptions. Your Murgo generals might very well also choose to misunderstand your instructions when they see a horde of Alorns bearing down on them."

"That's true, isn't it?" Urgit conceded. "What about the Tolnedran legions then? There have always been good relations between Tolnedra and Cthol Murgos."

Javelin coughed delicately and then looked around with some show of checking for unwanted listeners. Javelin knew that he must move with some care now. Urgit was proving to be far more shrewd than any of them had anticipated. Indeed, he was at times as slippery as an eel and he seemed to know instinctively exactly the way Javelin's fine-tuned Drasnian mind was working. "I trust this won't go any further, your Majesty?" he said in a half whisper.

"You have my word on it, Margrave," Urgit whispered back. "Although anyone who takes the word of a Murgo—*and* a member of the Urga Dynasty as well—shows very poor judgment. Murgos are notoriously untrustworthy, and all Urgas are quite mad, you know."

Javelin chewed on a fingernail, strongly suspecting that he was being outmaneuvered. "We've received some disquieting information from Tol Honeth."

"Oh?"

"You know how the Tolnedrans are—always alert for the main chance."

"Oh, my goodness, yes." Urgit laughed. "Some of the fondest memories of my childhood come from the times when Taur Urgas, my late, unlamented father, fell to chewing on the furniture when he received the latest proposal from Ran Borune."

"Now mind you, your Majesty," Javelin went on, "I'm not suggesting that Emperor Varana himself is in any way involved in this, but there are some fairly high-ranking Tolnedran nobles who've been in contact with Mal Zeth."

"That's disturbing, isn't it? But Varana controls the legions. As long as *he's* opposed to 'Zakath, we're safe."

"That's true—as long as Varana's alive."

"Are you suggesting the possibility of a coup?"

"It's not unheard of, your Majesty. Your own kingdom gives evidence of that. The great families in northern Tolnedra are still infuriated about the way the Borunes and Anadiles pulled a march on them and put Varana on the imperial throne. If something happens to Varana and he's succeeded by a Vordue or a Honeth or a Horbite, all assurances go out the window. An alliance between Mal Zeth and Tol Honeth could be an absolute disaster for Murgo and Alorn alike. More than that, though, if such an alliance were kept a secret and you had Tolnedran legions in force here in Cthol Murgos and they received sudden instructions to change sides, you'd be caught between an army of Tolnedrans and an army of Malloreans. That isn't my idea of a pleasant way to spend a summer."

Urgit shuddered.

"Under the circumstances, your Majesty," Javelin went on smoothly, "I'd advise the following course." He began ticking items off on his fingers. "One: There's a vastly diminished Mallorean presence here in Cthol Murgos. Two: An Alorn force inside your borders would be neither necessary nor advisable. You have enough troops of your own to drive the Malloreans out, and we'd be ill-advised to risk any accidental confrontations between your people and ours. Three: The rather murky political situation in Tolnedra makes it extremely risky to contemplate bringing the legions down here."

"Wait a minute, Khendon," Urgit objected. "You came here to Rak Urga with all sorts of glowing talk about alliances and commonality of interests, but now when it's time to put troops into the field, you back down. Why have you been wasting my time?"

"The situation has changed since we began our negotiations, your Majesty,"

Javelin told him. "We did not anticipate a Mallorean withdrawal of such magnitude, and we certainly didn't expect instability in Tolnedra."

"What am *I* going to get out of this then?"

"What is Kal Zakath likely to do the minute he gets word that you're marching on his strongholds?"

"He'll turn around and send his whole stinking army back to Cthol Murgos."

"Through a Cherek fleet?" Javelin suggested. "He tried that after Thull Mardu, remember? King Anheg and his berserkers sank most of his ships and drowned his troops by the regiment."

"That's true, isn't it?" Urgit mused. "Do you think Anheg might be willing to blockade the east coast to keep 'Zakath's army from returning?"

"I think he'd be delighted. Chereks take such childlike pleasure in sinking other people's boats."

"He'd need charts in order to make his way around the southern tip of Cthol Murgos, though," Urgit said thoughtfully.

Javelin coughed. "Ah—we already have those, your Majesty," he said deprecatingly.

Urgit slammed his fist down on the arm of his throne. "Hang it all, Khendon! You're here as an ambassador, not as a spy."

"Just keeping in practice, your Majesty," Javelin replied blandly. "Now," he went on, "in addition to a Cherek fleet in the Sea of the East, we're prepared to line the northern and western borders of Goska and the northwestern border of Araga with Algar cavalry and Drasnian pikemen. That would effectively cut off escape routes for the Malloreans trapped in Cthol Murgos, block Kal Zakath's favorite invasion route down through Mishrak ac Thull, *and* seal off the Tolnedran legions in the event of an accommodation between Tol Honeth and Mal Zeth. That way, everybody defends more or less his own territory, and the Chereks keep the Malloreans off the continent so that we can settle it all to our own satisfaction."

"It also totally isolates Cthol Murgos." Urgit pointed out the one fact that Javelin had hoped to gloss over. "I exhaust my kingdom pulling your chestnuts out of the fire, and then the Alorns, Tolnedrans, Arends, and Sendars are free to march in and eliminate the Angarak presence on the western continent."

"You have the Nadraks and Thulls as allies, your Majesty."

"I'll trade you," Urgit said dryly. "Give me the Arends and the Rivans, and I'll gladly give you the Thulls and Nadraks."

"I think it's time for me to contact my government on these matters, your Majesty. I've already overextended my authority. I'll need further instructions from Boktor."

"Give Porenn my regards," Urgit said, "and tell her that I join with her in wishing a mutual relative well."

Javelin felt a lot less sure of himself as he left.

The Child of Dark had smashed all the mirrors in her quarters in the Grolim Temple at Balasa that morning. It had begun to touch her face now. Dimly she had seen the swirling lights beneath the skin of her cheeks and forehead and then had broken the mirror that had revealed the fact to her—and all the others, as well. When it was done, she stared in horror at the gash in the palm of her hand. The lights were even in her blood. Bitterly she recalled the wild joy that had filled her when she had first read the prophetic words: "Behold: the Child of Dark shall be exalted above all others and shall be glorified by the light of the stars." But the light of the stars was no halo or glowing nimbus. The light was a creeping disease that encroached upon her inch by inch.

It was not only the swirling lights, however, that had begun to consume her. Increasingly her thoughts, her memories, and even her dreams were not her own. Again and again she awoke screaming as the same dream came again and again. She seemed to hang bodiless and indifferent in some unimaginable void, watching all unconcerned as a giant star spun and wobbled on its course, swelling and growing redder as it shuddered toward inevitable extinction. The random wobble of the off-center star was of no real concern until it became more and more pronounced. Then the bodiless and sexless awareness drifting in the void felt a prickle of interest and then a growing alarm. This was wrong. This had not been intended. And then it happened. The giant red star exploded in a place where that explosion was not supposed to happen; and, because it was in the wrong place, other stars were caught up in it. A vast, expanding ball of burning energy rippled outward, engulfing sun after sun until an entire galaxy had been consumed.

The awareness in the void felt a dreadful wrench within itself as the galaxy exploded, and for a moment it seemed to exist in more than one place. And then it was no longer one. "This must not be," the awareness said in a soundless voice.

"Truly," another soundless voice responded.

And that was the horror that brought Zandramas bolt upright and screaming in her bed night after night—the sense of another presence when always before there had been the perfect solitude of eternal oneness.

The Child of Dark tried to put those thoughts—memories, if you will—from her mind. There was a knock at the door of her chamber, and she pulled up the hood of her Grolim robe to hide her face. "Yes?" she said harshly.

The door opened, and the archpriest of this temple entered. "Naradas has departed, Holy Sorceress," he reported. "You wanted to be told."

"All right," she said in a flat voice.

"A messenger has arrived from the west," the archpriest continued. "He brings news that a western Grolim, a Hierarch, has landed on the barren west coast of Finda and now moves across Dalasia toward Kell."

Zandramas felt a faint surge of satisfaction. "Welcome to Mallorea, Agachak," she almost purred. "I've been waiting for you."

It was foggy that morning along the southern tip of the Isle of Verkat, but Gart was a fisherman and he knew the ways of these waters. He pushed out at first light, steering more by the smell of the land behind him and the feel of the prevailing current than by anything else. From time to time he would stop rowing, pull in his net, and empty the struggling, silver-sided fish into the large box beneath his feet. Then he would cast out his net again and resume his rowing while the fish he had caught thumped and flapped beneath him.

It was a good morning for fishing. Gart did not mind the fog. There were other boats out, he knew, but the fog created the illusion that he had the ocean to himself, and Gart liked that.

It was a slight change in the pull of the current on his boat that warned him. He hastily shipped his oars, leaning forward, and began to clang the bell mounted in the bow of his boat to warn the approaching ship that he was here.

And then he saw it. It was like no other ship Gart had ever seen before. It was long and it was big and it was lean. Its high bowsprit was ornately carved. Dozens of oars propelled it hissing through the water. There could be no mistaking the purpose for which that ship had been built. Gart shivered as the ominous vessel slid past.

Near the stern of the ship, a huge red-bearded man in chain mail stood leaning over the rail. "Any luck?" he called to Gart.

"Fair," Gart replied cautiously. He did not wish to encourage a ship with that big a crew to drop anchor and begin hauling in *his* fish.

"Are we off the southern coast of the Isle of Verkat yet?" the red-bearded giant asked.

Gart sniffed at the air and caught the faint scent of the land. "You're almost past it now," he told them. "The coast takes a bend to the northeast about here."

A man dressed in gleaming armor joined the big red-bearded fellow at the rail. The armored man held his helmet under one arm, and his black hair was curly. "Thy knowledge of these waters doth seem profound, friend," he said in an archaic form of address Gart had seldom heard before, "and thy willingness to share thy knowledge with others doth bespeak a seemly courtesy. Canst thou perchance advise us of the shortest course to Mallorea?"

"That would depend on exactly where you wanted to go in Mallorea," Gart replied.

"The closest port," the red-bearded man said.

Gart squinted, trying to recall the details of the map he had tucked on a shelf at home. "That would be Dal Zerba in southwestern Dalasia," he said. "If it were me, I'd go on due east for another ten or twenty leagues and then come about to a northeasterly course."

"And how long a voyage do we face to reach this port thou hast mentioned?" the armored man asked.

Gart squinted at the long, narrow ship alongside him. "That depends on how fast your ship goes," he replied. "It's three hundred and fifty leagues or so, but you have to swing back out to sea again to get around the Turim reef. It's very dangerous, I'm told, and no one tries to go through it."

"Peradventure we might be the first, my Lord," the armored man said gaily to his friend.

The giant sighed and covered his eyes with one huge hand. "No, Mandorallen," he said in a mournful voice. "If we rip out my ship's bottom on a reef, we'll have to swim the rest of the way, and you're not dressed for it."

The huge ship began to slide off into the fog.

"What kind of a ship is that?" Gart called after the disappearing vessel.

"A Cherek war boat," the rumbled reply came back with a note of pride. "She's the largest afloat."

"What do you call her?" Gart shouted between his cupped hands.

"Seabird," the reply came ghosting back to him.

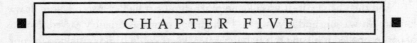

CHAPTER FIVE

It was not a large city, but its architecture was at a level of sophistication Garion had never seen before. It nestled in a shallow valley near the foot of the vast white peak, looking somehow as if it were resting in the mountain's lap. It was a city of slender white spires and marble colonnades. The low buildings spaced among the spires often had entire walls of glass. There were wide lawns around the buildings and groves of trees with marble benches beneath them. Formal gardens were spaced about the lawns—boxy hedges and beds of flowers lined by low, white walls. Fountains played in the gardens and in the courtyards of the buildings.

'Zakath gaped at the city of Kell in stunned amazement. "I never even knew this was here!" he exclaimed.

"You didn't know about Kell?" Garion asked him.

"I knew about Kell, but I didn't know it was like *this*." 'Zakath made a face. "It makes Mal Zeth look like a collection of hovels, doesn't it?"

"Tol Honeth, as well—and even Melcene," Garion agreed.

"I didn't think the Dals even knew how to build a proper house," the Mallorean said, "and now they show me something like this."

Toth had been gesturing to Durnik.

"He says that it's the oldest city in the world," the smith supplied. "It was built this way long before the world was cracked. It hasn't changed in almost ten thousand years."

'Zakath sighed. "They've probably forgotten how to do it, then. I was going to press some of their architects into service. Mal Zeth could use a bit of beautifying."

Toth gestured again, and a frown appeared on Durnik's face. "I can't have gotten that right," he muttered.

"What did he say?"

"The way I got it was that nothing the Dals have ever done has ever been forgotten." Durnik looked at his friend. "Is that what you meant?" he asked.

Toth nodded and gestured again.

Durnik's eyes went wide. "He says that every Dal alive today knows everything that every Dal who's ever lived knew."

"They must have very good schools then," Garion suggested.

Toth only smiled at that. It was a strange smile, tinged slightly with pity. Then he gestured briefly to Durnik, slid down from his horse, and walked away.

"Where's he going?" Silk asked.

"To see Cyradis," Durnik replied.

"Shouldn't we go with him?"

Durnik shook his head. "She'll come to us when she's ready."

Like all the Dals Garion had ever seen, the inhabitants of Kell wore simple white robes with deep cowls attached to the shoulders. They walked quietly across the lawns or sat in the gardens in groups of two or three engaged in sober discussion. Some carried books or scrolls. Others did not. Garion was somehow reminded of the University of Tol Honeth or the one at Melcene. This community of scholars, he was convinced, however, was engaged in studies far more profound than the often petty research that filled the lives of the professors at those exalted institutions.

The group of Dals who had escorted them to this jewel-like city led them along a gently curving street to a simple house on the far side of one of the formal gardens. An ancient, white-robed man leaned on a long staff in the doorway. His eyes were very blue, and his hair was snowy white. "We have long awaited your coming," he said to them in a quavering voice, "for the *Book of Ages* has foretold that in the Fifth Age the Child of Light and his company would come to us here at Kell to seek guidance."

"And the Child of Dark?" Belgarath asked him, dismounting. "Will she also come here?"

"No, Ancient Belgarath," the elderly man replied. "She may not come here, but will find direction elsewhere and in a different manner. I am Dallan, and I am bid to greet you."

"Do you rule here, Dallan?" 'Zakath asked, also dismounting.

"No one rules here, Emperor of Mallorea," Dallan said, "not even you."

"You seem to know us," Belgarath noted.

"We have known you all since the book of the heavens was first opened to us, for your names are written large in the stars. And now I will take you to a place where you may rest and await the pleasure of the Holy Seeress." He looked at the oddly placid she-wolf at Garion's side and the frolicking puppy behind her. "How is it with you, little sister?" he asked in formal tones.

"One is content, friend," she replied in the language of wolves.

"One is pleased that it is so," he replied in her own tongue.

"Does everyone in the whole world except me speak wolf?" Silk asked with some asperity.

"Would you like lessons?" Garion asked.

"Never mind."

And then with a tottering step the white-haired man led them across the verdant lawn to a large marble building with broad, gleaming steps at the front. "This house was prepared for you at the beginning of the Third Age, Ancient Belgarath," the old man said. "Its first stone was laid on the day when you recovered your Master's Orb from the City of Endless Night."

"That was quite some time ago," the sorcerer observed.

"The Ages were long in the beginning," Dallan agreed. "They grow shorter now. Rest well. We will attend to your mounts." Then he turned and, leaning on his staff, he went back toward his own house.

"Someday a Dal is going to come right out and say what he means without all the cryptic babble, and the world will come to an end," Beldin growled. "Let's go inside. If this house has been here for as long as he said it has, the dust's likely to be knee-deep in there, and it's going to need to be swept out."

"Tidiness, uncle?" Polgara laughed as they started up the marble steps. "From you?"

"I don't mind a certain amount of dirt, Pol, but dust makes me sneeze."

The interior of the house, however, was spotless. Gossamer curtains hung at the windows, billowing in the sweet-scented summer breeze, and the furniture, although oddly constructed and strangely alien-looking, was very comfortable. The interior walls were peculiarly curved, and there were no corners anywhere to be seen.

They wandered about this strange house, trying to adjust themselves to it. Then they gathered in a large, domed central room where a small fountain trickled water down one wall.

"There isn't any back door," Silk noted critically.

"Were you planning to leave, Kheldar?" Velvet asked him.

"Not necessarily, but I like to have that option open if the need should arise."

"You can always jump out a window if you have to."

"That's amateurish, Liselle. Only a first-year student at the academy dives out of windows."

"I know, but sometimes we have to improvise."

There was a peculiar murmuring sound in Garion's ears. At first he thought it might be the fountain, but somehow it didn't quite sound like running water. "Do you think they'd mind if we went out and had a look around?" he asked Belgarath.

"Let's wait a bit before we do that. We were sort of put here. I don't know yet if that means we're supposed to stay or what. Let's feel things out before we take any chances. The Dals here—and Cyradis in particular—have something we need. Let's not offend them." He looked at Durnik. "Did Toth give you any hints about when she'll be coming here?"

"Not really, but I got the impression it wouldn't be too long."

"That's not really too helpful, brother mine," Beldin said. "The Dals have a rather peculiar notion of time. They keep track of it in ages rather than years."

'Zakath had been rather closely examining the wall a few yards from the trickling fountain. "Do you realize that there's no mortar holding this wall together?"

Durnik joined him, took his knife from its sheath, and probed at the slender fissure between two of the marble slabs. "Mortise and tenon," he said thoughtfully, "and very tightly fit, too. It must have taken years to build this house."

"And centuries to build the city, if it's all put together that way," 'Zakath added. "Where did they learn how to do all this? And when?"

"Probably during the First Age," Belgarath told him.

"Stop that, Belgarath," Beldin snapped irritably. "You sound just the way they do."

"I always try to follow local customs."

"I still don't know any more than I did before," 'Zakath complained.

"The First Age covered the period of time from the creation of man until the day when Torak cracked the world," Belgarath told him. "The beginning of it is a little vague. Our Master was never very specific about when he and his brothers made the world. I expect that none of them want to talk about it because their Father disapproved. The cracking of the world is fairly well pinpointed, though."

"Were you around when it happened, Lady Polgara?" Sadi asked curiously.

"No," she replied. "My sister and I were born a while later."

"How long a while?"

"Two thousand years or so, wasn't it, father?"

"About that, yes."

"It chills my blood, the casual way you people shrug off eons." Sadi shuddered.

"What makes you think they learned this style of building before the cracking of the world?" 'Zakath asked Belgarath.

"I've read parts of the *Book of Ages*," the old man said. "It fairly well documents the history of the Dals. After the world was cracked and the Sea of the East rushed in, you Angaraks fled to Mallorea. The Dals knew that eventually they'd have to come to terms with your people, so they decided to pose as simple farmers. They dismantled their cities—all except this one."

"Why would they leave Kell intact?"

"There was no need to take it apart. The Grolims were the ones they were really worried about, and the Grolims can't come here."

"But other Angaraks can," 'Zakath noted shrewdly. "How is it that none of them has ever reported a city like this to the bureaucracy?"

"They're probably encouraged to forget," Polgara told him.

He looked at her sharply.

"It's not really that difficult, 'Zakath. A hint or two can usually erase memories." An expression of irritation crossed her face. "What *is* that murmuring sound?" she demanded.

"I don't hear anything," Silk said, looking slightly baffled.

"You must have your ears stopped up, then, Kheldar."

About sunset, several young women in soft white robes brought supper to them on covered trays.

"I see that things are the same the world over," Velvet said wryly to one of the young women. "The men sit around and talk, and the women do the work."

"Oh, we don't mind," the girl replied earnestly. "It's an honor to serve." She had very large dark eyes and lustrous brown hair.

"That's what makes it even worse," Velvet said. "First they make us do all the work, and then they persuade us that we like it."

The girl gave her a startled look, then giggled. Then she looked around guiltily and blushed.

Beldin had seized a crystal flagon almost as soon as the young women had entered. He filled a goblet and drank noisily. Then he began to choke, spraying a purplish liquid over half the room. "What is this stuff?" he demanded indignantly.

"It's fruit juice, sir," the young woman with the dark hair assured him earnestly. "It's very fresh. It was pressed only this morning."

"Don't you let it set long enough to ferment?"

"You mean when it goes bad? Oh, no. We throw it out when that happens."

He groaned. "What about ale? Or beer?"

"What are those?"

"I knew there was going to be something wrong with this place," the dwarf growled to Belgarath.

Polgara, however, had a beatific smile on her face.

"What was that all about?" Silk asked Velvet after the Dalasian women had left. "All that chitchat, I mean?"

"Groundwork," she replied mysteriously. "It never hurts to open channels of communication."

"Women." He sighed, rolling his eyes toward the ceiling.

Garion and Ce'Nedra exchanged a quick look, both of them remembering how often each of them had said approximately the same thing in the same tone early in their marriage. Then they both laughed.

"What's so funny?" Silk asked suspiciously.

"Nothing, Kheldar," Ce'Nedra replied. "Nothing at all."

Garion slept poorly that night. The murmuring in his ears was just enough of a distraction to bring him back from the edge of sleep over and over again. He arose the next morning sandy-eyed and out of sorts.

In the large round central room he found Durnik. The smith had his ear pressed against the wall near the fountain.

"What's the trouble?" Garion asked him.

"I'm trying to pinpoint that noise," Durnik said. "It might be something in the plumbing. The water in this fountain has to come from somewhere. Probably it's piped in, and then the pipe runs under the floor or up through the walls."

"Would water running through a pipe make that sort of noise?"

Durnik laughed. "You never know what sort of sounds are going to come out of the plumbing, Garion. I saw a whole town abandoned once. They all thought the place was haunted. The noise turned out to be coming from the municipal water supply."

Sadi came into the room once again wearing his iridescent silk robe.

"Colorful," Garion observed. For the past several months, the eunuch had been wearing a tunic, hose, and Sendarian half-boots.

Sadi shrugged. "For some reason I feel homesick this morning." He sighed. "I think I could live out my life in perfect contentment if I never saw another mountain. What are you doing, Goodman Durnik? Still examining the construction?"

"No. I'm trying to track down the source of that noise."

"What noise?"

"Surely you can hear it."

Sadi cocked his head to one side. "I hear some birds just outside the window," he said, "and there's a stream somewhere nearby, but that's about all."

Garion and Durnik exchanged a long, speculative look. "Silk couldn't hear it yesterday either," Durnik recalled.

"Why don't we get everybody up?" Garion suggested.

"That might make some of them a little unhappy, Garion."

"They'll get over it. I think this might be important."

There were some surly looks directed at Garion as the others filed in.

"What's this all about, Garion?" Belgarath asked in exasperation.

"It's what you might call an experiment, Grandfather."

"Do your experiments on your own time."

"My, aren't *we* cross this morning?" Ce'Nedra said to the old man.

"I didn't sleep very well."

"That's strange. I slept like a baby."

"Durnik," Garion said, "would you stand over there, please?" He pointed to one side of the room. "And Sadi, you over there." He pointed to the other side. "This will only take a few minutes," he told them all. "I'm going to whisper a question to each of you, and I want you to answer yes or no."

"Aren't you being just a bit exotic?" Belgarath asked sourly.

"I don't want to contaminate the experiment by giving all of you the chance to talk it over."

"It's a sound scientific principle," Beldin approved. "Let's humor him. He's stirred up my curiosity."

Garion went from person to person, whispering a single question: "Can you hear that murmuring sound?" Depending on the answer, he asked each of them to join either Sadi or Durnik. It did not take long, and the result confirmed Garion's suspicions. Standing with Durnik were Belgarath, Polgara, Beldin, and—somewhat surprisingly—Eriond. Standing with Sadi were Silk, Velvet, Ce'Nedra, and 'Zakath.

"Now do you suppose you could explain all this rigamarole?" Belgarath asked.

"I asked everybody the same question, Grandfather. The people standing with you can hear that sound. The people over there can't."

"Of course they can. It kept me awake half the night."

"Maybe that's why you're so dense this morning." Beldin grunted. "Good experiment, Garion. Now, why don't you explain it to our fuzzy-headed friend?"

"It's not difficult, Grandfather," Garion said deprecatingly. "It's probably so simple that you're overlooking it. The only people who can hear the sound are those with what you used to call 'talent.' Ordinary people can't."

"I'll be honest, Belgarath," Silk said. "I can't hear a sound."

"And I've been hearing it ever since we first caught sight of Kell," Durnik added.

"Now isn't that interesting?" Beldin said to Belgarath. "Shall we take it a few steps further, or did you want to go back to bed?"

"Don't be absurd," Belgarath replied absently.

"All right, then," Beldin continued, "we've got a sound that ordinary people can't hear, but that we can. I can think of another right offhand, as well, can't you?"

Belgarath nodded. "The sound of someone using sorcery."

"This is not a natural sound, then," Durnik mused. He suddenly laughed. "I'm glad you worked this out, Garion. I was right on the verge of tearing up the floor."

"What on earth for?" Polgara asked him.

"I thought the noise was coming from a water pipe somewhere."

"This isn't sorcery, though," Belgarath said. "It doesn't sound the same and it doesn't feel the same."

Beldin was scratching thoughtfully at his matted beard. "How does this idea strike you?" he said to Belgarath. "The people here have enough concentrated power to deal with any Grolim or group of Grolims who might come along, so why go to the trouble of laying down that curse of theirs?"

"I don't quite follow you."

"A large proportion of Grolims are sorcerers, right? So they'd be able to hear this sound. What if that enchantment is there to keep the Grolims far enough away so that they won't hear it?"

"Aren't you getting a little exotic, Beldin?" 'Zakath asked skeptically.

"Not really. Actually, I'm simplifying. A curse designed to keep away people you're not really afraid of doesn't make sense. Everybody's always thought that the curse was there to protect Kell itself, and that doesn't make any sense either. Isn't it simpler to assume that there's something more important that has to be protected?"

"What is there about this sound that would make the Dals so concerned about having it overheard?" Velvet asked, sounding perplexed.

"All right," Beldin said. "What is a sound?"

"Not *that* again." Belgarath sighed.

"I'm not talking about the noise in the woods. A sound is just a noise unless it's meaningful. What do we call a meaningful sound?"

"Talk, isn't it?" Silk ventured.

"Exactly."

"I don't understand," Ce'Nedra confessed. "What are the Dals saying that they want to keep secret? Nobody understands what they're saying anyway."

Beldin spread his hands helplessly, but Durnik was pacing up and down, his face creased with thought. "Maybe it's not so much *what* they're saying, but *how*."

"And you accuse *me* of being obscure," Beldin said to Belgarath. "What are you getting at, Durnik?"

"I'm groping," the smith admitted. "The noise, or sound—whatever you want to call it—isn't a signal that somebody's turning people into frogs." He stopped. "Can we really do that?" he asked.

"Yes," Beldin said, "but it's not worth the trouble. Frogs multiply at a ferocious rate. I'd rather have one person who irritated me instead of a million or so aggravating frogs."

"All right, then," Durnik continued. "It's not the noise that sorcery makes."

"Probably not," Belgarath agreed.

"And I think Ce'Nedra's right. Nobody really understands what the Dals are saying—except for other Dals. Half the time I can't follow what Cyradis is saying from one end of a sentence to the other."

"What does that leave?" Beldin asked intently, his eyes alight.

"I'm not sure. I've got the feeling though that 'How' is more important than 'What.'" Durnik suddenly looked slightly embarrassed. "I'm talking too much," he confessed. "I'm sure that some of the rest of you have more important things to say about this than I do."

"I don't really think so," Beldin told him. "I think you're right on the edge of it. Don't lose it."

Durnik was actually sweating now. He covered his eyes with one hand, trying to collect his thoughts. Garion noticed that everyone in the room was almost breathlessly watching his old friend labor with a concept that was probably far beyond the grasp of any of the rest of them.

"There has to be something that the Dals are trying to protect," the smith went on, "and it has to be something that's very simple—for them at least—but something they don't want anybody else to understand. I wish Toth were here. He might be able to explain it." Then his eyes went very wide.

"What is it, dear?" Polgara asked.

"It can't be that!" he exclaimed, suddenly very excited. "It couldn't be!"

"Durnik!" she said in exasperation.

"Do you remember when Toth and I first began to talk to each other—in gestures, I mean?" Durnik was suddenly talking very fast and he was almost breathless. "We'd been working together, and a man who works with someone else begins to know exactly what the other one is doing—and even what he's thinking." He stared at Silk. "You and Garion and Pol use that finger-language," he said.

"Yes."

"You've seen the gestures Toth makes. Would the secret language be able to say all that much with just a few waves of the hand—the way he does it?"

Garion already knew the answer.

Silk's voice was puzzled. "No," he said. "That would be impossible."

"But I know exactly what he's trying to say," Durnik told them. "The gestures don't mean anything at all. He does it just to make me—to give me some rational explanation for what he's really doing." Durnik's face grew awed. "He's been putting the words directly into my mind—without even talking. He has to, because he *can't* talk. What if that's what this murmuring we hear is? What if it's the sound of the Dals talking to one another? And what if they can do it over long distances?"

"And over time, too," Beldin said in a startled voice. "Do you remember what your big, silent friend said when we first got here? He said that nothing the Dals have ever done has ever been forgotten and that every Dal alive knows everything that every Dal who's ever lived knew."

"You're suggesting an absurdity, Beldin," Belgarath scoffed.

"No. Not really. Ants do it. So do bees."

"We aren't ants—or bees."

"I can do almost anything a bee can do." The hunchback shrugged. "Except make honey—and you could probably build a fairly acceptable anthill."

"Will one of you please explain what you're talking about?" Ce'Nedra asked crossly.

"They're hinting at the possibility of a group mind, dear," Polgara said quite calmly. "They're not doing it very well, but that's what they're groping toward." She gave the two old men a condescending sort of smile. "There are certain creatures—usually insects—that don't have very much intelligence individually, but as a group they're very wise. A single bee isn't too bright, but a beehive knows everything that's ever happened to it."

The she-wolf had come padding in, her toenails clicking on the marble floor, with the puppy scampering along behind her. "Wolves do it, as well," she supplied, indicating that she had been listening at the door.

"What did she say?" Silk asked.

"She said that wolves do the same thing," Garion translated. Then he remembered something. "I was talking with Hettar once, and he said that horses are the same way. They don't think of themselves as individuals—only as parts of the herd."

"Would it really be possible for *people* to do something like that?" Velvet asked incredulously.

"There's one way to find out," Polgara replied.

"No, Pol," Belgarath said very firmly. "It's too dangerous. You could be drawn into it and never be able to get back out."

"No, father," she replied quite calmly. "The Dals may not let me in, but they won't hurt me or keep me in if I want to leave."

"How do you know that?"

"I just do." And she closed her eyes.

CHAPTER SIX

They stood watching her apprehensively as she lifted her flawless face. Eyes closed, she concentrated. Then a strange expression came to her features.

"Well?" Belgarath asked.

"Quiet, father. I'm listening."

He stood drumming his fingers impatiently on the back of a chair, and the others watched breathlessly.

At last Polgara opened her eyes with a vaguely regretful sigh. "It's enormous," she said very quietly. "It has every thought these people have ever had—and every memory. It even remembers the beginning, and every one of them shares in it."

"And so did you?" Belgarath asked her.

"For a moment, father. They let me catch a glimpse of it. There are parts of it that are blocked off, though."

"We might have guessed that," Beldin said, scowling. "They're not going to provide access to anything that would give us the slightest advantage. They've been perched on *that* fence since the beginning of time."

Polgara sighed again and sat on a low divan.

"Are you all right, Pol?" Durnik asked with some concern.

"I'm fine, Durnik," she replied. "It's just that for a moment I saw something I've never experienced before, and then they asked me to leave."

Silk's eyes narrowed slightly. "Do you think they'd object if we left this house and had a look around?"

"No. They won't mind."

"I'd say that's our next step then," the little man suggested. "We know that the

Dals are the ones who are going to make the final choice—at least Cyradis is—but this oversoul of theirs is probably going to provide her some direction."

"That's a very interesting term, Kheldar," Beldin noted.

"What is?"

"Oversoul. How did you come up with it?"

"I've always had a way with words."

"There may be some hope for you after all. Someday we'll have to have a long talk."

"I shall place myself at your disposal, Beldin," Silk said with a florid bow. "Anyway," he continued, "since the Dals are going to decide things, I think we ought to get to know them better. If they're leaning in the wrong direction, maybe we can sway them back."

"Typically devious," Sadi murmured, "but probably not a bad idea. We should split up, though. We'll be able to cover more ground that way."

"Right after breakfast," Belgarath agreed.

"But, Grandfather," Garion protested, impatient to be off.

"I'm hungry, Garion, and I don't think well when I'm hungry."

"That might explain a lot," Beldin noted blandly. "We should have fed you more often when you were younger."

"You can be terribly offensive sometimes, do you know that?"

"Why, yes, as a matter of fact I do."

The same group of young women brought breakfast to them, and Velvet drew aside the large-eyed girl with the glossy brown hair and spoke with her briefly. Then the blond girl returned to the table. "Her name is Onatel," she reported, "and she's invited Ce'Nedra and me to visit the place where she and the other young women work. Young women talk a great deal, so we might pick up something useful."

"Wasn't Onatel the name of that seeress we met on the Isle of Verkat?" Sadi asked.

"It's a common name among Dalasian women," 'Zakath told him. "Onatel was one of their most honored seeresses."

"But the Isle of Verkat is in Cthol Murgos," Sadi pointed out.

"It's not all that strange," Belgarath said. "We've had some fairly strong hints that the Dals and the slave race of Cthol Murgos are closely related and keep in more or less constant contact. This is just some additional confirmation."

The morning sun was warm and bright as they emerged from the house and strolled off in various directions. Garion and 'Zakath had removed their armor and left their swords behind, although Garion prudently carried the Orb in a pouch tied to his belt. The two of them walked across a dewy lawn toward a group of larger buildings near the center of the city.

"You're always very careful with that stone, aren't you, Garion?" 'Zakath asked.

"I'm not sure that careful is the exact word," Garion replied, "but then again, maybe it is—in a broader sense. You see, the Orb is very dangerous, and I don't want it hurting people by accident."

"What does it do?"

"I'm not really sure. I've never seen it do anything to anybody—except possibly Torak—but that might have been the sword."

"And you're the only one in the world who can touch the Orb?"

"Hardly. Eriond carried it around for a couple of years. He kept trying to give it to people. They were mostly Alorns, so they knew better than to take it."

"Then you and Eriond are the only people who can touch it?"

"My son can," Garion said. "I put his hand on it right after he was born. It was very happy to meet him."

"A stone? Happy?"

"It's not like other stones." Garion smiled. "It can be a little silly now and then. It gets carried away by its own enthusiasm. I have to be very careful about what I think sometimes. If it decides I really want something, it might just take independent action." He laughed. "Once I was speculating about the time when Torak cracked the world, and it proceeded to tell me how to patch it."

"You're not serious!"

"Oh, yes. It has no conception of the word 'impossible.' If I really wanted it to, it could probably spell out my name in stars." He felt a small twitch in the pouch at his belt. "Stop that!" he said sharply to the Orb. "That was just an example, not a request."

'Zakath was staring at him.

"Wouldn't that look grotesque?" Garion said wryly. " 'Belgarion' running from horizon to horizon across the night sky?"

"You know something, Garion," 'Zakath said. "I've always believed that some-day you and I would go to war with each other. Would you be terribly disappointed if I decided not to show up?"

"I think I could bear it." Garion grinned at him. "If nothing else, I could always start without you. You could drop by from time to time to see how things were going. Ce'Nedra can fix you supper. Of course, she's not a very good cook, but we all have to make a few sacrifices, don't we?"

They looked at each other for a moment and then burst out laughing. The process that had begun at Rak Urga with the quixotic Urgit was now complete. Garion realized with a certain amount of satisfaction that he had taken the first few steps toward ending five thousand years of unrelenting hatred between Alorn and Angarak.

The Dals paid little attention to them as they strolled along marble streets and past sparkling fountains. The inhabitants of Kell went about their activities quietly and comtemplatively, their eyes lost in thought. They spoke but little, since speech among them was largely unnecessary.

"It's an eerie sort of place, isn't it?" 'Zakath observed. "I'm not used to cities where nobody does anything."

"Oh, they're doing something, all right."

"You know what I mean. There aren't any shops, and nobody's even out sweeping the streets."

"It is a little odd, I suppose." Garion looked around. "What's even odder is that we haven't seen a single seer since we got here. I thought this was the place where they lived."

"Maybe they stay indoors."

"That's possible, I suppose."

Their morning stroll gained them little information. They tried occasionally to strike up conversations with the white-robed citizens, and although the Dals were unfailingly polite, they volunteered little in the way of talk. They answered questions that were put to them, and that was about all.

"Frustrating, wasn't it?" Silk said when he and Sadi returned to the house that had been assigned to them. "I've never met a group of people so disinterested in talk. I couldn't even find anybody willing to discuss the weather."

"Did you happen to see which way Ce'Nedra and Liselle went?" Garion asked him.

"Someplace over on the other side of town, I think. I imagine they'll come back when those young women bring us our lunch."

Garion looked around at the others. "Did anybody happen to see any of the seers?" he asked.

"They aren't here," Polgara told him. She sat by a window mending one of Durnik's tunics. "One old woman told me they have a special place. It's not in the city."

"How did you manage to get an answer out of her?" Silk asked.

"I was fairly direct. You have to push the Dals a bit when you want information."

As Silk had predicted, Velvet and Ce'Nedra returned with the young women who were bringing their meals to them.

"You have a brilliant wife, Belgarion," Velvet said after the Dalasian women had left. "She sounded for all the world as if there weren't a brain in her head. She spent the morning babbling."

"Babbling?" Ce'Nedra objected.

"Weren't you?"

"Well, I suppose so, but 'babbling' is such an unflattering word."

"I presume there was a reason for it?" Sadi suggested.

"Of course," Ce'Nedra said. "I saw fairly soon that those girls weren't going to be very talkative, so I filled up the spaces. They began to loosen up after a bit. I talked so that Liselle could watch their faces." She smiled smugly. "It worked out fairly well, even if I do say it myself."

"Did you get anything out of them?" Polgara asked.

"A few things," Velvet replied. "Nothing all that specific, but a few hints. I think we should be able to get a bit more this afternoon."

Ce'Nedra looked around. "Where's Durnik?" she asked. "And Eriond?"

"Where else?" Polgara sighed.

"Where did they find any water to fish in?"

"Durnik can smell water from several miles away," Polgara told her in a resigned tone of voice, "and he can tell you what kind of fish are in it, how many, and probably even what their names are."

"I've never cared all that much for fish myself," Beldin said.

"I don't know that Durnik does either, uncle."

"Why does he bother them then?"

She spread her hands helplessly. "How should I know? The motives of fishermen are dreadfully obscure. I can tell you one thing, though."

"Oh? What's that?"

"You've said a number of times that you want to have some long conversations with him."

"Yes, I do."

"You'd better learn how to fish then. Otherwise, he probably won't be around."

"Has anybody come by to give us any kind of word about Cyradis?" Garion asked.

"Not a soul," Beldin replied.

"We don't really have time for an extended stay," Garion fretted.

"I might be able to stir an answer out of somebody," 'Zakath offered. "She commanded me to present myself to her here at Kell." He winced slightly. "I can't believe I just said that. Nobody's commanded me to do anything since I was about eight years old. Anyway, you know what I mean. I could insist that somebody take me to her so I can obey her orders."

"I think you might choke on that one, 'Zakath," Silk said lightly. "Obey is a difficult concept for someone in your position."

"He's an irritating little fellow, isn't he?" 'Zakath said to Garion.

"I've noticed."

"Why, your Majesties," Velvet said, all wide-eyed innocence, "what a thing to suggest."

"Well, isn't he?" 'Zakath said pointedly.

"Of course, but it's not nice to talk about it."

Silk looked slightly offended. "Would you people like for me to go away so you can talk freely?"

"Oh, that won't be necessary, Kheldar," Velvet said with a dimpled smile.

They gained little more in the way of information that afternoon, and the frustration of the fruitless quest made them all irritable. "I think perhaps we should follow up that idea of yours," Garion said to 'Zakath after supper. "First thing tomorrow morning, why don't we go see that old man, Dallan? We'll tell him right out that you're supposed to present yourself to Cyradis. I think it's time to start pushing a little."

"Right," 'Zakath agreed.

Dallan, however, proved to be as unresponsive as all the rest of the citizens of Kell. "Be patient, Emperor of Mallorea," he advised. "The Holy Seeress will come to you at the proper time."

"And when is that?" Garion asked bluntly.

"Cyradis knows, and that's all that's really important, isn't it?"

"If he wasn't so old and feeble, I'd shake some answers out of him," Garion muttered as he and 'Zakath walked back to the house.

"If this goes on much longer, I might just ignore his age and infirmity," 'Zakath said. "I'm not in the habit of having my questions evaded this way."

Velvet and Ce'Nedra were approaching the house from the other direction as Garion and 'Zakath reached the broad marble steps. The two young women were walking quickly, and Ce'Nedra's expression was triumphant.

"I think we managed to get something useful at last," Velvet said. "Let's go inside so we can tell everyone at once."

They gathered again in the domed room, and the blond girl spoke to them quite seriously. "This isn't too precise," she admitted, "but I think it might be all we're likely to get out of these people. This morning, Ce'Nedra and I went back to that house where those young women work. They were weaving, and that's the sort of thing that tends to make people a little less than alert. Anyway, that girl with the large eyes, Onatel, wasn't there, and Ce'Nedra put on her most empty-headed expression and—"

"I most certainly did not," Ce'Nedra said indignantly.

"Oh, but you did, dear—and it was absolutely perfect. She stood there all wide-eyed and innocent and asked the young women where we could find our 'dear friend,' and one of them let something slip that she probably wasn't supposed to have. She said that Onatel had been summoned to serve in 'the place of the seers.' Ce'Nedra's eyes went—if possible—even more vacant, and she asked where that might be. Nobody answered, but one of them looked at the mountain."

"How can you avoid looking at that monster?" Silk scoffed. "I'm a little dubious about this, Liselle."

"The girl was weaving, Kheldar. I've done that myself a few times, and I know you have to keep your eyes on what you're doing. She looked away in response to Ce'Nedra's question, and then she jerked her eyes back and tried to cover her mistake. I've been to the academy, too, Silk, and I can read people almost as well as you can. That girl might as well have screamed it out loud. The seers are somewhere up on that mountain."

Silk made a face. "She's probably right, you know," he admitted. "That's one of the things they stress at the academy. If you know what you're looking for, most people's faces are like open books." He squared his shoulders. "Well, 'Zakath," he said, "it looks as if we'll get to climb that mountain a little sooner than we'd expected."

"I don't think so, Kheldar," Polgara said firmly. "You could spend half a lifetime poking around in those glaciers and still not find the seers."

"Have you got a better idea?"

"Several, actually." She rose to her feet. "Come along, Garion," she said. "You, too, uncle."

"What are you up to, Pol?" Belgarath asked.

"We're going to go up and have a look."

"That's what I suggested already," Silk objected.

"There's one difference, though, Kheldar," she said sweetly. "You can't fly."

"Well," he said in an offended tone, "if you're going to be that way about it."

"I am, Silk. It's one of the advantages of being a woman. I get to do all sorts of unfair things, and you have to accept them because you're too polite not to."

"One for her side," Garion murmured.

"You keep saying that," 'Zakath said, puzzled. "Why?"

"It's an Alorn joke," Garion told him.

"Why don't you save yourself a bit of time, Pol?" Belgarath suggested. "See if you can get some confirmation from that group mind before you go swooping off."

"That's a very good idea, father," she agreed. She closed her eyes and lifted her face. After a moment she shook her head. "They won't let me back in." She sighed.

"That's a kind of confirmation in itself." Beldin chuckled.

"I don't exactly follow that," Sadi said, rubbing his freshly shaved scalp.

"The Dals may be wise," the hunchback told him, "but they're not very shrewd. These two girls of ours have picked up some information. If the information wasn't correct, there wouldn't be any reason to keep Pol out. Since they *did* keep her out, it indicates that we're on to something. Let's go outside of town," he suggested to Polgara, "so that we don't give away any secrets."

"I don't really fly all that well, Aunt Pol," Garion said dubiously. "Are you sure you need me?"

"Let's not take chances, Garion. If the Dals go out of their way to make this place inaccessible, we might need to use the Orb to break through. We'll save time if you come along with it in the first place."

"Oh," he said, "maybe you're right."

"Keep in touch," Belgarath said as the three of them started out the door.

"Naturally," Beldin grunted.

Once they were out on the lawn, the dwarf squinted around. "Over there, I think," he said, pointing. "That thicket on the edge of town should hide what we're doing."

"All right, uncle," Polgara agreed.

"One other thing, Pol," he added, "and I'm not trying to be offensive."

"That's a novelty."

"You're in good form this morning." He grinned. "Anyway, a mountain like that one breeds its own weather—and most particularly, its own winds."

"Yes, uncle, I know."

"I know how fond you are of snowy owls, but the feathers are too soft. If you get into a high wind, you could end up coming back naked."

She gave him a long, level look.

"Do you *want* all your feathers blown off?"

"No, uncle, as a matter of fact, I don't."

"Why don't you do it my way, then? You might even find that you like being a hawk."

"Blue-banded, I suppose?"

"Well, that's up to you, but you do look good in blue, Pol."

"You're impossible." She laughed. "All right, uncle, we'll do it your way."

"I'll change first," he offered. "Then you can use me as a model to make sure you get the shape right."

"I know what a hawk looks like, uncle."

"Of course you do, Pol. I'm just trying to be helpful."

"You're too kind."

It felt very strange to make a shape other than that of a wolf. Garion looked himself over carefully, making frequent comparisons to Beldin, who perched fierce-eyed and magnificent on a branch overhead.

"Good enough," Beldin told him, "but next time make your tail feathers a little fuller. You need them to steer with."

"All right, gentlemen," Polgara said from a nearby limb, "let's get started."

"I'll lead," Beldin said. "I've had more practice at this. If we hit a downdraft, sheer away from the mountain. You don't want to get banged up against those rocks." He spread his wings, flapped a few times, and flew off.

The only time Garion had been aloft before had been on the long flight from Jarviksholm to Riva after Geran had been abducted. He had flown that time as a speckled falcon. The blue-banded hawk was a much bigger bird, and flying over mountain terrain was much different from flying over the vast open expanse of the Sea of the Winds. The air currents eddied and swirled around the rocks, making them unpredictable and even dangerous.

The three hawks spiraled upward on a rising column of air. It was an effortless way to fly, and Garion began to understand Beldin's intense joy in flight.

He also discovered that his eyes were incredibly sharp. Every detail on the mountainside stood out as if it were directly in front of him. He could see insects and the individual petals of wildflowers. His talons twitched involuntarily when a small mountain rodent scurried across a rockfall.

"Pay attention to what we're here for, Garion," he heard Aunt Pol's voice in the silences of his mind.

"But—" The yearning to plummet down with his talons spread wide was almost irresistible.

"No buts, Garion. You've already had breakfast. Just leave the poor little creature alone."

"You're taking all the fun out of it for him, Pol," Garion heard Beldin protest.

"We're not here to have fun, uncle. Lead on."

The buffeting was sudden, and it took Garion by surprise. A violent downdraft hurled him toward a rocky slope, and it was only at the last instant that he was able to veer away from certain disaster. The downdraft pushed him this way and that, wrenching at his wings, and it was suddenly accompanied by a pelting rainstorm, huge, icy drops that pounded at him like large wet hammers.

"It isn't natural, Garion!" Aunt Pol's voice came to him sharply. He looked around desperately, but he could not see her.

"Where are you?" he called out.

"Never mind that! Use the Orb! The Dals are trying to keep us away!"

Garion was not entirely positive that the Orb could hear him in that strange place to which it went when he changed form, but he had no choice but to try. The driving rain and howling wind currents made settling to earth and resuming his own shape unthinkable. "Make it stop!" he called out to the stone, "the wind, the rain, all of it!"

The surge he felt when the Orb unleashed its power sent him staggering through the air, flapping his wings desperately to hold his balance. The air around him seemed suddenly bright blue.

And then the turbulence and the rain that had accompanied it were gone, and the column of warm air was back, rising undisturbed into the summer air.

He had lost at least a thousand feet in the downdraft, and he saw Aunt Pol and Beldin, each over a mile away in opposite directions. As he began again to spiral upward, he saw that they also were rising and veering through the air toward him. "Stay on your guard," Aunt Pol's voice told him. "Use the Orb to muffle anything else they try to throw at us."

It took them only a few minutes to regain the height they had lost, and they continued upward over forests and rockslides until they reached that region on the flanks of the mountain above the tree line and below the eternal snows. It was an area of steep meadows with grass and wildflowers nodding in the mountain breeze.

"There!" Beldin's voice seemed to crackle. "It's a trail."

"Are you sure it's not just a game trail, uncle?" Polgara asked him.

"It's too straight, Pol. A deer couldn't walk in a straight line if his life depended on it. That trail is man-made. Let's see where it goes." He tilted on one wing and swooped down toward the well-traveled track stretching up one of the meadows toward a gap in a rocky ridge. At the upper end of the meadow, he flared his wings. "Let's go down," he told them. "It might be better if we follow the rest of the way on foot."

Aunt Pol and Garion followed him down, and the three of them blurred back into their own forms. "It was touch and go there for a while," Beldin said. "I came within a few feet of bending my beak on a rockslide." He looked critically at Polgara. "Would you like to revise your theory about the Dals not hurting anybody?"

"We'll see."

"I wish I had my sword," Garion said. "If we run into trouble, we're pretty much defenseless."

"I don't know if your sword would be much use against the kind of trouble we're likely to come up against," Beldin told him. "Don't lose contact with the Orb, though. Let's see where this goes." He started up the steep trail toward the ridge.

The gap in the ridge was a narrow pass between two large boulders. Toth stood in the center of the trail, mutely blocking their way.

Polgara looked him coolly in the face. "We *will* go to the place of the seers, Toth. It is foreordained."

Toth's eyes grew momentarily distant. Then he nodded and stepped aside for them.

CHAPTER SEVEN

The cavern was vast, and there was a city inside. The city looked much like Kell, thousands of feet below, except, of course, for the absence of lawns and gardens. It was dim, since the blindfolded seers needed no light, and the eyes of their mute guides had, Garion surmised, become adjusted to the faint light.

There were few people abroad in those shadowy streets, and those they saw as Toth led them into the city paid no attention to them. Beldin was muttering to himself as he stumped along.

"What is it, uncle?" Polgara asked him.

"Have you ever noticed how much some people are slaves to convention?" he replied.

"I don't quite see what you're getting at."

"This town is inside a cave, but they still put roofs on the houses. Isn't that sort of an absurdity? It isn't going to rain in here."

"But it will get cold—particularly in the winter. If a house has no roof, it's a little hard to keep the heat in, wouldn't you say?"

He frowned. "I guess I didn't think of that," he admitted.

The house to which Toth led them was in the very center of this strange subterranean city. Although it was no different from those around it, its location hinted that the inhabitant was of some importance. Toth entered without knocking and led them to the simple room where Cyradis sat waiting for them, her pale young face illuminated by a single candle.

"You have reached us more quickly than we had expected," she said. In a peculiar way her voice was different from the way it had sounded in their previous meetings. Garion uneasily felt that the seeress was speaking in more than one voice, and the result was startlingly choral.

"You knew that we could come, then?" Polgara asked her.

"Of course. It was but a question of time before you would complete your threefold task."

"Task?"

"It was but a simple endeavor for one as powerful as thou art, Polgara, but it was a necessary test."

"I don't seem to recall—"

"As I told thee, it was so simple that doubtless thou hast forgotten it."

"Remind us," Beldin said gruffly.

"Of course, gentle Beldin." She smiled. "You have found this place; you have subdued the elements to reach it; and Polgara hath spoken correctly the words that gained you entry."

"More riddles," he said sourly.

"A riddle is sometimes the surest way to make the mind receptive."

He grunted.

"It was necessary for the riddle to be solved and the tasks to be completed ere I could reveal to you that which must be revealed." She rose to her feet. "Let us depart from this place then, and go down even unto Kell. My guide and dear companion will bear the great book that must be delivered into the hands of Ancient Belgarath."

The mute giant went to a shelf on the far side of the dimly lit room and took down a large book bound in black leather. He tucked it under his arm, took his mistress by the hand, and led them back out of the house.

"Why the secrecy, Cyradis?" Beldin asked the blindfolded girl. "Why do the seers hide up here on the mountain instead of staying at Kell?"

"But this *is* Kell, gentle Beldin."

"What's that city down in the valley, then?"

"Also Kell." She smiled. "It hath ever been thus among us. Unlike the cities of others, our communities are widespread. This is the place of the seers. There are many other places on this mountain—the place of the wizards, the place of the necromancers, the place of the diviners—and all are a part of Kell."

"Trust a Dal to come up with an unnecessary complication."

"The cities of others are built for different purposes, Beldin. Some are for commerce. Some are for defense. Our cities are built for study."

"How can you study if you have to walk all day in order to talk with your colleagues?"

"There is no need for walking, Beldin. We can speak to each other whenever we choose. Is this not the way in which thou and Ancient Belgarath converse?"

"That's different," he growled.

"In what way?"

"Our conversations are private."

"We have no need of privacy. The thoughts of one are the thoughts of all."

It was shortly before noon when they emerged from the cavern into the warm sunlight again. Gently guiding Cyradis, Toth led them back to the gap in the ridge and down the steep path that crossed the high meadows. After about an hour of descent, they entered a cool green forest where birds caroled from the treetops and insects whirled like specks of fire in the slanting columns of sunlight.

The trail was still steep, and Garion soon discovered one of the disadvantages of walking downhill for any extended period of time. A large and painful blister was forming atop one of the toes on his left foot, and a few twinges from his right clearly indicated that he would soon have a matched set. He gritted his teeth and limped on.

It was nearly sunset when they reached the gleaming city in the valley. Garion noticed with a certain satisfaction that Beldin was also limping as they walked along the marble street that led to the house Dallan had lodged them in.

The others were eating when they entered. As it chanced to happen, Garion was looking at 'Zakath's face when the Mallorean saw that Cyradis was with them. His olive-skinned face paled slightly, a pallor made more pronounced by the short black beard he had grown to conceal his identity. He rose to his feet and bowed slightly. "Holy Seeress," he said respectfully.

"Emperor of Mallorea," she responded. "As I promised thee in cloud-dark Darshiva, I surrender myself up to thee as thy hostage."

"There's no need to talk of hostages, Cyradis," he replied with a slightly embarrassed flush. "I spoke in haste in Darshiva, before I clearly understood what it is that I am to do. I am committed now."

"I am, nonetheless, thy hostage, for it is thus preordained, and I must accompany thee unto the Place Which Is No More to face the task that awaits me."

"You must all be hungry," Velvet said. "Come to the table and eat."

"I must complete one task first, Huntress," Cyradis told her. She held out both hands, and Toth placed the heavy book he had carried down from the mountain in them. "Ancient Belgarath," she said in that strangely choral voice, "thus do we commend into thy hands our holy book as the stars have instructed us to do. Read it carefully, for thy destination is revealed in its pages."

Belgarath rose quickly, crossed to her, and took the book, his hands trembling with eagerness. "I thank you, Cyradis. I know how precious the book is, and I will care for it while it is in my hands and return it once I've found what I need." Then he went to a smaller table near the window, sat, and opened the heavy volume.

"Move over," Beldin told him, stumping to the table and drawing up another chair. The two old men bent their heads over the crackling pages, oblivious to all around them.

"Will you eat now, Cyradis?" Polgara asked the blindfolded girl.

"Thou art kind, Polgara," the Seeress of Kell replied. "I have fasted since thine arrival here in preparation for this meeting, and mine hunger weakens me."

Polgara gently led her to the table and seated her between Ce'Nedra and Velvet.

"Is my baby well, Holy Seeress?" Ce'Nedra asked urgently.

"He is well, Queen of Riva, although he doth yearn to be returned to thee."

"I'm surprised he even remembers me." Ce'Nedra said it with some bitterness. "He was only a baby when Zandramas stole him." She sighed. "There's so much I've missed—so many things I'll never see." Her lower lip began to tremble.

Garion went to her and put his arms comfortingly around her. "It's going to be all right, Ce'Nedra," he assured her.

"Will it, Cyradis?" she asked in a voice near to tears. "Will everything really be all right again?"

"That I cannot say, Ce'Nedra. Two courses stand before us, and not even the stars know upon which we will place our feet."

"How was the trip?" Silk asked, more, Garion thought, to get past an uncomfortable moment than out of any burning curiosity.

"Nervous," Garion replied. "I don't fly very well, and we ran into some bad weather."

Silk frowned. "But it's been absolutely clear all day."

"Not where we were, it wasn't." Garion glanced at Cyradis and decided not to make an issue of the near-disastrous downdraft. "Is it all right to tell them about the place where you live?" he asked her.

"Of a certainty, Belgarion." She smiled. "They are of thy company, and thou shouldst conceal nothing from them."

"Do you remember Mount Kahsha in Cthol Murgos?" Garion asked his friend.

"I've been trying to forget."

"Well, the seers have a city that's sort of like the one the Dagashi built at Kahsha. It's inside a very large cave."

"I'm glad I didn't go there, then."

Cyradis turned her face toward him, a concerned little frown touching her forehead. "Hast thou not yet mastered this unreasoning fear of thine, Kheldar?"

"Not noticeably, no—and I'd hardly call it unreasoning. Believe me, Cyradis, I have reasons—lots and lots of reasons." He shuddered.

"Thou must summon up thy courage, Kheldar, for the time will surely come when thou must enter a place such as thou holdest in dread."

"Not if I can help it, I won't."

"Thou must, Kheldar. No choice is open to thee."

His face was bleak, but he said nothing.

"Tell me, Cyradis," Velvet said then, "were *you* the one who interrupted the progress of Zith's pregnancy?"

"Thou art shrewd to have perceived the pause in that most natural of events, Liselle," the Seeress told her, "but nay, it was not I. The wizard Vard on the Isle of Verkat bade her to wait until her task at Ashaba was completed."

"Vard is a wizard?" Polgara asked in some surprise. "I can usually detect them, but in his case, I didn't sense a thing."

"He is most subtle," Cyradis agreed. "Things stand so in Cthol Murgos that great care must be exercised in the practice of our arts. The Grolims in the land of the Murgos are ever alert to the disturbances such acts inevitably cause."

"We were quite put out with you on Verkat," Durnik told her. "That was before we understood the reason for what you did. I'm afraid I treated Toth very badly for a while. He was good enough to forgive me, though."

The big mute smiled at him and made a few gestures.

Durnik laughed. "You don't really have to do that anymore, Toth," he told his friend. "I finally figured out how you were talking to me."

Toth lowered his hands.

Durnik seemed to listen for a moment. "Yes," he agreed. "It's much easier this way—and faster, too—now that we don't have to wave our hands at each other. Oh, by the way, Eriond and I found a pond a little ways below the city here. It has some very nice trout in it."

Toth grinned broadly.

"I thought you might feel that way." Durnik grinned back.

"I'm afraid we've corrupted your guide, Cyradis," Polgara apologized.

"Nay, Polgara." The Seeress smiled. "This passion hath been upon him since boyhood. Ofttimes in our travels he hath found excuse to linger for a time by some lake or stream. I do not chide him for this, for I am fond of fish, and he doth prepare them exquisitely."

They finished their meal and sat, talking quietly to avoid disturbing Belgarath and Beldin who still sat poring over the *Mallorean Gospels*.

"How is Zandramas going to find out where we're all going?" Garion asked the Seeress. "Since she's a Grolim, she can't come here."

"That I may not tell thee, Child of Light. She will, however, arrive at the appointed place at the proper time."

"With my son?"

"As it hath been foretold."

"I'm looking forward to that meeting." He said it bleakly. "There are a great many things Zandramas and I have to settle."

"Let not thy hatred blind thee to thy tasks," she told him quite seriously.

"And what *is* my task, Cyradis?"

"That thou wilt know when it doth face thee."

"But not before?"

"Nay. Thy performance of that task would be marred shouldst thou consider it overlong."

"And what is *my* task, Holy Seeress?" 'Zakath asked her. "You said you would instruct me here at Kell."

"I must reveal that to thee in private, Emperor of Mallorea. Know, however, that thy task will begin when thy companions have completed theirs, and it will consume the balance of thy life."

"As long as we're talking about tasks," Sadi said, "perhaps you could explain mine to me."

"You have already begun it, Sadi."

"Am I doing it very well?"

She smiled. "Passing well, yes."

"I might do a little better if I knew what it is."

"Nay, Sadi. Even as Belgarion's, thy task would be marred shouldst thou know of it."

"Is this place we're going to very far?" Durnik asked her.

"Many leagues, and there is yet much to be done."

"I'll need to talk with Dallan about supplies, then. And I think I'll want to check the horses' hooves before we start. This might be a good time to get them shod again."

"That's impossible!" Belgarath suddenly burst out.

"What is it, father?" Aunt Pol asked him.

"It's Korim! The meeting is supposed to take place at Korim!"

"Where's that?" Sadi asked in puzzlement.

"It's no place," Beldin growled. "It's not there anymore. It was a mountain range that sank into the sea when Torak cracked the world. The *Book of Alorn* mentions it as 'The High Places of Korim, which are no more.' "

"There's a certain perverted logic to it," Silk observed. "That's what these assorted prophecies have meant all along when they talked about a Place Which Is No More."

Beldin tugged thoughtfully at one ear. "There's something else, too," he noted. "You remember the story Senji told us back at Melcene? About the scholar who stole the Sardion? His ship was last seen rounding the southern tip of Gandahar, and it never came back. Senji said he thought that it had gone down in a storm off the Dalasian coast. It's beginning to sound as if he was right. We have to go where the Sardion is, and I've got the uncomfortable feeling that it's resting on top of a mountain that sank into the sea over five thousand years ago."

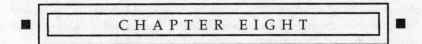

CHAPTER EIGHT

The Queen of Riva was in a pensive mood as they set out from the glowing marble city of Kell. A peculiar kind of languor seemed to come over her as they rode through the forest to the west of Kell, a languor that grew more pronounced with each passing mile. She took no part in the general conversation, but was content merely to listen.

"I don't see how you can be so calm about this, Cyradis," Belgarath was saying to the blindfolded Seeress as they rode along. "Your task will fail the same as ours will if the Sardion is lying at the bottom of the sea. And why are we making this side trip to Perivor?"

"It is there that the instruction thou received from the Holy Book will be made clear to thee, Ancient Belgarath."

"Couldn't you just explain it to me yourself? We're a little pressed for time, you know."

"That I may not do. I may not give thee any aid that I do not also give to Zandramas. It is thy task—and hers—to unravel this riddle. To aid one of thee and not the other is forbidden."

"Somehow I thought you might look at it that way," he said glumly.

"Where's Perivor?" Garion asked 'Zakath.

"It's an island off the south coast of Dalasia," the Mallorean replied. "The inhabitants there are very strange. Their legends say that they're descendants of some people from the west who were aboard a ship that was blown off course and wrecked on the island about two thousand years ago. The island's of little value, and the people there are fearsome fighters. The general opinion in Mal Zeth has always been that the place wouldn't be worth the trouble it would take to subdue it, and Urvon didn't even bother to send Grolims there."

"If they're so savage, won't it be sort of dangerous for us to go there?"

"No. Actually they're civil and even hospitable—as long as you don't try to land an army there. That's when things start to take a turn for the worse."

"Have we really got the time to go to this place?" Silk asked the Seeress of Kell.

"Ample time, Prince Kheldar," she replied. "The stars have told us for eons that the Place Which Is No More awaits the coming of thee and thy companions, and that thou and thy companions will come there upon the day appointed for the meeting."

"And so will Zandramas, I suppose?"

She smiled a gentle little smile. "How can there be a meeting if the Child of Dark be not also present?" she asked him.

"I think I detected a faint glimmer of humor there, Cyradis," he bantered. "Isn't that a bit out of character for one of the seers?"

"How little you know us, Prince Kheldar." She smiled again. "Ofttimes we have been convulsed with laughter at some message writ large in the stars and at the absurd lengths to which others go to ignore or avoid that which is preordained. Submit to the instruction of the heavens, Kheldar. Spare thyself the agony and turmoil of trying to evade thy fate."

"You throw the word 'fate' around awfully lightly, Cyradis," he said disapprovingly.

"Hast thou not come here in response to a fate laid down for thee at the beginning of days? All thy concern with commerce and espionage have been but a diversion to occupy thee until the appointed day."

"That's a polite way to tell someone he's been behaving like a child."

"We are all children, Kheldar."

Beldin came soaring through the sun-dappled forest, avoiding tree trunks with deft shifts of his wings. He settled to earth and changed form.

"Trouble?" Belgarath asked him.

"Not as much as I'd expected." The dwarf shrugged. "And that worries me a bit."

"Isn't that a little inconsistent?"

"Consistency is the defense of a small mind. Zandramas couldn't go to Kell, right?"

"As far as we know."

"Then she has to follow *us* to the meeting place, right?"

"Unless she's found some other way to find out where it is."

"That's what worries me. If she had to follow us, wouldn't it be logical for her to have ringed this forest with troops and Grolims to find out which way we were going?"

"I suppose so, yes."

"Well, there's no army out there—only a few patrols, and they're just going through the motions."

Belgarath frowned. "What's she up to?"

"My point exactly. I'd guess that she's got a surprise in store for us somewhere."

"Keep your eyes open, then. I don't want her slipping up behind me."

"It might simplify things if she did."

"I doubt it. Nothing about this entire affair has been simple, and I don't expect things to change at this stage."

"I'll go scout ahead." The dwarf blurred and soared away.

They made their encampment that evening beside a spring that gushed out of an outcropping of moss-covered rock. Belgarath seemed moody and out of sorts, so the rest of them avoided him as they worked at tasks they had repeated so many times that they had become habitual.

"You're very quiet this evening," Garion said to Ce'Nedra as they sat by the fire after supper. "What's the matter?"

"I just don't feel like talking." The peculiar lethargy that had come over the little queen had not diminished as the day wore on, and she had actually found herself dozing in her saddle several times during the late afternoon.

"You look tired," he observed.

"I am, a bit. We've been traveling for a long time now. I think it might be starting to catch up with me."

"Why don't you go to bed then? You'll feel better after a good night's sleep."

She yawned and held out her arms to him. "Carry me," she said.

He looked startled. Ce'Nedra enjoyed startling her husband. His face always looked so wide-eyed and boyish. "Aren't you feeling well?" he asked.

"I'm fine, Garion. I'm just sleepy, and I want to be babied a bit. Carry me to the tent, put me to bed, and tuck me in."

"Well, if that's what you want . . ." He rose, picked her up easily, and carried her across the encampment to their tent.

"Garion," she murmured drowsily after he had gently drawn their blankets up around her shoulders.

"Yes, dear?"

"Please don't wear your mail shirt when you come to bed. It makes you smell like an old iron pot."

Ce'Nedra's sleep that night was disturbed by strange dreams. She seemed to see people and places she had not seen or even thought of in years. She saw legionnaires guarding her father's palace, and Lord Morin, her father's chamberlain, hurrying down a marble corridor. Then she seemed to be at Riva, holding a long, incomprehensible conversation with Brand, the Rivan Warder, while Brand's blond niece sat spinning flax by the window. Arell seemed unconcerned about the dagger hilt protruding from between her shoulder blades. Ce'Nedra stirred, muttering to herself, and immediately began to dream again.

She seemed then to be a Rheon in eastern Drasnia. Casually she plucked a dagger from the belt of Vella, the Nadrak dancer, and just as casually drove it to the hilt into the belly of black-bearded Ulfgar, the head of the Bear-cult. Ulfgar was speaking sneeringly to Belgarath as Ce'Nedra sank the knife into him, and he did not even pay any attention to her as she slowly twisted the blade in his vitals.

And then she was at Riva again, and she and Garion were sitting naked beside a sparkling forest pool while thousands of butterflies hovered over them.

She traveled in her restless dream to the ancient city of Val Alorn in Cherek, and then went on to Boktor for the funeral of King Rhodar. And once again she saw the battlefield at Thull Mardu, and once more the face of her self-appointed protector, Brand's son Olban.

There was no coherence to the dream. She seemed to go from place to place without effort, moving through time and space looking for something, although she could not remember what it was she had lost.

When she awoke the next morning, she was as tired as she had been the previous evening. Every movement was an effort, and she kept yawning.

"What's the matter?" Garion asked her as they dressed. "Didn't you sleep well?"

"Not really," she replied. "I kept having the strangest dreams."

"Do you want to talk about them? Sometimes that's the best way to put them to rest so they don't keep coming back night after night."

"They didn't make any sense, Garion. They just kept jumping around. It was almost as if someone were moving me from place to place for some reason of her own."

"Her? Was this someone a woman?"

"Did I say 'her'? I can't imagine why. I never saw this person." Ce'Nedra yawned again. "I hope whoever it was got finished with it, though. I'd rather not go through another night like that." Then she gave him a sly, sidelong glance through her eyelashes. "There were some parts of the dream that were rather nice, though," she said. "Once we were sitting by that pool back at Riva. Do you want to know what we were doing?"

A slow blush crept up Garion's neck. "Uh, no, Ce'Nedra. I don't really think so."

But she told him anyway—in great detail—until he finally fled from the tent.

Her restless night increased the peculiar lassitude that had lain on her since they had left Kell, and she rode that morning in a half doze that, try though she might, she could not seem to shake off. Garion spoke with her several times to warn her that she was allowing her horse to stray, and then, apparently seeing that she just couldn't keep her eyes open, he took her reins from her hands and led her horse.

About midmorning, Beldin rejoined them. "I think you'd better take cover," he tersely told Belgarath. "There's a Darshivan patrol coming along this trail."

"Are they searching for us?"

"Who knows? If they are, they're not being very serious about it. Go back into the woods for a couple hundred yards and let them ride on by. I'll keep an eye on them and let you know when they've passed."

"All right." Belgarath turned aside from the trail and led the rest of them back into the concealment of the forest.

They dismounted and waited tensely. Soon they heard the jingling of the soldiers' equipment as they rode along the forest trail at a trot.

Even in this potentially dangerous situation, Ce'Nedra simply could not keep her eyes open. Dimly she could hear the whispered conversations of the others until she finally dozed off again.

And then she came awake—or at least partially so. She was walking alone through the forest, her mind all bemused. She knew that she should be alarmed at being separated from the others, but oddly, she was not. She walked on, not so much going anywhere in particular as following some sort of subtle summoning.

Then at last she reached a grassy clearing and saw a tall blond girl standing among the wildflowers and holding a blanket-wrapped bundle in her arms. The girl's blond braids were coiled at her temples, and her complexion was like new milk. It was Brand's niece, Arell. "Good morning, your Majesty," she greeted the Queen of Riva. "I've been waiting for you."

Something deep in Ce'Nedra's mind tried to scream at her that this was wrong—that the tall Rivan girl could not possibly be here. But Ce'Nedra could not remember why, and the moment passed. "Good morning, Arell," she said to her dear friend. "What on earth are you doing here?"

"I came to help you, Ce'Nedra. Look at what I've found." She turned back the corner of the blanket to reveal a tiny face.

"My baby!" Ce'Nedra exclaimed, almost overcome with joy. She ran forward, her arms extended hungrily, and took the sleeping infant from her friend and held him to her body, her cheek pressed against his soft curls. "How did you possibly find him?" she asked Arell. "We've been looking for him for the longest time now."

"I was traveling alone through this forest," Arell replied, "and I thought I smelled the smoke of a campfire. I went to investigate and I found a tent set up beside a little stream. I looked inside the tent, and there was Prince Geran. There was no one else around, so I picked him up and came looking for you."

Ce'Nedra's mind was still trying to scream at her, but she was too deliriously happy to pay any attention. She held her baby, rocking back and forth and crooning to him.

"Where is King Belgarion?" Arell asked.

"Back there someplace." Ce'Nedra gestured vaguely.

"You should go to him and let him know that his son is safe."

"Yes. He'll be very happy."

"I have something that I really have to attend to, Ce'Nedra," Arell said. "Do you think you'll be able to find your way back alone?"

"Oh, I'm sure I could, but couldn't you come along? His Majesty is sure to want to reward you for restoring our son to us."

Arell smiled. "The happiness on your face is all the reward I need, and this matter I must take care of is extremely important. I may be able to join you later, however. Which way will you be traveling?"

"South, I think," Ce'Nedra replied. "We have to get to the seacoast."

"Oh?"

"Yes. We're going to an island—Perivor, I think the name is."

"There's supposed to be a meeting of some kind very soon, isn't there? Is Perivor the place where it's going to happen?"

"Oh, no." Ce'Nedra laughed, still cuddling her baby. "We're just going to Perivor to get some more information about it. We'll be going on from there."

"I may not be able to join you at Perivor," Arell said, frowning slightly. "Perhaps you could tell me where the meeting's supposed to take place. I'm sure I'll be able to meet you there."

"Let me see," Ce'Nedra pondered. "What did they call it? Oh, now I remember. It's someplace that's called Korim."

"*Korim?*" Arell exclaimed in astonishment.

"Yes. Belgarath seemed dreadfully upset when he first found out about it, but Cyradis told him that everything would be all right. That's why we have to go to Perivor. Cyradis says that there's something there that will make everything clear. It seems to me that she said something about a chart or something." She laughed a bit giddily. "To be honest with you, Arell, I've been so sleepy for the last few days that I can barely keep track of what the people around me are saying."

"Of course," Arell said absently, her face creased in thought. "Why would Perivor be the key?" she mused to herself. "What could possibly be there to explain an absurdity? Are you absolutely certain the word was Korim? Perhaps you misunderstood."

"That was the way I heard it, Arell. I didn't read it for myself, but Belgarath and Beldin kept talking about 'the High Places of Korim, Which Are No More,' and isn't the meeting supposed to be at the Place Which Is No More? I mean, it does sort of fit together, doesn't it?"

"Yes," Arell replied, frowning strangely. "Now that I think about it, it does." Then she straightened, smoothing her gown. "I'll have to leave you now, Ce'Nedra," she said. "Take your baby back to your husband. Give him my regards." Her eyes seemed to glint in the sunlight. "Give my best to Polgara, as well," she added. There seemed to be something slightly malicious in the way she said it. She turned then and walked away, crossing the flowery meadow toward the dark edge of the forest.

"Good-bye, Arell," Ce'Nedra called after her, "and thank you so much for finding my baby."

Arell neither turned nor answered.

·　　·　　·

Garion was frantic. When he first discovered that his wife was missing, he leaped into his saddle and rode Chretienne off into the forest at a gallop. He had gone three hundred yards before Belgarath finally caught up with him. "Garion! Stop!" the old man shouted.

"But, Grandfather!" Garion shouted back. "I've got to find Ce'Nedra!"

"Where do you plan to start looking? Or are you just going to ride around in circles trusting to luck?"

"But—"

"Use your head, boy! We have another way that's much faster. You know what she smells like, don't you?"

"Of course, but—"

"Then we have to use our noses. Get down off that horse and send him back. We'll change form and follow her trail. It's faster and a great deal more certain."

Garion felt suddenly very foolish. "I wasn't thinking, I guess," he confessed.

"I didn't think you were. Get rid of that horse."

Garion slid down and slapped Chretienne sharply on the rump. The big gray bolted back toward where the others were still concealed. "What on earth was she thinking of?" Garion fumed.

"I'm not sure if she was," Belgarath grunted. "She's been acting strangely for the past few days. Let's get on with this. The quicker we find her, the quicker we can get her back to the others. Your aunt can get to the bottom of this." The old man was already blurring into the shape of the huge silver wolf. "You lead," he growled at Garion. "Her scent is more familiar to you."

Garion changed and cast back and forth until his nose caught Ce'Nedra's familiar fragrance. "She went this way," he cast his thought to Belgarath.

"How fresh is the trail?" the old wolf asked.

"It can't be much more than a half hour old," Garion replied, bunching himself to run.

"Good. Let's go find her." And the two of them ran smoothly through the woods, their noses to the ground in the manner of hunting wolves.

They found her after about a quarter of an hour. She was coming happily back through the forest, crooning softly to a bundle she was carrying tenderly in her arms.

"Don't startle her," Belgarath warned. "There's something very wrong here. Just go along with anything she tells you." The two of them shimmered and changed.

Ce'Nedra gave a little cry of delight when she saw them. "Oh, Garion!" she exclaimed, running toward them. "Look! Arell found our baby!"

"Arell? But Arell's—"

"Just let it lie!" Belgarath snapped under his breath. "Don't send her into hysterics!"

"Why—uh—that's wonderful, Ce'Nedra," Garion said, trying to make it sound natural.

"It's been so long," Ce'Nedra said, her eyes brimming with tears, "and he looks just the same as he did before. Look, Garion. Isn't he beautiful?"

She turned back the blanket, and Garion saw that what she was holding so tenderly was not a baby, but a bundle of rags.

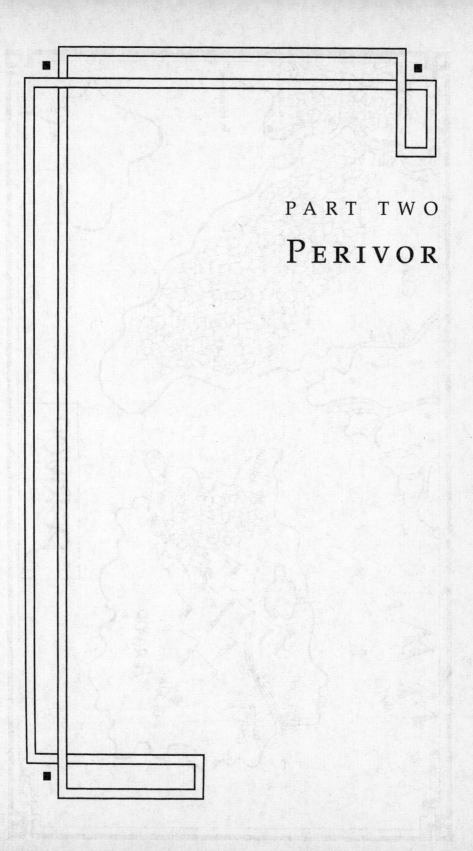

PART TWO
PERIVOR

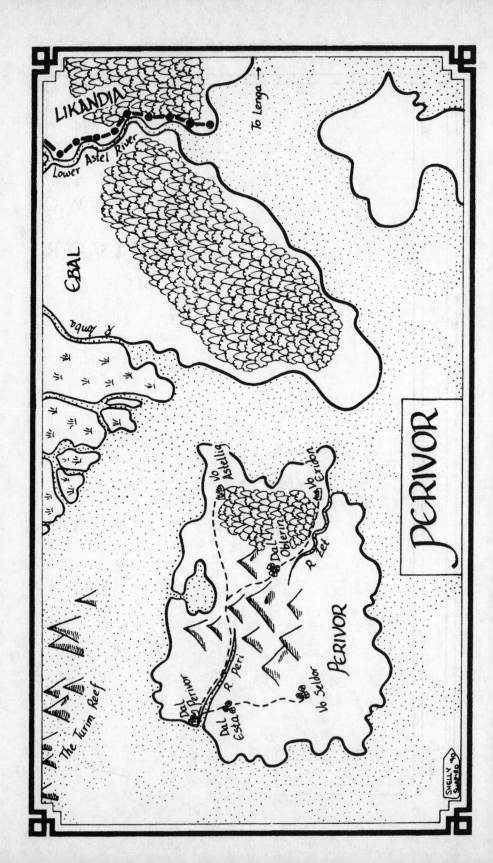

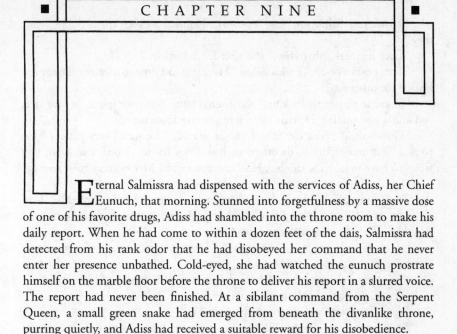

Eternal Salmissra had dispensed with the services of Adiss, her Chief Eunuch, that morning. Stunned into forgetfulness by a massive dose of one of his favorite drugs, Adiss had shambled into the throne room to make his daily report. When he had come to within a dozen feet of the dais, Salmissra had detected from his rank odor that he had disobeyed her command that he never enter her presence unbathed. Cold-eyed, she had watched the eunuch prostrate himself on the marble floor before the throne to deliver his report in a slurred voice. The report had never been finished. At a sibilant command from the Serpent Queen, a small green snake had emerged from beneath the divanlike throne, purring quietly, and Adiss had received a suitable reward for his disobedience.

And now Eternal Salmissra coiled pensively on her throne, idly contemplating her reflection in the mirror. The troublesome business of selecting a new Chief Eunuch still lay before her, and she was not really in the mood for it. She decided finally to forgo the chore for a time to give the palace eunuchs the opportunity to scramble for the position. That scramble usually resulted in a number of fatalities, and there were really too many eunuchs in the palace anyway.

From under the throne there was an irritated grumbling. Her pet green snake was obviously distressed about something. "What is it, Ezahh?" she asked him.

"Can't you have them washed before you ask me to bite them, Salmissra?" Ezahh replied plaintively. "You might have at least warned me what to expect." Although Ezahh and Salmissra were of different species, their languages were to some degree compatible.

"I'm sorry, Ezahh. It was inconsiderate of me, I suppose." In rather sharp contrast to her dealings with humans, whom she held more or less in general contempt, the Serpent Queen was unfailingly polite to other reptiles—particularly the venomous ones. This is considered the course of wisdom in the world of snakes.

"It was not entirely your fault, Salmissra." Ezahh was also a snake, and he was also very polite. "I just wish there was some way to get the taste out of my mouth."

"I could send for a saucer of milk. That might help."

"Thank you, Salmissra, but the taste of him might curdle it. What I'd really like is a nice fat mouse—alive, preferably."

"I'll see to it at once, Ezahh." She turned her triangular face around on her slender neck. "You," she hissed to one of the chorus of eunuchs kneeling in adoration at one side of the throne, "go catch a mouse. My little green friend is hungry."

"At once, Divine Salmissra," the eunuch replied obsequiously. He jumped to his feet and backed toward the door, genuflecting at every other step.

"Thank you, Salmissra," Ezahh purred. "Humans are such trivial things, aren't they?"

"They respond only to fear," she agreed, "and to lust."

"That raises a point," Ezahh noted. "Have you had time to consider the request I made the other day?"

"I have some people looking," she assured him, "but your species is very rare, you know, and finding a female for you might take some time."

"I can wait, if necessary, Salmissra," he purred. "We are all very patient." He paused. "I'm not trying to be offensive, but if you hadn't chased Sadi away, you wouldn't have to take the trouble. His little snake and I were on very good terms."

"I noticed that on occasion. You might even be a father by now."

The green snake slid his head out from under the throne and regarded her. Like all snakes of his kind, he had a bright-red stripe down his green back. "What's a father?" he asked in a dull, incurious tone.

"It's a difficult concept," she replied. "Humans make much of it for some reason."

"Does any real creature care about the perverse peculiarities of humans?"

"I certainly don't—at least not anymore."

"You were always a serpent at heart, Salmissra."

"Why, thank you, Ezahh," she said in a pleased hiss. She paused, her restless coils rubbing dryly against each other. "I must select a new Chief Eunuch," she mused. "It's a bothersome thing."

"Why trouble yourself? Select one at random. Humans are all alike, after all."

"Most of them, yes. I've been attempting to locate Sadi, however. I'd like to persuade him to come back to Sthiss Tor."

"That one is different," Ezahh agreed. "One might almost believe that he is somewhat akin to us."

"He does have certain reptilian qualities, doesn't he? He's a thief and a scoundrel, but he still managed the palace better than anyone else has ever been able to. If I hadn't been molting when he fell into disgrace, I might have forgiven him."

"Shedding one's skin is always a trying procedure," Ezahh agreed. "If you don't mind a bit of advice, Salmissra, you should probably make the humans stay away from you at those times."

"I need a few of them around me. If nothing else, it gives me someone to bite."

"Stick to mice," he advised. "They taste better, and at least they can be swallowed."

"If I can persuade Sadi to return, it may just solve both our problems," she hissed dryly. "I'll have someone to run the palace without bothering me, and you'll get your little playmate back."

"Interesting notion, Salmissra." He looked around. "Is that human you sent out to fetch my mouse raising it from infancy?" he asked.

Yarblek and Vella slipped into Yar Nadrak late one snowy evening just before the gates were closed for the night. Vella had left her lavender satin gowns at Boktor and had reverted to her traditional tight leather garb. Because it was winter, she wore in addition a sable coat that would have cost a fortune in Tol Honeth. "Why does this place always smell so bad?" she asked her owner as they rode through snow-clogged streets toward the riverfront.

"Probably because Drosta let the contract for the sewer system out to one of his cousins." Yarblek shrugged, pulling the collar of his shabby felt coat up around his neck. "The citizens paid a great deal in taxes for the system, but Drosta's cousin turned out to be a better embezzler than he was an engineer. I think it runs in the family. Drosta even embezzles from his own treasury."

"Isn't that sort of absurd?"

"We have an absurd sort of king, Vella."

"I thought the palace was over that way." She pointed toward the center of town.

"Drosta won't be in the palace at this time of night," Yarblek told her. "He gets lonesome when the sun goes down, and he usually goes out looking for companionship."

"He could be anywhere, then."

"I doubt it. There are only a few places in Yar Nadrak where he's welcome after dark. Our king isn't widely loved." Yarblek pointed up a littered alley. "Let's go this way. We'll stop by the office of our factor and get you some suitable clothing."

"What's wrong with what I'm wearing?"

"Sable attracts attention in the part of town we're going to visit, Vella, and we're trying to be inconspicuous."

The office in Yar Nadrak of Silk and Yarblek's far-flung commercial empire was in a loft over a cavernous warehouse filled with bales of furs and deep-piled Mallorean carpets. The factor was a squinty-eyed Nadrak named Zelmit, who was probably almost as untrustworthy as he looked. Vella had never really liked him and she customarily loosened her daggers in their sheaths whenever she came into his presence, making very sure that he saw her doing so to be certain that there would be no misunderstandings. Technically, of course, Vella was one of Yarblek's possessions, and Zelmit had a reputation for making rather free with things that belonged to his employer.

"How's business?" Yarblek asked as he and Vella entered the cluttered little office.

"We're getting by," Zelmit said in a rasping voice.

"Specifics, Zelmit," Yarblek said brusquely. "Generalities make my teeth itch."

"We've found a way to bypass Boktor and evade Drasnian customs."

"That's useful."

"It takes a bit longer, but we can get our furs to Tol Honeth without paying Drasnian duties. Our profits in the fur market are up by sixty percent."

Yarblek beamed. "If Silk ever comes back through here, I don't think you really need to tell him about it," he cautioned. "Sometimes he breaks out in a rash of patriotism, and Porenn *is* his aunt, after all."

"I wasn't really thinking of telling him. We still have to carry the Mallorean carpets through Drasnia, though. The best market for those is still the great fair in cen-

tral Arendia, and we can't pay anybody enough to get him to freight them across
Ulgoland." He frowned. "Someone's cutting the prices on us, though. Until we can
find out what's going on, it might not be a bad idea to curtail our imports."

"Did you manage to sell off those gemstones I brought back from Mallorea?"

"Naturally. We smuggled them out and sold them here and there on our way
south."

"Good. It always depresses the market when you show up in one place with a
bushel basket full of them. Do you know if Drosta's in the usual place tonight?"

Zelmit nodded. "He went there just before sundown."

"Vella's going to need a sort of nondescript cloak," Yarblek said then.

Zelmit squinted at the girl.

Vella opened her fur coat and put her hands on the hilts of her daggers. "Why
don't you go ahead and try it now, Zelmit?" she said. "Let's get it over with."

"I wasn't really planning anything, Vella," he said innocently. "I was just sizing
you up, that's all."

"I noticed," she said dryly. "Did that cut on your shoulder ever heal?"

"It aches a little in damp weather," he complained.

"You should have kept your hands to yourself."

"I think I've got an old cloak that'll fit you. It's a little shabby, though."

"So much the better," Yarblek said. "We're going to the One-Eyed Dog and
we'd like to sort of blend in."

Vella removed her sable and laid it across a chair. "Don't lose track of this,
Zelmit," she warned. "I'm fond of it, and I'm sure we'd both hate what would happen if it accidentally wound up on a caravan bound for Tol Honeth."

"You don't have to threaten him, Vella," Yarblek said mildly.

"That wasn't a threat, Yarblek," she retorted. "I just wanted to be sure that
Zelmit and I understood each other."

"I'll get that cloak," Zelmit offered.

"Do that," she said.

The cloak was not so much shabby as it was tattered, and it smelled as if it had
never been washed. Vella pulled it on over her shoulders with some reluctance.

"Put the hood up," Yarblek told her.

"I'll have to wash my hair if I do."

"So?"

"Do you know how long it takes hair like mine to dry in the wintertime?"

"Just do it, Vella. Why do you always argue with me?"

"It's a matter of principle."

He sighed mournfully. "Take care of our horses," he told Zelmit. "We'll walk
the rest of the way." And then he led Vella out of the office. When they reached the
street, he took a length of clinking chain with a leather collar on one end out of a
side pocket of his overcoat. "Put this on," he told her.

"I haven't worn a chain or collar in years," she said.

"It's for your own protection, Vella," he said wearily. "We're going into a very
rough part of town, and the One-Eyed Dog is the roughest place down there. If
you're chained, nobody will bother you—unless he wants to fight with me. If you're
loose, some of the men in the tavern might misunderstand."

"That's what my daggers are for, Yarblek."

"Please, Vella. Oddly enough, I sort of like you, and I don't want you getting hurt."

"Affection, Yarblek?" She laughed. "I thought the only thing you really liked was money."

"I'm not a *complete* scoundrel, Vella."

"You'll do until the real thing comes along," she said, fastening the collar around her neck. "As a matter of fact, I sort of like you, too."

His eyes widened, and he grinned.

"Not *that* much, though," she added.

The One-Eyed Dog was perhaps the foulest tavern Vella had ever entered and Vella had been in a large number of low dives and shabby taverns in her life. Since the age of twelve, she had always relied on her daggers to ward off unwanted attentions. Although she had seldom been obliged to kill anyone—except for a few enthusiasts—she had nonetheless established a reputation for being a girl no sensible man would attempt. Sometimes that rankled a bit, though, since there were times when Vella might have welcomed an attempt. A nick or two in some unimportant places upon an ardent admirer would sustain her honor, and then—well, who knows?

"Don't drink any of the beer here," Yarblek cautioned as they entered. "The vat is open, and there are usually a few drowned rats floating around in it." He wrapped her chain around his hand.

Vella looked around. "This is really a revolting place, Yarblek," she told him.

"You've been spending too much time with Porenn," he said. "You're starting to get delicate."

"How would you like to have me gut you?" she offered.

"That's my girl." He grinned. "Let's go upstairs."

"What's up there?"

"The girls. Drosta doesn't come here for rat-flavored beer."

"That's disgusting, you know?"

"You've never met Drosta, have you? Disgusting only begins to describe him. He even turns *my* stomach."

"Are you planning to just walk in on him? Aren't you going to snoop around a bit first?"

"You've been in Drasnia too long," he replied as they started up the steps. "Drosta and I know each other. He knows better than to try to lie to me. I'll get to the bottom of this right away, and then we can get out of this stinking town."

"I think you're starting to get delicate, as well."

There was a door at the end of the hall, and the pair of Nadrak soldiers standing at either side of it proclaimed by their presence that King Drosta lek Thun was inside.

"How many so far?" Yarblek asked them as he and Vella stopped in front of the door.

"Three, isn't it?" one of the soldiers asked the other.

"I lost count." The other soldier shrugged. "They all look the same to me. Three or four. I forget."

"Is he busy right now?" Yarblek asked.

"He's resting."

"He must be getting old. He never used to have to rest after only three. Do you want to tell him I'm here? I've got a business proposition for him." Yarblek suggestively shook Vella's chain.

One of the soldiers eyed Vella up and down. "She might be able to wake him up at that." He leered.

"And I can put him back to sleep just as fast," Vella said, opening her shabby cloak to reveal her daggers.

"You're one of those wild women from up in the forest, aren't you?" the other soldier asked. "We really shouldn't let you in there with him with those daggers."

"Would you like to try to take them away from me?"

"Not me, girl," he replied prudently.

"Good. Resharpening a dagger is very tedious, and I've been hitting bone a great deal lately."

The other soldier opened the door. "It's that Yarblek fellow again, your Majesty," he said. "He's got a girl he wants to sell you."

"I just bought three," a shrill voice replied with an obscene giggle.

"Not like *this* one, your Majesty."

"It's so nice to be appreciated," Vella murmured.

The soldier grinned at her.

"Yarblek, get in here!" King Drosta's high-pitched voice commanded.

"Right away, your Majesty. Come along, Vella." Yarblek tugged on her chain and led her into the room.

Drosta lek Thun, King of Gar og Nadrak, lay half dressed on a rumpled bed. He was by far the ugliest man Vella had ever seen. Even the hunchbacked dwarf Beldin was handsome by comparison. He was scrawny and had bulging eyes. His face was pockmarked, and his beard scraggly. "You idiot!" he snapped at Yarblek. "Yar Nadrak is overrun with Mallorean agents. They know that you're Prince Kheldar's partner and that you practically live in Porenn's palace."

"Nobody saw me, Drosta," Yarblek said, "and even if they did, I've got a perfectly legitimate reason to be here." He shook Vella's chain.

"Do you really want to sell her?" Drosta said, eyeing the girl.

"Hardly, but we can tell anybody curious about it that we couldn't agree on a price."

"Why are you really here, then?"

"Porenn's a little curious about your activities. Javelin's got some spies in your palace, but you're sneaky enough to hide what you're doing from them. I thought I'd save some time and come right to the source."

"What makes you think I've been up to something?"

"You usually are."

Drosta laughed shrilly. "That's true, I suppose, but why should I tell you?"

"Because if you don't, I'll set up camp in the palace, and the Malloreans will think you're crossing them."

"That's blackmail, Yarblek," Drosta accused.

"Some people call it that, yes."

Drosta sighed. "All right, Yarblek," he said, "but this is for Porenn's ears only, and I don't want you and Silk taking advantage of it. I've been trying to mend my fences with 'Zakath. He was very angry when I switched sides at Thull Mardu. It's only a question of time until he subdues all of Cthol Murgos, and I don't want him to get the idea of coming north looking for me. I've been negotiating with Brador, the chief of his bureau of internal affairs, and we've almost reached an accommodation. I get to keep my skin if I allow Brador's agents to pass through Gar og Nadrak to infiltrate the west. 'Zakath's pragmatic enough to forgo the pleasure of having me skinned alive if I'm useful to him."

Yarblek looked at him skeptically. "All right, Drosta, what else? That's hardly enough to keep 'Zakath from peeling you like an apple."

"Sometimes you're too smart for your own good, Yarblek."

"Give, Drosta. I don't want to have to spend the next month here in Yar Nadrak being conspicuous."

Drosta gave up. "I've cut the import duties on Mallorean carpets. 'Zakath needs tax revenue to continue the war in Cthol Murgos. If I cut those duties, Mallorean merchants can undersell you and Silk in the marketplaces to the west. The whole plan is to make myself so indispensable to his Imperial Majesty that he'll leave me alone."

"I was wondering why our profits in carpets have been falling off," Yarblek mused. "That's all?" he asked.

"I swear it is, Yarblek."

"Your oaths tend to be a little worthless, my King."

Drosta had been looking at Vella appreciatively. "Are you absolutely positive you don't want to sell this girl?" he asked.

"You couldn't really afford me, your Majesty," Vella told him, "and sooner or later your appetite would get the better of you. I'd have to take steps at that point."

"You wouldn't actually draw a knife on your own king, would you?"

"Try me."

"Oh, one other thing, Drosta," Yarblek added. "From now on, Silk and I will be paying the same import duties you're charging the Malloreans."

Drosta's eyes bulged even more. "That's out of the question!" he almost screamed. "What if Brador found out about it?"

"We'll just have to make sure he doesn't, then, won't we? That's my price for keeping my mouth shut. If you *don't* cut those fees, I'll just have to let it be known that you *have.* You'll stop being so indispensable to 'Zakath at that point, won't you?"

"You're robbing me, Yarblek."

"Business is business, Drosta," Yarblek said blandly.

King Anheg of Cherek had journeyed to Tol Honeth to confer with Emperor Varana. When he had been admitted to the imperial apartments, he got right to the point. "We've got a problem, Varana," he said.

"Oh?"

"You know my cousin, the Earl of Trellheim?"

"Barak? Of course."

"He hasn't been seen for quite some time. He's off with that oversized ship of his and he's got some friends with him."

"It's a free ocean, I suppose. Who are these friends?"

"Cho-Hag's son Hettar, that Mimbrate Mandorallen, and Lelldorin the Asturian. He also has his own son Unrak along and the Ulgo fanatic Relg."

Varana frowned. "That's a dangerous group," he noted.

"I couldn't agree more. It's sort of like a natural disaster looking for a place to happen."

"Any ideas about what they're doing?"

"If I knew which way they're going, I could make a few guesses."

There was a polite tap on the door. "There's a Cherek out here, your Imperial Majesty," one of the guards outside the door announced. "He's a sailor, I think, and he says he needs to talk with King Anheg."

"Send him in," the emperor instructed.

It was Greldik, and he was slightly drunk. "I think I've solved your problem, Anheg. After I dropped you off on that pier, I wandered around on the docks for a while to see what kind of information I could pick up."

"In taverns, I see."

"You don't find sailors in tearooms. Anyway, I came across the captain of a Tolnedran merchantman. He'd picked up a cargo of Mallorean goods, and he was coming south across the Sea of the East toward the southern end of Cthol Murgos."

"That's very interesting, but I don't quite see the point."

"He saw a ship, and when I described *Seabird* to him, he agreed that it had been the ship he saw."

"That's a start, anyway. Where's Barak going?"

"Where else? Mallorea, of course."

After about a week's voyage, the *Seabird* made port at Dal Zerba on the southwest coast of the Mallorean continent. Barak asked a few questions and then led his friends to the offices of Silk's factor in the port city.

The factor was a very thin man, not so much undernourished as he was emaciated.

"We're trying to locate Prince Kheldar," Barak rumbled to him. "It's a matter of some urgency, and we'd appreciate any information you might be able to give us as to his whereabouts."

The factor frowned. "The last I heard was that he was in Melcene on the other side of the continent, but that was over a month ago, and Prince Kheldar moves around a great deal."

"That's Silk, all right," Hettar murmured.

"Do you have any guesses about where he might have gone from Melcene?" Barak asked.

"This office is fairly new," the factor said, "and I'm sort of at the tail end of the route of any couriers." He made a sour face. "The factor up at Dal Finda was a bit put out when Kheldar and Yarblek set up this office. I guess he felt that I might be in competition with him. Sometimes he forgets to pass things on to me. His office has been well established for some time, so the couriers always stop there. If anybody in this part of Dalasia knows anything about Kheldar's location, he would."

"All right. Where's Dal Finda, then?"

"Upriver about forty leagues."

"Thanks for the help, friend. Do you happen to have a map of this part of Mallorea?"

"I believe I could find one for you, yes."

"I'd appreciate it. We're not familiar with this part of the world."

"So we go upriver?" Hettar said when Silk's factor was out of the room looking for the map.

"If it's the only place where we can find out where Garion and the others are, we'll have to," Barak replied.

The current in the Finda River was sluggish, and the oarsmen made good time as they rowed upstream. They reached the river town late the following day and went immediately to Silk's offices there.

The factor here was almost the reverse of the man in Dal Zerba. He was bulky more than fat and he had huge meaty hands and a florid face. He was not particularly cooperative. "How do I know you're the prince's friends?" he demanded suspiciously. "I'm not going to reveal his location to complete strangers."

"Are you trying to be difficult?" Barak asked.

The factor looked at the big red-bearded man and swallowed hard. "No, but sometimes the prince wants his whereabouts kept secret."

"Probably when he's planning to steal something," Hettar added.

"Steal?" the factor objected in a shocked voice. "The prince is a respectable businessman."

"He's also a liar, a cheat, a thief, and a spy," Hettar told him. "Now, where is he? We'd heard that he'd been in Melcene awhile back. Where did he go from there?"

"Can you describe him?" the factor countered.

"Short," Hettar replied, "sort of thin. He's got a face like a rat and a long, pointed nose. He's got a clever mouth and he thinks he's funny."

"That's a fair description of Prince Kheldar," the factor conceded.

"We have heard that our friend standeth in a certain amount of danger," Mandorallen said. "We have sailed many leagues to offer our assistance."

"I was sort of wondering why most of you were wearing armor. Oh, all right. The last I heard was that he was bound for a place called Kell."

"Show me," Barak said, unfolding his map.

"It's over here," the factor said.

"Is that river navigable?"

"As far north as Balasa."

"Good. We can sail around the southern end of the continent and go up that river. How far back from the main channel is this Kell place?"

"A league or so from the east bank. It's at the foot of a very big mountain. I'd be careful, though. Kell's got a very peculiar reputation. The seers live there, and they don't particularly welcome strangers."

"We'll have to chance it," Barak said. "Thanks for your help, friend. We'll give Kheldar your regards when we catch up with him."

They set out downriver the following morning. There was enough of a breeze so that the sails were able to aid the oarsmen, and they made excellent time. It was shortly before noon when they heard a number of cracking detonations coming from somewhere just ahead.

"Methinks we will encounter a storm ere long," Mandorallen said.

Barak frowned. "The sky's perfectly clear, Mandorallen," he disagreed, "and that doesn't sound exactly right for thunder." He raised his voice. "Ship oars and lower the sail," he commanded his sailors, swinging his tiller over sharply so that *Seabird* coasted to the bank.

Hettar, Relg, and Lelldorin came up from below. "Why are we stopping?" Hettar asked.

"There's something peculiar going on just up ahead," Barak replied. "I think we'd better go have a look before we blunder into anything."

"You want me to get the horses?"

"I don't think so. It's not very far, and men on horseback are kind of conspicuous."

"You're starting to sound like Silk."

"We've been together for quite a while. Unrak!" he shouted to his son, who had been riding in the bow. "We're going to go see what that noise is all about. You're in charge here until we get back."

"But, father!" the red-haired boy protested.

"That's an order, Unrak!" Barak thundered.

"Yes, sir." Unrak sounded slightly sullen.

The *Seabird* swung slowly around in the current and bumped gently against the brush-covered riverbank. Barak and the others jumped from the rail to the bank and started cautiously inland.

There were more of those strange detonations that did not sound exactly like thunder.

"Whatever it is, it's coming from just up ahead," Hettar said quietly.

"Let's stay out of sight until we find out what's going on," Barak said. "We've heard that kind of sound before—at Rak Cthol when Belgarath and Ctuchik were fighting."

"Sorcerers, thinkest thou?" Mandorallen suggested.

"I'm not positive, but I'm beginning to have some strong suspicions in that direction. I think we'd better stay under cover until we can see just who or what is out there."

They crept to the edge of a clump of scrubby trees and looked out at an open field.

A number of black-robed figures lay smoking on the turf. Others huddled fearfully near the edge of the field.

"Murgos?" Hettar sounded startled.

"Methinks not, my Lord," Mandorallen said. "If thou wilt look closely, thou wilt see that the hoods of their cloaks are lined in diverse colors. Those colors do indicate rank among the Grolims. Thou wert wise, my Lord of Trellheim, to advise caution."

"What's making them smoke like that?" Lelldorin whispered, nervously fingering his bow.

As if in answer to his question, a black-robed and hooded figure rose at the top of a knoll and gestured almost contemptuously. A ball of incandescent fire seemed to leap from the figure's hand, sizzled across the open field, and struck one of the frightened Grolims full in the chest with another of those cracking detonations. The Grolim shrieked and, clutching at his chest, fell to the earth.

"I guess that explains the noise," Relg observed.

"Barak," Hettar said quietly, "that one on top of the knoll is a woman."

"Are you sure?"

"I've got very good eyes, Barak, and I can tell the difference between a man and a woman."

"So can I, but not when they're all wrapped up in cloaks like that."

"Look at her elbows the next time she raises her arms. Women's elbows are hinged differently from ours. Adara says it has to do with carrying babies."

"Did you fear to come alone, Agachak?" the woman atop the little hill demanded with contempt. Then she flicked another fireball, and another Grolim crumpled to the ground.

"I fear nothing, Zandramas," a hollow voice came from the trees at the edge of the field.

"Now we know who they are," Hettar said. "But why are they fighting?"

"Zandramas is a woman?" Lelldorin asked in amazement.

Hettar nodded. "Queen Porenn found out about it some time back. She sent word to the Alorn kings, and Cho-Hag told me."

Zandramas almost casually felled the three remaining Grolims. "Well, Agachak," she said then, "will you come out of hiding now? Or must I come and find you?"

A tall, cadaverous-looking Grolim stepped out of the trees. "Your fire will have no effect on me, Zandramas," he said, advancing toward the hooded woman.

"I wasn't thinking of fire, Agachak," she almost purred. "*This* will be your fate." She suddenly seemed to blur and shimmer, and then standing in the place she had occupied was an enormous, hideous beast. It had a long, snakelike neck and huge bat wings.

"Belar!" Barak swore. "She just turned into a dragon!"

The dragon spread her wings and flapped into the air. The cadaverous Grolim shrank back, then raised both arms. There was a shocking sound, and the dragon was suddenly encased in a sheet of green fire. The voice that came thundering from the dragon's mouth was still the voice of Zandramas. "You should have paid more attention to your studies, Agachak. If you had, you'd know that Torak made dragons immune to sorcery." The dragon hovered over the now-terrified Grolim. "Incidentally, Agachak," she said, "you'll be happy to know that Urvon is dead.

Give him my regards when you see him." And then she struck, sinking her talons into Agachak's chest. He shrieked once before a sudden billow of sooty fire burst from the dragon's mouth and engulfed his face. And then the dragon bit his head off.

Lelldorin made a retching sound. "Great Chamdar!" he gasped in a revolted voice. "She's eating him!"

There was a horrid crunching sound as the dragon continued her ghastly feast. Then at last, with a shrill scream of triumph, she spread her huge wings and flew off to the east.

"Is it safe to come out now?" a shaking voice asked from nearby.

"You'd better," Barak said ominously, drawing his sword.

It was a Thull. He was young, with muddy-colored hair and a slack-lipped mouth.

"What's a Thull doing in Mallorea?" Lelldorin asked the stranger.

"Agachak brought me," the Thull replied, trembling violently.

"What's your name?" Relg asked him.

"I'm Nathel, King of Mishrak ac Thull. Agachak said he'd make me Overking of Angarak if I'd help him with something he had to do here. Please, don't leave me alone." Tears were streaming down his face.

Barak looked at his companions. They all had expressions of pity on their faces. "Oh, all right," he said grudgingly. "Come along, I guess."

CHAPTER TEN

"What's the matter with her, Aunt Pol?" Garion was looking at Ce'Nedra, who sat crooning over her blanket-wrapped bundle of rags.

"That's what I need to find out," Polgara said. "Sadi, I need some Oret."

"Is that really wise, Lady Polgara?" the eunuch asked. "In her present condition . . ." He spread his thin-fingered hands suggestively.

"If there's any danger, Aunt Pol—" Garion began.

"Oret is relatively harmless," she cut him off. "It stimulates the heart a bit, but Ce'Nedra's heart is strong. I can hear it beating half a continent away. We need to know what happened right now, and Oret is the fastest way."

Sadi had opened his red leather case and he handed Polgara one of his little vials. She judiciously tapped three drops of the yellow liquid into a cup and then filled the cup with water. "Ce'Nedra, dear," she said to the little queen, "you must be thirsty. This might help." She handed the cup to the red-haired girl.

"Why, thank you, Lady Polgara." Ce'Nedra drank deeply. "As a matter of fact, I was just about to ask someone for a drink of water."

"Very smooth, Pol," Beldin whispered.

"Rudimentary, uncle."

"Do you have any idea of what they're talking about?" 'Zakath asked Garion.

"Aunt Pol implanted the notion of thirst into Ce'Nedra's mind."

"You people can actually do that?"

"As she said, it's rudimentary."

"Can *you* do it?"

"I don't know. I've never tried." Garion's attention was, however, firmly fixed on his blissfully smiling little wife.

Polgara calmly waited.

"I think you can begin now, Lady Polgara," Sadi said after a few minutes.

"Sadi," she said absently, "we know each other well enough by now to skip the formalities. I'm not going to choke over 'your Excellency,' so why should you strangle on 'my Lady'?"

"Why, thank you, Polgara."

"Now, Ce'Nedra," Polgara said.

"Yes, Aunt Pol?" the tiny queen said, her eyes slightly unfocused.

"There's a first," Silk said to Beldin.

"She's been living with Garion for quite a while now," the dwarf replied. "Things do rub off after a bit."

"I wonder what Polgara'd do if *I* called her by that name?"

"I don't recommend experimentation," Beldin told him. "It's up to you, though, and you'd make a very interesting-looking radish."

"Ce'Nedra," Polgara said, "why don't you tell me exactly how you got your baby back?"

"Arell found him for me." Ce'Nedra smiled. "Now I have even more reason to love Arell."

"We all love Arell."

"Isn't he beautiful?" Ce'Nedra turned back the blanket to reveal her rags.

"He's lovely, dear. Did you and Arell have a chance to talk at all?"

"Oh, yes, Aunt Pol. She's doing something that's very important. That's why she couldn't join us just now. She said she might be able to catch up with us at Perivor—or maybe later at Korim."

"Then she knew where we're going?"

"Oh, no, Aunt Pol." Ce'Nedra laughed. "I had to tell her. She does *so* want to be with us, but she has this important thing to do. She asked me where we were going, and I told her about Perivor and Korim. She seemed a little surprised about Korim, though."

Aunt Pol's eyes narrowed. "I see," she said. "Durnik, why don't you set up a tent? I think Ce'Nedra and her baby should get a little rest."

"Right away, Pol," her husband agreed after a quick look at her.

"Now that you mention it, Aunt Pol," Ce'Nedra said happily, "I *do* feel a little tired, and I'm sure Geran needs a nap. Babies sleep so much, you know. I'll nurse him, and then he'll sleep. He always sleeps after he nurses."

"Steady," 'Zakath said quietly to Garion as the Rivan King's eyes filled with tears. The Mallorean Emperor put his hand firmly on his friend's shoulder.

"What's going to happen when she wakes up, though?"

"Polgara can fix it."

After Durnik had set up the tent, Polgara led the bemused girl inside. After a moment, Garion felt a slight surge and heard a whisper of sound. Then his aunt came out of the tent carrying Ce'Nedra's bundle. "Get rid of this," she said, pushing it into Garion's hands.

"Is she going to be all right?" he asked her.

"She's asleep now. She'll wake up in about an hour and, when she does, she won't remember that any of this happened. None of us will mention it to her, and that will be the end of it."

Garion took the bundle back into the woods and hid it under a bush. When he returned, he approached Cyradis. "It was Zandramas, wasn't it?" he demanded.

"Yes," Cyradis replied simply.

"And you knew it was going to happen, didn't you?"

"Yes."

"Why didn't you warn us?"

"To have done so would have been an interference in an event that had to occur."

"That was cruel, Cyradis."

"Necessary events sometimes are. I tell thee, Belgarion, Zandramas could not go to Kell as thou didst. Therefore, she had to find the location of the meeting from one of thy companions, else she would not be at the Place Which Is No More at the proper time."

"Why Ce'Nedra?"

"Zandramas, thou wilt recall, hath imposed her will upon thy queen in times past. It is not difficult for her to reimpose that bond."

"I'm not going to forgive this, Cyradis."

"Garion," 'Zakath said, "let it go. Ce'Nedra hasn't been hurt, and Cyradis was only doing what she had to do." The Mallorean seemed peculiarly defensive.

Garion turned and stalked away, his face livid with anger.

When Ce'Nedra awoke, she appeared to have no memory of the meeting in the woods and seemed to have returned to normal. Durnik struck the tent, and they rode on.

They reached the edge of the forest about sunset and set up for the night there. Garion rather studiously avoided 'Zakath, not trusting himself to be civil to his friend after he had jumped to the defense of the blindfolded Seeress. 'Zakath and Cyradis had engaged in a lengthy conversation before they had all left Kell, and now the Emperor seemed wholly committed to her cause. His eyes were sometimes troubled, though, and he frequently turned in his saddle to look at her.

That night, however, when they were both on watch, it was no longer possible for Garion to avoid his friend.

"Are you still angry with me, Garion?" 'Zakath asked.

Garion sighed. "No, I guess not," he said. "I don't think I was really angry—just a little irritated, is all. Most of all, I'm angry with Zandramas, not with you and Cyradis. I don't like people who play tricks on my wife."

"It really had to happen, you know. Zandramas had to find out where the meeting's going to take place. She has to be there, too."

"You're probably right. Did Cyradis give you any details about your task?"

"A few. I'm not supposed to talk about it, though. About all I can tell you is that somebody very important is coming, and I'm supposed to help him."

"And that's going to take you the rest of your life?"

"And probably the lives of a lot of others, as well."

"Mine, too?"

"I don't think so. I think your task will be over after the meeting. Cyradis sort of implied that you've done enough already."

They set out early that morning and rode out onto a rolling plain along the west side of the Balasa River. There were farm villages here and there, villages that looked rude, but in which the houses were really very well constructed. The Dalasian villagers labored in the fields with the simplest of tools.

"And it's all subterfuge," 'Zakath said wryly. "These people are probably far more sophisticated than even the Melcenes, and they've gone to a great deal of trouble to hide the fact."

"Would thy people or the priests of Torak have left them unmolested had the truth been known?" Cyradis asked him.

"Probably not," he admitted. "The Melcenes in particular would likely have pressed most of the Dals into service in the bureaucracy."

"That would not have been compatible with our tasks."

"I understand that now. When I get back to Mal Zeth, I think I'll make some changes in imperial policy toward the Dalasian Protectorates. Your people are doing something much, much more important than raising beets and turnips for the rest of Mallorea."

"If all goes well, our work will be done once the meeting hath taken place, Emperor 'Zakath."

"But your studies will continue, won't they?"

She smiled. "Inevitably. The habits of eons die very hard."

Belgarath pulled his horse in beside Cyradis. "Could you be a bit more specific about what we're supposed to be looking for when we get to Perivor?" he asked her.

"It is as I told thee at Kell, Ancient Belgarath. At Perivor thou must seek out the map that will guide thee to the Place Which Is No More."

"How is it that the people of Perivor know more about it than the rest of the world?"

She did not reply.

"I gather that this is another one of those things you're not going to tell me."

"I may not at this time, Belgarath."

Beldin came soaring in. "You'd better get ready," he said. "There's a patrol of Darshivan soldiers just ahead."

"How many?" Garion asked quickly.

"A dozen or so. They've got a Grolim with them. I didn't want to get too close, but I think it's White-eyes. They're hiding in ambush in a grove of trees in the next valley."

"How would he know we're coming this way?" Velvet asked in perplexity.

"Zandramas knows that we're going to Perivor," Polgara replied. "This is the shortest route."

"A dozen Darshivans don't really pose much of a threat," 'Zakath said confidently. "What's the purpose of this, then?"

"Delay," Belgarath told him. "Zandramas wants to hold us up so that she can get to Perivor before we do. She can communicate with Naradas over long distances. We can probably expect him to set traps for us every few miles all the way to Lengha."

'Zakath scratched at his short beard, frowning in concentration. Then he opened one of his saddlebags, took out a map, and consulted it. "We're still about fifteen leagues from Lengha," he said. He squinted at Beldin. "How fast could you cover that distance?"

"A couple hours. Why?"

"There's an imperial garrison there. I'll give you a message to the garrison commander with my seal on it. He'll move out with troops and spring those traps from behind. As soon as we join those forces, Naradas won't be bothering us anymore." Then he remembered something. "Holy Seeress," he said to Cyradis, "back in Darshiva, you told me to leave my troops behind when I came to Kell. Is that prohibition still in effect?"

"Nay, Kal Zakath."

"Good. I'll write that message."

"What about the patrol hiding just ahead?" Silk asked Garion. "Or are we just going to wait here until 'Zakath's troops arrive?"

"I don't think so. What's your feeling about a little exercise?"

Silk's answering grin was vicious.

"There's still a problem, though," Velvet said. "With Beldin on his way to Lengha, we won't have anyone to scout out any other ambushes."

"Tell the she with yellow hair not to be concerned," the wolf said to Garion. "One is able to move without being seen, or if one is seen, the man-things will pay no heed."

"It's all right, Liselle," Garion said. "The wolf will scout for us."

"She's a very useful person to have along." Velvet smiled.

"Person?" Silk said.

"Well, isn't she?"

He frowned. "You know, you might be right at that. She has a definite personality, doesn't she?"

The wolf wagged her tail at him and then loped off.

"All right, gentlemen," Garion said, loosening Iron-grip's sword in its sheath, "let's go pay these lurking Darshivans a visit."

"Won't Naradas cause some problems?" 'Zakath asked, handing his note to Beldin.

"I certainly hope he *tries*," Garion replied.

Naradas, however, proved to no longer be among the Darshivan soldiers hidden in the grove of trees. The skirmish was short, since most of the ambushers seemed to be much better at running than at fighting.

"Amateurs," 'Zakath said scornfully, wiping his sword blade on the cloak of one of the fallen.

"You're getting fairly competent with that, you know?" Garion complimented him.

"The training I was given when I was young seems to be coming back," 'Zakath replied modestly.

"He handles that sword almost the same way Hettar handles his saber, doesn't he?" Silk noted, pulling one of his daggers out of a Darshivan's chest.

"Much the same," Garion agreed, "and Hettar got his training from Cho-Hag, the finest swordsman in Algaria."

"Which Taur Urgas discovered the hard way," Silk added.

"I'd have given a great deal to watch that fight," 'Zakath said wistfully.

"So would I," Garion said, "but I was busy somewhere else at the time."

"Sneaking up on Torak?" 'Zakath suggested.

"I don't think 'sneaking' is the right word. He knew I was coming."

"I'll go get the ladies and Belgarath," Durnik said.

"Beldin spoke with me," Belgarath told them when he rode up. "Naradas flew out of this grove before you got here. Beldin considered killing him, but he had that parchment in his talons."

"What form did he take?" Silk asked. "Naradas, I mean?"

"A raven," Belgarath said with distaste. "Grolims are always fond of ravens for some reason."

Silk suddenly laughed. "Remember the time when Asharak the Murgo changed into a raven on the plain of Arendia, and Polgara called that eagle down to deal with him? It rained black feathers for almost an hour."

"Who's Asharak the Murgo?" 'Zakath asked.

"He was one of Ctuchik's underlings," Belgarath replied.

"Did the eagle kill him?"

"No," Silk said. "Garion did that later."

"With his sword?"

"No. With his hand."

"That must have been a mighty blow. Murgos are bulky people."

"Actually it was only a slap," Garion said. "I set fire to him." He hadn't thought of Asharak in years. Surprisingly, he found that the memory no longer bothered him.

'Zakath was staring at him in horror.

"He was the one who killed my parents," Garion told him. "The action seemed appropriate. He burned them to death, so I did the same thing to him. Shall we ride on?"

The tireless she-wolf ranged out ahead of them and located two more groups of ambushers before the sun went down. The survivors of the first, failed ambush had spread the word, however, and as soon as these other two groups of Darshivans saw Garion and his companions bearing down on them, they fled in panic.

"Disappointing," Sadi said after they had flushed out the second group. He slipped his small, poisoned dagger back into its sheath.

"I expect that Naradas is going to speak quite firmly with those fellows when he finds out that he's gone to all this trouble for nothing," Silk added gaily. "He'll probably sacrifice a goodly number of them just as soon as he can find an altar."

They met the men of 'Zakath's imperial garrison from Lengha about noon the following day. The commander of the garrison rode forward and stared at 'Zakath in some amazement. "Your Imperial Majesty," he said, "is that really you?"

'Zakath rubbed at his black beard. "Oh, you mean this, Colonel?" He laughed. "It was the suggestion of that old man over there." He pointed at Belgarath. "We didn't want people to recognize me, and my face is stamped on every coin in Mallorea. Did you have any trouble on your way north?"

"Nothing worth mentioning, your Majesty. We encountered a dozen or so groups of Darshivan soldiers—usually hiding in clumps of trees. We encircled each clump, and they all surrendered immediately. They're very good at surrendering."

"They run quite well, too, we've noticed." 'Zakath smiled.

The colonel looked at his emperor a bit hesitantly. "I hope you won't be offended at my saying this, your Majesty, but you seem to have changed since the last time I was in Mal Zeth."

"Oh?"

"I've never seen you under arms, for one thing."

"Troubled times, Colonel. Troubled times."

"And if you'll forgive my saying so, your Majesty, I've never heard you laugh before—or even seen you smile."

"I've had little reason before, Colonel. Shall we go on to Lengha?"

When they arrived in Lengha, Cyradis, with Toth's assistance, led them directly to the harbor, where a strangely configured ship awaited them.

"Thank you, Colonel," 'Zakath said to the garrison commander. "Providing this ship was most considerate of you."

"Excuse me, your Majesty," the colonel replied, "but I had nothing to do with the ship."

'Zakath gave Toth a startled look, and the big mute smiled briefly at Durnik.

Durnik frowned slightly. "Brace yourself, Kal Zakath," he said. "The arrangements for the ship were made several thousand years ago."

Belgarath's face was suddenly creased by a broad smile. "It would seem that we're right on schedule then. I do so hate to be late for an appointment."

"Really?" Beldin said. "I remember one time when you showed up five years after you were supposed to."

"Something came up."

"Something usually does. Wasn't that during the period when you were spending your time with the girls in Maragor?"

Belgarath coughed and cast a slightly guilty look at his daughter.

Polgara raised one eyebrow but didn't say anything.

The ship was manned by the same sort of mute crew as had conveyed them from the coast of Gorut in Cthol Murgos to the Isle of Verkat. Once again Garion was struck by that haunting sense of repetition. As soon as they were on board, the crew cast off all lines and made sail.

"Peculiar," Silk observed. "The breeze is coming in off the sea, and we're sailing directly into it."

"I noticed that," Durnik agreed.

"I thought you might have. It appears that normal rules don't apply to the Dals."

"Wilt thou, Belgarion, and thy friend 'Zakath accompany me to the aft cabin?" Cyradis said as they cleared the harbor.

"Of course, Holy Seeress," Garion replied. He noticed that as the three of them moved aft, 'Zakath took the blindfolded girl's hand to lead her, almost unconsciously duplicating Toth's solicitude. A peculiar notion crossed the mind of the Rivan King at that point. He looked rather closely at his friend. 'Zakath's face was strangely gentle, and his eyes had an odd look in them. The notion was absurd, of course, but as clearly as if he had seen directly into the Mallorean Emperor's heart, Garion knew that it was absolutely true. He rather carefully concealed a smile.

In the aft cabin stood two gleaming suits of armor, looking for all the world like those of the knights at Vo Mimbre.

"These must garb you at Perivor," Cyradis told them.

"There's a reason, I assume," Garion said.

"Indeed. And when we approach that coast, thou must each lower thy visor and under no circumstances raise it whilst we are on that isle unless I give thee leave."

"And you're not going to tell us what the reason is, are you?"

She smiled gently and laid one hand on his arm. "Know only that it is needful."

"I sort of thought she might take that position," Garion said to 'Zakath. He went to the door of the cabin. "Durnik," he called, "we're going to need some help down here."

"We don't have to put it on yet, do we?" 'Zakath asked him.

"Have you ever worn full armor before?"

"No. I can't say that I have."

"It takes a bit of getting used to. Even Mandorallen grunted a bit when he first put his on."

"Mandorallen? That Mimbrate friend of yours?"

Garion nodded. "He's Ce'Nedra's champion."

"I thought you were."

"I'm her husband. Different rules apply." He looked critically at 'Zakath's sword, a rather light and slim-bladed weapon. "He's going to need a bigger sword, Cyradis," he told the Seeress.

"In that cabinet, Belgarion."

"She thinks of everything," Garion said wryly. He opened the cabinet. Inside, standing almost to shoulder height, was a massive broadsword. He lifted it out with both hands. "Your sword, your Majesty," he said, extending the hilt to 'Zakath.

"Thank you, your Majesty." 'Zakath grinned. As he took the sword, his eyes suddenly went wide. "Torak's teeth!" he swore, almost dropping the huge weapon. "Do people actually use these things on each other?"

"Frequently. It's a major form of entertainment in Arendia. If you think that one's heavy, you should try mine." Then Garion remembered something. "Wake up," he said rather peremptorily to the Orb.

The murmur of the stone was slightly offended.

"Don't overdo this," Garion instructed, "but my friend's sword is just a bit heavy for him. Let's make it lighter—a little at a time." He watched as 'Zakath strained to raise the sword. "A little more," he instructed the Orb.

The sword point came up—slowly.

"How's that?" Garion asked.

"A bit more, maybe," 'Zakath grunted.

"Do it," Garion said to the Orb.

"That's better—" 'Zakath sighed "—but is it really safe to talk to that stone that way?"

"You have to be firm. It's like a dog or a horse sometimes—or even a woman."

"I will not forget thy remark, King Belgarion," Cyradis said in a crisp tone.

He grinned at her. "I didn't expect you to, Holy Seeress," he said mildly.

"One for your side," 'Zakath said.

"You see how useful that is?" Garion laughed. "I'll make an Alorn of you yet."

CHAPTER ELEVEN

The ship continued to move against the wind, and when they were perhaps three leagues out from the harbor, the albatross appeared, ghosting along on motionless, seraphlike wings. It made one solitary cry, and Polgara inclined her head in response. Then it took a position just in advance of the bowsprit as if it were leading the vessel.

"Isn't that peculiar?" Velvet said. "It's just like the one we saw on the way to the Isle of Verkat."

"No, dear," Polgara told her. "He's the same one."

"That's impossible, Lady Polgara. That was half a world away."

"Distance has no meaning to a bird with wings like that."

"What's he doing here?"

"He has a task of his own."

"Oh? What's that?"

"He did not choose to tell me, and it would have been impolite of me to ask."

'Zakath had been walking up and down the deck trying to set his armor into place. "This always *looks* so splendid, but it's really very uncomfortable, isn't it?"

"Not nearly as uncomfortable as not having it on when you really need it," Garion told him.

"You get used to it in time, though, don't you?"

"Not appreciably, no."

Although it was some distance to the island of Perivor, the strange ship with its silent crew made good time and landed them on a wooded coast about noon the following day.

"To be perfectly honest with you," Silk said to Garion as they unloaded the horses, "I'm just as happy to be off that vessel. A ship that sails against the wind and sailors who don't swear make me nervous somehow."

"There are a great many things about this entire business that are making *me* nervous," Garion replied.

"The only difference is that I'm just an ordinary man. You're a hero."

"What's that got to do with it?"

"Heroes aren't allowed to be nervous."

"Who made up that rule?"

"It's a known fact. What happened to that albatross?"

"He flew off as soon as we came in sight of land." Garion put his visor down.

"I don't care what Polgara says about them," Silk said with a shudder. "I've known a lot of sailors, and I've never heard one of them with anything good to say about those birds."

"Sailors are superstitious."

"Garion, there's some basis in fact for all superstitions." The little man squinted at the dark woods lining the upper end of the beach. "Not a very inviting coast, is it? I wonder why the ship didn't put us down in some seaport?"

"I don't think anybody really knows why the Dals do anything."

After the horses had been unloaded from the ship, Garion and the others mounted and rode up the beach into the woods. "I think I'd better cut you and 'Zakath some lances," Durnik said to Garion. "Cyradis had some reason for putting you two in armor, and I've noticed that an armored man usually looks a little undressed without a lance." He dismounted, took his axe, and went back among the trees. He returned a few moments later with two stout poles. "I'll put points on them when we stop for the evening," he promised.

"This is going to be awkward," 'Zakath said, fumbling with his lance and shield.

"You do it like this," Garion said, demonstrating. "Buckle the shield on your left arm and hold the reins in your left hand. Then set the butt of the lance in the stirrup beside your right foot and hold it in place with your free hand."

"Have you ever fought with a lance?"

"A few times, yes. It's fairly effective against another man wearing armor. Once you knock him off his horse, it takes him quite awhile to get back on his feet again."

Beldin, as usual, had been scouting ahead. He came drifting back, ghosting among the trees on almost motionless wings. "You're not going to believe this," he said to Belgarath after he had changed back into his own form.

"What's that?"

"There's a castle up ahead."

"A what?"

"A large building. They usually have walls, moats, and drawbridges."

"I know what a castle is, Beldin."

"Why did you ask then? Anyway, the one ahead looks almost as if it had been transplanted directly from Arendia."

"Do you suppose you could clarify this for us, Cyradis?" Belgarath asked the Seeress.

"It is really no mystery, Ancient Belgarath," she replied. "Some two thousand years ago, a group of adventurers from the west were shipwrecked on the coast of this island. Seeing that there was no way to make their ship whole again, they settled here and took wives from among the local populace. They have retained the customs and manners and even the speech of their homeland."

"Lots of thees and thous?" Silk asked her.

She nodded.

"And castles?"

She nodded again.

"And the men all wear armor? The same as Garion and 'Zakath are wearing?"

"It is even as thou hast said, Prince Kheldar."

He groaned.

"What's the problem, Kheldar?" 'Zakath asked him.

"We've traveled thousands of leagues only to find Mimbrates again."

"The reports I received from the battlefield at Thull Mardu all said that they're very brave. That might explain the reputation of this island."

"Oh, it does indeed, 'Zakath," the little man told him. "Mimbrates are the bravest people in the world—probably because they don't have brains enough to be afraid of anything. Garion's friend Mandorallen is totally convinced that he's invincible."

"He is," Ce'Nedra said in automatic defense of her knight. "I saw him kill a lion once with his bare hands."

"I've heard of his reputation," 'Zakath said. "I thought it was exaggerated."

"Not by very much," Garion said. "I heard him suggest to Barak and Hettar once that the three of them attack an entire Tolnedran legion."

"Perhaps he was joking."

"Mimbrate knights don't know *how* to joke," Silk told him.

"I will not sit here and listen to you people insult my knight," Ce'Nedra said hotly.

"We're not insulting him, Ce'Nedra," Silk told her. "We're describing him. He's so noble he makes my hair hurt."

"Nobility is an alien concept to a Drasnian, I suppose," she noted.

"Not alien, Ce'Nedra. Incomprehensible."

"Perhaps in two thousand years they've changed," Durnik said hopefully.

"I wouldn't count on it," Beldin grunted. "In my experience, people who live in isolation tend to petrify."

"I needs must warn ye all of one thing, however," Cyradis said. "The people of this island are a peculiar mixture. In many ways they are even as you have described them, but their heritage is also Dal, and they are conversant with the arts of our people."

"Oh, fine," Silk said sardonically, "Mimbrates who use sorcery. That's assuming they can figure out which way to point it."

"Cyradis," Garion said, "is this why 'Zakath and I are wearing armor?"

She nodded.

"Why didn't you just say so?"

"It was necessary for you to find that out for yourselves."

"Well, let's go have a look," Belgarath said. "We've dealt with Mimbrates before, and we've usually managed to stay out of trouble."

They rode on through the forest in golden afternoon sunshine and, when they reached the edge of the trees, they saw the structure Beldin had reported. It stood atop a high promontory, and it had the usual battlements and fortifications.

"Formidable," 'Zakath murmured.

"There's no real point in lurking here in the trees," Belgarath told them. "We can't get across all that open ground without being seen. Garion, you and 'Zakath take the lead. Men in armor are usually greeted with some courtesy."

"Are we just going to ride up to the castle?" Silk asked.

"We might as well," Belgarath said. "If they still think like Mimbrates, they'll almost be obliged to offer hospitality for the night, and we need a certain amount of information anyway."

They rode out onto an open meadow and proceeded at a walk toward the grim-looking castle. "You'd better let me do most of the talking when we get there," Garion said to 'Zakath. "I sort of know the dialect."

"Good idea," 'Zakath agreed. "I'd probably choke on all the thees and thous."

From inside the castle a horn blew a brazen note, announcing that they had been seen, and a few minutes later a dozen gleaming knights rode out across the drawbridge at a rolling trot. Garion moved Chretienne slightly to the front.

"Prithee, abate thy pace, Sir Knight," the man who appeared to be the leader of the strangers said. "I am Sir Astellig, baron of this place. May I ask of thee thy name and what it is that brings thee and thy companions to the gates of my keep?"

"My name I may not reveal, Sir Knight," Garion replied. "There are certain reasons, which I will disclose unto thee in due course. My fellow knight and I are embarked with these diverse companions on a quest of gravest urgency, and we have come here in search of shelter for the night, which shall descend upon us, methinks, within the next few hours." Garion was rather proud of the speech.

"Thou needst but ask, Sir Knight," the baron said, "for all true knights are compelled by honor, if not by courtesy, to offer aid and shelter to any fellow knight engaged in a quest."

"I cannot sufficiently express our gratitude to thee, Sir Astellig. We have, as thou canst see, ladies of quality with us whom the rigors of our journey have sorely fatigued."

"Let us proceed straightaway to my keep then, Sir Knights. Attending to the well-being of ladies is the paramount duty of all men of gentle birth." He wheeled his horse with a grand flourish and led the way up the long hill to his castle with his men close behind him.

"Elegant," 'Zakath commented admiringly.

"I spent some time at Vo Mimbre," Garion told him. "You can pick up their speech after a while. About the only problem with it is that the sentences are so involved that you sometimes lose track of what you're saying before you get to the bottom end of it."

Baron Astellig led the way across the drawbridge, and they all dismounted in a flagstoned courtyard. "My servants will see thee and thy companions to suitable quarters, Sir Knight," he said, "where you may all refresh yourselves. Then, an it please you, join me in the great hall and disclose unto me how I may aid thee in thy noble quest."

"Thy courtesy is most seemly, my Lord," Garion said. "Be assured that my brother knight and I will join you straightaway, as soon as we have seen to the comfort of the ladies."

They followed one of the baron's servants to comfortable quarters on the second floor of the main keep.

"I'm truly amazed at you, Garion," Polgara said. "I didn't think you had the faintest idea of how to speak a civilized language."

"Thank you," he said, "I think."

"Maybe you and 'Zakath should speak with the baron alone," Belgarath told Garion. "You've covered your own need for anonymity fairly well, but if the rest of us are around, he might start asking for introductions. Feel him out rather carefully. Inquire about local customs, that sort of thing, and ask him about any incidental wars going on." He looked at 'Zakath. "What's the capital of the island?"

"Dal Perivor, I think."

"That's where we'll want to go then. Where is it?"

"On the other side of the island."

"Naturally." Silk sighed.

"You'd better get started," Belgarath told the two armored men. "Don't keep our host waiting."

"When this is all over, would you consider hiring him out to me?" 'Zakath asked Garion as the two of them clanked down the hall. "You could make a tidy profit, you know, and I'd have the most efficient government in the world."

"Do you really want a man who's likely to live forever running your government?" Garion asked in an amused tone. "Not to mention the fact that he's probably more corrupt than Silk and Sadi put together? That is a very bad old man, Kal Zakath. He's wiser than whole generations, and he's got a large number of disgusting habits."

"He's your grandfather, Garion," 'Zakath protested. "How can you talk about him like that?"

"Truth is truth, your Majesty."

"You Alorns are a very strange people, my friend."

"We've never tried to hide that, my friend."

There was a clicking of toenails from behind, and the she-wolf slipped up between them. "One wonders where you are bound," she said to Garion.

"One and one's friend go to speak with the master of this house, little sister," he replied.

"One will accompany you and your friend," she said. "If needful, one may help to prevent missteps."

"What did she say?" 'Zakath asked.

"She's coming along to keep us from making any serious mistakes," Garion said.

"A wolf?"

"This is no ordinary wolf, 'Zakath. I'm beginning to have some suspicions about her."

"One is gratified that even a puppy may show some semblance of perception." The wolf sniffed.

"Thank you," he said. "One is happy to gain approval from one so dearly loved."

She wagged her tail at him. "One requests, however, that you keep your discovery to yourself."

"Of course," he promised.

"What was that all about?" 'Zakath asked.

"It's a wolfy sort of thing," Garion said. "It doesn't really translate."

Baron Astellig had removed his armor and sat in a massive chair before a crackling hearth. "It is ever thus, Sir Knights," he said. "Stone doth provide protection from foes, but it is forever cold, and the chill of winter is slow to seep away from its obdurate surface. Perforce we are required to maintain our fires even when summer doth bathe our isle with its gentle warmth."

"It is, my Lord, as thou sayest," Garion replied. "E'en the massive walls of Vo Mimbre do harbor this oppressive chill."

"And thou, Sir Knight, hath seen Vo Mimbre?" the baron asked in wonder. "I would give all that I own or ever will to behold that fabled city. What is it truly like?"

"Large, my Lord," Garion said, "and its golden stones do flash back the light of the sun as if to shame the heavens by its magnificence."

The baron's eyes filled with tears. "Blessed am I, Sir Knight," he said in a voice choked with emotion. "This unexpected encounter with a knight of noble purpose and passing fair eloquence hath been the crown of my life, for the memory of Vo Mimbre, echoing down through the endless progression of years, hath sustained those of us in lonely exile here, though its echoes grow more remote with each passing season e'en as dearly loved faces of those gone before us are remembered only in a dream that fades and dies as cruel eld creepeth upon us."

"My Lord," 'Zakath said a bit haltingly, "thy speech hath touched my heart. If I have power—and I do—I will convey thee at some future date even unto Vo Mimbre and present thee before the throne in the palace there, that we may reunite thee with thy kindred."

"You see," Garion murmured to his friend, "it gets to be habit-forming."

The baron wiped his eyes unashamed. "I note this hound of thine, Sir Knight," he said to Garion to ease them past an embarrassing moment, "a bitch, I perceive—"

"Steady," Garion said firmly to the she-wolf.

"That is a *very* offensive term," she growled.

"He didn't invent it. It's not his fault."

"She is of a lean and lithesome configuration," the baron continued, "and her golden eyes do bespeak intelligence far beyond that of the poor mongrels that do infest this kingdom. Canst thou perhaps, Sir Knight, identify her breed?"

"She is a wolf, my Lord," Garion told him.

"A wolf!" the baron exclaimed, leaping to his feet. "We must flee ere the fearsome beast fall upon us and devour us."

It was a bit ostentatious, but sometimes things like that impress people. Garion reached down and scratched the wolf's ears.

"Thou art brave beyond belief, Sir Knight," the baron said almost in wonder.

"She is my friend, my Lord," Garion replied. "We are linked by ties beyond thine imagining."

"One advises that you stop that," the wolf told him, "unless you have a paw to spare."

"You *wouldn't!*" he exclaimed, snatching his hand back.

"But you're not entirely sure, are you?" She bared her teeth almost in a grin.

"Thou speakest the language of beasts?" The baron gasped.

"Of a few, my Lord," Garion said. "They each have their own, thou knowest. I have not yet mastered the speech of the serpent. I think it has to do with the shape of my tongue."

The baron suddenly laughed. "Thou art a droll man, Sir Knight. Thou hast presented me here with much to ponder and much at which to marvel. Now, to the main point. What canst thou reveal to me of thy quest?"

"Be very careful here," the wolf warned Garion.

Garion considered. "As thou mayest know, my Lord," he began, "there is a great evil abroad in the world now." That was fairly safe. There was *always* a great evil abroad in the world.

"Truly," the baron agreed fervently.

"It is the sworn task of my steadfast companion here and myself to confront this evil. Know thou, however, that rumor, like a barking dog, would run before us, announcing—should they be known—our identities to the foul miscreant upon whom we mean to do war. Should, all forewarned, this vicious enemy learn of our approach, its minions would waylay us. Thus it is that we must conceal ourselves behind our visors and refrain from declaring before all the world our names—which have some smirch of honor upon them in diverse parts of the world." Garion was beginning to enjoy this. "We, neither one, fear any living thing." Mandorallen himself could not have said it more confidently. "We have, however, dear companions in this quest, whose lives we dare not endanger. Moreover, our quest is fraught with perilous enchantments that may even vaunt our prowess. Thus, though it is distasteful, we must, with thieflike stealth, approach this despised miscreant that we may administer suitable chastisement." He said the last word with something as close to the crack of doom as he could manage.

The baron got the point immediately. "My sword, and those of my knights, are at thine immediate disposal, my Lord. Let us eradicate this evil for good and all." The baron was a Mimbrate to the bone, all right.

Garion raised one regretful hand. "Nay, my Lord of Astellig," he said. "It may not be so, though I would welcome thee and thy brave companions with all my heart. This task hath been lain upon me and upon my dear companions. To accept thine aid in this endeavor would be to anger the minions of the spirit world, which, no less than we, do contend in this matter. We—all of us—are but mortal, and the spirit world is a world of immortals. To defy the commands of the spirits might well confound the purpose of those friendly spirits that take our part in this ultimate battle."

"Though it wounds my heart, Sir Knight," the baron said sadly, "I must agree that thine argument hath cogency. Know, moreover, that a kinsman of mine hath but recently arrived from the capital at Dal Perivor and hath advised me privately of a disturbing turn of events at court. No more than a few days ago, a wizard appeared at the king's palace. Doubtless using enchantments such as thou hast mentioned, he beguiled our king within the space of a few hours and gained the king's ear and is now his closest advisor. He now doth wield almost absolute authority in the kingdom. Guard yourselves well, Sir Knights. Should, perchance, this wizard be one of the minions of your foe, he now hath power to do thee gravest injury." The baron made a wry face. "Methinks the beguiling of the king was no serious task for him. It is improper of me to say it, perhaps, but his Majesty is not a man of profound intellectual gifts." This from a *Mimbrate*? "This wizard," the baron continued, "is a wicked man, and I must advise thee in the spirit of true comradeship to avoid him."

"I thank thee, my Lord," Garion said, "but our destiny, and that of our quest, compels us to Dal Perivor. If needs be, we will confront this wizard and rid the kingdom of his influence."

"May the Gods and the spirits guide thy hand," the baron said fervently. Then he grinned. "Mayhap, an it please thee, I might watch as thou and thy valiant, laconic companion administer such chastisement as thou seest fit."

"We would be honored, my Lord," 'Zakath assured him.

"With that end in view then, my Lords," the baron said, "be advised that I and diverse nobles journey on the morrow toward the king's palace at Dal Perivor, there to participate in the grand tourney that our Lord King hath ordained to select champions of the kingdom to deal with a certain recurrent problem which hath confronted us. Know, moreover, that by centuries-old tradition, misunderstandings and frictions are held in the abeyance of general truce during this period and we may expect general tranquility on our journey to the west. An it please you, my Lords, may I entreat you to accompany me to the capital?"

"My Lord," Garion said, bowing with a slight creaking of armor, "your suggestion and gracious invitation could not suit our purposes more. And now, if we may, we will retire to make our preparations."

As Garion and 'Zakath strode down the long hall, the wolf's toenails had an almost metallic ring to them. "One is pleased," she said. "You didn't do all that badly—for a couple of puppies."

■ ⌐ CHAPTER TWELVE ¬ ■

Perivor proved to be a pleasant island with rolling, emerald-green hills where sheep grazed and with dark plowed fields where meticulously straight rows of crops flourished. Baron Astellig looked about with some pride. "It is a fair land," he observed, "though doubtless not so fair as far-off Arendia."

"Methinks thou wouldst be somewhat disappointed by Arendia, my Lord," Garion told him. "Though the land be fair, the kingdom is much marred by civil turmoil and by the misery of the serfs."

"Doth that sad institution still prevail there? It was abolished here many centuries ago."

Garion was a bit surprised at that.

"The folk who inhabited this isle ere we came are a gentle people, and our forebears sought wives from among them. At first these common folk were bound in serfdom, as had always been the practice in Arendia, but our ancestors soon perceived that this was the grossest injustice, since the serfs were kinsmen by marriage." The baron frowned slightly. "Doth this civil discord thou spake of truly mar our ancestral homeland to any great extent?"

Garion sighed. "We have some small expectation that it may abate, my Lord. Three great duchies warred with each other for centuries until one—Mimbre—finally achieved nominal mastery. Rebellion lurked ever beneath the surface, however. Moreover, the barons of southern Arendia make bloody war upon each other for the most trivial of reasons."

"War? Truly? Such affairs arise here on Perivor, as well, but we have attempted to formalize the conflict to such degree that few are ever slain."

"How meanst thou 'formalize,' my Lord?"

"Such disputes as arise are—except in cases of outrage or gravest insult—customarily settled by tourneys." The baron smiled. "Indeed, I have known of a number of disputes that were counterfeited by the mutual contrivance of the principals merely as an excuse to hold such tourneys—which do entertain nobles and commons alike."

"How very civilized, my Lord," 'Zakath said.

The strain of phrasing such involuted sentences was beginning to wear on Garion. He asked the baron to excuse him, pleading the need to confer with his companions, and rode back to talk with Belgarath and the others.

"How are you and the baron getting along?" Silk asked him.

"Quite well, actually. The intermarriage with the Dals has altered certain of the more irritating Arendish tendencies."

"Such as?"

"Gross stupidity for one thing. They've abolished serfdom, and they usually settle disputes with tournaments rather than open war." Garion looked at the dozing Belgarath. "Grandfather."

Belgarath opened his eyes.

"Do you think we've managed to get here ahead of Zandramas?"

"There's no way to know for sure."

"I could use the Orb again."

"It's probably better if you don't just yet. If she's on the island, there's no way to know where she landed. She may not have come this way, so the Orb wouldn't react to her trail. I'm sure she can feel it, though, and about all we'd succeed in doing would be to let her know we're here. Besides, the Sardion is in this part of the world. Let's not wake it up just yet."

"You might ask your friend the baron," Silk suggested. "If she's here, he might have heard something about her."

"I doubt it," Belgarath said. "In the past she's usually gone to a great deal of trouble to remain unobserved."

"That's true," Silk conceded, "and I think she'll go to even more trouble now. She might have some difficulty trying to explain those lights under her skin."

"Let's wait until we get to Dal Perivor," Belgarath decided. "I want to sort things out there before we do anything irrevocable."

"Do you suppose it would do any good to ask Cyradis?" Garion asked quietly, glancing back at the Seeress, who rode in the splendid carriage the baron had provided for the ladies.

"No," Belgarath said. "She won't be permitted to answer us."

"I think we might have a certain advantage in all this," Silk observed. "Cyradis is the one who's going to make the choice, and the fact that she's traveling with us instead of with Zandramas bodes rather well, wouldn't you say?"

"I don't think so," Garion disagreed. "I don't think she's traveling with *us* so much as she's here to keep an eye on 'Zakath. He has something very important to do, and she doesn't want him to stray."

Silk grunted. "Where do you propose to start looking for this map you're supposed to find?" he asked Belgarath.

"A library probably," the old man replied. "This map is another one of those 'mysteries,' and I've had a fair degree of luck finding the others in libraries. Garion, see if you can persuade the baron to take us to the king's court in Dal Perivor. Palace libraries are usually the most complete."

"Of course," Garion agreed.

"I want to take a look at this wizard anyway. Silk, do you have an office in Dal Perivor?"

"I'm afraid not, Belgarath. There's nothing here worth trading in."

"Well, no matter. You're a businessman, and there'll be others in the city. Go talk business with them. Tell them you want to check over shipping routes. Look at every map you can lay your hands on. You know what we're looking for."

"You're cheating, Belgarath," Beldin growled.

"How do you mean?"

"Cyradis told you that *you* were supposed to find the map."

"I'm only delegating responsibility, Beldin. It's perfectly legitimate."

"I don't think she'd see it that way."

"You can explain it to her. You're much more persuasive than I am."

They traveled in easy stages, more to spare the horses, Garion felt, than for any other reason. The horses of Perivor were not large, and they labored under the weight of men in full armor. So it was that it was several days before they crested a hill and looked down at the seaport city which was the capital of Perivor.

"Behold Dal Perivor," the baron proclaimed, "the crown and the heart of the isle."

Garion saw immediately that the shipwrecked Arends who had arrived on this shore two thousand years ago had made a conscious effort to duplicate Vo Mimbre.

The city walls were high and thick and yellow, and brightly colored pennons flew from spires within those walls.

"Where did they find the yellow stone, my Lord?" 'Zakath asked the baron. "I have seen no such rock on our journey here."

The baron coughed a bit apologetically. "The walls are painted, Sir Knight," he explained.

"Whatever for?"

"To serve as a remembrance of Vo Mimbre," the baron said a bit sadly. "Our ancestors were homesick for Arendia. Vo Mimbre is the jewel of our ancestral home, and its golden walls speak to our blood even across the endless miles."

"Ah," 'Zakath said.

"As I have promised thee, Sir Knight," the baron said to Garion, "gladly will I convey thee and thy companions forthwith to the king's palace where he will doubtless honor thee and offer thee his hospitality."

"Once more we are in thy debt, my Lord," Garion replied.

The baron smiled a bit slyly. "I confess it to thee, Sir Knight, that my motives are not altogether magnanimous. I will accrue much credit by presenting at court stranger knights bent on a noble quest."

"That's quite all right, my friend." Garion laughed. "This way there's something for everybody."

The palace was almost identical to that in Vo Mimbre, a fortress within a fortress with high walls and a stout gate.

"At least this time I don't think my grandfather will have to grow a tree," Garion murmured to 'Zakath.

"Do what?"

"When we first went to Vo Mimbre, the knight in charge of the palace gate didn't believe Mandorallen when he introduced Grandfather as Belgarath the Sorcerer, so Grandfather took a twig from his horse's tail and made an apple tree grow right there in the square in front of the palace. Then he ordered the skeptical knight to spend the rest of his life taking care of it."

"Did the knight actually do it?"

"I assume so. Mimbrates take those kinds of commands very seriously."

"Strange people."

"Oh, yes, indeed. I had to force Mandorallen to marry a girl he'd loved since childhood, and I had to stop a war in the process."

"How do you stop a war?"

"I made some threats. I think they took me seriously." He thought about it. "The thunderstorm I created may have helped, though," he added. "Anyway, Mandorallen and Nerina had loved each other for years, but they'd been suffering in silence beautiful for all that time. I finally got tired of it, so I made them get on with it. I made some more threats. I've got this big knife back here." He poked his thumb over his shoulder. "It attracts a lot of attention sometimes."

"Garion!" 'Zakath laughed. "You're a peasant."

"Yes. Probably," Garion admitted. "But it got them married, after all. They're both deliriously happy now, and if anything goes wrong, they can always blame me, can't they?"

"You're not like other men, my friend," 'Zakath said very seriously.

"No." Garion sighed. "Probably not. I'd like to be, though. The world lies very heavily on you and me, 'Zakath, and it doesn't leave us any time for ourselves. Wouldn't you just like to ride out on a summer morning to look at the sunrise and see what lies over the next hilltop?"

"I thought that's what we've been doing."

"Not entirely. We're doing all this because we're compelled to. What I was talking about was doing it just for fun."

"I haven't done anything just for fun in years."

"Didn't you rather enjoy threatening to crucify King Gethel of the Thulls? Ce'Nedra told me about that."

'Zakath laughed. "That wasn't too bad," he admitted. "I wouldn't have done it, of course. Gethel was an idiot, but he was sort of necessary at that point."

"It always comes to that, doesn't it? You and I do what's necessary, not what we'd really prefer to do. Neither of us sought this eminence, but we'll do what's necessary and what's expected of us. If we don't, this world will die, and good, honest men will die with it. I won't permit that if I can help it. I won't betray those good, honest men, and neither will you. You're too good a man yourself."

"Good? Me?"

"You underestimate yourself, 'Zakath, and I think that very soon someone will come and teach you not to hate yourself anymore."

'Zakath started visibly.

"You didn't think I knew?" Garion said, boring in relentlessly. "But that's nearly over now. Your suffering and pain and remorse are almost done, and if you need any instructions in how to be happy, look me up. After all, that's what friends are for, aren't they?"

A choked sob came from behind 'Zakath's visor.

The she-wolf had been standing between their horses. She looked up at Garion. "Very well done," she said. "Perhaps one has misjudged you, young wolf. Perhaps you are not a puppy after all."

"One can but do one's best," Garion replied, also in the language of wolves. "One hopes that one has not been too much a disappointment."

"One feels that you have some promise, Garion."

And that confirmed something that Garion had suspected for some time now. "Thank you, Grandmother," he said, sure at last just to whom he was speaking.

"And it took you so very, very long to say it?"

"It might have been considered impolite."

"One believes that you have been too long with one's eldest daughter. She is, one has noticed, much caught up in propriety. One assumes you will continue to keep your discovery to yourself?"

"If you wish."

"It might be wiser." She looked at the palace gate. "What is this place?"

"It is the palace of the king."

"What are kings to wolves?"

"It is the custom among the man-things to pay respect to them, Grandmother. The respect is more to the custom than to the man-thing who wears the crown."

"How very curious," she sniffed.

At last, with a great deal of creaking and the clanking of chain, the drawbridge boomed down, and Baron Astellig and his knights led them into the palace court-yard.

As was the one in Vo Mimbre, the throne room here in Dal Perivor was a great, vaulted hall with sculptured buttresses soaring upward along the walls. Tall, narrow windows rose between the buttresses, and the light streaming through their stained-glass panels was jeweled. The floor was polished marble, and on the red-carpeted stone platform at the far end stood the throne of Perivor, backed by heavy purple drapes. Flanking the draped wall hung the massive antique weapons of two thou-sand years of the royal house. Lances, maces, and huge swords, taller than any man, hung among the tattered war-banners of forgotten kings.

Almost bemused by the similarities, Garion half expected to see Mandorallen in his gleaming armor come striding across the marble floor to greet them, flanked by red-bearded Barak and horse-maned Hettar. Once again, that strange sense of re-currence struck him. With a start he realized that in recounting past experiences to 'Zakath, he had in fact been reliving them. In some obscure way this seemed a kind of cleansing in preparation for the now almost inevitable meeting in the Place Which Is No More.

"An it please ye, Sir Knights," Baron Astellig said to Garion and 'Zakath, "let us approach the throne of King Oldorin that I may present ye to his Majesty. I will advise him of the diverse restrictions your quest hath lain upon ye."

"Thy courtesy and consideration become thee, my Lord of Astellig," Garion said. "Gladly will we greet thy king."

The three of them proceeded along the marble floor toward the carpeted plat-form. King Oldorin, Garion noticed, was a more robust-looking man than Koro-dullin of Arendia, but his eyes revealed a fearful lack of anything resembling thought.

A tall, powerfully built knight stepped in front of Astellig. "This is unseemly, my Lord," he said. "Instruct thy companions to raise their visors that the king may behold those who approach him."

"I will explain to his Majesty the reason for this necessary concealment, my Lord," Astellig replied a bit stiffly. "I assure thee that these knights, whom I dare to call friends, intend no disrespect to our Lord King."

"I'm sorry, Baron Astellig," the knight said, "but I cannot permit this."

The baron's hand went to his sword hilt.

"Steady," Garion warned, placing one gauntleted hand on Astellig's arm. "As all the world knows, it is forbidden to draw arms in the king's presence."

"Thou art well versed in propriety, Sir Knight," the man barring their way said, sounding a bit less sure of himself now.

"I've been in the presence of kings before, my Lord, and I am conversant with the customary usages. I do assure thee that we mean no disrespect to his Majesty by our visored approach to the throne. We are compelled to it, however, by a stern duty that hath been lain upon us."

The knight looked even more unsure of himself. "Thou art well spoken, Sir Knight," he admitted grudgingly.

"An it please you then, Sir Knight," Garion continued, "wilt thou accompany Baron Astellig, my companion, and myself to the throne? A man of thine obvious prowess can easily prevent mischief." A little flattery never hurt anything in difficult situations.

"It shall be as thou sayest, Sir Knight," the knight decided.

The four of them approached the throne and bowed somewhat stiffly. "My Lord King," Astellig said.

"Baron," Oldorin replied with an absent-seeming nod.

"I have the honor to present two stranger knights who have traveled here from afar in pursuit of a noble quest."

The king looked interested. The word "quest" rang bells in Mimbrate heads.

"As thou may have noticed, your Majesty," Astellig continued, "my friends are visored. This is not to be taken as a gesture of disrespect, but is a necessary concealment required by the nature of their quest. A foul evil is abroad in the world, and they journey with diverse companions to confront it. They each have some eminence in the world beyond the shores of our isle, and should they reveal their faces, they would instantly be recognized, and the evil one they seek would be forewarned of their coming and would seek to impede them. Thus it is that their visors must remain closed."

"A reasonable precaution," the king agreed. "Greetings, Sir Knights, and well met."

"Thou art kind, your Majesty," Garion said, "and we are grateful to thee for thy gracious understanding of our circumstances. Our quest is fraught with perilous enchantments, and I do fear me that should we reveal our identities, we might well fail, and the whole world would suffer as a result."

"I do fully understand, Sir Knight, and I will not press thee for further details of thy quest. The walls of any palace have ears, and some there are even here who might be in league with the villain thou seekest."

"Wisely spoken, my King," a rasping voice said from the back of the throne room. "As I myself know full well, the powers of enchanters are myriad, and even the prowess of these two brave knights may not be sufficient to match them."

Garion turned. The man who had spoken had absolutely white eyes.

"The wizard of whom I told thee," Baron Astellig whispered to Garion. "Be wary of him, Sir Knight, for he hath the king in thrall."

"Ah, good Erezel," the king said, his face lighting up, "an it please thee, approach the throne. Mayhap in thy wisdom thou mayest advise these two questors concerning the possibility of avoiding the perils posed by the enchantments certain to be strewn in their path."

"It shall be my pleasure, Lord King," Naradas replied.

"You know who he is, don't you?" 'Zakath murmured to Garion.

"Yes."

Naradas came down to the throne. "If I may be so bold as to suggest it, Sir Knights," he said in an unctuous tone, "a great tourney is planned not long hence. Should you not participate, it might arouse suspicion in the minions the one you seek hath doubtless placed here. My first advice to you, therefore, is that you enter our tourney and thus avoid that mischance."

"A most excellent suggestion, Erezel," the empty-headed king approved. "Sir Knights, this is Erezel, a great wizard and the closest advisor to our throne. Consider well his words, for they have great merit. We will, moreover, be greatly honored to have two such mighty men join with us in our forthcoming entertainment."

Garion ground his teeth together. With that one innocent-seeming suggestion, Naradas had effectively achieved the delay he had been seeking for weeks now. There was no way out, however. "We would be honored to join with thee and thy valiant knights in thy sport, your Majesty," he said. "Prithee, when are the games to begin?"

"Ten days hence, Sir Knight."

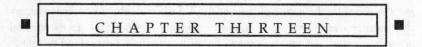

CHAPTER THIRTEEN

The quarters to which they were escorted were again hauntingly familiar. The displaced Arends who had been washed ashore here so many centuries ago had, it appeared, lovingly re-created the royal palace at Vo Mimbre down to the last detail—even including its inconveniences. Durnik, ever practical, noticed this immediately. "You'd think they'd have taken advantage of the opportunity to improve a few things," he observed.

"There's a certain charm in archaism, dear," Polgara said, smiling.

"It's nostalgic, perhaps, Pol, but a few modern touches wouldn't have hurt all that much. You *have* noticed that the baths are located down in the cellar, haven't you?"

"There's a point there, Lady Polgara," Velvet agreed.

"It *was* much more convenient in Mal Zeth," Ce'Nedra concurred. "A bath in one's own apartments offers all sorts of opportunities for fun and mischief."

Garion's ears turned bright red.

"I seem to be missing the more interesting parts of this conversation," 'Zakath said slyly.

"Never mind," Garion told him shortly.

And then the dressmakers arrived, and Polgara and the other ladies were whisked away to engage in that activity which, Garion had noticed, always seems to fill the feminine heart with a kind of dreamy bliss.

Immediately behind the dressmakers came the tailors, equally bent on making everyone look as old-fashioned as possible. Beldin, of course, adamantly refused their ministrations, even going so far as to show one insistent fellow a gnarled and very large fist to indicate that he was perfectly satisfied with the way he looked already.

Garion and 'Zakath, however, were under the constraint placed upon them by the Seeress of Kell, and so they remained buckled up in their armor.

When they were finally alone, Belgarath's expression grew grave. "I want you two to be careful in that tournament," he told the armored men. "Naradas knows who we are, and he's already managed to delay us. He may try to go a little further." He looked sharply toward the door. "Where are you going?" he demanded of Silk.

"I thought I'd nose around a bit," the little thief said innocently. "It never hurts to know what you're up against."

"All right, but be careful—and don't let anything slip into your pockets by mistake. We're walking on some fairly shaky ground here. If someone sees you pilfering, we could all get into a great deal of trouble."

"Belgarath," Silk replied in an offended tone, "no one has *ever* seen me steal anything." And then he went out muttering to himself.

"Is he trying to say that he *doesn't* steal?" 'Zakath asked.

"No," Eriond replied. "Only that no one ever sees him doing it." He smiled gently. "He has a few bad habits, but we've been trying to break him of them." It was the first time in quite a while that Garion had actually heard his young friend say anything. Eriond had grown increasingly reticent—one might even say withdrawn. It was troubling. He had always been a strange boy, and he seemed to be able to perceive things that none of the rest of them could. A chill came over Garion as he remembered the fateful words of Cyradis at Rheon: "Thy quest will be fraught with great peril, Belgarion, and one of thy companions shall lose his life in the course of it."

And then, almost as if his memory had summoned her, the blindfolded Seeress of Kell emerged from the room in which the ladies had been conferring with their dressmakers. Immediately behind her came Ce'Nedra, clad only in a *very* short chemise. "It's a perfectly suitable gown, Cyradis," she was protesting.

"Suitable for thee perhaps, Queen of Riva," the Seeress replied, "but such finery is not for me."

"Ce'Nedra!" Garion exclaimed in a shocked gasp. "You're not dressed!"

"Oh, bother that!" she snapped. "Everyone here has seen undressed women before. I'm just trying to reason with my mystical young friend here. Cyradis, if you don't put on the gown, I'll be very cross with you—and we really need to do something with your hair."

The Seeress unerringly took the tiny queen in her arms and embraced her fondly. "Dear, dear Ce'Nedra," she said gently, "thy heart is larger than thyself, and thy concern doth fill mine as well. I am content, however, in this simple garb. Mayhap in time my tastes will change, and then will I gladly submit to thy gentle ministrations."

"There's absolutely no talking to her," Ce'Nedra said, throwing her arms in the air. Then, with a charming flirt of the hem of her chemise, she stormed back into the room from which the two of them had emerged.

"You ought to feed her more," Beldin told Garion. "She's really very skinny, you know."

"I sort of like her the way she is," Garion replied. He looked at Cyradis. "Will you sit, Holy Seeress?"

"If I may."

"Of course." He waved off Toth's almost instinctive move to aid his mistress and guided the girl to a comfortable chair.

"I thank thee, Belgarion," she said. "Thou art as kind as thou art brave." She smiled, and it was like the sun coming up. She touched one hand to her hair. "Doth this really look so ugly?" she asked.

"It's just fine, Cyradis," he told her. "Ce'Nedra sometimes exaggerates, and she has an absolute passion for making people over—me, usually."

"And dost thou mind her efforts, Belgarion?"

"I suppose not. I'd probably miss them if she didn't try, at least."

"Thou art caught in the snare of love, King Belgarion. Thou art a mighty sorcerer, but methinks thy little queen hath a more powerful sorcery yet, for she holds thee in the palm of that tiny hand."

"That's true, I suppose, but I don't really mind all that much."

"If this gets any more cloying, I think I'll throw up," Beldin said gruffly.

And then Silk returned.

"Anything?" Belgarath asked.

"Naradas beat you to the library. I stopped by there, and the man in charge—"

"Librarian," Belgarath corrected absently.

"Whatever. Anyway, he said that as soon as Naradas arrived, he ransacked the library."

"So that's it, then," Belgarath said. "Zandramas isn't on the island. She sent Naradas here to do her looking for her, it seems. Is he still looking?"

"Apparently not."

"That means he's found it, then."

"And probably destroyed it to keep us from getting a look at it," Beldin added.

"Nay, gentle Beldin," Cyradis said. "The chart ye seek doth still exist, but it is not in the place where ye propose to seek."

"I don't suppose you could give us a few hints?" Belgarath asked her.

She shook her head.

"I didn't think so."

"You said *the* chart," Beldin said, approaching the subject obliquely. "Does that mean there's only one copy?"

She nodded.

The dwarf shrugged. "Oh, well," he said. "Looking for it gives us something to do while we're waiting for our two heroes here to go out and start denting other people's armor."

"That brings up a point," Garion said. He looked at 'Zakath. "You're not particularly familiar with the lance, are you?"

"Not really, no."

"Tomorrow morning, then, we'll have to go someplace so that I can give you some instruction."

"That seems like a sensible plan to me."

The two of them arose early the following morning and left the palace on horseback. "I think we'd better go out of town," Garion said. "There's a practice field near the palace, but there'll be other knights there. I'm not trying to be offensive, but the first few passes are usually very awkward. We're supposed to be great knights, so let's not let anybody get the idea that you're totally inept."

"Thanks," 'Zakath said dryly.

"Do you enjoy public embarrassment?"

"Not really."

"Let's do it my way, then."

They rode out of the city and to a meadow a few miles away.

"You've got two shields," 'Zakath noted. "Is that customary?"

"The other one is for our opponent."

"Opponent?"

"A stump or a tree probably. We need a target." Garion reined in. "Now," he began, "we're going to be involved in a formal tournament. The idea is not to kill anybody, since that's considered bad form. We'll probably be using blunted lances. That helps to keep down the fatalities."

"But sometimes people *do* get killed, don't they?"

"It's not unheard of. The whole purpose of a formal joust is to knock the other fellow off his horse. You ride at him and aim your lance at the center of his shield."

"And he does the same thing to me, I suppose."

"Exactly."

"It sounds painful."

"It is. After a few passes, you'll probably be bruised from head to hip."

"And they do this for entertainment?"

"Not entirely. It's a form of competition. They do it to find out who's the best."

"Now *that* I can understand."

"I thought the notion might appeal to you."

They buckled the spare shield to a springy lower limb of a cedar tree. "That's about the right height," Garion said. "I'll make the first couple of passes. Watch very closely. Then you can try."

Garion had become quite proficient with the lance and he hit the shield squarely on both passes.

"Why do you stand up at the last second?" 'Zakath asked him.

"I wasn't actually standing so much as leaning forward. The idea is to brace your feet in the stirrups, lean forward, and hold your body rigid. That way the weight of the horse is added to your own."

"Clever. Let me try it."

'Zakath completely missed the shield on his first attempt. "What did I do wrong?" he asked.

"When you raised up and leaned forward, the point of your lance dipped. You have to adjust your point of aim."

"Oh, I see. All right, let me try it again." On the next pass he struck the shield a glancing blow that made it spin around the limb. "Any better?" he asked.

Garion shook his head. "You'd have killed him. When you hit the top of the shield that way, your lance is deflected upward, and it drives right into his visor. It breaks his neck."

"I'll try it again."

By noon 'Zakath had made considerable progress.

"That's enough for today," Garion said. "It's starting to get hot out here."

"I'm still all right," 'Zakath objected.

"I was thinking about your horse."

"Oh. He *is* lathered a bit, isn't he?"

"More than just a bit. Besides, I'm starting to get hungry."

The day of the tourney dawned clear and sunny, and throngs of the citizens of Dal Perivor streamed through the streets in bright-colored clothing toward the field where the festivities were to take place. "A thought just occurred to me," Garion said to 'Zakath as they left the palace. "You and I aren't *really* interested in who gets proclaimed the winner of the tournament, are we?"

"I don't follow you."

"We have something much more important to do, and assorted broken bones would probably hinder us. We make a few passes and unhorse a few knights and then allow ourselves to get knocked out of the saddle. We'll have satisfied the requirements of honor without putting ourselves in any serious danger of injury."

"Are you suggesting that we deliberately lose?" 'Zakath asked incredulously.

"Approximately, yes."

"I've never lost a contest of any kind in my whole life."

"You're starting to sound more and more like Mandorallen every day." Garion sighed.

"Besides," 'Zakath went on, "I think you're overlooking something. We're supposed to be mighty knights embarked on a noble quest. If we don't try our very best, Naradas will fill the king's ears with all sorts of innuendo and suspicion. If we win, on the other hand, we pull his teeth."

"Win?" Garion snorted. "You've learned very quickly in the past week or so, but the knights we'll be facing have been practicing all their lives. I don't think we're in any real danger of winning."

"A compromise then?" 'Zakath asked slyly.

"What have you got in mind?"

"If we win the tournament, there's almost nothing the king won't grant us, right?"

"That's usually the way it works."

"Wouldn't he be more than happy to let Belgarath have a look at that chart? I'm sure he knows where it is—or he can compel Naradas to produce it."

"You've got a point there, I suppose."

"You're a sorcerer. You can fix it so that we win, can't you?"

"Wouldn't that be cheating?"

"You're very inconsistent, Garion. First you suggest that we deliberately fall off our horses, and that's cheating, too, isn't it? I'll tell you what, my friend. I'm the Emperor of Mallorea. You have my imperial permission to cheat. Now, is there a way you can do it?"

Garion thought about it and then remembered something. "Do you remember the time I told you that I had to stop a war in order to get Mandorallen and Nerina safely married?"

"Yes?"

"This is how I did it. Most lances break sooner or later. By the time this tournament is over, the lists will be ankle-deep in splinters. On the day I stopped that war, though, *my* lance would *not* break, and I sort of surrounded it with pure force. It was very effective. Nobody, not even the best knights in all of Mimbre, stayed on his horse that day."

"I thought you said you conjured up a thunderstorm."

"That was a little later. The two armies were facing each other across an open field. Not even Mimbrates would charge across a field where lightning was blowing big holes in the turf. They're not *that* stupid."

"You've had a remarkable career, my young friend." 'Zakath laughed.

"I had a bit of fun that day," Garion admitted. "It's not too often that one man gets to bully two complete armies. I got into a great deal of trouble about it later, though. When you tamper with the weather, you can't be sure just what the consequences are going to be. Belgarath and Beldin spent the next six months running around the world quieting things down. Grandfather was *very* cross when he got back. He called me all sorts of names, and 'blockhead' was about the mildest."

"You mentioned something called 'lists.' What are they?"

"They sink posts into the ground and fasten a long, heavy pole to the tops of them. The pole is about shoulder high on a horse. The knights who are jousting ride toward each other on opposite sides of the pole. I think the idea is to keep the horses from running into each other. Good horses are expensive. Oh, that reminds me of something else. We're going to have a certain advantage in this anyway. Our horses are quite a bit bigger and stronger than the local ones."

"That's true, isn't it? I'll still feel more comfortable if you cheat, though."

"I probably will, too. If we were to do it legitimately, we'd still pick up so many bruises that neither one of us would be able to get out of bed for a week, and we've got an appointment—if we can ever find out where it's supposed to take place."

The tournament field was gaily decorated with bright-colored buntings and flapping pennons. A stand had been erected for the king, the ladies of the court, and members of the gentry too old to participate on the field. The commoners stood on the far side of the lists, watching avidly. A pair of gaily dressed jugglers was entertaining the crowd while the knights made their preparations. Brightly striped pavilions stood at either end of the lists—places for knights to have their armor repaired and places where the injured could suffer out of sight, since watching people groaning and writhing tends to dampen an otherwise enjoyable afternoon.

"I'll be right back," Garion told his friend. "I want to talk with Grandfather for a moment." He dismounted and crossed the bright-green turf to the end of the stand where Belgarath sat. The old man was wearing a snowy white robe and a disgruntled expression.

"Elegant," Garion said.

"It's somebody's idea of a joke," Belgarath said.

"Your obvious antiquity shines in your face, old friend," Silk said impudently from just behind him. "People instinctively want to make you as dignified-looking as possible."

"Do you mind? What is it, Garion?"

" 'Zakath and I are going to cheat a little. If we win, the king will grant us a boon—like letting you look at that chart."

"That might actually work, you know."

"How do you cheat in a tournament?" Silk asked.

"There are ways."

"Are you *sure* you'll win?"

"I can almost guarantee it."

Silk jumped to his feet.

"Where are you going?" Belgarath demanded.

"I want to lay a few wagers." And the little man scurried off.

"He never changes," Belgarath observed.

"One thing, though. Naradas is here. He's a Grolim, so he'll know what we're doing. Please, Grandfather, keep him off my neck. I don't want him tampering with what I'm doing at some crucial moment."

"I'll handle him," Belgarath said bleakly. "Go out there and do your best, but be careful."

"Yes, Grandfather." Garion turned and went back to where 'Zakath waited with their horses.

"We'll stand in the second or third rank," Garion said. "It's customary to let the winners of previous tournaments joust first. It makes us look properly modest, and it'll give you a chance to see how to approach the lists." He looked around. "We'll have to surrender our lances before we joust; and they'll give us each one of those blunted ones from that rack over there. I'll take care of them as soon as we get our hands on them."

"You're a devious young man, Garion. What's Kheldar doing? He's running through those stands like a pickpocket hard at work."

"As soon as he heard what we're planning, he went out to place a few wagers."

'Zakath suddenly burst out laughing. "I wish I'd known. I'd have given him some money to wager for me, as well."

"Getting it back from him might have been a little difficult, though."

Their friend, Baron Astellig, was unhorsed on the second pass. "Is he all right?" 'Zakath asked with concern.

"He's still moving," Garion said. "He probably just broke one of his legs."

"At least we won't have to fight him. I hate hurting friends. Of course, I don't have all that many friends."

"You probably have more than you realize."

After the third pass of the front rank, 'Zakath said, "Garion, have you ever studied fencing?"

"Alorns don't use light swords, 'Zakath. Except for the Algars."

"I know, but the theory is similar. If you twist your wrist or elbow at the last instant, you could knock your opponent's lance aside. Then you could correct your aim and smash into the center of his shield when his lance is completely out of position. He wouldn't have a chance at that point, would he?"

Garion considered it. "It's highly unorthodox," he said dubiously.

"So's using sorcery, isn't it? Would it work?"

" 'Zakath, you're using a fifteen-foot lance, and it weighs about two pounds a foot. You'd need arms like a gorilla to move it around that fast."

"Not really. You don't really have to move it that far back and forth. Just a tap would do. Can I try it?"

"It's your idea. I'll be here to pick you up if it doesn't work."

"I knew I could count on you." 'Zakath's voice sounded excited—even boyish.

"Oh, Gods," Garion murmured almost in despair.

"Anything wrong?" 'Zakath asked.

"No, I guess not. Go ahead and try it, if you feel that you have to."

"What difference does it make? I can't get hurt, can I?"

"I wouldn't go entirely that far. Do you see that?" Garion pointed at a knight who had just been unhorsed and had come down on his back across the center pole of the lists, scattering bits and pieces of his armor in all directions.

"He's not really hurt, is he?"

"He's still moving—a little bit—but they'll need a blacksmith to get him out of his armor before the physicians can go to work on him."

"I still think it might work," 'Zakath said stubbornly.

"We'll give you a splendid funeral if it doesn't. All right. It's our turn. Let's go get our lances."

The blunted lances were padded at the tip with layer upon layer of woolly sheepskin tightly wrapped in canvas. The result was a round padded ball that looked totally humane, but which Garion knew would hurl a man from his saddle with terrific force, and it was not the impact of the lance that broke bones, rather it was the violent contact with the ground. He was a bit distracted at the point when he began to focus his will, and so the best words he could come up with as a release for that will was "Make it that way." He was not entirely positive that it worked exactly as he had planned. His first opponent was hurled from his saddle at a point some five feet before Garion's lance touched his shield. Garion adjusted the aura of force around their lances. 'Zakath's technique, Garion saw with some surprise, worked flawlessly. A single, almost unnoticeable, twist of his forearm deflected his opponent's lance, and then his own blunted lance smashed directly into the center of the knight's shield. A man hurled forcefully from the back of a charging horse flies through the air for quite some distance, Garion noticed, and the crash when he hits the ground sounds much like that which might come from a collapsing smithy. Both their opponents were carried senseless from the field.

It was a bad day for the pride of Perivor. As their experience with their enhanced weapons increased, the Rivan King and the Emperor of Mallorea quite literally romped through the ranks of the steel-clad knights of Perivor, filling the dispensaries with row upon row of groaning injured. It was more than a rout. It soon reached disastrous proportions. At last, with even their unthinking Mimbrate heritage sobered by the realization that they were facing an invincible pair, the knights of Perivor gathered and took counsel with each other. And then, en masse, they yielded.

"What a shame," 'Zakath said regretfully. "I was starting to enjoy this."

Garion decided to ignore that.

As the two started back toward the stands to make the customary salute to the king, white-eyed Naradas came forward with an oily smile. "Congratulations, Sir Knights," he said. "Ye are men of great prowess and extraordinary skill. Ye have won the field and the laurels of the day. Mayhap ye have heard of the great prize of honor and glory that is to be bestowed upon the champions of this field?"

"No," Garion said flatly. "I can't say that we have."

"Ye have contested this day for the honor of subduing a troublesome beast that betimes hath disturbed the peace of our fair kingdom."

"What kind of beast?" Garion asked suspiciously.

"Why, a dragon, of course, Sir Knight."

CHAPTER FOURTEEN

"He's tricked us again, hasn't he?" Beldin growled when they had returned to their quarters following the tourney. "White-eyes is beginning to irritate me just a bit. I think I'll take some steps."

"Too noisy," Belgarath told him. "The people here are not entirely Mimbrate." He turned to Cyradis. "There's a certain sound sorcery makes," he said.

"Yes," she replied. "I know."

"Can *you* hear it?"

She nodded.

"Are there other Dals here on the island who can hear it, as well?"

"Yes, Ancient Belgarath."

"How about these counterfeit Mimbrates? They're at least half Dal. Is it possible that some of them might be able to hear it, too?"

"Entirely so."

"Grandfather," Garion said in a worried tone, "that means that half the people in Dal Perivor heard what I did to the lances."

"Not over the noise of the crowd, they didn't."

"I didn't know that would make a difference."

"Of course it does."

"Well," Silk said grimly, "I won't use sorcery, and I can guarantee that there won't be any noise."

"But there *will* be a certain amount of evidence, Kheldar," Sadi pointed out, "and since we're the only strangers in the palace, there might be some embarrassing questions if they find Naradas with one of your daggers sticking out of his back. Why don't you let me handle it? I can make things look much more natural."

"You're talking about cold-blooded murder, Sadi," Durnik accused.

"I appreciate your sensibilities, Goodman Durnik," the eunuch replied, "but

Naradas has already tricked us twice and, each time he does, he delays us that much more. We have to get him out of the way."

"He's right, Durnik," Belgarath said.

"Zith?" Velvet suggested to Sadi.

He shook his head. "She won't leave her babies—not even for the pleasure of biting someone. I have a few other things that are just as effective. They're not quite as fast perhaps, but they get the job done."

" 'Zakath and I still have to come up against Zandramas," Garion said glumly, "and this time we'll have to do it alone—because of that stupid tournament."

"It won't be Zandramas," Velvet told him. "Ce'Nedra and I spoke with some of the young ladies here at court while you two were out there being magnificent. They told us that this 'fearsome beast' has been showing up from time to time for centuries now, and Zandramas has only been active for a dozen years, hasn't she? I really think the dragon you'll be fighting will be the real one."

"I'm not so sure, Liselle," Polgara disagreed. "Zandramas can take the form of that dragon at any time. If the real one is asleep in her lair, it could very well be Zandramas who's been out there terrorizing the countryside this time—all as a part of the scheme to force a confrontation *before* we get to the place of the meeting."

"I'll know which it is as soon as I get a look at it," Garion said.

"How?" 'Zakath asked him.

"The first time we met, I cut off about four feet of her tail. If the one we run into out there has a stub tail, we'll know it's Zandramas."

"Do we really *have* to go to this celebration tonight?" Beldin asked.

"It's expected, uncle," Aunt Pol told him.

"But I haven't got a single solitary thing to wear, don't y' know," he said roguishly, lapsing back into Feldegast's brogue.

"We'll take care of you, uncle," she said ominously.

The affair that evening had been weeks in the planning. It was the grand finale of the tournament, and it involved dancing—in which Garion and 'Zakath, still in armor, could not participate. It involved a banquet—which, visored, they could not eat. And it involved a great many flowery toasts to "these mighty champions, who have lent luster to our remote isle by their presence here," as the nobles in the court of King Oldorin vied with one another to heap extravagant praise on Garion and 'Zakath.

"How long is this likely to go on?" 'Zakath muttered to Garion.

"Hours."

"I was afraid you might say that. Here come the ladies."

Polgara, flanked by Ce'Nedra and Velvet, entered the throne room almost as if she owned it. Cyradis, strangely—or perhaps not—was not with them. Polgara, as usual, was gowned in royal-blue velvet trimmed with silver. She looked magnificent. Ce'Nedra wore a cream-colored gown much like her wedding dress, although the seed pearls that had adorned her nuptial gown were missing. Her wealth of copper-colored hair spilled down in curls over one shoulder. Velvet was gowned in lavender satin. Any number of the young knights of Perivor—those who could still walk after the day's entertainment—were hopelessly smitten by the sight of her.

"Time for some obscure introductions, I think," Garion muttered to 'Zakath. Pleading the necessity for anonymity, the ladies had remained in their quarters since their arrival. Garion stepped forward and escorted them to the throne. "Your Majesty," he said to King Oldorin, bowing slightly, "though I may not, by reason or our need for concealment, tell thee in fulsome detail of their lands of origin, it would be discourteous of me—to both thee and to the ladies themselves—not to present them. I have the honor to present her Grace, the Duchess of Erat." That was safe. Nobody on this side of the world would have the faintest idea where Erat was.

Polgara curtsied with exquisite grace. "Your Majesty," she greeted the king in her rich voice.

He rose to his feet with alacrity. "Your Grace," he replied with a deep bow. "Thy presence here illuminates our poor palace."

"And, your Majesty," Garion went on, "her Highness, Princess Xera." Ce'Nedra stared at him. "Your real name might be too well known," he whispered to her.

Ce'Nedra recovered instantly. "Your Majesty," she said with a curtsy every bit as graceful as Polgara's. After all, a girl can't grow up in an imperial court without learning a *few* things.

"Your Highness," the king responded. "Thy beauty doth rob my poor tongue of speech."

"Isn't he nice?" Ce'Nedra murmured.

"And lastly, your Majesty," Garion concluded, "but certainly not the least, the Margravine of Turia," he introduced Velvet, making the name up on the spur of the moment.

Velvet curtsied. "Your Majesty," she said. When she straightened, she was smiling, leveling the full impact of her dimples upon him.

"My Lady—" The king faltered, bowing once again "—thy smile doth stop my heart." He looked around, a bit puzzled. "Methinks I do remember another lady among thy companions, Sir Knight," he said to Garion.

"A poor blind girl, your Majesty," Polgara interceded, "who hath but recently joined us. Courtly entertainments, I fear, would be lost on one who lives in darkness perpetual. She is in the care of the enormous man in our company, one of her family's faithful retainers, who hath guided and protected her since the melancholy occasion when the light of day forever vanished from her eyes."

Two great tears of sympathy trickled down the king's cheeks. Arends, even transplanted ones, were, after all, an emotional people.

Then Garion's other companions entered, and Garion was glad that his visor hid his grin. Beldin's face was like a thundercloud. His hair and beard had been washed and combed, and he wore a blue robe not unlike Belgarath's white one. Garion proceeded with a group of introductions as fraudulent as the previous ones, concluding with, "And this, your Majesty, is Master Feldegast, a supremely talented jester, whose rare japes do lighten the weary miles for us all."

Beldin scowled at him and then made a cursory bow. "Ah, yer Majesty, 'tis overwhelmed I am by the splendor of yer city an' yer magnificent palace here. 'Tis a match fer Tol Honeth, Mal Zeth, an' Melcene—all of which places I have seen in th' plyin' of me trade an' demonstratin' me unspeakable talents, don't y' know."

The king was grinning broadly. "Master Feldegast," he said, inclining his head. "In a world full of sorrow, such men as thou art rare and precious."

"Ah, isn't it grand of y' t' say it, yer Majesty?"

Then, with the formalities over, Garion and the others drifted away to mingle. A determined-looking young lady advanced on Garion and 'Zakath. "You are the greatest knights on life, my Lords," she greeted them with a curtsy, "and the exalted stations of your companions do proclaim louder than words that ye are both men of high, mayhap even royal, rank." She gave Garion a smoldering look. "Art thou perchance betrothed, Sir Knight?" she asked.

Another one of those repetitions, Garion groaned inwardly. "Married, my Lady," he replied. This time he knew how to deal with the situation.

"Ah," she said, her eyes clearly disappointed. Then she turned to 'Zakath. "And thou, my Lord?" she asked. "Art thou espoused, as well—or betrothed, perchance?"

"Nay, my Lady," 'Zakath answered, sounding puzzled.

Her eyes brightened.

Garion stepped in at that point. "It is time, my friend, for thee to consume yet another draft of that admittedly foul-tasting potion."

"Potion?" 'Zakath asked in a baffled voice.

Garion sighed. "Thy malady worsens, I perceive," he said, feigning a sorrowful voice. "This forgetfulness of thine is, I fear me, a precursor of the more violent symptoms that will inevitably ensue. Pray to all seven Gods that we may conclude our quest ere the hereditary madness, the curse of thy family, o'erwhelms thee quite."

The determined-looking young lady backed away, her eyes wide with fright.

"What *are* you talking about, Garion?" 'Zakath muttered.

"I've been through this before. The girl was looking for a husband."

"That's absurd."

"Not to her, it wasn't."

And then the dancing started. Garion and 'Zakath drew off to one side to watch. "It's a silly pastime, isn't it?" 'Zakath observed. "I've never known why any sane man would choose to waste time on it."

"Because the ladies love to dance," Garion told him. "I've never met one who didn't. It's in their blood, I think." He looked toward the throne and saw that King Oldorin was unoccupied at the moment. He sat smiling and tapping his foot in time to the music. "Let's find Belgarath and go talk with the king. This might be a good time to ask about that chart."

Belgarath was leaning against one of the buttresses, watching the dancers with a slightly bored look on his face. "Grandfather," Garion said to him, "nobody's talking to the king right now. Why don't we go ask him about that map?"

"Good idea. This party's likely to last well into the night, so there won't be much chance for a private audience."

They approached the throne and bowed. "Might we have a word with thee, your Majesty?" Garion asked.

"Of course, Sir Knight. Thou and thy companion are my champions, and it would be churlish of me indeed not to lend an ear to thee. What is this matter that concerns thee?"

"It is but a small thing, your Majesty. Master Garath here—" Garion had dropped the "Bel" in making the introduction "—as I told thee earlier, is mine eldest advisor and he hath guided my steps since earliest childhood. In addition, he is a scholar of some note and hath recently turned his attention to the study of geography. There hath been a long-standing dispute among geographers concerning the configuration of the world of antiquity. By purest chance, Master Garath happened to hear of an ancient chart that, his informant assured him, is kept here in the palace in Dal Perivor. Beset by raging curiosity, Master Garath hath implored me to inquire of thee if thou knowest if such a chart doth indeed exist, and if perchance thou dost, if thou wilt give him permission to peruse it."

"Indeed, Master Garath," the king said, "I do assure thee that thine informant was not in error. The chart thou seekest is one of our most prized relics, for it is the selfsame chart that guided our ancestors to the shores of this isle eons ago. As soon as we have leisure, I will be most happy to provide thee access to it in furtherance of thy studies."

Then Naradas stepped from behind the purple drape at the back of the throne. "There will be, I fear me, scant time for studies for some while, your Majesty," he said, sounding just a bit smug. "Forgive me, my King, but I chanced to overhear thy last remark as I was hurrying to bring thee perhaps distressing news. A messenger hath arrived from the east advising that the foul dragon doth even now ravage the village of Dal Esta not three leagues from here. The beast is unpredictable in its depredations and may lurk in the forest for days ere it emerge again. It well may be that this tragic occurrence is to our advantage. Now is the time to strike. What better opportunity than this for our two brave champions to sally forth and rid us of this nuisance? And I do perceive that these powerful knights do rely heavily upon the advice of this ancient man, and it is fitting therefore that he should accompany them to guide their strategy."

"Well spoken, Erezel," the silly king agreed enthusiastically. "I had feared me that flushing the beast from hiding might have consumed weeks. Now it is accomplished in the space of a single night. Venture forth then, my champions and Master Garath. Rid my kingdom of this dragon, and no boon ye ask shall be denied thee."

"Thy happy discovery was timely, Master Erezel," Belgarath said. The words were bland, but Garion knew his grandfather well enough to recognize their implication. "As his Majesty hath said, thou hast saved us much time this night. As soon as I have leisure, I will think of some way to thank thee properly."

Naradas shrank back slightly, his face apprehensive. "No thanks are necessary, Master Garath," he said. "I did no more than my duty to my king and his realm."

"Ah, yes," Belgarath said, "duty. We all have many duties, don't we? Commend me to the Child of Dark when next thou prayest to her. Advise her that, as is fore-ordained, we shall meet anon."

Then he turned and, with Garion and 'Zakath close behind him, he strode out among the dancers and left the throne room. So long as he had been in the presence of strangers, the old man's expression had been neutral. Once they reached the deserted corridor, however, he began to swear savagely. "I was right on the verge of getting my hands on that chart," he fumed. "Naradas has done it to me again."

"Should I go back and get the others?" Garion asked.

"No. They'd all want to go along, and that'd only start an argument. We'll leave a note."

"Again?"

"These repetitions are cropping up more and more regularly, aren't they?"

"Let's hope Aunt Pol doesn't react the same way this time."

"What are you two talking about?" 'Zakath asked.

"Silk, Grandfather, and I slipped out of Riva when we went to meet Torak," Garion explained. "We left a note, but Aunt Pol didn't take it too well. As I understand it, there was a lot of swearing and a number of explosions."

"Lady Polgara? She's the very soul of gentility."

"Don't be deceived, 'Zakath," Belgarath told him. "Pol's got a vile temper when things don't go the way she wants them to go."

"It must be a family trait," 'Zakath said blandly.

"Are you trying to be funny? You two go down to the stables. Tell the grooms to saddle our horses and find out where this village is. I want to talk with Cyradis a moment before we leave. I'm going to get some straight answers out of that girl. I'll join you in the courtyard in a few minutes."

It was perhaps ten minutes later when they mounted. Garion and 'Zakath took their lances from the rack at the stable wall, and then the three of them rode out of the palace compound. "Any luck with Cyradis?" Garion asked Belgarath.

"Some. She told me that the dragon out there is *not* Zandramas."

"It's the real one then?"

"Probably. She got cryptic on me then, though. She said that there's some other spirit influencing the dragon. That means you'll both have to be very careful. The dragon's very stupid normally, but if some spirit's guiding her, she might be a bit more perceptive."

A shadow slunk from a dark side street. It was the she-wolf.

"How is it with you, little sister?" Garion greeted her formally. At the last instant, he avoided calling her "Grandmother."

"One is content," she replied. "You go to hunt. One will accompany you."

"One must advise you that the creature we seek is not fit for eating."

"One does not hunt only to eat."

"We will be glad of your company then."

"What did she say?" 'Zakath asked.

"She wants to go along."

"Did you warn her that it's going to be dangerous?"

"I think she already knows."

"It's up to her." Belgarath shrugged. "Trying to tell a wolf what to do is an exercise in futility."

They passed out through the city gate and took the road to which one of the grooms had directed Garion. "He said it's about eight miles," Garion said.

Belgarath squinted up at the night sky. "Good," he said, "there's a full moon. Let's try a gallop until we get to about a mile from that village."

"How will we know when we're that close?" 'Zakath asked.

"We'll know," Belgarath replied bleakly. "There'll be all kinds of fire."

"They don't *really* breathe fire, do they?"

"Yes, as a matter of fact, they do. You're both wearing armor, so that makes it a little safer. Her sides and belly are a bit softer than her back. Try to get your lances into her, then finish her off with your swords. Let's not drag this out. I want to get back to the palace and get my hands on that map. Let's ride."

It was about an hour later when they saw the red glow of fire just ahead. Belgarath reined in. "Let's go carefully," he said. "We'll want to pinpoint her location before we go charging in there."

"One will go look," the she-wolf said, and loped off into the darkness.

"I'm glad she came along," Belgarath said. "For some reason it's comforting to have her around."

Garion's visor concealed his smile.

The village of Dal Esta was perched on a hilltop, and they could see the sooty red flames shooting up out of burning barns and houses. They rode up the hill a ways and found the wolf waiting for them. "One has seen the creature we seek," she advised. "It is feeding just now on the other side of that hill where the dens of the man-things are."

"What's it feeding on?" Garion asked apprehensively.

"A beast such as the one upon which you sit."

"Well?" 'Zakath asked.

"The dragon's on the other side of the village," Belgarath told him. "She's eating a horse just now."

"A *horse*? Belgarath, this isn't a good time for surprises. Just how big is that thing?"

"About the size of a house—that's not counting the wings, of course."

'Zakath swallowed hard. "Could we perhaps reconsider this? I haven't taken much joy in my life until recently. I'd sort of like to savor it a little longer."

"I'm afraid we're committed now," Garion told him. "She doesn't fly very fast, and it takes her quite a while to get off the ground. If we can surprise her while she's eating, we might be able to kill her before she attacks."

They rode carefully around the hill, noting the trampled crops and the carcasses of half-eaten cows. There were a few other dead things, as well—things at which Garion carefully avoided looking.

And then they saw it. "Torak's teeth!" 'Zakath swore. "It's bigger than an elephant!"

The dragon was holding down the carcass of a horse with its front claws, and she was not so much feeding as she was ravening.

"Give it a try," Belgarath said. "She's usually a bit unwary when she's eating. Be careful, though. Get clear of her as soon as you sink your lances into her. And don't let your horses go down. She'll kill them if they do, and a man on foot is at a serious disadvantage when he's fighting a dragon. Our little sister and I will slip around to the rear and attack her tail. She's sensitive there, and a few bites might distract her." He dismounted, walked some distance away from the horses, and blurred into the shape of the great silver wolf.

"That still unnerves me," 'Zakath admitted.

Garion had been looking carefully at the feeding dragon. "Notice that she has her wings raised," he said quietly. "With her head down like that, they block her vision toward the rear. You go around to that side, and I'll go to this one. When we both get into position, I'll whistle. That's when we'll charge. Go in as fast as you can and try to stay behind that upraised wing. Sink your lance as deep into her as you can and leave it stuck in. A couple of lances hanging out of her should impede her movements a bit. Once you get the lance in, wheel and get out of there."

"You're awfully cold-blooded about this, Garion."

"In this kind of situation you almost have to be. If you stop to think about it, you'll never do it. This isn't the most rational thing we've ever done, you know. Good luck."

"You, too."

They separated and moved out slowly at some distance from the feeding dragon until they had flanked her on either side. 'Zakath dipped his lance twice to indicate that he was in position. Garion drew in a deep breath. He noticed that his hands were shaking slightly. He shook off all thought and concentrated on a spot just behind the dragon's front shoulder. Then he whistled shrilly.

They charged.

As far as it went, Garion's strategy worked quite well. The dragon's scaly hide, however, was much tougher than he had expected, and their lances did not penetrate as deeply as he might have wished. He wheeled Chretienne and rode away at a dead run.

The dragon shrieked, belching fire, and she tried to turn toward Garion. As he had hoped, the lances protruding from her sides impeded her movements. Then Belgarath and the she-wolf darted in, savagely biting and tearing at the scaly tail. Desperately the dragon began to flap her sail-like wings. She rose ponderously into the air, screeching and belching out fire.

"She's getting away!" Garion threw the thought at his grandfather.

"She'll be back. She's a very vindictive beast."

Garion rode past the dead horse and rejoined 'Zakath.

"The wounds we inflicted are probably mortal, aren't they?" the Mallorean said hopefully.

"I wouldn't count on it," Garion replied. "We didn't get the lances in deep enough, I'm afraid. We should have backed off another hundred yards to pick up more momentum. Grandfather says that we can expect her back."

"Garion," Belgarath's voice sounded in his mind, *"I'm going to do something. Tell 'Zakath not to panic."*

" 'Zakath," Garion said, "Grandfather's going to use sorcery of some kind. Don't get excited."

"What's he going to do?"

"I don't know. He didn't tell me." Then Garion felt the familiar surge and rush of sound. The air around them turned a pale azure.

"Colorful," 'Zakath said. "What's it supposed to do?" His voice sounded nervous.

Belgarath came padding out of the darkness. "Good enough," he said in the language of wolves.

"What is it?" Garion asked.

"It's a kind of a shield. It'll protect you from the fire—at least partially. The armor should take care of the rest. You might get singed a bit, but the fire won't really hurt you. Don't get *too* brave, though. She still has claws and fangs."

"It's a shield of sorts," Garion told 'Zakath. "It should help to protect us from the flame."

Then from off to the east there was a scream and a sooty belch of fire up in the sky. "Get ready!" Garion said sharply. "She's coming back!" Cautioning the Orb to behave itself, he drew Iron-grip's sword. 'Zakath also pulled his broadsword from its sheath with a steely hiss. "Spread out," Garion said. "Get far enough away so that she can attack only one of us at a time. If she comes at you, I'll attack her from behind. If she comes at me, you do the same. If you can manage it, try for her tail. She goes all to pieces when somebody attacks that. She'll try to turn around to protect it. Then whichever one of us is in front of her might be able to get a clear swing at her neck."

"Right," 'Zakath said.

They fanned out again, tensely awaiting the dragon's attack.

Their lances, Garion saw, had been bitten off, leaving only short stumps protruding from the dragon's sides. It was upon 'Zakath that she fell, and the force of her strike knocked him out of his saddle. He floundered, trying to get to his feet as the dragon bathed him in flames.

Again and again he struggled, trying to get up, but he instinctively flinched back from each billow of flame, and the dragon's raking talons dug at him, making it impossible for him to regain his feet. Snakelike, the dragon's head darted forward, her cruel fangs screeching across his armor.

Garion discarded his strategy at that point. His friend needed immediate protection. He leaped from his saddle to run to 'Zakath's aid. "I need some fire!" he barked at the Orb, and his sword immediately burst into bright-blue flame. He knew that Torak had made the dragon invincible to common sorcery on the day he had created her, but he hoped that she might not be immune to the power of the Orb. He stepped in front of 'Zakath's struggling body and drove the dragon back with great, two-handed strokes. Iron-grip's sword sizzled each time it bit into her face, and she shrieked in pain with every stroke. She did not, however, flee.

"Get up!" Garion shouted to 'Zakath. "Get on your feet!" Behind him he could hear the rattling of 'Zakath's armor as the Mallorean struggled to rise. Suddenly ignoring the pain Garion's blows were causing her, the dragon clawed at him with her talons, knocking him off balance. He stumbled backward and fell on top of 'Zakath. The dragon shrieked in triumph and lunged in. Desperately Garion stabbed with his sword, and with a great, sizzling hiss, her bulging left eyeball collapsed. Even as he struggled to get back up again, a strange notion came to Garion. It was the same eye. Torak's left eye had been destroyed by the power of the Orb, and now the same thing had happened to the dragon. Despite the dreadful danger they were in, Garion was suddenly certain that they would win.

The dragon had fallen back, bellowing in pain and rage. Garion took advantage of that. He scrambled to his feet and yanked 'Zakath up. "Get around to her left side!" he barked. "She's blind on that side now! I'll keep her attention! You swing at her neck!"

They separated, moving fast to get into position before the dragon could recover. Garion swung his great, blazing sword as hard as he could and opened a huge wound across the dragon's snout. The blood spurted out, drenching his armor, and the dragon answered his blow with a billow of flame that engulfed him. He ignored the fire and drove in, swinging stroke after stroke at her face. He could see 'Zakath directing two-handed blows at the snakelike neck, but the heavy, overlapping scales defeated his best efforts. Garion continued his attack with the burning sword. The half-blinded dragon clawed at him, and he struck at the scaly forepaw, half severing it. Injured now almost beyond endurance, the dragon began a grudging, step-by-step retreat.

"Keep on her!" Garion shouted to 'Zakath. "Don't give her time to set herself again!"

Grimly the pair drove the hideous beast back and back, alternating their blows. When Garion struck, the dragon turned her head to bathe him in fire. Then 'Zakath would swing at the unprotected back of her head. She would swivel her head to meet his attack, and then Garion would strike at her. Confused and frustrated by this deadly tactic, the dragon helplessly swung her head back and forth, her furnace-like breath singeing bushes and turf more often than it did her attackers. Finally, driven beyond her ability to bear the pain, she began to desperately flap her sail-like wings, clumsily attempting to rise from the earth.

"Don't let up!" Garion called. "Keep pushing her!" They continued their savage attack. "Try to get her wings!" Garion yelled. "Don't let her get away!"

They switched their attack to the batlike wings, desperately striving to cripple the dragon's final option, but her armored skin defeated their purpose. Ponderously she rose into the air, and still shrieking, belching flame, and streaming blood from her many wounds, she flew off toward the east.

Belgarath had resumed his own form and he strode up to them, his face livid with rage. "Are you two insane?" he almost screamed at them. "I told you to be careful!"

"Things got a little out of hand there, Belgarath," 'Zakath panted. "We didn't have much choice in the matter." He looked at the Rivan King. "You saved my life again, Garion," he said. "You're starting to make a habit of that."

"It sort of seemed like the thing to do," Garion replied, sinking exhausted to the ground. "We're still going to have to chase her down, though. If we don't, she'll only come back."

"One does not think so," the she-wolf said. "One has had much experience with wounded beasts. You poked sticks into her, put out her eye, and cut her face and forepaw with fire. She will return to her den and remain there until she heals—or dies."

Garion quickly translated for 'Zakath.

"It presents a problem, though," the emperor of Mallorea said dubiously. "How are we going to persuade the king that we've driven her off for good? If we'd have killed her, we'd have no further obligation, but the king—with Naradas prompting him—might very well insist that we stay here until he's sure she's not coming back."

Belgarath was frowning. "I think Cyradis was right," he said. "The dragon wasn't behaving exactly right. Each time Garion hit her with that burning sword, she flinched momentarily."

"Wouldn't you have?" 'Zakath asked him.

"This is a little different. The dragon herself wouldn't even feel fire. She was being directed by something—something that the Orb can injure. I'll talk it over with Beldin when we get back. As soon as you two get your breath, we'll round up the horses. I want to get back to Dal Perivor and have a look at that map."

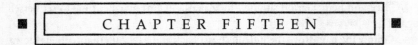

CHAPTER FIFTEEN

It was nearly dawn by the time they returned to the palace, and to their surprise, they found nearly everyone awake. A ripple of gasps ran through the throne room as Garion and 'Zakath entered. Garion's armor was scorched and red with the dragon's blood; 'Zakath's surcoat was charred, and great fang marks scarred one side of his breastplate. The condition of their armor gave mute testimony to the seriousness of the encounter.

"My glorious champions!" the king exulted as they entered the throne room. It appeared to Garion at first that the king was leaping to a conclusion—that because they had returned alive, they had succeeded in killing the dragon.

"In all the years that this foul beast hath been ravaging this realm," the king said, however, "this is the first time anyone hath forced it to flee." Then, noting Belgarath's puzzled look, he elaborated. "Not two hours ago, we observed the dragon flying over the city, shrieking in pain and fright."

"Which way did it go, your Majesty?" Garion asked.

"It was last seen flying out to sea, Sir Knight, and, as all men know, its lair lies somewhere to the west. The chastisement thou and thy valiant companion administered hath driven it from the realm. Doubtless it will seek shelter in its lair and lick its wounds there. Now, an it please ye, our ears hunger for an account of what transpired."

"Let me," Belgarath muttered. He stepped forward. "Thy two champions, your Majesty, are modest men, as befits their nobility. They would, I do fear me, be reticent in their description of their exploit out of a desire not to appear boastful. Better, perhaps, that I describe the encounter for them so that your Majesty and the members of thy court receive a truer version of what actually occurred."

"Well said, Master Garath," the king replied. "True humility is the crown of any man of noble birth, but it doth, as thou sayest, ofttimes obscure the truth of an encounter such as this knight hath witnessed. Say on, I pray thee."

"Where to begin?" Belgarath mused. "Ah, well. As your Majesty knoweth, Master Erezel's timely warning that the dragon was ravaging the village of Dal Esta came not a moment too soon. Directly upon our departure from this very hall, we took to horse and rode posthaste to the aforementioned village. Great fires burned there, graphic evidence of the dragon's fiery breath, and cattle and many of the inhabitants had already been slain and partially consumed by the beast—for whom all flesh is food."

"Piteous." The king sighed.

"His commiseration is all very pretty," 'Zakath murmured to Garion, "but I wonder if he'll be willing to dip into his treasury to aid the villagers in the reconstruction of their homes."

"You mean actually to give back some of the taxes after he's gone to all the trouble of extorting them from his people?" Garion asked in mock surprise. "What a shocking thing to suggest."

"Carefully thy champions reconnoitered the area around the village," Belgarath was saying, "and they soon located the dragon, which was at that very moment feeding on the bodies of a herd of horses."

"I only saw one," 'Zakath whispered.

"Sometimes he embellishes things to make his stories more exciting," Garion whispered back.

Belgarath was warming to his subject now. "Advised by me," he said modestly, "thy champions paused to take stock of the situation. At once we all perceived that the dragon's attention was wholly riveted upon its grisly feast, and of a certainty, because of its size and savagery, it had never been given reason to be wary. The champions separated and circled around the feeding dragon that they might attack one from either side, hoping thereby to drive their lances into its vitals. Cautiously, step by step, they moved, for though they are the bravest men on life, they are not foolhardy."

There was absolute silence in the throne room as the king's court listened to the old man with that same breathless fascination Garion had seen before in the dining hall at Faldor's farm.

"Isn't he laying it on a bit thick?" 'Zakath whispered.

"It's a compulsion, I think," Garion whispered back. "Grandfather's never been able to let a good story rest on its own merits. He always feels the need for artistic enhancement."

Certain now that he had his audience's full attention, Belgarath began to utilize all those subtle tricks of the storyteller's art. He altered pitch and volume. He changed cadences. Sometimes his voice dropped to a whisper. He was obviously enjoying himself enormously. He described the simultaneous charge on the dragon in glowing detail. He told of the dragon's initial retreat, adding gratuitously a wholly fictional feeling of triumph in the hearts of the two knights and their belief that they had struck mortal blows with their lances. Though this last was not entirely true, it helped to heighten the suspense.

"I wish I'd seen *that* fight," 'Zakath murmured. "Ours was a lot more prosaic."

The old man then went on to describe the dragon's vengeful return, and, just to make things interesting, he expanded hugely on 'Zakath's mortal peril. "And then," he went on, "heedless of his own life, his stalwart companion leaped into the fray. Sick with the fear that his friend might already have received fatal injury and filled with righteous rage, he hurled himself into the very teeth of the beast with great two-handed strokes of his mighty blade."

"Were you really thinking those things?" 'Zakath asked Garion.

"Approximately."

"And then," Belgarath said, "though it may have been some trick of the flickering light coming from the burning village, methought I saw the hero's blade come all aflame. Again and again he struck, and each stroke was rewarded with rivers of bright blood and with shrieks of agony. And then, horror of horrors, a chance blow from the dragon's mighty talons hurled our champion back, and then he stumbled, and then he fell—full upon the body of his companion, who was still vainly striving to rise."

Groans of despair came from the throng crowding the throne room, even though the presence of the two heroes plainly said that they had survived.

"I admit it freely," Belgarath continued, "that I felt dark despair in my heart. But as the savage dragon sought to slay our champions, the one—I may not say his name—plunged his burning sword into the very eye of the loathsome beast."

There was a great roar of applause.

"Shrieking in pain, the dragon faltered and fell back. Our champions took advantage of this momentary opportunity to regain their feet. And then what a mighty battle ensued." Belgarath proceeded in loving detail to describe at least ten times more sword strokes than Garion and 'Zakath had actually delivered.

"If I'd swung that sword that many times, my arms would have fallen off," 'Zakath said.

"Never mind," Garion said. "He's enjoying himself."

"At last," Belgarath concluded, "unable to any longer bear the dreadful punishment, the dragon, which had never known fear before, turned and cravenly fled from the field, to pass, as your Majesty hath said, directly over this fair city toward its hidden lair, where the fear it hath learned this night will, methinks, canker far more than the wounds it received. It will, I believe, never return to thy kingdom, your Majesty, for, stupid though it may be, it will not willingly return to the place that hath been the site of so much pain. And that, your Majesty, is exactly what happened."

"Masterful!" the king said delightedly. And from the assemblage there in the throne room came thunderous applause. Belgarath turned and bowed, signaling to Garion and 'Zakath to do likewise, generously permitting them to share in the adulation.

The nobles of the court, some of them with actual tears in their eyes, pressed forward to congratulate the trio, Garion and 'Zakath for their heroism and Belgarath for his lurid description of it. Naradas, Garion noticed, stood at the king's elbow, his dead white eyes burning with hatred. "Brace yourselves," Garion warned his friends. "Naradas is planning something."

When the hubbub had died down, the white-eyed Grolim stepped to the front of the dais. "I, too, join my voice with these others in this hall to heap praise upon these mighty heroes and their brilliant advisor. Never hath this kingdom seen their match. Methinks, however, that caution is indicated here. I do fear me that Master Garath, fresh from the scene of this unutterably magnificent struggle and understandably exhilarated by what he hath witnessed, may have been too sanguine in his assessment of the dragon's present state of mind. Truly, most normal creatures would shun a place that hath been the locale of such desperate agony, but this foul, loathsome brute is no normal creature. Might it not be more probable that, given what we know of it, it will instead be consumed with rage and a hunger and a thirst for revenge? Should these mighty champions depart now, this fair and beloved kingdom would lie defenseless beneath the vengeful depredations of a creature consumed with hatred."

"I *knew* he was going to do that," 'Zakath grated.

"I am honor bound, therefore," Naradas added, "to advise his Majesty and the members of his court to consider long and well rather than make hasty decision concerning the disposition of these knights. We have seen that they are perhaps the only two on life who can face this monster with any hope of success. Of what other knights in all this land are there any of whom we can make the same statement with any degree of certainty?"

"What thou sayest may well be true, Master Erezel," the king said with surprising coolness, "but it would be churlish of me to hold them here against their will in view of the sacred nature of the quest in which they are engaged. We have delayed them here too long already. They have rendered us amply sufficient service. To insist on more would be ungrateful of us in the extreme. I thereby decree that tomorrow will be a day of celebration and of gratitude throughout the realm and shall culminate with a royal banquet at which we will honor these mighty champions and bid them a regretful farewell. I do perceive that the sun hath risen, and our champions are doubtless greatly fatigued by the rigors of the tourney of yesterday and by their encounter last night with the loathsome dragon. This day, therefore, will be a day of preparation, and tomorrow will be a day of joy and thanksgiving. Let us then to our beds for a time to refresh ourselves that we may more assiduously turn to our several tasks."

"I thought he'd never get around to that," 'Zakath said as the three of them moved through the packed throne room. "Right now I could sleep standing up."

"Please don't," Garion said. "You're wearing armor, and you'd make an awful clatter when you toppled over. I don't want to be startled out of sleep. I'm as tired as you are."

"At least you have someone to sleep with."

"Two someones, actually, counting the puppy. Puppies take an unwholesome interest in toes, I've noticed."

'Zakath laughed.

"Grandfather," Garion said, "up until now, the king has blithely gone along with anything Naradas suggested. Did you tamper with him at all?"

"I made a couple of suggestions," Belgarath admitted. "I don't usually like to do that, but the situation was a bit unusual."

It was in the corridor outside that Naradas caught up with them. "You haven't won yet, Belgarath," he hissed.

"No, probably not," Belgarath admitted with aplomb, "but then, neither have you, Naradas, and I imagine Zandramas—you've heard the name before, I trust— will be a bit cross with you when she finds out how miserably you've failed here. Maybe, if you start running right now, you can get away from her—for a while, at least."

"This isn't the end of this, Belgarath."

"Never thought it was, old boy." Belgarath reached out and insultingly patted Naradas on the cheek. "Run along now, Grolim," he advised, "while you still have your health." He paused. "Unless, of course, you'd like to challenge *me*. Considering your limited talents, I don't advise it, but that's entirely up to you."

After one startled look at the Eternal Man, Naradas fled.

"I enjoy doing that to his kind," Belgarath gloated.

"You *are* a dreadful old man, aren't you?" 'Zakath said.

"Never pretended not to be, 'Zakath." Belgarath grinned. "Let's go talk with Sadi. Naradas is starting to become an inconvenience. I think it's high time he left us."

"You'll do anything, won't you?" 'Zakath asked as they continued down the corridor.

"To get the job done? Of course."

"And when I interfered with you back in Rak Hagga, you could have blown me into nothingness, couldn't you?"

"Probably, yes."

"But you didn't. Why not?"

"Because I thought I might need you, and I saw more in you than others did."

"More than Emperor of half the world?"

"That's trash, 'Zakath," Belgarath said scornfully. "Your friend here is Overlord of the West, and he still has trouble getting his boots on the right feet."

"I do *not*!" Garion objected vehemently.

"That's probably because you've got Ce'Nedra to help you figure it out. That's what you really need, 'Zakath—a wife, someone to keep you looking reasonably presentable."

"I'm afraid that's quite out of the question, Belgarath." 'Zakath sighed.

"We'll see," the Eternal Man said.

The greetings they received in their quarters in the royal palace at Dal Perivor were not cordial.

"You old fool!" Polgara began, speaking to her father. Things deteriorated quite rapidly from there.

"You idiot!" Ce'Nedra shrieked at Garion.

"Please, Ce'Nedra," Polgara said patiently, "let *me* finish first."

"Oh, of course, Lady Polgara," the Rivan Queen agreed politely. "Sorry. You have many more years of aggravation than I do. Besides, I can get *this* one alone in bed and give him a piece of my mind."

"And you wanted *me* to get married?" 'Zakath asked Belgarath.

"It has its drawbacks," Belgarath replied calmly. He looked around. "The walls are still standing, I see, and there doesn't seem to be any evidence of explosions. Maybe, eventually, you'll grow up after all, Pol."

"Another note?" she half shrieked. "A miserable note?"

"We were pressed for time."

"The three of you went up against the dragon alone?"

"More or less—yes. The she-wolf was with us, however."

"An *animal*? That's your idea of protection?"

"She was very helpful."

At that point, Polgara began to swear—in several different languages.

"Why, Pol," he objected mildly, "you don't even know what those words mean—at least I *hope* you don't."

"Don't underestimate me, old man. This isn't over yet. All right, Ce'Nedra, it's your turn."

"I think I'd prefer to conduct my discussions with his Majesty in private—where I can be much more direct," the tiny queen said in an icy tone.

Garion winced.

Then, surprisingly, Cyradis spoke. "It was discourteous of thee, Emperor of Mallorea, to hurl thyself into mortal danger without first consulting me." Belgarath, it appeared, had been characteristically obscure in his discussion with her before they had gone forth to face the dragon, conveniently forgetting to mention what they proposed to do.

"I beg thy forgiveness, Holy Seeress," 'Zakath apologized, lapsing, perhaps unconsciously, into archaic language. "The urgency of the matter was such that there was no time for consultation."

"Nicely spoken," Velvet murmured. "We'll make a gentleman out of him yet."

'Zakath raised his visor and grinned at her—a surprisingly boyish grin.

"As it may be, Kal Zakath," Cyradis continued sternly, "know that I am wroth with thee for thy hasty and unthinking rashness."

"I am covered with confusion, Holy Seeress, that I have offended thee, and I hope that thou canst find it in thy heart to forgive mine error."

"Oh," Velvet sighed, "he'll be *just* fine. Kheldar, were you taking notes?"

"Me?" Silk sounded surprised.

"Yes. You."

There were *far* too many things going on, and Garion was hovering on the verge of exhaustion. "Durnik," he said a bit plaintively, "can you help me out of this?" He rapped his knuckles on the breastplate of his armor.

"If you wish." Even Durnik's voice sounded cold.

"Does he really *have* to sleep with us?" Garion complained about midmorning.

"He's warm," Ce'Nedra replied in a snippy tone, "which is more than I can say for some others. Besides, he sort of fills the vacancy I have in my heart—in a small way, of course."

The wolf puppy under the covers was enthusiastically licking Garion's toes, then, inevitably, fell to nibbling.

They slept for a goodly part of the day, rising about midafternoon. They sent a servant to the king, asking to be excused from this night's festivities, pleading extreme fatigue.

"Wouldn't this be a good time to ask to see that map?" Beldin asked.

"I don't think so," Belgarath replied. "Naradas is getting desperate now. He knows how unforgiving Zandramas can be, so he'll do just about anything to keep us away from that chart. He still has the king's ear, and he'll come up with all kinds of excuses to stop us. Why don't we just let him wonder about what we're up to? It might help to keep him off balance until Sadi has the chance to put him to sleep."

The eunuch bowed a bit mockingly.

"There's an alternative, Belgarath," Silk volunteered. "I could slip around a bit and fish for information. If I can pinpoint the location of the map, a bit of burglary could solve our problem."

"What if you got caught?" Durnik asked.

"Please, Durnik," Silk said in a pained voice, "don't be insulting."

"It's got some possibilities," Velvet said. "Kheldar could steal a man's teeth even if the man had his mouth closed."

"Better not chance it," Polgara told her. "Naradas is a Grolim, and he may very well have laid a few traps around that chart. He knows all of us, by reputation at least, and I'm sure he's fully aware of Silk's specialized talents."

"Do we really have to kill him?" Eriond asked sadly. "Naradas, I mean?"

"I don't think we have any choice, Eriond," Garion said. "As long as he's still alive, we'll be stumbling over him at every turn." He frowned. "It may be my imagination, but Zandramas seems very reluctant to leave the choice to Cyradis. If she can block us, she'll win by default."

"Thy perception is not altogether awry, Belgarion," Cyradis told him. "Zandramas indeed hath done all in her power to thwart my task." She smiled briefly. "I tell thee truly, she hath caused me much vexation, and were the choice to be between her and thee, well might I be tempted to choose against her by way of retribution."

"I never thought I'd hear that from one of the seers," Beldin said. "Are you actually coming down off that fence, Cyradis?"

She smiled again. "Dear, gentle Beldin," she said affectionately, "our neutrality is not the result of whim, but of duty—a duty laid upon us before even thou wast born."

Since they had slept most of the day, they talked well into the night. Garion awoke refreshed the next morning and prepared to face the day's festivities.

The nobles at the court of King Oldorin had utilized the previous day and probably half the night preparing speeches—long, flowery, and generally tedious speeches—in praise of "our heroic champions." Protected by his closed visor, Garion frequently found himself dozing—a languor brought on not by weariness, but by boredom. At one point he heard a light clang on the side of his armor.

"Ouch!" Ce'Nedra said, rubbing her elbow.

"What's the matter, dear?"

"Do you *have* to wear all that steel?"

"Yes, but you know I'm wearing it. What possessed you to try to gouge me in the ribs?"

"Habit, I suppose. Stay awake, Garion."

"I wasn't sleeping," he lied.

"Really? Why were you snoring then?"

Following the speeches, the king assessed the glassy-eyed condition of his court and called upon "Good Master Feldegast" to lighten things up.

Beldin was at his outrageous best that day. He walked on his hands; he did astonishing backflips; he juggled with amazing dexterity—all the while telling jokes in his lilting brogue. "I hope I've managed in me small way t' add t' the festivities, yer Majesty," he concluded the performance after bowing in response to the enthusiastic applause of the assemblage.

"Thou art truly a virtuoso, Master Feldegast," the king complimented him. "The memory of thy performance this day will warm many a dreary winter evening in this hall."

"Ah, yer too kind t' say it, yer Majesty." Beldin bowed.

Before the banquet got under way, Garion and 'Zakath went back to their quarters for a light meal, since they would be unable to eat in the main dining hall without raising their visors. As guests of honor, however, it was incumbent upon them to be present.

"I've never gotten very much entertainment out of watching other people eat," 'Zakath said quietly to Garion after they had entered the banquet hall and taken their seats.

"If you want entertainment, watch Beldin," Garion replied. "Aunt Pol spoke very firmly with him last night. She told him to mind his manners today. You've seen the way he usually eats. The strain of behaving himself should come very close to making him fly apart."

Naradas sat at the king's right elbow. His white eyes were uncertain—even slightly baffled. The fact that Belgarath had made no attempt to get his hands on the map obviously confused him.

And then the serving men began to bring in the banquet. The smells made Garion's mouth water, and he began to wish that he'd eaten a bit more earlier.

"I must talk with the king's chef before we leave," Polgara said. "This soup is exquisite."

Sadi chuckled slyly.

"Did I say something amusing, Sadi?"

"Just watch, Polgara. I wouldn't want to spoil it for you."

Suddenly there was a commotion at the head of the table. Naradas had half risen, clutching at his throat with his hands. His white eyes were bulging, and he was making strangling noises.

"He's choking!" the king cried out. "Someone help him!"

Several of the nobles near the head of the table leaped to their feet and began to pound the Grolim on the back. Naradas, however, continued to strangle. His tongue protruded from his mouth, and his face started to turn blue.

"Save him!" the king almost screamed.

But Naradas was beyond saving. He arched backward, stiffened, and toppled to the floor.

There were cries of dismay from all over the dining hall.

"How did you do that?" Velvet murmured to Sadi. "I'd take an oath that you were never anywhere near his food."

Sadi smirked wickedly. "I didn't have to go near his food, Liselle," he said. "The other night I took a rather careful note of his customary place at the table. He always sits to the king's right. I slipped in here an hour or so ago and anointed his spoon with a little something that makes a man's throat swell shut." He paused. "I hope he enjoyed his soup," he added. "I know *I* certainly did."

"Liselle," Silk said, "when we get back to Boktor, why don't you have a chat with your uncle? Sadi's out of work just now, and Javelin could use a man with his talents."

"It snows in Boktor, Kheldar," Sadi said with some distaste, "and I really don't like snow that much."

"You wouldn't necessarily have to be stationed in Boktor, Sadi. How would Tol Honeth suit you? You'd have to let your hair grow, though."

'Zakath leaned forward, chuckling. "Brilliant, Sadi," he added his congratulations, "and so perfectly appropriate. Naradas poisoned *me* back in Rak Hagga, and you poisoned *him* here. I'll tell you what, I'll double any offer Javelin makes you if you'll come to work for me in Mal Zeth."

" 'Zakath!" Silk exclaimed.

"The employment opportunities seem to be cropping up in all quarters of the world," Sadi observed.

"Good men are hard to find, my friend," 'Zakath told him.

The king, shaking and with his face white, was being slowly escorted from the room. As he passed their table, Garion could hear him sobbing.

Belgarath began to swear under his breath.

"What's the matter, father?" Polgara asked him.

"That idiot will be in mourning for weeks. I'll *never* get my hands on that map."

CHAPTER SIXTEEN

Belgarath was still swearing when they returned to their quarters. "I think I've outsmarted myself," he fumed. "We should have exposed Naradas before we killed him. There's no way to discredit him in the king's eyes now."

Cyradis sat at the table eating a simple meal with Toth standing protectively over her. "What hath thou wrought, Ancient One?" she asked.

"Naradas is no longer with us," he replied, "and now the king's in mourning for him. It could be weeks before he recovers his composure enough to show me that map."

Her face grew distant and Garion seemed to hear the murmur of that strange group mind. "I am permitted to aid thee in this, Ancient One," she said. "The Child of Dark hath violated the commandment we laid upon her when we assigned her this task. She sent her henchman here rather than coming to seek the chart herself. Thus certain strictures upon me are relaxed."

She leaned back in her chair and spoke briefly to Toth. He nodded and quietly left the room. "I have sent for one who will assist us," she said.

"What exactly are you going to do?" Silk asked her.

"It might be unwise of me to tell thee in advance, Prince Kheldar. Canst thou, however, discover the location of the remains of Naradas for me?"

"I should be able to do that," he replied. "I'll go ask around a bit." Then he left the room.

"And when Prince Kheldar returns with the location of dead Naradas, thou, King of Riva, and thou, Emperor of Mallorea, go even unto the king and prevail upon him in the strongest of terms to accompany you at midnight to that place, for certain truths shall be revealed to him there which may lessen his grief."

"Cyradis," Beldin sighed, "why must you always complicate things?"

She smiled almost shyly. "It is one of my few delights, gentle Beldin. To speak obscurely doth cause others to ponder my words more carefully. The dawning of understanding in them causes me a certain satisfaction."

"Not to mention the fact that it's very irritating."

"That perhaps is also a part of the delight," she agreed impishly.

"You know," Beldin said to Belgarath, "I think she's a human being after all."

It was about ten minutes later when Silk returned. "Found him," he said a bit smugly. "They've got him laid out on a bier in the chapel of Chamdar on the main floor of the palace. I looked in on him. He's really much, much more attractive with his eyes closed. The funeral's scheduled for tomorrow. It's summer, and he probably won't keep."

"What would be thine estimate of the hour, Goodman?" Cyradis asked Durnik.

The smith went to the window and looked up at the stars. "I make it about an hour before midnight," he replied.

"Go then now, Belgarion and 'Zakath. Use all the powers of persuasion at your command. It is absolutely essential that the king be in that chapel at midnight."

"We'll bring him, Holy Seeress," 'Zakath promised her.

"Even if we have to drag him," Garion added.

"I wish I knew what she was up to," 'Zakath said as he and Garion walked down the hall outside. "It might make the king a bit easier to persuade if we could tell him what to expect."

"It might also make him skeptical," Garion disagreed. "I think Cyradis is planning something fairly exotic, and some people have difficulty accepting that sort of thing."

"Oh, my, yes." 'Zakath grinned.

"His Majesty does not wish to be disturbed," one of the guards at the king's door said when they asked admission.

"Tell him, please, that it is a matter of extremest urgency," Garion said.

"I'll try, Sir Knight," the guard said dubiously, "but he is much distraught at the death of his friend."

The guard returned a few moments later. "His Majesty consents to see thee and thy companion, Sir Knight, but prithee, be brief. His suffering is extreme."

"Of course," Garion murmured.

The king's private chambers were ornate. The king himself sat in a deeply cushioned chair reading a slender volume by the light of a single candle. His face looked ravaged, and there were signs that he had been weeping. He held up the book after they had presented themselves to him. "A volume of consolation," he said. "It doth not offer much of that to me, however. How may I serve ye, Sir Knights?"

"We have come in part to offer thee our condolences, your Majesty," Garion began carefully. "Know that first grief is always sharpest. The passage of time will dull thy pain."

"But never banish it entirely, Sir Knight."

"Undoubtedly true, your Majesty. What we have come to ask of thee may seem cruel in the light of present circumstances, and we would not presume to intrude upon thee were the matter not of such supreme urgency—not to us so much as it is to thee."

"Say on, Sir Knight," the king said, a faint interest showing in his eyes.

"There are certain truths which must be revealed unto thee this very night, your Majesty," Garion went on, "and they can be revealed only in the presence of thy late friend."

"Unthinkable, Sir Knight," the king said adamantly.

"We are assured by the one who will reveal these truths that they may in some measure assuage thy sorrow. Erezel was thy dearest friend, and he would not have thee suffer needlessly."

"Truly," the king conceded. "He was a man with a great heart."

"I'm sure," Garion said.

"There is perhaps another, more personal reason for thee to visit the chapel where Master Erezel lies in state, your Majesty," 'Zakath added. "His funeral will be held, we are told, tomorrow. The ceremony will be attended by most of thy court. This night provides thee thy last opportunity to visit with him privately and to fix his well-loved features in thy memory. My friend and I will guard the chapel door to insure that thy communion with him and with his spirit shall be undisturbed."

The king considered that. "It may be even as thou sayest, Sir Knight," he conceded. "Though it may wring my heart, I would indeed look upon his face one last time. Very well, then, let us repair to the chapel." He rose and led them from the chamber.

The chapel of Chamdar, the Arendish God, was dimly lighted by a lone candle standing on the bier at the body's head. A gold-colored cloth covered the immobile form of Naradas to the chest, and his face was calm, even serene. Knowing what he did of the Grolim's career, Garion found that apparent serenity a mockery.

"We will guard the chapel door, your Majesty," 'Zakath said, "and leave thee alone with thy friend." He and Garion stepped back out into the corridor and closed the door.

"You were very smooth back there," Garion told his friend.

"You weren't so bad yourself, but smooth or rough, at least we got him here."

They stood at the door awaiting Cyradis and the others. After about a quarter of an hour, they arrived.

"Is he in there?" Belgarath asked Garion.

"Yes. We had to do a bit of fast talking, but he finally agreed."

Standing beside Cyradis was a figure robed and hooded in black. It appeared to be a woman, a Dal most likely, but it was the first time Garion had ever seen one of that race clad in any color but white. "This is the one who will aid us," the Seeress said. "Let us go in unto the king, for the hour is nigh."

Garion opened the door, and they filed in.

The king looked up in some surprise.

"Be not dismayed, King of Perivor," Cyradis said to him, "for, as thy champions have told thee, we have come to reveal truths to thee, truths which will lessen thy sorrow."

"I am grateful for thine efforts, Lady," the king replied, "but that is scarce possible. My sorrow may neither be lessened nor banished. Here lieth my dearest friend, and my heart lieth on that cold bier with him."

"Thine heritage is in part Dal, your Majesty," she said to him, "so thou art aware that many of us possess certain gifts. There are things the one you called Erezel did not tell thee ere he died. I have summoned one who will question him ere his spirit doth sink into the darkness."

"A necromancer? Truly? I have heard of such, but have never seen the art practiced."

"Knowest thou that one with such gifts cannot misspeak what the spirits reveal?"

"I understand so, yes."

"I assure thee that it is true. Let us then probe the mind of this Erezel, and see what truths he will reveal to us."

The dark-robed and hooded necromancer stepped to the bier and laid her pale, slender hands on Naradas' chest.

Cyradis began posing the questions. "Who art thou?" she asked.

"My name was Naradas," the figure in black replied in a halting, hollow voice. "I was Grolim Archpriest of the Temple of Torak at Hemil in Darshiva."

The king stared first at Cyradis and then at the body of Naradas in stunned astonishment.

"Whom didst thou serve?" Cyradis asked.

"I served the Child of Dark, the Grolim Priestess Zandramas."

"Wherefore camest thou to this kingdom?"

"My mistress sent me hither to seek out a certain chart and to impede the progress of the Child of Light to the Place Which Is No More."

"And what means didst thou use to accomplish these ends?"

"I sought out the king of this isle, a vain and foolish man, and I beguiled him. He showed me the chart which I sought, and the chart revealed to me a wonder which my shadow conveyed immediately to my mistress. Now she knows precisely where the final meeting is to take place. I prevailed upon the king's gullibility and was able to lead him into various acts which delayed the Child of Light and his companions so that my mistress might arrive at the Place Which Is No More before him and thereby avoid the necessity of leaving the issue in the hands of a certain seeress whom my mistress distrusts."

"How is it that thy mistress did not herself perform this task, which was lain upon *her* and not upon thee?" Cyradis' voice was stern.

"Zandramas had other concerns. I was her right hand, and all that I did was as if she had done the deeds herself."

"His spirit doth begin to sink out of reach, Holy Seeress," the necromancer said in a more normal tone of voice. "Ask quickly, for soon I will no longer be able to wrest further answers from him."

"What were these concerns of thy mistress which prevented her from seeking the answer to the last riddle herself as she was commanded to do?"

"A certain Grolim Hierarch from Cthol Murgos, Agachak by name, had come to Mallorea seeking the Place Which Is No More, hoping to supplant my mistress. He was the last of our race with enough power to challenge her. She met him near the barrens of Finda and killed him there." The hollow voice broke off, and then there came a despairing wail. "Zandramas!" the voice cried. "You said that I would not die! You promised, Zandramas!" The last word seemed to fall away into some unimaginable abyss.

The dark-hooded necromancer's head slumped forward, and she was shuddering violently. "His spirit has gone, Holy Seeress," she said in a weary voice. "The midnight hour is past, and he can no longer be reached."

"I thank thee," Cyradis said simply.

"I but hope, Holy Seeress, that I have been able in some small way to aid thee in thine awesome task. May I retire now? For contact with this diseased mind hath distressed me beyond measure."

Cyradis nodded briefly, and the necromancer quietly left the chapel.

The King of Perivor, his face ashen but firmly set, walked to the bier. He took hold of the golden cloth that covered Naradas to the chest and hurled it to the floor. "Some rag perhaps," he said from between clenched teeth. "I would not look upon the face of this foul Grolim more."

"I'll see what I can find, your Majesty," Durnik said sympathetically. He stepped out into the hall.

The rest stood silently by as the king, his back to the bier and his jaws clenching and unclenching, stared at the back wall of the chapel.

After a few moments, the smith returned with a torn piece of burlap, rusty and mildewed. "There was a storeroom just down the hall, your Majesty," he said. "This was plugging up a rat hole. Was it more or less what you had in mind?"

"Perfect, my friend. An it please thee, throw it over the face of that piece of carrion. I declare here unto ye all, there will *be* no funeral for this miscreant. Some ditch and a few spadefuls of earth shall be his grave."

"More than a few spadefuls I think, your Majesty," Durnik suggested prudently. "He's corrupted your kingdom enough already. We wouldn't want him to pollute it any more, would we? I'll take care of it for you."

"I like thee, my friend," the king said. "An it please thee, bury the Grolim facedown."

"We'll see to it, your Majesty," Durnik promised. He nodded to Toth, and the two of them roughly lifted the body of Naradas from the bier by the shoulders and dragged it from the chapel with its sandal-shod feet bouncing unceremoniously across the floor.

Silk stepped closer to 'Zakath. "So now we know that Agachak is dead," he said quietly to the Mallorean. "Urgit will be delighted to hear it. I don't suppose you'd be willing to send a messenger to him to let him know about it?"

"The tensions between your brother and myself have not relaxed all *that* much, Kheldar."

"Who *are* ye all?" the king demanded. "Was this so-called quest of thine mere subterfuge?"

"The time hath come for us to reveal ourselves," Cyradis said gravely. "The need for concealment is now past, for the other spies Zandramas hath set in this place without the knowledge of Naradas cannot commune with her without his aid."

"That's Zandramas, all right," Silk said. "She doesn't even trust herself."

Garion and 'Zakath raised their visors with some relief. "I know that your kingdom is isolated, your Majesty," Garion said in his normal dialect. "How much do you know of the outside world?"

"There are times when seafarers call upon this harbor," the king replied. "They bring us news as well as goods."

"And what of the events that shaped the world in times past?"

"Our forebears brought many books with them, Sir Knight, for the hours at sea are long and tedious. Among those volumes were those of history, which I have read."

"Good," Garion said. "That should make things a bit easier to explain. I am Belgarion, King of Riva," he introduced himself.

The king's eyes widened. "The Godslayer?" he asked in an awed voice.

"You've heard about that, I see," Garion said wryly.

"All the world hath heard of it. Didst thou indeed slay the God of Angarak?"

"I'm afraid so. My friend here is Kal Zakath, Emperor of Mallorea."

The king began to tremble. "What event is of such magnitude that it persuaded ye two to put aside thy hereditary enmity?"

"We'll get to that in a moment, your Majesty. The helpful fellow who's out burying Naradas is Durnik, the most recent disciple of the God Aldur. The short one there is Beldin, also a disciple, and the one with the whiskers is Belgarath the Sorcerer."

"The Eternal Man?" The king's voice was choked.

"I wish you wouldn't throw that around so much, Garion," Belgarath said in a pained tone. "Sometimes it upsets people."

"It saves time, Grandfather," Garion replied. "The tall lady with the lock of white hair is Belgarath's daughter, Polgara the Sorceress. The little one with the red hair is Ce'Nedra, my wife. The blond girl is the Margravine Liselle of Drasnia, niece to the chief of Drasnian intelligence, and the blindfolded girl who exposed Naradas is the Seeress of Kell. The big fellow who's helping Durnik is Toth, her guide, and this one is Prince Kheldar of Drasnia."

"The richest man in the world?"

"The reputation might be a trifle exaggerated, your Majesty," Silk said modestly, "but I'm working on it."

"The young fellow with blond hair is named Eriond, a very close friend."

"I am awed to be in such august company. Which of ye is the Child of Light?"

"That's the burden I bear, your Majesty," Garion told him. "Now, though it's largely a part of Alorn history and prophecy, you may know that from time to time in the past there have been meetings between the Child of Light and the Child of Dark. We're going toward the last one there's ever going to be. The meeting's going to decide the fate of the world. Our problem at the moment is discovering where the meeting's supposed to take place."

"Thy quest then is even more awesome than I had imagined, King Belgarion. I will aid thee in whatsoever way I can. The foul Grolim Naradas misled me into hindering thee. Whatever small way in which I might assist thee may serve as partial recompense for that error. I will send forth my ships to seek out the place of the meeting for thee wheresoever it may be, from the beaches of Ebal to the reef of Korim."

"The reef of *what?*" Belgarath exclaimed.

"Korim, Ancient Belgarath. It doth lie to the northwest of this isle. Its location is clearly marked upon that chart which thou hast sought. Let us repair to my chambers, and I will show thee."

"I think we've just about come to the end of it, Belgarath," Beldin said. "As soon as you take a look at that map, you'll be able to go home."

"What are you talking about?"

"That's the end of your task, old man. We certainly appreciate your efforts, though."

"You wouldn't mind *too* much if I came along, would you?"

"That's up to you, of course, but we wouldn't want to keep you from anything important you've been neglecting." Beldin's grin grew vicious. Needling Belgarath was one of his favorite forms of entertainment.

As they turned toward the chapel entrance, Garion saw the she-wolf sitting in the doorway. Her golden eyes were intent, and her tongue lolled out in a wolfly smile.

CHAPTER SEVENTEEN

They followed the king through the dimly lighted and deserted midnight halls of the palace at Perivor. A tense excitement filled Garion. They had won. No matter how hard Zandramas had tried to prevent it, they had still won. The answer to the riddle lay no more than a few yards away, and once it was answered, the meeting would take place. No power on earth could prevent it now.

"*Stop that,*" the voice in his mind told him. "*You have to be calm now—very calm. Try to think about Faldor's farm. That always seems to settle you.*"

"*Where have you—*" Garion started, then broke off.

"*Where have I what?*"

"*Never mind. The question always irritates you.*"

"*Amazing. You actually remembered something I said. Faldor's farm, Garion. Faldor's farm.*"

He did as he had been told. Though the memories had seemed to fade over the years, they suddenly returned with startling clarity. He saw the shape of the place, the sheds and barns and the kitchen, smithy, and dining hall on the lower floor, and the gallery on the second floor where the sleeping chambers were—all surrounding that central yard. He could hear the steely ring of Durnik's hammer coming from the smithy and smell the warm fragrance of freshly baked bread coming from Aunt Pol's kitchen. He saw Faldor and old Cralto and even Brill. He saw Doroon and Rundorig and, last, Zubrette—blond and pretty and artfully deceitful. A vast kind of calm came over him, not unlike the calm that had engulfed him when he had stood in the tomb of the one-eyed God in the City of Endless Night so long ago.

"That's better," the voice said. *"Try to hold on to that. You're going to have to think very clearly in the next few days and you can't do that with your mind racing every which way. You can fly to pieces after it's all over."*

"That's if I'm still around."

"We can hope." Then the voice was gone.

The guards at the king's door admitted them, and the king went directly to a cabinet, unlocked it, and removed a roll of ancient, crackling parchment. "It is much faded, I do fear," he said. "We have tried to protect it from the light, but it is very old." He went to a table and carefully unrolled the chart, weighting down the corners with books. Once again Garion felt the tense excitement as he held back slightly, reaching back into his memories of Faldor's farm to steady himself.

The King of Perivor pointed with his finger. "Here lieth Perivor," he told them, "and here doth lie the reef of Korim."

Garion knew that if he looked too long at that fateful spot on the map, the wild excitement and sense of triumph would return, so he merely glanced at it, then let his eyes rove over the rest of the map. The spellings were strangely archaic. His eyes automatically sought his own kingdom. "Ryva" it was spelled. There were also "Aryndia," "Kherech," and "Tol Nydra" as well as "Draksnya" and "Chthall Margose."

"It's misspelled," 'Zakath noted. "The proper name is the Turim reef."

Beldin began to explain, but Garion already knew the answer. "Things change," the dwarf said, "and among those things are the way we say certain words. The sounds of words shift over the centuries. The name of that reef has probably changed several times over the last few thousand years. It's a common phenomenon. If Belgarath were to speak in the language the people spoke in the village where he grew up, for example, none of us would be able to understand him. I'd guess that for a time the reef was called Torim or something like that, and it finally settled into Turim. It may change again a few times. I've made a study of that sort of thing. You see, what happens is that—"

"Will you get on with it?" Belgarath demanded in exasperation.

"Aren't you interested in expanding your education?"

"Not at the moment, no."

Beldin sighed. "Anyway," he continued, "what we call writing is just a way to reproduce the sound of a word. As the sound changes, so does the spelling. The difference is easily explained."

"Thine answer to the question was cogent, gentle Beldin," Cyradis said, "but in this particular case, the change of the sound was imposed."

"Imposed?" Silk said, "by who—whom?"

"It was the two prophecies, Prince Kheldar. In furtherance of their game, they altered the sound of the word to conceal the location from Ancient Belgarath and from Zandramas. These two were both required to solve the riddle ere the final meeting could take place."

"Game?" Silk asked incredulously. "They were playing games with something this important?"

"These two eternal awarenesses are not as we, Prince Kheldar. They contend with each other in myriad ways. Ofttimes, one will attempt to alter the course of a star, while the other strives to hold it in place. At other times, one will attempt to move a grain of sand while the other exerts all its energy to keep the grain motionless. Such struggles ofttimes consume whole eons. The riddle game they have played with Belgarath and Zandramas is but another of the ways they have used to formalize their contention, for should it ever come to pass that they confront each other directly, they would rend the universe apart."

Garion suddenly remembered an image that had come to him in the throne room at Vo Mimbre just before he had exposed the Murgo Nachak to King Korodullin. He had seemed to see two faceless players seated at a game where the moves had been so complex that his mind could not follow them. With absolute certainty now he saw that he had caught a momentary glimpse of the higher reality Cyradis had just described. *"Did you do that on purpose?"* he asked the voice in his mind.

"Naturally. You needed a bit of encouragement to get you to do something that was necessary. You're a competitive sort of boy, so I thought the image of the great game might get you started."

Then something else occurred to Garion. "Cyradis," he said, "why is it that there are so many of *us* while Zandramas appears to be almost totally alone?"

"It hath ever been thus, Belgarion. The Child of Dark is solitary, even as was Torak in his pride. Thou, however, art humble. Thou hast never pushed thyself forward, for thou knowest not thine own worth. This is endearing in thee, Child of Light, for thou art not puffed up with thine own importance. The Prophecy of Dark hath ever chosen one and one only, and hath infused that one with all its power. The Prophecy of Light, however, hath chosen to disperse its power among many. Although thou art the principal bearer of the burden, all of thy companions share it with thee. The difference between the two prophecies is simple, but it is profound."

Beldin was frowning. "You're saying that it's sort of like the difference between absolutism and shared responsibility, then?"

"It is much as thou hast said. The difference is more complex, however."

"I was just trying to be concise."

"Now that's a first," Belgarath said. Then he looked at the King of Perivor. "Can you describe this reef to us, your Majesty?" he asked. "The representation on the map isn't too precise."

"Gladly, Ancient Belgarath. In my youth I sailed thither, for the reef is something of a marvel. Seafarers assert that there is none like it in all the world. It doth consist of a series of rocky pinnacles rising from the sea. The pinnacles themselves are easy to see and therefore to avoid. Other dangers, however, lurk beneath the surface. Savage currents and tides do rush through gaps in the reef, and the weather there is ever unsettled. By reason of these perils, the reef hath never been charted in any detail. All prudent sailors avoid it entirely, giving that dangerous obstruction wide berth."

Durnik and Toth entered. "We've taken care of it, your Majesty," Durnik reported. "Naradas is safely in the ground now. He won't trouble you—or us—ever again. Did you want to know where we put him?"

"Methinks not, my friend. Thou and thy massive companion have done me a service this night. I implore thee, if ever I can do thee service in return, hesitate not to call upon me."

"Cyradis," Belgarath said, "is this the last part of the riddle? Or are there other bits and pieces lurking about?"

"Nay, Ancient One. The game of the riddles is finished. Now the game of deeds doth begin."

"Finally," Belgarath said with some relief. Then he and Beldin fell to studying the map.

"Did we find it?" Durnik asked Silk. "I mean, does the map show the location of Korim?"

Silk led him to the table. "It's right here," he said, pointing. "This is a very old map. Modern maps misspell the name. That's why we had to come here."

"We've been doing a lot of running around chasing after scraps of paper," the smith observed.

"We have indeed, my friend. According to Cyradis, it's all been part of a game being played by the friend Garion's got inside his head and the other one, who's probably inside Zandramas' head."

"I hate games."

"I don't mind them."

"That's because you're Drasnian."

"That could be part of it, I suppose."

"It's in the approximate location where the mountains of Korim were, Belgarath," Beldin said, measuring off distances with his fingers. "They were probably moved a bit when Torak cracked the world."

"A lot of things were moved that day, as I recall."

"Oh, yes," Beldin agreed fervently. "I had trouble standing up, and I'm built closer to the ground than you are."

"You know something? I've noticed that myself. Your Majesty," the old man addressed the king, "could you be a bit more specific about the reef? Trying to land on the side of a rock pinnacle from a boat that's pitching around in the surf would be difficult and dangerous."

"If memory doth serve me, Ancient Belgarath, I do seem to recall a few rocky beaches, built up, doubtless, from shards and boulders tumbled from the sides of the peaks and then pounded to bits by the restless sea. When the tide is low, this rubble, accumulated over the eons, doth rise above the surface of the sea, providing means whereby one may move freely from one pinnacle to the next."

"Sort of like that land bridge from Morindland to Mallorea," Silk recalled sourly. "That wasn't a very pleasant trip."

"Are there any landmarks of any kind?" Belgarath pressed. "That reef goes on for quite a ways. It could take a lot of wading to find the exact place we need to reach."

"I cannot attest to this from mine own true knowledge," the king said cautiously, "but certain seafarers have asserted that there appears to be a cave mouth on the north side of the highest pinnacle. On occasion, more adventurous ones have sought to go ashore to explore its depths, for, as is widely known, remote caves ofttimes serve as repositories for the ill-gotten gains of freebooters and pirates. The pinnacle, however, hath ever repulsed their most valiant efforts. Each time one of these brave souls attempts landing there, the sea becomes angry, and sudden storms do appear from a cloudless sky."

"That's it, Belgarath." Beldin chortled exultantly. "Something's been going out of its way to keep casual explorers out of that cave."

"*Two* somethings, I gather," Belgarath agreed. "You're right, though. We've finally located the exact place of the meeting. It's in that cave."

Silk groaned.

"Art thou ill, Prince Kheldar?" the king inquired.

"Not yet, your Majesty, but I think I'm going to be."

"Our Prince Kheldar has difficulties with caves, your Majesty," Velvet explained, smiling.

"There's nothing difficult about it at all, Liselle," the rat-faced little man disagreed. "It's really very simple. Every time I see a cave, I go into an absolute panic."

"I have heard of this malady," the king said. "One wonders what may be its mysterious source."

"There's nothing mysterious about the source of mine, your Majesty," Silk said dryly. "I know *exactly* where it came from."

"If it is thine intent to dare the perilous reef, Ancient Belgarath," the king said then, "I will provide thee and thy companions with a stout ship to convey thee thither. I will give orders that the ship be ready to sail with the morning tide."

"Your Majesty is very kind."

"It is but small payment for the service thou hast rendered to me this night." The king paused, his face reflective. "It may be even as the spirit of foul Naradas proclaimed," he mused. "I may indeed be a vain and foolish man, but I am not immune to the promptings of gratitude. You all have preparations to make," he said then. "I will not delay you more. We shall meet again on the morrow ere you depart."

"We thank you, your Majesty," Garion said, his armor creaking as he bowed. Then he led the others from the chamber. He was not at all surprised to see the she-wolf sitting just outside the door.

"The time is exactly right, isn't it, Cyradis?" Polgara said to the Seeress once they were all out in the corridor. "At Ashaba, you said it would be nine months until the meeting. As I make it, the exact time will be the day after tomorrow."

"Thy calculations are correct, Polgara."

"It works out precisely then. It should take us one full day to reach the reef, and we'll go to the cave on the following morning." Polgara smiled a bit wryly. "All this time we've been fretting about arriving late, and now we get there precisely on time." She laughed. "What a waste of all that perfectly good worrying."

"Well, now we know where and when," Durnik said. "All that's left to do is to go there and get on with it."

"That sums it up, I'd say," Silk agreed.

Eriond sighed, and Garion felt a chill suspicion that was not quite a certainty. *"Is it going to be he?"* he asked the dry voice. *"Is Eriond going to be the one who dies?"*

But the voice would not answer.

They entered their quarters with the wolf close behind them.

"It's been a long time getting here," Belgarath said wearily. "I'm getting a little old for these extended journeys."

"Old?" Beldin snorted. "You were born old. I still think you've got a few miles left in you, though."

"I think that when we get home, I'll spend a century or so in my tower."

"That's an idea. It should take you about that long to get it cleaned up—oh, one other thing, Belgarath. Why don't you fix that loose step?"

"I'll get around to it."

"Aren't we all assuming that we're going to win?" Silk said. "I think that making plans for the future at this point might be a bit premature—unless the Holy Seeress might see fit to let slip a hint or two about the outcome?" He looked at Cyradis.

"I would not be permitted to do that, Prince Kheldar—even if I knew the answer."

"You mean you don't know?" he asked incredulously.

"The Choice hath not yet been made," she said simply. "It may not be made until I stand in the presence of the Child of Light and the Child of Dark. Until that moment, the outcome doth still hang in the balance."

"What good is it being a Seeress if you can't predict the future?"

"This particular Event is not susceptible to prediction, Kheldar," she said tartly.

"I think we'd all better get some sleep," Belgarath said. "The next couple of days are going to be hectic."

The she-wolf followed Garion and Ce'Nedra to their room and entered with them. Ce'Nedra looked a bit startled at that, but the wolf went directly to the bed and put her forepaws up on it to look critically at the puppy, who lay sleeping on his back with all four of his paws in the air.

The wolf gave Garion a slightly reproachful look. "One notes that he has grown fat," she said. "Your mate has ruined him with overfeeding and pampering. He is no longer fit to be a wolf. He no longer even smells like a wolf."

"One's mate bathes him from time to time," Garion explained.

"Bathes," the wolf said in a tone loaded with contempt. "A wolf should be bathed only by the rain or in the course of swimming across a river." She dropped to her haunches. "One would ask a favor of your mate."

"One will convey your request to her."

"One had hoped you might. Ask your mate if she will continue to care for the young one. One believes you need not add that she has spoiled him so badly that he is unfit to be anything but a lapdog."

"One will phrase your request cautiously."

"What's she saying?" Ce'Nedra asked.

"She wants to know if you'd be willing to take care of the puppy."

"Of course I will. I've wanted to do that all along." Then she knelt and impulsively put her arms about the she-wolf's neck. "I will care for him," she promised.

"One notes that her scent is not unpleasant," the wolf said to Garion.

"One has also noticed that."

"One was fairly certain that you had." Then the wolf rose to her feet and silently left the room.

"She's going to leave us now, isn't she?" Ce'Nedra said wistfully. "I'm going to miss her."

"What makes you think that?"

"Why else would she give up her baby?"

"I think there's a bit more to it than that. She's preparing for something."

"I'm very tired, Garion. Let's go to bed."

Later, in the velvet darkness as they lay close together in the bed, Ce'Nedra sighed. "Two more days and I'll see my baby again. It's been so very, very long."

"Try not to dwell on it, Ce'Nedra. You need your rest, and thinking too much about it will keep you awake."

She sighed again, and after a few moments, she drifted off to sleep.

"*Cyradis is not the only one who has to make a choice,*" the voice in his mind told him. "*You and Zandramas also have choices to make.*"

"*What choices are those?*"

"*You have to choose your successors. Zandramas has already chosen hers. You should be giving some thought to your last task as the Child of Light. It's going to be fairly significant.*"

"*I suppose that in a way, I'll sort of miss having that to carry around, but I'll be glad to get rid of it. Now I'll be able to go back to being ordinary again.*"

"*You never were ordinary, you know. You've been the Child of Light since the moment you were born.*"

"*I know I'm going to miss you.*"

"*Please don't get sentimental, Garion. I may stop by from time to time, just to see how you're doing. Now get some sleep.*"

When he awoke the next morning, Garion lay in bed for quite some time. He had tried for very long not to think about something, but now he had no choice but to face it squarely. He had every reason in the world to hate Zandramas, but . . .

Finally, he slipped out of bed, dressed himself, and went looking for Belgarath.

He found the old man in the central room, seated with Cyradis. "Grandfather," he said, "I've got a problem."

"There's nothing unusual about that. What's got you worked up this time?"

"Tomorrow I'm going to meet Zandramas."

"Why, do you know? I think you're right."

"Please don't do that. This is serious."

"Sorry, Garion. I'm feeling whimsical today."

"I'm afraid that the only way we're going to be able to stop her is to kill her, and I'm not sure I'll be able to do that. Torak was one thing, but Zandramas is a woman."

"Well, she *was*. I think her gender has become irrelevant now, though—even to herself."

"I still don't think I'll be able to do it."

"There will be no need, Belgarion," Cyradis assured him. "Another fate doth lie in store for Zandramas, no matter what my choice may be. Thou wilt not be required to shed her blood."

A vast wave of relief came over Garion. "Thank you, Holy Seeress," he said. "I've been afraid to face up to that. It's good to know that it's not one of the tasks I've got ahead of me. Oh, by the way, Grandfather, my friend up here—" He tapped his forehead "—has been visiting again. Last night he told me that my final task will be to choose my successor. I don't suppose I could get you to help me, could I?"

"No, Garion, I'm afraid not. I don't think I'm supposed to, am I, Cyradis?"

"Nay, Ancient Belgarath. That task lieth on the Child of Light alone."

"I was afraid you might look at it that way," Garion said glumly.

"Oh, one thing, Garion," Belgarath said. "The one you choose has a fair chance of becoming a God. Don't choose me. I'm not suited for the job."

The others drifted in singly or in pairs. As each one entered, Garion considered their faces, trying to picture each of his friends as a divinity. Aunt Pol? No, that didn't seem right somehow, and that automatically excluded Durnik. He could not deprive her of her husband. Silk? That idea very nearly caused Garion to collapse in helpless laughter. 'Zakath? It had some possibilities. 'Zakath was an Angarak, and the new God would be the God of that race. 'Zakath was a bit unpredictable, however. Until recently, he had been obsessed with power. A sudden onset of Godhood might unsettle his mind and make him revert. Garion sighed. He'd have to think about it some more.

The servants brought in breakfast, and Ce'Nedra, obviously remembering her promise of the previous night, fixed a plate for the puppy. The plate contained eggs, sausage, and a generous dollop of jam. The she-wolf looked away with a shudder.

They deliberately avoided the subject of tomorrow's meeting as they ate. The meeting was inevitable now, so there was no point in talking about it.

Belgarath pushed back his plate with a look of contentment on his face. "Don't forget to thank the king for his hospitality," he told Garion.

And then the she-wolf came over and laid her head in the old man's lap. Belgarath looked startled. The wolf had usually avoided him. "What is it, little sister?" he asked her.

Then, to everyone's astonishment, the wolf actually laughed and spoke quite plainly in the language of humans. "Your brains have gone to sleep, old wolf," she said to Belgarath. "I thought you'd have known me weeks ago. Does this help?" A sudden blue nimbus surrounded her. "Or this?" She shimmered, and then the wolf was gone. Standing in its place was a tawny-haired, golden-eyed woman in a brown dress.

"Mother!" Aunt Pol exclaimed.

"You're no more observant than your father, Polgara," Poledra said reprovingly. "Garion has known for quite some time now."

Belgarath, however, was staring in horror at the puppy.

"Oh, don't be silly, old man," his wife told him. "You know that we're mated for life. The puppy was weak and sick, so the pack had to leave him behind. I cared for him, that's all."

The smile on the face of the Seeress of Kell was gentle. "This is the Woman Who Watches, Ancient Belgarath," she said. "Now is thy company complete. Know, however, that she is ever with thee, as she has always been."

PART THREE

THE HIGH PLACES
OF KORIM

THE KORIM REEF

KORIM

PERIVOR

DAL PERIVOR

VO ASTELLIG

DAL ESTALAN

R. PERI

THE HIGH PLACES OF KORIM

SHELLY SHAPIRO '40

Garion had seen his grandmother—or her image—several times, but the similarity of her features to Aunt Pol's seemed uncanny. There were differences, of course. Aunt Pol's hair, except for that white lock at her brow, was dark, almost black, and her eyes were a deep, deep blue. Poledra, on the other hand, had tawny hair, hovering nearly on the verge of being as blond as Velvet's, and her eyes were as golden as the eyes of a wolf. The features of the two women, however, were almost identical, as had been, the one time Garion had seen her image, the features of Aunt Pol's sister, Beldaran. Belgarath, his wife, and his daughter had withdrawn to the far side of the room, and Beldin, his tears glistening through his scowl, had placed himself squarely between them and the others in the room to guard their privacy during their reunion.

"Who is she?" 'Zakath asked Garion in puzzlement.

"She's my grandmother," Garion replied simply. "Belgarath's wife."

"I didn't know he *had* a wife."

"Where did you think Aunt Pol came from?"

"I guess I hadn't thought of that." 'Zakath looked around, noting that both Ce'Nedra and Velvet were dabbing at their eyes with wispy little handkerchiefs.

"Why is everyone so misty-eyed?" he asked.

"We all thought that she had died in childbirth when Aunt Pol and her sister Beldaran were born."

"And how long ago was that?"

"Aunt Pol is over three thousand years old." Garion shrugged.

'Zakath began to tremble. "And Belgarath's been grieving all that time?"

"Yes." Garion didn't really want to talk just then. All he wanted to do was to drink in the radiant faces of his family. The word came to him unbidden, and he suddenly remembered that bleak time after he had first learned that Aunt Pol was not, strictly speaking, his aunt. He had felt then so terribly alone—an orphan in the most dreadful sense of the word. It had taken years, but now everything was all right. His family was nearly complete. Belgarath, Poledra, and Aunt Pol did not speak, for speech was largely unnecessary. Instead they simply sat in chairs drawn closely together gazing into each other's faces and holding hands. Garion could only faintly begin to understand the intensity of their emotions. He did not, however, feel cut off from them, but rather seemed somehow to share their joy.

Durnik crossed the room to the rest of them. Even solid, practical Durnik's eyes shone with unshed tears. "Why don't we leave them alone?" he suggested. "It's a good time to get the packing done anyway. We have a ship to catch, you know."

"She said you knew," Ce'Nedra said accusingly to Garion when they had returned to their room.

"Yes," he admitted.

"Why didn't you tell me?"

"She asked me to keep it to myself."

"That doesn't apply to your own wife, Garion."

"It doesn't?" he asked in feigned surprise. "When did they pass that rule?"

"I just made it up," she admitted. "Oh, Garion," she said then, throwing her arms about his neck and kissing him, "I do love you."

"I certainly hope so. Shall we pack?"

The corridors of the royal palace here in Perivor were cool as Garion and Ce'Nedra returned to the central room, and the arched embrasures admitted golden morning sunlight as if even the elements were bestowing a benediction on what was, after all, a special, even sacred, day.

When they had all gathered once again, Belgarath and his wife and daughter had composed themselves enough so that they welcomed company.

"Would you like to have me introduce them, mother?" Aunt Pol asked.

"I know all of them, Polgara," Poledra replied. "I've been with you for quite some time, remember?"

"Why didn't you tell me?"

"I wanted to see if you could figure it out for yourself. You disappointed me just a bit, Polgara."

"Mother," Aunt Pol protested, "not in front of the children."

They both laughed that same warm, rich laugh. "Ladies and gentlemen," Polgara said then, "this is my mother, Poledra."

They crowded around the tawny-haired legend. Silk extravagantly kissed her hand. "I suppose, Lady Poledra," he said slyly, "we should congratulate Belgarath. All things considered, I think *you* got the worst of that bargain. You daughter's been trying to reform him for about three eons now without much notable success."

Poledra smiled. "One has perhaps greater resources at one's command than one's daughter, Prince Kheldar." She lapsed, it seemed, unconsciously into her previous mode of speech.

"All right, Poledra," Beldin growled, stumping forward, "what *really* happened? After the girls were born, our Master came to us and told us that you were no longer with us. We all thought he meant that you had died. The twins cried for two straight months, and that left me to try to cope with the babies. What really happened?"

"Aldur didn't lie to you, Beldin," she replied calmly. "In a very real sense, I *was* no longer with you. You see, shortly after the girls were born, Aldur and UL came to me. They said they had a great task for me but that it would involve an equally great sacrifice. I would have to leave you all behind to prepare for the task. At first, I refused, but when they explained the task to me, I had no choice but to agree. I turned my back on the Vale and went with UL to Prolgu to receive instruction. From time to time he'd relent and let me go unobserved out into the world to see how my family was doing." She looked rather firmly at Belgarath. "You and I have much to discuss, Old Wolf," she told him.

Belgarath winced.

"I don't suppose you could give us some enlightenment about this momentous task?" Sadi suggested mildly.

"I'm afraid not."

"I didn't think so," the eunuch murmured.

"Eriond," Poledra said then, greeting the blond-haired young man.

"Poledra," he responded. Eriond, as always, seemed unsurprised by this turn of events. Eriond, Garion had noticed, was never surprised.

"You've grown since we last met," she noted.

"I suppose I have," he agreed.

"Are you ready?"

The question sent a chill through Garion as he suddenly remembered the strange dream he had had the night before his true identity had been revealed.

There was a polite knock on the door. Durnik answered it and found an armored knight standing outside. "His Majesty hath dispatched me to advise thee and thy companions that thy ship awaiteth thee in the harbor, my Lord," the knight said.

"I'm not a—" Durnik started.

"Let it lie, Durnik," Silk told him. "Sir Knight," he said to the armored man at the door, "where might we find his Majesty? We would take our leave of him and thank him for his many kindnesses."

"His Majesty doth await thee and thy companions at the harbor, my Lord. He would bid ye all farewell there and see ye off on the great adventure which doth lie in store for ye."

"We will make haste then, Sir Knight," the little man promised. "It were discourteous of us in the extreme to keep one of the paramount monarchs of the world awaiting our arrival. Thou hast performed thine appointed task in manner which does thee credit, Sir Knight, and we are all in thy debt."

The knight bowed, beaming. Then he went back down the hallway.

"Where did you ever learn to speak like that, Kheldar?" Velvet asked in some surprise.

"Ah, dear Lady," Silk replied with outrageous extravagance, "knowest thou not that the poet doth lurk beneath the most common exterior? An it please thee, I will deliver unto thee fulsome compliments upon thine every ravishing and unsurpassed part." He eyed her up and down suggestively.

"Kheldar!" she exclaimed, blushing bright red.

"That's sort of fun, you know," Silk said, referring to the archaic speech—at least Garion *hoped* that was what he was referring to. "Once you learn how to wrap your tongue around the 'haths,' and 'doths,' and 'forasmuches,' it has a certain ring and cadence to it, doesn't it?"

"We're surrounded by charlatans, mother." Polgara sighed.

"Belgarath," Durnik said seriously, "there's not much point in taking the horses, is there? What I mean is that we're going to be clambering over rocks and wading in surf when we get to the reef. Wouldn't the horses just be in the way?"

"You're probably right, Durnik," the old man agreed.

"I'll go down to the stables and talk with the grooms," the smith said. "The rest of you go on ahead. I'll catch up." He turned and left the room.

"An eminently practical man," Poledra observed.

"The poet, however, doth lurk beneath that most practical of exteriors, Mother—" Polgara smiled "—and thou wouldst not believe how much pleasure I take in that aspect of him."

"I think it's time for us to get off this island, Old Wolf," Poledra said wryly. "Two more days and they'll all be sitting around composing bad poetry."

Servants arrived then to carry their packs to the harbor, and Garion and his companions trooped through the halls of the palace and out into the streets of Dal Perivor. Although the morning had dawned bright and sunny, a bank of heavy clouds had begun to build up off to the west, heavy, purple clouds that spoke eloquently of the likelihood of bad weather over Korim.

"I suppose we should have known." Silk sighed. "Once—just once—I'd like to see one of these stupendous events happen in good weather."

Garion fully understood what lay behind the apparently lighthearted banter. None of them approached tomorrow without a certain apprehension. The pronouncement Cyradis had made at Rheon that one of them would not survive the meeting lay heavily on each of their minds, and in the fashion as old as man himself, each tried to make light of his fears. That reminded him of something, and he dropped back to have a word with the Seeress of Kell. "Cyradis," he said to the blindfolded girl, "should 'Zakath and I wear our armor when we get to the reef?" He plucked at the front of the doublet he had put on with some relief that morning in the hope that he might never again be obliged to encase himself in steel. "What I'm getting at is that if the meeting is going to be entirely spiritual, there's no real need for it, is there? But if there's a possibility of some fighting, we should probably be prepared, shouldn't we?"

"Thou art as transparent as glass, Belgarion of Riva," she said, chiding him gently. "Thou thinkest to trick answers from me to questions which I am forbidden to discuss with thee. Do as it pleaseth thee, King of Riva. Prudence, however, doth suggest that a bit of steel here and there in thine apparel might not be inappropriate when approaching a situation where surprises might await thee."

"I will be guided by thee." Garion grinned. "Thy prudent advice seemeth to me the course of wisdom."

"Makest thou a rather feeble attempt at humor, Belgarion?"

"Would I do that, Holy Seeress?" He grinned at her and strode back to where Belgarath and Poledra walked hand in hand just behind 'Zakath and Sadi. "Grandfather, I think I just managed to sneak an answer out of Cyradis," he said.

"That might be a first," the old man replied.

"I think there might be some fighting when we get to the reef. I asked her if 'Zakath and I should wear armor when we get there. She didn't answer me directly, but she said that it might not be a bad idea—just in case."

"You might want to pass that on to the others. Let's not have them walking into something blind."

"I'll do that."

The king, along with most of his gaily clad court, awaited them on a long wharf extending out into the choppy waters of the harbor. Despite the temperate morning, the king wore an ermine robe and a heavy gold crown. "Gladly do I greet thee and thy noble companions, Belgarion of Riva," he declaimed, "and in sadness do I await thy departure. Many here have pled with me that I might permit them also to speak to this matter, but in thy behalf I have steadfastly refused such permission, knowing full well the urgency of thy quest."

"Thou art a true and faithful friend, your Majesty," Garion said with genuine gratitude at being spared a morning of windy speeches. He clasped the king's hand warmly. "Know that if the Gods grant us victory on the morrow, we will return straightaway to this happy isle so that we may more fulsomely express our gratitude to thee and the members of thy court who have all treated us with such noble courtesy." Besides, they had to come back for the horses anyway. "And now, your Majesty, our fate awaits us. We must, with scant and niggard farewell, take ship to go forth with resolute hearts to meet that fate. An it please the Gods, we shall return anon. Good-bye, my friend."

"Fare thee well, Belgarion of Riva," the king said in a voice near to tears. "May the Gods grant thee and thy companions victory."

"Pray that it may be so." Garion turned with a rather melodramatic swirl of his cloak and led his friends up the gangway. He glanced back over his shoulder and saw Durnik pushing his way through the crowd. That would help. As soon as the smith was on board, Garion could give the order to cast off all lines and thus avoid the necessity of more extended farewells shouted across the ship's rail.

Directly behind Durnik came the several carts carrying their packs. Their belongings were quickly transferred to the ship, and Garion went aft to speak with the captain, a grizzled old seaman with a weathered face.

Unlike western vessels, whose bare plank decks were usually holystoned into some semblance of whiteness, the quarterdeck and its surrounding railings were finished with a dark, glossy varnish, and snowy ropes hung in neat coils from highly polished belaying pins. The effect was almost ostentatiously neat, evidence that the vessel's master took great pride in his ship. The captain himself wore a somewhat weathered blue doublet. He was, after all, in port. A jaunty velvet cap was cocked rakishly over one of his ears.

"I guess that's everything, Captain," Garion said. "We may as well cast off and get clear of the harbor before the tide turns."

"You've been to sea before, I see, young master," the captain said approvingly. "I hope your friends have, as well. It's always a trial to have landsmen aboard. They never seem to realize that throwing up into the wind isn't a good idea." He raised his voice to an ear-splitting bellow. "Cast off all lines! Prepare to make sail!"

"Your speech doesn't seem to be that of the island, Captain," Garion observed.

"I'd be surprised if it were, young master. I'm from the Melcene Islands. About twenty years ago, there were some ugly rumors about me being circulated in some quarters back home, so I thought it might be prudent to absent myself for a while. I came here. You wouldn't believe what these people were calling a ship when I got here."

"Sort of like a seagoing castle?" Garion suggested.

"You've seen them then?"

"In another part of the world."

"Make sail!" the captain roared at his crew. "There, young master." He grinned at Garion. "I'll have you out of earshot in no time at all. That should spare us all that drasty eloquence. Where was I? Oh, yes. When I got here, the ships of Perivor were so top-heavy that a good sneeze would capsize them. Would you believe it only took me five years to explain that to these people?"

"You must have been amazingly eloquent, Captain." Garion laughed.

"A bout or two with belaying pins helped a bit," the captain conceded. "Finally I had to issue a challenge, though. None of these blockheads can refuse a challenge, so I proposed a race around the island. Twenty ships started out, and only mine finished. They started listening about then. I spent the next five years in the yards supervising construction. Then the king finally let me go back to sea. I got me a baronetcy out of it—not that it matters. I think I've even got a castle somewhere."

A brazen blast came from the wharf as, in true Mimbrate fashion, the knights of the king's court saluted them on their horns. "Isn't that pitiful?" the captain said. "I don't think there's a man on the whole island who can carry a tune." He looked appraisingly at Garion. "I heard tell that you're making for the Turim reef."

"Korim reef," Garion corrected absently.

"You've been listening to the landsmen, I see. They can't even pronounce the name right. Anyway, before you get your mind set in stone about where you want to land, send for me. There's some very ugly water around that reef. It's not the sort of place where you want to make mistakes, and I've got some fairly accurate charts."

"The king told us there weren't any charts of the reef."

The captain winked slyly. "The rumors I mentioned earlier stirred some ship captains to try to follow me," he admitted, "although 'chase' would probably be a more accurate word. Rewards cause that sort of thing sometimes. Anyhow, I was passing near the reef in calm weather once, and I decided to take some soundings. It never hurts to have a place to hide where others are afraid to follow you."

"What's your name, Captain?" Garion asked him.

"Kresca, young master."

"I think we can drop that. Garion will do just fine."

"Whatever you like, Garion. Now get off my quarterdeck so I can maneuver this old tub out of the harbor."

The speech was different, and it was halfway around the world, but Captain Kresca was so much like Barak's friend Greldik that Garion felt suddenly very secure. He went below to join the others. "We've had a bit of luck," he told them. "Our captain is a Melcene. He's not overburdened with scruples, but he *has* got charts of the reef. He's probably the only man in these waters who does. He's offered to advise us when the time comes to decide on where we want to land."

"That was helpful of him," Silk said.

"Maybe, but I think his main concern is not ripping the bottom out of his ship."

"I can relate to that," Silk said. "As long as I'm on board, anyway."

"I'm going back up on deck," Garion said then. "Staying in a stuffy compartment on the first day of a voyage always makes me a little queasy for some reason."

"And *you're* the ruler of an island?" Poledra said.

"It's just a question of getting adjusted, Grandmother."

"Of course."

The sea and sky were unsettled. The heavy cloud bank was still coming in from the west, sending long, ponderous combers rolling in from that direction, waves that had in all probability started somewhere off the east coast of Cthol Murgos. Although, as king of an island nation, Garion knew that the phenomenon was not unusual, he nonetheless felt a certain sense of superstitious apprehension when he saw that the surface winds were moving westward while those aloft, as proclaimed by the movement of the clouds, moved east. He had seen this happen many times before, but this time he could not be positive that the weather was responding to natural causes or to something else. Idly he wondered what those two eternal awarenesses might have done had he and his friends not found a ship. He had a momentary vision of the sea parting to provide a broad highway across its bottom, a highway littered with startled fish. He began to feel less and less in charge of his own destiny. Even as he had on the long trek to Cthol Mishrak, he became increasingly certain that the two prophecies were herding him toward Korim for a meeting that, though he himself might not have chosen it, was the ultimate Event toward which the entire universe had been yearning since the beginning of days. A plaintive "Why me?" hovered on his lips.

And then Ce'Nedra was there, burrowing under his arm as she had during those first few heady days when they had finally discovered that they did, in fact, love each other. "What are you thinking about, Garion?" she asked softly. She had changed out of the antique green satin gown she had worn at the palace and now wore a gray dress of utilitarian wool.

"I'm not, really. Probably worrying comes a lot closer."

"What's there to worry about? We're going to win, aren't we?"

"That hasn't been decided yet."

"Of course you're going to win. You always do."

"This time's a little different, Ce'Nedra." He sighed. "It's not just the meeting, though. I've got to choose my successor, and the one I choose is going to be the new Child of Light—and most probably a God. If I pick the wrong person, it's possible that I'll create a God who'll be an absolute disaster. Could you imagine Silk as a God? He'd be out there picking the pockets of the other Gods and inscribing off-color jokes in the constellations."

"He doesn't really seem to have the right kind of temperament for it," she agreed. "I *like* him well enough, but I'm afraid UL might disapprove very strongly. What else is bothering you?"

"You know what else. One of us isn't going to live through tomorrow."

"You don't really have to concern yourself about that, Garion," she said wistfully. "It's going to be me. I've known that from the very beginning."

"Don't be absurd. I can make sure it's not you."

"Oh? How?"

"I'll just tell them that I won't make the Choice if they hurt you in any way."

"Garion!" she gasped. "You can't do that! You'll destroy the universe if you do!"

"So what? The universe doesn't mean anything to me without you, you know."

"That's very sweet, but you can't do it. You wouldn't do it anyway. You've got too great a sense of responsibility."

"What makes you think you're going to be the one?"

"The tasks, Garion. Every one of us has a task—some of us more than one. Belgarath had to find out where the meeting's going to take place. Velvet had to kill Harakan. Even Sadi had a task. He had to kill Naradas. I have no task—except to die."

Garion decided at that point to tell her. "You *did* have a task, Ce'Nedra," he told her, "and you did it very well."

"What are you talking about?"

"You wouldn't remember it. After we left Kell, you were very drowsy for several days."

"Yes, I remember that."

"It wasn't because you were sleepy. Zandramas was tampering with your mind. She's done it before. You remember that you got sick on your way to Rak Hagga?"

"Yes."

"It was a different kind of sickness, but it was Zandramas again. She's been trying to take control of you for more than a year now."

Ce'Nedra stared at him.

"Anyway, after we left Kell, she managed to put your mind to sleep. You wandered off and, out there in the forest, you thought you met Arell."

"Arell? She's dead."

"I know, but you thought you met her all the same, and she gave you what you thought was our baby. Then this supposed Arell asked you some questions, and you answered them."

"What kind of questions?"

"Zandramas had to find out where the meeting was supposed to take place, and she couldn't go to Kell. She posed as Arell so she could ask you those questions. You told her about Perivor, about the map, and about Korim. That was your task."

"I betrayed you?" Her look was stricken.

"No. You saved the universe. Zandramas absolutely *has* to be at Korim at the right time. Somebody had to tell her where to go, and that was *your* task."

"I don't remember any of this."

"Of course not. Aunt Pol erased the memory of it from your mind. It wasn't really your fault, and you'd have been overcome with remorse if you'd been able to remember what happened."

"I still betrayed you."

"You did what had to be done, Ce'Nedra." Garion smiled a bit wistfully. "You know, both sides in this have been trying to do the same thing. We—and Zandramas, of course—have been trying to find Korim and to keep the other side from finding out where it is so that we can win by default. It was never going to happen that way, though. The meeting absolutely *has* to take place before Cyradis can choose. The prophecies weren't going to let it happen any other way. Both sides have wasted a great deal of effort trying to do something that simply could not be done. We should have all realized that from the very beginning. We could have saved ourselves a lot of trouble. About the only consolation I have is that Zandramas wasted a lot more effort than we did."

"I'm still certain that it's going to be me."

"Nonsense."

"I just hope they let me hold my baby before I die," she said sadly.

"You're *not* going to die, Ce'Nedra."

She ignored him. "I want you to take care of yourself, Garion," she said firmly. "Be sure that you eat right, dress warmly in winter, and make sure that our son doesn't forget me."

"Ce'Nedra, will you stop this?"

"One last thing, Garion," she plowed on relentlessly. "After I've been gone for a while, I want you to marry again. I don't want you moping around the way Belgarath has for the last three thousand years."

"Absolutely not. Besides, nothing's going to happen to you."

"We'll see. Promise, Garion. You weren't meant to be alone, and you need somebody to take care of you."

"Have you almost finished with this?" It was Poledra. She stepped out from behind the foremast in a businesslike way. "It's all very pretty and sweetly melancholy, I'm sure, but isn't it just a trifle overdramatic? Garion's right, Ce'Nedra. Nothing's going to happen to you, so why don't you fold up all this nobility and put it away in a closet someplace?"

"I know what I know, Poledra," Ce'Nedra said stubbornly.

"I hope you won't be too disappointed when you wake up the day after tomorrow and find that you're in perfect health."

"Who's it going to be, then?"

"Me," Poledra said simply. "I've known about it for over three thousand years now, so I've had time to get used to it. At least I have this day with the ones I love before I have to leave for good. Ce'Nedra, that wind is very chilly. Let's go below before you catch cold."

"She's just like your Aunt Pol, isn't she?" Ce'Nedra said over her shoulder as Poledra firmly led her toward the stair leading belowdecks.

"Naturally," Garion called back.

"It's started, I see," Silk said from not far away.

"What's started?"

"The gushy farewells. Just about everybody's convinced that he's the one who won't see the sun go down tomorrow. I'd imagine that they'll all come up here one by one to say good-bye to you. I thought I'd be first—sort of to get it out of the way—but Ce'Nedra beat me to it."

"You? Nothing could kill you, Silk. You're too lucky."

"I've made my own luck, Garion. It's not that hard to tamper with dice." The little man's face grew reflective. "We've really had some good times, haven't we? I think they outweigh the bad ones, and that's about all a man can hope for."

"You're as maudlin as Ce'Nedra and my grandmother were."

"It does sort of seem that way, doesn't it? And that's very unbecoming. Don't be too sad about it, Garion. If I *do* happen to be the one, it should spare me the discomfort of making a *very* unpleasant decision."

"Oh? What decision is that?"

"You know my views on marriage, don't you?"

"Oh, yes. You've spoken on the subject many, many times."

Silk sighed. "All that to the contrary, I think I'm going to have to make up my mind about Liselle."

"I wondered how long that would take you."

"You knew?" Silk looked surprised.

"Everybody knew, Silk. She set out to get you, and she did exactly that."

"That's depressing—to get trapped finally when I'm in my dotage."

"I'd hardly say you're *that* far gone."

"I must be even to be considering something like this," Silk said moodily. "Liselle and I could continue to go on the way we have been, I suppose, but sneaking down hallways to her bedroom in the middle of the night seems a little disrespectful for some reason, and I'm too fond of her for that."

"Fond?"

"All right then," Silk snapped. "I'm in love with her. Does it make you feel better to have me come right out and say it?"

"I just wanted to get it clear, that's all. Is this the first time you've admitted it—even to yourself?"

"I've been trying to avoid that. Do you suppose we could talk about something else?" He looked around. "I wish he'd go find another piece of air to fly in," he said in a grouchy tone of voice.

"Who?"

"That blasted albatross. He's back again." Silk pointed. Garion turned and saw the white seabird with its enormous wings on station once more just ahead of the bowsprit. The cloud bank to the west had grown more and more purple as the morning had progressed, and against that backdrop the snowy bird seemed almost to glow with an unearthly incandescence.

"That's very strange," Garion said.

"I just wish I knew what he was up to," Silk said. "I'm going below. I don't want to look at him anymore." He took Garion's hand in his. "We've had fun," he said gruffly. "Take care of yourself."

"You don't have to leave."

"I have to make room for all the others waiting in line to see you, your Majesty." Silk grinned. "I think you're in for a depressing day. I'm going to go find out if Beldin's found an ale barrel yet." With a jaunty wave, the little man turned and went to the stairway leading below.

Silk's prediction proved to be all too accurate. One by one, Garion's friends came up on deck to take leave of him, each firmly convinced that *he* would be the one to die. All in all, it was a very gloomy day.

It was almost twilight when the last of the self-composed epitaphs had been completed. Garion leaned on the rail, looking back at the phosphorescent wake glowing behind their ship.

"Bad day, I take it?" It was Silk again.

"Dreadful. Did Beldin find any ale?"

"I don't recommend any of that for you. You'll need your wits about you tomorrow. I just came up to make sure that all the gloom your friends have been piling on you doesn't make you start thinking about drowning yourself." Silk frowned. "What's that?" he asked.

"What's what?"

"That booming noise." He looked toward the bow. "There it is," he said tensely.

The purple sky had turned almost black with the onset of evening, a black pierced here and there with patches of angry red, the light of the setting sun glowing through the clouds. There was a rusty-colored blur low on the horizon, a blur that seemed to be wearing a white necklace of frothy surf.

Captain Kresca came forward with the rolling walk of a man who spends little time ashore. "That's it, good masters," he told them. "That's the reef."

Garion stared out at the Place Which Is No More, his thoughts and emotions stumbling over each other.

And then the albatross gave a strange cry, a cry that seemed almost triumphant. The great pearly-white bird dipped its pinions once, then continued toward Korim on seemingly motionless wings.

CHAPTER NINETEEN

Oskatat the Seneschal moved with a certain deliberate speed through the corridors of the Drojim Palace toward the throne room of Urgit, High King of Cthol Murgos. Oskatat's scarred face was bleak, and his mind was troubled. He stopped before the closely guarded door to the throne room. "I will speak with his Majesty," he declared.

The guards hastily opened the door for him. Although by mutual agreement between himself and King Urgit, Oskatat still bore only the title of Seneschal, the guards, like everyone else in the palace, recognized the fact that he was second only to the king himself in authority in Cthol Murgos.

He found his rat-faced monarch in light conversation with Queen Prala and Queen Mother Tamazin, Oskatat's own wife. "Ah, there you are, Oskatat," Urgit said. "Now my little family is complete. We've been discussing some extensive remodeling of the Drojim Palace. All these jewels and the tons of gold on the ceilings are in terribly bad taste, wouldn't you say? Besides, I need the money I'll be able to get for all that trash for the war effort."

"Something important has come up, Urgit," Oskatat told his king. By royal command, Oskatat always called his king by his first name in private conversations.

"That's depressing," Urgit said, sprawling deeper into the cushions on his throne. Taur Urgas, Urgit's supposed father, had scornfully rejected such comforts as cushions, preferring to set an example of Murgo hardihood by sitting for hours on cold stone. About all that brainless gesture had gained the mad king had been a fistula, which had added quite noticeably in the later years of his life to his irritability.

"Sit up straight, Urgit," Lady Tamazin, the king's mother, said absently.

"Yes, mother," Urgit replied, straightening slightly on his throne. "Go ahead, Oskatat," he said, "but please drop it on me gently. Lately I've noticed that 'important things' usually turn out to be disasters."

"I've been in contact with Jaharb, Chief Elder of the Dagashi," Oskatat reported. "At my request, he's been trying to pinpoint the location of Agachak the Hierarch. We've finally found him—or at least found the port he sailed from when he left Cthol Murgos."

"Astonishing," Urgit said with a broad grin. "For once you've actually brought me some good news. So Agachak has left Cthol Murgos. We can hope that it's his intention to sail off the edge of the world. I'm glad you told me about this, Oskatat. I'll sleep much better now that that walking corpse no longer contaminates what's left of my kingdom. Were Jaharb's spies able to find out his intended destination?"

"He's bound for Mallorea, Urgit. Judging from his actions, he appears to believe that the Sardion is there. He went to Thull Mardu and pressured King Nathel into accompanying him."

Urgit suddenly laughed uproariously. "He actually did it!" he exclaimed with delight.

"I don't quite follow you."

"I suggested to him once that he take Nathel instead of me when he went after the Sardion. Now he's saddled himself with that cretin. I'd give a great deal to listen to some of their conversations. If he happens to succeed, he'll make Nathel Overking of Angarak, and Nathel can't even tie his own shoes."

"You don't actually think Agachak will succeed, do you?" Queen Prala said, a slight frown creasing her flawless brow. Queen Prala was several months gone with child, and she'd taken to worrying about things lately.

"Win?" Urgit snorted. "He hasn't got a chance. He has to get past Belgarion first—not to mention Belgarath and Polgara. They'll incinerate him." He smiled sardonically. "It's so nice to have powerful friends." He stopped, frowning slightly. "We really ought to warn Belgarion, though—and Kheldar," he added. He sprawled down into his cushions again. "The last we heard, Belgarion and his friends had left Rak Hagga with Kal Zakath. Our best guess was that they were going to Mal Zeth, either as guests or as prisoners." He pulled at his long, pointed nose. "I know Belgarion well enough to know that he's not the sort to stay a prisoner for very long, though. 'Zakath probably knows where he is, however. Oskatat, is there any way we can get a Dagashi to Mal Zeth?"

"We could try, Urgit, but our chances of success wouldn't be too good, and a Dagashi might have some difficulty getting in to see the Emperor. 'Zakath's got a civil war on his hands, so he's likely to be a bit preoccupied."

"That's true, isn't it?" Urgit tapped his fingers on the arm of his throne. "He's still keeping abreast of what's happening here in Cthol Murgos, though, wouldn't you say?"

"Undoubtedly."

"Why not let *him* be our messenger to Belgarion then?"

"You're moving a little fast for me, Urgit," Oskatat confessed.

"What's the nearest town occupied by the Malloreans?"

"They still have a reduced garrison at Rak Cthaka. We could overwhelm them in a few hours, but we haven't wanted to give 'Zakath any reason to return to Cthol Murgos in force."

Urgit shuddered. "I'm very strongly inclined toward that line of thinking myself," he admitted, "but I owe Belgarion several favors, and I want to protect my brother as much as I can. I'll tell you what you do, Oskatat. Take about three army corps and run on down to Rak Cthaka. Malloreans out in the countryside will run off to Rak Hagga to pass the word on to Kal Zakath that we're beginning to attack his cities. That should get his attention. Mill around outside the city for a while, then surround the place. Ask for a parlay with the garrison commander. Explain the situation to him. I'll compose a letter to Kal Zakath pointing out a certain community of interest in this affair. I'm sure he doesn't want Agachak in Mallorea any more than I want the old magician here in Cthol Murgos. I'll suggest in the strongest terms that he pass the word on to Belgarion. The word he'll have already received about our hostile actions will guarantee that he'll at least look at my letter. He'll get in touch with Belgarion, and then we can both sit back and watch the Godslayer solve our problem for us." He grinned suddenly. "Who knows? This might even be the first step toward a reconciliation between his Imperial Implacableness and me. I really think it's time for Angaraks to stop killing each other."

"Can't you squeeze any more speed out of her?" King Anheg demanded of Captain Greldik.

"Of course, Anheg," Greldik growled. "I could crowd on more sail, and we'll be as swift as an arrow—for about five minutes. Then the masts will break, and we'll go back to rowing. Which shift should I put you down for?"

"Greldik, have you ever heard the term 'lèse-majesté'?"

"You've mentioned it frequently, Anheg, but you should take a look at maritime law sometime. When we're on board this ship and at sea, I have even more absolute authority than you've got in Val Alorn. If I tell you to row, you'll row—or swim."

Anheg walked away, muttering curses under his breath.

"Any luck?" Emperor Varana asked as the Alorn king approached the bow.

"He told me to mind my own business," Anheg grunted. "Then he offered to let me man an oar if I was in such a hurry."

"Have you ever manned an oar before?"

"Once. Chereks are a seagoing people, and my father thought it would be educational for me to make a voyage as a deckhand. I didn't mind the rowing so much. It was the flogging that irritated me."

"They actually flogged the crown prince?" Varana asked incredulously.

"It's very hard to see an oarsman's face when you're coming up behind him." Anheg shrugged. "The oarsmaster was trying to get more speed out of us. We were pursuing a Tolnedran merchantman at the time, and we didn't want her to reach the safety of Tolnedran territorial waters."

"Anheg!" Varana exclaimed.

"That was years ago, Varana. I've given orders now that Tolnedran vessels are not to be molested—at least not in the sight of witnesses. The whole point of this is that Greldik's probably right. If he puts on all sail, the wind will uproot his masts, and you and I'll both wind up rowing."

"We don't have much chance of catching up with Barak, then, do we?"

"I'm not so sure. Barak's not nearly as good a sailor as Greldik is, and that oversized tub of his isn't very responsive to the helm. We're gaining on him every day. When he gets to Mallorea, he's going to have to stop in every port to ask questions. Most Malloreans wouldn't recognize Garion if he walked up and spat in their eyes. Kheldar's another matter, though. I understand that the little thief has branch offices in most of the cities and towns in Mallorea. I know how Barak thinks. As soon as he gets to Mallorea, he's going to go looking for Silk, since Silk and Garion are obviously going to be together. I don't have to ask about Silk, though. All I've got to do is describe the *Seabird* to waterfront loafers in just a few towns. For the price of a few tankards of ale, I'll be able to follow Barak wherever he goes. Hopefully we'll catch up with him before he finds Garion and ruins everything. I just wish that blind girl hadn't told him he couldn't go along. The fastest way I know of to get Barak to do something is to forbid him to do it. If he was with Garion, at least Belgarath would be there to keep him under control."

"How do you propose to stop him even if we do catch up with him? His ship may be slower than this one, but it's also bigger, and it carries more men."

"Greldik and I have worked that out," Anheg replied. "Greldik's got a special piece of equipment in his forward hold. It bolts to the bow of this ship. If Barak refuses to come about when I order him to, Greldik's going to ram him. He won't go very fast in a sinking ship."

"Anheg, that's monstrous!"

"So's what Barak's trying to do. If he succeeds in breaking through to Garion, Zandramas will win, and we'll all end up under the heel of somebody worse than Torak was. If I have to sink *Seabird* to avoid that, I'll do it ten times over." He sighed. "I'll miss my cousin, though, in case he gets drowned," he admitted.

Queen Porenn of Drasnia had summoned Margrave Khendon, the chief of her intelligence service, to her private chambers that morning and issued her commands in no uncertain terms. "Every one of them, Javelin," she had said in a peremptory tone. "I want every single spy out of this wing of the palace for the rest of the day."

"Porenn!" Javelin had gasped. "That's unheard of!"

"Not really. You just heard it—from me. Tell your people to sweep all the unofficial spies out, as well. I want this wing of the palace totally unpopulated within the hour. I have spies of my own, Javelin, and I know where all the usual hiding places are. Clean out every one of them."

"I'm bitterly disappointed in you, Porenn. Monarchs simply don't treat the intelligence service in this fashion. Have you any idea of what this is going to do to my people's morale?"

"Frankly, Khendon, I couldn't care less about the morale of your professional snoops. This is a matter of supreme urgency."

"Has my service ever failed you, your Majesty?" Javelin's tone had been a bit offended.

"Twice that I recall. Didn't the Bear-cult infiltrate your service? And didn't your people fail abysmally to warn me about General Haldar's defection?"

Javelin had sighed. "All right, Porenn, sometimes a few minor things have escaped us."

"You call Haldar's going over to the Bear-cult minor?"

"You're being unnecessarily critical, Porenn."

"I want this wing cleared, Javelin. Would you like to have me summon my son? We'll draw up a proclamation making the prohibition against spying on the royal family permanent."

"You wouldn't!" Javelin's face had turned absolutely white. "The whole service would collapse. The right to spy on the royal family has always been the highest reward for exemplary service. Most of my people jump at the chance." He frowned slightly. "Silk's turned it down three times already, though," he added.

"Then clear them out, Javelin—and don't forget the closet hidden behind the tapestry in the corridor just outside."

"How did you find out about *that*?"

"I didn't. Kheva did, actually."

Javelin had groaned.

A few hours after that, Porenn sat impatiently in her sitting room with her son, King Kheva. Kheva was maturing rapidly now. His voice had settled into a resonant baritone, and a downy beard had begun to sprout on his cheeks. His mother, in somewhat marked contrast to most regents, had been gradually introducing him into state councils and negotiations with foreign powers. It would not be long now until she could gently guide him to the forefront and gradually withdraw herself from her unwanted position of authority. Kheva would be a good king, she thought. He was very nearly as shrewd as his father had been and he had that most necessary trait in a reigning monarch, good sense.

There was a rather heavy-handed pounding on the sitting-room door. "Yes?" Porenn replied.

"It's me, Porenn," a brash-sounding voice said. "Yarblek."

"Come in, Yarblek. We've got something to talk about."

Yarblek pushed the door open, and he and Vella entered. Porenn sighed. During the course of her visit to Gar og Nadrak, Vella had reverted. She had shed the shallow veneer of gentility Porenn had labored so long to create, and her garb indicated that she had once again become the wild, untamable creature she had always been before.

"What's all the rush, Porenn?" Yarblek said gruffly, dumping his shabby felt coat and shaggy hat in the corner. "Your messenger almost killed his horse getting to me."

"Something urgent has come up," the Queen of Drasnia replied. "I think it concerns us all. I want you to keep it in strictest confidence, however."

"Confidence." Yarblek laughed derisively. "You know there aren't any secrets in your palace, Porenn."

"There is this time," Porenn said a bit smugly. "This morning I ordered Javelin to clear all the spies out of this wing of the palace."

Yarblek grinned. "How did he take it?"

"Badly, I'm afraid."

"Good. He's been getting just a little too sure of himself lately. All right, let's get down to business. What's this problem?"

"In a moment. Did you find out what Drosta's been up to?"

"Of course. He's trying to make peace with 'Zakath. He's been dealing—at a distance—with the Mallorean who's in charge of their Bureau of Internal Affairs; Brador, I think his name is. Anyway, Drosta's been letting Mallorean agents funnel through Gar og Nadrak to infiltrate the west."

It was Yarblek's tone of voice more than anything that warned Porenn that there was more. "All of it, Yarblek. You're holding things back."

Yarblek sighed. "I *hate* dealing with a clever woman," he complained. "It seems so unnatural for some reason." Then he prudently skipped out of the range of Vella's daggers. "All right." He gave up. " 'Zakath needs money and lots of it to deal with the wars he's got on two different fronts. Drosta's cut the import duties on Mallorean carpets—at least to the merchants who pay taxes to Mal Zeth. Those Malloreans have been scalping Silk and me in the Arendish markets."

"I assume you took advantage of that information?"

"Naturally." He thought a moment. "Here's your chance to make a tidy profit, Porenn," he suggested. "Drosta's cut the import duties to the Malloreans by fifteen percent. You could raise *your* duties by the same amount. You'll make money, and Silk and I can stay competitive."

"I think you're trying to swindle me, Yarblek," Porenn said suspiciously.

"Me?"

"We'll talk about it later. Now, listen very carefully. This is the reason I sent for you. Barak, Mandorallen, Hettar, Lelldorin, and Relg are sailing to Mallorea. We're not entirely positive, but we think they plan to intrude themselves in Belgarion's quest. You were there at Rheon, and you know what that Dalasian Seeress told us. Those hotheads absolutely *have* to stay out of it."

"I'll certainly agree about that."

"How fast can you get a message to your people in Mallorea?"

"A few weeks. Maybe a little faster if I make it a top priority."

"This matter has the highest priority, Yarblek. Anheg and Varana are chasing Barak, but we can't be sure they'll catch him in time. We have to delay Barak, and the best way to do that is to feed him misinformation. I want you to instruct your people in Mallorea to tell Barak lies. Keep him going off in the wrong direction every chance you get. Barak will be following Kheldar, so he'll be checking in at every one of your branch offices in Mallorea for information. If Kheldar and the others are going to Maga Renn or Penn Daka, have your people tell Barak that he's going to Mal Dariya."

"I know the procedure, Porenn," Yarblek said. He squinted at her speculatively. "You'll be turning authority here in Drasnia over to his Majesty here fairly soon, won't you?" he asked her.

"In a few years, yes."

"When this business in Mallorea is concluded, I think Silk and I might want to have a long discussion with you."

"Oh?"

"What's your feeling about accepting a junior partnership in our operation—after your obligations here in Boktor have all been satisfied?"

"I'm very flattered, Yarblek. What possessed you to raise such a possibility?"

"You're very shrewd, Porenn, and you've got all sorts of contacts. We might even be prepared to go as high as a five percent share."

"Absolutely out of the question, Yarblek," King Kheva interrupted surprisingly. "The percentage would have to be at least twenty."

"*Twenty?*" Yarblek almost screamed.

"I have to protect my mother's interests," Kheva said blandly. "She won't always be young, you know, and I'd hate to see her spend her declining years scrubbing floors."

"This is highway robbery, Kheva!" Yarblek's face had turned bright red.

"I'm not holding a knife to your throat, Yarblek," Kheva said. "It might really be better in the long run if mother went into business for herself anyway. She should be able to do very well—particularly in view of the fact that all members of the royal family are exempt from Drasnian import duties."

"I think you just stabbed yourself in the hand, Yarblek." Vella smirked. "As long as you're getting bad news today anyway, I might as well add my share. When this is all over, I want you to sell me."

"Sell you? To whom?"

"I'll tell you when the time comes."

"Has he got any money?"

"I really don't know, but that doesn't matter. I'll pay you your share of the price myself."

"You must really think a lot of him to make that kind of an offer."

"You have absolutely no idea, Yarblek. I was made for this man."

"We were told to stay here, Atesca," Brador said stubbornly.

"That was before this long silence," General Atesca said, nervously pacing up and down in the large pavilion they shared. Atesca wore his uniform and his gold-inlaid steel breastplate. "The Emperor's well-being and safety are *my* responsibility."

"They're as much mine as they are yours." Brador was absently rubbing the furry tummy of the half-grown cat lying ecstatic in his lap.

"All right, why aren't you doing something about it then? We haven't had word of him in weeks. Not even your intelligence network can tell us where he is."

"I know that, Atesca, but I'm not going to disobey an imperial command just because you're getting nervous—or bored."

"Why don't you stay here and take care of the kittens, then?" Atesca said acidly. "I'm going to move the army out tomorrow morning."

"I didn't deserve that, Atesca."

"Sorry, Brador. This long silence is making me a little edgy, and I'm losing my grip on civility."

"I'm as concerned as you are, Atesca," Brador said, "but all of my training rises up in protest at the notion of flying directly in the face of an imperial command." The kitten in Brador's lap nuzzled at his fingers affectionately. "You know," he said, "I think that when his Majesty returns, I'll ask him if I can have this kitten. I'm really growing rather fond of her."

"That's up to you," Atesca said. "Trying to find homes for two or three litters of kittens every year might keep you out of trouble." The broken-nosed general tugged thoughtfully at one earlobe. "How about a compromise?" he suggested.

"I'm always willing to listen."

"All right. We know that Urvon's army has largely disbanded, and there's fairly strong presumptive evidence that Urvon is dead."

"I'd say so, yes."

"And Zandramas has moved her forces into the Dalasian protectorates."

"That's what my people report."

"Now then, we're both senior officials in his Majesty's government, aren't we?"

"Yes."

"Doesn't that mean that we're expected to use our own initiative to take advantage of tactical situations that arise in the field without consulting Mal Zeth?"

"I suppose so. You've spent more time in the field than I have, though."

"It's standard practice, Brador. All right, then. Darshiva is virtually undefended. What I'm suggesting is that we restore order across the river in Peldane and move in to occupy Darshiva. That way we cut Zandramas off from her base of support. We set up a main line of resistance along the edge of those mountains to repel her forces if they try to return. We'll have effectively brought these two provinces back under imperial control. We might even get a few medals out of it."

"His Majesty *would* be rather pleased if that happened, wouldn't he?"

"He'd be overjoyed, Brador."

"I still don't see how occupying Darshiva is going to get us any closer to locating his Majesty."

"That's because you're not a military man. We have to keep track of the enemy. In this case, that means the Darshivan army. Standard military procedure in such situations is to send out patrols in force to make contact with the enemy to determine his strength and probable intentions. If those patrols should just *happen* to encounter the Emperor in the process, well—" He spread his hands eloquently.

"You'd have to brief the officers in command of those patrols rather thoroughly," Brador pointed out cautiously. "A green lieutenant might get flustered and blurt out things we'd rather not have the Emperor aware of."

"I said patrols in *force,* Brador." Atesca smiled. "I was thinking along the lines of full brigades. A brigade is commanded by a colonel, and I've got a number of fairly intelligent colonels."

Brador grinned at his friend. "When do we start?" he asked.

"Did you have anything planned for tomorrow morning?"

"Nothing that I can't postpone," Brador said.

·   ·   ·

"But *why* didn't you know it was coming?" Barak demanded of Drolag, his bosun. The two of them stood on the aft deck with the wind-driven rain sheeting almost horizontally across the rail to tear at their beards.

Drolag mopped at his face with one hand. "I haven't got the faintest idea, Barak," he admitted. "That leg has never failed me before." Drolag was one of those unfortunates who at some time in the past had broken one of his legs—in Drolag's case it had happened in a tavern brawl. He had discovered not long after the bone had knit that the leg was extraordinarily sensitive to weather changes. He was able to predict the onset of bad weather with uncanny accuracy. His shipmates always watched him very closely. When Drolag winced with every step, they began search-ing the horizons for oncoming storms; when he limped, they shortened sail and began rigging safety lines; and when he fell down with a surprised cry of pain, they immediately battened down all hatches, rigged the sea anchor, and went below. Drolag had turned a temporary inconvenience into a lifetime career. He always commanded top pay, and nobody ever expected him to do any real work. All he had to do was pace the deck where everybody could watch him. The miraculous leg even made it possible for him to predict with some degree of certainty just exactly when a given storm would hit. But not this time. The storm that swept the *Seabird*'s decks with wind and pelting rain had come unannounced, and Drolag was as surprised by its arrival as any man on board.

"You didn't get drunk and fall down and break it again, did you?" Barak de-manded suspiciously. Barak had very little knowledge of human anatomy—except about where to hit someone with an axe or to run a sword through him that would have the desired, and usually fatal, results. The big red-bearded man reasoned some-what foggily that if Drolag had achieved his weather sensitivity by breaking his leg, a second break might very well have taken it away again.

"No, of course I didn't, Barak," Drolag said disgustedly. "I'm not going to risk my livelihood for a few tankards of bad ale."

"How did the storm sneak up on you, then?"

"I don't know, Barak. Maybe it's not a natural storm. Some wizard may have summoned it. I don't know if my leg would react to something like that."

"That's always an easy excuse, Drolag," Barak scoffed. "Anytime an ignorant man can't explain something, he blames it on magic."

"I don't have to take this, Barak," Drolag said hotly. "I earn my way, but I'm not responsible for supernatural forces."

"Go below, Drolag," Barak told him. "Have a long talk with your leg and see if it can come up with a better excuse."

Drolag staggered down the pitching deck talking to himself.

Barak was in a foul humor. Everything seemed to be conspiring to delay him. Not long after he and his friends had witnessed Agachak's unpleasant demise, *Seabird* had struck a submerged log and sprung a seam. It had only been by dint of herculean bailing that they had been able to limp downriver to Dal Zerba and to haul the leaky ship up onto a mud bar for repairs. That chore had cost them two weeks, and now this storm from nowhere added to the delay. Then Unrak came up from below, trailed by the dull-faced King of the Thulls. Unrak looked around with the wind clawing at his bright red hair. "It doesn't seem to be letting up, does it, father?" he observed.

"Not noticeably."

"Hettar wants to talk with you."

"I've got to steer this big brute."

"The mate can do it, father. All he has to do is keep her bow into the wind. Hettar's been studying that map, and he thinks we're in danger."

"From this little storm? Don't be silly."

"Is *Seabird*'s bottom strong enough to take on rocks?"

"We're in deep water."

"Not for long, I don't think. Just come below, father. Hettar can show you."

Grumbling, Barak turned the tiller over to the first mate and followed his son to the companionway leading below. Nathel, the King of the Thulls, trailed along behind them, his face incurious. Nathel was a bit older than Unrak, but he had taken to following Barak's red-haired son about like a stray puppy. Unrak was none too gracious to his unwanted companion.

"What's this all about, Hettar?" Barak demanded of his friend as he entered the cramped cabin.

"Come over here and have a look," the tall Algar said.

Barak strode to the bolted-down table and looked down at the map.

"We left Dal Zerba yesterday morning, right?"

"Yes. We'd have gotten away sooner if somebody'd been paying attention to what was lying under the surface of that river. I think I'll find out who was on bow watch that day and have him keel-hauled."

"What's keel-hauled?" Nathel asked Unrak.

"Something very unpleasant," the red-haired boy replied.

"I'd rather you didn't tell me, then. I don't like unpleasant stuff."

"Whatever you want, your Majesty." Unrak *did* have a *few* manners.

"Couldn't you just call me Nathel?" the Thull asked plaintively. "I'm not really a king anyway. Mother's the one who makes all the decisions."

"Anything you want, Nathel." Unrak said it with a certain pity.

"How far would you estimate we've come since yesterday?" Hettar asked Barak.

"Oh, maybe twenty leagues. We had to heave to last night because we're in strange waters."

"That puts us almost right here, doesn't it?" Hettar pointed at an ominous symbol on the map.

"We aren't anywhere near that reef, Hettar. We came about to southeast as soon as we came out of that estuary at the mouth of the river."

"But we haven't been *going* southeast, Barak. There seems to be a current that comes down along the west coast of Mallorea, and it's a fairly strong one. I've checked a few times. Your bow is pointed southeast, but the *Seabird* has been drifting sideways almost due south because of that current."

"When did you suddenly become such an expert on sailing?"

"I don't have to be, Barak. Take a stick of wood and throw it off your starboard side. Your ship will catch up with the stick in just a few minutes. We're definitely drifting south in spite of whichever direction your bow is pointed. I'd guess that within an hour we'll be able to hear the surf breaking on that reef."

"I do confirm that our friend speaketh truth, my Lord of Trellheim," Mandorallen assured him. "I myself have witnessed his experiment with the stick. Truly, we are tending southward."

"What can we do?" Lelldorin asked a bit apprehensively.

Barak stared gloomily at the map. "We don't have any choice," he said. "We can't get back out into open sea in this storm. We'll have to drop both anchors and hope that we can find a bottom that'll hold us. Then we sit tight and ride it out. What's the name of that reef, Hettar?"

"Turim," the Algar replied.

CHAPTER TWENTY

Like almost every other ship's cabin in all the world, the one on Captain Kresca's vessel was low and had dark-stained beams overhead. The furniture was bolted to the floor, and oil lamps swung from the beams as the ship, swinging at anchor, rolled heavily in the combers coming in off the Sea of the East. Garion rather liked being at sea. There was a calmness, a kind of suspension of care out on deep water. When he was ashore it seemed that he was always scurrying from place to place through crowds of people, all filling his ears with distractions. At sea, however, there was time to be alone with his thoughts, and the even, patient roll of waves and the slow movement of the sky made those thoughts long and deep.

Their evening meal had been simple, a hearty bean soup and thick slices of dark, rich bread, and they sat on the benches around the plain table after they had eaten, talking idly and awaiting the arrival of the captain, who had promised to join them as soon as he had secured his ship.

The half-grown wolf lay under the table near where Ce'Nedra sat, and his eyes had a studied, pleading look in them. Ce'Nedra slipped him tidbits when she thought no one was watching her. Wolves are not stupid, after all.

"The surf seems to be heavy," 'Zakath said, cocking his head to one side to listen to the booming of the waves against the rocks of the reef. "That's likely to cause some problems when we try to land, isn't it?"

"I rather doubt it," Belgarath said. "This storm has probably been brewing since the day the earth was made. It's not going to interfere with us in any way."

"Aren't you being just a little fatalistic, Belgarath?" Beldin suggested. "And perhaps slightly overconfident?"

"I don't think so. The two prophecies *must* have this meeting. They've been coming toward this place since the beginning of time. They're not going to let anything interfere with the arrival of anyone who's supposed to be here."

"Why raise a storm like this, then?"

"The storm wasn't designed to hinder us—or Zandramas."

"What is its purpose?"

"It's probably out there to keep others away. There are only certain people who are supposed to be on that reef tomorrow. The prophecies are going to see to it that no one else can set foot on it until after our business has been completed."

Garion looked at Cyradis. The blindfolded girl's face was calm, even serene. The half concealment of the strip of cloth across her eyes had always at least partially concealed her features from him. In this light, however, he suddenly realized just how extraordinarily beautiful she really was. "That raises something rather interesting, Grandfather," he said. "Cyradis, didn't you tell us that the Child of Dark has always been solitary? Doesn't that mean that she'll have to face us alone tomorrow?"

"Thou hast misread my meaning, Belgarion of Riva. Thou and each of thy companions have had your names writ large in the stars since the beginning of days. Those who will accompany the Child of Dark, however, are of no moment. Their names do not stand in the book of the heavens. Zandramas is the only emissary of the dark prophecy of any significance. The others she will bring with her were doubtless chosen at random, and their numbers are limited to match your force."

"A fair fight, then," Velvet murmured approvingly. "I think we can probably cope."

"That doesn't bode too well for me, though," Beldin said. "Back at Rheon, you rather carefully listed the people who were supposed to come here with Garion. As I recall, my name wasn't on the list. Do you suppose they forgot to send me an invitation?"

"Nay, gentle Beldin. Thy presence here is necessary now. Zandramas hath included in her forces one who is beyond the prophecies. Thou art here to offset that one, though in numbers only."

"Zandramas can't ever play a game without cheating, can she?" Silk said.

"Can you?" Velvet asked him.

"That's different. I'm only playing for worthless counters—bits and pieces of unimportant metal. The stakes in this game are a lot higher."

The cabin door opened, and Captain Kresca entered with several rolls of parchment under his arm. He had changed out of his doublet and now wore a tar-stained canvas sea coat and no hat. Garion saw that his short-cropped hair was as silvery as Belgarath's, a startling contrast to his deeply tanned and weathered face. "The storm seems to be abating," he announced. "At least around the reef it is. I don't think I've ever seen a storm like this."

"I'd be surprised if you had, Captain," Beldin told him. "As closely as we can determine, this is the first one—and probably the last—of its kind."

"I think you're wrong, friend," Captain Kresca disagreed. "There's nothing new in the way of weather in the world. It's all happened before."

"Just let it lie," Belgarath said quietly to Beldin. "He's a Melcene. He's not really prepared for this sort of thing."

"All right," the captain said, pushing their soup bowls out of the way and laying his charts on the table. "We're here." He pointed. "Now, which part of the reef was it you propose to land on?"

"The highest pinnacle," Belgarath told him.

Kresca sighed. "I might have known," he said. "That's the one part of the reef where my charts aren't too accurate. About the time I got to taking soundings around that one, a squall came out of nowhere, and I had to back off." He thought about it. "No matter," he decided. "We'll stand a half mile or so offshore and go in with the longboat. There's something you ought to know about that part of the reef, though."

"Oh?" Belgarath said.

"I think there are some people there."

"I sort of doubt it."

"I don't really know of any other creature that builds fires, do you? There's a cave on the north side of that pinnacle, and sailors have been seeing the light of fires coming out of the mouth of it for years now. It's my guess that there's a band of pirates living in there. It wouldn't be all that hard for them to come out in small boats on dark nights and waylay merchantmen in the straits on the landward side of the reef."

"Can you see the fire from where we are right now?" Garion asked him.

"I'd guess so. Let's go topside and have a look."

The ladies, Sadi, and Toth remained in the cabin, and Garion and his other friends followed Captain Kresca up the companionway to the deck. The wind, which had been howling through the rigging when the sailors had dropped anchor, had fallen off, and the surf along the reef was no longer frothy.

"There," Kresca said, pointing. "It's not quite as visible from this angle, but you can make it out. When you're standing out to sea from the cave mouth, it's really bright."

Dimly, Garion could see a sooty red glow a short way up the side of a bulky-looking peak jutting up out of the sea. The other rocks that formed the reef appeared to be little more than slender spires, but the central peak had a different shape. For some reason, it reminded Garion of the truncated mountain that was the site of far-off Prolgu in Ulgoland.

"Nobody's ever explained to my satisfaction how the top of that mountain got sliced off like that," Kresca said.

"It's probably a very long story," Silk told him. The little man shivered. "It's still a little chilly out here," he noted. "Why don't we go below again?"

Garion fell back to walk beside Belgarath. "What's making that light, Grandfather?" he asked quietly.

"I'm not entirely sure," Belgarath replied, "but I think it might be the Sardion. We know it's in that cave."

"We do?"

"Of course we do. At the time of the meeting, the Orb and the Sardion have to come into each other's presence in the same way you and Zandramas do. That Melcene scholar who stole the Sardion—the one Senji told us about—sailed around the southern tip of Gandahar and disappeared into these waters. That was all too convenient to be mere coincidence. The Sardion was controlling the scholar, and the scholar delivered the stone to the precise place it wanted to go. It's probably been waiting for us in that cave for about five hundred years."

Garion looked back over his shoulder. The hilt of his sword was covered by the leather sleeve, but he was still fairly certain that he'd be able to see the muted glow of the Orb. "Doesn't the Orb usually react to the presence of the Sardion?" he asked.

"We may not be close enough yet, and we're still at sea. Open water confuses the Orb. Then, too, maybe it's trying to conceal itself from the Sardion."

"Could it actually think its way through that complex an idea? It's usually fairly childish, I've noticed."

"Don't underestimate it, Garion."

"Everything's fitting together, then, isn't it?"

"It all has to, Garion. Otherwise what's going to happen tomorrow couldn't happen."

"Well, father?" Polgara asked as they reentered the cabin.

"There's a fire of some kind in that cave, all right," he told her. His fingers, however, were telling her something else.—*We'll talk about it in more detail after the captain leaves.*—He turned toward Kresca. "When's the next low tide?" he asked the seaman.

Kresca squinted, calculating. "We just missed one," he said. "The tide's coming in now. The next low tide will come about daybreak and, if my observations are correct, it should be a neap tide. Well, I'll leave you to get some rest now. I sort of gather that you've got a full day ahead of you tomorrow."

"Thank you, Captain Kresca," Garion said, shaking the seaman's hand.

"Don't mention it, Garion." Kresca grinned. "The King of Peldane paid me very handsomely for this voyage, so being helpful doesn't really cost me anything."

"Good." Garion grinned back. "I like to see friends get ahead in the world."

The captain laughed and went back out with a hearty wave.

"What was he talking about?" Sadi asked. "What's a neap tide?"

"It only happens a few times a year," Beldin explained. "It's an extreme low tide. It has to do with the positions of the sun and moon."

"Everything seems to be going out of its way to make tomorrow a very special day," Silk observed.

"All right, father," Polgara said crisply. "What's the story on the fire in that cave?"

"I can't be positive, Pol, but I rather strongly suspect that it's not a group of pirates—not after all the trouble the prophecies have gone to to keep people away from the cave."

"What do you think it is, then?"

"It's probably the Sardion."

"Would it give off a red glow?"

He shrugged. "The Orb glows blue. I suppose there's a sort of logic to the Sardion's glowing a different color."

"Why not green?" Silk asked.

"Green's an in-between color," Beldin told him. "It's a mixture of blue and yellow."

"You're a real gold mine of useless information, you know that, Beldin?" Silk said.

"There's no such thing as useless information, Kheldar." Beldin sniffed.

"All right," 'Zakath said, "how are we going to go about this?"

"Cyradis," Belgarath said to the Seeress, "I'm guessing about this, but I think I'm fairly close. Nobody is going to reach that cave first, are they? What I mean is that the prophecies aren't going to let Zandramas get there before we do—or let us get there first either."

"Astounding," Beldin murmured. "That actually sounded like real logic. Aren't you feeling well, Belgarath?"

"Would you please?" Belgarath growled. "Well, Cyradis?"

She paused, her expression distant. Garion seemed to hear that faint choral murmuring. "Thy reasoning is correct, Ancient One. The same perception came to Zandramas some time ago, so I am not revealing anything unto thee which she doth not already know. Zandramas, however, hath rejected the fruits of her reasoning and hath striven to circumvent her conclusions."

"Very well, then," 'Zakath said, "since we're all going to get there at the same time anyway, and since everybody knows about it, there's not much point in being coy, is there? I say we just land on the beach and march straight to the cave."

"Stopping only long enough for you and me to put on our armor," Garion added. "It probably wouldn't be a good idea to dress up here on board ship. It might make Kresca nervous."

"Your plan sounds good to me, 'Zakath," Durnik agreed.

"I'm not so sure," Silk said dubiously. "There's a certain advantage to sneaking."

"Drasnians," Ce'Nedra sighed.

"Listen to his reasons before you throw the notion out, Ce'Nedra," Velvet suggested.

"It's sort of like this," Silk went on. "Zandramas *knows*—deep down—that she can't beat us to that cave, but she's been trying for months all the same, hoping that there's some way she can bypass the rules. Now, let's try to think the way she does."

"I'd sooner take poison," Ce'Nedra said with a shudder.

"It's only for the sake of understanding your opponent, Ce'Nedra. Now, Zandramas has been hoping against hope that she can beat us to that cave and avoid the necessity of coming up against Garion. He *did* kill Torak, after all, and nobody in his right mind would willingly confront the Godslayer."

"I'm going to have that removed from my title when I get back to Riva," Garion said sourly.

"You can do that later," Silk told him. "What would Zandramas most likely feel if she arrived at the cave mouth, looked around, and didn't see us?"

"I think I see where you're going, Kheldar," Sadi said admiringly.

"You would," 'Zakath said dryly.

"It's really rather brilliant, you know, Kal Zakath," the eunuch said. "Zandramas is going to feel a wild exultation. She'll believe that she's succeeded in circumventing the prophecies and that she's won in spite of them."

"Then what's going to happen to her when we all step out from behind a boulder and she finds out that she still has to face Garion and submit to the choice of Cyradis after all?" Silk asked.

"She's probably going to be very disappointed," Velvet said.

"I think disappointment might be too mild a term," Silk suggested. "I think chagrin might come closer. Couple that with exasperation and a healthy dose of fear, and we'll be looking at somebody who's not going to be thinking too clearly. We're fairly sure there's going to be a fight when we get there, and you've always got an advantage in a fight when the opposing general is distracted."

"It's sound tactical reasoning, Garion," 'Zakath conceded.

"I'll go along with it," Belgarath said. "If nothing else, it should give me the opportunity to pay Zandramas back for all the times she's upset me. I think I still owe her just a bit for slicing pieces out of the Ashabine Oracles. I'll talk with Captain Kresca early tomorrow morning and find out if there's a beach on the east side of the peak. With a neap tide, our chances should be pretty good. Then we'll work our way up along the side of the peak, staying out of sight. We'll take cover near the cave mouth and wait for Zandramas to put in an appearance. Then we'll step out and surprise her."

"I can add an even bigger advantage," Beldin said. "I'll scout on ahead and let you know when she lands. That way, you'll be ready for her."

"Not as a hawk, though, uncle," Polgara suggested.

"Why not?"

"Zandramas isn't stupid. A hawk wouldn't have any business on that reef. There wouldn't be anything there for him to eat."

"Maybe she'll think the storm blew me out to sea."

"Do you want to risk your tail feathers on a maybe? A seagull, uncle."

"A seagull?" he objected. "But they're so stupid—and so dirty."

"*You?* Worried about dirt?" Silk asked him, looking up. Silk had been busily counting on his fingers.

"Don't push it, Kheldar," Beldin growled ominously.

"What day of the month was Prince Geran born on?" Silk asked Ce'Nedra.

"The seventh, why?"

"We appear to have another one of those things that's setting out to make tomorrow very special. If I've counted right, tomorrow will be your son's second birthday."

"It can't be!" she exclaimed. "My baby was born in the wintertime."

"Ce'Nedra," Garion said gently, "Riva's up near the top of the world. This reef is near the bottom. It *is* winter in Riva right now. Count up the months since Geran was born—the time he spent with us before Zandramas stole him, the time we spent marching on Rheon, the trip to Prolgu then to Tol Honeth and on to Nyissa and all those other places where we had to stop. I think if you count rather closely, you'll find that it *has* been very close to two years."

She frowned, ticking the months off. Finally, her eyes went very wide. "I think he's right!" she exclaimed. "Geran will be two years old tomorrow!"

Durnik laid his hand on the little queen's arm. "I'll see if I can make something for you to give as a present, Ce'Nedra," he said gently. "A boy ought to have a birthday present after he's been separated from his family for so long."

Ce'Nedra's eyes filled with tears. "Oh, Durnik!" She wept, embracing him. "You think of everything."

Garion looked at Aunt Pol, his fingers moving slightly.—*Why don't you ladies take her in and put her to bed?*—he suggested.—*We're all through here, and if she thinks too much about this, she's going to get herself worked up. Tomorrow's going to be hard enough for her anyway.*—

—*You might be right.*—

After the ladies had left, Garion and the other men sat around the bolted-down table reminiscing. They covered in some detail the various adventures they had shared since that wind-tossed night so long ago when Garion, Belgarath, Aunt Pol, and Durnik had crept out through the gate of Faldor's farm into the world where the possible and the impossible inexorably merged. Again Garion felt that sense of cleansing, coupled with something else. It was as if, by recapitulating all that had happened in their long journey to the reef lying out there in the darkness, they were somehow bringing everything into focus to strengthen their resolve and their sense of purpose. It seemed to help for some reason.

"I think that's about enough of that," Belgarath said finally, rising to his feet. "Now we all know what's behind us. It's time to pack all that away and start looking ahead. Let's get some sleep."

Ce'Nedra stirred restlessly when Garion slipped into bed. "I thought you were going to stay up all night," she said sleepily.

"We were talking."

"I know. I could hear the murmur of voices even in here. And men think women talk all the time."

"Don't you?"

"Probably, but a woman can talk while her hands are busy. A man can't."

"You might be right."

There was a moment of silence. "Garion," she said.

"Yes, Ce'Nedra?"

"Can I borrow your knife—the little dagger Durnik gave you when you were a boy?"

"If you want something cut, point it out. I'll cut it for you."

"It's nothing like that, Garion. I just want to have a knife tomorrow."

"What for?"

"As soon as I see Zandramas, I'm going to kill her."

"Ce'Nedra!"

"I have every right to kill her, Garion. You told Cyradis you didn't think you could do it because Zandramas is a woman. I don't suffer from the same kind of delicacy as you do. I'm going to carve out her heart—if she has one—slowly." She said it with a fierceness he had never heard in her voice before. "I want blood, Garion! Lots of blood, and I want to hear her scream as I twist the knife in her. You'll lend me your dagger, won't you?"

"Absolutely not!"

"That's all right, Garion," she said in an icy tone. "I'm sure Liselle will lend me one of hers. Liselle's a woman and she knows how I feel." Then she turned her back on him.

"Ce'Nedra," he said placatingly.

"Yes?" Her tone was sulky.

"Be reasonable, dear."

"I don't want to be reasonable. I want to kill Zandramas."

"I'm not going to let you put yourself in that kind of danger. We have much more important things to do tomorrow."

She sighed. "I suppose you're right. It's just—"

"Just what?"

She turned back and put her arms around his neck. "Never mind, Garion," she said. "Let's go to sleep now." She nestled down against him, and after a few moments her regular breathing told him that she had drifted off.

"You should have given her the knife," the voice in his mind told him. *"Silk could have stolen it back from her sometime tomorrow."*

"But—"

"We've got something else to talk about, Garion. Have you been thinking about your successor?"

"Well—sort of. It doesn't really fit any of them, you know."

"Have you given serious consideration to each of them?"

"I suppose I have, but I haven't been able to make any decisions yet."

"You're not supposed to make your choice yet. All you had to do was think about each one of them and get them all firmly fixed in your mind."

"When do I make the choice then?"

"At the last possible moment, Garion. Zandramas might be able to hear your thoughts, but she can't hear what you haven't decided yet."

"What if I make a mistake?"

"I really don't think you can, Garion. I really don't."

Garion's sleep was troubled that night. His dreams seemed chaotic, disconnected, and he woke often only to sink back into a restless doze. There was at first a kind of distorted recapitulation of the strange dreams that had so disturbed him that night long ago on the Isle of the Winds just before his life had been unalterably changed. The question "Are you ready?" seemed to echo again and again in the vaults of his mind. Again he faced Rundorig with Aunt Pol's matter-of-fact instruction to kill his boyhood friend roaring in his mind. And then the boar he had encountered in the snowy wood outside Val Alorn was there, pawing at the snow, its eyes aglow with rage and hate. "Are you ready?" Barak asked him before releasing the beast. Then he stood on the colorless plain surrounded by the pieces of the incomprehensible game trying to decide which piece to move while the voice in his mind urged him to hurry.

The dream subtly changed and took on a different tone. Our dreams, no matter how bizarre, have a familiarity to them, since they are formed and shaped by our own minds. Now it seemed as if Garion's dreams were being formed by a different and unfriendly awareness almost in the same way that Torak had intruded himself in dreams and in thoughts before the meeting at Cthol Mishrak.

Again he faced Asharak the Murgo in the loamy Wood of the Dryads, and once again he unleashed his will with that single, open-handed slap and the fatal word, "Burn!" This was a familiar nightmare. It had haunted Garion's sleep for years. He saw Asharak's cheek begin to seethe and smoke. He heard the Grolim shriek and saw him clutch at his burning face. He heard the dreadful plea, "Master, have mercy!" He spurned that plea and intensified the flame, but this time the act was not overlaid with the sense of self-loathing that had always accompanied the dream, but a kind of cruel exultation, a hideous joy as he watched his enemy writhe and burn before him. Deep within him something cried out, trying to repudiate that unholy joy.

And then he was at Cthol Mishrak, and his flaming sword slid again and again into the body of the One-Eyed God. Torak's despairing "Mother!" did not this time fill him with pity but with a towering satisfaction. He felt himself laughing, and the savage, unpitying laughter erased his humanity.

Soundlessly shrieking in horror, Garion recoiled, not so much from the awful images of those whom he had destroyed, but more from his own enjoyment of their despairing agony.

■ CHAPTER TWENTY-ONE ■

They were a somber group when they gathered in the main cabin before daybreak the following morning. With a sudden, even surprising, insight, Garion was very certain that the nightmares had not been his alone. Insight and intuitive perception were not normal for Garion. His sensible Sendarian background rejected such things as questionable, even in some peculiar way, immoral. *Did you do that?* he asked the voice.

"No. Rather surprisingly, you came up with it all on your own. You seem to be making some progress—slowly, of course, but progress all the same."

"Thanks."

"Don't mention it."

Silk looked particularly shaken as he entered the cabin. The little man's eyes were haunted, and his hands were shaking. He slumped onto a bench and buried his face in his hands. "Have you got any of that ale left?" he asked Beldin in a hoarse voice.

"A little quivery this morning, Kheldar?" the dwarf asked him.

"No," Garion said. "That's not what's bothering him. He had some bad dreams last night."

Silk raised his face sharply. "How did you know that?" he demanded.

"I had some myself. I got to relive what I did to Asharak the Murgo, and I killed Torak again—several times. It didn't get any better as we went along."

"I was trapped in a cave," Silk said with a shudder. "There wasn't any light, but I could feel the walls closing in on me. I think the next time I see Relg, I'm going to hit him in the mouth—gently, of course. Relg's sort of a friend."

"I'm glad I wasn't the only one," Sadi said. The eunuch had placed a bowl of milk on the table, and Zith and her babies were gathered around it, lapping and purring. Garion was a bit surprised to note that no one really paid any attention to Zith and her brood anymore. People, it seemed, could get used to almost anything. Sadi rubbed his long-fingered hand over his shaved scalp. "It seemed to me that I was adrift in the streets of Sthiss Tor, and I was trying to survive by begging. It was ghastly."

"I saw Zandramas sacrificing my baby," Ce'Nedra said in a stricken voice. "There was crying and so much blood—so very much blood."

"Peculiar," 'Zakath said. "I was presiding over a trial. I had to condemn a number of people. There was one of them I cared a great deal about, but I was forced to condemn her anyway."

"I had one, too," Velvet admitted.

"I rather expect we all did," Garion told them. "The same thing happened to me on the way to Cthol Mishrak. Torak kept intruding in my dreams." He looked at Cyradis. "Does the Child of Dark always fall back on this?" he asked her. "We've found that events keep repeating themselves when we're leading up to one of these meetings. Is this one of those events that keeps happening over and over again?"

"Thou art very perceptive, Belgarion of Riva," the Seeress told him. "In all the uncounted eons since these meetings began, thou art the first Child of either Light or Dark to have realized that the sequence must be endlessly repeated until the division hath ended."

"I am not sure I can take much credit for it, Cyradis," he admitted. "As I understand it, the meetings are getting closer and closer together. I'm probably the first in history to have been the Child of Light—or Dark—during *two* meetings, and even then it took me awhile to realize that it was happening. The nightmares are part of that pattern then?"

"Thy guess is shrewd, Belgarion." She smiled gently. "Unfortunately, it is not correct. It seemeth to me a shame to waste such a clever perception, though."

"Are you trying to be funny, Holy Seeress?"

"Would I do that, noble Belgarion?" she said, perfectly imitating Silk's inflection.

"You could spank her," Beldin suggested.

"With that human mountain standing guard over her?" Garion said, grinning at Toth. His eyes narrowed. "You're not permitted to help us with this, are you, Cyradis?" he asked her.

She sighed and shook her head.

"That's all right, Holy Seeress," he said. "I think we can come up with a workable answer to the question by ourselves." He looked at Belgarath. "All right," he said. "Torak tried to frighten me with nightmares, and now it looks as if Zandramas is trying to do the same thing, except that this time, she's doing it to all of us. If it's not one of those usual repetitions, what is it?"

"That boy's beginning to develop a rather keen analytical mind, Belgarath," Beldin said.

"Naturally," the old man said modestly.

"Don't wrench your shoulder out of its socket trying to pat yourself on the back," Beldin said sourly. He rose to his feet and started pacing up and down, his forehead creased in thought. "Now then," he began, "first: This isn't just one of the tedious repetitions that have been dogging us since the beginning, right?"

"Right," Belgarath agreed.

"Second: It happened in about the same way last time." He looked at Garion. "Right?" he asked.

"Right," Garion said.

"That's only two times. Twice can be a coincidence, but let's assume that it's not. We know that the Child of Light always has companions, but that the Child of Dark is always solitary."

"So Cyradis tells us," Belgarath agreed.

"She doesn't have any reason to lie to us. All right, if the Child of Light has companions but the Child of Dark is alone, wouldn't that put the Dark at a serious disadvantage?"

"You'd think so."

"But the two have always been so evenly matched that not even the Gods can predict the outcome. The Child of Dark is using something to offset the apparent advantage of our side. I think these nightmares might be part of it."

Silk rose and came over to Garion. "Discussions like this make my head ache," he said quietly. "I'm going up on deck for a while." He left the cabin, and for no apparent reason the gangly young wolf followed him.

"I don't really think a few nightmares would make that much difference, Beldin," Belgarath disagreed.

"But what if the nightmares are only a part of it, Old Wolf?" Poledra asked him. "You and Pol were both at Vo Mimbre, and that was one of these meetings, too. You two have been companions of the Child of Light twice already. What happened at Vo Mimbre?"

"We *did* have nightmares," Belgarath conceded to Beldin.

"Anything else?" the dwarf asked intently.

"We saw things that weren't there, but that could have come from all the Grolims in the vicinity."

"And?"

"Everybody went sort of crazy. It was all we could do to keep Brand from trying to attack Torak with his teeth, and at Cthol Mishrak I entombed Belzedar in solid rock, and then Pol wanted to dig him up so that she could drink his blood."

"Father! I did *not*!" she objected.

"Oh, really? You were *very* angry that day, Pol."

"It fits the same pattern, Old Wolf," Poledra said somberly. "Our side fights with normal weapons. Garion's sword might be a little abnormal, but it's still just a sword."

"You wouldn't say that if you'd been at Cthol Mishrak," her husband told her.

"I *was* there, Belgarath," she replied.

"You *were*?"

"Of course. I was hiding in the ruins watching. Anyway, the Child of Dark doesn't attack the body; it attacks the mind. That's how it manages to keep everything so perfectly balanced."

"Nightmares, hallucinations, and ultimately madness," Polgara mused. "That's a formidable array of things to throw against us. It might even have worked—if Zandramas hadn't been so clumsy."

"I don't quite follow that, Pol," Durnik said.

"She blundered." Polgara shrugged. "If only one person has a nightmare, he'll probably try to shrug it off and he certainly won't mention it on the morning of the meeting. Zandramas sent nightmares to all of us, though. This conversation probably wouldn't have taken place if she hadn't."

"It's nice to know that she can stumble, too," Belgarath said. "All right then, we know that she's been tampering with us. The best way to defeat that tactic is to put those nightmares out of our minds."

"*And* to be particularly wary if we start seeing things that shouldn't be there," Polgara added.

Silk and the wolf came back down the stairs to the cabin. "We've got absolutely beautiful weather this morning," he reported happily, bending slightly to scratch the pup's ears.

"Wonderful," Sadi murmured dryly. Sadi was carefully anointing his small dagger with a fresh coating of poison. He was wearing a stout leather jerkin and leather boots that reached to midthigh. Back in Sthiss Tor, Sadi had appeared, despite his slender frame, to be soft, even in some peculiar way flabby. Now, however, he looked lean and tough. A year or more without drugs and with an enforced regimen of hard exercise had changed him a great deal.

"It's perfect," Silk told him. "We have fog this morning, ladies and gentlemen," he said, "a nice, wet, gray fog almost thick enough to walk on. That fog would be a burglar's delight."

"Trust Silk to think of that." Durnik smiled. The smith wore his usual clothing, but he had given Toth his axe, while he himself carried the dreadful sledge with which he had driven off the demon Nahaz.

"The prophecies are leading us around by the noses again," Beldin said irritably, "but at least it appears that we made the right decision last night. A good thick fog makes sneaking almost inevitable." Beldin looked the same as always, tattered, dirty, and very ugly.

"Maybe they're just trying to help," Velvet suggested. Velvet had shocked them all when she had entered the cabin a half hour earlier. She wore tight-fitting leather clothing not unlike that normally worn by the Nadrak dancer, Vella. It was a peculiarly masculine garb and bleakly businesslike. "They've done a great deal to assist Zandramas. Maybe it's our turn to get a little help."

"*Is she right?*" Garion asked the awareness that shared his mind. "*Are you and your opposite helping us for a change?*"

"*Don't be silly, Garion. Nobody's been helping anybody. That's forbidden at this particular stage of the game.*"

"*Where did the fog come from then?*"

"*Where does fog usually come from?*"

"*How would I know?*"

"*I didn't think so. Ask Beldin. He can probably tell you. The fog out there is perfectly natural.*"

"Liselle," Garion said, "I just checked with my friend. The fog isn't the result of any playing around. It's a natural result of the storm."

"How disappointing," she said.

Ce'Nedra had risen that morning fully intent on wearing a Dryad tunic. Garion had adamantly rejected that idea, however. She wore instead a simple gray wool dress with no petticoats to hinder her movements. She was quite obviously stripped down for action. Garion was fairly certain that she had at least one knife concealed somewhere in her clothing. "Why don't we get started?" she demanded.

"Because it's still dark, dear," Polgara explained patiently. "We have to wait for at least a little bit of light." Polgara and her mother wore almost identical plain dresses, Polgara's gray and Poledra's brown.

"Garion," Poledra said then, "why don't you step down to the galley and tell them that we'll have breakfast now? We should all eat something, since I doubt that we'll have time or maybe even the need for lunch." Poledra sat at Belgarath's side, and the two of them were almost unconsciously holding hands. Garion was a bit offended at her suggestion. He *was* a king, after all, not an errand boy. Then he realized just how silly that particular thought was. He started to rise.

"I'll go, Garion," Eriond said. It was almost as if the blond young man had seen into his friend's thoughts. Eriond wore the same simple brown peasant clothes he always wore, and he had nothing even resembling a weapon.

As the young man went out through the cabin door, Garion had an odd thought. Why was he paying so much attention to the appearance of each of his companions? He had seen them all before, and for the most part, he had seen the clothing they wore this morning so many times that the garments should not even have registered on his mind. Then, with dreadful certainty, he knew. One of them was going to die today, and he was fixing them all in his mind so that he could remember for the rest of his life the one who was to make that sacrifice. He looked at 'Zakath. His Mallorean friend had shaved off his short beard. His slightly olive skin was no longer pale, but tanned and healthy-looking save for the now-lighter patch on his chin and jaw. He wore simple clothing much like Garion's own, since as soon as they reached the reef, the two of them would be putting on their armor.

Toth, his face impassive, was dressed as always—a loincloth, sandals, and that unbleached wool blanket slung across one shoulder. He did not, however, have his heavy staff. Instead, Durnik's axe lay in his lap.

The Seeress of Kell was unchanged. Her hooded white robe gleamed, and her blindfold, unwrinkled and unchanged, smoothly covered her eyes. Idly Garion wondered if she removed the cloth when she slept. A chilling thought came to him then. What if the one they would lose today was going to be Cyradis? She had sacrificed everything for her task. Surely the two prophecies could not be so cruel as to require one last, supreme sacrifice from this slender girl.

Belgarath, of course, was unchanged and unchangeable. He still wore the mismatched boots, patched hose, and rust-colored tunic he had worn when he had appeared at Faldor's farm as Mister Wolf the storyteller. The one difference about the old man was the fact that he did not hold a tankard in his free hand. At supper the previous evening, he had almost absently drawn himself one that brimmed with foaming ale. Poledra, just as absently, had firmly removed it from his hand and had emptied it out a porthole. Garion strongly suspected that Belgarath's drinking days had come rather abruptly to an end. He decided that it might be refreshing to have a long conversation with his grandfather when the old man was completely sober.

They ate their breakfast with hardly any conversation, since there was nothing more to say. Ce'Nedra dutifully fed the puppy, then looked rather sadly at Garion. "Take care of him, please," she said.

There was no point in arguing with her on that score. The idea that she would not survive this day was so firmly fixed in her mind that no amount of talking would erase it. "You might want to give him to Geran," she added. "Every boy should have a dog, and caring for him will teach our son responsibility."

"I never had a dog," Garion said.

"That was unkind of you, Aunt Pol," Ce'Nedra said, lapsing unconsciously—or perhaps not—into that form of address.

"He wouldn't have had time to look after one, Ce'Nedra," Polgara replied. "Our Garion has had a very busy life."

"Let's hope that it gets less so when this is all over," Garion said.

After they had eaten, Captain Kresca entered the cabin carrying a map. "This isn't very precise," he apologized. "As I said last night, I was never able to take very accurate soundings around that peak. We can inch our way to within a few hundred yards of the beach, and then we'll have to take to the longboat. This fog is going to make it even more complicated, I'm afraid."

"Is there a beach along the east side of the peak?" Belgarath asked him.

"A very shallow one," Kresca replied. "The neap tide should expose a bit more of it, though."

"Good. There are a few things we'll need to take ashore with us." Belgarath pointed at the two stout canvas bags holding the armor Garion and 'Zakath would wear.

"I'll have some men stow them in the boat for you."

"When can we get started?" Ce'Nedra asked impatiently.

"Another twenty minutes or so, little lady."

"So long?"

He nodded. "Unless you can figure out a way to make the sun come up early."

Ce'Nedra looked quickly at Belgarath.

"Never mind," he told her.

"Captain," Poledra said, "could you have someone look after our pet?" She pointed at the wolf. "He's a bit overenthusiastic sometimes, and we wouldn't want him to start howling at the wrong time."

"Of course, Lady." Kresca, it appeared, had not spent enough time ashore to recognize a wolf when he saw one.

"Inching" proved to be a very tedious process. The sailors raised the anchors and then manned the oars. After every couple of strokes, they paused while a man in the bow heaved out the lead-weighted sounding line.

"It's slow," Silk observed in a low voice as they all stood on deck, "but at least it's quiet. We don't know who's on that reef, and I'd rather not alert them."

"It's shoaling, Captain," the man with the sounding line reported, his voice no louder than absolutely necessary. The obviously warlike preparations of Garion and his friends had stressed the need for quiet louder than any words. The sailor cast out his line again. There was that interminable-seeming wait while the ship drifted up over the weighted line. "The bottom's coming up fast, Captain," the sounder said then. "I make it two fathoms."

"Back your oars," Kresca commanded his crew in a low voice. "Drop the hook. This is as close as we can go." He turned to his mate. "After we get away in the long-boat, back out about another hundred yards and anchor there. We'll whistle when we come back—the usual signal. Guide us in."

"Aye, aye, Cap'n."

"You've done this before, I see," Silk said to Kresca.

"A few times, yes," Kresca admitted.

"If all goes well today, you and I might want to have a little talk. I have a business proposition that I think might interest you."

"Is that all you ever think about?" Velvet asked him.

"A missed opportunity is gone forever, my dear Liselle," he replied with a certain pomposity.

"You're incorrigible."

"I suppose you could say that, yes."

An oil-soaked wad of burlap in the hawsehole muffled the rattling of the anchor chain as the heavy iron hook sank down through the dark water. Garion felt rather than heard the grating of the points of the anchor on the rocks lying beneath the heavy swells.

"Let's board the longboat," Kresca said. "The crew will lower her after we're all on board." He looked apologetically at them. "I'm afraid you and your friends are going to have to help with the rowing, Garion. The longboat only holds so many people."

"Of course, Captain."

"I'll come along to make sure you get ashore safely."

"Captain," Belgarath said then, "once we're ashore, stand your ship out to sea a ways. We'll signal you when we're ready to be picked up."

"All right."

"If you don't see a signal by tomorrow morning, you might as well go on back to Perivor, because we won't be coming back."

Kresca's face was solemn. "Is whatever it is you're planning to do on that reef really *that* dangerous?" he asked.

"Probably even more so," Silk told him. "We've all been trying very hard not to think about it."

It was eerie rowing across the oily-seeming black water with the grayish tendrils of fog rising from the heavy swells. Garion was suddenly reminded of that foggy night in Sthiss Tor when they had crossed the River of the Serpent with only the unerring sense of direction of the one-eyed assassin Issus to guide them. Idly, as he rowed, Garion wondered whatever had happened to Issus.

After every ten stokes or so, Captain Kresca, who stood in the stern at the tiller, signaled for them to stop, and he cocked his head, listening to the sound of the surf. "Another couple hundred yards now," he said in a low voice. "You there," he said to the sailor in the bow who held another sounding line, "keep busy with that lead. I don't want to hit any rocks. Sing out if it starts shoaling."

"Aye, aye, Cap'n."

The longboat crept on through dark and fog toward the unseen beach where the long wash and slither of the waves on graveled shingle made that peculiar grating sound as each wave lifted pebbles from the beach to carry them up to the very verge of land and then, with melancholy and regretful note, to draw them back again as if the ever-hungry sea mourned its inability to engulf the land and turn all the world into one endless ocean where huge waves, unimpeded, could roll thrice around the globe.

The heavy fog bank lying to the east began to turn lighter and lighter as dawn broke over the dark, mist-obscured waves.

"Another hundred yards," Kresca said tensely.

"When we get there, Captain," Belgarath said to him, "keep your men in the boat. They won't be permitted to land anyway, and they'd better not try. We'll push you back out as soon as we get ashore."

Kresca swallowed hard and nodded.

Garion could hear the surf more clearly now and catch the seaweed-rank smell of the meeting of sea and land. Then, just before he was able to make out the dark line of the beach through the obscuring fog, the heavy, dangerous swells flattened, and the sea around the longboat became as flat and slick as a pane of glass.

"That was accommodating of them," Silk observed.

"Shh," Velvet told him, laying one finger to her lips. "I'm trying to listen."

The bow of the longboat grated on the gravel strand, and Durnik stepped out of the boat and drew it farther up onto the pebbles. Garion and his friends also stepped out into the ankle-deep water and waded ashore. "We'll see you tomorrow morning, Captain," Garion said quietly as Toth prepared to push the boat back out. "I hope," he added.

"Good luck, Garion," Kresca said. "After we're all back on board, you'll have to tell me what this was all about."

"I may want to forget about it by then," Garion said ruefully.

"Not if you win," Kresca's voice came back out of the fog.

"I like that man," Silk said. "He's got a nice optimistic attitude."

"Let's get off this open beach," Belgarath said. "In spite of what Garion's friend told him, I sense a certain tenuousness about this fog. I'll feel a lot better if we've got some rocks to hide behind."

Durnik and Toth picked up the two canvas bags containing the armor, and Garion and 'Zakath drew their swords and led the way up from the gravel strand. The mountain they approached seemed composed of speckled granite, fractured into unnatural blocks. Garion had seen enough granite in the mountains here and there around the world to know that the stone usually crumbled and weathered into rounded shapes. "Strange," Durnik murmured, kicking with one still-wet boot at the perfectly squared-off edge of one of the blocks. He lowered the canvas bag and drew his knife. He dug for a moment at the rock with his knife point. "It's not granite," he said quietly. "It *looks* like granite, but it's much too hard. It's something else."

"We can identify it later," Beldin told him. "Let's find some cover just in case Belgarath's suspicion turns out to be accurate. As soon as we get settled, I'll drift around the peak a few times."

"You won't be able to see anything," Silk predicted.

"I'll be able to hear, though."

"Over there," Durnik said, pointing with his sledge. "It looks as if one of these blocks got dislodged and rolled down to the beach. There's a fairly large niche there."

"Good enough for now," Belgarath said. "Beldin, when you make the change, do it very slowly. I'm sure Zandramas landed at almost the exact same time we did, and she'll hear you."

"I know how it's done, Belgarath."

The niche in the side of the strange, stair-stepped peak was more than large enough to conceal them, and they moved down into it cautiously.

"Neat," Silk said. "Why don't you all wait here and catch your breath? Beldin can turn into a seagull and go have a look around the island. I'll go on ahead and pick out a trail for us."

"Be careful," Belgarath told him.

"Someday you're going to forget to say that, Belgarath, and it'll probably wither every tree on earth." The little man climbed back up out of the niche and disappeared into the fog.

"You *do* say that to him a lot, you know," Beldin said to Belgarath.

"Silk's an enthusiast. He needs frequent reminding. Did you plan to leave sometime during the next hour?"

Beldin spat out a very unflattering epithet, shimmered very slowly, and sailed away.

"Your temper hasn't improved much, Old Wolf," Poledra said to him.

"Did you think it might have?"

"Not really," she replied, "but there's always room for hope."

Despite Belgarath's premonition, the fog hung on. After about a half hour, Beldin returned. "Somebody's landed on the west beach," he reported. "I couldn't see them, but I could certainly hear them. Angaraks seem to have some trouble keeping their voices down—sorry, 'Zakath, but it's the truth."

"I'll issue an imperial command that the next three or four generations converse in whispers, if you'd like."

"No, that's all right, 'Zakath." The dwarf grinned. "As long as I'm on the opposite side from at least *some* Angaraks, I like to be able to hear them coming. Did Kheldar make it back yet?"

"Not yet," Garion told him.

"What's he doing? These stone blocks are much too big to steal."

Then Silk slipped over the edge of the niche and dropped lightly to the stone floor. "You're not going to believe this," he said.

"Probably not," Velvet said, "but why don't you go ahead and tell us anyway?"

"This peak is man-made—or at least *something* made it. These blocks encircle it like terraces, all straight and smooth. The thing formed steps up to that flat place on top. There's an altar up there and a huge throne."

"So *that's* what it meant!" Beldin exclaimed, snapping his fingers. "Belgarath, have you ever read the Book of Torak?"

"I've struggled through it a few times. My Old Angarak isn't really all that good."

"You can speak Old Angarak?" 'Zakath asked with some surprise. "It's a forbidden language here in Mallorea. I suspect Torak was changing a few things, and he didn't want anyone to catch him at it."

"I learned it before the prohibition went into effect. What's the point of this, Beldin?"

"Do you remember that passage near the beginning—in the middle of all that conceited blather—when Torak said he went up into the High Places of Korim to argue with UL about the creation of the world?"

"Vaguely."

"Anyway, UL didn't want anything to do with it, so Torak turned his back on his father and went down and gathered up the Angaraks and led them back to Korim. He told them what he had in mind for them, and then, in true Angarak fashion, they fell down on their faces and started butchering each other as sacrifices. There's a word in that passage, 'Halagachak.' It means 'temple,' or something like that. I always thought that Torak was speaking figuratively, but he wasn't. This peak is that temple. The altar up there more or less confirms it, and these terraces were where the Angaraks stood to watch while the Grolims sacrificed people to their God. If I'm right, this is also the place where Torak spoke with his father. Regardless of how you feel about old Burnt-Face, this is one of the holiest places on earth."

"You keep talking about Torak's father," 'Zakath said, looking puzzled. "I didn't know that the Gods *had* fathers."

"Of course they do," Ce'Nedra said loftily. "Everybody knows that."

"I didn't."

"UL is their father," she said in a deliberately offhand manner.

"Isn't he the God of the Ulgos?"

"Not by choice exactly," Belgarath told him. "The original Gorim more or less bullied him into it."

"How do you bully a God?"

"Carefully," Beldin said. "Very, very carefully."

"I've met UL," Ce'Nedra supplied gratuitously. "He sort of likes me."

"She can be very irritating at times, can't she?" 'Zakath said to Garion.

"You've noticed."

"You don't have to like me," she said with a toss of her curls, "either one of you. As long as the Gods like a girl, she'll do all right."

Garion began to have some hope at that point. If Ce'Nedra was willing to banter with them, it was a fair indication that she did not take her supposed intimations of her own incipient demise all that seriously. He *did*, however, wish that he could get that knife away from her.

"During the course of your fascinating explorations, did you by any chance happen to locate that cave?" Belgarath asked Silk. "I more or less thought that's why you were out there sneaking around in the fog."

"The cave?" Silk said. "Oh, that's around on the north side. There's a sort of amphitheater in front of it. It's almost exactly in the middle of that face. I found that in the first ten minutes."

Belgarath glared at him.

"It's not exactly a cave, though," Silk added. "There may be a cave back inside the peak, but the opening is more like a wide doorway. It's got pillars on each side and a familiar face above the lintel."

"Torak?" Garion said with a sinking feeling.

"None other."

"Hadn't we better get started then?" Durnik suggested. "If Zandramas is already on the island . . ." He spread his hands.

"So what?" Beldin said.

They all stared at the grotesque little hunchback.

"Zandramas can't go into the cave until we get there, can she?" he asked Cyradis.

"Nay, Beldin," she replied. "That is forbidden."

"Good. Let her wait, then. I'm sure she'll enjoy the anticipation. Did anybody think to bring anything to eat? I may have to be a seagull, but I *don't* have to eat raw fish."

CHAPTER TWENTY-TWO

They waited for almost an hour until Beldin decided that by now Zandramas must be keyed to a fever pitch. Garion and 'Zakath took advantage of the delay to put on their armor. "I'll take a look," the dwarf said finally. He slowly slipped into the shape of a seagull and drifted away into the fog. When he returned, he was chuckling evilly. "I've never heard a woman use that kind of language," he said. "She even puts you to shame, Pol."

"What's she doing?" Belgarath asked him.

"She's standing outside the cave mouth—or door, or whatever you want to call it. She had about forty Grolims with her."

"*Forty?*" Garion exclaimed. He turned on Cyradis. "I thought you said we'd be evenly matched," he accused.

"Art thou not a match for at least five, Belgarion?" she asked simply.

"Well—"

"You said *had*," Belgarath said to his brother.

"I'd say that our star-speckled friend tried to force several of her Grolims to push through whatever it is that has the door sealed against her. I'm not sure if it was the force holding the door or if Zandramas lost her temper when the Grolims failed. About five of them are noticeably dead at the moment, and Zandramas is stalking about outside inventing swear words. All of her Grolims have purple linings on the insides of their hoods, by the way."

"Sorcerers, then," Polgara said bleakly.

"Grolim sorcery is not all that profound." Beldin shrugged.

"Could you see if she's got those lights under her skin?" Garion asked.

"Oh, my, yes. Her face looks like a meadow full of fireflies on a summer evening. I saw something else, too. That albatross is out there. We nodded, but we didn't have time to stop and speak."

"What was he doing?" Silk asked suspiciously.

"Just hovering. You know how albatrosses are. I don't think they move their wings more than once a week. The fog is starting to thin. Why don't we just ease around and stand on one of these terraces just above that amphitheater and let this murk dissipate. Seeing a group of dark figures emerging out of the fog should give her quite a turn, wouldn't you think?"

"Did you see my baby?" Ce'Nedra asked, her heart in her voice.

"He's hardly a baby anymore, little girl. He's a sturdy little lad with curls as blond as Eriond's used to be. I gathered from his expression that he's not very fond of the company he's in, and judging from the look of him, he's going to grow up to be as bad-tempered as the rest of his family. Garion could probably go down there and hand him the sword, and then we could all sit back and watch him deal with the problem."

"I'd rather not have him start killing people until after he loses his baby teeth," Garion said firmly. "Is there anybody else there?"

"Judging from his wife's description, the Archduke Otrath is among the group. He's wearing a cheap crown and sort of secondhand royal robes. There's not too much in the way of intelligence in his eyes."

"That one is mine," 'Zakath grated. "I've never had the opportunity to deal with high treason on a personal level before."

"His wife will be eternally in your debt." Beldin grinned. "She might even decide to journey to Mal Zeth to offer her thanks—among other things—in person. She's a lush wench, 'Zakath. I'd advise that you get plenty of rest."

"Methinks I care not for the turn this conversation hath taken," Cyradis said primly. "The day wears on. Let us proceed."

"Anythin' yer heart desires, me little darlin'." Beldin grinned.

Cyradis smiled in spite of herself.

Again they all spoke with that jocular bravado. They were approaching what was probably the most important Event in all of time, and making light of it was a natural human response.

Silk led the way out of the niche, his soft boots making no sound on the wet stones under their feet. Garion and 'Zakath, however, had to move with some care to avoid clinking. The sharply mounting stone terraces were each uniformly about ten feet tall, but at regular intervals there were stairways leading from one terrace to the one above. Silk led them up about three levels and then began circling the truncated pyramid. When they reached the northeast corner, he paused. "We'd better be very quiet now," he whispered. "We're only about a hundred yards from that amphitheater. We don't want some sharp-eared Grolim to hear us."

They crept around the corner and made their way carefully along the north face for several minutes. Then Silk stopped and leaned out over the edge to peer

down into the fog. "This is it," he whispered. "The amphitheater's a rectangular in-
dentation in the side of the peak. It runs from the beach up to that portal or whatever you want to call it. If you look over the edge, you'll see that the terraces below
us break off back there a ways. The amphitheater is right below us. We're within a
hundred yards of Zandramas right now."

Garion peered down into the fog, almost wishing that by a single act of will he
could brush aside the obscuring mist so that he could look at the face of his enemy.

"Steady," Beldin whispered to him. "It's going to come soon enough. Let's not
spoil the surprise for her."

Disjointed voices came up out of the fog—harsh, guttural Grolim voices. The
fog seemed to muffle them, so Garion could not pick out individual words, but he
didn't really have to.

They waited.

The sun by now had risen above the eastern horizon, and its pale disk was
faintly visible through the fog and the roiling cloud that was the aftermath of the
storm. The fog began to eddy and swirl. Gradually the mist overhead dissolved, and
now Garion could see the sky. A thick blanket of dirty-looking scud lay over the reef
but extended only a few leagues to the east. Thus it was that the sun, low on the
eastern horizon, shone on the underside of the clouds and stained them an angry
reddish orange with its light. It looked almost as if the sky had taken fire.

"Colorful," Sadi murmured, nervously passing his poisoned dagger from one
hand to the other. He set his red leather case down and opened it. Then he took up
the earthenware bottle, worked the stopper out, and laid it on its side. "There
should be mice on this reef," he said, "or the eggs of seabirds. Zith and her babies
will be all right." Then he straightened, carefully putting a small bag he had taken
from the case in the pocket of his tunic. "A little precaution," he whispered by way
of explanation.

The fog now lay beneath them like a pearly gray ocean in the shadow of the
pyramid. Garion heard a strange, melancholy cry and raised his eyes. The albatross
hovered on motionless wings above the fog. Garion peered intently down into the
obscuring mist, almost absently working the leather sleeve off the hilt of his sword.
The Orb was glowing faintly, and its color was not blue, but an angry red, almost
the color of the burning sky.

"That confirms it, Old Wolf," Poledra said to her husband. "The Sardion's in
that cave."

Belgarath, silvery hair and beard glowing red in the light reflected from the
clouds overhead, grunted.

The fog below began to swirl, its surface looking almost like an angry sea. It
thinned even more. Garion could now see shadowy forms beneath them, hazy, indistinct, and uniformly dark.

The fog was now no more than a faintly obscuring haze.

"Holy Sorceress!" a Grolim voice exclaimed in alarm. "Look!"

A hooded figure in a shiny black satin robe spun about, and Garion looked full
into the face of the Child of Dark. He had heard the lights beneath her skin described several times, but no description had prepared him for what he now saw.
The lights in Zandramas' face were not stationary, but swirled restlessly beneath her

skin. In the shadow of the ancient pyramid, her features were dark, nearly invisible, but the swirling lights made it appear, in the cryptic words of the Ashabine Oracles, as if "all the starry universe" were contained in her flesh.

Behind him he heard the sharp hiss of Ce'Nedra's indrawn breath. He turned his head and saw his little queen, dagger in hand and eyes ablaze with hatred, starting toward the stairs leading down into the amphitheater. Polgara and Velvet, obviously aware of her desperate plan, quickly restrained and disarmed her.

Then Poledra stepped to the edge of the terrace. "And so it has come at last, Zandramas," she said in a clear voice.

"I was but waiting for thee to join thy friends, Poledra," the sorceress replied in a taunting tone. "I was concerned for thee, fearing that thou hadst lost thy way. Now it is complete, and we may proceed in orderly fashion."

"Thy concern with order is somewhat belated, Zandramas," Poledra told her, "but no matter. We have all, as was foretold, arrived at the appointed place at the appointed time. Shall we put aside all this foolishness and go inside? The universe must be growing impatient with us."

"Not just yet, Poledra," Zandramas replied flatly.

"How tiresome," Belgarath's wife said wearily. "That's a failing in thee, Zandramas. Even after something obviously isn't working, thou must continue to try. Thou hast twisted and turned and tried to evade this meeting, but all in vain. And all of thine evasion hath only brought thee more quickly to this place. Thinkest thou not that it is time to forgo thine entertainments and to go along gracefully?"

"I do not think so, Poledra."

Poledra sighed. "All right, Zandramas," she said in a resigned tone, "as it pleaseth thee." She extended her arm, pointing at Garion. "Since thou art so bent on this, thus I summon the Godslayer."

Slowly, deliberately, Garion reached back across his shoulder and wrapped his hand about the hilt of his sword. It made an angry hiss as it slid from its sheath and it was already flaming an incandescent blue as it emerged. Garion's mind was icy calm now. All doubt and fear were gone, even as they had been at Cthol Mishrak, and the spirit of the Child of Light possessed him utterly. He took the sword hilt in both hands and slowly raised it until the flaming blade was pointed at the fiery clouds overhead. "This is thy fate, Zandramas!" he roared in an awful voice, the archaic words coming unbidden to his lips.

"That has yet to be determined, Belgarion." Zandramas' tone was defiant, as might be expected, but there was something else behind it. "Fate is not always so easily read." She made an imperious gesture, and her Grolims formed up into a phalanx around her and began to intone a harsh chant in an ancient and hideous language.

"Get back!" Polgara warned sharply, and she, her parents, and Beldin stepped to the edge of the terrace.

Flickering faintly, an inky shadow began to appear at the very edge of Garion's vision, and he began to feel an obscure sense of dread. "Watch yourselves," he quietly warned his friends. "I think she's starting one of those illusions we were talking about last night." Then he felt a powerful surge and heard a roar of sound. A wave of sheer darkness rolled out from the extended hands of the Grolims massed around Zandramas, but the wave shattered into black fragments that sizzled and skittered around the amphitheater like frightened mice as the four sorcerers blew it apart almost contemptuously with a single word spoken in unison. Several of the Grolims collapsed writhing to the stone floor, and most of the rest of them staggered back, their faces suddenly pasty white.

Beldin cackled evilly. "An' would ye like t' try it again, darlin'?" he taunted Zandramas. "If that's yer intent, ye should have brought more Grolims. Yer usin' 'em up at a fearful rate, don't y' know."

"I *wish* you wouldn't do that," Belgarath said to him.

"So does *she*, I'll wager. She takes herself very seriously, and a little ridicule always sets that sort off their pace."

Without changing expression, Zandramas hurled a fireball at the dwarf, but he brushed it aside as if it were no more than an annoying insect.

Garion quite suddenly understood. The sudden sheet of darkness and the fireball were not intended seriously. They were no more than subterfuge, a way to distract attention from that shadow at the edge of vision.

The Sorceress of Darshiva smiled a chill little smile. "No matter." She shrugged. "I was only testing you, my droll little hunchback. Keep laughing, Beldin. I like to see people die happy."

"Truly," he agreed. "Smile a bit yerself, me darlin', an' have a bit of a look around. Y' might say good-bye t' the sun while yer at it, fer I don't think ye'll be seein' it fer much longer."

"Are all these threats really necessary?" Belgarath asked wearily.

"It's customary," Beldin told him. "Insults and boasting are a common prelude to more serious business. Besides, she started it." He looked down at Zandramas' Grolims, who had started to move menacingly forward. "I guess it's time, though. Shall we go downstairs then and prepare a big pot of Grolim stew? I like mine chopped rather fine." He extended his hand, snapped his fingers, and wrapped the hand around the hilt of a hook-pointed Ulgo knife.

With Garion in the lead, they walked purposefully to the head of the stairs and started down as the Grolims, with a variety of weapons in their hands, rushed to the bottom.

"Get back!" Silk snapped at Velvet, who had resolutely joined them with one of her daggers held professionally low.

"Not a chance," she said crisply. "I'm protecting my investment."

"What investment?"

"We can talk about it later. I'm busy right now."

The Grolim leading the charge was a huge man, almost as big as Toth. He was swinging a massive axe, and his eyes were filled with madness. When he was perhaps five feet from Garion, Sadi stepped up to the Rivan King's shoulder and hurled a fistful of strangely colored powder full into the ascending Grolim's face. The Grolim shook his head, pawing at his eyes. Then he sneezed. And then his eyes filled with horror, and he screamed. Howling in terror, he dropped his axe, spun, and bolted back down, shouldering his companions off the steps as he fled. When he reached the floor of the amphitheater, he did not stop, but ran toward the sea. He floundered out into waist-deep water and then stepped off the edge of an unseen terrace lurking beneath the surface. It did not appear that he knew how to swim.

"I thought you were out of that powder," Silk said to Sadi even as he made a long, smooth, overhand cast with one of his daggers. A Grolim stumbled back, plucking at the dagger hilt protruding from his chest, missed his footing, and fell heavily backward down the stairway.

"I always keep a bit for contingencies," Sadi replied, ducking under a sword swipe and deftly slicing a Grolim across the belly with his poisoned dagger. The Grolim stiffened, then slowly toppled off the side of the staircase. A number of black-robed men, seeking to surprise them from the rear, were clambering up the rough sides of the stairway. Velvet knelt and coolly drove one of her daggers into the upturned face of a Grolim on the verge of reaching the top. With a hoarse cry he clutched at his face and fell backward, sweeping several of his companions off the wall as he plunged down.

Then the blond Drasnian girl darted to the other side of the stairs, shaking out her silken cord. She deftly looped it about the neck of a Grolim in the act of scrambling up onto the steps. She stepped under his flailing arms, turned until they were back to back, and leaned forward. The helpless Grolim's feet came up off the step, and he clutched at the cord about his neck with both hands. His feet kicked futilely at the air for a few moments, his face turning black, and then he went limp. Velvet turned back, unlooped her cord, and coolly kicked the inert body off the edge.

Durnik and Toth had moved up to take positions beside Garion and 'Zakath, and the four of them moved implacably down the stairs, step by step, chopping and smashing at the black-robed figures rushing up to meet them. Durnik's hammer seemed only slightly less dreadful than the sword of the Rivan King. The Grolims fell before them as they moved inexorably down the stairs. Toth was chopping methodically with Durnik's axe, his face as expressionless as that of a man felling a tree. 'Zakath was a fencer, and he feinted and parried with his massive, though nearly weightless, sword. His thrusts were quick and usually lethal. The steps below the dreadful quartet were soon littered with twisted bodies and were running with rivulets of blood.

"Watch your footing," Durnik warned as he crushed another Grolim's skull. "The steps are getting slippery."

Garion swept off another Grolim head. It bounced like a child's ball down the steps even as the body toppled off the side of the stairway. Garion risked a quick look back over his shoulder. Belgarath and Beldin had joined Velvet to help the girl repel the black-robed men scrambling up the sides of the steps. Beldin seemed to take vicious delight in driving his hook-pointed knife into Grolim eyes, then, with a sharp twist and a jerk he would pull out sizable gobs of brains. Belgarath, his thumbs tucked into his rope belt, waited calmly. When a Grolim's head appeared above the edge of the stair, the old man would draw back his foot and kick the priest of Torak full in the face. Since it was a thirty-foot drop from the stairs to the stones of the amphitheater, few of the Grolims he kicked off the side of the stairs tried the climb a second time.

When they reached the foot of the stairs, scarcely any of Zandramas' Grolims survived. With his usual prudence, Sadi darted around first one side of the stairway and then the other, coolly sinking his poisoned dagger into the bodies of those Grolims who had fallen to the amphitheater floor, the inert dead as well as the groaning injured.

Zandramas seemed somewhat taken aback by the sheer violence of her foes' descent. She held her ground nonetheless, drawing herself up in scornful defiance. Standing behind her, his mouth agape with terror, stood a man in a cheap crown and somewhat shopworn regal robes. His features bore a faint resemblance to those of 'Zakath, so Garion assumed that he was the Archduke Otrath. And then at last, Garion beheld his own young son. He had avoided looking at the boy during the bloody descent, since he had been unsure of what his own reaction might have been at a time when his concentration was vital. As Beldin had said, Geran was no longer a baby. His blond curls gave his face a softness, but there was no softness in his eyes as he met his father's gaze. Geran was quite obviously consumed with hatred for the woman who firmly held his arm in her grasp.

Gravely, Garion raised his sword to his visor in salute, and, just as gravely, Geran lifted his free hand in response.

Then the Rivan King began an implacable advance, pausing only long enough to kick an unattached Grolim head out of his way. The uncertainty he had felt back in Dal Perivor had vanished now. Zandramas stood no more than a few yards away, and the fact that she was a woman no longer mattered. He raised his flaming sword and continued his advance.

The flickering shadow along the periphery of his vision grew darker, and he hesitated as his sense of dread increased. Try though he might, he could not stifle it. He faltered.

The shadow, vague at first, began to coalesce into a hideous face that towered behind the black-robed sorceress. The eyes were soullessly blank, and the mouth gaped open in an expression of unspeakable loss as if the owner of the face had been plunged into a horror beyond imagining from a place of light and glory. That loss, however, bespoke no compassion or gentleness, but rather expressed the implacable need of the hideous being to find others to share its misery.

"Behold the King of Hell!" Zandramas cried triumphantly. "Flee now and live a few moments longer ere he pulls you all down into eternal darkness, eternal flames, and eternal despair."

Garion stopped. He could not advance on that ultimate horror.

And then a voice came to him out of his memories, and with the voice there came an image. He seemed to be standing in a damp clearing in a forest somewhere. A light, drizzling rain was falling from a heavy, nighttime sky, and the leaves underfoot were wet and soggy. Eriond, all unconcerned, was speaking to them. It had happened, Garion realized, just after their first encounter with Zandramas, who had assumed the shape of the dragon to attack them. "But the fire wasn't real," the young man was explaining. "Didn't you all know that?" He looked slightly surprised at their failure to understand. "It was only an illusion. That's all evil ever really is— an illusion. I'm sorry if any of you were worried, but I didn't have time to explain."

That was the key, Garion understood now. Hallucination was the product of derangement; illusion was not. He was not going mad. The face of the King of Hell was no more real than had been the illusion of Arell that Ce'Nedra had encountered in the forest below Kell. The only weapon the Child of Dark had to counter the Child of Light with was illusion, a subtle trickery directed at the mind. It was a powerful weapon, but very fragile. One ray of light could destroy it. He started forward again.

"Garion!" Silk cried.

"Ignore the face," Garion told him. "It isn't real. Zandramas is trying to frighten us into madness. The face isn't there. It doesn't even have as much substance as a shadow."

Zandramas flinched, and the enormous face behind her wavered and vanished. Her eyes darted this way and that, lingering, Garion seemed to perceive, upon the portal leading into the cave. As surely as if he could see it, Garion *knew* that there was something in that cave—something which was Zandramas' last line of defense. Then, seemingly all unconcerned by the obliteration of the weapon that had always served the Child of Dark so well, she made a quick gesture to her remaining Grolims.

"No." It was the light, clear voice of the Seeress of Kell. "I cannot permit this. The issue must be decided by the Choice, not by senseless brawling. Put up thy sword, Belgarion of Riva, and withdraw thy minions, Zandramas of Darshiva."

Garion found that the muscles of his legs had suddenly cramped, and that he could no longer move even one step. Painfully, he twisted around. He saw Cyradis descending the stairs, guided now by Eriond. Immediately behind her came Aunt Pol, Poledra, and the Rivan Queen.

"The task you both share here," Cyradis continued in an echoing choral voice, "is not to destroy each other, for should it come to pass that one of you destroyeth the other, your tasks will remain uncompleted, and I also will be unable to complete mine. Thus, all that is, all that was, and all that is yet to be will forever perish. Put up thy sword, Belgarion, and send away thy Grolims, Zandramas. Let us go even into the Place Which Is No More and make our choices. The universe grows weary of our delay."

Regretfully, Garion sheathed his sword, but the Sorceress of Darshiva's eyes narrowed. "Kill her," she commanded her Grolims in a chillingly flat voice. "Kill the blind Dalasian witch in the name of the new God of Angarak."

The remaining Grolims, their faces filled with religious exaltation, started toward the foot of the stairs. Eriond sighed and resolutely stepped forward to place his body in front of that of Cyradis.

"That will not be necessary, Bearer of the Orb," Cyradis told him. She bowed her head slightly, and the choral voice swelled to a crescendo. The Grolims faltered, and then began to grope around, staring with unseeing eyes at the daylight around them.

"It's the enchantment again," 'Zakath whispered, "the same one that surrounded Kell. They're blind."

This time, however, what the Grolims saw in their blindness was not the vision of the Face of God that the gentle old priest of Torak, who they had met in the sheep camp above Kell, had seen, but something altogether different. The enchantment, it appeared, could cut two ways. The Grolims cried out first in alarm, then in fright. Then their cries became screams, and they turned, stumbling over each other and even crawling on hands and knees to escape that which they saw. They scrambled blindly down to the water's edge, obviously bent on following the hulking Grolim into whose face Sadi had thrown that strange powder of his. They floundered out into the now gently rolling waves, and one by one stepped off into deep water.

A few could swim, but not very many. Those who could swam desperately out to sea and inevitable death. Those who could not sank beneath the surface, their imploring hands reaching upward even after their heads had gone under. Columns of bubbles rose to the top of the dark water for a few moments, and then they stopped.

The albatross, its great wings motionless, drifted over them for a moment and then returned to hover over the amphitheater.

CHAPTER TWENTY-THREE

"And now art thou, as thou hast ever chosen to be, alone, Child of Dark," Cyradis said sternly.

"The ones who were here with me were of no moment, Cyradis," Zandramas replied indifferently. "They have served their purpose, and I no longer need them."

"Art thou then ready to enter through the portal into the Place Which Is No More to stand in the presence of the Sardion, there to make thy choice?"

"Of course, Holy Seeress," Zandramas acquiesced with surprising mildness. "Gladly will I join with the Child of Light that together we may enter the Temple of Torak."

"Watch her, Garion," Silk whispered. "The whole tone of this is wrong. She's up to something."

But Cyradis, it appeared, had also detected the ruse. "Thy sudden acceptance is puzzling, Zandramas," she said. "Vainly hast thou striven for all these weary months to avoid this meeting, and now thou wouldst rush eagerly into the grotto. What hath so altered thee? Doth perchance some unseen peril lurk within yon grot? Seekest thou still to lure the Child of Light to his doom, thinking thereby to avoid the necessity of the Choice?"

"The answer to thy question, blind witch, doth lie behind that portal," Zandramas replied in a harsh voice. She turned her glittering face toward Garion. "Surely the great Godslayer is without fear," she said. "Or is he who slew Torak become of a sudden timid and fearful? What threat could I, a mere woman, pose to the mightiest warrior in the world? Let us then investigate this grotto together. Confidently will I deliver my safety into thy hands, Belgarion."

"It may not be so, Zandramas," the Seeress of Kell declared. "It is too late now for subterfuge and deceit. Only the Choice will free thee now." She paused and briefly bowed her head. Again Garion heard that choral murmuring. "Ah," she said at last, "now we understand. The passage in the book of the heavens was obscure, but now it is clear." She turned toward the portal. "Come forth, Demon Lord. Lurk not in darkness awaiting prey, but come forth that we may see thee."

"*No!*" Zandramas cried hoarsely.

But it was too late. Reluctantly, almost as if being driven, the battered and half-crippled dragon limped out of the grotto, roaring and belching billows of flame and smoke.

"Not again," 'Zakath groaned.

Garion, however, saw more than just the dragon. Even as in the snow-clogged forest outside Val Alorn when he had seen the image of Barak superimposed upon that of the dreadful bear rushing to his rescue after he had speared the boar when he was no more than fourteen, he now saw the form of the Demon Lord Mordja within the shape of the dragon. Mordja, archfoe of Nahaz, the demon that had borne the shrieking Urvon into the eternal pit of Hell. Mordja, who with a half-dozen snakelike arms grasped a huge sword—a sword that Garion recognized all too well. The Demon Lord, encased in the form of the dragon, strode forward with monstrous steps wielding Cthrek Goru, Torak's dread sword of shadows.

The burning red clouds overhead erupted with lightning as the hideously twinned beast came at them. "Spread out!" Garion shouted. "Silk! Tell them what to do!" He drew a deep breath as great bolts of lightning streaked down from the roiling red sky above to crash against the sides of the terraced pyramid with earth-shattering claps of thunder. "Let's go!" Garion cried to 'Zakath as he once more drew Iron-grip's sword. But then he paused, dumbfounded. Poledra, as calmly as she would if crossing a meadow, approached the awful monstrosity. "Thy Master is the Lord of Deception, Mordja," she said to the suddenly immobilized creature before her, "but it is time for deceit to end. Thou wilt speak only truth. What is thy purpose here? What is the purpose of all of thy kind in this place?"

The Demon Lord, frozen within the form of the dragon, snarled its hatred as it twisted and writhed, attempting to break free.

"Speak, Mordja," Poledra commanded. Did *anyone* have that kind of power?

"I *will* not." Mordja spat out the words.

"Thou wilt," Garion's grandmother said in a dreadfully quiet voice.

Mordja shrieked then, a shriek of total agony.

"What is thy purpose?" Poledra insisted.

"I serve the King of Hell!" the demon cried.

"And what is the purpose of the King of Hell here?"

"He would possess the stones of power," Mordja howled.

"And why?"

"That he may break his chains, the chains in which accursed UL bound him long ere any of this was made."

"Wherefore hast thou then aided the Child of Dark, and wherefore didst thy foe Nahaz aid the Disciple of Torak? Didst not thy Master know that each of them sought to raise a God? A God which would even more securely bind him?"

"What they sought was of no moment," Mordja snarled. "Nahaz and I contended with each other, in truth, but our contention was *not* on behalf of mad Urvon or sluttish Zandramas. In the instant that either of them gained Sardion would the King of Hell reach forth with my hands—or with the hands of Nahaz—

and seize the stone. Then, using its power, would the one of us or the other wrest Cthrag Yaska from the Godslayer and deliver both stones to our Master. In the instant that *he* took up the two stones would *he* become the new God. His chains would break and he would contend with UL as an equal—nay, an even mightier—God, and all that is, was, or will be would be his and his alone."

"And what then was to be the fate of the Child of Dark or the Disciple of Torak?"

"They were to be our rewards. Even now doth Nahaz feed eternally upon mad Urvon in the darkest pit of Hell, even as I shall feed upon Zandramas. The ultimate reward of the King of Hell is eternal torment."

The Sorceress of Darshiva gasped in horror as she heard her soul's fate so cruelly pronounced.

"Thou canst not stop me, Poledra," Mordja taunted, "for the King of Hell hath strengthened my hand."

"Thy hand, however, is confined in the body of this rude beast," Poledra said. "Thou hast made thy choice, and in *this* place, a choice, once made, cannot be unmade. Here wilt thou contend alone, and thine only ally will *not* be the King of Hell, but no more than this mindless creature which thou hast chosen."

The demon raised its dreadful, fang-filled muzzle with a great howl, and it struggled, heaving its vast shoulders this way and that as it desperately tried to wrench itself free of the shape that enclosed it.

"Does this mean we have to fight them *both*?" 'Zakath asked Garion in a shaking voice.

"I'm afraid so."

"Garion, have you lost your mind?"

"It's what we do, 'Zakath. At least Poledra has limited Mordja's power—I don't know how, but she has. Since he doesn't have his full powers, we at least have a chance against him. Let's get at it." Garion clapped down his visor and strode forward, swinging his flaming sword before him.

Silk and the others had separated, and they were approaching the dragon from the sides and from the rear.

As he and 'Zakath warily moved in, Garion saw something that might be an even greater advantage. The melding of the primitive mind of the dragon and the age-old one of the demon was not complete. The dragon, with stubborn stupidity, could only focus her single eye upon those enemies who stood directly before her, and she charged on, unmindful of Garion's friends moving toward her flanks. Mordja, however, was all too much aware of the dangers advancing from the sides and from the rear. The division of the unnaturally joined mind of the vast, bat-winged creature gave it a kind of uncharacteristic hesitation, indecision even. Then Silk, the sword of a fallen Grolim in his hands, darted in from the rear and chopped manfully at the writhing tail.

The dragon bellowed in pain, and flames burst from her gaping mouth. Overriding what little control Mordja exerted upon her, she wheeled clumsily to respond to Silk's attack. The little thief, however, skipped nimbly out of her way even as the others dashed in to attack her flanks. Durnik rhythmically hammered on one exposed flank while Toth chopped no less rhythmically at the other.

A desperate plan came unbidden to Garion as he saw that the dragon had turned almost completely around to meet Silk's attack. "Work on her tail!" he shouted to 'Zakath. He backed off a few paces to give himself running room, then lumbered forward, his movements made awkward by his armor. He leaped over the slashing tail and ran up the dragon's back.

"Garion!" he heard Ce'Nedra scream in horror. He ignored her frightened cry and continued to scramble up the scaly back until he was finally able to plant his feet on the dragon's shoulders between the batlike wings. The dragon, he knew, would not fear or even feel the strokes of his burning sword. Mordja, however, would. He raised Iron-grip's sword and struck a two-handed blow at the base of the scaly neck. The dragon, weaving her fearsome head and breathing fire and smoke as she sought out those who were attacking her, paid no heed. Mordja, however, screamed in agony as the power of the Orb seared him. That was their advantage. Left to herself, the dragon was incapable of meeting their many-pronged attack. It was the added intelligence of the Demon Lord that made her so dangerous in this situation, but Garion had seen evidence in the past that the Orb could inflict intolerable agony upon a demon. In that respect, it had even more power than did a God. Demons fled from the presence of the Gods, but they could not flee from the chastisement of Aldur's Orb. "Hotter!" he commanded the stone as he raised his blade again. He struck and struck and struck again. The great blade no longer bounced off the dragon's scales but seared its way through them to bite into the dragon's flesh. The half-indistinct image of Mordja, encased in the dragon, shrieked as the sword cut into *his* neck even as it slashed at that of the dragon. Almost in mid-stroke, Garion reversed his sword and, grasping the crosspiece of the hilt, drove it down into the dragon's back between the vast shoulders.

Mordja screamed.

Garion wrenched the sword back and forth, tearing the wound even wider.

Even the dragon felt that. She screamed.

Garion raised his sword again, and once again sank it into the bleeding wound, deeper this time.

The dragon and Mordja screamed in unison.

Ludicrously, Garion remembered a time in his bygone youth when he had watched old Cralto digging holes for fence posts. He consciously imitated the old farm worker's rhythmic motion, raising his reversed sword high overhead as Cralto had his shovel, and driving the blade down into the dragon's flesh. With each driving blow the wound grew deeper, and blood gushed and spurted from the quivering flesh. He momentarily saw the white of bone and altered his point of aim. Not even Iron-grip's sword could shear through that tree–trunksized backbone.

His friends had momentarily fallen back, astonished at the Rivan King's insane-appearing audacity. Then they saw that the dragon's almost serpentlike head was raised high in the air as she tried desperately to writhe her neck around to bite at the tormenter digging a huge hole between her shoulder blades. They rushed back into the attack, hacking and stabbing at the softer scales covering the dragon's throat, belly, and flanks. Darting in and out quickly to avoid being trampled by the huge beast, Silk, Velvet, and Sadi attacked the unprotected underside of the distracted dragon. Durnik was steadily pounding on the dragon's side, methodically breaking ribs one by one as Toth chopped at the other side. Belgarath and Poledra, once again as wolves, were gnawing on the writhing tail.

Then Garion saw what he had been searching for—the hawserlike tendon leading down into one of the dragon's huge wings. "Hotter!" he shouted again at the Orb.

The sword flared anew, and this time Garion did not strike. Instead he set the edge of his weapon against the tendon and began to saw back and forth with it, burning through the tough ligament rather than chopping. The tendon, finally severed, snapped, its cut ends slithering snakelike back into the bleeding flesh.

The bellow of pain that emerged from that flame-filled mouth was shattering. The dragon lurched, then fell, thrashing its huge limbs in terrible agony.

Garion was thrown clear when the dragon fell. Desperately he rolled, trying to get away from those flailing claws. Then 'Zakath was there, yanking him to his feet. "You're insane, Garion!" he shouted in a shrill voice. "Are you all right?"

"I'm fine," Garion said in a tight voice. "Let's finish it."

Toth, however, was already there. In the very shadow of the dragon's huge head he stood, his feet planted wide apart, chopping at the base of the dragon's throat. Great gushes of blood spurted from severed arteries as the huge mute, his heavy shoulders surging, sought to find and cut the barrel-like windpipe. Despite the concerted efforts of Garion and his friends, there had been little more than pain before. Toth's singleminded attack, however, threatened the dragon's very life. Were he to succeed in severing or even broaching the thick gristle of that windpipe, the dragon would die, choking for lack of breath or drowning in her own blood. She clawed her way back onto her forelegs and reared high over the huge mute.

"Toth!" Durnik shouted. "Get out of there! She's going to strike!"

But it was not the fanged mouth that struck. Dimly, within the bleeding body of the dragon, Garion saw the indistinct shape of Mordja desperately raise Cthrek Goru, the sword of shadows. Then the Demon Lord thrust out with the sword. The blade, as if insubstantial, emerged from the dragon's chest and, as smoothly, plunged into Toth to emerge from his back. The mute stiffened, then slid limply off the sword, unable even in death to cry out.

"No!" Durnik roared in a voice filled with indescribable loss.

Garion's mind went absolutely cold. "Keep her teeth off me," he told 'Zakath in a flat, unemotional tone. Then he dashed forward, reversing his sword once again in preparation for a thrust such as he had never delivered before. He aimed that thrust not at the wound Toth had opened but at the dragon's broad chest instead.

Cthrek Goru flickered out to ward him off, but Garion parried that desperate defensive stroke, then set his shoulder against the massive crosspiece of his sword's hilt. He fixed the now-shrinking demon with a look of pure hatred and then he drove his sword into the dragon's chest with all his strength, and the great surge as the Orb unleashed its power almost staggered him.

The sword of the Rivan King slid smoothly into the dragon's heart, like a stick into water.

The awful bellowing from both the dragon and the Demon Lord broke off suddenly in a kind of gurgling sigh.

Grimly, Garion wrenched his sword free and stepped clear of the convulsing beast. Then, like a burning house collapsing in on itself, the dragon crumpled to the ground, twitched a few times, and was still.

Garion wearily turned.

Toth's face was calm, but blind Cyradis knelt on one side of his body and Durnik on the other. They were both weeping openly.

High overhead, the albatross cried out once, a cry of pain and loss.

Cyradis was weeping, her blindfold wet with her tears.

The smoky-looking orange sky roiled and tumbled overhead, and inky black patches lay in the folds of the clouds, shifting, coiling, and undulating as the clouds, still stained on their undersides by the new-risen sun, writhed in the sky above and flinched and shuddered as they begot drunken-appearing lightning that staggered down through the murky air to strike savagely at the altar of the One-Eyed God on the pinnacle above.

Cyradis was weeping.

The sharply regular stones that floored the amphitheater were still darkly wet from the clinging fog that had enveloped the reef before dawn and the downpour of yesterday. The white speckles in that iron-hard stone glittered like stars under their sheen of moisture.

Cyradis was weeping.

Garion drew in a deep breath and looked around the amphitheater. It was not as large perhaps as he had first imagined—certainly not large enough to contain what had happened here—but then, all the world would probably not have been large enough to contain that. The faces of his companions, bathed in the fiery light from the sky and periodically glowing dead white in the intense flashes of the stuttering lightning, seemed awed by the enormity of what had just happened. The amphitheater was littered with dead Grolims, shrunken black patches lying on the stones or sprawled in boneless-looking clumps on the stairs. Garion heard a peculiar, voiceless rumble that died off into something almost like a sigh. He looked incuriously at the dragon. Her tongue protruded from her gaping mouth, and her reptilian eyes stared blankly at him. The sound he had heard had come from that vast carcass. The beast's entrails, still unaware that they, like the rest of the dragon, were dead, continued their methodical work of digestion. Zandramas stood frozen in shock. The beast she had raised and the demon she had sent to possess it were both dead, and her desperate effort to evade the necessity of standing powerless and defenseless in the place of the Choice had crumbled and fallen as a child's castle of sand crumbles before the encroaching waves. Garion's son looked upon his father with unquestioning trust and pride, and Garion took a certain comfort in that clear-eyed gaze.

Cyradis was weeping. All else in Garion's mind was drawn from reflection and random impressions. The one incontrovertible fact, however, was that the Seeress of Kell was crushed by her grief. At this particular time she was the most important person in the universe, and perhaps it had always been so. It might very well be, Garion thought, that the world had been created for the one express purpose of bringing this frail girl to this place at this time to make this single Choice. But could she do that now? Might it not be that the death of her guide and protector—the one person in all the world she had truly loved—had rendered her incapable of making the Choice?

Cyradis was weeping, and so long as she wept, the minutes ticked by. Garion saw now as clearly as if he were reading in that book of the heavens which guided the seers that the time of the meeting and of the Choice was not only this particular day, but would come in a specific instant of this day, and if Cyradis, bowed down by her unbearable grief, were unable to choose in that instant, all that had been, all that was, and all that was yet to be would shimmer and vanish like an ephemeral dream. Her weeping must cease, or all would be forever lost.

It began with a clear-toned single voice, a voice that rose and rose in elegiac sadness that contained within it the sum of human woe. Then other voices emerged singly or in trios or in octets to join that aching song. The chorus of the group mind of the seers plumbed the depths of the grief of the Seeress of Kell and then sank in an unbearable diminuendo of blackest despair and faded off into a silence more profound than the silence of the grave.

Cyradis was weeping, but she did not weep alone. Her entire race wept with her.

That lone voice began again, and the melody was similar to the one that had just died away. To Garion's untrained ear, it seemed almost the same, but a subtle chord change had somehow taken place, and as the other voices joined in, more chords insinuated themselves into the song, and the grief and unutterable despair were questioned in the final notes.

Yet once again the song began, not this time with a single voice but with a mighty chord that seemed to shake the very roots of heaven with its triumphant affirmation. The melody remained basically the same, but what had begun as a dirge was now an exultation.

Cyradis gently laid Toth's hand on his motionless chest, smoothed his hair, and groped across his body to touch Durnik's tear-wet face consolingly.

She rose, no longer weeping, and Garion's fears dissolved and faded as the morning fog that had obscured the reef had faded beneath the onslaught of the sun. "Go," she said in a resolute voice, pointing at the now-unguarded portal. "The time approaches. Go thou, Child of Light, and thou, Child of Dark, even into the grot, for we have choices to make which, once made, may never be unmade. Come ye with me, therefore, into the Place Which Is No More, there to decide the fate of all men." And with firm and unfaltering step, the Seeress of Kell led the way toward that portal surmounted by the stony image of the face of Torak.

Garion found himself powerless in the grip of that clear voice and he fell in beside satin-robed Zandramas to follow the slender Seeress. He felt a faint brush against his armored right shoulder as he and the Child of Dark entered the portal. It was almost with a wry amusement that he realized that the forces controlling this meeting were not so entirely sure of themselves. They had placed a barrier between him and the Sorceress of Darshiva. Zandramas' unprotected throat lay quite easily within the reach of his vengeful hands, but the barrier made her as unassailable as if she had been on the far side of the moon. Faintly, he was aware that the others were coming up behind, his friends following him, and Geran and the violently trembling Otrath trailing after Zandramas.

"This need not be so, Belgarion of Riva," Zandramas whispered urgently. "Will we, the two most powerful ones in all the universe, submit to the haphazard choice of this brain-sickly girl? Let us bestow our choices upon ourselves. Thus will we both become Gods. Easily will we be able to set aside UL and the others and rule all creation jointly." The swirling lights beneath the skin of her face spun faster now, and her eyes glowed red. "Once we have achieved divinity, thou canst put aside thine earthly wife, who is not, after all, human, and thou and I could mate. Thou couldst father a race of Gods upon me, Belgarion, and we could sate each other with unearthly delights. Thou wilt find me fair, King of Riva, as all men have, and I will consume thy days with the passion of Gods, and we will share in the meeting of Light and Dark."

Garion was startled, even a little awed by the single-mindedness of the Spirit of the Child of Dark. The thing was as implacable and as unchangeable as adamantine rock. He perceived that it did not change because it *could* not. He began to grope his way toward something that seemed significant. Light could change. Every day was testimony to that. Dark could not. Then it was at last that he understood the *true* meaning of the eternal division which had rent the universe apart. The Dark sought immobile stasis; the Light sought progression. The Dark crouched in a perceived perfection; the Light, however, moved on, informed by the concept of perfectability. When Garion spoke, it was not in reply to the blatant inducements of Zandramas, but rather to the Spirit of Dark itself. "It *will* change, you know," he said. "Nothing you can do will stop me from believing that. Torak offered to be my father, and now Zandramas offers to be my wife. I rejected Torak, and I reject Zandramas. You cannot lock me into immobility. If I change only one little thing, you've lost. Go stop the tide if you can, and leave me alone to do my work."

The gasp that came from the mouth of Zandramas was more than human. Garion's sudden understanding had actually stung the Dark, not merely its instrument. He felt a faint, almost featherlike probing, and made no effort to repel it.

Zandramas hissed, her eyes aflame with hate-filled frustration.

"Didn't you find what you wanted?" Garion asked.

The voice that came from her lips was dry, unemotional. "You'll have to make your choice eventually, you know," it said.

The voice that came from Garion's lips was not his own, and it was just as dry and clinical. "There's plenty of time," it replied. "My instrument will choose when it is needful."

"A clever move, but it does not yet signify the end of the game."

"Of course not. The last move lies in the hands of the Seeress of Kell."

"So be it, then."

They were walking down a long, musty-smelling corridor.

"I absolutely hate this," Garion heard Silk murmur from behind him.

"It's going to be all right, Kheldar," Velvet told the little man comfortingly. "I won't let anything happen to you."

Then the corridor opened out into a submerged grotto. The walls were rough, irregular, for this was not a construction but a natural cavern. Water oozed down a far wall to trickle endlessly with silvery note into a dark pool. The grotto had a faintly reptilian smell overlaid by the odor of long-dead meat, and the floor was littered with gnawed white bones. By some ironic twist, the lair of the Dragon God had become the lair of the dragon herself. No better guard had been necessary to protect this place.

On the near wall stood a massive throne carved from a single rock, and before the throne there was one of the now all-too-familiar altars. Lying on the center of that altar was an oblong stone somewhat larger than a man's head. The stone glowed red, and its ugly light illuminated the grotto. Just to one side of the altar lay a human skeleton, its bony arm extended in a gesture of longing. Garion frowned. Some sacrifice to Torak, perhaps? Some victim of the dragon? Then he knew. It was the Melcene scholar who had stolen the Sardion from the university and fled with it to this place to die here in unthinking adoration of the stone that had killed him.

Just over his shoulder, Garion heard a sudden animal-like snarl coming from the Orb, and a similar sound came from the red stone, the Sardion, which lay on the altar. There was a confused babble of sound in a multitude of languages, some drawn, for all Garion knew, from the farthest reaches of the universe. Flickering streaks of blue shot up through the milky-red Sardion, and similarly, angry red bathed the Orb in undulant waves as all the conflicts of all the ages came together in this small, confined space.

"Control it, Garion!" Belgarath said sharply. "If you don't they'll destroy each other—and the universe, as well!"

Garion reached back over his shoulder and placed his marked palm over the Orb, speaking silently to the vengeful stone. "Not yet," he said. "All in good time." He could not have explained why he had chosen those precise words. Grumbling almost like a petulant child, the Orb fell silent, and the Sardion also grudgingly broke off its snarl. The lights, however, continued to stain the surfaces of both stones.

"You were quite good back there," the voice in Garion's mind congratulated him. *"Our enemy is a bit off balance now. Don't get overconfident, though. We're at a slight disadvantage here because the Spirit of the Child of Dark is very strong in this grotto."*

"Why didn't you tell me that before?"

"Would you have paid any attention? Listen carefully, Garion. My opposite has agreed that we should leave the matter in Cyradis' hands. Zandramas, however, has made no such commitment. She's very likely to make one last attempt. Put yourself between her and the Sardion. No matter what you have to do, don't let her reach that stone."

"All right," Garion said bleakly. He reasoned that attempting to edge into position inch by inch would not deceive the Sorceress of Darshiva as to his intent. Instead, quite calmly and deliberately, he simply stepped in front of the altar, drew his sword, and set its point on the floor of the grotto in front of him with his crossed hands resting on the pommel.

"What art thou about?" Zandramas demanded in a harsh, suspicious tone of voice.

"You know exactly what I'm doing, Zandramas," Garion replied. "The two spirits have agreed to let Cyradis decide between them. I haven't heard you agree yet. Do you still think you can avoid the Choice?"

Her light-speckled face twisted with hatred. "Thou wilt pay for this, Belgarion," she answered. "All that thou art and all that thou lovest will perish here."

"That's for Cyradis to decide, not you. In the meantime, nobody's going to touch the Sardion until *after* Cyradis makes her choice."

Zandramas ground her teeth in sudden, impotent fury.

And then Poledra came closer, her tawny hair stained by the light of the Sardion. "Very well done, young wolf," she said to Garion.

"Thou no longer hast the power, Poledra." The strangely abstracted words came from Zandramas' unmoving mouth.

"Point." The familiar dry voice spoke through Poledra's lips.

"I perceive no point."

"That's because you've always discarded your instruments when you were finished with them. Poledra was the Child of Light at Vo Mimbre. She was even able to defeat Torak there—if only temporarily. Once that power is bestowed, it can never be wholly taken away. Did not her control over the Demon Lord prove that to you?"

Garion was almost staggered by that. Poledra? The Child of Light during that dreadful battle five hundred years ago?

The voice went on. "Do you acknowledge the point?" it asked its opposite.

"What difference can it make? The game will be played out soon."

"I claim point. Our rules require that you acknowledge it."

"Very well. I acknowledge the point. You've really become quite childish about this, you know."

"A rule is a rule, and the game isn't finished yet."

Garion went back to watching Zandramas very closely so that he might meet any sudden move she made toward the Sardion.

"When is the time, Cyradis?" Belgarath quietly asked the Seeress of Kell.

"Soon," she replied. "Very soon."

"We're all here," Silk said, nervously looking up at the ceiling. "Why don't we get on with it?"

"This is the day, Kheldar," she said, "but it is not the instant. In the instant of the Choice, a great light shall appear, a light which even *I* will see."

It was the strange detached calm that came over him that alerted Garion to the fact that the ultimate Event was about to take place. It was the same calm that had enveloped him in the ruins of Cthol Mishrak when he had met Torak.

Then, as if the thought of his name had aroused, if only briefly, the spirit of the One-Eyed God from its eternal slumber, Garion seemed to hear Torak's dreadful voice intoning that prophetic passage from the last page of the Ashabine Oracles:

"Know that we *are* brothers, Belgarion, though our hate for each other may one day sunder the heavens. We are brothers in that we share a dreadful task. That thou art reading my words means that thou hast been my destroyer. Thus must I charge *thee* with the task. What is foretold in these pages is an abomination. Do not let it come to pass. Destroy the world. Destroy the universe if need be, but do not permit this to come to pass. In thy hand is now the fate of all that was, all that is, and all that is yet to be. Hail, my hated brother, and farewell. We will meet—or have met—in the City of Endless Night, and there will our dispute be concluded. The task, however, still lieth before us in the Place Which Is No More. One of us must go there to face the ultimate horror. Should it be thou, fail us not. Failing all else, thou must reave the life from thine only son, even as thou hast reft mine from me."

This time, however, the words of Torak did not fill Garion with weeping. They simply intensified his resolve as he finally began to understand. What Torak had seen in the vision that had come to him at Ashaba had been so terrifying that in the moment of his awakening from his prophetic dream the maimed God had felt impelled to lay the possibility of the dreadful task upon his most hated foe. That momentary horror had surpassed even Torak's towering pride. It had only been later, after the pride had reasserted itself, that Torak had mutilated the pages of his prophecy. In that one bleak moment of sanity, the maimed God had spoken truly for perhaps the one time in his life. Garion could only imagine the agony of self-abasement that single moment of truth had cost Torak. In the silence of his mind Garion pledged his fidelity to the task his most ancient foe had lain upon him. "I will do all that is in my power to keep this abomination from coming to pass, my brother," he threw out his thought to the spirit of Torak. "Return to thy rest, for here *I* take up the burden."

The dusky red glow of the Sardion had muted the swirling lights in the flesh of Zandramas, and Garion could now see her features quite clearly. Her expression was troubled. She had quite obviously been unprepared for the sudden acquiescence of the spirit that dominated her. Her drive to win at any cost had been frustrated by the withdrawal of the support of that spirit. Her own mind—or what was left of it—still strove to evade facing the Choice. The two prophecies had agreed at the beginning of time to place the entire matter in the hands of the Seeress of Kell. The evasions, the trickery, and the multitudinous atrocities that had marked the passage of the Child of Dark through the world had all come from the twisted Grolim perceptions of the Sorceress of Darshiva herself. At this moment, Zandramas was more dangerous than she had ever been.

"Well, Zandramas," Poledra said, "and is *this* the time thou hast chosen for our meeting? Shall we destroy each other now when we have come so close to the ultimate instant? If thou but await the Choice of Cyradis, thou wilt stand an even chance of obtaining that which thou hast so desperately sought. If thou shouldst confront *me*, however, thou wilt cast the entire matter into the lap of pure chance. Wilt thou throw away thy half chance of success in exchange for an absolute uncertainty?"

"I am stronger than thou art, Poledra," Zandramas declared defiantly. "I am the Child of Dark."

"And I *was* the Child of Light. How much art thou willing to gamble on the possibility that I can still call forth the strength and power? Wilt thou gamble *all*, Zandramas? All?"

Zandramas' eyes narrowed, and Garion could clearly feel the clenching of her will. Then, with a blasting surge of energy and a vast roar, she released it. An aura of darkness suddenly surrounded her, and she seized Garion's son and lifted him. "*Thus* will I conquer, Poledra!" she hissed. She closed her hand about the struggling boy's wrist and pushed his Orb-marked hand out in front of her. "In the instant the hand of Belgarion's son touches the Sardion, I will triumph." Implacably, step by step, she started forward.

Garion raised his sword and leveled its point at her. "Push her back," he commanded the Orb. A bolt of intense blue light shot from the sword point, but it divided as it struck that dark aura, encasing the shadow but in no way interfering with Zandramas' advance. *"Do something!"* Garion shouted silently.

"I can't interfere," the voice told him.

"Is that really the best thou canst do, Zandramas?" Poledra asked calmly. Garion had often heard that same note in Aunt Pol's voice, but never with quite such indomitable determination. Poledra raised her hand almost indifferently and released her will. The surge and the sound nearly buckled Garion's knees. The aura of dark surrounding Zandramas and Geran vanished. The Sorceress of Darshiva, however, did not falter, but continued her slow advance. "Wilt thou kill thy son, Belgarion of Riva?" she asked. "For thou canst not strike at me without destroying him."

"I can't do it!" Garion cried out, his eyes suddenly full of tears. *"I can't!"*

"You must. You've been warned that this might happen. If she succeeds and puts your son's hand on the Sardion, he will be worse than dead. Do what must be done, Garion."

Weeping uncontrollably, Garion raised his sword. Geran looked him steadily in the face, his eyes unafraid.

"No!" It was Ce'Nedra. She dashed across the floor of the grotto and threw herself directly in front of Zandramas. Her face was deathly pale. "If you intend to kill my baby, you'll have to kill me, too, Garion," she said in a broken voice. She turned her back on Garion and bowed her head.

"So much the better," Zandramas gloated. "Wilt thou kill thy son and thy wife both, Belgarion of Riva? Wilt thou carry that with thee to thy grave?"

Garion's face twisted in agony as he gripped the hilt of his flaming sword more firmly. With one stroke, he would destroy his very life.

Zandramas, still holding Geran, stared at him incredulously. "Thou *wilt* not!" she exclaimed. "Thou *canst* not!"

Garion clenched his teeth and raised his sword even higher.

Zandramas' incredulity suddenly turned to fright. Her advance stopped, and she began to shrink back from that awful stroke.

"Now, Ce'Nedra!" Polgara's voice cracked like a whip.

The Rivan Queen, who had been coiled like a spring beneath her apparent mute submission to her fate, exploded. With a single leap, she snatched Geran from the arms of Zandramas and fled with him back to Polgara's side.

Zandramas howled and tried to follow, her face filled with rage.

"No, Zandramas," Poledra said. "If thou turnest away, I will kill thee—or Belgarion will. Thou hast inadvertently revealed thy decision. Thy choice hath been made, and thou art no longer the Child of Dark, but are only an ordinary Grolim priestess. There is no longer any need for thee here. Thou art free now to depart—or to die."

Zandramas froze.

"Thus all thy subterfuge and evasion have come to naught, Zandramas. Thou hast no longer any choice. Wilt thou now submit to the decision of the Seeress of Kell?"

Zandramas stared at her, the expression on her star-touched face a mixture of fear and towering hatred.

"Well, Zandramas," Poledra said, "what is it to be? Wilt thou die this close to thy promised exaltation?" Poledra's golden eyes were penetrating as she looked into the face of the Grolim priestess. "Ah, no," she said quite calmly, "I perceive that thou wilt not. Thou canst not. But I would hear the words from thine own mouth, Zandramas. Wilt thou *now* accept the decision of Cyradis?"

Zandramas clenched her teeth. "I will," she grated.

CHAPTER TWENTY-FOUR

The thunder still cracked and rumbled outside, and the wind accompanying the storm that had been brewing since the earth had been made moaned in the passageway leading into the grotto from the amphitheater outside. In an abstract sort of way as he resheathed his sword, Garion recognized precisely what his mind was doing. It had happened so often in the past that he wondered why he had not expected it. The circumstances required that he make a decision. The fact that he no longer even considered the decision, but concentrated instead on a meticulous examination of his surroundings, indicated that he had already made his choice somewhere so deep in his mind that it did not even register on the surface. There was, he conceded, a very good reason for what he was doing. Dwelling upon an impending crisis or confrontation would only rattle him, lead him into that distracting series of "what ifs," and make him begin to have those second thoughts that could quite easily lock him into an agonized indecision. Right or wrong, the choice had been made now, and to continue to worry at it would serve no purpose. The choice, he knew, was based not only on careful reasoning but also on deep feelings. He had that serene inner peace which flowed from the knowledge that the choice, whatever it was, was right. Calmly, he turned his attention to the grotto itself.

The stones of the walls appeared, though it was hard to be sure in the pervading red light of the Sardion, to be a kind of basalt that had fractured into a myriad of flat surfaces and sharp edges. The floor was peculiarly smooth, either as a result of eons of patiently eroding water or of a single thought of Torak during his sojourn in this cave while he had contended with and ultimately rejected UL, his father. The trickle of water into the pool on the far side of the grotto was something of a mystery. This was the highest peak of the reef. Water should run *down* from here, not up to the hidden spring in the wall. Beldin could probably explain it—or Durnik. Garion knew that he needed to be alert in this strange place, and he did not want to break his concentration by pondering the ins and outs of hydraulics.

And then, since it was the only source of light in this dim grotto, Garion's almost indifferent eyes were drawn inevitably to the Sardion. It was not a pretty stone. It was streaked with pale orange and milky white in alternating stripes banded closely together, and it was now stained with the wavering blue light emanating from the Orb. It was as smooth and polished as the Orb. The Orb had been polished by the hand of Aldur, but who had polished the Sardion? Some God unknown? Some shaggy clan of the brutish precursors of man squatting in dull-eyed patience over the stone, devoting generation after generation to the single incomprehensible task of rubbing the orange and white surface smooth with calloused and broken-nailed hands that were more like paws than human appendages? Even such unthinking creatures would have felt the power of the stone, and, feeling it to be a God—or at the very least, some object descended from a God—might not their mindless polishing have been some obscure act of worship?

Then Garion let his eyes wander over the faces of his companions, the familiar faces of those who had, in response to destinies that had been written large in the stars since the beginning of days, accompanied him to this place on this particular day. The death of Toth had answered the one unanswered question, and now all was in place.

Cyradis, her face still tearstained and marked by her grief, stepped to the altar to face them. "The time draws nigh," she said in a clear, unwavering voice. "Now must the choices of the Child of Light and the Child of Dark be made. All must be in readiness when the instant of *my* Choice arrives. Know ye both that your choices, once made, cannot be unmade."

"My choice was made at the beginning of days," Zandramas declared. "Adown all the endless corridors of time hath the name of Belgarion's son echoed, for he hath touched Cthrag Yaska, which spurneth all other hands save the hand of Belgarion himself. In the instant that Geran touches Cthrag Sardius, will he become an omnipotent God, higher than all the rest, and he shall have lordship and dominion over all of creation. Stand forth, Child of Dark. Take thy place before the altar of Torak to await the Choice of the Seeress of Kell. In the instant that she chooses thee, reach forth thy hand and seize thy destiny."

It was the last clue. Now Garion knew what the choice he had made in the deep silences of his mind had been, and he knew why it was so perfectly right. Reluctantly, Geran walked toward the altar, stopped and then turned, his small face grave.

"And now, Child of Light," Cyradis said, "the time hath come for thee to make *thy* choice. Upon which of thy companions wilt thou lay the burden?"

Garion had little sense of the melodramatic. Ce'Nedra, and even on occasion Aunt Pol, were, he knew, quite capable of extracting the last ounce of theatricality from any given situation, whereas he, a solid, practical Sendar, was more inclined toward matter-of-fact unostentation. He was quite certain, however, that Zandramas somehow knew what his choice *should* be. He also knew that, despite her reluctant agreement to leave the Choice in the hands of the Seeress of Kell, the black-robed sorceress was still perfectly capable of some desperate final ploy. He had to do something to throw her off balance so that she would hesitate at the crucial moment. If he *appeared* to be on the verge of making the wrong choice, the Sorceress would exult and she would think that she had finally won. Then, at the last possible instant, he could make the *correct* choice. The Child of Dark's momentary chagrin might well freeze her hand and give him time to block her. Carefully, he noted her position and that of Geran and Otrath. Geran stood perhaps ten feet in front of the altar with Zandramas no more than a few feet from him. Otrath was cowering back against the rough stone wall at the back of the grotto.

It would have to be exactly right. He would have to build up an almost unbearable suspense in the mind of Zandramas, then dash her hopes all at once. Rather artfully, he drew his face into an expression of agonized indecision. He wandered among his friends, his face filled with a purely feigned bafflement. He stopped from time to time to look deeply into their faces, even going so far as to occasionally half raise his hand as if on the very verge of choosing the wrong person. Each time he did that, he clearly felt a wild surge of glee coming from Zandramas. She was not even attempting to hide her emotions. Better and better. His enemy by now was no longer even rational.

"What are you doing?" Polgara whispered when he stopped in front of her.

"I'll explain later," he murmured. "It's necessary—and important. You've got to trust me, Aunt Pol." He moved on. When he reached Belgarath, he felt a momentary apprehension emanating from Zandramas. The Eternal Man was certainly someone to be reckoned with, and should the eminence of the Child of Light be added to that—*and* the potential for divinity, as well—the old man could be a serious adversary.

"*Will* you move on with it, Garion?" his grandfather muttered.

"I'm trying to push Zandramas off balance," Garion whispered. "Please watch her closely after I choose. She might try something."

"Then you know who it's going to be?"

"Of course. I'm trying not to think about it, though. I don't want her to pick it out of my mind."

The old man made a face. "Do it your way, Garion. Just don't drag it out *too* long. Let's not irritate Cyradis as well as Zandramas."

Garion nodded and moved past Sadi and Velvet, letting his mind push out toward that of Zandramas as he did. Her emotions were veering around wildly now, and it was clear that she was at a fever pitch. To draw things out any further would serve no purpose. He stopped at last in front of Silk and Eriond. "Keep your face straight," he warned the rat-faced little man. "Don't let Zandramas see any change of expression no matter what I seem to be doing."

"Don't make any mistakes here, Garion," Silk warned. "I'm not looking for a sudden promotion of any kind."

Garion nodded. It was nearly over now. He looked at Eriond, a young man who was almost his brother. "I'm sorry about this, Eriond," he apologized in a low murmur. "You probably won't want to thank me for what I'm about to do."

"It's all right, Belgarion." Eriond smiled. "I've known it was going to happen for quite some time now. I'm ready."

And that clinched it. Eriond had answered the ubiquitous question "Are you ready?" for probably the last time. Eriond, it appeared, *was*—and probably had been since the day he was born. Everything now slipped into place to fit together so tightly that nothing could ever take it apart again.

"Choose, Belgarion," Cyradis urged.

"I have, Cyradis," Garion said simply. He stretched out his hand and laid it on Eriond's shoulder. "Here is my choice. Here is the Child of Light."

"Perfect!" Belgarath exclaimed.

"Done!" the voice in Garion's mind agreed.

Garion felt a peculiar wrench followed by a kind of regretful emptiness. He was no longer the Child of Light. It was Eriond's responsibility now, but Garion knew that he still had one last responsibility of his own. He turned slowly, trying to make it look casual. The expression on the light-speckled face of Zandramas was a mixture of rage, fear, and frustration. It confirmed that what Garion had just done had been the right thing. He had made the proper choice. He had never actually done what he tried to do next before, although he had seen and felt Aunt Pol do it many times. This was not, however, a time for random experimentation. Carefully, he sent his mind out again, looking this time not so much for overall emotional responses from Zandramas as for specifics. He had to know exactly what she was going to try to do before she could put it into motion.

The mind of the Sorceress of Darshiva was filled with a confused welter of thoughts and emotions. The wild hope Garion's subterfuge had raised in her seemed to have done its work. Zandramas floundered, unable to concentrate now on her next step. But step she must. Garion perceived that she simply *could* not leave the matter wholly in the hands of the Seeress of Kell.

"Go thou then, Child of Light, to stand beside the Child of Dark that I may choose between ye," Cyradis said.

Eriond nodded. Then he turned and crossed the grotto to stand beside Geran.

"It's done, Cyradis," Poledra said. "All the choices have been made but yours. This is the appointed place and the appointed day. The moment for you to perform your task has arrived."

"Not quite yet, Poledra," Cyradis said, her voice trembling with anxiety. "The signal that the instant of the Choice hath come must be delivered from the book of the heavens."

"But you cannot see the heavens, Cyradis," Garion's grandmother reminded her. "We stand beneath the earth. The book of the heavens is obscured."

"I need not go to the book of the heavens. It will come to me."

"Consider, Cyradis," Zandramas urged in a wheedling tone. "Consider my words. There is no possible choice but Belgarion's son."

Garion's mind suddenly became very alert. Zandramas had made a decision. *She* knew what she was going to do, but she had somehow managed to conceal it from him. He almost began to admire his enemy. She had prepared each of her moves from the very beginning—and each of her defenses in this place, as well—

with an almost military precision. As each defense failed, she withdrew to the next. That was why he could not pick her thought from her mind. She already knew what she was going to do, so there was no need for her even to think about it. He could feel, however, that her next move had something to do with Cyradis herself. *That* was Zandramas' last line of defense. "Don't do that, Zandramas," he told the sorceress. "You know it's not the truth. Leave her alone."

"Then choose, Cyradis," the sorceress commanded.

"I may not. The instant hath not yet arrived." The face of Cyradis was twisted with an inhuman agony.

Then Garion felt it. Wave upon wave of indecision and doubt were emanating from Zandramas, all focusing on the blindfolded Seeress. *This* was the final desperate attempt. Failing to attack *them* successfully, Zandramas was now attacking Cyradis. *"Help her, Aunt Pol,"* Garion threw the thought out desperately. *"Zandramas is trying to keep her from making the Choice."*

"Yes, Garion," Polgara's voice came back calmly, *"I know."*

"Do something!"

"It's not time yet. It has to come at the moment of the Choice. If I try to do anything earlier, Zandramas will feel it and take steps to counteract me."

"Something's happening outside," Durnik said urgently. "There's a light of some kind coming down the corridor."

Garion looked quickly. The light was still dim and indistinct, but it was like no other light he had ever seen.

"The time for the Choice hath come, Cyradis," Zandramas said, her voice cruel. "Choose!"

"I cannot!" the Seeress wailed, turning toward the growing light. "Not yet! I'm not ready yet!" She stumbled across the floor, wringing her hands. "I'm not ready! I can't choose! Send another!"

"Choose!" Zandramas repeated implacably.

"If only I could see them!" Cyradis sobbed. "If only I could see them!"

And then at last, Polgara moved. "That's easily arranged, Cyradis," she said in a calm and oddly comforting tone. "Your vision has clouded your sight, that's all." She reached out and gently removed the blindfold. "Look then with human eyes and make your choice."

"That is forbidden!" Zandramas protested shrilly as her advantage crumbled.

"No," Polgara said. "If it were forbidden, I would not have been able to do it."

Cyradis had flinched back from even the faint light in the grotto. "I cannot!" she cried, covering her eyes with her hands. "I cannot!"

Zandramas' eyes came suddenly alight. "I triumph!" she exulted. "The Choice *must* be made, but now will it be made by another. It no longer lieth in the hands of Cyradis, for the decision not to choose is also a choice."

"Is that true?" Garion quickly asked Beldin.

"There are two schools of thought on that."

"Yes or no, Beldin."

"I don't know. I really don't, Garion."

There was suddenly a soundless burst of intense light from the mouth of the passageway leading to the outside. Brighter than the sun, the light swelled and grew. It was so impossibly intense that even the cracks between the stones in the grotto blazed incandescently.

"It has come at last," Garion's inner companion said unemotionally through Eriond's lips. "It is the instant of the Choice. Choose, Cyradis, lest all be destroyed."

"It has come," another equally unemotional voice spoke through the lips of Garion's son. "It is the instant of the Choice. Choose, Cyradis, lest all be destroyed."

Cyradis swayed, torn by indecision, her eyes darting back and forth to the two faces before her. Again she wrung her hands.

"She cannot!" the Emperor of Mallorea exclaimed, starting forward impulsively.

"She *must*!" Garion said, catching his friend's arm. "If she doesn't, everything will be lost!"

Again the eyes of Zandramas filled with that unholy joy. "It is too much for her!" the priestess almost crowed. "Thou hast made thy choice, Cyradis," she cried. "It cannot be unmade. Now will *I* make the Choice for thee, and I will be exalted when the Dark God comes again!"

And that may have been Zandramas' last and fatal error. Cyradis straightened and, eyes flashing, she looked full into the starry face of the sorceress. "Not so, Zandramas," the Seeress said in an icy voice. "What passed before was indecision, not choice, and the moment hath not yet passed." She lifted her beautiful face and closed her eyes. The vast chorus of the Seers of Kell swelled its organ note in the tight confines of the grotto, but it ended on a questioning note.

"Then the decision is wholly mine," Cyradis said. "Are all the conditions met?" She addressed the question to the two awarenesses standing unseen behind Eriond and Geran.

"They are," the one said from Eriond's lips.

"They are," the other said from Geran's.

"Then hear my Choice," she said. Once again she looked full into the faces of the little boy and the young man. Then with a cry of inhuman despair, she fell into Eriond's arms. "I choose thee!" she wept. "For good or for ill, I choose thee!"

There was a titanic lateral lurch—not an earthquake certainly, for not one single pebble was dislodged from the walls or ceiling of the grotto. For some reason, Garion was positive that the entire world had moved—inches perhaps, or yards or even thousands of leagues—to one side. And as corollary to that certainty, he was equally sure that the same movement had been universal. The amount of power Cyradis' agonized decision had released was beyond human comprehension.

Gradually, the blazing light diminished somewhat, and the Sardion's glow became wan and sickly. In the instant of the Choice of the Seeress of Kell, Zandramas had shrunk back, and the whirling lights beneath the skin of her face seemed to flicker. Then they began to whirl and to glow more and more brightly. "No!" she shrieked. *"No!"*

"Perhaps these lights in thy flesh are thine exaltation, Zandramas," Poledra said. "Even now it may be that thou wilt shine brighter than any constellation. Well hast thou served the Prophecy of Dark, and it may yet find some way to exalt thee." Then Garion's grandmother crossed the grotto floor to the satin-robed sorceress.

Zandramas shrank back even more. "Don't touch me," she said.

"It is not thee I would touch, Zandramas, but thy raiment. I would see thee receive thy reward and thine exaltation." Poledra tore back the satin hood and ripped the black robe away. Zandramas made no attempt to conceal her nakedness, for indeed, there was no nakedness. She was now no more than a faint outline, a husk filled with swirling, sparkling light that grew brighter and brighter.

Geran ran on sturdy little legs to his mother's arms, and Ce'Nedra, weeping with joy, enfolded him and held him close to her. "Is anything going to happen to him?" Garion demanded of Eriond. "He's the Child of Dark, after all."

"There *is* no Child of Dark anymore, Garion." Eriond answered the question. "Your son is safe."

Garion felt an enormous wave of relief. Then something that he had felt since the moment in which Cyradis had made her Choice began to intrude itself increasingly upon his awareness. It was that overwhelming sense of *presence* which he had always felt when he had come face to face with a God. He looked more closely at Eriond, and that sense grew stronger. His young friend even looked different. Before, he had appeared to be a young man of probably not much over twenty. Now he appeared to be about the same age as Garion, although his face seemed strangely ageless. His expression, which before had been sweetly innocent, had now become grave and even wise. "We have one last thing to do here, Belgarion," he said in a solemn tone. He motioned to 'Zakath and then gently placed the still-weeping Cyradis into the Mallorean's arms. "Take care of her, please," he said.

"For all of my life, Eriond," 'Zakath promised, leading the sobbing girl back to the others.

"Now, Belgarion," Eriond continued, "give me my brother's Orb from off the hilt of Iron-grip's sword. It's time to finish what was started here."

"Of course," Garion replied. He reached back over his shoulder and put his hand on the pommel of his sword. "Come off," he told the Orb. The stone came free in his hand, and he held it out to the young God.

Eriond took the glowing blue stone and turned to look at the Sardion and then down at the Orb in his hand. There was something inexplicable in his face as he looked at the two stones that were at the center of all division. He raised his face for a moment, his expression now serene. "So be it then," he said finally.

And then to Garion's horror, he gripped the Orb even more tightly and pushed his hand quite deliberately, Orb and all, into the glowing Sardion.

The reddish stone seemed to flinch. Like Ctuchik in his last moment, it first expanded, then contracted. Then it expanded one last time. And then, like Ctuchik, it exploded—and yet that explosion was tightly confined, enclosed somehow within some unimaginable globe of force that came perhaps from Eriond's will or from the power of the Orb or from some other source. Garion knew that had that force not been in place, all the world would have been torn apart by what was happening in this tightly confined place.

Even though it was partially muffled by Eriond's immortal and indestructible body, the concussion was titanic, and they were all hurled to the floor by its force. Rocks and pebbles rained down from the ceiling, and the entire pyramidal islet that was all that was left of Korim shuddered in an earthquake even more powerful than that which had destroyed Rak Cthol. Confined within the grotto, the sound was beyond belief. Without thinking, Garion rolled across the surging floor to cover Ce'Nedra and Geran with his armored body, noting as he did so that many of his companions were also protecting loved ones in the same fashion.

The earth continued its convulsive shuddering, and what lay confined on the altar now with Eriond's hand still buried within it was no longer the Sardion but an intense ball of energy a thousand times brighter than the sun.

Then Eriond, his face still calm, removed the Orb from the center of the incandescent ball that once had been the Sardion. As if the removal of Aldur's Orb had also removed the constraint that had held the Sardion in one shape and place, the blazing fragments of Cthrag Sardius blasted upward through the roof of the grotto, ripping the top off the shuddering pyramid and sending the huge stone blocks out in all directions as if they were no more than pebbles.

The suddenly revealed sky was filled with a light brighter than the sun, a light that extended from horizon to horizon. The fragments of the Sardion streamed upward to lose themselves in that light.

Zandramas wailed, an inhuman, animal-like sound. The faint outline that was all that was left of her was writhing, twisting. *"No!"* she cried, "It cannot be! You promised!" Garion did not know, could not know, to whom she spoke. She extended her hands to Eriond in supplication. "Help me, God of Angarak!" she cried. "Do not let me fall into the hands of Mordja or the foul embrace of the King of Hell! Save me!"

And then her shadowy husk split apart, and the swirling lights that had become her substance streamed inexorably upward to follow the fragments of the Sardion into that vast light in the sky.

What was left of the Sorceress of Darshiva fell to the floor like a discarded garment, shriveled and tattered like a rag no longer of any use to anyone.

The voice that came from Eriond's lips was very familiar to Garion. He had been listening to it for all his life.

"Point," it said in a detached, emotionless tone, as if merely stating a fact. "Point and game."

■ CHAPTER TWENTY-FIVE ■

The sudden silence in the grotto was almost eerie. Garion rose and helped Ce'Nedra to her feet. "Are you all right?" he asked her, his voice hushed. Ce'Nedra nodded absently. She was examining their little boy, a look of concern on her smudged face. Garion looked around. "Is everyone all right?" he asked.

"Is that earthquake finished yet?" Silk demanded, still covering Velvet's body with his own.

"It's passed, Kheldar," Eriond told him. The young God turned and gravely handed the Orb back to Garion.

"Aren't you supposed to keep it?" Garion asked him. "I thought—"

"No, Garion. You're still the Guardian of the Orb."

For some reason, that made Garion feel better. Even in the midst of what had just happened, he had felt an empty sense of loss. Somehow he had become convinced that he would be obliged to give up the jewel now. Covetousness was not a part of Garion's nature, but over the years the Orb had become more a friend than a possession.

"May we not go forth from this place?" Cyradis asked, her voice filled with a deep sadness. "I would not leave my dear companion alone and untended."

Durnik touched her shoulder gently, and then they all turned and silently left the shattered grotto.

They emerged from the portal into the light that was more than the light of day. The intense brilliance that had even penetrated the dim grotto behind them had faded to the point where it was no longer blinding. Garion looked around. Though the time of day was certainly different, there was that peculiar sense that he had been through all of this before. The storm and lightning that had raged over the Place Which Is No More had passed. The clouds had rolled back, and the wind that had swept the reef during the fight with the dragon and the demon Mordja had subsided to a gentle breeze. Following the death of Torak at Cthol Mishrak, Garion had felt in a strange way that he had been witnessing the dawn of the first day. Now it was noon—years later, to be sure—but somehow the noon of that selfsame day. What had begun at Cthol Mishrak was only now complete. It was over, and he felt a vast sense of relief. He also felt a bit light-headed. The emotional and physical energy he had expended since the first light of this most momentous of days had crept slowly over a fogbound sea had left him weak and near to exhaustion. More than anything right now he wanted to get out of his armor, but the thought of the amount of effort that would cost made him almost quail. He settled for wearily removing his helmet. He looked around again at the faces of his friends.

Although Geran could obviously walk now, Ce'Nedra had insisted on carrying him, and she kept her cheek pressed tightly to his, pulling back only long enough to kiss him from time to time. Geran did not seem to mind.

'Zakath had placed his arm about the shoulders of the Seeress of Kell, and the look on his face rather clearly indicated that he had no real intention of ever removing it. Garion remembered with a smile how, in the first moments of their openly avowed love for each other, Ce'Nedra had continually wormed her way into a very similar embrace. He walked wearily over to where Eriond stood looking out across the sun-splashed waves. "Can I ask you something?" he asked.

"Of course, Garion."

Garion looked pointedly at 'Zakath and Cyradis. "Is that more or less a part of the way things are supposed to be?" he asked. "What I'm getting at is that 'Zakath lost someone very dear to him when he was young. If he loses Cyradis now, it might destroy him. I wouldn't want that to happen."

"Put your mind at rest, Garion." Eriond smiled. "Nothing will separate those two. It's one of the things that are preordained."

"Good. Do they know?"

"Cyradis does. She'll explain it to 'Zakath in time."

"She's still a seeress then?"

"No. That part of her life ended when Polgara removed her blindfold. She *has* looked into the future, though, and Cyradis has a very good memory."

Garion thought about that for a moment, and then his eyes opened very wide. "Are you trying to say that the fate of the entire universe depended on the choice of an ordinary human being?" he asked incredulously.

"I'd hardly call Cyradis ordinary. She's been preparing for that choice since infancy. But in a way you're right. The Choice *had* to be made by a human being, and it had to be made without any help. Not even her own people could help Cyradis at that moment."

Garion shuddered. "That must have been terrifying for her. She had to have been desperately lonely."

"She was, but the people who make choices always are."

"She didn't just select at random, did she?"

"No. She wasn't really choosing between your son and me, though. She was choosing between the Light and the Dark."

"I can't see where all the difficulty was then. Doesn't everybody prefer the light to the dark?"

"You and I might, but the Seers have always known that Light and Dark are simply opposite sides of the same thing. Don't worry too much about 'Zakath and Cyradis, Garion," Eriond said, returning to the original subject. He tapped his forehead with one finger. "Our mutual friend here has made a few arrangements about those two. 'Zakath's going to be very important for most of the rest of his life, and our friend has a way of encouraging people to do necessary things by rewarding them—sometimes in advance."

"Like Relg and Taiba?"

"Or you and Ce'Nedra—or Polgara and Durnik, for that matter."

"Can you tell me what it is that 'Zakath's supposed to do? What could you possibly need from him?"

"He's going to complete what you started."

"Wasn't I doing it right?"

"Of course you were, but you're not an Angarak. You'll understand in time, I think. It's not really very complicated."

A thought came to Garion, and in the instant it emerged he was sure it was absolutely correct. "You knew all along, didn't you? Who you really are, I mean."

"I knew that the potential was there. It didn't really happen until Cyradis made the Choice, though." He looked over to where the others were sadly gathering around Toth's still form. "I think they need us now," he said.

Toth's face was in repose, and his hands, folded across his chest, covered the wound Cthrek Goru had made when Mordja had killed him. Cyradis stood enfolded in 'Zakath's arms, her face wet with new tears.

"Are you sure this is the right idea?" Beldin asked Durnik.

"Yes," the smith said simply. "You see—"

"You don't have to explain it, Durnik," the hunchback told him. "I just wanted to know if you're sure. Let's build a litter for him. It has more dignity." He made a brief gesture, and a number of smooth, straight poles and a coil of rope appeared beside Toth's body. The two of them carefully lashed the poles together to form a litter and then lifted the mute's massive body onto it. "Belgarath," Beldin said, "Garion, we'll need some help here."

Although any one of them could have translocated Toth's body into the grotto, the four sorcerers chose instead to carry it to its final resting place in a ceremony as old as mankind.

Since the upward explosion of the Sardion had unroofed the grotto, the noon sun filled the formerly dim cave with light. Cyradis quailed slightly when she saw the grim altar upon which the Sardion had lain. "It seemeth to me so dark and ugly," she mourned in a small voice.

"It isn't really very attractive, is it?" Ce'Nedra said critically. She turned to look at Eriond. "Do you suppose—?"

"Of course," he agreed. He glanced only briefly at the roughly squared-off altar. It blurred slightly and then became a smooth bier of snowy-white marble.

"That's much nicer," she said. "Thank you."

"He was my friend, too, Ce'Nedra," the young God responded.

It was not a formal funeral in any sense of the word. Garion and his friends simply gathered about the bier to gaze upon the face of their departed friend. There was so much concentrated power in the small grot that Garion could not be sure exactly who created the first flower. Tendrils of ivylike vines grew suddenly up the walls, but unlike ivy, the vines were covered with fragrant white flowers. Then, between one breath and another, the floor was covered with a carpet of lush green moss. Flowers in profusion covered the bier, and then Cyradis stepped forward to lay the simple white rose Poledra had provided her upon the slumbering giant's chest. She kissed his cold forehead and then sighed. "All too soon, methinks, the flowers will wither and fade."

"No, Cyradis," Eriond said gently, "they won't. They'll remain fresh and forever new until the end of days."

"I thank thee, God of Angarak," she said gratefully.

Durnik and Beldin had retired to a corner near the pool to confer. Then they both looked up, concentrated for a moment, and roofed the grotto with gleaming quartz that refracted the sunlight into rainbows.

"It's time to leave now, Cyradis," Polgara told the slim girl. "We've done all we can." Then she and her mother took the still-weeping Seeress by the arms and slowly led her back to the passage with the others following behind.

Durnik was the last to leave. He stood at the bier with his hand lying on Toth's motionless shoulder. Finally, he put out his hand and took Toth's fishing pole out of midair. He carefully laid it on the bier beside his friend's body and patted the huge crossed hands once. Then he turned and left.

When they were outside again, Beldin and the smith sealed the passageway with more quartz.

"There's a nice touch," Silk observed sadly to Garion, pointing to the image above the portal. "Which one of you thought of that?"

Garion turned to look. The face of Torak was gone, and in its place the image of Eriond's face smiled its benediction. "I'm not really sure," he replied, "and I don't think it really matters." He tapped his fingers against the breastplate of his armor. "Do you suppose you could help me out of this?" he asked. "I don't think I need it anymore."

"No," Silk agreed, "probably not. From the look of things, I'd say you've run out of people to fight."

"Let's hope so."

It was much later. They had removed the Grolims from the amphitheater and cleaned up the debris that had littered the stone floor. There was very little they could do about the vast carcass of the dragon, however. Garion sat on the lowest step of the stairway leading down into the amphitheater. Ce'Nedra, still holding her sleeping child, dozed in his arms.

"Not bad at all," the familiar voice said to him. This time, however, the voice did not echo in the vaults of his mind, but seemed instead to be right beside him.

"I thought you were gone," Garion said, speaking quietly to avoid waking his wife and son.

"No, not really," the voice replied.

"I seem to remember that you once said that there was going to be a new voice—awareness, I suppose would be a better term—after this was decided."

"There is, actually, but I'm a part of it."

"I don't quite understand."

"It's not too complicated, Garion. Before the accident there was only one awareness, but then it was divided in the same way everything else was. Now it's back, but since I was part of the original, I've rejoined it. We're one again."

"*That's* your idea of not too complicated?"

"Do you really want me to explain further?"

Garion started to say something but then he decided against it. "You can still separate yourself, though?"

"No. That would only lead to another division."

"Then how—" Garion decided at the last instant that he didn't really want to ask that question. "Why don't we just let this drop?" he suggested. "What was that light?"

"That was the accident, the thing that divided the universe. It also divided me from my opposite and the Orb from the Sardion."

"I thought that happened a long time ago."

"It did—a *very* long time ago."

"But—"

"Try to listen for a change, Garion. Do you know very much about light?"

"It's just light, isn't it?"

"There's a little more. Have you ever stood a long way from somebody who's chopping wood?"

"Yes."

"Did you notice that he'd chop and that then, a moment or so later, you heard the sound?"

"Yes, now that you mention it, I did. What causes that?"

"The interval is the amount of time the sound takes to reach you. Light moves much faster than sound, but it still takes time to go from one place to another."

"I'll take your word for it."

"Do you know what the accident was?"

"Something out among the stars, I understand."

"Exactly. A star was dying, and it died in a place where that wasn't supposed to happen. The dying star was in the wrong place when it exploded, and it ignited an entire cluster of stars—a galaxy. When the galaxy exploded, it tore the fabric of the universe. She protected herself by dividing. That's what led to all of this."

"All right. Why were we talking about light then?"

"That's what that sudden light was—the light from that exploding galaxy—the accident. It only just now reached this place."

Garion swallowed hard. "Just how far away *was* the accident?"

"The numbers wouldn't mean anything to you."

"How long ago did it happen?"

"That's another number you wouldn't understand. You might ask Cyradis. She could probably tell you. She had a very special reason to have it calculated rather precisely."

Garion slowly began to understand. "That's it then," he said, excited in spite of himself. "The instant of the Choice was the instant when the light from the accident reached this world."

"Very good, Garion."

"Did that cluster of stars that exploded come back again after Cyradis made the Choice? I mean there has to be *something* to patch that hole in the universe, doesn't there?"

"Better and better. Garion, I'm proud of you. You remember how the Sardion and Zandramas broke up into little flecks of intense light when they blew the roof off the grotto?"

"It's not the sort of thing I'd be likely to forget." Garion shuddered.

"There was a reason for that. Zandramas and the Sardion—or the pieces of them, at any rate—are on their way back toward that 'hole,' as you put it. They're going to be the patch. They'll get bigger along the way, of course."

"And how long—" Garion broke off. "Another meaningless number, I suppose?"

"Very meaningless."

"I noticed some things about Zandramas back there. She had this all worked out, didn't she? Right from the very beginning?"

"My opposite was always very methodical."

"What I'm getting at is that she made all of her arrangements in advance. She had everything in place in Nyissa before she ever went to Cherek to pick up those Bear-cultists. Then, when she went to Riva to steal Geran, everything was ready. She'd even put things in place so that we all suspected the cult instead of her."

"She'd have probably made a very good general."

"But she went even further. No matter how good her plans were, she always had a contingency to fall back on in case the original plan failed." A thought came to him. "Did Mordja get her? I mean, she blew all apart when the Sardion exploded, didn't she? Is her spirit still mixed up in those stars, or did it get pulled down into Hell? She sounded so very much afraid just before she dissolved."

"I really wouldn't know, Garion. My opposite and I dealt with *this* universe, not with Hell—which, of course, is a universe all its own."

"What would have happened if Cyradis had chosen Geran instead of Eriond?"

"You and the Orb would be moving to a new address about now."

Garion felt his skin begin to crawl. "And you didn't warn me?" he demanded incredulously.

"Would you really have wanted to know? And what difference would it have made?"

Garion decided to let that pass. "Was Eriond always a God?" he asked.

"Weren't you listening earlier when he explained? Eriond was intended to be the seventh God. Torak was a mistake caused by the accident."

"He's always been around then? Eriond, I mean?"

"Always is a long time, Garion. Eriond was present—in spirit—since the accident. When you were born, he began to move around in the world."

"We're the same age then?"

"Age is a meaningless concept to the Gods. They can be any age they choose to be. It was the theft of the Orb that started things moving toward what happened here today. Zedar wanted to steal the Orb, so Eriond found him and showed him how to do it. That's what got you moving in the first place. If Zedar hadn't stolen the Orb, you'd probably still be at Faldor's farm—married to Zubrette, I'd imagine. Try to keep your perspective about this, Garion, but in a very peculiar way this world was created just to give you something to stand on while you were fixing things."

"Please stop joking."

"I'm not joking, Garion. You're the most important person who's ever lived—or ever will—with the possible exception of Cyradis. You killed a bad God and replaced him with a good one. You did a lot of floundering around in the process, but you finally managed to get it all done. I'm sort of proud of you, actually. All in all, you turned out rather well."

"I had a lot of help."

"Granted, but you're entitled to a bit of conceit—for a moment or two, anyway. I wouldn't overdo it, though. It's not a very becoming sort of thing."

Garion concealed a smile. "Why me?" he asked, making it sound as plaintive and imbecilic as possible.

There was a startled silence, and then the voice actually laughed. "Please don't go back to asking that, Garion."

"I'm sorry. What happens now?"

"You get to go home."

"No, I mean to the world?"

"A lot of that's going to depend on 'Zakath. Eriond is the God of Angarak now, and despite Urgit and Drosta and Nathel, 'Zakath's the real Overking of Angarak. It might take a bit of doing and he may have to use up a large number of Grolims in the process, but before he's done, 'Zakath is going to have to ram Eriond down the throats of all the Angaraks in the world."

"He'll manage." Garion shrugged. " 'Zakath's very good at ramming things down people's throats."

"Cyradis will be able to soften that side of him, I expect."

"All right, then. What about afterward? After all the Angaraks have accepted Eriond?"

"The movement will spread. You'll probably live long enough to see the day when Eriond is the God of the whole world. That's what was intended from the beginning."

" 'And he shall have Lordship and Dominion'?" Garion quoted with a sinking feeling, remembering certain Grolim prophecies.

"You know Eriond better than that. Can you possibly see him sitting on a throne gloating over sacrifices?"

"No, not really. What happens to the other Gods then? Aldur and the rest of them?"

"They'll move on. They've finished with what they came here to do, and there are many, many other worlds in the universe."

"What about UL? Will he leave, too?"

"UL doesn't leave any place, Garion. He's everywhere. Does that more or less answer all the questions? I have some other things that need to be attended to. There are a number of people I have to make arrangements for. Oh, incidentally, congratulations on your daughters."

"Daughters?"

"Small female children. They're devious, but they're prettier than sons, and they smell better."

"How many?" Garion asked breathlessly.

"Quite a few, actually. I won't tell you the exact number. I wouldn't want to spoil any surprises for you, but when you get back to Riva, you'd better start expanding the royal nursery." There was a long pause. "Good-bye for now, Garion," the voice said, its tone no longer dry. "Be well."

And then the voice was gone.

The sun was slipping down, and Garion, Ce'Nedra, and Geran had rejoined the others near the portal to the grotto. They were all subdued as they sat not far from the vast carcass of the dragon.

"We ought to do something about her," Belgarath murmured. "She wasn't really a bad brute. She was just stupid, and that's not really a crime. I've always felt rather sorry for her, and I'd sort of hate to just leave her out here in the open for the birds to pick over."

"You've got a sentimental streak in you, Belgarath," Beldin noted. "That's very disappointing, you know."

"We all get sentimental as we get older." Belgarath shrugged.

"Is she all right?" Velvet asked Sadi as the eunuch returned with Zith's little bottle. "You took quite a long time."

"She's fine," Sadi replied. "One of the babies wanted to play. He thought it was funny to hide from me. It took me awhile to locate him."

"Is there any real reason for us to stay here?" Silk asked. "We could light that beacon, and maybe Captain Kresca could pick us up before dark."

"We're expecting company, Kheldar," Eriond told him.

"We are? Whom are we expecting?"

"Some friends are planning to stop by."

"Your friends or ours?"

"Some of each, actually. There's one of them now." Eriond pointed out to sea. They all turned to look.

Silk suddenly laughed. "We should have known," he said. "Trust Barak to disobey orders."

They all looked out at the gently rolling ocean. The *Seabird* looked a bit the worse for weather, but she wallowed through the waves ponderously on a starboard tack that was taking her on a course past the reef. "Beldin," Silk suggested, "why don't we go down to the shore and light a signal for him?"

"Can't you do it yourself?"

"I'll be happy to—just as soon as you teach me how to set fire to rocks."

"Oh, I hadn't thought of that, I guess."

"Are you sure you're not older than Belgarath? Your memory seems to be slipping a bit, old boy."

"Don't belabor it, Silk. Let's go see if we can signal that oversized barge into shore."

The two of them started down to the edge of the water.

"Was that arranged?" Garion asked Eriond. "Barak showing up, I mean?"

"We had a hand in it, yes," Eriond admitted. "You're going to need transportation back to Riva, and Barak and the others are sort of entitled to find out what happened here."

"The others, too? Is that all right? I mean, at Rheon, Cyradis said—"

"There's no problem now." Eriond smiled. "The Choice has been made. There are quite a number of people on their way to meet us, actually. Our mutual friend has a passion for tying up loose ends."

"You've noticed that already, I see."

The *Seabird* hove to on the lee side of the reef, and a longboat put out from her starboard side to glide across what seemed to Garion to be a molten stretch of water made golden by the setting sun. They all went down to the shore to join Silk and Beldin as the longboat ran smoothly toward the shore of the reef.

"What kept you?" Silk called across the intervening water to Barak, who stood, his beard aflame in the light of the setting sun, in the prow of the boat.

Barak was grinning broadly. "How did things turn out?" he shouted.

"Quite well, actually," Silk called back. Then he seemed to think of something. "Sorry, Cyradis," he said to the Seeress. "That was insensitive of me, wasn't it?"

"Not entirely, Prince Kheldar. My companion's sacrifice was made willingly, and methinks his spirit doth rejoice in our success even as we do."

They were all in the boat with Barak, Garion saw. Mandorallen's armor gleamed just behind the huge Cherek. Hettar, lean and whiplike, was there, and Lelldorin, and even Relg. Barak's son Unrak was chained in the stern. Unrak had grown, but the restraints upon him were puzzling.

Barak placed one huge foot on the gunwale, preparing to leap from the boat.

"Careful," Silk told him. "It's deep right there. There are a fair number of Grolims who found that out the hard way."

"Did you throw them out into the water?" Barak asked.

"No. They volunteered."

The longboat's keel grated on the wave-eroded stones of the amphitheater, and Barak and the others clambered out. "Did we miss very much?" the big man asked.

"Not really," Silk replied with a shrug. "It was just your average, run-of-the-mill saving of the universe. You know how those things are. Is your son in trouble?" Silk looked at Unrak, who seemed a bit crestfallen in his chains.

"Not exactly that," Barak replied. "Along about noon, he turned into a bear, that's all. We sort of thought it was significant."

"It runs in your family, I see. But why chain him now?"

"The sailors refused to get into the longboat with him until we did."

"I didn't follow that at all," 'Zakath murmured to Garion.

"It's a hereditary sort of thing," Garion explained. "Barak's family members are the protectors of the Rivan King. When the situation demands it, they turn into bears. Barak did it several times when I was in danger. It appears that he passed it on to Unrak—his son."

"Unrak's your protector now? He seems a little young, and you don't really need that much protection."

"No. He's probably Geran's protector, and Geran was in a certain amount of danger back there in the grotto."

"Gentlemen," Ce'Nedra said then in a triumphant voice, "may I introduce the Crown Prince of Riva?" She held Geran up so that they could see him.

"He's going to forget how to walk if she doesn't put him down one of these days," Beldin muttered to Belgarath.

"Her arms should start getting tired before too much longer," Belgarath said.

Barak and the others crowded around the little queen even as the sailors who had been rowing reluctantly removed the chains from Barak's son.

"Unrak!" Barak roared, "Come here!"

"Yes, father." The boy stepped out of the boat and came forward.

"This young fellow is your responsibility," Barak told him, pointing at Geran. "I'll be very cross if you let anything happen to him."

Unrak bowed to Ce'Nedra. "Your Majesty," he greeted her, "you're looking well."

"Thank you, Unrak." She smiled.

"May I?" Unrak asked, holding out his arm toward Geran. "His Highness and I should probably get to know each other."

"Of course," Ce'Nedra said, giving her son to the youthful Cherek.

"We've missed you, your Highness." Unrak grinned at the little boy he held in his arms. "The next time you plan one of these extended trips, you should let us know. We were a little worried."

Geran giggled. Then he reached out and tugged on Unrak's scarcely fledged red beard.

Unrak winced.

Ce'Nedra embraced each of their old friends in turn, bestowing kisses at random. Mandorallen, of course, was weeping openly, too choked up to even deliver a flowery greeting, and Lelldorin was in virtually the same condition. Relg, peculiarly, did not even shrink from the Rivan Queen's embrace. Relg, it appeared, had undergone certain philosophical modifications during the years of his marriage to Taiba.

"There seem to be a few strangers here," Hettar noted in his quiet voice.

Silk smacked his forehead with an open palm. "How remiss of me," he said. "How could I have been so forgetful? This is Lady Poledra, Belgarath's wife and Polgara's mother. The rumors about her demise appear to have been exaggerations."

"Will you be serious?" Belgarath muttered as their friends greeted the tawny-haired woman with a certain awe.

"Not a chance," Silk said roguishly. "I'm having too much fun with this, and I'm just starting to get warmed up. Please, gentlemen," he said to their friends, "let me get on with this. Otherwise the introductions are likely to last until midnight. This is Sadi. You should remember him—Chief Eunuch in the palace of Queen Salmissra."

"*Formerly* Chief Eunuch, Kheldar," Sadi corrected. "My Lords." He bowed.

"Your Excellency," Hettar replied. "I'm sure there'll be all sorts of explanations later."

"You all remember Cyradis, of course," Silk went on, "the Holy Seeress of Kell. She's a little tired just now. She had to make a fairly important decision about noon today."

"Where's that big fellow who was with you at Rheon, Cyradis?" Barak asked her.

"Alas, my Lord of Trellheim," she said. "My guide and protector gave up his life to insure our success."

"I'm deeply sorry," Barak said simply.

"And this, of course," Silk said in an offhand voice, "is his Imperial Majesty, Kal Zakath of Mallorea. He's been rather helpful from time to time."

Garion's friends looked at 'Zakath warily, their eyes filled with surprise.

"I'd assume that we can set aside certain unpleasantnesses from the past," 'Zakath said urbanely. "Garion and I have more or less resolved our differences."

"It pleaseth me, your Imperial Majesty," Mandorallen said with a creaking bow, "to have lived to see near-universal peace restored to all the world."

"Thy reputation, the marvel of the known world, hath preceded thee, my Lord of Mandor," 'Zakath replied in an almost perfect Mimbrate dialect. "I do perceive now, however, that reputation is but a poor shade of the stupendous reality."

Mandorallen beamed.

"You'll do just fine," Hettar murmured to 'Zakath.

'Zakath grinned at him. Then he looked at Barak. "The next time you see Anheg, my Lord of Trellheim, tell him that I'm still going to send him a bill for all those ships of mine he sank in the Sea of the East after Thull Mardu. I think some reparations might be in order."

"I wish you all the luck in the world, your Majesty—" Barak grinned "—but I think you'll find that Anheg's *very* reluctant to open the doors of his treasury."

"Never mind," Garion said quietly to Lelldorin, who had drawn himself up, pale-faced and furious at the mention of 'Zakath's name.

"But—"

"It wasn't his fault," Garion said. "Your cousin was killed in a battle. Those things happen, and there's no point in holding grudges. That's what's kept things stirred up in Arendia for the last twenty-five hundred years."

"And I'm sure you all recognize Eriond—formerly Errand," Silk said once again in a deliberately offhand manner, "the new God of Angarak."

"The *what*?" Barak exclaimed.

"You really should try to keep abreast of things, my dear Barak," Silk said, buffing his nails on the front of his tunic.

"Silk," Eriond said reprovingly.

"I'm sorry." Silk grinned. "I couldn't resist. Can you find it in your heart to forgive me, your Divinityship?" He frowned. "That's really very cumbersome, you know. What *is* the correct form of address?"

"How about just Eriond?"

Relg had gone deathly pale and he almost instinctively fell to his knees.

"Please don't do that, Relg," Eriond told him. "After all, you've known me since I was just a little boy, haven't you?"

"But—"

"Stand up, Relg," Eriond said, helping the Ulgo to his feet. "Oh, my father sends his best, by the way."

Relg looked awed.

"Oh, well," Silk said wryly, "we might as well get it out into the open, I suppose. Gentlemen," he said, "I'm sure you all remember the Margravine Liselle, my fiancée."

"Your *fiancée*?" Barak exclaimed in amazement.

"We all have to settle down sometime." Silk shrugged.

They gathered around to congratulate him. Velvet, however, did not look pleased.

"Was something the matter, dear?" Silk asked her, all innocence.

"Don't you think you've forgotten something, Kheldar?" she asked acidly.

"Not that I recall."

"You neglected to ask me about this first."

"Really? Did I actually forget that? You weren't planning to refuse, were you?"

"Of course not."

"Well, then—"

"You haven't heard the last of this, Kheldar," she said ominously.

"I seem to be getting off to a bad start here," he observed.

"Very bad," she agreed.

They built a large bonfire in the amphitheater not too far from the huge carcass of the dragon. Durnik had rather shamefacedly translocated a sizable stack of driftwood in from various beaches here and there on the reef. Garion looked critically at the stack. "I seem to remember a number of very wet evenings when Eriond and I spent hours looking for dry firewood," he said to his old friend.

"This is sort of a special occasion, Garion," Durnik explained apologetically.

"Besides, if you'd have wanted it done this way, you could have done it yourself, couldn't you?"

Garion stared at him, then he suddenly laughed. "Yes, Durnik," he admitted, "I suppose I could have at that. I don't know that we have to tell Eriond, though."

"Do you really think he doesn't know?"

They talked until quite late. A great deal had happened since they had last seen each other, and they all had a lot of catching up to do. Finally, one by one, they drifted off to sleep.

It was still a few hours before dawn when Garion came suddenly awake.

It was not a sound that had awakened him, but a light. It was a single beam of intense blue that bathed the amphitheater in its radiance, and it was soon joined by others that streamed down from the night sky in great glowing columns, red and yellow and green and shades for which there were no names. The columns stood in a semicircle not far from the edge of the water, and there in the center of their rainbow-hued light, the pristine white albatross hovered on seraphlike wings. The incandescent forms that Garion had seen before at Cthol Mishrak began to appear in the columns of pure light. Aldur and Mara, Issa and Nedra, Chaldan and Belar, the Gods stood, their faces filled with the joy of welcome.

"It's time," Poledra sighed from where she sat enfolded in Belgarath's arms. She firmly took his arms from about her shoulders and rose to her feet.

"No," Belgarath protested in an anguished tone, his eyes filled with tears. "There's time yet."

"You knew this was going to happen, Old Wolf," she said gently. "It has to be this way, you know."

"I'm not going to lose you twice," he declared. He also rose. "There's no longer any meaning to any of this." He looked at his daughter. "Pol," he said.

"Yes, father," she replied, rising to her feet with Durnik at her side.

"You'll have to look after things now. Beldin and Durnik and the twins will help you."

"Will you orphan me in one single stroke, father?" Her voice was throbbing with unshed tears.

"You're strong enough to bear it, Pol. Your mother and I are not displeased with you. Be well."

"Don't be foolish, Belgarath," Poledra said firmly.

"I'm not. I won't live without you again."

"It's not permitted."

"It can't be prevented. Not even our Master can prevent me now. You won't leave alone, Poledra. I'm going with you." He put his arms about his wife's shoulders and looked deeply into her golden eyes. "It's better this way."

"As you decide, my husband," she said finally. "We must act now, however, before UL arrives. *He* can prevent it, no matter how much you bend your will to its accomplishment."

Then Eriond was there. "Have you really considered this, Belgarath?" he said.

"Many times in the last three thousand years, yes. I had to wait for Garion, though. Now he's here, and there's nothing to hold me any longer."

"What would make you change your mind?"

"Nothing. I *won't* be separated from her again."

"Then I'll have to see to that, I suppose."

"That's forbidden, Eriond," Poledra objected. "I agreed to this when my task was laid upon me."

"Agreements are always subject to renegotiation, Poledra," he said. "Besides, my father and my brothers neglected to advise me of their decision, so I'll have to deal with the situation without their advice."

"You *can't* defy your father's will," she objected.

"But I don't *know* my father's will as yet. I'll apologize, of course. I'm sure he won't be *too* angry with me, and no one stays angry forever—not even my father— and no decision is irrevocable. If necessary, I'll remind him of the change of heart he had at Prolgu when Gorim persuaded him to relent."

"That sounds awfully familiar," Barak murmured to Hettar. "It looks as if the new God of Angarak has spent a little too much time with our Prince Kheldar."

"It might be contagious," Hettar agreed.

An impossible hope had sprung up in Garion's heart.

"May I borrow the Orb again, Garion?" Eriond asked politely.

"Of course." Garion almost snatched the Orb from the pommel of the sword and offered it to the youthful God.

Eriond took the glowing jewel and approached Belgarath and his wife. Then he reached out with it and gently touched it to each of their foreheads. Garion, know- ing that the touch of the jewel meant death, leaped forward with a strangled cry, but it was too late.

Belgarath and Poledra began to glow with a blue nimbus as they looked deeply into each other's eyes. Then Eriond handed the Orb back to the Rivan King.

"Won't you get into trouble about this?" Garion asked.

"It's all right, Garion," Eriond assured him. "I'm probably going to have to break all kinds of rules in the next several years, so I might as well get into practice."

A deep organ note came from the incandescent columns of light at the edge of the water. Garion looked quickly at the assembled Gods and saw that the albatross had become so intensely bright that he could not bear to look at it.

And then the albatross was gone, and the Father of the Gods stood where it had hovered, and he was surrounded by his sons. "Very well done, my Son," UL said.

"It took me a little while to perceive what thou hadst in thy mind, Father," Eriond apologized. "I'm sorry to have been so dense."

"Thou art unaccustomed to such things, my Son," UL forgave him. "Thy use of thy brother's Orb in this was unanticipated, however, and most ingenious." A faint smile touched the Eternal Face. "Even had I been inclined not to relent, that alone would have forestalled me."

"I thought such might be the case, Father."

"I pray thee, Poledra," UL said then, "forgive me my cruel-seeming subterfuge. Know that the deception was not meant for thee, but for my son. He hath ever been of a retiring nature, reluctant to exercise his will, but his will shall prevail upon this world, and he must learn now to unleash it or to restrain it as seemeth him best."

"It was a test, then, Most Holy?" Belgarath's voice had a slight edge to it.

"All things which happen are tests, Belgarath," UL explained calmly. "Thou mayest take some satisfaction in the knowledge that thou and thine espoused wife did very well in this. It was the decisions of you two which compelled my son to make his. Still do you both serve even now, when all seems complete. And now, Eriond, join with me and thy brothers. Let us go apart a ways that we may welcome thee unto this world which we now deliver into thy hands."

CHAPTER TWENTY-SIX

The sun had risen, a golden disc hanging low on the eastern horizon. The sky was intensely blue and the light breeze blowing steadily in from the west touched the tops of the waves with white. There was still the faint, damp smell of the previous day's fog lingering on the stones of the strangely shaped pyramid that jutted up out of the sea to form the center of the reef.

Garion was light-headed with exhaustion. His body screamed for rest, but his mind skittered from impression to thought to image and back again, keeping him awake but all bemused on the very edge of sleep. There would be time later to sort out everything that had happened here in the Place Which Is No More. And then he rearranged his thinking about that. If ever there was a place that *was,* it was Korim. Korim was more eternally real than Tol Honeth, Mal Zeth, or Val Alorn. He gathered his sleeping wife and his son closer in his arms. They smelled good. Ce'Nedra's hair had its usual, flowerlike fragrance, and Geran smelled like every little boy who had ever lived—a small creature probably at least marginally in need of a bath. Garion's own need for bathing was, he concluded, somewhat more than marginal. Yesterday had been very strenuous.

His friends were gathered in strange little groupings here and there around the amphitheater. Barak, Hettar, and Mandorallen were talking with 'Zakath. Liselle sat with a look of abstract concentration on her face, combing Cyradis' hair. The ladies all seemed quite determined to take the Seeress of Kell in hand. Sadi and Beldin sprawled on the stones near the carcass of the dragon, drinking ale. Sadi's expression was polite, but it nonetheless revealed that he was consuming the bitter brew more out of politeness than from any sense of gusto. Unrak was exploring, and close on his heels was Nathel, the slack-faced young King of the Thulls. The Archduke Otrath stood alone near the now-sealed portal to the grotto, his face filled with apprehensive dread. Kal Zakath had not yet seen fit to discuss certain matters with his kinsman, and Otrath was obviously not looking forward to their conversation. Eriond was talking quietly with Aunt Pol, Durnik, Belgarath, and Poledra. The young God had a strange nimbus of pale light about him. Silk was nowhere in sight.

And then the little man came around the shoulder of the pyramid. Behind him, on the far side of the peak, rose a column of dark smoke. He came down the stairway to the floor of the amphitheater and crossed to where Garion was sitting.

"What were you doing?" Garion asked him.

"I set out a signal for Captain Kresca," Silk replied. "He knows the way back to Perivor, and I've seen Barak navigate in confined waters before. *Seabird*'s meant for the open sea, not for close quarters."

"You'll hurt his feelings if you tell him that, you know."

"I wasn't planning to tell him." The rat-faced little man sprawled on the stones beside Garion and his family.

"Did Liselle have that little chat with you as yet?" Garion asked.

"I think she's saving it up. She wants to have plenty of uninterrupted time for it. Is marriage always like this? I mean, do you always live in perpetual apprehension, waiting for these conversations?"

"It's not uncommon. You're not married yet, though."

"I'm closer to it than I ever thought I'd be."

"Are you sorry?"

"No, not really. Liselle and I are suited for each other. We have a great deal in common. I just wish she wouldn't keep things hanging over my head is all." Silk looked sourly around the amphitheater. "Does he *have* to glow like that?" he asked, pointing at Eriond.

"He probably doesn't even know he's doing it. He's new at this. He'll get better at it as he goes along."

"Do you realize that we're sitting around criticizing a God?"

"He was a friend first, Silk. Friends can criticize us without giving offense."

"My, aren't *we* philosophical this morning? My heart almost stopped when he touched Belgarath and Poledra with the Orb, though."

"Mine, too," Garion admitted, "but it appears he knew what he was doing." He sighed.

"What's the problem?"

"It's all over now. I think I'm going to miss it—at least I will just as soon as I get caught up on my sleep."

"It *has* been a little hectic for the past few days, hasn't it? I suppose that if we put our heads together, we can come up with something exciting to do."

"I know what *I'm* going to be doing," Garion told him.

"Oh? What's that?"

"I'm going to be very busy being a father."

"Your son won't stay young forever, Garion."

"Geran isn't going to be an only child. My friend up here in my head warned me to expect large numbers of daughters."

"Good. It might help to settle you down a bit. I don't want to seem critical, Garion, but sometimes you're awfully flighty. Hardly a year goes by when you're not running off to some corner of the world with that burning sword in your hand."

"Are you trying to be funny?"

"Me?" Silk leaned back comfortably. "You're not going to have all *that* many daughters, are you? What I'm getting at is that women are only of childbearing age for just so long."

"Silk," Garion said pointedly, "do you remember Xbell, that Dryad we met down near the River of the Woods in southern Tolnedra?"

"The one who was so fond of men—all men?"

"That's the one. Would you say that she's still of childbearing age?"

"Oh, my yes."

"Xbell is over three hundred years old. Ce'Nedra's a Dryad, too, you know."

"Well, maybe *you'll* get too old to—" Silk broke off and looked at Belgarath. "Oh, dear," he said. "You *have* got a bit of a problem, haven't you?"

It was almost noon when they boarded the *Seabird.* Barak had agreed, although somewhat reluctantly, to follow Captain Kresca to Perivor. After the two men had met and inspected each other's ships, however, things went more smoothly. Kresca had been lavish in his praise of *Seabird,* and that was always a way to get on the good side of Barak.

As they weighed anchor, Garion leaned on the starboard rail gazing at the strange-looking pyramid sticking out of the sea with a pillar of greasy smoke rising from the amphitheater on its north side.

"I'd have given a great deal to have been there," Hettar said quietly, leaning his elbows on the rail beside Garion. "How was it?"

"Noisy," Garion told him.

"Why did Belgarath insist on burning that dragon?"

"He felt sorry for her."

"Belgarath's funny sometimes."

"He is indeed, my friend. How are Adara and the children?"

"Fine. She's with child again, you know."

"*Again?* Hettar, you two are almost as bad as Relg and Taiba."

"Not quite," Hettar said modestly. "They're still a few ahead of us." He frowned critically, his hawklike face outlined against the sun. "I think somebody's cheating, though. Taiba keeps having babies in twos and threes. That makes it very hard for Adara to keep up."

"I wouldn't want to point any fingers, but I'd suspect that Mara's been interfering there. It's going to take awhile to repopulate Maragor." He looked over to where Unrak stood in the bow with his shadow, Nathel, just behind him. "What's that all about?" he asked.

"I'm not sure," Hettar said. "Nathel's a pathetic sort of boy, and I think Unrak feels sorry for him. I gather there hasn't been too much kindness in Nathel's life, so he'll even accept pity. He's been following Unrak around like a puppy ever since we picked him up." The tall Algar looked at Garion. "You look tired," he said. "You should get some sleep."

"I'm exhausted," Garion admitted, "but I don't want to get my days and nights turned around. Let's go talk with Barak. He seemed just a bit surly when he came ashore."

"You know how Barak is. Missing a fight always makes him discontent. Tell him some stories. He likes a good story almost as much as he likes a good fight."

It was good to be back among his old friends again. There had been a sort of emptiness in Garion since he had left them behind at Rheon. The absence of their burly self-confidence had been part of it, of course, but even more than that, perhaps, had been the camaraderie, that sense of good-natured friendship that lay under all the apparent bickering. As they started aft to where Barak stood with one beefy hand on the tiller, Garion saw 'Zakath and Cyradis standing on the lee side of a longboat. He motioned to Hettar to stop and laid one finger to his lips.

"Eavesdropping isn't very nice, Garion," the tall Algar whispered.

"It's not exactly eavesdropping," Garion whispered back. "I just need to be sure that I won't have to take steps."

"Steps?"

"I'll explain later."

"And what will you do now, Holy Seeress?" 'Zakath was asking the slim girl, his heart in his voice.

"The world lies open before me, Kal Zakath," she replied a little sadly. "The burden of my task hath been lifted, and thou needst no longer address me as 'Seeress,' for, indeed, that burden hath also been lifted. Mine eyes are now fixed on the plain, ordinary light of day, and I am now no more than a plain, ordinary woman."

"Hardly plain, Cyradis, and far from ordinary."

"Thou art kind to say so, Kal Zakath."

"Let's drop that 'Kal,' shall we, Cyradis? It's an affectation. It means King and God. Now that I've seen *real* Gods, I know just how presumptuous it was of me to encourage its use. But let's return to the point. Your eyes have been bound for years, haven't they?"

"Yes."

"Then you haven't had occasion to look into a mirror lately, have you?"

"Neither occasion nor inclination."

'Zakath was a very shrewd man and he fully realized when the time had come for extravagance. "Then let mine eyes be thy mirror, Cyradis," he said. "Look into them and see how fair thou art."

Cyradis blushed. "Thy flattery doth quite catch my breath away, 'Zakath."

"It's not exactly flattery, Cyradis," he said clinically, lapsing back into his usual speech. "You're by far the most beautiful woman I've ever met, and the thought of having you go back to Kell—or anywhere else, for that matter—leaves a vast emptiness in my heart. You've lost your guide and your friend. Let me become both for you. Return with me to Mal Zeth. We've got much to discuss, and it may take us the rest of our lives."

Cyradis turned her pale face away slightly, and the faintly triumphant smile which touched her lips said quite clearly that she saw a great deal more than she was willing to reveal. She turned back to the Mallorean Emperor, her eyes innocently wide. "Wouldst thou indeed take some small pleasure in my company?" she asked.

"Thy company would fill my days, Cyradis," he said.

"Then gladly will I accompany thee to Mal Zeth," she said, "for thou art now my truest friend and dearest companion."

Garion motioned with his head, and he and Hettar went on aft.

"What were we doing?" Hettar asked. "That seemed like a fairly private conversation."

"It was," Garion told him. "I just needed to be sure that it took place, that's all. I was told that it was going to happen, but I like a little verification now and then."

Hettar looked puzzled.

" 'Zakath's been the loneliest man in the world," Garion told him. "That's what made him so empty and soulless—and so dangerous. That's changed now. He isn't going to be lonely anymore, and that should help him with something he has to do."

"Garion, you're being awfully cryptic. All I saw was a young lady rather skillfully wrapping a man around her finger."

"It did sort of look that way, didn't it?"

Early the next morning, Ce'Nedra bolted from her bed and ran up the stairs to the deck. Alarmed, Garion followed her. "Excuse me," she said to Polgara, who was leaning out over the rail. Then she took her place beside the ageless woman, and the two of them stood for some time retching over the side.

"You, too?" Ce'Nedra said with a wan smile.

Polgara wiped her lips with a kerchief and nodded.

Then the two of them embraced each other and began to laugh.

"Are they all right?" Garion asked Poledra, who had just come up on deck with the ubiquitous wolf pup again at her side. "Neither one of them *ever* gets seasick."

"They aren't seasick, Garion," Poledra said with a mysterious smile.

"But why are they—"

"They're just fine, Garion. More than fine. Go on back down to your cabin. I'll take care of this."

Garion had just awakened, and his mind was a little foggy. So it was that it was not until he was halfway down the stairs before it slowly dawned on him. He stopped, his eyes very wide. *"Ce'Nedra?"* he exclaimed. "And *Aunt Pol?"* Then he, too, began to laugh.

The appearance of Sir Mandorallen, the invincible Baron of Vo Mandor, in the court of King Oldorin caused an awed silence. Because of Perivor's remote location, Mandorallen's towering reputation had not reached the island, but his very presence—that overpowering sense of his nobility and perfection—stunned the king's court. Mandorallen was the ultimate Mimbrate, and it showed.

Garion and 'Zakath, once again in full armor, approached the throne with the stupendous knight between them. "Your Majesty," Garion said with a bow, "it pleaseth me beyond measure to announce that our quest hath come to a happy and successful conclusion. The beast which plagued thy shores is no more, and the evil which beset the world is quelled for good and all. Fortune, which sometimes doth bestow blessings with open-handed generosity, hath also seen fit to reunite my companions and me with old and well-loved friends—most of whom I shall present to thee anon. A keen awareness, however, of a fact that, methinks, will be of supreme importance to thee and to thy court doth impell me to present at once a puissant knight from far-off Arendia, who doth ever stand at the right hand of his Majesty, King Korodullin, and who, doubtless, will greet thee in kinship and love. Your Majesty, I have the honor to present Sir Mandorallen, Baron of Vo Mandor and the paramount knight in all the world."

"You're getting better at that," 'Zakath said quietly.

"Practice," Garion said deprecatingly.

"Lord King," Mandorallen said in his resonant voice, bowing to the throne, "gladly do I greet thee and the members of thy court, and dare to call ye all kinsmen. I presume to bear thee warmest greetings from their Majesties, King Korodullin and Queen Mayaserana, monarchs of well-loved Arendia, for, doubtless, as soon as I return to Vo Mimbre and reveal that those who were once lost are now joyfully found again, their Majesties' eyes will fill to overflowing with tears of thanksgiving, and they shall embrace thee from afar, if needs be, as a brother, and, as great Chaldan gives me strength, shall I presently return to thy magnificent city with missives top-filled with their regard and affection which shall, methinks, presage a soon-to-be accomplished reunion—may I dare even hope, a reunification—of the disseevered branches of the holy blood of sacred Arendia."

"He managed to say all that in one sentence?" 'Zakath murmured to Garion with some awe.

"Two, I think," Garion murmured back. "Mandorallen's in his element here. This is liable to take awhile—two or three days, I'd imagine."

It did not take quite *that* long, but almost. The speeches of the nobles of Perivor were at first somewhat rudimentary, since the members of King Oldorin's court had been taken by surprise by Mandorallen's sudden appearance and had been rendered almost tongue-tied by his eloquence. A sleepless night spent in fevered composition, however, remedied that. The following day was given over to flowery speeches, an extended banquet, and assorted entertainments. Belgarath was prevailed upon to present an only slightly embellished account of the events that had transpired on the reef. The old man rather judiciously avoided references to some of the more incredible incidents. The sudden appearance of divinities in the middle of an adventure story sometimes stirs skepticism in even the most credulous audience.

Garion leaned forward to speak quietly to Eriond, who sat across the banquet table from him. "At least he protected your anonymity," he said quietly.

"Yes," Eriond agreed. "I'll have to think of some way to thank him for that."

"Restoring Poledra to him is probably all the thanks he can handle right now. It's going to come out eventually though, you know—your identity, I mean."

"I think it's going to need a bit of preparation, though. I'll need to have a long talk with Ce'Nedra, I think."

"Ce'Nedra?"

"I want some details on how she got started when she raised the army she took to Thull Mardu. It seems to me she began on a small scale and then worked her way up. That might be the best way to go at it."

"Your Sendarian background is starting to show, Eriond." Garion laughed. "Durnik left his mark on both of us, didn't he?" Then he cleared his throat a little uncomfortably. "You're doing it again," he cautioned.

"Doing what?"

"Glowing."

"Does it show?"

Garion nodded. "I'm afraid so."

"I'll have to work on that."

The banquets and entertainments lasted well into the night for several days, but since nobles are not customarily early risers, this left the mornings free for Garion and his friends to discuss all that had happened since they had separated at Rheon. The accounts of those who had remained at home were filled with domesticity—children, weddings, and affairs of state. Garion was quite pleased to hear that Brand's son Kail was managing the Kingdom of Riva probably at least as well as he might have himself. Moreover, since the Murgos were preoccupied with the Mallorean presence in southeastern Cthol Murgos, peace by and large prevailed among the western kingdoms, and trade flourished there. Silk's nose began to twitch at that information.

"This is all well and good," Barak rumbled. "But could we possibly skip over what's happening back home and get down to the real story? I'm dying of curiosity."

And so they began. No attempt to gloss things over was permitted. Every detail was savored.

"Did you really do that?" Lelldorin asked Garion at one point after Silk had luridly described their first encounter with Zandramas, who had assumed the form of the dragon in the hills above the Arendish plain.

"Well," Garion replied modestly, "not her *whole* tail, only about four feet of it. It seemed to get her attention, though."

"When he gets home, our splendid hero here is going to look into the career opportunities available in the field of dragon-molesting." Silk laughed.

"But there aren't any more dragons, Kheldar," Velvet pointed out.

"Oh, that's all right, Liselle." He grinned. "Maybe Eriond can make a few for him."

"Never mind," Garion told him.

Then, at a certain point in the narrative, they all had to see Zith, and Sadi rather proudly displayed his little green snake and her wriggling brood.

"She doesn't look all that dangerous to me," Barak grunted.

"Go tell that to Harakan." Silk grinned. "Liselle threw the little dear into his face at Ashaba. Zith nipped him a few times and absolutely petrified him."

"Was he dead?" the big man asked.

"I've never seen anybody any deader."

"You're getting ahead of the story," Hettar chided.

"There's no way we're going to be able to tell you about everything that happened in one morning, Hettar," Durnik said.

"That's all right, Durnik," Barak said. "It's a long way back home. We'll have plenty of time at sea."

That afternoon, by more or less popular demand, Beldin was obliged to repeat the performance he had given prior to their departure for the reef. Then, simply to demonstrate some of the gifts of his companions, Garion suggested that they adjourn to the tournament grounds to give them more room. Lelldorin showed the king and his court some of the finer points of archery, culminating the demonstration by showing them an entirely new way to pick plums from a distant tree. Barak bent an iron bar into something resembling a pretzel, and Hettar put them into a state verging on stunned amazement by a dazzling display of horsemanship. The culmination of the affair did not come off too well, however. When Relg walked through a solid stone wall, many ladies fainted, and some of the younger members of the audience fled screaming.

"They don't seem to be ready for that yet," Silk said. Silk had resolutely turned his back when Relg had approached the wall. "I know *I'm* not," he added.

About noon a few days later, two ships entered the harbor from different directions. One of the ships was a familiar Cherek war boat, and General Atesca and Bureau Chief Brador disembarked from the other. Greldik led King Anheg and Emperor Varana down the gangway of the war boat.

"Barak!" Anheg roared as he came down the gangway. "Can you think of any reason I shouldn't take you back to Val Alorn in chains?"

"Testy, isn't he?" Hettar observed to the red-bearded man.

"He'll calm down after I get him drunk." Barak shrugged.

"I'm sorry, Garion," Anheg said in a booming voice. "Varana and I tried to catch him, but that big scow of his moves faster than we thought."

"Scow?" Barak protested mildly.

"It's all right, Anheg," Garion replied. "They didn't arrive until after everything was finished."

"You got your son back, then?"

"Yes."

"Well, trot him out, boy. We all invested a lot of effort in trying to find him for you."

Ce'Nedra came forward carrying Geran, and Anheg enfolded them both in a bear hug. "Your Majesty," he greeted the Rivan Queen, "and you, your Highness." He grinned and tickled the little boy. Geran giggled.

Ce'Nedra tried a curtsy.

"Don't do that, Ce'Nedra," Anheg told her. "You'll drop the baby."

Ce'Nedra laughed and then smiled at Emperor Varana. "Uncle," she said.

"Ce'Nedra," the silvery-haired emperor replied. "You're looking well." He squinted at her. "Is it my imagination, or are you putting on a little weight?"

"It's just temporary, uncle," she replied. "I'll explain later."

Brador and Atesca approached 'Zakath. "Why, your Imperial Majesty," Atesca said to his emperor in feigned surprise. "Imagine meeting you here—of all places."

"General Atesca," 'Zakath said to him, "don't we know each other well enough to ignore these subterfuges?"

"We were worried about you, your Majesty," Brador said. "Since we were in the vicinity anyway . . ." The bald man spread his hands.

"And just what were you two doing in this vicinity? Didn't I leave you back on the banks of the Magan?"

"Something came up, your Majesty," Atesca put in. "Urvon's army fell all apart, and the Darshivans seemed to be distracted. Brador and I seized the opportunity to bring Peldane and Darshiva back into the empire, and we've been pursuing the remnants of the Darshivan army all over eastern Dalasia."

"Very good, gentlemen," 'Zakath approved. "Very, very good. I should take a vacation more often."

"*This* was his idea of a vacation?" Sadi murmured.

"Of course," Silk replied. "Fighting dragons can be very invigorating."

'Zakath and Varana had been eyeing each other speculatively.

"Your Imperial Majesties," Garion said politely, "I should probably introduce you. Emperor Varana, this is his Imperial Majesty, Kal Zakath of Mallorea. Emperor 'Zakath, this is his Imperial Majesty, Ran Borune XXIV of the Tolnedran Empire."

"Just Varana will do, Garion," the Tolnedran said. "We've all heard a lot about you, Kal Zakath," he said, extending his hand.

"None of it good, I'm sure, Varana." 'Zakath smiled, shaking the other emperor's hand warmly.

"Rumors are seldom accurate, 'Zakath."

"We have much to discuss, your Imperial Majesty," 'Zakath said.

"Indeed we do, your Imperial Majesty."

King Oldorin of Perivor appeared to be in a state verging on nervous prostration. His island kingdom, it seemed, was quite suddenly awash with royalty. Garion made the introductions as gently and, he hoped, as painlessly as possible. King Oldorin mumbled a few greetings, almost forgetting his thees and thous. Garion drew him to one side. "This is a momentous occasion, your Majesty," he said. "The presence in one place of 'Zakath of Mallorea, Varana of Tolnedra, and Anheg of Cherek doth presage the possibility of tremendous steps toward that universal peace for which the world hath longed for eons."

"Thine own presence doth not diminish the occasion, Belgarion of Riva."

Garion bowed his acknowledgment. "Though the courtesy and hospitality of thy court are the marvel of the known world, your Majesty," he said, "it were foolish of us not to seize this opportunity in so noble a cause. Thus I implore thee that my friends and I may closet separately for some time to explore the possibilities of this chance meeting, although it seemeth to me that chance hath had but small part in this coming to pass. Surely the Gods themselves have had a hand in it."

"I am certain of it, your Majesty," Oldorin agreed. "There are council chambers on the topmost floor of my palace, King Belgarion. They are at the immediate disposal of thyself and thy royal friends. I have no doubt that momentous things may emerge from this meeting, and the honor I shall accrue that it is to take place beneath my roof doth overwhelm me quite."

It was an impromptu meeting that was held in the upper chambers of the palace. Belgarath, by common consent, presided. Garion agreed to look after the interests of Queen Porenn, and Durnik to those of King Fulrach. Relg spoke for Ulgo—and Maragor. Mandorallen represented Arendia, and Hettar spoke for his father. Silk stood in for his brother, Urgit. Sadi spoke for Salmissra, and Nathel spoke for the Thulls, although very seldom. No one was particularly interested in taking the part of Drosta lek Thun of Gar og Nadrak.

Right at the outset there was, to Varana's obvious disappointment, an agreement that matters of trade be excluded from the discussion, and then they got down to business.

About midway through the second day, Garion leaned back in his chair, only half listening as Silk and 'Zakath haggled incessantly over a peace treaty between Mallorea and Cthol Murgos. Garion sighed pensively. Only a few days ago, he and his friends had witnessed—and participated in—the most momentous Event in the history of the universe, and now they sat around a table deeply involved in the mundane matters of international politics. It seemed so anticlimactic somehow, and yet Garion knew that most of the people in the world would be far more concerned about what happened around this table than what had happened at Korim—for a while, anyway.

Finally, the Accords of Dal Perivor were reached. They were tentative, to be sure, and couched in broad generalities. They were subject, of course, to ratification by those monarchs not actually present. They were tenuous and based more on goodwill than on the rough give-and-take of true political negotiation. They were nonetheless, Garion felt, the last, best hope of mankind. Scribes were summoned to copy from Beldin's copious notes, and it was decided that the document should be issued over the seal of King Oldorin of Perivor as host monarch.

The ceremony of the signing was stupendous. Mimbrates are very good at stupendous ceremonies.

Then, on the following day, came the good-byes. 'Zakath, Cyradis, Eriond, Atesca, and Brador were to depart for Mal Zeth while the rest of them were to board the *Seabird* for the long voyage home. Garion spoke at some length with 'Zakath. They both promised to correspond and, when affairs of state permitted it, to visit. The correspondence would be easy, they both knew. The visits, however, were far more problematical.

Then Garion joined his family while they took their leave of Eriond. Garion then walked the young and as-yet-unknown God of Angarak down to the quay where Atesca's ship waited. "We've come a long way together, Eriond," he said.

"Yes," Eriond agreed.

"You've got a lot ahead of you, you know."

"Probably more than you can even imagine, Garion."

"Are you ready?"

"Yes, Garion, I am."

"Good. If you ever need me, call on me. I'll come to wherever you are as quickly as I can."

"I'll remember that."

"And don't get so busy that you let Horse get fat."

Eriond smiled. "No danger of that," he said. "Horse and I still have a long way to go."

"Be well, Eriond."

"You, too, Garion."

They clasped hands and then Eriond went up the gangway to his waiting ship.

Garion sighed and made his way to where *Seabird* was moored. He went up the gangway to join the others as they watched Atesca's ship sail slowly out of the harbor, veering slightly around Greldik's ship, which waited with the impatience of a leashed hound.

Then Barak's sailors cast off all lines and rowed out into the harbor. The sails were raised, and *Seabird* turned her prow toward home.

CHAPTER TWENTY-SEVEN

The weather held clear and sunny, and a steady breeze filled *Seabird*'s sails to drive her northwesterly in the wake of Greldik's patched and weather-beaten war boat. At Unrak's insistence, the two vessels were making a side trip to Mishrak ac Thull to deposit Nathel in his own kingdom.

The days were long and filled with sunshine and the sharp smell of brine. Garion and all his friends spent most of those days in the sunny main cabin. The story of the quest to Korim was long and involved, but those who had not been with Garion and the others wanted as much in the way of detail as they could possibly get. Their frequent interruptions and questions led to extended digressions, and the story jumped back and forth in time, but it proceeded, albeit at a frequently limping pace. There was much in the story that an average listener might have found incredible. Barak and the others, however, accepted it. They had spent enough time with Belgarath, Polgara, and Garion to know that almost nothing was impossible. The only exception to this rule was Emperor Varana, who remained adamantly skeptical—more on philosophical grounds, Garion suspected, than from any real disbelief.

Unrak gave Nathel some very extended advice before the King of the Thulls was deposited in a seaport town in his own kingdom. The advice had to do with the need for Nathel to assert himself and to break free of the domination of his mother. Unrak didn't look all that optimistic after the young Thull departed.

The *Seabird* turned her course southward then, still following Greldik's wake as they ran along the barren, rocky coast of Goska in northeastern Cthol Murgos. "That's disgraceful, you know that?" Barak said to Garion one day, pointing at Greldik's vessel. "It looks like a floating shipwreck."

"Greldik uses his ship rather hard," Garion agreed. "I've sailed with him a few times."

"The man has no respect for the sea," Barak grumbled, "and he drinks too much."

Garion blinked. "I beg your pardon?" he said.

"Oh, I'll be the first to admit that I take a tankard of ale now and then, but Greldik drinks at sea. That's revolting, Garion. I think it might even be irreligious."

"You know more about the sea than I do," Garion admitted.

Greldik's ship and *Seabird* sailed through the narrow strait between the Isle of Verkat and the southern coasts of Hagga and Gorut. Since it was summer in the southern latitudes, the weather continued fair and they made good time. After they had passed through the dangerous cluster of rocky islets strung down from the tip of the Urga penninsula, Silk came up on deck. "You two have taken to living up here," he observed to Garion and Barak.

"I like to be on deck when we're in sight of land," Garion said. "When you can see the shoreline slipping by, it gives you the sense that you're getting somewhere. What's Aunt Pol doing?"

"Knitting." Silk shrugged. "She's teaching Ce'Nedra and Liselle how it's done. They're creating whole heaps of little garments."

"I wonder why," Garion said with a perfectly straight face.

"I've got a favor to ask, Barak," Silk said.

"What do you need?"

"I'd like to stop at Rak Urga. I want to give Urgit a copy of those accords, and 'Zakath made a couple of proposals at Dal Perivor that my brother really ought to know about."

"Will you help chain Hettar to the mast while we're in port?" Barak asked him.

Silk frowned slightly, then he seemed to suddenly understand. "Oh," he said. "I'd sort of forgotten that. It wouldn't be a very good idea to take Hettar into a city full of Murgos, would it?"

"A bad idea, Silk. Disastrous might come even closer."

"Let me talk with him," Garion suggested. "Possibly I can calm him down a bit."

"If you can manage that, I'll have you come up on deck and talk to the next gale we run into," Barak said. "Hettar's *almost* as reasonable as the weather where Murgos are concerned."

The tall Algar, however, did not, in fact, go stony-faced and reach for his saber at the mention of the word "Murgo." They had told him about Urgit's real background during the voyage, and his hawklike face became alive with curiosity when Garion rather hesitantly told him of the plan to stop at Rak Urga. "I'll control my instincts, Garion," he promised. "I think I'd really like to meet this Drasnian who's managed to become the King of the Murgos."

Because of the hereditary and by now almost instinctive animosity between Murgos and Alorns, Belgarath advised caution in Rak Urga. "Things are quiet now," he said. "Let's not stir them up. Barak, run up a flag of truce, and when we get to within hailing distance of the wharves, I'll send for Oskatat, Urgit's Seneschal."

"Can he be trusted?" Barak asked dubiously.

"I think so, yes. We won't all trek up to the Drojim, though. Have *Seabird* and Greldik's ship pull back out into the harbor after we go ashore. Not even the most rabid Murgo sea captain would attack a pair of Cherek war boats in open water. I'll keep in touch with Pol, and we'll send for help if the occasion arises."

It took some fairly extensive shouting between ship and shore to persuade a Murgo colonel to send to the Drojim Palace for Oskatat. The colonel's decision may have been tipped in that direction when Barak ordered his catapults loaded. Rak Urga was not a very attractive town, but the colonel quite obviously didn't want it burned to the ground.

"Are you back already?" Oskatat bellowed across the intervening water when at last he arrived on the wharf.

"We were in the vicinity and we thought we'd pay a call," Silk said lightly. "We'd like to speak with his Majesty if possible. We'll control these Alorns if you can keep your Murgos leashed."

Oskatat gave a number of very abrupt commands that were accompanied by some fairly grisly threats, and Garion, Belgarath, and Silk took to *Seabird*'s longboat. They were accompanied by Barak, who had left Unrak in charge, and by Hettar and Mandorallen.

"How did it go?" Oskatat asked Silk as the party, accompanied by a contingent of King Urgit's black-robed household guard, rode up from the harbor to the Drojim.

"Things turned out rather well," Silk smirked.

"His Majesty should be pleased to hear that."

They entered the garish Drojim Palace, and Oskatat led them down a smoky, torch-lit hall toward the throne room. "His Majesty has been expecting these people," Oskatat said harshly to the guards. "He will see them now. Open the door."

One of the guards seemed to be new. "But they're Alorns, Lord Oskatat," he objected.

"So? Open the door."

"But—"

Oskatat coolly drew his heavy sword. "Yes?" he said in a deceptively mild tone.

"Ah—nothing, my Lord Oskatat," the guard repeated. "Nothing at all."

"Why is the door still closed then?"

The door was quickly snatched open.

"Kheldar!" It was a ringing shout, and it came from the far end of the throne room. King Urgit bolted down the steps of the dais, flinging his crown over one shoulder as he ran. He caught Silk in a rough embrace, laughing uncontrollably. "I thought you were dead," he crowed.

"You're looking well, Urgit," Silk said to him.

Urgit made a slight face. "I'm married now, you know," he said.

"I was afraid Prala might get you eventually. I'm getting married myself shortly."

"The blond girl? Prala told me about how she felt about you. Imagine that, the invincible Prince Kheldar, married at last."

"Don't make any large wagers on it just yet, Urgit," Silk told his brother. "I may still decide to fall on my sword instead. Are we sort of alone here? We've got some things to tell you, and our time's a bit short."

"Mother and Prala are here," Urgit told him, "and my stepfather here, of course."

"Stepfather?" Silk exclaimed, looking at Oskatat in surprise.

"Mother was getting lonely. She missed all the playful abuse Taur Urgas used to bestow on her. I used my influence to marry her off to Oskatat. I'm afraid he's been a terrible disappointment to her, though. So far as I know, he hasn't knocked her down a single flight of stairs or kicked her in the head even once."

"He's impossible when he's like this," Oskatat apologized for his king.

"Just brimming over with good spirits, Oskatat." Urgit laughed. "By Torak's boiling eye, I've missed you, Kheldar." Then he greeted Garion and Belgarath and looked inquiringly at Barak, Mandorallen, and Hettar.

"Barak, Earl of Trellheim," Silk introduced the red-bearded giant.

"He's even bigger than they say he is," Urgit noted.

"Sir Mandorallen, Baron of Vo Mandor," Silk went on.

"The Gods' own definition of the word 'gentleman,' " Urgit said.

"And Hettar, son of King Cho-Hag of Algaria."

Urgit shrank away, his eyes suddenly fearful. Even Oskatat took a step backward.

"Not to worry, Urgit," Silk said grandly. "Hettar came all the way through the streets of your capital, and he didn't kill even one of your subjects."

"Remarkable," Urgit murmured nervously. "You've changed, Lord Hettar," he said. "You're reputed to be a thousand feet tall and to wear a necklace of Murgo skulls."

"I'm on vacation," Hettar said dryly.

Urgit grinned. "We aren't going to be unpleasant to each other, are we?" he asked, still slightly apprehensive.

"No, your Majesty," Hettar told him, "I don't think we are. For some reason, you intrigue me."

"That's a relief," Urgit said. "If you find yourself getting edgy, though, be sure to let me know. There are still a dozen or so of my father's generals lurking about the Drojim. Oskatat hasn't found a reason to have them beheaded yet. I'll send for them, and you can settle your nerves. They're just a bother to me anyway." He frowned. "I wish I'd known you were coming," he said. "I've wanted to send your father a present for years now."

Hettar looked at him, one eyebrow raised.

"He did me the greatest service any man can ever do for another. He ran his saber through Taur Urgas' guts. You might tell him that I tidied up for him afterward."

"Oh? My father doesn't usually need to be tidied up after."

"Oh, Taur Urgas was dead enough all right," Urgit assured him, "but I didn't want some Grolim to come along and accidentally resurrect him, so I cut his throat before we buried him."

"Cut his throat?" Even Hettar seemed startled by that.

"From ear to ear," Urgit said happily. "I stole a little knife when I was about ten, and I spent the next several years sharpening it. After I slit his weasand, I drove a stake through his heart and buried him seventeen feet deep—head down. He looked better than he had in years with just his feet sticking up out of the dirt. I paused to enjoy that sight while I was resting from all the shoveling."

"You buried him yourself?" Barak asked.

"I certainly wasn't going to let anybody else do it. I wanted to be sure of him. After I had him well planted, I stampeded horses across his grave several times to conceal the spot. As you may have guessed, my father and I were not on the best of terms. I take some pleasure in knowing that not a single living Murgo knows exactly where he's buried. Why don't we go join my queen and my mother? Then you can tell me your splendid news—whatever it is. Dare I hope that Kal Zakath rests in the arms of Torak?"

"I wouldn't think so."

"Pity," Urgit said.

As soon as they found out that Polgara, Ce'Nedra, and Velvet were still on board *Seabird*, Queen Prala and Queen Mother Tamazin excused themselves and left the throne room to renew old acquaintances.

"Find seats, gentlemen," Urgit said after they had left. He sprawled on his throne with one leg cocked up over the arm. "What are these things you wanted to tell me, Kheldar?"

Silk sat down on the edge of the dais and reached inside his tunic.

"Please don't do that, Kheldar," Urgit told him, shying away. "I know how many daggers you carry."

"Not a dagger this time, Urgit," Silk assured him. "Only this." He handed over a folded parchment packet.

Urgit opened it and scanned it quickly. "Who's Oldorin of Perivor?" he asked.

"He's the king of an island off the south coast of Mallorea," Garion told him. "A group of us met in his palace."

"*Quite* a group, I see," Urgit said, looking over the signatures. He frowned. "I *also* see that you spoke for me," he said to Silk.

"He protected your interests rather well, Urgit," Belgarath assured him. "The details we hammered out are mostly generalities, you'll notice, but it's a start."

"It is indeed, Belgarath," Urgit agreed. "I notice that no one spoke for Drosta."

"The King of Gar og Nadrak was unrepresented, your Majesty," Mandorallen told him.

"Poor old Drosta." Urgit chuckled. "He always seems to get left out. This is all very nice, gentlemen, and it might even insure a decade or so of peace—provided you promised to let 'Zakath have my head on a plate to decorate some unimportant room in his palace at Mal Zeth with."

"That's the main thing we came to discuss with you," Silk told him. " 'Zakath returned to Mal Zeth when we all left Perivor, but I talked with him for quite a while before we separated, and he finally agreed to accept peace overtures."

"Peace?" Urgit scoffed. "The only peace 'Zakath wants is eternal peace—for every living Murgo, and I'm at the top of his list."

"He's changed a bit," Garion told him. "He has something more important on his mind right now than exterminating Murgos."

"Nonsense, Garion. *Everybody* wants to exterminate the Murgos. Even *I* want to exterminate them, and I'm their king."

"Send some ambassadors to Mal Zeth," Silk advised him. "Give them enough power to negotiate in good faith."

"Give a Murgo power? Kheldar, are you out of your mind?"

"I can find some trustworthy men, Urgit," Oskatat assured him.

"In Cthol Murgos? Where? Under some damp rock?"

"You're going to have to start trusting people, Urgit," Belgarath told him.

"Oh, of course, Belgarath," Urgit said with heavy sarcasm. "I sort of *have* to trust you, but that's because you'll turn me into a frog if I don't."

"Just send your ambassadors to Mal Zeth, Urgit," Silk said patiently. "You may be pleasantly surprised at the outcome."

"Any outcome that doesn't leave me without my head would be pleasant." Urgit squinted shrewdly at his brother. "You've got something else on your mind, Kheldar," he said. "Go ahead and spit it out."

"The world's right on the verge of breaking out in a bad case of peace," Silk told him. "My partner and I have been on a wartime footing for years now. Our enterprises are very likely to collapse if we don't find new markets—and markets for peacetime goods. Cthol Murgos has been at war for a generation now."

"Longer than that, actually. Technically, we've been at war since the ascension of the Urga Dynasty—which I have the distinct displeasure of representing."

"There must be quite a hunger for peacetime amenities in your kingdom then—little things, like roofs for the houses, pots to cook in, something to cook in them—things like that."

"I'd imagine so, yes."

"Good. Yarblek and I can ship goods to Cthol Murgos by sea and turn Rak Urga into the largest commercial center on the southern half of the continent."

"Why would you want to? Cthol Murgos is bankrupt."

"The bottomless mines are still there, aren't they?"

"Of course, but they're all in territories controlled by the Malloreans."

"But if you conclude a peace treaty with 'Zakath, the Malloreans will be leaving, won't they? We'll have to move fast on this, Urgit. As soon as the Malloreans withdraw, you'll have to move in, not only with troops, but also with miners."

"What do I get out of it?"

"Taxes, brother mine, taxes. You can tax the gold miners, you can tax me, and you can tax my customers. You'll be rolling in money in just a few years."

"And the Tolnedrans will swindle me out of all of it in just a few weeks."

"Not too likely." Silk smirked. "Varana's the only Tolnedran in the world who knows about this, and he's on Barak's ship out in the harbor right now. He won't get back to Tol Honeth for several weeks."

"What difference does that make? Nobody can make a move of any kind until I conclude a peace treaty with 'Zakath, can they?"

"That's not entirely true, Urgit. You and I can draw up an agreement guaranteeing me exclusive access to the Murgo market. I'll pay you handsomely for it, of course, and the agreement will be perfectly legal—and ironclad. I've drawn up enough trade agreements to be able to see to that. We can hammer out the details later, but the important thing right now is to get something down in writing with both our names on it. And then, when peace breaks out, the Tolnedrans will swarm down here. You can show them the document and send them all home again. If I've got exclusive access, we'll make millions. Millions, Urgit, millions!"

Both of their noses were twitching violently now.

"What sort of provisions would we want to put in this agreement of exclusivity?" Urgit asked cautiously.

Silk grinned broadly at him and reached inside his doublet again. "I've taken the liberty of drawing up an interim document," he said, pulling out another parchment, "just to save time, of course."

Sthiss Tor was still a very unattractive city, Garion noticed as Barak's sailors moored *Seabird* to the familiar wharf in the Drasnian trade enclave. The hawsers were no sooner tied off than Silk leaped across to the wharf and hurried up the street. "Is he likely to have any trouble?" Garion asked Sadi.

"Not too likely," Sadi, who was crouched down behind a longboat, replied.

"Salmissra knows who he is, and I know my queen. Her face doesn't show any emotion, but her curiosity is very strong. I've spent the last three days composing that letter. She'll see me. I can practically guarantee that. Could we go below, Garion? I'd really rather not have anybody see me."

It was perhaps two hours later when Silk returned accompanied by a platoon of Nyissan soldiers. The platoon leader was familiar.

"Is that you, Issus?" Sadi called out through the porthole of the cabin in which he was hiding. "I thought you'd be dead by now."

"Hardly," the one-eyed assassin said.

"You're working at the palace now?"

"Yes."

"For the queen?"

"Among others. I take on a few odd jobs for Javelin now and then."

"Does the queen know about that?"

"Of course. All right, Sadi. The queen's agreed to a two-hour amnesty for you. We'd better hurry. I'm sure you'll want to be gone from here before those two hours run out. The queen's fangs start to itch every time she hears your name, so let's go—unless you'd like to reconsider and start running right now."

"No," Sadi said. "I'll be right up. I'm bringing Polgara and Belgarion with me, if that's all right."

"That's up to you," Issus said with an indifferent shrug.

The palace was still infested with snakes and with dreamy-eyed eunuchs. A pimply-faced official with broad hips and a grotesquely made-up face met them at the palace door. "Well, Sadi," he said in a piping soprano voice, "I see you've returned."

"And I see you've managed to stay alive, Y'sth," Sadi replied coldly. "That's a shame, really."

Y'sth's eyes narrowed with undisguised hatred. "I'd be a little careful about what I say, Sadi," he squeaked. "You're not Chief Eunuch anymore. As a matter of fact, I may soon hold that position myself."

"May the heavens defend poor Nyissa then," Sadi murmured.

"You've heard of the queen's command that Sadi be given safe conduct?" Issus asked the eunuch.

"Not from her own lips."

"Salmissra doesn't have lips, Y'sth, and you've just heard about it—from me. Now, are you going to get out of our way? Or am I going to have to slit you up the middle?"

Y'sth backed away. "You can't threaten me, Issus."

"I wasn't threatening you. I was just asking a question." Then the assassin led the way up the polished stone corridor leading to the throne room.

The room they entered was unchanged and probably unchangeable. Thousands of years of tradition had seen to that. Salmissra, her coils stirring restlessly and her blunt, crowned head weaving sinuously in front of her mirror, occupied the throne.

"Sadi the eunuch, my Queen," Issus announced with a bow. Issus, Garion noted, did not prostrate himself before the throne as did other Nyissans.

"Ah," Salmissra hissed, "and the beautiful Polgara and King Belgarion. You've fallen in with important people since you left my service, Sadi."

"Pure chance, my Queen," Sadi lied glibly.

"What is this vital matter that impelled you to risk your life by coming into my presence again?"

"Only this, Eternal Salmissra," Sadi replied. He set his red leather case on the floor, opened it, and removed a folded parchment. He casually kicked a groveling eunuch in the ribs. "Take this to the queen," he commanded.

"You're not enhancing your popularity here, Sadi," Garion cautioned quietly.

"I'm not running for public office, Garion. I can be as disagreeable as I choose to be."

Salmissra quickly perused the Accords of Dal Perivor. "Interesting," she hissed.

"I'm sure your Majesty can see the opportunities implicit in those accords," Sadi said. "I felt it was my responsibility to make you aware of them."

"Of course I can see what's involved, Sadi," she said. "I'm a snake, not a cretin."

"Then I'll bid you good-bye, my Queen. I've performed my last duty to you."

Salmissra's eyes had gone flat with concentration. "Not just yet, my Sadi," she said in a whisper that was almost a purr. "Come a little closer."

"You gave your word, Salmissra," he said apprehensively.

"Oh, *do* be sensible, Sadi," she said. "I'm not going to bite you. It was all a ploy, wasn't it? You had discovered the possibility that these accords might be in the making and you deliberately set out to have yourself disgraced so that you could pursue them. Your negotiations on my behalf were brilliant, I must say. You have done very well, Sadi—even if your actions involved deceiving me. I am well pleased with you. Would you consent to resume your former position here in the palace?"

"Consent, my Queen?" he blurted almost boyishly. "I'd be overjoyed. I live but to serve you."

Salmissra swiveled her head around to regard the prostrated eunuchs. "You will all leave me now," she commanded them. "I want you to go throughout the palace and spread the word that Sadi has been rehabilitated and that I've reinstated him. If anyone cares to dispute my decision, send him to me, and I'll explain it to him."

They stared at her, and Garion noticed that not a few faces were filled with chagrin.

"How tiresome," Salmissra sighed. "They're too delighted to move. Please drive them out, Issus."

"As my Queen desires," Issus said, drawing his sword. "Did you want them all to survive?"

"A few of them, Issus—the more nimble ones."

The throne room was vacated almost immediately.

"I cannot sufficiently thank your Majesty," Sadi said.

"I'll think of a way, my Sadi. First of all, we'll both pretend that the motives I suggested a moment ago were genuine, won't we?"

"I understand perfectly, Divine Salmissra."

"After all," she added, "we must protect the dignity of the throne. You will assume your former duties and your former quarters. We'll think of suitable honors and rewards later." She paused. "I've missed you, my Sadi. I don't think anyone can ever know how much." Her head moved slowly around, and she regarded Polgara. "And how did your encounter with Zandramas go, Polgara?" she asked.

"Zandramas is no longer with us, Salmissra."

"Splendid. I never really liked her. And is the universe restored again?"

"It is, Salmissra."

"I think I'm glad of that. Chaos and disruption are irritating to a snake, you know. We're partial to calm and to order."

Garion noticed that a small green snake had slithered out from under Salmissra's throne to approach Sadi's red leather case, which lay open and forgotten on the marble floor. The little snake reared up to regard the earthenware bottle. He was purring seductively.

"And did you recover your son, your Majesty?" Salmissra asked Garion.

"We did, your Majesty."

"Congratulations. Give my regards to your wife."

"I will, Salmissra."

"We must leave now," Polgara said. "Good-bye, Sadi."

"Good-bye, Lady Polgara." Sadi looked at Garion. "Good-bye, Garion," he said. "It's been a lot of fun, hasn't it?"

"Yes, it has," Garion agreed, shaking the eunuch's hand.

"Say good-bye to the others for me. I rather imagine we'll all see each other from time to time on state business, but it won't be exactly the same, will it?"

"No, probably not." Garion turned to follow Aunt Pol and Issus from the throne room.

"A moment, Polgara," Salmissra said.

"Yes?"

"You've changed many things here. At first, I was very angry with you, but now I've had time to reconsider. Everything's turned out for the best after all. You have my thanks."

Polgara inclined her head.

"Congratulations on your forthcoming blessing," Salmissra added.

Polgara's face gave no hint of surprise at the Serpent Queen's perception of her condition. "Thank you, Salmissra," she said.

They stopped off in Tol Honeth to deliver Emperor Varana to the palace. The heavy-shouldered professional soldier seemed a bit abstracted, Garion noticed. He spoke briefly with a palace functionary as the group moved toward his quarters, and the official scurried away.

Their farewells were brief, almost abrupt. Varana was, as always, the soul of courtesy, but he obviously had other things on his mind.

Ce'Nedra was fuming as they left the palace. She was, as she almost always was now, carrying her young son and was absently running her fingers through his blond curls. "He was almost rude," she said indignantly.

Silk looked down the broad marble drive leading up to the palace. Spring was approaching in these northern latitudes, and the leaves were beginning to appear on the huge old trees lining the drive. A number of richly dressed Tolnedrans was almost running up the drive toward the palace. "Your uncle—or brother, whichever you want to call him—has something very important to attend to just now," the little man told Ce'Nedra.

"What could possibly be more important than common courtesy?"

"Cthol Murgos, at the moment."

"I don't understand."

"If 'Zakath and Urgit work out a peace treaty, there'll be all sorts of commercial opportunities in Cthol Murgos."

"I understand that," she said tartly.

"Of course you do. You're a Tolnedran, after all."

"Why aren't *you* doing something about it?"

"I already have, Ce'Nedra." He smiled, polishing a large ring on the front of his pearl-gray doublet. "Varana may be very cross with me when he finally finds out what I've done to him."

"What exactly *did* you do?"

"I'll tell you once we're back out to sea. You're still a Borune and you might have some residual family loyalties. I wouldn't want you to spoil the surprise for your uncle."

They sailed north along the west coast, and then up the River Arend to the shallows a few leagues west of Vo Mimbre. Then they took to horse and rode through spring sunshine to the fabled city of the Mimbrate Arends.

The court of King Korodullin was thunderstruck by Mandorallen's announcement that Mimbrate Arends had been discovered on the far side of the world. Courtiers and functionaries were sent scurrying off to various libraries to compose suitable replies to the greetings sent from King Oldorin.

The copy of the Accords of Dal Perivor delivered to the throne by Lelldorin, however, evoked troubled expressions on the faces of several of the more seasoned members of the court. "I do fear me, your Majesties," one elderly courtier observed to Korodullin and Mayaserana, "that our poor Arendia hath once more fallen behind the rest of the civilized world. Always in the past have we taken some comfort in the well-nigh eternal strife between Alorn and Angarak and the more recent conflict between Mallorean and Murgo, thinking perhaps that *their* discord in some measure excused ours. This scant comfort, methinks, will not be available to us. Shall we let it be said that only in this most tragic of kingdoms doth rancor and rude war still prevail? How may we hold up our heads in a peaceful world so long as childish bickering and idiotic intestine war do mar our relationships with each other?"

"I find thy words highly offensive, my Lord," a stiff-necked young baron denounced the old man. "No true Mimbrate could ever refuse to heed the stern urgings of honor."

"I speak not of Mimbrates only, my Lord," the old man replied mildly. "I speak of all Arends, Asturians as well as Mimbrates."

"Asturians *have* no honor," the baron sneered.

Lelldorin immediately went for his sword.

"Nay, my young friend," Mandorallen said, restraining the impetuous youth. "The insult hath been delivered here—on Mimbrate soil. Thus it is *my* responsibility—and pleasure—to answer it." He stepped forward. "Thy words were perhaps hasty, my Lord," he said politely to the arrogant baron. "I pray thee, reconsider them."

"I have said what I have said, Sir Knight," the young hothead declared.

"Thou hast spoken discourteously to a revered counselor of the king," Mandorallen said firmly, "and thou hast delivered a mortal insult unto our brethren of the north."

"I *have* no Asturian brethren," the knight declared. "I do not deign to acknowledge kinship with miscreants and traitors."

Mandorallen sighed. "I pray thee, forgive me, your Majesty," he apologized to the king. "Mayhap thou wouldst have the ladies withdraw, for I propose to speak bluntly."

No force on earth, however, could have dragged the ladies of the court from the throne room at that time.

Mandorallen turned back toward the insolently sneering baron. "My Lord," the great knight said distantly, "I find thy face apelike and thy form misshapen. Thy beard, moreover, is an offense against decency, resembling more closely the scabrous fur which doth decorate the hinder portion of a mongrel dog than a proper adornment for a human face. Is it possible that thy mother, seized by some wild lechery, did dally at some time past with a randy goat?"

The baron went livid and he spluttered, unable to speak.

"Thou seemeth wroth, my Lord," Mandorallen said to him in that same deceptively mild tone, "or mayhap thine unseemly breeding hath robbed thy tongue of human speech." He looked critically at the baron. "I do perceive, my Lord, that thou art afflicted with cowardice as well as lack of breeding, for, in truth, no man of honor would endure such deadly insult as those which I have delivered unto thee without some response. Therefore, I fear I must goad thee further." He removed his gauntlet.

As all the world knew, it was customary to hurl one's gauntlet to the floor when issuing a challenge. Mandorallen somehow missed the floor. The young baron staggered backward, spitting teeth and blood. "Thou art no longer a youth, Sir Mandorallen," he raged. "Long hast thou used thy questionable reputation to avoid combat. Methinks it is time for thee to be truly tried."

"It speaks," Mandorallen said with feigned astonishment. "Behold this wonder, my Lords and Ladies—a talking dog."

The court laughed at that.

"Let us proceed to the lower court, my Lord of Fleas," Mandorallen continued. "Mayhap a pass at arms with so elderly and feeble a knight shall give thee entertainment."

The next ten minutes were very long for the insolent young baron. Mandorallen, who could undoubtedly have split him down the middle with one stroke, toyed with him instead, inflicting numerous painful and humiliating injuries. None of the bones the great knight broke were absolutely essential, however, and none of the cuts and contusions were incapacitating. The baron reeled about, trying desperately to protect himself as Mandorallen skillfully peeled his armor off him in chunks and pieces. Finally, apparently growing bored with the whole business, the champion of Arendia broke both of the young man's shinbones with a single stroke. The baron howled with pain as he fell.

"Prithee, my Lord," Mandorallen chided, "modulate thy shrieks of anguish, lest thou alarm the ladies. Groan quietly, an it please thee, and keep this unseemly writhing to a minimum." He turned sternly to a hushed and even frightened crowd. "And," he added, "should any other here share this rash youth's prejudices, let him speak now, ere I sheath my sword, for truly, it is fatiguing to draw the weapon again and again." He looked around. "Let us proceed then, my Lords, for this foolishness doth weary me, and presently I shall grow irritable."

Whatever their views were, the knights of the royal court chose at that point to keep them to themselves.

Ce'Nedra gravely stepped out into the courtyard. "My knight," she said proudly to Mandorallen. Then her eyes sparkled with mischief. "I do perceive that thy prowess doth remain undiminished even though cruel eld doth palsy thy limbs and snow down silvery hair upon thy raven locks."

"Eld?" Mandorallen protested.

"I'm only teasing, Mandorallen." She laughed. "Put away your sword. No one else wants to play with you today."

They bade farewell to Mandorallen, Lelldorin, and Relg, who intended to return to Taiba and their children in Maragor from Vo Mimbre.

"Mandorallen!" King Anheg bellowed as they rode away from the city. "When winter gets here, come up to Val Alorn, and we'll take Barak and go boar hunting."

"I surely will, your Majesty," Mandorallen promised from the battlements.

"I *like* that man," Anheg said expansively.

They took ship again and sailed north to the city of Sendar to advise King Fulrach of the Accords of Dal Perivor. Silk and Velvet were to sail north on *Seabird* with Barak and Anheg, and the rest of them planned a leisurely ride across the mountains to Algaria and from thence down into the Vale.

The farewells at wharfside were brief, in part because they would all see each other again shortly, and in part because none of them wanted to appear overemotional. Garion took his leave of Silk and Barak in particular with a great deal of reluctance. The two oddly matched men had been his companions for more than half his life, and the prospect of being separated from them caused him an obscure kind of pain. The earthshaking adventures were over now, and things would not ever really be the same.

"Do you think you can stay out of trouble now?" Barak asked him gruffly, obviously feeling the same way. "It upsets Merel when she wakes up in the morning to find that she's been sharing her bed with a bear."

"I'll do my best," Garion promised.

"Do you remember what I told you that time just outside Winold—when it was so frosty that morning?" Silk asked.

Garion frowned, trying to remember.

"I said that we were living in momentous times, and that now was the time to be alive to share in those events."

"Oh, yes, now I remember."

"I've had some time to think about it, and I believe I'd like to reconsider." Silk grinned suddenly, and Garion knew that the little man did not mean one word he said.

"We'll see you at the Alorn Council later this summer, Garion," Anheg shouted across the rail as *Seabird* prepared to depart. "It's at your place this year. Maybe if we work on it, we can teach you to sing properly."

They left the city of Sendar early the next morning and took the high road to Muros. Although it was not, strictly speaking, necessary, Garion had decided to see his friends all home. The gradual eroding of their company as they had sailed north had been depressing, and Garion was not quite ready yet to be separated from *all* of them.

They rode across Sendaria in late-spring sunshine, crossed the mountains into Algaria, and reached the Stronghold a week or so later. King Cho-Hag was overjoyed at the outcome of the meeting at Korim, and startled at the results of the impromptu conference at Dal Perivor. Because Cho-Hag was far more stable than the brilliant but sometimes erratic Anheg, Belgarath and Garion went into somewhat greater detail about the astonishing elevation of Eriond.

"He always was a strange boy," Cho-Hag mused in his deep, quiet voice when they had finished, "but then, this entire series of events had been strange. We've been privileged to live in important times, my friends."

"We have indeed," Belgarath agreed. "Let's hope that things quiet down now— for a while, at least."

"Father," Hettar said then, "King Urgit of the Murgos asked me to convey his appreciation to you."

"You met the Murgo King? And we're not at war?" Cho-Hag was amazed.

"Urgit's not like any other Murgo you've ever met, Father," Hettar told him. "He wanted to thank you for killing Taur Urgas."

"That's a novel sentiment coming from a son."

Garion explained Urgit's peculiar background, and the normally reserved King of Algaria burst out in peal after peal of laughter. "I knew Prince Kheldar's father," he said. "That's exactly the kind of thing he *would* have done."

The ladies were gathered about Geran and about Adara's growing brood of children. Garion's cousin was at the ungainly stage of her pregnancy, and she sat most of the time now with a dreamy smile on her face as she listened to the inexorable changes nature was imposing on her body. The revelation of the dual pregnancies of Ce'Nedra and Polgara filled Adara and Queen Silar with wonder, and Poledra sat among them, smiling mysteriously. Poledra, Garion was sure, knew far more than she was revealing.

After about ten days, Durnik grew restless. "We've been away from home a long while, Pol," he said one morning. "There's still time to put in a crop, and I'm sure we'll need to tidy up a bit—mend fences, check the roof, that sort of thing."

"Anything you say, dear," she agreed placidly. Pregnancy had notably altered Polgara. Nothing seemed to upset her now.

On the day of their departure, Garion went down to the courtyard to saddle Chretienne. Although there were plenty of Algar clansmen here in the Stronghold who would have been more than willing to have performed the task for him, he feigned a desire to attend to it himself. The others were engaged in extended farewells, and Garion knew that about one more good-bye right now would probably reduce him to tears.

"That's a very good horse, Garion."

It was his cousin Adara. Her face had the serenity that pregnancy bestows upon women, and looking at her convinced Garion once again just how lucky Hettar really was. Since he had first met her, there had always been a special bond and a special kind of love between Garion and Adara. " 'Zakath gave him to me," he replied. If they confined their conversation to the subject of horses, he was fairly certain that he'd be able to keep his emotions under control.

Adara, however, was not there to talk about horses. She put one hand gently to the back of his neck and kissed him. "Farewell, my kinsman," she said softly.

"Good-bye, Adara," he said, his voice growing thick. "Good-bye."

CHAPTER TWENTY-EIGHT

King Belgarion of Riva, Overlord of the West, Lord of the Western Sea, Godslayer, and general all-round hero, had an extended argument with his coruler, Queen Ce'Nedra of Riva, Imperial Princess of the Tolnedran Empire and Jewel of the House of Borune. The subject of their discussion hinged on the question of just who should have the privilege of carrying Crown Prince Geran, Heir to the Throne of Riva, hereditary Keeper of the Orb, and, until recently, the Child of Dark. The conversation lasted for quite some time as the royal pair rode with their family from the Stronghold of the Algars to the Vale of Aldur.

Ultimately, albeit somewhat reluctantly, Queen Ce'Nedra relented. As Belgarath the Sorcerer had predicted, Queen Ce'Nedra's arms had at last grown tired of continually carrying her young son, and she relinquished him with some relief.

"Make sure he doesn't fall off," she warned her husband.

"Yes, dear," Garion replied, settling his son on Chretienne's neck just in front of the saddle.

"And don't let him get sunburned."

Now that he had been rescued from Zandramas, Geran was a good-natured little boy. He spoke in half phrases, his small face very serious as he tried to explain things to his father. Very importantly, he pointed out deer and rabbits as they rode south, and he dozed from time to time, resting his blond, curly head against his father's chest in absolute contentment. He was restive one morning, however, and Garion, without really thinking about it, removed the Orb from the pommel of his sword and gave it to his son to play with. Geran was delighted, and with a kind of bemused wonder he held the glowing jewel between his hands to stare with fascination into its depths. Often he would hold it to his ear to listen by the hour to its song. The Orb, it appeared, was even more delighted than the little boy.

"That's really very disturbing, Garion," Beldin chided. "You've turned the most powerful object in the universe into a child's plaything."

"It's his, after all—or it will be. They ought to get to know each other, wouldn't you say?"

"What if he loses it?"

"Beldin, do you really think the Orb *can* be lost?"

The game, however, came rather abruptly to an end when Poledra reined in her horse beside the Overlord of the West.

"He's too young to be doing this sort of thing, Garion," she said reprovingly. She reached out her arm and a curiously twisted and knotted stick appeared in her hand. "Put the Orb away, Garion," she said. "Give him this to play with instead."

"That's the stick with only one end, isn't it?" he said suspiciously, remembering the toy Belgarath had once shown him in the cluttered tower—the toy that had occupied Aunt Pol's mind during her babyhood.

Poledra nodded. "It should keep him busy," she said.

Geran willingly gave up the Orb for the new toy. The Orb, however, muttered complaints in Garion's ear for the next several hours.

They reached the cottage a day or so later. Poledra looked rather critically down from the hilltop above it. "You've made some changes, I see," she said to her daughter.

"Do you mind, mother?" Aunt Pol asked.

"Of course not, Polgara. A house should reflect the character of its owner."

"I'm sure there are a million things to do," Durnik said. "Those fences really need attention. We'll have hundreds of Algar cows in the dooryard if I don't mend them."

"And I'm sure the cottage needs a thorough cleaning," his wife added.

They rode down the hill, dismounted, and went inside. "Impossible," Polgara exclaimed, looking about in dismay at the negligibly thin film of dust lying over everything. "We'll need some brooms, Durnik," she said.

"Of course, dear," he agreed.

Belgarath was rummaging through the pantry.

"None of that now, father," Polgara told him crisply. "I want you and Uncle Beldin and Garion to go out there and clear the weeds out of my kitchen garden."

"*What?*" he demanded incredulously.

"I'll want to plant tomorrow," she told him. "Open the ground for me, father."

Garion, Beldin, and Belgarath rather disconsolately went out to the lean-to where Durnik kept his tools.

Garion looked with a sense of defeat at Aunt Pol's kitchen garden, which seemed quite large enough to provide food for a small army.

Beldin gave the ground a few desultory chops with his hoe. "This is ridiculous!" he burst out. He threw down his hoe and pointed one finger at the ground. As he moved the finger, a neat furrow of freshly plowed earth moved resolutely across the garden.

"Aunt Pol will be angry," Garion warned the hunchback.

"Not if she doesn't catch us," Beldin growled, looking at the cottage where Polgara, Poledra, and the Rivan Queen were busy with brooms and dustcloths. "Your turn, Belgarath," he said. "Try to keep the furrows straight."

"Let's see if we can coax some ale from Pol before we rake it," Beldin suggested when they had finished. "This is hot work—even doing it this way."

As it happened, Durnik had also returned to the house briefly to refresh himself before returning to the fence line. The ladies were busily wielding their brooms, stirring up the dust, which, Garion observed, stubbornly settled back on places already swept. Dust was like that sometimes.

"Where's Geran?" Ce'Nedra suddenly exclaimed, dropping her broom and looking around in dismay.

Polgara's eyes went distant. "Oh, dear," she sighed. "Durnik," she said quite calmly, "go fish him out of the creek, please."

"What?" Ce'Nedra almost screamed as Durnik, moving rapidly, went outside.

"He's all right, Ce'Nedra," Polgara assured her. "He just fell into the creek, that's all."

"That's all?" Ce'Nedra's voice went up another octave.

"It's a common pastime for little boys," Polgara told her. "Garion did it, Eriond did it, and now Geran's doing it. Don't worry. He swims rather well, actually."

"How did he learn to swim?"

"I haven't the faintest idea. Maybe little boys are born with the ability—some of them, anyway. Garion was the only one who tried drowning."

"I was starting to get the hang of swimming, Aunt Pol," he objected, "before I came up under that log and hit my head."

Ce'Nedra stared at him in horror, and then she quite suddenly broke down and began to cry.

Durnik was carrying Geran by the back of his tunic when he returned. The little boy was dripping wet, but seemed quite happy, nonetheless. "He's really very muddy, Pol," the smith noted. "Eriond used to get wet, but I don't think he ever got this muddy."

"Take him outside, Ce'Nedra," Polgara instructed. "He's dripping mud on our clean floor. Garion, there's a washtub in the lean-to. Put it in the dooryard and fill it." She smiled at Geran's mother. "It's about time for him to have a bath anyway. For some reason, little boys always seem to need bathing. Garion used to get dirty even while he was asleep."

On one perfect evening, Garion joined Belgarath just outside the cottage door. "You seem a bit pensive, Grandfather. What's the problem?"

"I've been thinking about living arrangements. Poledra's going to be moving back into my tower with me."

"So?"

"We're probably going to become involved in a decade or so of cleaning—and hanging window curtains. How can a man look out at the world with window curtains in his way?"

"Maybe she won't make such an issue of it. Back on Perivor, she said that wolves aren't as compulsively tidy as birds are."

"She lied, Garion. Believe me, she lied."

Two guests rode up a few days later. Despite the fact that it was almost summer now, Yarblek still wore his shabby felt overcoat, his shaggy fur hat, and a disconsolate expression. Vella, the overwhelmingly sensual Nadrak dancer, wore her usual tight-fitting black leather.

"What are you up to, Yarblek?" Belgarath asked Silk's partner.

"This wasn't my idea, Belgarath. Vella insisted."

"All right," Vella said in a commanding voice, "I haven't got all day. Let's get on with this. Get everybody out of the house. I want witnesses to this."

"What exactly are we witnessing, Vella?" Ce'Nedra asked the dark-haired girl.

"Yarblek's going to sell me."

"*Vella!*" Ce'Nedra exclaimed, outraged. *"That's revolting!"*

"Oh, bother that," Vella snapped. *Bother* was not precisely the word Vella used. She looked around. "Are we all here?"

"That's everybody," Belgarath told her.

"Good." She slid down from her saddle and sat cross-legged on the grass. "Let's get down to business. You—Beldin, or Feldegast, or whatever you want to call yourself—one time back in Mallorea, you said you wanted to buy me. Were you serious?"

Beldin blinked. "Well—" he floundered. "I suppose I was, sort of."

"I want a yes or a no, Beldin," she said crisply.

"All right then, yes. You're not a bad-looking wench, and you curse and swear rather prettily."

"Good. What are you prepared to offer for me?"

Beldin choked, his face going suddenly red.

"Don't dawdle, Beldin," she told him. "We haven't got all day for this. Make Yarblek an offer."

"Are you serious?" Yarblek exclaimed.

"I've never been more serious in my life. How much are you willing to pay for me, Beldin?"

"Vella," Yarblek protested, "this is absolute nonsense."

"Shut up, Yarblek. Well, Beldin? How much?"

"Everything I own," he replied, his eyes filled with a kind of wonder.

"That's a little unspecific. Give me a number. We can't haggle without a number."

Beldin scratched at his matted beard. "Belgarath," he said, "have you still got that diamond you found in Maragor that time before the Tolnedran invasion?"

"I think so. It's somewhere in my tower, I believe."

"So's half the clutter in the world."

"It's in the bookcase on the south wall," Poledra supplied, "behind that rat-chewed copy of the Darine Codex."

"Really?" Belgarath said. "How did you know about that?"

"Remember what Cyradis called me at Rheon?"

"The woman who watches?"

"Does that answer your question?"

"Would you lend it to me?" Beldin asked his brother. "I suppose 'give' would be a better word. I doubt that I'll ever be in a position to repay you."

"Certainly, Beldin," Belgarath said. "I wasn't really using it anyway."

"Could you get it for me?"

Belgarath nodded, and then he concentrated, holding out his hand.

The diamond that suddenly appeared in his hand was almost like a chunk of ice, except that it had a definite pinkish cast to it.

It was also somewhat larger than an apple.

"Torak's teeth and toenails!" Yarblek exclaimed.

"An' would th' two of ye, consumed with greed though ye may be, consider this triflin' thing a suitable price fer this beguilin' wench yer both so set on sellin'?" Beldin said, lapsing into Feldegast's brogue and pointing at the stone resting on Belgarath's hand.

"That's worth a hundred times more than has ever been paid for any woman since time began," Yarblek said in an awed tone.

"Then that ought to be about the right price," Vella said triumphantly. "Yarblek, when you get back to Gar og Nadrak, I want you to spread that word around. I want every woman in the kingdom for the next hundred years to cry herself to sleep every night just thinking about the price I brought."

"You're a cruel woman, Vella." Yarblek grinned.

"It's a question of pride," she said, tossing her blue-black hair. "There, now, that didn't take too long at all, did it?" She rose to her feet and dusted off her hands. "Yarblek," she said, "have you got my ownership papers?"

"Yes."

"Get them and sign me over to my new owner."

"We have to divide up the price first, Vella." He looked mournfully at the pink stone. "It's really going to be a shame to split that beauty," he said.

"Keep it," she said indifferently. "I don't need it."

"Are you sure?"

"It's yours. Get those papers, Yarblek."

"Are you *really* sure about all this, Vella?" he asked her again.

"I've never been more sure of anything in my life."

"But he's so *ugly*—sorry, Beldin, but it's the truth. Vella, what could possibly have made you choose *him*?"

"Only one thing," she said.

"What's that?"

"He can fly." Her tone was filled with a kind of wonder.

Yarblek shook his head and went to his saddlebag. He brought back the ownership papers and signed them over to Beldin.

"An' what would I be wantin' with these?" Beldin asked. The brogue, Garion realized, was a way to hide emotions so deep that the hunchback was almost afraid of them.

"Keep them or throw them away." Vella shrugged. "They don't have any meaning for me anymore."

"Very well then, me darlin'," he said. He crumpled the papers up into a ball and held the ball out on the palm of his hand. The wad of paper burst into flame and burned down to ashes. "There," he said, blowing the ashes away. "Now they won't be troublin' us anymore. Is that it? Is that all there is to it?"

"Not quite," she said. She bent and removed the two daggers from her boot tops. Then she took the other two from her belt. "Here," she said, her eyes now very soft, "I won't be needing these anymore." She handed the daggers to her new owner.

"Oh," Polgara said, her eyes filling with tears.

"What is it, Pol?" Durnik asked, his face filled with concern.

"That's the most sacred thing a Nadrak woman can do," Polgara answered, touching at her eyes with the hem of her apron. "She just totally surrendered herself to Beldin. That's just beautiful."

"An' what would I be needin' knives fer?" Beldin asked with a gentle smile. One by one he tossed the daggers into the air, where they vanished in little puffs of smoke. He turned. "Good-bye, Belgarath," he said to the old sorcerer. "We've had some fun, haven't we?"

"I've enjoyed it." Belgarath had tears in his eyes.

"And Durnik," Beldin said, "it looks as if you're here to replace me."

"You talk like a man about to die," Durnik said.

"Oh, no, Durnik, I'm not going to die. I'm just going to change a bit. You two say good-bye to the twins for me. Explain things to them. Enjoy your good fortune, Yarblek, but I still think I got the better of that bargain. Garion, try to keep the world running."

"Eriond's supposed to take care of that."

"I know, but keep an eye on him. Don't let him get into trouble."

Beldin didn't say anything to Ce'Nedra. He simply kissed her rather noisily. Then he also kissed Poledra. She regarded him fondly, her golden eyes filled with love.

"Good-bye, old cow," he said at last to Polgara, slapping her familiarly on the bottom. He looked meaningfully at her waist. "I told you that you were going to get fat if you kept eating all those sweets."

She kissed him then with tears in her eyes.

"An' now, me darlin'," he said to Vella, "let's be walkin' a bit apart. There's much t' be said before we leave." Then the two of them walked hand in hand toward the top of the hill. When they reached it, they stopped and spoke together for a while. Then they embraced and exchanged a long, fervent kiss, and then, while they were still locked in each other's arms, they shimmered and seemed almost to dissolve.

The one hawk was very familiar. The bands on his wings were electric blue. The other hawk, however, had lavender bands on *her* wings. Together, they thrust themselves into the air and rose in an effortless spiral up and up through the glowing air. Higher and higher they spun in that formal wedding dance until they were no more than a pair of specks winging up and out over the Vale.

And then they were gone, never again to return.

· · ·

Garion and the others remained at the cottage for another two weeks. Then, noting that Polgara and Durnik were beginning to show signs of wanting to be alone, Poledra suggested that the rest of them go on to the Vale. Promising to return that evening, Garion and Ce'Nedra took their son and the nearly grown wolf pup and accompanied Belgarath and Poledra down into the heart of the Vale.

They reached Belgarath's familiar squat tower about noon and started up the stairway to the circular room at the top. "Watch that step," the old man said absently as they climbed. This time, however, Garion stopped, letting the rest go on ahead. He reached down, heaved up the stone slab that was the step, and looked under it. A round stone about the size of a hazelnut lay under the slab. Garion removed the stone, put it in his pocket, and replaced the slab. He noticed that the other steps were worn in the center, but this one was not, and he wondered just how many centuries—or eons—the old man had been stepping over it. He went on up, feeling rather pleased with himself.

"What were you doing?" Belgarath asked him.

"Fixing that step," Garion replied. He handed the old man the round pebble. "It was rocking because this was under it. It's steady now."

"I'm going to miss that step, Garion," his grandfather complained. He stared at the pebble, frowning. "Oh," he said, "now I remember. I put this under the step on purpose."

"Whatever for?" Ce'Nedra asked him.

"It's a diamond, Ce'Nedra." Belgarath shrugged. "I wanted to find out how long it would take to grind it down to a powder."

"A diamond?" she gasped, her eyes widening.

"You can have it, if you'd like," he said, tossing it to her.

Then, taking into account her Tolnedran heritage, Ce'Nedra performed an act of sheer unselfishness. "No, thanks, Belgarath," she said. "I wouldn't want to separate you from an old friend. Garion and I can put it back where it was when we leave."

Belgarath laughed.

Geran and the young wolf were playing together near one of the windows. There was a fair amount of mauling involved in their play, and the wolf was cheating outrageously, seizing every chance to lick Geran's neck and face, which always sent the little boy into uncontrolled giggling.

Poledra was looking around at the cluttered circular room. "It's good to be home," she said. She was fondly caressing the back of the owl-clawed chair. "I spent almost a thousand years perched on this chair," she told Garion.

"What were you doing, Grandmother?" Ce'Nedra asked her. Ce'Nedra had begun, perhaps without realizing it, to mimic Garion's customary forms of address.

"Watching *him*," the tawny-haired woman replied. "I knew that eventually he'd get around to noticing me. I didn't really think it would take him all that long, though. I really had to do something out of the ordinary to get his attention."

"Oh?"

"I chose *this* form," Poledra said, touching one hand to her breast. "He seemed more interested in me as a woman than he did when I was an owl—or a wolf."

"There was something I always meant to ask you," Belgarath said. "There weren't any other wolves around when we met. What were you doing out there?"

"Waiting for you."

He blinked. "You knew I was coming?"

"Of course."

"When was that?" Ce'Nedra asked.

"Just after Torak stole the Orb from Aldur," Belgarath replied, his mind obviously on something else. "My Master had sent me north to advise Belar of what had happened. I took the form of the wolf to make better time. Poledra and I met somewhere in what's now northern Algaria." He looked at his wife. "Who told you I was coming?" he asked her.

"No one had to tell me, Belgarath," she replied. "I was born knowing you'd come—someday. You certainly took your time about it, though." She looked around critically. "I think we should tidy up a bit here," she suggested, "and those windows definitely need some curtains."

"See?" Belgarath said to Garion.

There were kisses and embraces and handshakes and a few tears—although not really very many of those. Then Ce'Nedra picked up Geran, and Garion, the wolf, and they started down the stairs.

"Oh," Garion said when they were halfway down, "give me the diamond. I'll put it back where it belongs."

"Wouldn't an ordinary pebble work just as well, Garion?" Her eyes were suddenly calculating.

"Ce'Nedra, if you want a diamond so badly, I'll buy you one."

"I know, Garion, but if I keep this one I'll have two."

He laughed, firmly took the diamond from her tightly clenched little fist, and returned it to its place under the step.

They mounted their horses and rode slowly away from the tower in the bright sunshine of a spring noon. Ce'Nedra held Geran, and the wolf scampered alongside, dashing out from time to time to chase rabbits.

After they had gone a little way, Garion heard a familiar whisper of sound. He reined Chretienne in. "Ce'Nedra," he said, pointing back at the tower, "look."

She looked back. "I don't see anything."

"Wait. They'll be out in a moment."

"They?"

"Grandmother and Grandfather. There they come now."

Two wolves bounded out through the open door of the tower and ran across the grassy plain, matching stride for stride as they ran. There was a kind of unbridled freedom and an intense joy in the way they ran.

"I thought they were going to get started with the cleaning," Ce'Nedra said.

"This is more important, Ce'Nedra. Much, much more important."

They reached the cottage just as the sun was going down. Durnik was still busy in the fields, and they could hear Polgara singing softly in the kitchen. Ce'Nedra went inside, and Garion and the wolf crossed the field to join Durnik.

The meal that evening consisted of a roast goose and everything that went with it: gravy, dressing, three kinds of vegetables, and freshly baked bread, still hot from the oven and dripping with butter.

"Where did you get the goose, Pol?" Durnik asked.

"I cheated," she admitted calmly.

"Pol!"

"I'll explain it some other time, dear. Let's eat it before it all gets cold."

After supper they sat near the fire. They didn't really need a fire—indeed, the doors and windows were even open—but fire and hearth were a part of home, sometimes necessary even when not, strictly speaking, needed.

Polgara held Geran, her cheek against his curls and a dreamy look of contentment on her face. "Just practicing," she said quietly to Ce'Nedra.

"There's no way you could ever forget that, Aunt Pol," the Rivan Queen said. "You've raised hundreds of little boys."

"Well, not quite *that* many, dear, but it never hurts to keep one's hand in."

The wolf lay sound asleep on the hearth before the fire. He was making small yipping noises, however, and his feet were twitching.

"He's dreaming." Durnik smiled.

"I wouldn't be surprised," Garion said. "He spent the whole time while we were coming back from Grandfather's tower chasing rabbits. He didn't catch any, though. I don't think he was really trying."

"Speaking of dreaming," Aunt Pol said, rising to her feet. "You two and your son and your puppy will want an early start in the morning. Why don't we all go to bed?"

They arose at first light the next morning, ate a hearty breakfast, and then Durnik and Garion went out to saddle the horses.

The farewells were not prolonged. There was no real need for extended farewells among these four, because they would never really be apart. There were a few brief words, a few kisses, and a gruff handshake between Durnik and Garion, and then the Rivan King and his family rode up the hill.

Halfway to the top, Ce'Nedra turned in her saddle. "Aunt Pol," she called, "I love you."

"Yes, dear," Polgara called back, "I know. I love you, too."

And then Garion led the way on up the hill and toward home.

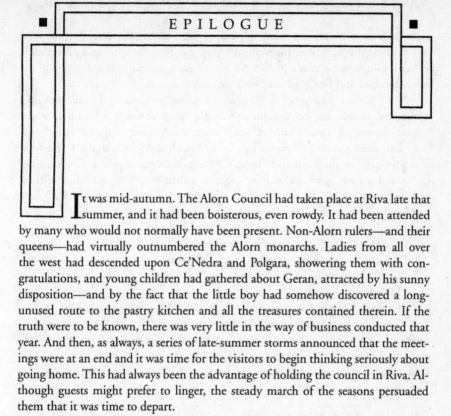

It was mid-autumn. The Alorn Council had taken place at Riva late that summer, and it had been boisterous, even rowdy. It had been attended by many who would not normally have been present. Non-Alorn rulers—and their queens—had virtually outnumbered the Alorn monarchs. Ladies from all over the west had descended upon Ce'Nedra and Polgara, showering them with congratulations, and young children had gathered about Geran, attracted by his sunny disposition—and by the fact that the little boy had somehow discovered a long-unused route to the pastry kitchen and all the treasures contained therein. If the truth were to be known, there was very little in the way of business conducted that year. And then, as always, a series of late-summer storms announced that the meetings were at an end and it was time for the visitors to begin thinking seriously about going home. This had always been the advantage of holding the council in Riva. Although guests might prefer to linger, the steady march of the seasons persuaded them that it was time to depart.

Affairs had settled down in Riva. There had been a wild celebration when the king and his wife had at last returned with Crown Prince Geran, but no people, no matter how emotional, could celebrate forever, and after a few weeks things had returned to normal.

Garion spent most days closeted with Kail now. Many decisions had been made in his absence. Although, almost without exception, he approved of Kail's handling of those matters, he still needed to be briefed on them and some of those decisions needed to be ratified by the royal signature.

Ce'Nedra's pregnancy was proceeding along expected lines. The little queen bloomed and swelled and became increasingly short-tempered. The peculiar hungers for exotic foods that sometimes beset ladies in that delicate condition were not nearly as much fun for the Rivan Queen as they were for most other ladies. There has long been a suspicion in the male half of the population that these gastronomical yearnings are nothing more than a peculiar form of entertainment for their wives. The more exotic and unobtainable a given food might be and the more extreme the lengths to which a doting husband must go to put his hands on it, the more the ladies would insist that they would absolutely *die* if it were not provided in abundance. Garion privately suspected that the whole business involved little more than a desire for reassurance. If a husband proved willing to disassemble the known world to obtain strawberries out of season or strange seafoods normally found only in waters half a world away, it was a sure sign that he still loved his wife, despite her disappearing waistline. It was not nearly as much fun for Ce'Nedra, because each time she made a seemingly impossible request, Garion simply stepped into the next room, created the foodstuff in question on the spot, and presented it to her—usually on a silver platter. Ce'Nedra grew increasingly sulky about the whole business and finally gave up on it entirely.

And then late on a very frosty autumn evening, an ice-coated Mallorean ship entered the harbor, and her captain delivered a packet of neatly folded parchment bearing the seal of 'Zakath of Mallorea. Garion thanked the seaman profusely, offered him and his crew the hospitality of the Citadel, and then immediately carried 'Zakath's letter to the royal apartment. Ce'Nedra was sitting by the fire, knitting. Geran and the young wolf were lying together on the hearth, both of them dozing and twitching slightly as they dreamed. The two always slept together. Ce'Nedra had finally given up the idea of trying to keep them separate at night, since no door in the world could be effectively locked from both sides.

"What is it, dear?" she asked as Garion entered.

"We just received a letter from 'Zakath," he replied.

"Oh? What does he say?"

"I haven't read it yet."

"Open it, Garion. I'm dying to find out what's happening in Mal Zeth."

Garion broke the seal and unfolded the parchment. "For his Majesty, King Belgarion of Riva," he read aloud, "Overlord of the West, Godslayer, Lord of the Western Sea, and for his revered Queen, Ce'Nedra, coruler of the Isle of the Winds, Princess of the Tolnedran Empire, and Jewel of the House of Borune—from 'Zakath, Emperor of all of Angarak.

"I hope this finds you both in good health and I send greetings to your daughter, whether she has already arrived or if her birth be still impending. (I have not, I hasten to assure you, become suddenly clairvoyant. Cyradis said once that she was no longer blessed with her vision. I have come to suspect that she was not entirely truthful on that score.)

"A great deal has happened here since we parted. The imperial court, I suspect, was more than a little pleased by the alteration in my personality which was the direct result of our journey to Korim and by what happened there. I must have been an impossible ruler to deal with. This is not to suggest that all here in Mal Zeth has become a fairy tale of good feeling and felicity. The general staff was mightily upset when I declared my intention to conclude a peace treaty with King Urgit. You know how generals are. If you take their favorite war away from them, they snivel and complain and pout like spoiled children. I had to step on a few necks quite firmly. Incidentally, I recently promoted Atesca to the position of commander-in-chief of the armies of Mallorea. This also enraged the other members of the general staff, but no one can please everybody.

"Urgit and I have been in communication with each other, and I find him to be a rare fellow—quite nearly as droll as his brother. I think we'll get on well together. The bureaucracy very nearly went into collective apoplexy when I announced the autonomy of the Dalasian Protectorates. It's my feeling that the Dals must be permitted to go their own way, but many members of the bureaucracy have vested interests there, and they sniveled and complained and pouted almost as much as the generals did. That came to an abrupt halt however, when I announced my intention to have Brador conduct a thorough audit of the affairs of every bureau chief in the government. The sound of a massive divestiture of all holdings in the protectorates was well-nigh deafening.

"Rather surprisingly, an ancient Grolim arrived at the palace shortly after we returned from Dal Perivor. I was about to send him away, but Eriond insisted rather firmly that he remain. The old fellow had some unpronounceable Grolim name, but Eriond changed it to Pelath for some reason. The old boy has a sweet disposition, but he sometimes speaks very strangely. The language he uses sounds very much like that of the Ashabine Oracles or the *Mallorean Gospels of the Dals*. Very peculiar."

"I'd almost forgotten that," Garion interrupted his reading.

"What's that, dear?" Ce'Nedra asked him, looking up from her knitting.

"Do you remember that old Grolim we met in Peldane? That night when the chicken bit you?"

"Yes. He seemed like a very nice old man."

"He was more than that, Ce'Nedra. He was also a prophet, and the Voice told me that he was going to become Eriond's first disciple."

"Eriond has a very long arm, hasn't he? Keep reading, Garion."

"Cyradis, Pelath, and I have conferred extensively with Eriond and we've all agreed that his status should remain concealed for the time being at least. He is such an innocent that I don't want to expose him to the depths of human depravity and chicanery just yet. Let's not discourage him so early in his career. We all remembered Torak and his overpowering hunger for worship, but when we offered to worship Eriond, he just laughed at us. Did Polgara perhaps leave something out when she was raising him?

"We did make one exception, however. A group of us, accompanied by the third, seventh, and ninth armies, visited Mal Yaska. The Temple Guardmen and Chandim attempted to flee, but Atesca rather effectively rounded them up. I waited until Eriond was off for his morning ride on that unnamed horse of his and spoke quite firmly with the assembled Grolims. I didn't want to cause Eriond any distress, but I indicated to the Grolims that I would be *most* unhappy if they did not change their religious affiliation forthwith. Atesca stood at my side, playing with his sword, so they immediately got my drift. Then, with no warning at all, Eriond appeared in the Temple. (How *does* that horse of his move so fast? The last time he had been observed that morning, he had been more than three leagues from the city.) He told them that black robes were not really all that attractive and that white ones would become them much more. Then, with no more than a faint smile, he actually changed the color of every Grolim robe in the temple. So much for his anonymity in that part of Mallorea, I'm afraid. Next he told them that they'd no longer need their knives, and every dagger in the place disappeared. Then he extinguished the fires in the sanctum and decorated the altar with flowers. I have since been advised that these trifling modifications are universal here in Mallorea. Urgit is presently investigating to determine if similar conditions prevail in Cthol Murgos. Our new God, I think, will take a bit of getting used to.

"To make it short, the Grolims all fell down on their faces. I still suspect that at least *some* of those conversions may have been fraudulent, so I'm not contemplating a demobilization of the army just yet. Eriond told them to get back on their feet and go out and care for the sick, the poor, the orphaned, and the homeless.

"On our way back to Mal Zeth, Pelath pulled his horse in beside mine, smiled that sickeningly sweet smile of his at me, and said, 'My Master believes that it's time for you to change your status, Emperor of Mallorea.' That gave me a bit of a turn. I was about half afraid that Eriond might suggest that I abdicate and take up sheepherding or something. Then Pelath went on. 'My Master believes that you've delayed something for quite long enough.'

"Oh?" I said cautiously.

"The delay is causing the Seeress of Kell a certain distress. My Master strongly suggests that you ask her to marry you. He wants that settled before anything comes along to interfere."

"So, when we got to Mal Zeth, I made what I thought was a very sensible proposal—and Cyradis turned me down flat! I thought my heart would stop. Then our mystic little Seeress waxed eloquent. She told me—at great length—what she thought of sensible. I've never seen her behave that way before. She was actually passionate, and some of the words she used, though archaic, were hardly flattering. I had to look some of them up, they were so obscure."

"Good for her," Ce'Nedra said fiercely.

"Just to make peace," the letter went on, "I fell to my knees and made a fatuous and embarrassingly gushy proposal, and she was moved by my eloquence to relent and accept me."

"Men!" Ce'Nedra snorted.

"The cost of the wedding very nearly bankrupted me. I even had to borrow money from one of Kheldar's business associates—at an outrageous rate of interest. Eriond officiated, of course, and having a God perform the ceremony really nailed down the lid on my coffin. At any rate, Cyradis and I were married last month, and I can truly say that I've never been happier in my life."

"Oh," Ce'Nedra said with that familiar catch in her voice, "that's just lovely." She went to the handkerchief.

"There's more," Garion told her.

"Keep going," she said, dabbing at her eyes.

"The Angarak Malloreans were not really pleased that I had chosen to marry a Dal, but they're wisely keeping their displeasure to themselves. I've changed a great deal, but not *that* much. Cyradis is having some difficulty adapting to her new status, and I simply cannot convince her that jewels are a necessary adornment for an empress. She wears flowers instead, and the slavish imitation of the ladies of the court has caused universal despair in the hearts of the jewelers here in Mal Zeth.

"I was going to have my distant cousin, the Archduke Otrath, shortened by the length of his head, but he's such a pathetic fool that I discarded the idea and sent him home instead. Following a suggestion your friend Beldin made in Dal Perivor, I ordered the cretin to set his wife up in a palace in the City of Melcene and never to go near her again for the rest of his life. I understand that the lady is something of a scandal in Melcene, but she probably deserves *some* recompense for putting up with that silly ass for all those years.

"That's about all from here, Garion. We're really hungry for news of all our friends and we send them our warmest greetings and affection.

"Sincerely,

"Kal Zakath and Empress Cyradis

"Note that I'm deleting that ostentatious prefix. Oh, by the way, my cat was unfaithful to me again a few months ago. Would Ce'Nedra like a kitten?—or maybe one for your new daughter? I can send two, if you'd like.

"Z"

In the early winter of that year, the Rivan Queen grew increasingly discontent, a discontentment and a waspish temper almost in direct proportion to her increasing girth. Some ladies might be uniquely suited for pregnancy; the Rivan Queen was uniquely not. She was snippy with her husband; she was short with her son; and on one occasion she even made an awkward attempt to kick the unoffending young wolf. The wolf nimbly dodged the kick, then looked with some puzzlement at Garion. "Has one somehow given offense?" he asked.

"No," Garion told him. "It is only that one's mate is in some distress. The time of her whelping is approaching, and this always makes the shes of the man-things uncomfortable and short-tempered."

"Ah," the wolf said. "The man-things are very strange."

"Truly," Garion agreed.

It was Greldik, naturally, who delivered Poledra to the Isle of the Winds in the middle of a howling blizzard.

"How did you find your way?" Garion asked the fur-clad seaman as the two of them sat before the fire in the low-beamed dining hall with tankards of ale in their hands.

"Belgarath's wife pointed the way." Greldik shrugged. "That's a remarkable woman, do you know that?"

"Oh, yes."

"Do you know that not one man in my whole crew took a single drink while we were at sea? Not even me. For some reason, we just didn't want any."

"My grandmother has strong prejudices. Will you be all right here? I want to go up and have a chat with her."

"That's all right, Garion." Greldik grinned, patting the nearly full ale keg affectionately. "I'll be just fine."

Garion went upstairs to the royal apartments.

The tawny-haired woman sat by the fire, idly stroking the young wolf's ears. Ce'Nedra was sprawled rather awkwardly on a divan.

"Ah, there you are, Garion," Poledra said. She sniffed the air rather delicately. "I notice you've been drinking." Her tone was disapproving.

"I had one tankard with Greldik."

"Would you please sit over there on the other side of the room then? One's sense of smell is quite acute, and the odor of ale turns one's stomach."

"Is that why you disapprove of drinking?"

"Of course. What other reason could there be?"

"I think Aunt Pol disapproves on some sort of moral grounds."

"Polgara has some obscure prejudices. Now then," she went on seriously. "My daughter is in no condition to travel just now, so I'm here to deliver Ce'Nedra's baby. Pol gave me all sorts of instructions, most of which I intend to ignore. Giving birth is a natural process, and the less interference the better. When it starts, I want you to take Geran and this young wolf here and go to the extreme far end of the Citadel. I'll send for you when it's all over."

"Yes, Grandmother."

"He's a nice boy," Poledra said to the Rivan Queen.

"I rather like him."

"I certainly hope so. All right, then, Garion, just as soon as the baby's born and we're sure everything's all right, you and I are going to return to the Vale. Polgara's a few weeks behind Ce'Nedra, but we really don't have too much time to waste. Pol wants you to be there when she gives birth."

"You *have* to go, Garion," Ce'Nedra said. "I only wish *I* could."

Garion was a bit dubious about leaving his wife so soon after she was delivered, but he definitely *did* want to be in the Vale when Aunt Pol had her baby.

It was three nights later. Garion was having a splendid dream that involved riding down a long, grassy hill with Eriond.

"Garion," Ce'Nedra said, nudging him in the ribs.

"Yes, dear?" He was still about half asleep.

"I think you'd better go get your grandmother."

He was fully awake immediately. "Are you sure?"

"I've been through this before, dear," she told him.

He rolled quickly out of bed.

"Kiss me before you go," she told him.

He did that.

"And don't forget to take Geran and the puppy when you go off to the other end of the building. Put Geran back to bed when you get there."

"Of course."

A strange expression came over her face. "I think you'd better hurry, Garion," she suggested.

Garion bolted.

It was nearly dawn when the Queen of Riva was delivered of a baby girl. The infant had a short crop of deep-red hair and green eyes. As it had for so many centuries, the Dryad strain bred true. Poledra carried the blanket-wrapped baby through the silent halls of the Citadel to the rooms where Garion sat before a fire and Geran and the wolf slept in a tangle of arms, legs, and paws on a divan.

"Is Ce'Nedra all right?" Garion asked, coming to his feet.

"She's fine," his grandmother assured him, "a little tired is all. It was a fairly easy delivery."

Garion heaved a sigh of relief, then turned back the corner of the blanket to look at the small face of his daughter. "She looks like her mother," he said. People the world over always make that first observation, pointing out the similarities of a newborn to this parent or that as if such resemblances were somehow remarkable. Garion gently took the baby in his arms and looked into that tiny red face. The baby looked back at him, her green-eyed gaze unwavering. It was a familiar gaze. "Good morning, Beldaran," Garion said softly. He had made that decision quite some time ago. There would be other daughters, and they would be named after a fair number of female relatives on both sides of the family, but it somehow seemed important that his first daughter should be named for Aunt Pol's blond twin sister, a woman who, though Garion had seen only her image and then only once, was still somehow central to all their lives.

"Thank you, Garion," Poledra said simply.

"It seems appropriate somehow," Garion told her.

Prince Geran was not too impressed with his baby sister, but boys seldom are. "Isn't she awfully little?" he asked when his father woke him to introduce them.

"It's the nature of babies to be little. She'll grow."

"Good." Geran looked at her gravely. Then, apparently feeling that he should say *something* nice about her, he added, "She has nice hair. It's the same color as mother's, isn't it?"

"I noticed that myself."

The bells of Riva pealed out that morning in celebration, and the Rivan people rejoiced, although there were some, many perhaps, who secretly wished that the royal infant might have been another boy, just for the sake of dynastic security. The Rivans, kingless for so many centuries, were nervous about that sort of thing.

Ce'Nedra, of course, was radiant. She expressed only minimal dissatisfaction with Garion's choice of a name for their daughter. Her Dryad heritage felt rather strongly the need for a name beginning with the traditional "X." She worked with it a bit, however, and came up with a satisfactory solution to the problem. Garion was fairly certain that in her own mind she had inserted an "X" somewhere in Beldaran's name. He decided that he didn't really want to know about it.

The Rivan Queen was young and healthy, and she recovered from her confinement quickly. She remained in bed for a few days—largely for the dramatic effect on the stream of Rivan nobility and foreign dignitaries who filed through the royal bedchamber to view the tiny queen and the even tinier princess.

After a few days, Poledra spoke with Garion. "That more or less takes care of business here," she said, "and we really should get started back to the Vale. Polgara's time is coming closer, you know."

Garion nodded. "I asked Greldik to stay," he told her. "He'll get us back to Sendaria faster than anybody else can."

"He's a very undependable man, you know."

"Aunt Pol said exactly the same thing. He's still the finest sailor in the world. I'll make arrangements to have horses put on board his ship."

"No," she said shortly. "We're in a hurry, Garion. Horses would only slow us down."

"You want to run all the way from the coast of Sendaria to the Vale?" he asked her, a little startled.

"It's not really all that far, Garion." She smiled.

"What about supplies?"

She gave him an amused look, and he suddenly felt very foolish.

Garion's good-byes to his family were emotional, though brief. "Be sure to dress warmly," Ce'Nedra instructed. "It's winter, you know."

He decided not to tell her exactly how he and his grandmother intended to travel.

"Oh," she said, handing him a parchment sheet, "give this to Aunt Pol."

Garion looked at the sheet. It was a rather fair artist's sketch, in color, of his wife and daughter.

"It's quite good, isn't it?" Ce'Nedra said.

"Very good," he agreed.

"You'd better run along now," she said. "If you stay much longer, I won't let you go at all."

"Keep warm, Ce'Nedra," he said, "and look after the children."

"Naturally. I love you, your Majesty."

"I love you, too, your Majesty." He kissed her and his son and daughter and quietly left the room.

The weather at sea was blustery, but the militantly impetuous Greldik paid almost no attention to weather, no matter how foul. His patched and decidedly scruffy-looking ship ran before the wind across a stormy sea under far more sail than even a marginally prudent sea captain would have crowded onto his masts, and two days later, they reached the coast of Sendaria.

"Any empty beach will do, Greldik," Garion told him. "We're in sort of a hurry, and if we stop at Sendar, Fulrach and Layla will tie us up with congratulations and banquets."

"How do you propose to get off a beach without horses?" Greldik asked bluntly.

"There are ways," Garion told him.

"More of *that* sort of thing?" Greldik said with a certain distaste.

Garion nodded.

"That's unnatural, you know."

"I come from an unnatural sort of family."

Greldik grunted disapprovingly and ran his ship in close to a windswept beach bordered on its upper edge with the rank grass of a salt flat. "Does this one suit you?" he asked.

"It's just fine," Garion said.

Garion and his grandmother waited on the windy beach with their cloaks whipping around them until Greldik was well out to sea. "I suppose we can get started now," Garion said, shifting his sword into a more comfortable position.

"I don't know why you brought that," Poledra said.

"The Orb wants to see Aunt Pol's baby." He shrugged.

"That may just be the most irrational thing I've ever heard anyone say, Garion. Shall we go?"

They shimmered and blurred, and then two wolves loped up the beach to the bordering grass and ran smoothly inland.

It took the two of them a little more than a week to reach the Vale. They stopped only rarely to hunt and even more infrequently to rest. Garion learned a great deal about being a wolf during that week. Belgarath had given him a certain amount of instruction in the past, but Belgarath had come into wolfhood when he had been full grown. Poledra, on the other hand, was the genuine article.

They crested the hill overlooking the cottage one snowy evening and looked down at the tidy farmstead with its fence lines half buried in snow and the windows of the cottage glowing a warm, welcoming yellow.

"Are we in time?" Garion asked the golden-eyed wolf beside him.

"Yes," Poledra replied. "One suspects, however, that the decision not to burden ourselves with the beasts of the man-things was wise. The time is very close. Let us go down and find out what is happening."

They loped on down the hill through swirling snowflakes and changed back into their own forms in the dooryard.

The interior of the cottage was warm and bright. Polgara, more than a little ungainly, was setting places for Garion and her mother at the table. Belgarath sat near the fire, and Durnik was patiently mending harness.

"I saved some supper for you," Aunt Pol told Garion and Poledra. "We've already eaten."

"You knew we'd get here this evening?" Garion asked.

"Of course, dear. Mother and I always stay more or less in constant contact. How's Ce'Nedra?"

"She and Beldaran are just fine." He said it in an offhand sort of way. Aunt Pol had surprised *him* often enough in the past. Now it was his turn.

She almost dropped a plate, and her glorious eyes grew wide. "Oh, Garion," she said, embracing him suddenly.

"Does the name please you? Just a little?"

"More than you could ever know, Garion."

"How are you feeling, Polgara?" Poledra asked, removing her cloak.

"Fine—I think." Aunt Pol smiled. "I know about the procedure, of course, but this is the first time I've experienced it personally. Babies spend a great deal of time kicking at this stage, don't they? A few minutes or so ago, I think mine kicked me in three separate places at once."

"Maybe he's punching, too," Durnik suggested.

"He?" She smiled.

"Well—the word's just for the sake of convenience, Pol."

"If you'd like, I could have a look and tell you if it's a he or a she," Belgarath offered.

"Don't you dare!" Polgara told him. "I want to find out for myself."

The snow let up shortly before daybreak, and the clouds blew off by midmorning. The sun came out, and it glittered brightly on the new-fallen blanket of white around the cottage. The sky was intensely blue, and, though it was cold that day, the bitter chill of midwinter had not yet set in.

Garion, Durnik, and Belgarath had been banished from the house at dawn, and they wandered about with that odd sort of uselessness men usually feel in such circumstances. At one point they stopped on the bank of the small stream that threaded its way through the farmstead. Belgarath looked down into the clear water, noting a number of dark, slim shapes just below the surface. "Have you had time to do any fishing?" he asked Durnik.

"No," Durnik said a bit sadly, "and I don't seem to have the enthusiasm for it I used to."

They all knew why, but none of them mentioned it.

Poledra brought their meals to them, but firmly insisted that they remain outside. Late in the afternoon, she put them to work boiling water over Durnik's forge, which sat in the toolshed.

"I've never seen any reason for this," Durnik confessed, lifting another steaming kettle from his forge. "Why do they always need boiling water?"

"They don't," Belgarath told him. Belgarath was comfortably sprawled on a woodpile and was examining the intricately carved cradle Durnik had built. "It's just a way to keep the menfolk out from underfoot. Some female genius came up with the idea thousands of years ago, and women have been honoring the custom ever since. Just boil water, Durnik. It makes the women happy, and it's not that big a chore."

The moon had been rising late, but the stars touched the snow with a fairy light, and all the world seemed somehow bathed in a gentle blue-white glow. It was, of all nights, among the closest to perfect Garion had ever seen, and all of nature seemed to be holding its breath.

Garion and Belgarath, noting Durnik's increasing edginess, suggested that they walk to the top of the hill to settle their suppers. They had both observed in the past that Durnik usually banished uncomfortable emotions by keeping busy.

The smith looked up at the night sky as they trudged through the snow toward the top of the hill. "It's really a special sort of night, isn't it?" He laughed a little sheepishly. "I suppose I'd feel that way even if it were raining," he said.

"I know I always do," Garion said. Then he, too, laughed, his breath steaming in the chill night air. "I don't know that twice qualifies as much of an always, though," he conceded, "but I know what you mean. I was feeling sort of the same way myself earlier." He looked beyond the cottage across the snowy plain lying white and still beneath the icy stars. "Does it seem very, very quiet to you two, as well?"

"There's not a hint of a breeze," Durnik agreed, "and the snow muffles all the sound." He cocked his head. "Now that you mention it, though, it does seem awfully quiet, and the stars are really bright tonight. There's a logical explanation for it, I suppose."

Belgarath smiled at them. "There's not a single ounce of romance in either one of you, is there? Didn't it ever occur to you that this might just *be* a very special night?"

They looked at him oddly.

"Stop and think about it," he said. "Pol's devoted most of her life to raising children that weren't hers. I've watched her do it, and I could feel an obscure kind of pain in her each time she took a new baby in her arms. That's going to change tonight, so in a very real sense this *is* a special night. Tonight Polgara's going to get a baby of her very own. It may not mean all that much to the rest of the world, but I think it does to us."

"It does indeed," Durnik said fervently. Then a thoughtful expression came into the good man's eyes. "I've been sort of working on something lately, Belgarath."

"Yes. I've heard you."

"Doesn't it seem to you that we're all sort of coming back to the places where we started? It's not exactly the same, of course, but things sort of feel familiar."

"I've been thinking sort of the same thing," Garion admitted. "I keep getting this strange feeling about it."

"It's only natural for people to go home after they've been on a long journey, isn't it?" Belgarath said, kicking at a lump of snow with one foot.

"I don't think it's that simple, Grandfather."

"Neither do I," Durnik agreed. "This seems more important for some reason."

Belgarath frowned. "I think it does to me, as well," he admitted. "I wish Beldin were here. He could explain it in a minute. Of course none of us would understand the explanation, but he'd explain it all the same." He scratched at his beard. "I've found something that *might* explain it," he said a bit dubiously.

"What's that?" Durnik asked him.

"Garion and I have had an extended conversation over the last year or so. He'd noticed that things kept happening over and over again. You probably heard us talking about it."

Durnik nodded.

"Between us, we came up with the notion that things kept repeating themselves because the accident made it impossible for the future to happen."

"That makes sense, I guess."

"Anyhow, that's changed now. Cyradis made her Choice, and the effects of the accident have been erased. The future *can* happen now."

"Then why is everybody going back to the place where he started?" Garion asked.

"It's only logical, Garion," Durnik told him quite seriously. "When you're starting something—even the future—you almost have to go back to the beginning, don't you?"

"Why don't we just assume that's the explanation," Belgarath said. "Things got stopped. Now they're moving again, and everybody got what he deserved. We got the good things, and the other side got the bad ones. It sort of proves that we picked the right side, doesn't it?"

Garion suddenly laughed.

"What's so funny?" Durnik asked him.

"Just before our baby was born, Ce'Nedra got a letter from Velvet—Liselle. She's managed to push Silk into naming a day. It's probably what he deserves, all right, but I imagine his eyes get a little wild every time he thinks about it."

"When's the wedding?" Durnik asked.

"Next summer sometime. Liselle wants to be sure that everybody can be in Boktor to witness her triumph over our friend."

"That's a spiteful thing to say, Garion," Durnik reproved.

"It's probably the truth, though." Belgarath grinned. He reached inside his tunic and drew out an earthenware flagon. "A touch of something to ward off the chill?" he offered. "It's some of that potent Ulgo brew."

"Grandmother won't like that," Garion warned.

"Your grandmother isn't here right now, Garion. She's a little busy at the moment."

The three of them stood atop the snowy hill looking down at the farmstead. The thatched roof was thick with snow, and icicles hung like glittering jewels from the eaves. The small panes of the windows glowed with golden lamplight that fell softly out over the gently mounded snow in the dooryard, and the ruddy glow from the forge where the menfolk had spent the afternoon boiling unneeded water came softly from the shed. A column of blue woodsmoke rose straight and unwavering from the chimney, reaching so high that it seemed almost to be lost among the stars.

A peculiar sound filled Garion's ears, and it took him awhile to identify it. It was the Orb, and it was singing a song of unutterable longing.

The silence seemed almost palpable now, and the glittering stars seemed to draw even closer to the snowy earth.

And then from the cottage there came a single cry. It was an infant voice, and it was not filled with that indignation and discomfort so common in the cries of most newborns but rather with a kind of wonder and ineffable joy.

A gentle blue light suddenly came from the Orb, and the longing in its note turned to joy.

As the song of the Orb faded, Durnik drew in a deep breath. "Why don't we go down?" he said.

"We'd better wait a bit," Belgarath suggested. "There's always some cleaning up to do at this point, and we should give Pol a chance to brush her hair."

"I don't care if her hair's a little mussed," Durnik said.

"*She* does. Let's wait."

Strangely, the Orb had renewed its yearning melody. The silence remained as palpable as before, broken now only by the thin, joyous wail of Polgara's baby.

The three friends stood on the hilltop, their breath steaming in the cold night air as they listened to that distant, piping song.

"Good healthy lungs," Garion complimented the new father.

Durnik grinned briefly at him, still listening to the cry of his child.

And then that single cry was not alone. Another voice joined in.

This time the light that burst from the Orb was a sudden blaze of blue that illuminated the snow around them, and its joyous song was a triumphant organ note.

"I *knew* it!" Belgarath exclaimed with delight.

"Two?" Durnik gasped. *"Twins?"*

"It's a family trait, Durnik." Belgarath laughed, catching the smith in a rough embrace.

"Are they boys or girls?" Durnik demanded.

"What difference does it make right now? But we might as well go on down there and find out, I suppose."

But as they turned, they saw that something seemed to be happening in the vicinity of the cottage. They stared at the single shaft of intensely blue light descending from the starry sky, a shaft that was soon joined by one of a paler blue. The cottage was bathed in their azure light as the two lights from the heavens touched the snow. Then those lights were joined by other lights, red and yellow and green and lavender and a shade Garion could not even put a name to. Last, the lights from the sky were joined by a single shaft of blinding white. Like the colors of the rainbow, the lights stood in a semicircle in the dooryard, and the brilliant columns from which they had descended rose above them to fill the night sky with a pulsing curtain of many-hued, shifting light.

And then the Gods were there, standing in the dooryard with their song joining with that of the Orb in a mighty benediction.

Eriond turned to look up the hill at them. His gentle face glowed with a smile of purest joy. He beckoned to them. "Join us," he said.

"Now it is complete." UL's voice was also joyous. *"All* is well now."

Then, with the God-light bathing their faces, the three friends started down from the snowy hilltop to view that miracle, which, though it is most commonplace, is a miracle nonetheless.

And so, my children, the time has come to close
the book. There will be other days and other stories,
but this tale is finished.

ABOUT THE AUTHOR

DAVID EDDINGS published his first novel, *High Hunt,* in 1973, before turning to the field of fantasy with The Belgariad, soon followed by The Malloreon. Born in Spokane, Washington, in 1931, and raised in the Puget Sound area north of Seattle, he received his bachelor of arts degree from Reed College in Portland, Oregon, in 1954, and a master of arts degree from the University of Washington in 1961. He has served in the United States Army, has worked as a buyer for the Boeing Company, and has been a grocery clerk and a college English teacher. He now lives with Leigh, his wife and collaborator, in Nevada.